The Blessed Farm

The Blessed Farm

Hermann Stehr

K A Nitz

ALBANY, NEW ZEALAND

Der Heiligenhof first published
in German 1918

This translation into NZ English
Copyright © K A Nitz 2017
All rights reserved

ISBN: 978-0-473-39813-2

Contents

BOOK ONE

The Blessed Farm

1

The Westphalian country around Münster throws up a wave of low hills towards the Rhine. It looks as if a widely strewn herd of giant cows had decamped from the fertile plain an unthinkably long time ago to wander over to the river for a drink. But on the way, so close to the goal, yet before the first could descend to the waters of the Rhine, the immeasurable herd had been overcome by weariness with the world. They had lain down as if it were only to rest a little. Only their sleep merged imperceptibly into the great calm of the earth which breathes in and out only once a year, in spring and autumn. The heads of the primeval cows sank into the ground, their wide horns rotted away, and only their misshapen bodies still protruded as hills from the level countryside. Their flesh turned to earth, their skeletons turned to stone. Grass grew on them, small forests drove their roots into them, and finally the men came and settled on them. It is the region between Emmerich and Wesel. Though the people who live there belong to the Rhine provinces, they must still be counted amongst the Westphalian tribes. Their settlements have already closed ranks into closed villages. But enough solitary farms still stand on the strung-out heights and in the wide, flat depressions.

Hermann Stehr

No further than three good hours of travel from the Rhine stood two stately farmsteads, each set on a knoll at a distance opposite each other so that you could recognise from the yard gate in clear visibility the condition of the clothes and the hair colour of the people of the other estate. You could hear the tone of a powerful, man's voice only as a vague sound, whereas a not all too loud, woman's song was distinctly heard in still air. But it seldom sounded around the broad, massive thatched rooves. The farms lay opposite each other as though with a bated breath of distrust and covert suspicion, and they awkwardly guarded the borders of the fields, although down in the little valley where they could have touched, a little path ran, leading out of the village to the Rhine and separating them. That is why it was impossible for a boundary stone to be able to stray overnight into the other's field. Cropped meadows, and here and there an oak, disorderly on both sides of the narrow strip of road, guarded over the area of the two properties as well. It was not in fact hostility which had separated the two farms in living memory. No, and yet everyone from the Sintlinger farm, which lay to the north towards Emmerich, made a large arc around the hill on which the farming family of Brindeisener had resided for centuries, if they had to go past the other farm because of some business.

This mutual diffidence as though before something dangerously ignoble seemed to not only lie in the blood of the families, it was fixed in the foundations of the walls, flowed from the udders of the cows, was unconsciously strewn every spring with the seeds into the furrows of the fields, and hardly had the new servants helped consume the second baking of bread than they were inwardly torn apart by this stream of blind discord.

The Blessed Farm

The two families were separated like certain breeds of animal which can never live with one another, or like species of plant which perish from their mutual evaporations.

Now there was also no greater contrast than a Brindeisener and a Sintlinger.

The former, tall, even somewhat overgrown, dragged his menacing taciturnity about slowly in a bony body, a taciturnity which was kept cool under an oblong skull by almost snow white blond hair and guarded over by steel blue defiant eyes.

The Sintlingers must have obtained through marriage in the earliest times such a powerful dash of Walloon that they looked as if they had immigrated across the Rhine from Brabant. Rather less than medium height, small and delicate as a throwing stick, sharp as a knife, always making a racket like a rolling barrel, these brown-haired, unsaintly people not only raged in the furrows of their fields, but also about the entire district, mindless of the encroachments they incurred on those neighbouring them, but also indifferent towards the almost contemptuous diffidence with which they were met everywhere.

The mutual aversion of the two families had become proverbial in the wider neighbourhood and tempted each limb of the sundered families to impress from childhood on the antipathy towards every custom of the other farm like a venerable bequest. And yet it was awkward to avoid smudging the cleft separating them through business.

At most they tolerated it with contemptuous smiles if the cowherds sang libellous rhymes with the autumn move to the meadows or tangled with each other with their whips.

Each had a different sun, a different air, a different God.

Even the blooming and wilting of the generations obeyed a different rhythm in each place. The wedding songs on the one sounded into the silence of the greying marriage on the other farm; while the one farmer's wife was rocking the first cradle, the other was dressing the corpse. The men never prospered at the same time; the youths on both farms never danced their fluttering hopes at the same time. When life on the Brindeisener hill sat at full tables and sang, death climbed from the churchyard to the Sintlinger house, sat on its threshold and cut his little pipe to size. So it is surely possible that next to the distinctiveness of the races, the difference of ages formed the reason for the estrangement of the two families.

In the entire district, the Sintlinger and Brindeisener farms also carried the name of the estranged farms, and it was even maintained that the smoke fled the chimneys, and if the animals of the estranged accidentally mixed, a deformed animal invariably arose.

The purring of the willows and oaks which separated their fields in the valley was not capable of bringing an inkling of peaceful moods to their dreams; the expanses of crops waved across the same hill in vain; the church bells of the village called out from the forest in vain.

It also stirred no one when, on quite sunken evenings in the direction of the Rhine, that great oppressive silence rose up which went along soundlessly in the sky over every powerful stream, and can bring contemplative natures close to the thoughts of eternity. At most, it was a young fellow perhaps from over there, or an icy grey man from over here who endured such a mysterious arrival at the bench under the yard gate's lime tree, stood up with heavy breaths, becoming overwhelmed for a moment, pondered the ground, and then shook his head.

"Yes, we cannot run after them", he then murmurs, "they shun us everywhere. There is nothing doing there ever since I can remember." With that he goes to sleep. And the farmsteads cannot come together because the valley lies between them, and the people remain apart because a chasm was torn between them which they neither comprehend nor are to blame for.

Over the blame, admittedly, many of the residents of the village of Hemsterhus to which both homesteads belonged were of a different opinion. The estranged farms were the most secluded, though most important properties of the small district whose kernel consisted of a small number of modest houses amongst trees and, if you want to say so, lay further into the countryside. For that reason, the fate of the two wealthy families provided the principal material for the stories which ran through the winter's fireside evenings.

It was said that once upon a time a farmer wild as a wolf had resided on the Sintlinger farm, the mad Jakob, a paragon for whom law and custom were worth no more than the dirt on his boots. When it once rained for weeks and the grain began to spoil on its stalks, he became so angry that he went to a crossroads and, amidst profanities, bombarded the crucifix with stones. He smelt the maidens on heat from miles away, and because a young wife was working at the time inside and outside at the Brindeisener farm, and her virtue was also not cut all too close to her body, he waited in ambush for her in the absence of her husband one evening and raped her. On returning home, the Brindeisener heard of the incident, tore the shirt from his wife's body the following night, tied her naked to a steer and chased the animal with the blows of a whip out into the darkness. But when after the harvest, the barn was stuffed full to the roof, he sent his servant and, on a stormy night, had his neighbour's farmstead lit at its four corners so that it was all burnt down to the ground. Not a hoof and not a tail, not a whisk and not a button could be saved. But this fierce retribution ate every infamous action from mad Jakob's body. Before the morning came, he had become a different man, had the scene of the fire blessed by the Hemsterhus Pastor and then began the rebuilding of his incinerated farmstead. On the roof of the homestead, he placed a little tower with a bell. As long as the malefactor lived, he faithfully rang it every hour of the day and also died an honest death with the thin notes in the air. In the course of time, the Sintlingers, however, strayed again into the old wildness. The tolling fell away, the stairs to the little tower collapsed, and the access to it was nailed up with boards. From now on, the little bell was left to itself, and the legend went that it began to toll every time a misfortune was imminent for the farm.

Thus the people told the story. But it is not certain that these events, and especially as they were carried as stories from mouth to mouth, actually happened.

It could very well be possible that the folk invented it to explain the ineradicable estrangement of the two farming families.

But the Hemsterhus folk went still further.

Many a one had claimed to have seen on a bright night, yes even in the middle of the bright light of day, something like a small child being driven naked, stumbling, but whirlingly quick about the Sintlinger farmstead and vanishing in the area towards the Rhine as if it were blown into the air. But this sort of clear sightedness did not descend from the prudent segment of the residents, but rather that guild of men who by nature have come up short in some way intellectually.

Lastly these stories were rife from a man whom the Hemsterhus cartwright had found on his doorstep as a small child. The childless old man adopted this poor worm, who had probably been left in this way by travelling folk, gave him the name Joseph Nobody and set about with his aged wife to make a useful man out of him. But all their efforts were in vain. The older poor Nobody became, the deeper he grew into a thousand strange tempers and oddities. Thus he claimed to feel the growing of finger and toe nails as a swishing in his body, ran after all the birds to listen to their song because he affected to understand them; talked to the trees like they were men; often listened all night long to the voices of the wind, and watched the changing shapes of the clouds as if they were profound images.

Although everyone laughed over these sorts of prophets, it was undeniable that the folk believed firmly that a child from the Sintlinger farm would one day bring together the estranged families, but find its own death at the same time.

2

The Hemsterhus incubus, as Joseph Nobody was known by everyone, had carried on his outerworldly juggling right past the death of his adopted parents until towards his thirtieth year. The cartwright's little house in which he had led his reclusive life had long ago rotted away and collapsed, and Nobody wandered about as a vagabond without getting any further than Brederode and Querhoven. Out of unacknowledged fear, the farmers tolerated him spending the night in a corner of the stalls and the day in a corner of the servants' room.

At this time, Andreas Sintlinger at barely twenty years of age came into possession of his farm. The little bell had demanded his grandfather unexpectedly early. He had fallen down dead during the harvest just when he had wanted to plunge in fury at an insubordinate servant, and drunkenness had hounded his father on his nocturnal journey home into a deep brick farm pool where he had drowned.

Andreas acceded to the mastery of the Sintlinger farm entirely in the manner of his forebears. On the first day of his possession, he gathered together the servants and had the tall fire ladder placed up to the high thatched roof. Then he grasped a rung, climbed up to the little tower, and laughingly tolled the bell so that it cried confusedly and hollowly over the hills. Now it had bleated its verdict, he suggested exuberantly, and will now surely spare him. After that he sat down with his people in the large living room, had dish after dish served, and drank and sang until deep into the night.

Mad Jakob Sintlinger seemed with him to have moved into the farmstead again. When the apron strings sat looser on a girl, he presented himself as the first at dusk. No prank succeeded without him, he lent his wit to every ridicule. At the festivities, he was the instigator of the riots, fomented disagreements with the greatest skill, and then, laughing derisively, drowned the overhasty hostilities in streams of wine. But his madness was ameliorated by a trace of chivalrousness, and what appeared in others as vulgarity received through his being the appearance of frivolous temerity. He never fraternised with fools, and when he stood up from a drinking bout in the circle of his classy drinking fellows, it happened that he poured the rest of his glass in their faces, and went away laughing. Despite these ceaseless explosions with which he was burdened, he did not neglect his business in the least. His small body possessed the indestructibility of a steel machine. He apparently needed the lack of restraint as much as other men needed rest to recover from their work. When he came home towards morning, he rose after three hours sleep as fresh as if he had snored an entire day long. The furrows could hardly keep up when he ploughed; the grain fell already at the whistle of his scythe, and once, when, at a cutting competition, a reaper well known over the entire district fell after two hours the length of two men behind Andreas, it had been all up with the little devil by a hair; for suddenly the enormous man, for whom it was just as much about the taler that was bet as the lost reputation and the ample mockery, lunged from behind at the Sintlinger, and if he had not at the last moment flown to the side like a smacked ball, the scythe of the other would have shoved him without a look before the gravedigger's door. The spectators seized the raging man, and when he had stopped foaming, Andreas stuck one sausage in his right trouser pocket and said it had good veal in it, the other in the left and assured him that it was mutton, pressed two talers in his hand, and confessed that it had not been fair with the competition, because he, Sintlinger, had furtively rubbed fat on the other man's scythe. He planted such ingratiating guile again and again next to the goat's beard of irritating debaucheries, and the farmers of the district never really knew how to take the madman — they swelled with indignation, overflowed with delight, and shook with laughter. In particular, the girls looked out their windows with a feeling mixed with horror, regret, and desire when the venturesome brat raced through a village on his wagon. But he sat hidden behind his horses' tails, and apparently thought more of aprons and jokes than hearts. Until one time he came through Brederode, a place perhaps half an hour's travel from Hemsterhus. There he saw on a spring morning the beautiful Johanna Klim, daughter of the Superintendent of Brederode, in the meadow next to the path bleaching linen. She was walking next to the long greyish white stretch and sprinkling from a watering can on the fabric which she had helped spin on the winter evenings. The sunny wind of May blew now and then against the thousandfold dispersed stream of water and scattered it in silvery shimmering drops about the blond, delicate girl so that she seemed more like a heavenly apparition in a transfigured light than a human. Hardly had Andreas Sintlinger seen her once than he pulled his horses up and waited with held breath until the shimmering sprayed about the young woman again, then he climbed down from the wagon as if in a dream, tied the horses to a tree, and sat and stared enraptured at the miracle which had unexpectedly stepped into his life. When the girl became aware of the puzzling behaviour of the mad fellow, her hands lowered the can in fright, for it could always be that he, still groggy from a night of drinking, was sitting by the ditch and pondering a prank which he could do to her. But she fastened onto the thought that she had never said anything bad against the young farmer, not even in secret, grasped the can, seemingly looked calmly over her work and strode fearlessly along the field margin towards him so as to pass across into her father's farmstead. As she neared him, he hurriedly plucked a few flowers, rose, and walked towards her. She saw already from a distance that the fire in his large, deep brown eyes and the red blaze over his entire face had its source in a different sort of intoxication, and doubly regretted her overconfidence. They already stood eye to eye opposite each other. She saw how the man, shaken by an inner storm, was trembling all over and offering her the flowers beseechingly, and she heard him stammering incomprehensible words. In extreme confusion, the girl wanted to slip past him. Then an abrupt wildness jerked through the Sintlinger so that he momentarily stood like an iron rod rammed into the earth before her. With impassioned decisiveness, he asked her permission to be able to pin the flowers to her breast. If she denied it, he could not compel her. But he would then race his team careering straight into the quarry which had been driven into the hill hard next to the road behind Brederode. Even if Andreas had not also turned pale to his gums, she definitely knew that he would have kept his word in his boldness, and she tolerated what he asked of her. Trembling all over, she still felt half faint as he covered her hand with ardent kisses. Then the way was free, and the Sintlinger, all his business over at once, travelled back to Hemsterhus in a jubilant gallop.

When he was out of sight, Johanna unpinned the flowers again and hid them in a woodpile. In the evening, however, the girl furtively retrieved them and placed them under her pillow because she thought that it was ignoble not to keep a promise she had given. For she was one of those rare godly good souls who slipped into the earthly life from their playing in the heavenly meadows behind the Lord's back, and hence walk in the light free from that stigma which, according to the opinions of many Christians, every person carries as liege follower in the guilt and sins of his forebears. Such people are led only by the concern for the hardship of others, and know through their charity nothing but the quaking over the suffering of their neighbours. This and the fact that love subsists in the desire for fulfillment which our being is denied bound the quietest, purest girl so firmly to Andreas Sintlinger, who only seemed to be brewed together from unshackled bluster, that old Klim in Brederode, after the first shock over the fate of his beloved only child, began to unpick the wisdom of his own long life, and by and by to turn so that he prised out where the error lay for which he would be punished thus. While he was occupied with this matter in all sorts of inner hardship, and his daughter talked full of sorrow to her conscience, he attained nothing more than increasing her helplessness over the incomprehensible providence so that she felt insolubly shackled to a man who had passed by days before as a colourful, wild shock to her life. Secret meetings, before which she shook sobbing, and which then left her blissfully numb, bound her still faster to the subterranean storm of her forbidden love, the more so as Andreas had suddenly become the tenderest, most devoted man, and pulled her ever deeper into the rapture of a transfiguration which had come over him. Finally the resistance of old Klim slackened, and barely a year after he had seen Johanna bleaching in the meadow, Sintlinger led her as his wife to his homestead by Hemsterhus. The blaze had vanished from his look, his face no longer twitched with ungovernability. The newly weds sat like peaceful, happy children amongst the wedding party, who did not at all lose their astonishment that an unruly fellow had so quickly become such a measuredly amiable man. For even the distrustful did not notice any exaggerated sweetness in Andreas through which an only arduously suppressed wildness would most easily have betrayed itself. Yes, he had even sent an invitation over to the Brindeisener farmstead at Johanna's request, so as to offer a hand for bridging the cleft dividing the two families according to the wish of his beloved, and had not flared up either when the guests from the other estranged farm stayed away. For the grown daughter lay there in a dangerous illness, and Anton Brindeisener had not only sent a respectable wedding wreath, but also an apology in the words of which you could read the good will for laying aside the unnatural hostility. At the instigation of the bride, a basket was packed full of the best dishes, a bottle of wine also included, and sent over to Brindeisener so that he could take part in the wedding in this way with his own family. Andreas Sintlinger assented to all this in a good mood, and when it was reported to him after some time that his neighbour was standing on the other hill before his yard gate and holding a glass in his hand, he laughingly filled his own glass too, hurried out, shouted a cheers over and emptied his glass in one draught as the other farmer also replied festively with his wine.

A part of the wedding party had followed the groom, and accompanied the ceremony of fraternal drinking with loud, happy applause. Just then the evening sun also appeared out of the clouds and poured its reddish light over the beautiful picture as if heaven itself were confirming the good intentions of the long divided.

In the first night in which Johanna slept under Sintlinger's roof, a mad storm fell upon the farmstead so that the lime trees at the gate had to brace with all their might to stand still, but the clairvoyant from Hemsterhus, who wanted to see the nightly chase of the child about the farmstead, that timid, foolish listener to everything, crept about the walls in vain, and listened to the racket of the wind. The bell hung soundlessly in the tower and slept.

***

Now farmers never carry friendship home in cart loads, and with the Brindeiseners and Sintlingers it was also an especially peculiar case. With all good will, each just sat too deeply in inherited shadows which, a little surly, just played around every congenial gesture, every open-minded word, before it let out these good messengers to the other man. Life also turned far too apart in

areas of existence during this time of their goodwill. For
the illness pressed Brindeisener's daughter deeper and
deeper into the pillows, and secretly poured into every
medicine its creeping poison so that every remedy
turned into just as many deferments of suffering, and
the poor being suffered breathing like a hardship and
her heartbeat like a pain. Thus to the little Brindeisener
it felt almost overwhelming to send greetings affectionately over this black wall by which she was enclosed into
the light garden of delight through which the young
Sintlinger was strolling with his even younger wife.
Their farmstead now lay in constant sunlight, and if a
breathless, scourged industry had earlier shaken it deep
into the night with its racket, the liveliness now passed
with bright sounds into the day, looked peaceful at the
end of the day from windows reddened by evening, and
listened on starry nights to the silence which passed
along with it over the distant, great currents high in the
heavens.

The servants teased each other mockingly over the
transformation which they perceived by the change in
themselves, and when such a stab met a raw spot then
the master lapsed into the old Sintlinger rage as proof of
his indifference to the new spirit; but when the young
farmer's wife merely walked across the yard and turned
her kindly face to him, the flaring man did indeed continue grumbling, but as if in apology, and only over the
cord which had caught in the wheels, or at the horse
which frisked about when being harnessed, and he then
guided the wagon out the gate in calm attentiveness as if
he had been accustomed since childhood to biting off
every swearword with his teeth before it had passed
over his lips.

The farmer himself naturally plunged deepest into
the bright magic which Johanna had brought to his
farm. Just like on the first day when he had seen her in

the meadow by Brederode, her figure was surrounded by a shimmer. The rooms gleamed with hidden promises; his property seemed like a new estate to him, the entire district was transformed; its boundlessness had struck at his inner being. He was expecting something extraordinary which he did not comprehend, and something wonderful which he approached only through passionate guesses. When he heard his wife breathing next to him at night, that rising and falling soon went all through the house, became a surging with which the darkness outside rested over the world, yes, it seemed to him as if he were himself borne by it up and down to some mysterious place, and the next morning, he awoke with astonishment just to find himself in his own room. In the evenings, when he sat with Johanna before the yard gate on the little bench under the oak, and listened to the calm and pure stories of her childhood, he saw fairy tales playing around him, always rolling past as precious unobtainable things.

3

The most wondrous thing befell him one morning, however. He was mowing a meadow which extended to the end of his farm next to the forest which ran down a hill through a gentle dip and a good way yet up the other slope. The birds were singing so loudly that their song drowned out the gentle swishing of the tree tops; the exultation of the larks lay like a resounding cloud over the fields, and Andreas became so stormily addicted to the rhythm in which he drew his scythe through the dewy grass that it seemed to him as if it were swinging him over the earth. Suddenly the birds fell silent, the forest stood quiet as a leaf, something tore the scythe back from him; he started from the rapture, and stared in silence, holding his breath in horror. The next moment, he knew his wife was dying. Thinking this, tossing the scythe aside, and running in mad fear across the fields was all one motion. When he stormed into the living room, and saw his wife plying the butter churn quietly and happily, he seized her about the body, swung her through the air, and cheered and laughed so that the maid who was present withdrew from embarrassment.

But as such ebullience induces, it purchased the shoes in which it trotted from the letdown, and Andreas Sintlinger had barely set his Johanna down next to the butter churn when the world which he had just seen pitifully collapse in his thoughts at her loss stood leisurely as ever, revolved around the sun, and let the rivers run as if what had made him tremble in the turmoil of fear, this sunlit being, his Johanna, were no more than a fly which ran over his hand, and it occurred to him that he would have been just like someone who would have danced on the tip of an inflated paper bag thinking it to be a mountain. He sat for a while on the bench which ran along the wall, looked agitated, suspicious, full of the most painful bewilderment at his wife, and became paler and paler in his face, the deeper he sank into this despondency. But before his soul could be swamped by such swirling waters as far as the edge of his eyes, he abruptly sprang up, shook himself with laughter, and went through the doorway with a shrill whistle on his lips.

From now on, it occurred more often that the veil tore before Andreas's eyes. His wondrous expectations, which till then had seemed the most certain and natural of things to him, appeared at first doubtful to him, then touch-and-go, and finally sank like distantly lit clouds paler and paler, until they had vanished completely behind the horizon of his soul. But this hidden wilting away of an invisible, glorious harvest lasted more than a year, and Johanna felt it sometimes like a fleeting frost in the warmest sun, sometimes like a darkening in the midst of light, and often also saw it as a chalky brightness drawing through sleepless nights.

When he did not return from a market in the evening, as was his custom, but stayed away the following and next day, and his bed still stood empty on the third day, his wife knew that the mad whirl of the Sintlinger blood had shattered over her Andreas again. But she did not say it the way you tear the clothes from your body, she recognised it like a man who bangs a nail into the darkest wall of his twilit house so as to not mislay the most precious holy picture of his devotion in the coming darkness, but to have it always securely before his eyes. Hence when, eight days afterward on the Sunday morning, she heard a desolate male singing approaching from the village, she stepped before the yard gate, and looked down the path which wound past between the willows and oaks from Hemsterhus finally to the Sintlinger farmstead. The picture which presented to her the next moment was not a comforting one — a wagon full of shouting belchers tumbling in confusion with every jolt, and her Andreas on the front seat, with his head uncovered, with fluttering hair and restlessly cracking whip. He was driving like a satan. In the place where the entrance way to the farm turned away from the avenue of coppiced willows and oaks, the wagon tipped up, and the boozers tumbled and fell clumsily and untowardly over the sides into the ditch. The young farmer shoved the last man, who had held himself half up above, quickly into the others, and then whipped his horses laughing scornfully up the hill so that they stopped foaming before her with flying flanks. Sintlinger was still laughing, threw aside his whip and reins, fell into his wife's arms, tore himself away, ran through the gate, across the yard into the house so that Johanna was un-able to follow him, and only stood still once he was in the bedroom. There she met him finally, choking with shrill laughter. He shook with delight and cried con-stantly, "Wonderful! Wonderful!" But his face was pale, and tears were running over his cheeks. Then he sank onto his bed, and Johanna stroked his sticky temples, soothed his forehead with her cool hands, and wiped away with a cloth the spit which the stormy, raw rattle of his breath drove out his mouth.

She undressed him then during his sleep so carefully that he did not awake, but only reached out a few times with dithering hands as if begging for and thanking the gentle goodness which he felt through the haze of his drunkenness. Then she placed his work clothes on the chair next to his bed so that on awakening he would sense the relapse into his wastefulness not as reality, but as a bad dream and not suffer any harm from the at-tempt to stray from the path through pure days. But no precaution of the dear soul helped at all. After light, confident weeks, he vanished again unexpectedly into the abyss which he carried around in himself, and dur-ing the nights, Johanna lay lonely and brooding in her bed, looked at the reflection of the fire from the stove scurrying along the wall in all sorts of fragmented vis-ions, struggled often in tears against deep despondency, and succumbed not infrequently to the thoughts that the storm which had tormented the yard's lime trees to breaking on her wedding night had not been without significance. Nevertheless all that only ran like a black cloud through her soul, and she did not begin at all at-tempting a bitter word or a disapproving look when her husband stumbled into the room slurring and with glazed eyes. At most, her hands trembled imperceptibly when she took his stick and cap from him and hung them by the coat stand next to the tall grandfather clock. "Still no good weather, Andreas?" she then asked, smiling and stroked the dislodged man's hair from his face so that the sympathetic caress startled him like a slap and drove him into some corner where, after he had slept off the intoxication, his wife found him in painful, silent brooding, his elbows propped on his knees, his head hanging down between his hunched shoulders. Then she sat silently for a while next to him, and pondered over how to help the bowed man. But whenever she strained to find something properly refreshing and strong for his benefit, the same thing always occurred to her simple childlike soul. She loosened his clenched hands, lifted his face up to herself, kissed him on the forehead, and said, "Do not despair, Andreas! You will succeed one day!" After that she shoved her arm under his, and led the confusedly smiling man again into the white light of her life.

And yet, new nights always came in which she had to sit alone under the lime tree before the yard gate as her husband went out on his whirling boat into the maelstrom which she knew through nothing else but the blackness which rose in her when she thought of it. The starry nights were often. The moon lay battered in a corner behind the world or hung eclipsed in the sky. Nothing had a shadow. The black outlines of things, that distorted repetition of their being through which they first become apprehensible to our eyes and our souls were dissolved in a uniform darkness in which they quivered as though torn, as if all life were being whirled about aimlessly. She heard the quietly fluttering, timorous sleep of the willows down on the boundary path, the cows rattling the chains and now and then emitting a longing, dull sound; the striking of the hours by the tower clock in the village fading away in the air. All that hounded her from her seat sometimes, and drove her for a bit from the farmstead into the fields so that noth-ing lay around her other than the night and nothing over her but the stars which had quivered, twitched, and fevered since eternity in red, green, and deathly pale light. "Why all that? Why?" the young wife then asked, went back to her little bench, pondered for a long time, struggling, and at last threw herself against the trunk of the lime tree, clasping it like a drunkard because her kind heart was sore, but could not accuse though. On such nights, she dreaded one thing with a strange fear, that on top of all that the little bell in the tower might begin to toll, and she fled to her bed, and drew the cov-ers up to her ears so that she heard nothing.

But once even that was not spared her. Late in the night, she passed from the flight to sleep into awaking. To start with she saw nothing. But when she had sent her eyes for a while insistently into the darkness next to her bed, her husband was standing before her. About his figure it flowed as if smouldering, like the hazy glow which plays from rotting wood. He has that from the light of the stars, Johanna thought, still dreamily con-fused, and felt a seething current migrate from him to her. In a whirl, mixed up of fear and happiness, dread and merciful kindness, she drew him in to herself with shaking arms, and the two melted into each other in ar-dent, dark waves like none they had ever been carried by. At this moment, she touched that mysterious hand at whose wave a new life sinks into the bodies of wo-men, and as she then lay, the whirl from which she had been led by the eyeless became weaker and ever weaker, and sounded in the end high and gentle like little bell chimes in boundless space. When Johanna heard that, she thought the sounds were stirring from the little tower on the roof, sprang from her bed to the window, brought her hands down, and stared through silent tears for a long time out into the darkness in which the day was gradually emerging on the distant horizon as if with the light of extinguished eyes. The coolness finally cleared her flying thoughts. She pulled herself together, and listened tensely for the high tinkling which had just then sounded to her; but she heard only the lime trees quietly rustling against the morning. Nothing else, and what passed over her seemed to her like the indistinct, warm whirl of a dream. Ashamed over her superstitious shock, she sought out her bed again, and smiled too that it had all just been an illusion. The deep sleep of morning erased it completely, and on awaking, the events of the night only lay as lustful exhaustion in the young farmer's wife.

After this transformation had taken place with her, Johanna lost the darknesses of sorrow entirely. Her blue eyes took on a deepened brilliance and always passed with a distracted look into the endless distance, without any heartache, full of rapturous expectation. The shimmer which had seemed extinguished for many a dark week flourished more fully around her. Her kind-heartedness had usually been almost of unreal tenderness. Now this predominant side of her being moved ever further into the maternal sun of summer. And Andreas was often seized by timidity and hesitation at the sight of his transformed wife, lit by a distant glow like in the time of their first love. Then he did not spring up as usual in the midst of loading the fodder, did not leave the plough standing halfway down the furrows so as to hurry abruptly out onto his path of frenzy. He stole secretly like a thief to the din of bottomless paths. He went as it were on tip toes through the mire. A secret fear of which he never spoke, which he never confessed, also hindered him from entering his house as usual in full drunkenness, and if it were not otherwise possible, he first slept off his intoxication in a hidden grove, or on a secluded slope, and then greeted his wife affectionately and cheerfully as if he were returning from a happily concluded business. Johanna never gave him the slightest taste of the sadness which this creeping voracity of his caused her. She drew more and more into the shimmer of her expectancy, in which she sat until late in the night as though in the light of rapture, sewed almost endlessly, and sang quiet songs of her childhood.

***

On a spring evening, already in the depths of the twilight, when the last sparks of light had sunk dully into darkness from the tip of Hemsterhus's church steeple, the old Brindeisener farmer's wife, their grown daughter, the one who had had to struggle with a difficult illness on the Sintlinger's wedding day, and little Peter, a four year old boy, the very late straggler of the Brindeisener marriage, were standing by the window in the living room of the Brindeisener farmstead and watching silently as the evening slowly crept up the hills from the valleys. The willows and oaks already stood grey and misshapen like forgotten hay down on the boundary path. The road smouldered wanly, and seemed to sway in the uncertain light like a grey ribbon. The Sintlinger farmstead soon lay in darkness too. Just then the farmer's wife intended to conclude this short pause of rest and contemplation and, already half turned to go, was placing her large hand caressingly on little Peter's pale blond head, when a light flared up over in the other estranged farmstead, expired, barely lit, twitched again, and died away again. "That is a clean lighter", Mrs Brindeisener said with a smile. "If the matchsticks must be ruined by skimping, then you can throw them straight away. Then you save yourself the trouble, and it remains even better dark." But finally the light flared securely, but not to stand calmly in one place. It began to drift. Sometimes it flickered at one window, sometimes at another, now it appeared deeper in the room, ran by an entire row of windows, and then seemed to turn in circles. "The Sintlingers are funny people", the daughter said, for she thought someone was dancing with the candle through the room. The mother made no other answer, instead opening the window, and leaning out listening. "Be completely quiet please", she said hastily. A wagon was heard hurriedly rattling, the clatter of horses' hooves. Then the yard gate flew open with a crack, and a vehicle plunged madly down the steep hill, careered onto the road to Hemsterhus, and vanished like a whirling shadow.

The farmer's wife returned hesitantly, with a strange stiffness, from the window, nodded distressingly, and then sat down in a chair as if her knees had weakened, and said with a dark voice after a short, dazed pondering, more to herself, "There is something not right over there! — Well now — really —." And as she looked out again, something like a red dress whirled down the Sintlinger hill, sprang across the road, and panted across the fields to the Brindeisener farmstead. "It is a woman from over there", the farmer's wife said, and rose. At the door to the living room, she met the maid who reported breathlessly and shaking with tears that her lady was in labour. Sintlinger had been out of his mind, hitting the wall trembling, and fleeing the farmstead as if chased from here to eternity, and the lady was asking her to help her in her need. Mrs Brindeisener threw a shawl over her head wordlessly and without hesitation, and followed the hurriedly departing servant.

Her daughter, a tall built, pale being, and little Peter remained at the open window, and they listened out apprehensively into the night. Then it seemed not long afterwards to the boy as if someone were whistling high and fearfully in the distance, and he asked his sister fearfully what it was. But she shut the window, trem-bling, and began crying softly.

Towards morning, Andreas, driven from there by pity and love, dared to return home. He cautiously led his horse up the hill; he opened and shut the gate as noiselessly as he could. But a sort of agitation governed him still so that he dared not ask the old labourer hurry-ing past about how his wife was faring. He only took the lantern from his hand and illuminated his face. Then he recognised from the impish, somewhat mocking grin of the servant the fortunate outcome of the danger, threw the lantern down on the ground with delight so that the light was extinguished amidst clattering glass shards, and crept cautiously into the house. The darkness of the hall and living room surged round him with the storm of his mood, and he constantly said jubilantly to him-self, "A Sintlinger! A Sintlinger!" Thus he arrived in the bedroom which was filled by the light from the pendant lamp as if by exhausted trembling. The midwife rose from her chair in the darkness where she had been sleeping, and indicated to him by hasty gestures to be-have calmly, since the young mother lay asleep. For she had misinterpreted the farmer's uncertain poise and the large, bright eyes in his pale face, stepped noiselessly up to him, and whispered in his ear that everything had been happily overcome, if not also easily. It goes with a girl just like with a boy. The main thing was that everything was alright, and she congratulated him on becoming a father for the first time. Now he understood why old Zenker, the labourer, had smiled so mockingly. A gentle disappointment arose in him. He nodded si-lently to the midwife, and hung his cap on the back of a chair. Then he stood there in aching indecisiveness, and did not know whether he should leave or stay there. It occurred to him that he had driven about all night, up and down hills, through villages, past forests, along the desolate main road, into stony defiles, and all that for the sake of a girl. But through the shadows of his bitterness, he saw the pained, pale face of his beautiful wife, heard her painful whimpering, and was overcome by merciful love. He stepped to her bed, and looked at the sunken features of the exhausted woman; but he was incapable of throwing a glance at the being which lay next to her. Johanna was not asleep though. She was watching her husband from under her lids, was surely happy that the haze of taverns did not lie about him, sucked in the scent which he had brought in with him of forests and fields yearningly, and was shaken to the core by his one-sided tenderness which met her amplified, helpless sensitivity like a reproach. Large tears swelled quietly through her eyelashes, and rolled down her cheeks. Then she stretched her hand out to him, and said imploringly, "Andreas, don't be cross at our child, I could not help it." Then his unsettled, boundless heart melted entirely. Without consideration for the midwife, he knelt next to the bed, kissed his wife's bloodless lips again and again, assured her of his delight, and tried to disperse her suspicions through caresses. He also had the child brought over, and pressed a timid kiss on the forehead of the unbelievably small, red stained being. But when he was alone in the room where his bed had been set up, he could not bring himself to light a candle, undress, and get into bed. He moved his chair to the window, and stared into the darkness without finding a anchorage in the whirl of his conflicted soul. Deep in the morning, the maid who was to wake him found him collapsed on the window sill, fast asleep.

4

It stayed that way for months, it may perhaps have been a year. Andreas moved hand in hand through the days in tender love with his wife, and secretly carried, without denying it, but also without stressing it, that joylessness in himself which every disappointing fulfillment of our soul leaves behind as an inheritance, even when we have overcome it. He was too clever, conscious too little in his depths of the dull narrowness of the rural existence, to have tolerated forever in himself the aggrieved vanity of having become the father of a girl and not a boy as being the explicit reason for his trepidation and unease. And yet he did not establish any relationship with his child, named Helene according to the will of the mother, but that of compelled playfulness, trifling tendernesses, and superficial caresses. He found himself in the position of a man who in the storms of a wild, long winter longs for the full release of its pent up powers, and is then betrayed in his hopes by a poor spring.

He felt his madness, which had assaulted him again in the marriage, more and more distinctly as the impatience of a man who beats on a wall so that it will open up a broad gate to incomprehensible enlightenment. Now it had been shut, and nothing other than the delicate, blond child had been gifted to him, the child who floated in a world in which it was not worth the effort to enter. Perhaps he just suffered an incapacity for quiet, paternal feelings next to this intemperance of his being. But it is in vain to want to ladle out a human soul to the last drops. Enough that the faith in the legitimation of his previous lifestyle was so shocked that his dissipations also bored him to the point that his exuberance became empty habit and his colourful jokes grimaces. Thus he drove himself ill-temperedly, dimly through the paths of his old life; no, also alone, quite alone; only a great, incomprehensible longing as his companion.

Yes, alone, for love is too impersonal a thing, too much an all encompassing feeling for it to be able to wrest the soul of worldly loneliness out from the storms of embraces into the sand dunes of our everyday life. Hardly does the fire in our eyes burn weaker again than the being which our love refers to is unreachable, already transported again into the strangeness of its own life. And if Andreas had always looked at his wife outdoors, wandering as it were far from his world, now, since she had been walking with the child on her arm through those quiet raptures, she was further from him than usual. Then the undivided commonalities of their work and worries were no help, all tendernesses were in vain. When he opened his arms and released her, she glided away from him according to the rules of an un-fathomable magic. When, striding across the farm, he heard Johanna talking intimately with the little one, her voice sounded to him as if from another life. When he watched from the bench in the evening, sitting resting, as she walked through the living room, cradling the child on her arm, he would have liked to have lifted his hand to brush the white shroud from the air which both veiled and beautified her. At the same time, he noticed that his wife was often seized by happiness at being a mother, almost to the point of anguish. Then she finally had to cover with her hand the girl's face which she had looked at penetratingly, no imploringly, and go outside sobbing, as if it exceeded her powers to watch so much loveliness for a long time. Yes, sometimes it even seemed to him as if his wife were depriving him of his child. Then he would creep to the cradle when Johanna was overseeing the milking in the stalls or busy elsewhere, send the nursemaid out on some pretext, and immerse himself in looking at the child so as to at least fathom something of the miracle which gripped his wife so deeply in her soul. But the little being lay still and white on the cushions, the little cheeks with a breath of red over them, silken locks playing about her forehead, and directing her eyes above herself motionlessly and wide open with a rapturous attention in her face. Hardly a twitch went through her eyelids when he stepped up to the cradle or stirred. None of the fervour of a glance twitched in the blue of her eyes, over which an amber yellow shimmer lay like the reflection of invisible, golden blossoming bushes. These eyes were deep, clear, and remote, bright to their depths like the water of still ponds on the heath which are nothing but mirrors of light. But as soon as he spoke to the child, it was startled by the sound of his voice as though pained, beat with its little hands as if fending him away, and began to scream. Then he crept away, and was troubled in his solitary labour with imagining those rare, strange eyes of his child, but he achieved nothing other than arriving at a feeling of distant, mysterious emotion.

One evening he stepped into the hallway and heard Johanna's voice talking to the child again. He noise-lessly opened the door, and stepped into the living room which was empty, and the last light of the day lay aslant and grey within. His wife stood bent raptly over the cradle. She was passing her hand closer and closer through the air over little Helene's face, as if she were teasing the child with the breath of the motion, and each time she called its name, but not caressingly, not in rapt composure, no, with an insistent achingly helpless voice, like that you woo someone with who wanders on unreachably distant hills. And a grey clutching, yes even something like fear came over Andreas so that he asked apprehensively, "What are you doing, Johanna?" Then his wife spun around in shock, and he saw that tears were streaming down her face. But she pulled herself together quickly, passed her apron over her eyes, and answered, sighing as if emerging from the forgetfulness of her happiness, "Oh, Andreas, I am playing with the child. She is so beautiful, so beautiful!" Then she grasped his hand, and drew him out of the room and into the yard. There she stood, and spoke of the sky, the twilit hills which lay around them, of Hemsterhus, and of her childhood home. She talked quickly, precipitately, and coldly, and he sensed how she was shaking all over.

Something secret which concerned him and the child was besetting her soul. But Andreas had in the years of his coexistence with his wife acquired so much of the gentle ways of her being that he desisted from some futile urging to learn the reason for her great agitation, slung his right arm around her shoulders, and led her back on a detour behind the barn, through the flower garden to the living room. Johanna thanked him for his chivalrous restraint by a quiet, warm nestling against him, and her words took on their calm undertone again. But at the door behind which the child lay, she released herself from his embrace in a way which bid him not to enter. As if she were putting him off with the words, 'let it be', she squeezed his hand, and glided into the room, and Sintlinger stepped back, and roamed about for a long time in the stalls, through the sheds and lofts. His thinking in the meantime seesawed fervently in the half dark which also lay about his inner being, and laboured to comprehend the secrets by which women are transformed by motherhood. And yet he had to pause again and again to spring back to himself from these general considerations as if from poetic subterfuges, and ask, "Why does she not take me with her to her child? Why?" Finally he said that to himself in the granary. He was standing next to the great pile of grain, and stirring into it with the tip of his boot, meditating. Then he went, raised up the dormer window, and bound it fast so that the wind skimmed over the grain; for a warm, musty, stuffy air prevailed. As he came to the end of this work, before going, he stepped once more to that window from which you could look out over the broad stream of hills to far beyond Hemsterhus. But the waves of earth rolling lower and lower already lay deep in the evening shadows so that they looked like greyish black, indistinctly separated clouds lying motionless on the earth. The same clouds stood in the sky silently and dissolved like their mirror image. In between hung thick, ash coloured twilight as far as the horizon where the darkness of above and below butted together. There, but so far away that it looked as if it were already on the other side of the world, the last light of day was quivering, a tiny, pale blue spot. Like the eyes of my child, the young farmer thought, oblivious to his surroundings, and was startled by it as strangely as if he were to blame for it all, for the twofold darkness and the powerless, dull sparks of light in it. When he looked up, it too had been extinguished, and the darkness had transformed into night.

Since that evening, he had not endeavoured anymore to creep alone to the cradle of his child, and when the child started crying, not so wrenchingly as is the way of children, no, with almost melodic wavering of its silvery little voice, more a singing of distress than a crying, and the little hands of the girl floundered about her little head, then Andreas's face always became a tad paler, and finally he had to go out. How often during this time did Johanna also feel his hand fumbling over her face, and when she asked him what was there, he turned with a relieved sigh to his dream side again and answered, "Oh, it is okay there." Or she heard him springing from his sleep as if plunging out a window, searching for the keys to all the doors and the pegs for all the windows, and then crawling under the covers again amidst irritated murmuring about disturbances. At threshing time, he often had the horses driven so that the machine ate up the grain howling and the thresher went like a furious drum roll. But he leant on the barn wall and, with pale face, devoured the racket of the feverishly shaken machine with the gleam of a seeming voracity in his eye.

It was said that this state Sintlinger was in lasted three weeks, and the people of simple villages observe well. According to the patrons at the Hemsterhus tavern, the peculiar behaviour of the young farmer stopped, and on the Sintlinger farm, that mysterious life began which brought the property and its owners to such high renown.

In that decisive night, Andreas had, half by despair and half tempted by contrariness, been led away once more down the hill, and sat in the village's single inn amidst jovial company. At first jolly teasing went the rounds, they delighted over the fools of the district, told droll stories, and drew the bolt on many a hidden foolishness, and Sintlinger behaved more wildly than usual, the checkerboard of his witty ideas, fitting malices, and funny anecdotes did not stand still, and next to him, two men in particular excelled in sputtering futility, the fat miller from Querhoven, more a barrel than a man, with a misshapen head and a cart load of blazing red hair on it, and the Royal Arenberg forester, a correct, infinitely tall, noisy beanpole. And after some hours, the entire party had fallen into the loud, empty din of drunkenness. But the more rashly the others dipped their voices deeper and deeper into the fervour of intoxication, the more distant Andreas became, the cooler, paler and more taciturn. The landlord said a glass of schnaps was at fault. A Hemsterhus small farmer, a tolerated hanger-on, so as to place himself in the favour of the powers amongst his drinking companions, had had a round of juniper brandy brought out, that watery clear schnaps which is so strong it turns to burning desire halfway down the throat. Weary of beer, everyone greeted the event with a loud cheer, and the tall forester rose to hold an amusing eulogy for the drink. But whilst the others, hands on glasses, all rewarded the witty ideas of the toast maker in advance with laughter, and impatiently convened for what was to come, to inter the contribution behind their tongues; Sintlinger was staring with growing horror at the small, shiny mirror of the schnaps which, turning yellow from the hazy light of the ceiling lamp, lay in the glass, and trembled constantly amidst the vibrations of the table. The young farmer's eyes had become absent; he was silent, and did not stir. Even when the others sprang up at the end of the address, and tilted the schnaps down their throats amidst a roar, Sintlinger sat motionless with bowed head, and when they finally intruded on him mockingly, he rose noiselessly, and looked at the circle, one after the other, wordlessly with such an expression of aggrieved astonishment in his pale face that everyone was silenced by its weightiness. Those sitting next to him rose at his wave as though under a spell. Andreas tilted his head in farewell, and went out silently.

At home he encountered his wife still awake. She was kneeling by the cradle in the glow of a little lamp, her arms thrown over the little bed, her face pressed in the pillows. When he entered quietly, she lifted her head exhaustedly, and surveyed her husband in an insistent, aching manner. He hung his cap on a hook, and embraced his wife with a long look. And as he thus stood and watched, Johanna, the cradle with the child, and that entire corner of the room was bathed in a blissful light. He walked into it as though on a bridge which spanned high over dark air. When he arrived at the cradle, his wife rose, took the girl from the cradle, and placed her in his arms, and Andreas spoke with such a soft voice to the child that it opened its sightless eyes and, for the first time, reached smiling for his face.

"How do you know that our child is blind?" Johanna asked suddenly, and lowered her eyes at the same time. Sintlinger passed his hand over her hair, and embraced her trembling in his arms.

When Johanna considered the wondrously poignant, though curt manner with which her husband had taken in the knowledge of their child's fate, she was shocked. For she, overlooking it so much in the vagaries of his fluctuating will, and doing justice to the childlike nature of his being through her angelic goodness, knew nothing of the emergencies and exaggerations through which he was able to remain at all alive. In the certain air of farmer's days, he suffered pain like a suffocating man. He was like a wanderer who only believes in progressing through constantly jumping into abysses. His debauched raging, his berserker-like industry, the frenzies of his abrupt love, all had been such abysses in which he had plunged in the belief that he would emerge again to a life on a peak, high and distant, which contained not a trace anymore of the accustomed forms of his past. And he always awoke from his whirl to the accustomed, idle gait of his occupation, which he pursued with the dogged fury of his heart until the grey air almost choked him again. The life of his child, however, about which he had drawn hidden circles helplessly for months, disgusted by the bleakness of his vices, overpowered by the eternally present sweetness of his marriage, sparkling unbelievably, allured into darkness by intuitions, depressed by incomprehensible emotion, incited anew by the strange conduct of his wife; all this agonising twilight through which he had waveringly gone had put his existence under such subterranean tension that the mysterious, lightning-like knowledge of the cruel miracle in which his child had been born had the effect of a bombshell. It had instantly flung him through the darkness in a high arc into the incomprehensible light which went out from the sightless eyes of his child. When he fell to earth again, he no longer found himself in his accustomed life, but as if on an unknown island in the middle of the ocean. Thus everything had also suddenly changed within him.

In the early morning, even before his wife awoke, the thin, wavering little voice of Helene rang out, delicate as the sound of the morning's first bird. Then Andreas sprang out of bed with a tentative leap as if he had waited all night for this cry, hurried to the small bed, and bent over it with stormy devotion so that a fright passed over the child's face. It's little hands went apart and its eyes closed. But as soon as Sintlinger let his breath brush caressingly and soft over the little one's cheeks, the eyelids opened again. Her eyes blossomed into still clarity, and stood motionless like listening mirrors. There was the seeing of listening in her inwardly turned sight, such as if the world did not spread out externally before them but everything passed through the depths of their interior. And when he spoke, the fire of seeing did not awake in them, no happy twitch of understanding, none of the fluctuating clouds of light came and went through the firmament of the iris. On their surface, a radiance awoke of such blessed beauty that it was as if the shimmer which emanates according to the pious from the gates of heaven was poured into their depths. No, this, his child was not blind, she was seeing in a different, more mysterious way than the common man. We look with the help of things into the world, in these eyes shimmered clearly the light which we others guess at arduously and darkly through the forms of existence. The longer Andreas sank into them, the more he was shackled by them. They carried him away into another world, and in the end, he could not bear looking into them anymore. What he had not understood about Johanna happened to him — he had to cover them with his hand. Then it troubled him no more in the living room and in the yard. Noiseless and with flying hands, he clothed himself, and took himself far out into the fields.

When, after awakening, his wife found the bed next to her empty and almost cold, she believed no less than that Andreas had been torn from the bed before the outbreak of day by the child's misfortune, and had been driven out of the house on a new wandering from tavern to tavern.

Thus the day moved on up to midday. Then she resolved finally to take the old labourer into her confidence. He reassured her with a mocking smile, and suggested that it was not bad, as from the window where he was standing and getting dressed, he had seen the farmer go down the hill early in the morning in the direction of the forest and vanish into the fields. Perhaps, as he added smirking, the impulse had come over him again, and then nothing worse would result. His loyalty and his natural tact hindered the man from asking the reason for the fuss which had come over his master. He slapped his cap jovially on his knee so that a thick cloud of dust burst out, and started off on the search without objection. He had gone across the five fields which ran the length of the Brindeisener boundary, and had reached the last wave of ground, the high butte, from which he could look over the large, depressed meadow which stretched beside the forest, intersected only by the way to Hemsterhus. There he noticed a man in the autumn's short grass, not all too distant from the edge of the forest. He lay stretched out and, with his upper body propped up on his elbows, was looking rigidly and motionlessly up into the pale blue

sky in which a few high little white clouds were constantly dwindling away dreamily and forming together
again. Cautiously, always keeping the man in sight, he
climbed down the gentle slope to the Hemsterhus way
which climbed the hill here and passed through the
forest towards the Rhine. "Hey there!" he finally
shouted to the unknown man, and waved in a friendly
way with his cap. The cry hit the recumbent man like a
kick, rolled him up, and then threw him in a few fleeing
leaps through the bushes into the forest from which he
did not surface again. The labourer rummaged about
amongst the trees for probably an hour, peered about
keenly and, whenever he heard a suspicious sound anywhere, called out the farmer's name. But when in
returning he had strode across the Hemsterhus way
again, and turned around on the high butte, he saw the
unknown man lying in the same position in the grass
and staring raptly at the sky as if he had not stirred from
the spot, but had remained there all along, made invisible, throughout this foolish ado. Now it seemed to him
as if the strange man was really none other than Sintlinger, but an inexplicable shyness, almost a reverent
shiver, held him back from setting off once more with
loud cries towards him. Arriving home, he remained silent, even towards the farmer's wife, about the
experience, spoke only of his futile roaming about, and
toddled away from Johanna to his work with a murmur
which had a note of solace and apology. The poor woman concluded the day now sorrowfully, and made an
honest effort to deal once more with the irreversibility
of her fate without cumbering the figure of Andreas with
complaints or reproaches. But when she finally lay in
bed, she thought she heard weakly and dully in the far
distance the unpitying thuds of a weaving loom. With
each of these humming, dissolving sounds, the darkness
around her seemed to become blacker and thicker. In

her anxiety, she groped for the cradle, rocked it carefully, and began singing a lullaby quite high and soft. At the same time, she constantly thought, my child is blind, my child is blind, and could not restrain her tears anymore.

The last note of the song was still hovering between her trembling lips like the stem of a pale flower which they were about to let fall, when she heard her husband returning home. If it had not been listening to her heart, her ear would not have divined it. The door moved so gently, long strides swept so evenly, almost sparingly down the hall. Now he entered the living room, and walked quietly to its middle. There he stopped. She heard him breath a few times loudly and stormily like the way it besets someone before an important undertaking. Although Johanna now knew that he was not drunk, her heart suddenly went like a falling leaf before the deeper worry that open fury was ruling over her husband. And really. Already the door was opened soundlessly, paused lurking, and before the opening which thrust up to her as a dark abyss out of the night, she slowly saw the pale face of her husband emerge and pause a while, scenting before the spring. She rose up horrified, and had to prop up her weary body with stiffened arms. Then, she did not know how, Sintlinger was lying on her breast, and had tied his arms like a cord around her ,and was breathing stiflingly and seethingly hot on her neck. He spoke haltingly and endlessly, but she did not understand any of the rapturous whirl by which she was pulled up and carried away from her despondency by his words. At once he loosened his arms, laid his wife carefully in the bed, undressed silently, and lay down. Although Johanna did not look at him, she sensed though that he was lying on his back, and staring wide-eyed into the night. After a long time, he said shakily and almost inaudibly, "I do not have a child, I have an angel." Then he turned around, and fell asleep.

5

From now on they both behaved no differently than if they had been seized by a deep current and been carried far from their old life into a new existence. Sint-linger especially walked about as if lit up by a difficult blessing. He guarded the secret which was spun around his child as if he were worried that the magic of its life could be disturbed by the knowledge and words of men. The district learnt nothing of little Helene's condition other than the great clemency which took possession of Sintlinger after this foreordination, the cheerful serious-ness of his industry, and the almost timid tenderness with which he embraced his wife. He moved in the laws of the new earth which the fate of his child had shoved around his feet, as if next to his steps never a stalk of ryegrass nor a stem of goatsbeard had grown, but in-stead as if even those stones which he stumbled over had sung a comforting song. All sorts of rumours brewed in the village, which, sometimes with malice, sometimes with schadenfreude, groped about for the reason by which his life had been lifted from the old ef-fervescent angling. There was talk of a bloody argument in which he had been torn from his drunkenness; of an offence against a delicate girl; of an extortionate busi-ness whose baleful results he had buried right before the prison door under a sack full of gold, and they even

claimed to know about marital strife and a nocturnal escape by the appalled wife.

Sintlinger let this squalid cloud of suspicion calmly
play about his farmstead, walked confidently and full of
amicable dignity about his business, and devoted himself to all the traits of his new existence. Old, frail
people, and children who carried loads too heavy for
them were invited from the road onto his wagon, and
were even carried, often enough on a detour, up to the
doors of their houses.

Even the little bell listener from Hemsterhus, that
simple-minded man who had contributed so much to
damage the Sintlingers' reputation through his talkativeness over unearthly tales which he entertained, was
shown kindness without a shadow of forbearance. Yes,
when, on a rainy autumn day, the half-witted man, in
ragged clothing, freezing from a long begging walk on
groundless paths, knocked wearily on the yard gate,
Sintlinger did not turn him away, but shoved the old labourer roughly to the side who was about to dispatch
the irritating fool with a powerful kick down the hill. He
affectionately drew the fearfully groaning man into the
house, stuffed a solid, warm meal into his body, and
also had an old suit and all sorts of underclothes tied up
into a large bundle for him. No beggar, and be they even
notorious drinkers or professional sun lovers, went un-
furnished from the farm, no unfortunate man remained
without aid. And if Sintlinger also often overshot the
goal in his manner of doing good, he was also torn away
by his impassioned being which just drove every action
so easily into immoderation. But no trace of morbid
sentimentality, unhealthy delight, or pious sanctimony
clung to him. Manifestly nothing guided him but the
emotion of a man who has gotten serious about his
goodness. His wife, however, did not need to change at
all. She simply went as always on distant, bright paths

through life, certainly sometimes with a light cloud about her forehead, but calmly and steadily, soberly and gently. And when her husband returned home from a work of charity too quickly, so that his fire dabbed his face from within with almost hectically red stains, then she brushed his hair up over his forehead like in the days of his derailment through intoxication, as if she were saying like then, 'let it be, Andreas, you will succeed still,' and smiled encouragingly and reassuringly at his exuberance again being on the straight and narrow.

It was also in that period that someone named the Sintlinger farmstead on the hill the blessed farm. This name was probably originally supplied by the mocking of a disapproving soul, and hence to start with had only a savoury flavour in people's mouths, but it slowly took on earnestness and prudence, especially when it was learnt why the farmstead's life had turned to such earnest beauty. For since the blind girl had taken to her feet, the farmer and his wife had not been able to keep secret her condition anymore. Now everyone became aware that the poor child wavered about, locked in deep night. The hearts of the entire district were startled at this news, and all the parents no longer carelessly presumed the health of their children as a necessity, but saw it as undeservedly endowed. Only the unworthy possessed the vile audacity to see in the child's fate the punishment for the many aberrations of the family line and for the mad urges of Andreas Sintlinger. Most were seized by the strange force with which the two bore the misfortune and wisely took advantage of it. It followed by itself that among many moved by it, enough busybodies were found who were pressed to carry unbidden help and advice to the blessed farm. And as is the way of people, especially country people, they did not fall on the obvious ideas of advising the Sintlinger couple of the skill of a doctor, but assailed them with the offering of all sorts of secret remedies. The white membrane which sat under the hard shell of the goshawk's egg would certainly open the girl's sight to the light because this bird was the only one which could dwell so close to the sun for its entire life without being blinded. Clever women approached with many herbs, spoke ancient prayers over the child, conjured the evil amidst strange gestures, and dispelled it into the waning moon, the whirlwind, or the flowing water so that it would not find its way back again. Even a pastor from a poor village on a heath a long way off sent a little bottle of his never-failing eye healing water. Many a one was driven to the Sintlinger's farmstead by sheer curiosity. These overeager people washed in a flood of foolish talk through the living rooms, gawked at everything with sharp eyes, and did not go away from the place until they had warmed themselves up well from the lady of the house's coffee-pot. To start with, the honest concern of so many worthy people did the father and mother well in their souls. They enjoyed with secret pride the astonishment of strangers over the angelically pure face of Helene, over the puzzle of the clear and yet engaged eyes, and the bright bell-like voice of the child, which seemed to resound from further away than her chest. Of their silent belief in a possibly higher calling through the miracle which had happened to their child, they said nothing. With due thanks, they accepted all remedies and then secretly placed the mixtures unused to the side. But when the swarm of sympathetic corner sitters streamed over the threshold, they hid the child and dispatched the empty tongue wigglers

But the old man's fury and his question, which had hit his chest like a blow, did not plunge Sintlinger deeper into inextricable doubt and unease. Not long after the old man's departure, he stepped into the living room, took the child from his wife's arms, swung it up high in the light of the window, and looked up into its face for a long time. With a hearty kiss, he then placed Helene on the floor, and watched her as she went with delicately wavering, little steps to Johanna's hand.

"What?" he cried suddenly in his old way, broken and loud. "What? Should I be outraged that the child is as she is? If it has no meaning, why did God give her to me thus? A nice way of believing and stony eyes! No? Then in the end, everything which has occurred to me at night would also be just such a gleaming, cobwebbed accident. No, no!" He smacked his fist protestingly against his chest with a blow, and went to his work, laughing derisively.

He remained in this belief, even when Pastor Ardelt of Hemsterhus, probably pushed by old Klim, appeared at the blessed farm on the pretext of interesting Sintlinger in a contribution for the painting of the little old church. Andreas and his wife sat and listened attentively to the moving words with which the priest described the many hidden defects of the house of God. The farmer even accepted the indirect reproaches of unchurchliness indifferently, and just drummed his fingers gently on the table top in answer. But when the Pastor in closing adroitly turned to the misfortune which had come over the couple, and soon lapsed into the role of penitential sermoniser, Sintlinger tore his hand from the table. His eyes flared up. Stiff and pale of face, he leant forward as if he wanted to make some retort, but took a hold of himself, stood up smiling, and carried the Pastor's hat and stick into the hall. Then a maid appeared, and reported that the spiritual lord's things were already outside. On the next day, however, Sintlinger sent a respectable donation to the parsonage. Andreas tolerated nobody's breath, the beliefs of no one other than his wife, and those only at a certain distance, on the path which he had himself taken to his astonishment.

Not long afterwards, his feet were taken out from under him.

One evening he came home from the fields with a cart load of green fodder and heard the maids speaking about him across the yard and saying that the Hemsterhus fool had been there. He had crept into the living room to the sleeping child, pulled a red rag from his pocket, and torn it up into small strips over the child amidst tears and imprecations. A maid had seen the incident through the open window from the garden, but not dared to intervene for fear of the weird man. When the farmer's wife appeared in the room, she had found the bell listener leaning in a corner, his face contorted by grievous pain, his eyes riveted on the child. At her cry it had been as if he were slowly emerging from a dream. But hardly had he recognised the farmer's wife than his crying and lamenting began anew. Only through kind persuasion had they succeeded in getting him out of the house, and now he sat down on the boundary path, and continued incessantly to bury and scrape out the red scraps.

Sintlinger threw the horse's reins over its back, went down under the lime tree by the yard gate, and immediately caught sight of the bell listener. The man was cowering, hunched up in the ditch, and still burrowing in the ground, more like a grey animal, a giant mole.

The farmer saw precisely the sinews of the long, thin neck, and in the deep groove between them the shock of hair flowed in a scraggly tail down to his coat collar — perhaps down his entire back, the farmer pondered, and the fellow is no man at all. Thus something like a horror assaulted Sintlinger after all the excitements of the preceding weeks, as the foolish incubus burrowed down there at the base of the hill on which his farm stood, a horror that if he let him, then one day everything would collapse unexpectedly over his head and bury him in the rubble. It flared up in him abruptly, a frightfully real dream. He had to take off his cap, for in the moment he did not know what to do. Finally fury overcame him. He straightened up, and he flung such a shrill shout at him that the halfwit flew up as if struck by a whip and ran away in long, jerking strides to Hemsterhus.

The same night, Sintlinger suddenly sprang from his bed, tore a horse from the stables, and galloped out into the darkness. Like that time when the child was born, Johanna heard the horse's hooves whirling down the hill and fading away ever weaker into the distance.

When she awoke in the grey of morning, her husband lay deathly pale on the pillows beside her. His face was shrunken, looked ploughed up, but bore the features of collected, if also painful earnesty, and his breathing was calm. He lay like an overly weary soldier, and sometimes his forehead twitched as if he had to clench his teeth over the burning of hidden wounds.

A woman knows nothing of the grey animals of the air with which a man must struggle if he wants to remain on the path on which high expectation has placed him. What he must always reach for in restlessness, she bears as innate certainty in her soul. Hence Johanna also believed her husband had been frightened by the appearance and strange behaviour of the bell listener, just like she had, and no differently from a child, and been driven into the night by all sorts of ominous concerns. But with these thoughts, she only very slightly touched on the need which had come over Andreas, and was shocked deeper than ever before in her life, when he awoke. He started abruptly, looked around his room as though it were strange to him, and then gazed for a long time darkly at his wife. After that he rose to talk. Without preamble, from the midst of his agitation, he spoke of the nonsense of life, when you must think that men are nothing but lightning rods which fate sometimes strikes, sometimes does not; that no effort is rewarded, neither by the good nor the wicked; that it would be better to fool about like the Hemsterhus fool, were there to be something like such a bestial power which is capable of punishing parents by shoving an innocent child into misfortune. That he would not bear a day longer. Here everything must be made pure. Early in the morning, he would travel to Münster to a great doctor. He would have to tell whether it was just about a nasty blow to his child's face. What then has to happen, he would know and he was resolved not to hesitate for a moment with what was needed then. She should prepare everything. Then he gently touched his wife's pale forehead with his lips, and sprang from his bed.

All these events did not at all run through the farm with the old Sintlinger bustle; they took place in measured and calm forms so that the servants did not at once notice anything of the storm which had seized the farmer.

Like every morning, on this day too, he stepped into the yard at the same time, pushed his cap back, and let his eyes wander all around attentively. He did it with deliberate leisureliness. If he could not manage the quiet whistling which usually pushed by itself out from between his lips, he at least gave the impression of a man who was accustomed to inspiring himself before activity with a look at his orderly prosperity. Then he called the old labourer over, who just then was coming bent over out of the barn's low backdoor with a wooden fodder carrier in his arms. The ponderous servant just nodded at the call as a sign of understanding to his master, and then carried his oats in unquickened strides into the stables. Andreas meanwhile moved slowly to the yard gate. There the labourer found him, and

without a word, both struck out into the fields. Sintlinger walked with his face turned to the ground, his
hands behind his back. The countryside drew in gentle
waves from the farmstead's hill to the forest which in
the trappings of the young oaks' foliage sometimes grew
out from the earth as a reddish green cloud, sometimes
sank back into it according to whether the two taciturn
men were striding over a rise or through a depression.
On the highest wave of ground, the high butte, the place
from where you could almost see over the entire Sintlinger estate, Andreas stopped, and began giving the
labourer instructions over the work which was needed
in the next few days. He spoke calmly, even with a sort
of cold casualness. Even when he, only in a roundabout
way, trailed off into considerations over the course of
the harvest, yes even the sale of the expected grain, it
happened so casually, so completely in playful completion of the actual tasks that the greyed servant found
nothing surprising in why his master was worrying himself already now over this far off time.

"You must know", Sintlinger finally said, "I am travelling to Münster tomorrow. I may be a week, even
longer. My wife and child are going with me, and if I
don't return on the same day as them, then it will be of
no significance. Understood? Meanwhile, you will manage everybody as if I were standing behind you. You do
not need to say anything to the other servants, especially the women. They would make out of a skin a cat
and out of a cat a cow."

Suddenly he fell silent. The last word had seemingly
been torn from his mouth. He offered the labourer his
hand, which he shook, and turned hastily around to the
long meadow which rolled out in the trappings of its
May flowers like a broad golden stream from the forest
through the sloping depression to the boundary path.
Then he hastily and passionately took in the entire view

of his well-managed, fertile estate in his brown eyes, which were filled to bursting with a deeper darkness, and strode almost running to the farmstead so that the labourer was barely capable of following. Then he immediately began a tour through all the buildings. He hastily devoured the midday meal. He threw the bites down his throat without chewing, looked heedlessly past his wife and child, and then again rummaged restlessly until evening, upstairs and down, through lofts, stalls, sheds and barns. At bedtime, he had vanished; Johanna found him, after searching for a long time, in the small garden which lay towards the Rhine. It was already night, but only half dark; for the sickle moon was just then squinting wanly over the hill. When the farmer's wife noiselessly opened the garden gate, and had made a few steps hovering on her toes on the path towards the arbour which stood at the gable end of the stalls, she had to stop in bewilderment. She heard something there, which she would never have held for possible. Her husband's voice sounded quite quietly, quite raptly in the arbour, like someone from a distant dream, from lost sunlight, singing. Certainly he spoke the words more elongated and thoughtfully weighted:

> If I now had three wishes,
> Three wishes too many.
> I would then go and wish:
> Three roses on a stem.

It was the first of the two verses of a song which very young people sung in that district when they stood in the first astonishment of life and love.

Johanna was so choked up by it that she made an inadvertently loud step.

Then her husband stepped across the threshold of the arbour towards her, and said, "Good, I am coming." He grasped her hand, and led her into the house.

***

The next morning started long before daybreak. Sintlinger took his place on the raised driver's seat of the hunting carriage, the old labourer and Johanna placed the child between themselves. She whimpered quietly and drowsily. As the vehicle dropped down the hill carefully, and then ran in quick rolling to the narrow trot of the nags, Helene fell silent. Her little face assumed an expression of fearfully tense expectation, and she drew her arms and legs close to her body. Sintlinger sat without stirring, let the whip swish whistling over the horses' heads when they wanted to drop into a slower tempo, did not turn around, but looked silently and constantly erect straight-ahead. Johanna could not look at him without feeling a certain horror. He seemed sinister to her, strange, almost like someone who had forced their soul violently out of themselves and, now dying away, chased behind it to fetch it back, whatever the cost.

After two hours of quick travel, they had reached the stretch of railway which came down from Bocholt. The transfer to the train was effected in silence. Then the farmer once more quickly faced the labourer who had taken his place on the driver's seat of the carriage and was just then reaching for the whip to travel back. "You remember everything still that I said to you?" he asked, and looked at him threateningly. The old man just nodded, doffed his hat, and set the horses into a trot. Andreas sprang onto the train, and immediately withdrew again into his inner depths where he remained for almost the entire journey. No dispute over the choice of doctor, over his probable diagnosis and the possibly conclusive measures, no attempt to come to the help of one another through the sound of words. Johanna made an attempt a few times to release the trepidation in her heart through talking. Sintlinger just shut his eyes in answer each time, leant back, and shook his head dismissively. Like someone carrying about a cocked pistol, the finger always on the trigger, he kept his intentions safe behind a silence which was also without any friendliness towards himself. It was a cool, unpitying waiting which shrouded him in darkness and menace in the midst of light, but a menace only towards an incomprehensible thing which waited in ambush for him as if behind the heavens. Towards his wife, the darkened insularity had the effect of an unexpressed assurance of deep love.

Only the railway station whirl, first in Wesel and then in Dorstel, was able to give back to Sintlinger for a moment something of his old being. Then he ran in the midst of the travellers hastening to and fro, shoved himself deliberately into massing tangles, dispensed pushes and shoves with his elbows, scared people pushing forwards out of the way by the blaze in his eyes, and sucked from the faces of the obliging so much restive hope, laughing decisiveness, and careless exuberance that his cheeks were reddened. Johanna sat with Helene on the bench before the waiting room, and watched the bustle of her husband with distress. He calmed her on returning though with the excuse that he had to enquire about the departure of the train, but lost in speaking every semblance of borrowed pleasure, and when they sat in the train, he crept back again completely into his inner depths.

Only once during the journey was he enticed out of this withdrawal into the darkness. After Haltern it was. The train seemed, rattling and wheezing, to have stopped in the same place on the monotonous plain as if if were feeding on the ground with its wheels. Hills appeared in the great distance. At first they peeked over the horizon, small and timid, as if they dared not approach because of the racket from the wheels. Suddenly, however, they were all sent into motion, and wandered joltingly, but noiselessly, ever nearer. Each brandished on its back several trees like green flags, and finally the train was surrounded by them. The clamour which enveloped it completely gaped apart sometimes in the wind, and you could hear that the entire May air out there was filled to bursting with lark song. Crows were walking through the young shoots. But you could only see their heads like little, black balls rolling waggling over the green surface. High in the sky stood a swarm of little white clouds, listening motionless to the earth below.

The environment carried so completely the features of his Hemsterhus home that Andreas was drawn out of his inner darkness for a moment. He brought it to Johanna's attention. They both looked out, and as they gazed, a fervent fever came over the high clouds. They began to quickly draw back in the sky, became smaller and smaller, and had vanished without trace before they had both blinked their eyes a second time. This incident happened so unexpectedly that the farmer and his wife fetched a deep breath. Johanna smiled instinctively. Sintlinger, however, sat there with eyes dark in dream, and when his wife asked him what was there, he answered, forgetting himself, "So like the clouds ... if it must already be, dying would be beautiful."

Then his wife realised which abyss her husband was daydreaming in, but contained herself, and gave the appearance of still having divined nothing of his inner state. She just asked him with insistent kindness to not hurt her anymore with such words. Hence, she placed her hand on his, as was her habit, and said, "Andreas, you won't say such a thing ever again, will you? For whoever wants the night as it were, will be overcome by it unexpectedly in the middle of the day."

In quiet, she intended to not let her husband out of her sight anymore.

Now the train was rolling through the boring Münster plains. Marshes with their thick bushes approached right up to the stretch of track, and finally the old cathedral city appeared on the distant horizon. When Sintlinger saw it emerge black and jagged from the reddish evening air, a touch of grim hostility flew over his face. He murmured something, and looked to the side. They took a room in a small hotel not far from Romburger Station, a hotel where farmers tended to alight on their visits to the big city, and whose name was known to Sintlinger from his father. As the farmer had not looked at his wife and child during the entire journey, probably so as not to be diverted from his hidden resolve by the sight of his nearest and dearest, he also attended to them calmly now, but from a distance, led them after a simple, light meal to the appointed room, and then went to seek out a doctor who was trustworthy enough to decide over the condition of his child and thereby over his own life. Fortune led him favourably, and after some running here and there, he stood in Ägidistraße before the tall, magnificent house of that great doctor who, according to Sintlinger's violent imagination, had to live in the cathedral city. The distinguished building belonged to Doctor Flöreck, a famous eye specialist all across Westphalia at that time, who had received the title of professor from a Thüringian prince because of an unprecedentedly bold operation on a princess. Sintlinger forced himself with the impetuousness of his passionate disposition past the last patients through the waiting room into the consulting room of the Professor and, suddenly seized by deep fear, brought up his request in a sort of painful defiance. Doctor Flöreck, a quite slender, taciturn man, nodded, smiling indulgently over the behaviour and manner of

Andreas's telling, and when the farmer had finished and now stood there shaking with dark eyes and pale face, he looked earnestly over the small, sinewy man, stepped to a window, and looked out at the evening bustle of the street. Then he went to his desk, made a few notes, read them thoughtfully, and finally handed over to Sintlinger a card with the remark that he was to present himself there with the patient at eight o'clock in the morning and to hand over the little card to the lady at the little desk in the front room.

When Andreas returned to the hotel, Johanna, who had been restlessly looking out for him constantly, was sitting with Helene in the dark room by the window. The child was listening with large, fearful eyes to the din which surged around the house from everywhere, and when the bells now all started to toll, she burrowed tearfully into her mother.

The next morning, Sintlinger's darkness overcame him more deeply again in the doctor's waiting room. For when he arrived, the long, narrow room, which only received light through a single, if also high window, was almost full of people, and an apprehensive stillness reigned like that which the aching hopes of many half-despondent people induces. Sintlinger was directed with his family quite a long way from the entrance to the consulting room, and took his child protectively between his wife and himself. He behaved towards those present in a sort of hostile repudiation, and sat there with his face turned to the floor. But when he straightened up, it finally occurred to him that he must throw a glance against his will at those sitting around.

Some were sitting as though ready to spring up, bent over on the extreme edge of their chairs, and groping about from time to time with trembling hand at the black bandage which lay over their eyes. Others kept themselves motionless on their seats in the stiff posture of the already completely blind, and sometimes groped, overcome by sudden fright, for their companions who had taken their places indifferently next to them. He looked into eyes which were like dead balls of milk in their sockets, and others again hung like bloody bubbles between their lids. He would have liked most of all to have covered his child's face with his hands to prevent the devastation which had befallen them all from leaping over to the clear irises of Helene.

Then he heard a door open in the consulting room, rose with a jerk, and gave Johanna a sign to take the child in her arms. Tense straightening up came over all the others, the collapsed and the stiffly seated, like over the accused before the pronouncement of the verdict. A few turned their faces disapprovingly at Andreas, offended by the loud start. But he paid no attention to them, instead moving with slow, firm strides towards the entrance to the consulting room. Now, as he stood on his feet, he was far away from the power of these ill-treated lives, and the certainty filled him that now there was only the doctor to get the better of. Then his child would be saved for him, and with her everything. Here it meant being on guard so as not to lose any gesture, any expression, not the slightest shadow of the glance with which doctors secretly confessed their conviction before their patients. Professor Flöreck opened the door to give the sign for the beginning of the consultation, and Sintlinger strode across the threshold without giving a thought to his right to it. The practice nurse tried to hold the farmer back because two patients were still pencilled in before him. Andreas just turned around with threatening face, ignored her words of explanation, said over his shoulder, "Good then!" and shut the door firmly behind him without taking notice of the laughter and cries of indignation in the waiting room. Doctor Flöreck ignored with a sparing smile this unaccustomed scene, let his look pass in astonishment from the gently quiet woman to the flickeringly dark man, and mean- while made all the preparations for an examination. Sintlinger moved with a chair to the wall, and followed it all with his dark eyes standing in his wide-awake face like the barrel ends of two rifles. His violent will en- gaged its attentiveness so exclusively on the vital moment that the apprising questions of the doctor over the age of the little patient, possible mishaps, presumed beginning of the incapacity of sight and several others almost flittered to him like an extraneous noise from afar. Suddenly the timbre of the doctor's voice changed. All severity drained away from it, the normally gentle organ became still more melodious. The words sounded like a pleasant play. He talked thus to little Helene, and already after a few moments, she was so taken by the man's gentle power that all shyness drained away from her. She let her little hands be clasped, happily tolerated the Professor stroking her hair and cheeks, and finally did whatever the clever doctor wished. The touch of the strange hands felt like her own gestures, and his inten- tions like her own wishes. Without making a sound, she endured every pressure on her eyes, moved according to his command, shut them, opened them, and held still in happy expectation as he examined with the mirror every corner of the mysterious clarity of her barred eyes. He nowhere discovered an injury, nowhere a morbid change. The iris was unclouded, the lens hung like an immaculate drop of dew before the divine darkness of the retina. Even the adaptiveness of the pupils was present in limited measure.

Sintlinger sat bent forward as though pushed, had seized the seat of his chair convulsively with both hands, and followed every movement of the doctor with a threatening look as though he were ready to pounce on him. He did not know where he was. Everything he saw happened behind a grey veil. Then he finally noticed that the Professor had straightened up, taken a thoughtful step to his desk, fumbled about deliberating, and then, as he had done the day before, had gone to the window and stared out onto the street.

"Good, now it comes", Sintlinger thought and, without realising what he did, sprang up.

"Doctor," he stuttered so that it sounded as if he were burrowing with his tongue in a mouth full of pebbles.

The Professor, used to all forms of human despair, turned around, and looked at Sintlinger, the fingers of his right hand on his chin. Sintlinger was shaking like a tense rope in a storm. But the doctor did not mind.

He spoke with a mild voice of the boundaries of human knowledge, the mysteries of the human body, the unexplained miracles and moods of nature, and confided that a case like this, where the capacity for sight was, with the complete intactness of the outer and inner eye, limited to a certain sensitivity to light, had never been seen by him before. All that he could do was give the advice to wait patiently for nature to pull away again the veil which it had mysteriously hung in such a hidden way before this child.

It seemed to Sintlinger as if he were hearing a heavenly voice speaking to him. To restrain himself so that he did not run and fall at the man's feet, he closed his hands together like claws, smiled madly, and did not realise that tears were running down his cheeks.

The doctor thought he was seeing the expression of deepest desperation, stepped up to Sintlinger, placed his hand on his shoulder, and spoke to him consolingly. The farmer, because of his inner jubilation, did not hear what the doctor said, and nodded to everything mechanically, even when the doctor asked permission for his assistant to undertake a short eye examination of this phenomenal case.

Hardly had the Professor vanished behind the door to the adjoining room, however, than Andreas quickly gathered up the mass of gold pieces from his pouch, threw them on the desk, and pulled his unsuccessfully resisting wife from the room. Laughing, he sprang down the stairs, and at the door took little Helene from his somewhat embarrassedly following wife's arms. Then he stepped onto the street as though in triumph. The doctor called something down to him from above, and the head of his assistant also appeared at the window.

Sintlinger probably heard his name called, but did not turn around, just doffed his hat and, intoxicated by great joy, sought out his hotel room.

6

After these hidden storms, the light of life implanted itself again in every space of the Sintlinger farm. Not that in the days of the struggle which had driven the farmer and his wife to Münster, something of the dark temperament or swift severity of the earlier time had unexpectedly preyed on the residents of the northern hill, no, but love had been obscured, kindness somewhat duller, and the poor and needy received gifts in those days as if they were placed in their hands silently from a shadowy hole in a wall. Now there was a kindhearted look with the piece of bread again as before, a good wish in the bowl of soup, a word of encouragement afterwards on the path, and the exhortation not to go past the hill in their need. The farmer himself excelled in particular at this fraternisation with all the door knockers. He was not repelled by any morbid deformation of the figure, was not provoked to disgust by any disfigurement, and was never driven to fury by one of those avaricious ones who seem tormented by half a dozen illnesses so long as they are in the sight of the giver, but are jovial and good things as soon as they think themselves out of sight. Yes, actually, the more unnatural and hopeless the condition of a poor person, the livelier Andreas's sympathy. He liked most of all to engage in a conversation with these burdened people, how they had been before, in what way the plague had overcome them, and how the world and their life now appeared to them, no differently than if the aches and pains were the right path to secret knowledge. And sometimes even, after such a dialogue, the farmer stood on the spot lost in silent meditation for a long time, or walked about for days with an absent look, and did his work as if in a dream. However he never took his wife with him into these secret dealings of his soul, instead brushing her away as if the views from such paths were not for the eyes of his wife.

One day she met him out in the fields on the edge of a steep slope next to a heap of field stones, rapt and quite alone. From time to time, he stooped, grasped one of the round stones, and let it roll down through the short grass into the meadow. Always, when the stone ran down without stopping, quicker and quicker, and then came to rest between the blades of grass, his face brightened as if it signified the revelation of a precious secret.

"I don't understand you", Johanna said.

"That I believe, little Klim, certainly", he answered. "But the stone, I tell you, knows more than all the doctors and pastors put together." And when she pressured him to tell her what he meant, he took her face in both hands, looked for a long time seriously into her eyes and, instead of answering, just shook his head with a smile.

Another time, they were both walking home from the fields in the evening. Sintlinger was having one of his quiet days, and was striding next to his wife in the rapt silence to which he had become accustomed. She attempted this and that to bring him into a conversation, but won from him no more than a word of agreement or dismissal, or even just a lingering look in his eye. A dark cloud, darkening more and more, began dumping its water down on the two, at first hesitantly, and then more and more heavily. Johanna quickened her gait at the first drops and finally sprang with a loud laugh into the protection of a tree standing by the path. Sintlinger, however, remained standing in the pouring rain, looked with a sort of devotion up into the flickering of the falling drops, and nothing could move him to go next to her under the shelter of the branches. After times of long drought, farmers certainly have a sort of pious reverence for rain, and even step out of the house into the gushing from heaven to slurp in the blessing as it were with their skin. But this enjoyment was not keeping Sintlinger out in the wet. The same joyful fire arose in his eyes as had ignited his look so deeply and strangely when playing with the stones. As if a revelation was dripping down on him, he observed how the drops ran over the back of his hands and fell from the tips of his fingers to the earth. At last he sprang to his wife under the roof of leaves, embraced her quickly, and rubbed his wet cheeks in her face. Johanna responded well to the fun, but noticed that Andreas wanted at the same time to avoid her questions about the meaning of his strange behaviour. When she had thus extricated herself, she asked him whether the rain was perhaps also cleverer than doctors and pastors the way the stones had been.

For she meant perhaps with the teasing to be able to get behind his secret running about. But a curtain seemed to fall over Sintlinger's face, and he answered full of impassioned earnesty, "Just so, Johanna! I tell you, you have something there for which in astonishment you cannot find words." He did not say anything more. Suddenly he interrupted himself as if caught, and drew her silently along the path because it had stopped raining.

Johanna probably felt that her husband's strange manner was connected with thoughts that revolved about Helene. But she did not understand in what ways unease could still torment him after the doctor in Münster had given them a comforting reassurance that the suffering of blindness would one day slip away from their little daughter like sleep from someone resting or the smoke over the roof of a house. The doctor had indeed said that. What in all the world was driving her Andreas into silence and grinding up many of his nights? And Johanna continued to follow her husband in all the secrecies of his strange unease with the sensing of her soul so as to at least capture the tip of a certainty. Her suppositions had to always turn back at the door of his hidden worries, shoved back by a kindness which sometimes tasted like compassion. And when Andreas had properly bored into himself like a pond which constantly swallows itself with quiet eddies, he either blossomed into his old laughingly mad cheerfulness, seized Helene under the arms, and danced singing through the living room, or lifted the child carefully in his arms, carried her into the sunny grass of the garden, and did not tire from sitting next to her and raptly caressing the girl's blond hair — according to the current that carried him, which had led his thinking into light or darkness; for that next to the paternal love, something deeper still led her husband's heart to such passionate entanglements with the life of the child, she noticed something which often stood like a distant air about Andreas and her girl. Johanna saw her husband's eyes, and did not understand their look, heard his heart beating, and did not really know what was driving it, felt the breath of his soul, and did not see the spirit land over which it skimmed.

7

In that time, a maid heard several nights one after the other a restless trotting of cautious steps from afar floundering around the Sintlinger farmstead, and if, in her opinion, it lasted hours, it stopped sometimes towards Hemsterhus, sometimes Brederode, sometimes the Rhine, or the Brindeisener's hill, paused for a while, and then began with short breath powerlessly emitting piteous sounds as if someone was perhaps blowing into a cracked horn, quieter and quieter, more and more achingly, further and further away. The farm labourers laughed at her, and suggested cynically that she had perhaps heard her own cuckoo calling. But the following night, it first struck loudly against the big yard gate and then at the back door by the flower garden, so blusteringly that both yard dogs began barking furiously, the farm labourers sprang from their beds and advanced amidst ample cursing with some hurriedly gathered clubs towards the unknown disturber of the peace. They thought they saw him strike out before them in a wide arc like a tall bundle, panted after him for a stretch, and returned to bed, weakened by the cold night air, half in disbelief whether they had in the end perhaps just been struck a little bit by their own imaginations.

But one of the farm labourers who had run out with them on that nocturnal rogue's hunt maintained after he had rolled it about in his head for a day that it had not been one person who had steamed them up in the dark, but rather, if you forced him he was ready to swear to it, he had seen two figures, a male and a female. The man, none other than the Hemsterhus incubus, had sprung away like a giant grasshopper, and always behind him, like a grey expiring will-o'-the-wisp, a woman's figure, mute and scurrying, had made off. Now at that time, in the forests around Brederode and Hemsterhus, a homeless woman was really present who, quite afraid of people, resided in the most secluded thickets, going out in the day after berries, roots and mushrooms, and on people's approach, running away hissing like a cat. A few had tried to look at her more closely, and described her as fat-necked, bestially stupid and ugly as a witch. Others claimed, never anything nice, but that they had never set eyes on such a wild-devilish woman as this vagrant in all their life, only they also admitted that she certainly possessed no more understanding than a stake and no language but only cooing like a pigeon and shrieking like a squirrel.

Not long after these events, some beggar carried the news to the Sintlinger farmstead that the Nobody incubus had strewn the rumour over the entire district that he was no longer sure of his life around Andreas Sintlinger. The farmer had spellbound him in a witch-like way, enticed him near to his farmstead, and then followed him all night long through the fields. And if he had not taken off, it would have been all up for him. For the past forty eight hours, he had also actually vanished from the district.

The woman had probably lured him out of the district. A carter from Brederode, who had unloaded logs for Dingden in Westphalia twice that week at the railway station, claimed to have met him two days later with the "human" by the edge of the forest. They had been sitting in front of each other, looking at themselves in wonder like images of the saints and had then, laughing and crying at once, run away in opposite directions as though possessed, but only to start the game of sitting in front of each other and gazing raptly from the beginning again.

The Blessed Farm

When the farmer was brought this news, he broke out into raucous laughter. But in the midst of this mad cheerfulness, it seemed as if he swallowed. The laughter had suddenly been torn from his throat. He changed colour, and the lost gleam came into his eyes. He stood thus for a while, shook his head barely perceptibly, let an incredulous smile play about his mouth, then snapped his fingers, and strode away. That same afternoon, he had led out of the stable the horse on which he had roamed about on the night after the appearance of the Hemsterhus incubus. The old labourer had to groom it, comb its mane, and put on the saddle and bridle which it had worn in those dark hours. Then the farmer called the old labourer to climb on the beautiful, bold animal, and gave the command to go as far as possible from there, to Bocholt, Haltern or wherever he wanted, even to Wesel if it occurred to him, to sell of the horse at the market somewhere at any price, and to only keep in mind that it did not return under any circumstances to the local district. The aged labourer, for whom this rare horse formed his pride and love, sprang furiously into the saddle, as he knew that objecting would be of no use with Sintlinger, lashed full of fury at the horse, and flew without word through the gate and down the hill. When the hoofbeats sounded no louder in the distance than the tapping of two fingernails against each other, the farmer grasped a shovel, and took himself to that place in the forest where he had once lain and, in looking at the autumn sky, struggled for an understanding of the wonder in which his life had been enclosed by the fate of his child. There he lifted with four deep thrusts a piece of turf from the ground, and carried it carefully down to the boundary path. He widened the ditch in which the Nobody incubus had once buried the red rags, placed the little crust of turf into it, trod it all down firmly, and purged the spot of the excess earth so that no person would notice any change or be able to doubt in the least that the grass had been growing in this place forever.

In the evening, he sat on the bench by the yard gate, and dreamt in the warm May evening.

Johanna now thought nothing else but that her husband was again filled with a secret fear of the bell listener and was led to these measures by the effort to blot out the paths on which the baneful power of this halfwit could creep into his fate. In any case, she held the time to be eminently favourable to perhaps let some air into the doorway to his secret thoughts, and tear him away from such dangerous isolation of the soul. After finishing her evening activities, she thus went to him, taking her place next to him and, after some to and fro about the weather, the farm, the state of the cattle and the servants, told small tales about people who had gotten into hardship through their life having touched the baneful circle of hellish people.

Sintlinger sensed quite soon where his wife wanted to go. But he also calmly let her talk, yes, not once pulling up at some derailment, and the loving, beset woman did not know exactly whether he was interested in her tales, or whether his barred senses were only devoted to the vanishing of the day which was going its way over the waves of hills with the light of squinting eyes and a humming like the quiet tones of a harp. When she finished, he slowly lifted his eyes from the darkening heavens, and said, "You are mistaken"; he said nothing more, and sank again into silence.

After a while, she noticed how he bent down, and threw something away from himself.

"Well, what did I let fall from my hand?" he asked.

"A stone, a piece of grass, something. I cannot tell in the darkness", Johanna answered.

"... and what I think and what is in me, you want to know that though. Right, dear wife? And it is much much darker around that than the evening around us."

"Perhaps, if you told me something about it, it would not always be so dark. — Well, Andreas!" Johanna spoke very insistently.

Sintlinger did not answer immediately, but put his hands between his knees, and fell into brooding.

Finally he shook his head dismissively, straightened up, and caressed his wife's forehead gently. "Oh, no", he said at the same time, "the bird which does not want to get giddy on the tall tree must be bred up there. — But I will tell you so much — there is much brightness which does not come from light, and many scents which do not come from flowers. And many mountains stand quite without foundation in us. — Yes. For that reason, there are also souls which can see without eyes. You can perhaps also strike without raising the arm, and push someone without standing up. The Nobody knows that *because* he is a fool, and I do because I can confound myself, that is, even though I am not one."

Johanna was beset at these strange words by a grave fear, for her husband was speaking almost as he had often done previously when intoxicated.

Sintlinger sensed how she was shaking, and said with mild reproof, "Look, Johanna, hardly do you step onto my threshold than you stumble, and then you want to go into my house. No, no! I beg you, don't creep after me always with your fears, promise me! Someday, when there is no helping it, I will talk. But it would be better that you heard nothing."

His wife had placed her head on his knee, her hands placed over her face. He caressed along her back whilst he spoke, and felt the gentle tremors of restrained tears. Then he fell silent, and when her body was completely still, he spoke reassuringly, "I suggested before that you were mistaken. By that I wanted to say that you were mistaken if you believed that I would have done what I did with the horse and the hole by the boundary path out of fear of the Nobody incubus. Nothing of the sort. But I don't want to be constantly reminded that I was once so stupid as to have the wind put up me by a fool. — And now come to bed. It is already late."

Sintlinger raised Johanna up from his knee. Over on the Brindeisener hill, the yard gate was being bolted. The rough, deep bass of the farmer rung out in an ill-tempered conversation with a second person who never answered. The pattering of heavy booted steps strayed drowsily over the red bricks of the yard and staggered into a corner behind the creaking of a door. After that nothing more was awake but breathless darkness.

Sintlinger suddenly said dejectedly, "That was old Brindeisener."

Then they both went into the house.

In the hallway, Johanna let go of her husband's arm, and hurried once more out before the gate on the pretence of having to fetch her forgotten headscarf. There she just stood, and listened for whether Sintlinger had followed her. But she heard him calmly open and close the door to the living room.

Then she spread her arms into the night, embraced the trunk of the lime tree, and began crying silently.

In this state of her soul, the return of the old labourer occurred. He had ridden the horse reluctantly to market, actually in open fury. He returned home dejectedly, without saddle, without bridle, only with a stick which he had cut from a bush along the way, the cash in his pouch, entirely according to Sintlinger's instructions. But what he had to report about the strange events which had taken place after the sale of the horse did not just warrant his trepidation, which sat on his neck like the blow of a fist, but was really suited to throwing an intimidated heart into confusion.

As the old labourer told it, he had put his mind to the sale of the horse from the beginning. Only in Wesel, in a small square at the end of the town, had there been anything like a horse market. Only this was actually just the rendezvous of the worst manger sitters, raging hounds, and bellyachers of the district, and at the halter of each nag hung two rogues, the owner and the buyer, both dealers who toiled amidst the mobilisation of every trick to entice an unsuspecting person, and then work the mechanism of their tongues for as long as it took until he could not differentiate a goat from a horse anymore. The old labourer had barely pulled the brown with him once around the swarm of half and total scoundrels and crocks than he had worked out what sort of kitchen he had arrived in, swung into the saddle, and whirled as inconspicuously as possible out of the town. But this sojourn of barely half an hour in the market at Wesel had been sufficient to inform every horse comb in the district of his brown and him, and wherever he entered, he was greeted with the same shoulder shrugs, the same faults were ascribed to his animal, and they behaved to him in such a way that he did not really know in the end whether he was justly leading his horse by the rein or had stolen it. In the end, the entire district had truly stunk of lies and deceit, and such a fury overpowered him that he had just ridden straight for an entire day to get away from this band of stranglers again and arrive amongst honest Christian men. On the evening of the same day, it was the fourth after his departure from the Sintlinger farm, he rode ill-temperedly into a small town, and next to him went a friendly, well-dressed man, half gentleman, half farmer. The latter again and again looked furtively at the beautiful nag and then to the side as if it were nothing, and the labourer thought to himself that he was another of the many who buy horses with their eyes, and pay with their yearning, and began irritably to add up all the expenses which he had up to then. As he placed item after item on top of each other and was just coming to the conclusion, come what may, to put the horse up for sale to all the world for just one more day, the stranger who had always remained alongside him tapped the horse on the cheeks. Thus they came into conversation. The talk turned into haggling and the haggling into a deal, and before the bellringer went across the market for the evening bells, they were sitting at the window of the tavern, and peacefully clinking their pints together over the agreed deal. The labourer carried the seven hundred marks charged in coins in his pouch, and the servant held the brown ready outside for its new master who wanted to ride him home that night, just two hours from there. Children arrived, an entire swarm, and admired the beautiful, unfamiliar animal. Even men and women interrupted their walks and parked themselves for a short, unhurried gawking. Suddenly a fellow stood there amidst all the people, thin and tall like a harvest pitchfork, dressed like a scarecrow, with a head no larger than a goose's, and he almost devoured the nag with his restive, burning, monkey eyes. At this moment, the servant was called by someone into the tavern. He tied the horse to a tree, and left it. At once an uproar arose amongst the crowd. Before someone could prevent it, the tall vagrant had torn the horse from the tree, and was graceless as a frog, yet quicker than a cat, in the saddle. Then he raced like a madman across the market, and before the two were instantly outside, even though flying out the door like thrown stones, he was away. They could do nothing but run after him like the others, and saw the thief already down the street riding into the open fields. The fellow was being tossed back and forth so that you would think that he would fall off any moment. But he remained on top as though tethered, and the next moment, as though smeared with devil's oil, he vanished around the corner.

That was the old labourer's tale, and when he had finished, he looked at the farmer and his wife, noticed from the quick breath of the woman, her pallor, the lowering of her eyes, and the gentle smile which played about Sintlinger's mouth, that both knew as well as he did who had ridden the brown away that evening never to be seen again. For that reason, he considered that it was better to bury the entire tale in silence, swallowed on his part the name which was tickling his tongue, and dawdled circuitously according to old habit out the door.

But the joiner is yet to be born who knows how to make a cabinet in which you can hide shadows. And the more each endeavoured to play at being harmlessly in-different before the others, the louder it screamed through the entire Sintlinger house, through every hall-way, through stalls and lofts, around the yard, roared in the tree tops and whirred with the birds' wings about the roof — the Nobody fool stole the brown. It agitated Johanna deepest of all. From the lower workings of her past climbed the memory of the mad storm during her wedding night; for dark reasons, she was overcome by the trembling from when after Helene's conception she had heard the unfortunate sound of the little bell; she suffered once more the torments amidst which she had had to confess the knowledge of her child's blindness. And when she considered the strange behaviour of this deluded fool at the cradle of her child, his mysterious disappearance from the district, and this foiling of the secret intentions of her husband for his defence, she felt her and her husband's fate was tied up by the tentacles of an infernal power, and she racked her mind to stave off this danger or to comprehend this menace from the darkness as her imagination, as a sudden ache in the brain. It was in vain. Not long after and she was constantly hearing the hoofbeats of a rider roaming about the farmstead at night, at first in quite distant circles, then closer and closer, and in the end she often heard the stamping and snorting of a stallion as distinctly as if the Nobody incubus was riding past her bed through the middle of the bedroom; and when he had roared out the window, and she saw his long, dangling legs vanish into the air, she lay for a while at first and recovered from the anxiety of fear; then she felt about herself cautiously, or lit a candle to convince herself of whether her husband and her child had been tormented by the same vision as her and still lay safe in their beds.

Once Johanna took it to heart, and when the trotting began again towards the twelfth hour, and then increased so that she thought she heard sand flying at the window panes, she quietly stood up, crept into the servants' room, quickly threw on a petticoat and jacket there, made the sign of the cross three times, and then began toddling through the pitch black hallway towards the front door. She was resolved to confront the unkindly one and, if it could be done no other way, break the fury of these subterranean powers with her life. Her heart was pounding as though it wanted to burst; but she pulled herself together, turned the key in the door, which to her astonishment was not locked, and stepped out into the yard. But hardly had she stepped into the open than the riding about the walls stopped as if it had been blown out of the air.

The night was moving its dark shawls soundlessly about the rooves, and Johanna was so taken aback by the sudden silencing of the ghostly racket that she could not distinguish left from right, nor front from back. For that reason, she began groping about herself for good luck. At the same time, she came closer to a dark figure which was standing motionless next to her in the darkness, and looming menacingly towards her. She wanted to quickly say, "In the name of the Father, the Son and the Holy Ghost, who are you?", but nothing came over her lips but the fearful whistling of a dying hare, and she began to sway. Strong arms caught the sinking woman, and when she had recovered, the old labourer was standing next to her. From him she learnt that he too, night after night, had heard the riding of the incubus, and like her had just come down to make an end to the mischief. She obtained the promise from him to remain silent over what he had heard, and went back to bed.

From this night on, Johanna was definite that she must no longer hesitate anymore to find a way out from this state which was becoming unbearable. But since she had in this striving laboured her soul into a proper whirl without espying the most distant twinkle of a deliverance, she realised that it would be most advisable to entrust her worries to a wise, discreet soul for advice and help. Only as someone carelessly skims a fence in passing did she touch the possibility of unburdening herself to Pastor Ardelt of Hemsterhus; but she soon drew back the emotional threads of her soul, and plunged into action the plan of going to her father and spreading out without reserve all her hardship and fear before him.

From that day when old Klim, so as not to choke on his fury, had left so quickly from the Sintlinger farmstead because his children had wanted nothing to do with the healing of their blind girl, the old man had stayed in his retirement house in Brederode without again stirring a foot towards Hemsterhus, and lived, as far as one could tell, only in the service of the memory of his late wife. Without fury, but seemingly also without love, upright and quiet, he bore the thought of irreconcilable separation from his children.

This averted old man's countenance, only moving painfully in its unfathomable deeps, appeared now before Johanna's seeking eyes, and shaken by the indifference of her own heart, she not only recognised the wrong of having left one of her nearest standing for so long before the slammed door of her fate, but also realised that it was high time to lead as much blessing as possible into her existence from the treasures of this homely soul.

For that reason, she waited for a day in which her husband was kept in business from morning until evening at the county seat. On the Sintlinger fields which bordered on Brederode, the crops were to be cleared of ground ivy and thistles, and Johanna knew how to arrange a visit to her father without the maids noticing. She let the work break off halfway through the afternoon, and sent the servants home, their carry cloths stuffed full of thistles. The farmwife herself wanted, as she pretended, to proceed by the detour over the Rhine hill to the driveway. But hardly had the maids with their high packs of thistles disappeared jogging behind the first bump of ground, than Johanna gathered up her skirt, and ran down the slope to Brederode. When she had reached the safety of the trees down in the beech stand, she sprang straight ahead as if someone was chasing behind her with a whip. Thus she was soon in her father's house. He was sitting at the table, the blue sackcloth and the silver snuffbox next to the book, and was reading a book of the lives of the saints. When Johanna entered unexpectedly, the old man lifted his

head, recognised her, put his finger on the page in his
confusion, so as to keep his place, and took his glasses
from his eyes. The farmwife had hesitated in the door
for a moment in shame and love; but when she saw the
old man's hand falling trembling with the glasses
through the air, she grasped it, because it looked as if
her father was waving to her one last time with the frail
hand from the grave. Then the usually so composed woman lost her reticence entirely, and with a laugh which
sounded more like a quiet cry, she plunged onto the old
man's chest. He noticed immediately on what leaves her
life was chewing, and when the first commotions were
over, the two sat down on the bench, and the daughter
poured out before her father everything which had oppressed and haunted her, but not as if she were bearing
her lot with pain or asking weakly for forgiveness. No,
as she in truth understood it, from the worry about her
husband outward, she spoke of everything which had
taken place on the Sintlinger hill since the old man's departure — of the appearance of the Hemsterhus incubus
and his rag scratching, her husband's night of madness,
the journey to Münster, of the Nobody fool's disappearing from the district and his ghostly appearance four
days later so far into the country at the sale of the horse.
She spoke the truth in everything, only deviating from
the facts in that she described her husband as depressed, fearful and lost, not desperate, but like
someone who lacks the advice of a clever, good man so
that he can feel secure in his way again.

Old Klim listened to all that in kindly sympathy, and
prized the chance that he could be useful to them once
more before his demise. It was all arranged for the following Sunday. The old man wanted to celebrate then
something like a party, naturally only for them and himself. Everything would be straightened out then as far as
he was capable.

During the conversation of the parties so-long separated, the evening had crept up unexpectedly like a thief outside and was squinting through the window before the two had arrived completely at the end, and Johanna had to leave in order to be at the farmstead before the arrival of her husband. She had slipped in unseen, and she also left her father unnoticed by his neighbour. She was seemingly chased up the field margins. She suddenly felt light-headed and frivolous, and when she came out of the beech stand, the last lark just then climbed up singing to the clouds lying in the deepened sky, clouds edged by the smouldering twilight. She took that as a favourable sign, and so forgot herself with joy that she bent down, plucked a handful of flowers, and threw the petals in the air according to the song.

Meanwhile on the same evening, in this wine of rising hopes, more than one drop of water was poured which placed her otherwise so secure soul into a whirl again.

Sintlinger had on the way received from the postman a letter from the man to which the brown had been sold by the old labourer. In this letter was enclosed the page of a newspaper in which a report about the success of the police's investigations over the whereabouts of the stolen horse was contained.

Woodcutters of the baronial forest at Deckertschen had on the morning walk to their work places in the middle of the forest heard the weak whinnying of a horse. When they followed the sound, they found behind a thicket and tied to a tree the horse which the unknown man had ridden out of the little town on that evening. It still wore the saddle, bridle, and fittings with which it had been provided at sale, but was found in such a state of misery, being emaciated with shuddering legs and head hanging down so that it could barely move its eyes at the shout of the pitying men. It was so weak it was incapable of chewing anymore. On the way out of the forest, it broke down and expired. The report added that the supposed thief was in all probability an artiste whom the director of a travelling circus had laid off because of signs of mental disturbance.

Following this news, Sintlinger reassured his wife with mild and insistent words from which ensued that he not only knew about her fear, but even about her and the labourer's attempt at driving away the imagined midnight rider. He advised her of how people go under the wheels of such spirit wagons only through weakness of soul, but otherwise wander undisturbed on the paths prescribed for them.

Only, instead of pandering to her husband's words of comfort, Johanna did not manage to wipe the fact of these repeated nightly disturbances from her mind as a delusion, for one, because in her opinion the witness of the old labourer spoke for its reality, for another, because she then saw herself pushed entirely into pathlessness. For, if not from the influence of this incubus-like Nobody, then from where did the anxiety and fear stir in her, and from where this transformation of Sintlinger from which every welling of effervescence, every possibility of a derailment into his previous errors had subsided so completely into wistful stillness that he often seemed to her to be an incomprehensible and unfamiliar man.

On the night which followed her visit to old Klim, Johanna dreamt of a man whom she saw running on all the paths in the world in the dark. He hurried through the villages and towns of the world, and tried to unlock the houses, but he possessed a key which did not fit anywhere. She did not know the man, nevertheless she was behind him in her dream every hour of her sleep, for when she was so near to him that she must succeed in

seeing his face, he turned away, and struck off on another path.

On awakening, the vividness of her dream life certainly sank, but the pain of not having recognised the
unusual man had probably become even stronger in
waking. That is why she walked behind the yard to collect herself, and immersed herself in the sight of the
heavens. She climbed with her eyes from cloud to cloud,
higher and higher up, and reached into those depths of
the blue chasm of the universe where the purest clouds
gave up hope. When they ventured there, they had to
immediately pine away. There, quite, quite high, Johanna heard a humming; but she heard it with that
mysterious hearing which is usually only detected by
people in dream. A quite quiet rustling went across all
the clouds at this infinite distance, and it sounded as if
it had been going on up there since eternity. But that
was not the strangest thing. What the farmwife took in
most vitally consisted in that the unease of the man
whose key did not fit any lock in the world was somehow contained in the quiet humming.

As she made the futile attempt for a moment to get
closer to the connection between her dream and this
mysterious sound in the heights, her husband suddenly
stood next to her, and reminded her with a smile of the
trip to her father.

At these everyday words, Sintlinger saw his wife start
and blanch. Then she shut her eyes a little, and went
back into the living room with him.

They did not take the road through Hemsterhus, but
the farmer instead steered for the child's sake around
the farm, and drove at a leisurely pace uphill, downhill
through the fields, and the little blind girl sat reclining
in her mother's arms and enjoyed with rapt little face
the coating of the soft light of July. When the wagon
sank down a slope, a joyful fear came into her mien as if

she were going into the open air. When the travelled
past trees, the child asked who was standing so tall and
motionless by the way. And when they turned into the
beech stand, the little forest which had belonged to the
estate previously belonging to Klim, Helene was astonished at how such a high, broad room was able to be
made that you could travel into.

Sintlinger did not tire of his child's wonder in which
everything familiar and known to him acted in a way
that he saw transformed behind the things a new meaning, a different life, and he often stopped to listen with
her to the quiet sound which a gentle breeze drove
through the crop fields, or to sample with the child the
high flittering of a bird's song. And when he then spoke
to Helene, his voice sounded even more deepened than
merely from astonishment and paternal love. This tone
came from such a clear chasm that Johanna leant back,
and had to look at her husband's face unobserved. At
once it seemed to her as if it were not her husband
speaking but rather as if she were hearing the gentle
humming above the clouds, and that sitting next to her
was the man who possessed the key which fitted no lock
in the world. Then she was overcome by a fear of what
would happen if Sintlinger stepped into her father's
house and began speaking in this tone.

Hence she immediately grasped at the reins, and
asked her husband to turn around for she had suddenly
become unwell. Johanna's face was really very pale. Just
a few steps, and the old man's house would emerge from
behind the fruit trees. For that reason, he drove the
horses on. The old man was looking from behind the
window at the quick approach of the carriage. He hesitated as to whether he should receive the visitors outside
or let himself be surprised in the living room, did not
sort it out, grasped his stick, let it go, put on his cap,
hung it up again, went to the door, leant out the win-

dow, and was sitting almost embarrassed at his table as Sintlinger entered quickly from outside.

Whip and hat in his right hand, holding the door to the room open with stiff arms, the young farmer remained standing on the threshold, called a casual, cheerful greeting to the old man, and informed him with a short remark that his wife was unwell. Then he hurried with a nod of his head out again to his carriage.

He unhitched it with the help of a labourer whom the new owner of the farm had immediately sent over, then had the animals led into the stables, and stood chatting a while with the new owner out of politeness. For the way to his father-in-law's retirement home, he chose in a sort of mischievous jesting the path through the little gate. By the gable wall of the home, the same woodpile seemingly still stood in which his Johanna had hidden that bouquet of flowers which he had stuck in her breast in the first intoxication of love. In walking past, he brushed the front of the pile, and smiled at the same time.

On entering his father-in-law's living room, he found the pale frailty had already been wiped from Johanna's face. The old man called to him amused from the adjoining room that the unwellness of his daughter was nothing in itself.

She had beamed with joy when Helene had attached herself to her grandfather so entirely without awe, and walked in happily behind the two as they wandered through the rooms without stopping. The old man was silently astonished over the confident, dauntless steps of the little blind girl, over the fine feeling with which she eluded objects, over her cleverness and joyfulness, but most of all over the expression of her eyes as she turned her head up to him listening when he spoke, but he locked away to himself every remark which concerned even from a distance the deplorable state of his grand-child.

To begin with, Helene was absolutely the centre, and the old man and Johanna especially, when the conversation started to take a different turn, shoved the little girl into the foreground of conversation again and again as if they, like two schemers, were frightened of betraying their plan through imprudence. But Sintlinger devoted himself without any restraint entirely to the feeling of joy which ruled over him. He even danced singing with Helene through the rooms, and the farmer's wife perceived that his voice no longer possessed any of the sound which had shaken her so on the journey there. His words sounded in contrast sometimes as if they had remained behind in him from his wild times — they had the tone of bronze balls being tossed with a short flip into a metal basin. In this quick, spirited igniting of her husband's talk lay something exceedingly comforting for the young woman. A colourful wave of youth poured out of it over her. Almost in a sort of rapt whirl, her heart rushed from the shadows and afflictions of the present into the light of her most beautiful period, but without her thinking a word about those days. She just *spoke* more inspired, *walked* more poised, *laughed* more melodiously, and secretly did not comprehend to what end and why she could have called on her father for help.

Old Klim, however, tired in the end of the walking through rooms with Helene, sat down in an armchair, and moved his snuffbox from one hand to the other. He was determined in view of the cheerfulness of Sintlinger and his daughter rather to give the benefit of his doubt to the permanent assuredness of the serious lifestyle of his son-in-law, than to believe in the worries and helplessness his daughter had spoken of to him.

"Oh, you children, now then, here!" he called during the course of the day with the happy mockery of his old, wise soul, and smiled, shaking his head, at the two who were meant to be unhappy and looked absolutely enviable in their seemingly light-hearted cheerfulness, and if he were not deceived, his daughter jumped at every cough that sounded as though he were reaching for weighty words, and made an assuaging look over to him. For that reason, the old man also decided by himself to leave to chance or, even better, to concede to the couple whether to touch on a shadow which perhaps only existed in his daughter's imagination.

The midday meal came and went. The easy colourfulness sank away from everyone. The new owner of the farm, and his wife, wholesome and nice, amiable people came for a short chat and left again. Helene wanted to sleep, and was accommodated in the adjoining room. Old Klim dozed off in his armchair.

Sintlinger went off to the new owner again, and took a tour through the cattle stalls. But Johanna walked among the hazel trees on the slope, a bit away from the house, to her childhood dreaming place. There she sat in the deep shadows of the round, oily leaves, drew her legs up like when she was a child, propped her elbows on her knees, and sank into a dreamy survey of the meadow in which she had met Sintlinger whilst bleaching.

"No, no!" she said after a long time with a happily smiling fending off; but then her head had already sunk onto her arms, and she fell asleep.

The sleep of old men is more divine than that of men in the middle of the strongest time of life; for during this even in the hours of rest the bonds of their plans are not entirely escaped, and after awakening, the conclusion to their day's work is found without hesitation; dream, that dark cloud of eternity, still hangs for a while about the alert eyes of the old so that they are bewildered by the familiar images of their surroundings as if they were apparitions from a strange world, yes, so that it may well seem that such a quietly wandering soul thinks the visit of sleep has unexpectedly opened the gates to death, and what treasure they left on earth, now greets them transfigured in heaven.

When old Klim awoke, his widower's home, the white-washed little room with the dark green garland under the ceiling, lay in the somewhat overspilling light of the brimming afternoon, and in this brightness the reflection of restive, white clouds quivered. A wavering lay about the old man. The walls did not seem to be steady at all. They swayed with the linen which a sedate wind billowed, the garland swung like a proper thread of foliage, and it seemed to the farmer no different than if he were floating billowing through the heights above the earth in a flying canvas tent, and before the windows which sat somewhere in it, he was seeing sunlit clouds streaming past.

"Yes, someday it will pass like that", the old man pondered half in dream and half awake, and let his eyes sink into the quiet relishing of the beautiful vision again. When he opened them again, the awakening was complete, and he recognised his room as it always was. On the bench which ran around two sides of the room, his blind grandchild was crouching in attentively devoted pose, and next to her sat Sintlinger, his elbows on the windowsill, and his head propped in his hand so that he could watch his daughter's face.

Now the old man watched as Helene bent back and held her hand to the light just as if the shimmering beams of the sun were not a fleeting trembling through

the air but a little arc of water which was filling her hollowed little hand with prickling warmth. What we
comprehend with our eyes, she embraced with the far
blunter sense of feeling. As if sitting invisibly under
those little finger tips there was an eye hungry for light
which was drinking the sunbeams. Thus Helene also
held each hand to the light like a slurping mouth, and
her face had an expression of fulfilled rapture, no differently than if she were a seeing person who stood in the
blessing of a still light.

As Sintlinger was observing this mysterious manner
of seeing that Helene had, he was at once again in that
astonished feeling of a deep living and weaving which
hastened behind the accustomed forms and processes of
the world to a goal which is perhaps deeper and more
glorious than we seeing people can ever experience. The
young farmer bent forward still further so as to discover
if possible something in the eyes of his child by which
his surmising could grope further into the magic. He received at the same time that touch of worry and pain in
his face which digs into the forehead and around the
mouths of men whose deep meditation takes unusual
effort.

Old Klim, however, who had observed all this, misunderstood the expression in the face of his son-in-law,
and thought that now Sintlinger had been seized by the
sorrow over his child's misfortune which he had kept so
adroitly and bravely hidden until then amidst the colourful racket. He recalled his promise to Johanna,
thought that now the right moment for intervention had
arrived, started by clearing his throat, and when, as a
result, Andreas turned around from his watching, and
looked questioning at the old man, he nodded to him
consolingly, and said kindly, "Let it well be, Andreas!"

"Oh, it is well, incomprehensibly well", the young
farmer answered in a flustered way.

"But it will get better and better, you don't need to give up hope. Yes. Giving up hope is like loading up — the more you load up, the stronger the wagon must be."

At the old man's calm way of talking, Helene ceased catching the sunbeams with her hands, sought fumbling for the table, slipped a little way along the bench, and sat upright listening.

"Little Lena thinks a story is starting", Sintlinger said with a smile, and passed his hand caressingly over his child's locks.

"There she is certainly right now", old Klim continued. "For it is a long, long story which I have spun as I was sitting in the chair here. Well, well, dear little Helene! Yes, yes. — But when you try as a human to comprehend God's decisions, then you are no different than a fly which wakes in the night and wants to leave the room. It constantly flies against the wall until it has knocked itself groggy, and next to it, perhaps not three hand-breadths away, the window stands open. With such a thing, my dear, you should seek the window calmly. Well, and with people it is also a little different — you should not grasp more despair than you can bear."

Sintlinger had meanwhile turned to the window again, and was looking out it.

"Look at me please, Sintlinger", the old man said gently urging, for he thought his son-in-law was hiding his face in pain.

"Talk with ease, Klim-father. When I turn my eyes away, I actually see you better than usual."

With these words of Sintlinger's, his wife had entered. When she heard the deep sound of his voice, the expression of unhurried drowsiness instantly vanished from her face. As she entered, she had paused quietly on the threshold, looked from one to the other, and apprehended the situation. Her father pointed to

her husband, and made a sign to her to skip away somewhere noiselessly and above all to be silent.

But then Sintlinger turned around.

"Ah, there you are too", he said with a smile.

"No? — It is a pity. Until now I have been sleeping
under the hazels", she answered, and sat down at the
table.

"He will not answer me", the old man burst out, "he
won't even look at me."

The young farmer smiled, and said to his wife, "If I
have stuck a candle in a lantern, why would I need to
light a second one?" With that he indicated with kindly
mockery and stiff thumb over his shoulder to the old
man.

"I am not understanding you, Andreas, what do you
mean?", Johanna answered, and shot a look at her
father who nodded to her encouragingly.

"Well yes, yes", Sintlinger said, taking a long breath,
and rose from his place by the window. "Come, little
Lena, we will look at the weather."

The two saw him go calmly and upright through the
door, and then looked at one another helplessly.

"He has become unearthly", old Klim said, "Hanna,
he gives answers like a house. He has lost his voice too,
did you hear how he talks?"

His daughter sat at the table, picked at her fingers,
and could barely quell the tears.

Even the old man fell into a fixed gaze. But at once
he pulled himself together, "No, no, he has really caught
himself in a black mill. But that means knocking, and if
nothing else, thundering, and the like. — Today — now
— for I am chewing so to speak on the last straws. There
is nothing to delay. Lord, my goodness!"

Johanna agreed with her father, called for the housekeeper, and sent the old woman after her husband with

instructions to take the child from him and send him in-side.

Even as they were eagerly taking counsel with each other on how to reach the poor man, Sintlinger walked in again. Johanna rose, and looked out the window. The old man rocked out of embarrassment with his eyes directed at the ceiling and the snuff box in his right hand. An oppressive mood reigned. Andreas sat down on the bench, folded his hands between his knees, and looked calmly at the floor. Then he said dreamily, "You should not have called me in. It would have been better not to. For now it is possible that you must run out. But perhaps it shall finally be so!"

"Dear Andreas", old Klim now said, "I was just thinking that too. See, when I awoke before, I did not in fact know straightaway whether I had died or was still living. Well, and if I should continue and knew you had still not gotten over your misfortune, then you can believe me that I would not find any rest in the grave. — Andreas, you must get a hold of yourself! Don't shake your head at me. You cannot make me mad, old man that I am. As the coal house burns down, the farmer stands in the midst of the corn and whistles. I know all about that! You can even whistle from fear. You see, and you stand in about that spot."

Johanna had returned to her chair. Sintlinger propped his elbows on the free place by the window, and covered his eyes with his hands.

"Keep talking", he said when the old man paused.

"Now, I think, as Johanna told me, the Münster doctor said that it would not last forever with Helene. Then you should not burrow into the darkness, but leave it all up to the Lord God, cut a stick from the ordeal so that you progress more easily, and not a switch for torment-ing yourself. Our Lord made old Tobias blind and made him see again. He will manage it with the child too, rely on it."

During the last words, Sintlinger had sprung up, and paced through the room with every sign of impatience. Now, when the old man had finished, he stepped up to him, placed his hand on his shoulder, and said with re-strained emotion, "Dear father, we do not understand each other at all. I cannot do anything wicked to a beg-gar or a vagrant. What thing then should I take away from you. Let it be. Do not worry about me. I will go and order the hitching of the carriage, and we will part in peace. The furrow which I have cultivated is going somewhere else. Adieu. Come, Johanna, and fetch the child."

The young farmer bore a luminous pallor in his face, and his eyes burned with a deep fire.

"Give me your hand, Andreas", old Klim said to him poignantly.

Sintlinger did so. "Farewell", he said.

The old man shook his head.

"No, I did not mean it like that", he said, "we are men, and can discuss with each other in peace. You have not hurt me. Go. Go, sit down and say what you have on your soul. Then we will see who is right."

His wife also insisted lovingly to him that he not shut himself off. Thus he walked hesitantly to his seat, and sat down and shook his head.

After that he waited a while, holding his face turned away, and looking at the open door into the next room as if someone would walk through it. That lasted a long time.

Unexpectedly he began to talk. To begin with, the other two did not actually realise that it was Sintlinger's voice. Johanna heard in shock the sound of the hum-ming above the clouds, and the words were as unrecognisable and incomprehensible to the old man as your own talking in a nocturnal dream which you hear but can neither prevent nor understand.

"The sparrow hawk eats the sparrow, the sparrow the beetle, the beetle the leaf. None does wrong, for it must live, and what is stronger has the power, and what has the power, prevails. So it goes in all of us. The stronger thoughts consume the weaker. In that way our power increases, and what otherwise tied us as though with cords, soon torments us no worse than a midge flying into our eye.

All that you say, father, to console me, has long been consumed in me, even solace itself. For someone who needs consoling is unhappy, but I am not.

In earlier times, I danced across the street, through the taverns, and into the halls. Now I dance within myself. Nobody notices that. But I go deeper and deeper, and only know now where the world begins."

Thus the young farmer spoke.

The two gradually came out of the whirl in which they had been enmeshed by these unexpected words, and they sat and dared not look at each other.

Sintlinger, however, had propped his elbows on his knees, and pressed his hands before his eyes. He sat there hunched up like that and, since he had stopped talking, breathed slowly and deeply as if he were sleeping.

"But the child", old Klim said because he did not rightly know what Sintlinger meant.

"Not even for the child's sake", Andreas answered in the same sleep-walking way, without changing his pose. "If someone needs consoling, it is not me, but God."

"But she is blind", the old man interjected helplessly.

"If she were blind, yes, all the more would God need consoling like someone to whom a folly or something wrong has happened."

"Andreas", Johanna cried, wrestling with herself.

Old Klim had clasped his hands together tightly, and was looking desperately with deathly pale face into emptiness.

"Well now", Sintlinger answered his wife, "it's okay. *If* she were. But she *is* not blind at all. She just does not need them, she looks out *over* her eyes.

You have noticed, Johanna, that our girl saw the tree on the way, and the forest, and the birds in the air. Didn't you? Answer me."

"Yes, certainly, but not with her eyes."

"And with what then?"

Johanna leant back painfully, drew her shoulders up, and said, "Oh God, heaven knows!"

"Well, with what then, father? Tell me!"

The old man gave no answer. He had propped his chin on his fist, and looked sombrely at the table.

"Now, I will tell you. With the soul. — So, with it we see everything. The eyes are only a detour. And what we see in the soul is a different thing to the world in our eyes. For that reason, there is behind the world of the eyes *another* world. And each thing is duplicated. And while I live, I live at the same time here and as though behind distant bushes ... and from that side of existence, my child looks at the world, at me, at you, Johanna, and at you, father. And for that reason, I would like to sing when she looks at something and life has come to it. No unease torments me anymore."

Sintlinger had, without knowing it, stood up, and as his streaming words became quieter and ever quieter as though from their own repletion, he made a few unconscious steps towards the door of the adjoining room. —

That was too much.

Old Klim started now, set his snuffbox audibly on the table, and said, laughing derisively, "Haha. Yes. Good. And what did the doctor say? The doctor also had ideas! Right?"

The entire old antipathy, the suppressed loathing to-wards the "robber" and "torturer" of his only child somersaulted into the aged man who saw his deepest certainties in life threatened by his son-in-law.

"Now *I* am asking and *you* will answer!" the old man added still shaking, and prodded the table a few times with his stiff forefinger. Sintlinger started from his rap-ture, and paused over the unaccustomed tone of the old man.

"The doctor?" he asked calmly and coldly.

"Yes, the doctor", Klim repeated belligerently.

"The doctor? — is a fool", the young farmer finally answered dismissively, and leant gently against the doorpost.

"But Andreas, you yourself skipped when he said our little Lena will see again", Johanna meanwhile joined in.

"Then I was also foolish, dear", Sintlinger answered with a smile.

"So, and you think then, because it fits so in your mad head, the doctor is wrong, and your child shall re-main blind all her life!" Klim cried more and more agitatedly.

A flash came from Sintlinger's eyes. But he mastered himself, and said calmly, "Dear old man! She just *is* not blind. It is more than sight, nobody makes a round wheel rectangular. So. Selah! Come, Johanna! You can-not thresh with the potato machine."

"Yes, certainly not, haha", the old man replied deris-ively, "and a wagon without long reins falls apart. And you are missing the long reins, Sintlinger, the lifelong reins, faith!"

Andreas paid no attention to the old man's words; with a wrenching jolt, he left his place by the door to the adjoining room, and went skipping through the room, collecting together his things. He looked to the pot cup-board, next to the clock case, on the bench, under the bench, hummed as if singing constantly to himself, "Where? — Where? — Where?", sometimes whistling softly, coughed curtly, laughing through clenched teeth, clasped shaking hands, swallowed his breath like a hot soup, and finally could not hold himself anymore.

He paused in the middle of the room, then threw a glance past old Klim like a sparkling knife, and asked stingingly, "Well?", and then passed with blazing eyes to his wife. But both dared not make a sound anymore. The old man had grasped the table top with one hand, with the other he clasped the snuffbox, and stared in disbelief and somewhat dully at Sintlinger. Johanna looked imploringly at him.

The young farmer had slogged doggedly up a steep mountain.

"Well?" he asked to the old man's face again, and then burst out into a laughter which lasted until he was ashen-faced and had the gleam of tears in his eyes.

"You think, old man, I have a fool's drum for a skull. Otherwise you would not dare to speak to me like I'm a child", he then said dully.

"I have my duty as a Christian", the old man answered coldly, "to set the straying on the right path."

Again Sintlinger burst out into a raucous laughter. After that it was deathly still in the room.

"I have my Christian faith, my precious Christian faith ...", the old man stuttered. Then the clock struck the hour.

Sintlinger sprang to it, stopped the pendulum, and seized the weight as if he were on the point of pulling the clock down and tossing it away in a great arc.

"For God's sake, what has suddenly gotten into you, Andreas?" his wife cried out.

"Let it be", he said, reassuring her, and looked rigidly, his lips tightly pressed together, with consuming eyes at the old man.

Finally he spoke in an unnaturally soft voice to old Klim, "You, with your Christian faith, you, you — if I lift a stone and release it from my hand, it falls down ... doesn't it ...?"

The old man bent his head, and fell silent.

"Yes, and when the rain steps off the cloud, it must fall to the earth. — Well? — Or could perhaps the clouds in the sky remain where they are when the wind blows? — Or the stone fly into the air again of its own accord, and water run upstream?"

He let go of the pendulum's chain, and took a step closer to old Klim.

"Hey, you, if that could be, if it could just be for a single time, then at once we would not be able to reckon with certainty on day and night and summer and winter anymore, and the stars in the sky would be as insecure as the tiles on the roof."

Sintlinger's breath went like a storm through him, and when he now fell silent, and his head sank onto his chest, it was now plunging up and down like surging waves.

Johanna was hit by the thought that madness had seized her husband, paralysing him like a blow to the head. She rose staggering to hurry to him.

"Stay sitting, dear wife", he began anew with iron calmness. "It is neither about my collar nor about yours. — But the straying man must be set on the right path. Right, Klim-father? Was it not so? — Now, and do you perhaps think someone of the world or outside the world would have the power to have the released stone not fall and the clouds not flee when the wind blows? — A single one?"

Then the old man jumped up like a gaunt tree which an earthquake has tossed up.

"Sintlinger", he cried beseechingly, "... you ...! Think what you are saying! There is a God in heaven!" But now a radiant smile came into Andreas's face.

"Yes", he inserted sharply, "not even God. Not a dust mote can he alter by it! — Nothing! — Haha. — Or if he did, he would be like a man who takes his own life. You all don't realise that; you don't, the Pastor doesn't, and the Münster doctor not really at all. — Johanna, if fate sent us an angel in our Helene, it will not make a person with eyes like we have out of her again. It is not even possible. Or stones will first have to fly into the air by themselves, and the Lord must make himself out of dust."

Johanna sank to the floor, numbed.

The old man groped at the table, his lips flew, but they did not catch any words.

Sintlinger set the clock into motion again, and said, "So, and now the clock can go again. For now is the correct time."

Then he bent down to his wife, took her head in the palms of his hands, lifted her up to himself, and asked kindly, "Hanna, dear, do you still like me? Dear wife?"

"Push him away from you!" the old man suddenly cried fearfully.

"Will you tell me?" Sintlinger whispered.

"He is a devil, Johanna! Stay with me!" the old man called beseechingly.

"Do you want to be with him or with me? Do what you must. I will not count it as a disgrace to you", the young farmer continued talking in quiet amicability.

Then the poor woman closed her despairing eyes, and embraced him around the neck.

Thus Sintlinger lifted her up, led her through the rooms, and helped her gather her things.

Then he stepped up to the old man who was still standing chalk-white and motionless on the same spot.

"Why did you not let me go, father?" he spoke calmly. "I asked you to. So, adieu!"

With that he stretched out his hand to him.

Klim made a powerless push against him, and sank sagging, with averted face, into his armchair.

"Then at least offer your hand to your daughter", Andreas said.

But the old man remained sitting turned away, and said with a voice choked with hate, "Out! Everyone out!"

And when the door had closed behind both of them, he obstinately turned his head, looked blindly at nothing for a long time with wide-open eyes, and murmured as though in a dream, "You sod ... You sod ... God forgive me my sins."

Then he sank onto the table, and began to sob.

In the night after the Sintlinger family's departure, the old housekeeper heard the old farmer crying, not rattling the way pain arduously struggles free from aged souls, but high, helpless, almost singing, like a lonely child crying. The woman, a well-tested old piece of furniture from Klim's short marriage, had set up her bed for the purpose of quicker help in the room next door to the widower's bedroom, whose door was left slightly ajar. As the old woman heard the powerless crying, she at first thought the night wind was sighing through the chimney. But when it repeated, she went with a candle and held its light to the face of her master. But he was sound asleep. He lay placid and pale on the pillows, and looked as though in vigil. The torturous dream must have left him on the approach of the candlelight. Only a trace of deep, almost desperate sorrow had remained behind, and without shaking, tears were running from the outer corners of his eyes over his furrowed cheeks, not in drops, but in uninterrupted soundless streams.

She carefully dabbed his face clean, and ducked into bed again. But the faithful soul lay for hours half between sleep and listening, and suffered from that strangely oppressive silence which listening itself produces in the darkness of the night. Only she could not repel the dreamlike doubt as to whether old Klim was not demandingly exhausting himself under the mask of sleep in this oppressive vigil, and to her it seemed as if she saw him sitting upright in bed, his frail hands entwined, and his eyes riveted to the door as though sucking on it. But the grey bonnet of sleep finally sank over her head. She still heard vaguely as if through a thick wall the old farmer calling, "Hanna, come in. Come in at your ease. I did not mean you, Hanna, dear!" Then everything sank into the ghostly quiet swishing with which dreams move into our souls.

When she opened her eyes, the cockcrow was already bursting loudly into the bright morning. Everywhere the sharpening of scythes played in the air. Had someone called her? But now, as she threw her clothes on in drowsiness, she realised that she herself, from within, had shaken herself awake with this cry. No sound could be heard from the farmer's bedroom. Dressed scantily, she tiptoed in. The bed was empty. The door into the living room stood torn wide open. She continued in just as quietly. There she met old Klim already in his Sunday-best, dressed perfectly from the polished boots to the carefully tied silk tie. He was sitting upright at the table like a traveller who lingers for hours in the waiting room of a railway station, waiting for the departure call. He sat with his cap next to him, one arm propped on the table, his stick in his right hand. His furrowed face was pale, and directed undisturbed, as if seeking something, towards the floor. He had obviously not heard the entrance of his housekeeper, for he did not stir in his pose, and seemed to be watching out for whether something would not spring out of the floor. The old woman was so taken aback by the unaccustomed sight that she did not dare to call out to her master. Suddenly the old man shook his head disbelievingly, and said quietly to himself, "Trine ... Trine ... Wagner Trine ... get up ...!"

They were the same words which the housekeeper had heard in her sleep, and then taken for a waking call from her own will.

"Here I am, Klim-father!" the old woman answered hesitantly, for she was frightened for a reason she did not understand that the old man would break down at her words or begin to cry as he had done during the night.

But Klim did not change his pose, instead just raising his head, and looking past Trine. His eyes stood still and had a look as if someone had spoken to him from a great distance.

"Why did you let me call you for so long?" he then said irritably and in a monotone. "Go and call the farmer. I must travel into town, and straightaway."

After that he let his head sink again. Trine assailed him with questions as to what it was about, whether he felt ill, and whether it would not be better to get undressed, crawl into bed, and take a fever remedy. The old farmer paid no attention to her words, and looked constantly at the floor. When she had stopped talking, he looked at her with a smile, and said gently and imploringly, "It doesn't matter, dear. Go and do what I told you."

He declined breakfast, sat there upright as if ready to jump up, and goaded her with quiet words to hurry.

Within half an hour, the farmer had rushed in front of the door with the carriage, and Klim stepped decisively out the door.

In the carriage's cushions, he grasped the handle of his stick tightly with both hands, and shut his eyes.

The horses pulled, and drew away from there.

The rolling of the wheels rumbled and rattled around him. The old farmer lay in the corner of the carriage constantly with lowered eyes.

When old Klim opened his eyes, the town was before him. It lay in the light of morning colourful and radiant amidst the green. But to the old man's clouded eyes, it looked like a grey phantom swaying in an inaudible wind.

The hooves of the horses now rang out brightly on the cobblestones. The carriage stopped before the inn. The old farmer had lapsed again into his dull soliloquy. His lips moving incessantly as if they were bubbling with a fever, he endeavoured to get down from the carriage. He did not notice that the young farmer helped him and talked to him about where he wanted to go, how long his business would last, and whether he should not go with him. Klim shook his head, endeavoured to smile, and said to himself, "The blind child ... the blind child ..." Thus he went down the street with faltering steps, and sometimes staggered like he was half drunk.

When the young farmer saw that, he threw the reins to the porter, and followed the old man at some distance to be at hand if something happened to him. But the deeper Klim went into the town, the more certain his gait became. At the little market square planted with lime trees, he suddenly pulled up, and stepped, stiffly upright, with rigid steps into the house of a well-known notary.

Now the young farmer knew the bells the sound of which had so transformed old Klim into unrecognisability. For the sake of certainty, he reread the sign next to the front door — Doctor Mende, Lawyer and Notary.

"Well then", he pondered to himself, "some are swept by pain before the gravedigger's feet, others by happiness. Yes, and yesterday they were all still as happy as fairgoers. But a child only needs to touch the ripe apple for it to fall."

Depressed, he then returned to the inn.

The old man, meanwhile, was sitting in the notary's room which, lit only by one window, lay half in darkness. Like the day before after waking up in the armchair, he had the feeling of floating through the clouds high above the earth. The aged lawyer, who had dealt all his life with the few legal matters he had been enmeshed in, without action on his part, sat on the half turned desk chair before him and chatted, as was his way, without stopping in a rasping voice at him. Klim looked at him sitting far below him, and it sounded as if he were speaking up from the street. With nods and shakes of the head and some ambiguous fillers, the farmer helped himself into a comfortable situation so that the other did not notice how it stood with him. He was scared of just the one thing — that Mende might now stop talking and ask what he was after. The sweat appeared on the old man's forehead. Then instantly everything foundered. The walls of the room moved in grey waves at him. Everything turned sharply distinct around him. The humming in his head also stopped, and it was cold, clear, and still in him like on a hard winter's morning. With steady voice, he cut through the midst of the unremitting stream of talk, and asked for the handing over of his deposited testament.

"A codicil, hmhm, old man, a codicil", the notary mocked with a smile, "can imagine, certainly. The hen does not stop scratching. And now the little heap shall also be housed. It is all the same to me. But you should at least think of *yourself* for once during these last years, not always of others."

During these words, Mende had stood up, had un-locked his desk, and was now rummaging about in it.

The farmer sat stiffly, and thought, "Now I will bury my daughter's fortune. Now everything must go down-hill, there is no more stopping it."

With superhuman effort, he held himself upright, but had barely felt the document in his hands when a trembling began to rattle his body. Everything in the room skipped. Only a spot on the wall, diagonally across from him and at the height of a cupboard, was still, he could distinguish exactly the small greyish-black loz-enges on the green background of the wallpaper.

"I just want to step over for a moment to that spot on the wall", he thought to himself, "then I will rip up my testament."

He rose laboriously from the chair, and smiled imp-ishly at Mr Mende. That is, he thought he did. In truth, his face was painfully distorted.

"What are you doing?" the notary asked in shock.

"My legs are falling asleep", Klim answered with great effort.

He only had two more steps to go to the wall. — Only suddenly he saw the wall torn apart from top to bottom with a crunch which went painfully through his body like a knife. — He staggered, and sank with a cry to the floor.

His eyes stood wide open. His lips moved constantly without making a sound, as if he were praying, and his wilted face smiled in despair.

He returned thus to his house, and was taken to bed.

His housekeeper wanted to immediately send to Hemsterhus for the Sintlingers, but he forbade it be-cause it was only a passing thing.

The farmer then lay for two days and two nights, and looked incessantly at the door as if he were expecting someone.

Nobody learnt whom his eyes were longing for. On the third morning, something had been overcome in him. He was cheerful, sat up in bed, and asked for food.

Halfway through the afternoon, he had himself dressed, and went on the housekeeper's arm out to the little bench before the house.

There he sat in the sun, his hands folded in his lap, and looked over to the meadow from where Sintlinger had once enticed away his only child.

The old man let his eyes drop, and devoted himself to the soundless, radiant flooding apart which filled the entire world. When he rose again, he saw not all too dis-tantly through a path between the fields a farmwife coming down the hill to him with lusty strides. She had her skirt drawn up, the red headscarf tied deep over her forehead, and carried a bright sickle in her right hand. In walking, her left hand brushed through the crops. Now she was in the meadow. Suddenly she stopped, looked over to him for a long time, nodded to him ami-ably, bent down, and picked a white flower. She came with it over the road, straight towards him. He saw her more and more exactly, the red headscarf, the drawn up skirt, the sickle, and could not deceive himself anymore that it was the young wife of the farmer to whom he had sold his property. But, in rapt horror, he did not bring himself to look straight in her shaded face, for it seemed to him that if he did that then he would see the counten-ance of his long dead wife. His heart began to flutter, and he lowered his face in bashful joy.

Now he could hear her skirt rustling next to him. Now she stood by him, and he felt how she pushed the cool stem of a flower between his fingers. Then it was humming around him, and the old man's senses depar-ted.

When the housekeeper went to see her master, he sat lifelessly on the little bench. A rapt smile lay on the face of the dead man, and the fingers of his right hand were still set as though they were holding a flower.

8

Johanna had not indeed, in the four days which lay between the Brederode discussion and the passing away of old Klim, come to any clarity over her heavily depressed soul, but had pushed herself up to the unbreakable calm of her husband as far as the extent of her old trust, and considered her most fervent wish to be attainable, that time would not only drive the wild ghosts from her husband's head, but also bridge the chasm which had opened up between her father and everyone who lived on the Sintlinger farm. Above all, she was reassured by the secret intention to set off at the first friendly sign to shimmer over to her hill from the Brederode retirement home, and to induce by love that reconciliation which the stubbornness of the men had not achieved.

On the evening of the day on which old Klim had with a smile enticed forever the breath from his chest, the two were leaning on the fence of the little flower garden behind the barn and looking through the glassy darkening at the endless rows of scarecrows swaying over the hill like a procession of masked men. Then Trine, the old housekeeper, stood unexpectedly next to the two, as if carried soundlessly out of the darkness. Her headscarf had fallen to her neck, her sweat-covered hair hung over her forehead. She struggled for words, but managed nothing but a stream of tears, and finally lifted up her struggling hands. "Come in, Trine", Sintlinger said, taking her by the arm and leading the old woman, who continued softly sobbing, across the darkened yard to the large, servants' room. It was empty, for the tired servants had already sought out their rooms or were sitting on the bench under the lime trees by the gate. The farmer sat the old woman down behind the table and, while he lit the little table lamp, Johanna also came in.

White as paper, stiff, soundless, she walked across the floor, took a seat next to Trine, and looked rigidly at her hands lying folded in her lap. Andreas closed the door to the bedroom where Helene was resting in her little bed, and then said, "Well, Trine, now tell us how it happened."

He placed himself opposite the two woman on the other side of the table, propped his hand with folded fingers on the table top, and looked attentively at the old housekeeper. She staggered at first with half sentences through a row of disconnected exclamations and asseverations, and when she had in this way somewhat relieved herself of the burden of her pain, she succeeded by and by to find her way into her memory, and she told in a long-winded way, right down to every look and half sigh, precisely of the misery by which the old man had been afflicted during his last days. Johanna did not move an inch, and seemed not to take a single breath. Only at the telling of the silent longing with which her father had looked at the door, constantly waiting, did an almost animal-like cry of pain erupt from her. Then she sat motionless again, without any tears. She just sank more and more into herself, and finally slipped soundlessly under the table when she heard the description of the gleam with which her father had been blinded from the living.

The endeavours of the two succeeded in tearing her from her faint, and when she opened her eyes, the first tears came forth. They flowed quietly, without sobs, over her pale cheeks and past her closed, discoloured mouth. Thus Johanna looked at her husband with eyes which dug almost devouringly into his deepest parts until the despairing pain of her face was transformed into such a horror that she could not bear the sight of her husband anymore. She shut her eyes, and turned towards the wall on the bench where she had been laid. She remained thus for a long time with breaths which sounded as if her body were being torn apart at every seam.

Finally she turned around again.

"You cannot stay here today", Sintlinger said. She shook her head.

Then the farmer waited earnestly for an answer. But she looked past him at the ceiling, and remained silent.

"Hm, hm", he spoke after some thought. "You must go to the vigil, I know … I know everything."

And without waiting for a response, he went and harnessed the horses, and the old labourer drove the women down the hill through the shadowy heavy summer night over to Brederode.

✳✳✳

For three days and two nights, Johanna stayed with her dead father and wrestled with herself. Sometimes it came over her that Andreas had pushed her father into the grave. Then she felt the horror running like a film of frost over her eyes, and her vision was turned out of her head. Her feet took flight, and she found herself in the hazels on the slope or by a tree in the fields. Sometimes she also had the sensation of not herself talking, seeing, thinking, walking, and resting. It seemed to her as if a force whose existence and intentions she could not grasp was taking hold of her will and life. For the discussion between her father and Andreas which should have freed her and him from the shadows had turned into a path which had just led deeper into the darkness.

From this darkening, she hurried to the dead man's bier, sank to her knees in silent tears, and asked the dead man whether she or Andreas had pushed him out of the world, whether he was angry with her. She could not help it, and he might at least help her from eternity so that she did not give up hope. But when she rose from such impassioned laments, and looked in the dead man's face, she was overcome by the shame at having disturbed his peace. For the beauty in which the old man had dreamt himself away still blossomed on his countenance, and he did not lie there like a dead man, but like one who had stretched out on his bed so as to enjoy with closed eyes the deep meaning of a wondrous story which is just then fading away in his ears.

Thus the anguished flickering of her moods reassured itself ever anew. But when she was on the point of setting her feet on the way to the blessed farm, she was turned back from within in despondency and covert horror.

When, on the evening of the third day, Sintlinger appeared in Brederode, because the burial was to take place on the next morning, he encountered his wife with a hidden apprehension no longer surrounded by such heavy shadows like when she had left him, only her eyes still wandered about in an unsettled way, she looked at him fearfully from the side, and while the two treated the days-long absence of Johanna as something quite natural, and talked about the state of the housekeeping, the development of Helene, and the progress of the harvest, he felt how she weighed the sound of his voice for a painfully long time in her ear, paid attention to his striding along, and almost reproachfully examined the calm with which he strode under the trees next to her to the threshold of the house of mourning.

Thus they stepped together into the room where old Klim was laid out, lit by only a night candle. Johanna immediately began crying softly, moving her lips, and sprinkling the dead man with holy water.

Suddenly she asked with shrouded voice, "Where will my father be now?" and turned her pale, shaking face to him.

She saw how her husband's lips stirred, but he did not answer, instead gazing in deep thought and placing his hand on the dead man's forehead in farewell.

After that he said the incomprehensible words, "The sea has drawn back."

Then they climbed silently to their farmstead.

Perhaps Sintlinger was thinking to himself, 'She is like someone who, suddenly overcome by fright in a wide forest, runs in all directions. If I now start calling to her to lead her onto my proper path, who knows if her fear will skew the sound of my voice so that she only scents a new danger in it, and instead of finding me runs still deeper into the madness.' That or something similar must have seized Sintlinger. For he neither stirred her soul with a lightening word on this evening, nor did he come to her help on the following morning other than by the fact of his indestructible confidence.

Steadily and freely, seriously, but quite unclouded, he stood next to her before the open grave, opposite the Hemsterhus Pastor who recited the responsories with his droning voice. The mournful bells of the little Brederode church let their sounds stray incessantly into the grey air, and the hills drew all around, exhausted in inconsolable expanses.

Johanna had folded her hands below her breast, and did not raise her eyes from the wall of earth which was heaped up around the grave. It looked as if she were endeavouring with her eyes to burrow a sense of her fate out of the ground. She remained in this position during the Pastor's funeral sermon, which began by speaking of the fullness of midsummer, of the sorrow of the heavens and the abrupt jolt of the sun out of the clouds. Then he spoke of the mature fruit of a man's life which death has calmly harvested here. For that reason, it behove everyone who was still filled by the steady faith in the reward of eternal joy on the other side to be full of joy, even if achingly. For if there was one certainty for our weak understanding here on earth, it was that for the dead man, who had himself been a friend to him, almost a paternal brother, the gates to blessedness had been opened willingly and widely.

The red-haired, large hands of the clergyman trembled whenever he lifted them in blessing or stretched them out, and several times his voice even faltered with emotion.

Here and there a quiet lament came from the funeral train. The men made sombre faces because they did not want to cry. Johanna stood deeply bowed, and her tears flowed soundlessly. She inconspicuously scanned Sintlinger with a glance to convince herself as to whether the sorrow had also seized him. Only he had still not had his upright pose handicapped by any gesture. Even if pale of face, he looked with his eyes straight ahead as if into the far-off distance. With a furtive shiver, she turned back again to her anguish. Yes, her posture even spoke somewhat of hopelessness.

The Pastor had allowed a pause to occur, and sent his gaze around, mulling the continuation.

It is probable that Sintlinger, standing there stiff and unmoved, affronted him, perhaps he was also only seized by the vanity of so many eulogists who seek the worth of their oratorical efforts in the ferocity of the anguish which they unleash. He began abruptly to speak of the lot of those piteous men who in the blindness of pride do not accept the fate of life, but, to evade the remorse over their sins, fool themselves over the nature of God, with crazy thoughts and all sorts of bold explanations of eternal dispensation. But he did not content himself with that. Once in the swing of it, it drove him deeper and deeper into the dismal circling, and he described with all the colours of fanatical, unrestrained imagination the end of the Godless.

Sintlinger, however, suddenly, with an abrupt cough which sounded like a mocking laugh, cut this heathen tumult through the middle so that the Pastor fell silent as if a stone had flown into his mouth.

But the blessed farmer paid no attention to the effect of his indignation — he leant over to his wife, whispered something kindly into her ear, and touched her shoulder soothingly with his hand. Johanna turned her twitching, streaming face to him, and looked at him sadly. And in the opinion that his wife was therefore so overwhelmed by her despair because she believed he was defying her father's death out of hostility, he bent down, picked a few red flowers next to his feet, and threw them onto the dead man's coffin instead of dirt.

But Johanna was so deep in the whirl of her anguish that she did not appear to notice this act of her husband's at all; she groped about in the fresh earth with dulled fingers, and threw it onto the coffin. At the same time, she said almost out loud and menacingly, "God give you eternal peace."

When the funeral entourage approached the two to express to them their condolences with the usual few words, her mood was still so unsettled that she obviously did not entirely grasp what all these people were aiming at in grasping her hand and addressing her. She looked at the people who stood before her no differently than like a runner who unexpectedly stands before a wall; a turbid helplessness was in her gaze. Sintlinger knew how to shorten the process in every way, and so he succeeded in the end quite quickly to twist himself with Johanna through the crowd to the exit. Certainly he had to almost carry his wife, for hardly had a new word of comfort forcibly lifted her head than her face fell to the ground again, and it seemed as if her life depended upon finding something between the other people's feet.

Already they stood perhaps six steps away from the crumbling gate arch which vaulted over the churchyard entrance, and except for a few small farmers from Hemsterhus, only Brindeisener and his family were still to be overcome. The were leaning quite compressed in the corner of the wall behind the gate; Anton Brindeisener, although slightly stooped, with his head almost touching the tiles of the little roof over the gate, more like a giant pyramid of ungainly human bones with inexorably cold eyes under a protruding squared-off forehead, awaiting the approach of the Sintlinger couple; and, almost obscured by the high wall of his back, his wife with her large, flat face and a painfully squinting look in her eye; next to her Amalie, her daughter, that one who had lain at death's door on the Sintlinger's wedding day, still pale, gaunt, ill.

Something like a happy fear radiated more and more passionately from the girl's large, hectically sparkling eyes when she saw Sintlinger leading his wife, sleepwalking with mourning, towards her at the exit. Yes, she seemingly fell into confusion, smiled and cried all-in-one, and already began nodding to testify to her agreement when her father had hardly begun saying with his gruff bass his words of regret and comfort.

Only suddenly something extraordinary happened. Johanna started from her sunken stooping, looked with horror into Brindeisener's face, tore away from her husband, and hurried down the steps to the path. Andreas

was unable to call her back, apologised for her behaviour as being a result of her agitation, and quickly
followed her.

9

Johanna had fallen under the wheels of the ghost
wagons which Sintlinger had warned her about long
before. She no longer possessed any power over her
strength of mind which had fallen into hopeless disorder. The death of her father had torn open a cleft next
to her, and she was convinced by her fear that her life
and that of her family must perish into it. Rumours over
her disinheritance in favour of Helene — which had
probably been strewn in the district by the notary, if
also only out of chattiness, and, misunderstood and exaggerated, and ran from house to house — burdened her
heart anew with the agonising certainty that her father,
if not with a soul averse to her, had parted in death
without any trust in a good outcome for her life. And
when after the elapse of three weeks, the reading of the
will made lies of all the rumours, she did not emerge
from her fear.

She had the greater part of her father's furniture
brought to the blessed farm, and distributed it amongst
the many rooms so as to plant in every room, in every
corner a breath and sound of the blessings of her youth,
of her father and mother, and thereby banish the perdi-
tion which haunted the hill. For the same reason, she
took her father's old housekeeper to the farmstead, and

entrusted her with tending to Helene. She herself, however, ran almost every morning behind her husband's back to the church at Hemsterhus, squeezed herself into the darkest corner, and barely looked up once during the entire mass from the Book which she imbibed from, selecting randomly like a child from it all, but preferring, trembling, most of all that prayer in which the talk was of the lowness, baseness, and corruption of human nature. And always, when she had so completely destroyed and trod herself down, she no longer felt the menace so darkly over herself and over the heads of her family.

Once, on reading the "prayer for our enemies", from the great whirl which had filled her inner being there emerged the memory of the way in which she had torn away from Brindeisener and his family at her father's funeral, and hurried down the churchyard steps. She saw the cold face of the gigantic, old farmer, his closed forehead, and his pale blue, cold eyes suddenly so starkly before herself that she obtained the conviction of having excited anew by her behaviour the hostility of the residents of the other estranged farm, and if she did nothing for their reconciliation, the superficially buried hate on the neighbouring hill would break out again and increase the danger which she saw lurking around her family.

On that same day, before Sintlinger had returned home from the fields, she set off under the protection of evening on the path to the Brindeisener farmstead. A few missing geese gave the pretext for her visit. But when she sat opposite the old farmwife by the window, heard her dry, brittle voice, and saw her kindly squinting eyes, she could not bring herself to speak of her lapse in the churchyard. She compelled herself with force to be friendly, and treated the nearness of the farms like a nearness of the families, thought of every concurrent stepping out of the yard gate as a greeting, and talked of the general work on the farm as if of the execution of plans advised in harmony. Brindeisener approached the chatting women at moments, listened to them with half squinting eyes as if in mocking amuse-ment; his oldest son walked heavily with long strides through the room a few times, stood and listened and, on Johanna's turning around, made himself busy and left sheepishly. On every staircase, ungainly steps rumbled, the entire homestead was as if filled by the dull racket of a hulking machine; everything was joyless and earnest.

Little Peter, now already a seven year old solid and white-haired boy, the one who on the day of Helene's birth had heard Johanna's high cry of distress, was the only ringing, the only light in this taciturn, dismal home.

Johanna Sintlinger had now risen, and was walking slowly next to the old farmwife to the door. Then he sprang laughing over the threshold, and pulled behind him a young dog who was playfully biting firmly onto a rope which he shook back and forth growling. When he became aware of Johanna, he immediately fell silent, and hid behind his mother's skirt. He could not be moved to a greeting, but burrowed both hands as if pro-tectively with stiff arms deep into his trouser pockets; but as Mrs Brindeisener immediately began to overflow delightedly in his praise, he looked quite astonished into Johanna's face the way children marvel at images of which they have heard in fairy tales. In the doorway, he plucked at his mother's skirt, drew her down, and whispered something in her ear. The farmwife closed his mouth, pushed him back into the house, and smiled meaningfully at Johanna. In striding across the yard, she told her about the little boy's request. He had wanted to know whether Johanna would fly home now.

For since he had heard her shrill cry in the air that evening, whose meaning he could not comprehend, he had considered her to be a wondrous being who, whenever it occurred to her, could sometimes walk the earth as a human and sometimes fly as a bird in the air.

Shaking her head, Johanna descended the Brindeisener hill, and thought to herself, 'Oh yes, the child is right, it sometimes takes you and leads you through the air to where you don't want to go.'

Down by the boundary path, she suddenly felt a warm child's hand in her right hand. When, startled from her thoughts, she looked down next to her, Peter stood with her, and was looking up at her in wishful happiness. But before she could say something to him, he stormed back laughing until he had gotten himself to safety. Then he turned around, and called her name jubilantly for a long time until she vanished under the gate of the blessed farm.

"Sintlinger! Sint—liiing—er!" the little Brindeisener sang over the little valley between the two estranged farms. The boundary path flowed like a soundless, yellow stream through the falling darkness. The willows stood like bowed load bearers resting a little by the edge of the ditch. The giant lime trees by the gate of the Sintlinger homestead were already like dark clouds.

Little Peter saw Johanna disappear inside, and thought with happy shivers that now she would become a bird again and fly into the heavens.

Then his singing became softer and softer, and at last he just bore it like a ringing shimmer inside himself.

Before falling asleep, he toddled over once more as if drunk, and grasped at the dormer window, for he slept with his sister in the upstairs room.

"What stupid thing are you doing again?" she asked, and immediately went back to sleep.

But Peter opened the little window, and looked up into the sky. The stars were wandering like glow worms in thick swarms through the sky, and the moon's white balloon swayed gently in the wind.

"Sintlinger", the little boy said in quiet yearning, and saw the name smoking as a white ribbon from his mouth up into the sky, for it was already autumn. Then Peter held it for certain that he had blown the farmwife a silver thread in the sky by which she could find him if she wanted, and he felt his way back happily through the darkness of the room past his sister's bed to his own.

**

Only for Mrs Sintlinger, this visit to the Brindeisener farmstead had only resulted in new trouble. Since she had not found the courage to confess her lapse in the churchyard, but had not neglected the request for forgiveness either — her quite amiable, ingratiating way must have been understood by the Brindeiseners as an admission of the guilty — she suffered alike under both, under the failed admission and the half execution. She could think only with anxiety of the Brindeisener farmstead with its many dim nooks, unfriendly corners, threatening shadowy stairs, and the grey living room, as if she had done something with the visit alone which could not be set right again, and even if she also established the intention of never setting a foot in the other estranged farmstead again, it was of no use. She heard herself constantly be enticed over by little Peter's voice. It rang so jubilantly, as if it were impossible for her to be able to permanently withstand it. The thought of their fateful interweaving and the legend of the terrible denouement of the two families did its thing to deepen this uncertain blackening of the fear so that she was led at once hard up against the whirling threshold of madness.

The Blessed Farm

That day she strode through the long, half-dark corridor of the second storey of the Sintlinger house. Only
the two staircase openings, one from the hall, the other
from the ground floor, breathed a weak light into the
broad passage. The doors to the rooms were stuck to the
left and right like dark cupboards in the wall. And when
Johanna looked down the corridor, as always befogged
by the constant seething of her life worries, she noticed
three doors away from her towards the stairs to the
ground floor a shadow stepping out of the wall. It came
out of the wall, quietly and effortlessly, like a man leaving his room through the door, and carried itself
upright, without steps, towards her, towards the stairs
to the ground floor, but as if it wanted to go past her.

Johanna thought it was her own shadow, although
she could not comprehend how it was at all possible in
the dark hallway, but stepped hard against the wall,
since it was gliding nearer and nearer to her, yes, she
not only pressed her back flat against the wall, but even
placed her hands on the cold plaster, and drew her feet
back so that she by necessity stood on her toes. Hardly
had she thus secured herself than the black, tall, soundless movement was also already close to her.

Horrified, Johanna stared at the hallucination of her
overwrought imagination ,and did not notice that Sintlinger was climbing up the stairs from the hall thinking
to himself. When he arrived on the landing where the
turn of the stairs finished, he caught sight of his wife
standing as if nailed to the wall, pale and motionless.
She was desperately staring at something which must
have been standing before her. With two gentle skips,
he was in the passage. No soul other than her was found
above, no scurrying of fleeing steps, no creaking of the
door was heard.

Then he called her name, and suddenly, like a picture
falling from the wall, she detached from the wall, and if

he had not sprung over to her, she would have crashed lengthwise onto the floor. He was able to catch her in his arms though. But hardly had he begun to lovingly reproach her over this persistent collapsing in anguish, and to scold her kindheartedly, than her breath began to rattle, and she sought violently to writhe out of his arms and plunge to his feet. Andreas gathered his poor wife up, pressed the next door open with his elbow, and preserved her from the curiosity of the servants. From the lower floor, a woman's skirt was already flying hurriedly up the steps. Sintlinger kicked the door shut quickly with his foot, and laid Johanna on the sofa. But he had barely let go of her when she sank to her knees before him, and begged imploringly amidst sobs, "Andreas, dear Andreas, don't be angry, I beg you, don't take it badly ... I was at the Brindeisener's farmstead."

It took him effort to calm her down. To start with, he used turns of phrase which it was the custom to use in mollifying excited people — wrongly burrowing monotonously into the pain, with goodwill as sole saviour, and what presented itself easily in a hurry, and sensed though that he was not achieving anything with these words, although her breast moved more easily, and her tears began to dry up.

Her hand pressed to her face, turned to the sofa back, Johanna heard Sintlinger's words of comfort, he having half taken a seat on the sofa and caressing her left hand with his own. She burrowed deeper and deeper into the corner of the sofa as if she were seeking protection from his words. Finally she turned around, looked imploringly at him, and said, shaking her head, nothing but this: "Dear husband!", reproachfully, almost bitterly, as if she wanted to say, 'I am your wife, and you talk to me like to a girlfriend.'

Sintlinger fell silent, taken aback, and looked at her inquiringly. Johanna took in his look with large eyes, and nodded to him affirmatively.

"I am alone", she said very softly, "entirely alone, Andreas, and know no counsel anymore. I sent my father below ground ... and did not bring Helene, our child, into life ... I don't know! I don't know!! ... And someone keeps your and my door shut from outside so that we are caught ..."

Shaking her head, she broke off, turned again to the back of the sofa, and continued speaking incoherently.

Sintlinger saw that he had acted wrongly in leaving his wife to the forces of her nature. He begged her to say aloud everything which oppressed her so that he could at least answer her.

"Johanna, look, when you lie like that and talk quietly, I cannot help you", he said insistently.

Then she suddenly threw herself around again, and asked him, almost shouting, "Yes, and what does it mean, 'the sea has drawn back', as you said to father when we stood by his bier in Brederode on the day before the burial?"

"Dear, dear Johanna", Sintlinger said after some thought. "You know, that meant nothing. It was like when someone says that it is a good path or a beautiful flower."

"And who gave you peace! You! Everywhere. By the coffin, by the grave, afterwards, along the way, in the house, at work ... who?"

Sintlinger looked at his wife, deliberating.

"And your peace lay in a deeper pit than mine?" Johanna continued talking in fits when her husband did not answer straightaway.

"What do you mean by that?" Andreas asked softly.

"Dear husband, I am not reproaching you!" Johanna said, threw her arms around his neck, drew him down to herself, and kissed him passionately.

When she had let go of him again, he stroked her hair from her face, and said, "Little wife, you are a child. Death is something over which men have no power. It is bound entirely in darkness, entirely in the depths of the world. When it is time with a man, it releases itself, steps into the house, and comes over him. You know, wife, it is not so, you cannot speak of such a thing any other way, you have to be a painter who paints a picture. — Oh, Johanna, life and death! No, no. Be at ease, I did not kill your father."

"But why did you say 'the sea has drawn back'?" the farmwife asked helplessly.

Sintlinger deliberated for a while, and then, looking at her earnestly, he asked in reply, "Will you be strong, and not be frightened?"

Johanna blanched even more, and nodded in confirmation.

The two found themselves in the same room in which Sintlinger had spent the night after Helene's birth. In the single windowed room, there was, apart from a bed, a cupboard, and a few bamboo chairs, a simple high desk at which the farmer concluded the few clerical tasks which were needed.

While he approached this primitive furniture, unlocked it, and searched in it, he said to his wife in explanation, "Don't think that my head has been a barn floor on which there has been no threshing over these weeks. But that is how it always is with meditating. When you want to winnow, it seems then as if you have been beating the chaff for hours. Right? — You see, and yet I know that I have been merely stirring husks with my thoughts. But when I wanted to know my thoughts, they were gone. For that reason, I started again, and wrote down what I ... not actually I, but what Helene brought to me. Only I will explain that another time."

With a sheet of paper in the hand, he returned, sat down at Johanna's feet, and looked at her a little concerned, even with a breath of self-mockery in his face.

His wife, however, did not pay any attention to his embarrassment; she had propped her head in her hand, and was observing the flower pattern on the sofa cover.

"I know already", Sintlinger began speaking, "all people have a great fear of death. I also had it, and not a little. Perhaps it was merely this, that drove me about so for years. My father and grandfather too. Every Sintlinger. You see, and yet such a fear is pure foolishness. Then life just lives off death. In addition, whoever has fear of death must also be frightened of life. In this way, you die all the time. The one after a year, another after forty or eighty years. Is it not so, Johanna? If you really think it over?"

Sintlinger's wife slowly bent her head, and looked at her husband quiet dreamily. But he continued speaking, "It cannot be so. For then the joy of parents over the birth of a child would be pure nonsense."

Johanna nodded to him. Her eyes immersed themselves in a dark shimmer, and then stared again at the pattern on the sofa. Andreas, who had spoken freely up to then, now read over what was written on the paper, accompanying the reading with nods of his head. After that, he continued talking, "I deliberated over all that. And it is wrong. Men say, 'I live and die', just like they say, 'I dig' or 'I travel'. Digging and travelling have as much and as little to do with them as living and dying do. The man is not more when he travels and digs, and not less when he stops with it. In the same way, it relates to living and dying. It is like the fire which does not stop manifesting itself even if the wood crumbles into ashes."

Johanna started quietly but vigorously, seized his arm imploringly, and had an expression in her face and in her eyes like a child who is held in the air above an abyss.

"And does the fire never burn again, which has stopped burning?" she asked breathlessly. "Are men forever dead when they have died?"

"Oh, dearest Johanna", Sintlinger answered. "I threw flowers on your father's grave. I would not have done it if it were so. Believe me. I cannot toss my hand from my body. And death does not tear us from the world. Little wife, with you, with all men and with me, it is thus — I know that I sleep, wake, am young and old, work and rest, live and die. For that reason, something must be in me which neither sleeps nor wakes, knows neither youth nor old age, no work and rest, not life and not death."

"But what then?" Johanna asked fearfully.

"Just be quite still. Then you are like one who looks over the entire world through a high window", Sintlinger answered softly, and lightly touched her hair. But because he noticed that she was pondering his words, he walked with quiet steps, noiselessly locked the sheet with the notes into the high desk, and left the room inaudibly.

After a long time, the farmwife started, and asked, "But the Brindeisener people, what if they harm us though?"

Then she saw that she was alone. And she did not comprehend the affair with the shadows, nor how she had come into this room. Her husband's words and everything were like a dream which she could not grasp. She rose, and stepped to the high desk, and touched it with her hands.

But the unrealness did not go away from her.

And when she looked out the window, she caught sight of the entire earth filled by the fathomless dream which came from her husband's talk. The hills were covered everywhere by the white cocoon of the Indian summer. The slanting sunbeams were caught in it, and ran trembling over it so that a tremor came over the entire rolling countryside as if it were a sea stirring imperceptibly in the light. This silvery play reached to the limits of the distant horizon.

She flung the window open, and shouted his name over the hills into the boundless emptiness, "Sintlinger? — Sintlinger!! —"

But as she called softer and softer into the slopes with a passionate sinking into herself, her voice assumed the sound of little Peter Brindeisener when he had let her name flutter through the valley over the boundary path in the twilight, and it seemed to Johanna as if the enticing to the estranged farm was coming from her own body.

10

Johanna had thus whirled through darkness the entire winter, and had found no lasting salvation. Hardly did a amiably good image from confident days dawn over her soul, though only like a passing bird in flight, than she was wrenched again from behind into all the grey entanglements. Then her father died again through her and her husband, there was actually neither life nor death, but only the shoreless existence of her

husband. Helene was barely her child, rather a mysterious, ghostly being; the entire Sintlinger farmstead with
all its inhabitants hung onto the hill as if over an abyss.

The days swished like inaudible hammer blows down
on her, and pounded her certainties. She often got up at
one o'clock at night, illuminated all the rooms, and
began working so passionately that her industry looked
like the desperate defence of a defeated person; she
swept and cleaned in all the dark loft rooms from morning until evening; sat with an absent look behind the
table, and hurried her sewing work with trembling
hands without being able to finish a stitch; ran far out
into the fields in the snow with Helene, but not on the
paths, instead back and forth on an invisible hare trail
as if she wanted to go away forever with the child, and
then anxiously held herself apart from her again for
days as if she were frightened of her like of something
dangerous.

Sintlinger, however, did not venture anymore to
show to her for comfort the endless expanse into which
he had climbed through the eyes of his child. Even if she
gauged him often with strange looks, and caught fright
when he talked to her, he never became mad at the life
for which fate had inwardly overcome him, and did not
slacken in being nice to his wife and hoping that after
many hardships the shadows would have to fall from
her and she would receive the light which glowed behind the mirror of her child's eyes.

Certainly from this time originated a great part of the
pages which together amounted to a slender bundle,
and remain as sparse milestones for the rarest of paths
through a high world which has ever been taken by a
man.

Probably in view of the frequent covert churchgoing
of his wife, the blessed farmer wrote a page in his diary

which read, expressing itself in our way under the protection of powerful imagery:

> Whoever believes man would have need of penance, atonement, and self-torment to be just is like a bleacher that the water lashes in order to clean. The most squalid pool becomes clear by itself when it comes to rest.

But he never disturbed anymore this process of "self-healing", as he called it on one page, by an abrupt taking hold, or even with a sort of sententiousness. Only, approaching spring, Johanna's state assumed forms as if she had been half sprung out of the world and her life, and Sintlinger often leant out the window and made a survey across the wave of hills which swelled greenly about the farm for whether the shimmer of salvation was not to be spotted somewhere. Sometime it was so bad with Johanna that he had to fear that the spirit of his poor wife was already rambling in aimless flitting behind the walls of madness.

A day in May finally brought the solution, and indeed from an area in which it had not occurred to Sintlinger to look.

On the morning of that day which would bring her salvation from all the rumpled and wistful entanglements, old Zenker went into the forest with the oxen boy Wendelin to fetch a load of coppiced wood. The boy was leading the team up the farm trail, and the old man was following the wagon by Sintlinger's side at a leisurely pace. The two men spoke about business matters, and came thus by themselves to the lamentable state of the farmer's wife. Actually Zenker raised the dispute to dispose once and for all the worries which had been tormenting him in secret. After the manner of simple souls, he spoke in terse sentences of the many strange things which had ruled over his usually so sweet-tempered master's wife for months, but provoked Sintlinger no more than that a shadow blurred his eyes, a rigid gaze petered out into the distance, or a weight slowed his steps. Even when Zenker told of how he saw her standing one evening on the pitch-black floor under the little clock tower, and staring up with eyes which, on his soul, were seemingly smoking green like sulphurous coal after lighting, the blessed farmer just closed his eyes, and brushed his hand over his forehead as if he were pushing his hat back to his neck because of the heat.

During this conversation, they had come half the distance to the high butte, to that place where the path, following a gentle depression, dropped a little for a stretch, and overlooked part of the slope which had been previously concealed from them by the curve of the hill. There they caught sight of Johanna with Helene motionless under the pear tree in the field, and sitting so raptly by the field margin that they had not once noticed the clatter of the approaching wooden wagon.

The old servant threw a sorrowfully understanding look at Sintlinger. The farmer stopped suddenly as if seized by the chest, and called out clenched, forgetting himself, "Truly, if it was known that it would make a difference, I would ignore everything here as it stands and grows, take my wife in the one arm and my child in the other, and run out into the wide world." Then he came to himself again, smiled in a peculiar way, and repeated, nodding his head, "If it would make a difference." And after some thought, he added, "But with us humans, it is probably no different than it is with any tree — they grow from within and also wither from within." Then he gave the old man directions over the site of the load of wood, sent him alone after the wagon, and approached his wife who was staring motionlessly and impassively at the wagon.

The Blessed Farm

The old man had soon caught up with the wagon, and travelled at a quick gait up the hill. For this anguished breaking out from the farmer's usual obstinate deliberations had confused the grey head quite frightfully at first and, in fear of a catastrophe, he sought to bring the gossipy boy as soon as possible out of the vicinity of the couple. Arriving at the high butte, he cracked the whip a few times in the lightly humid May air, waved the whip encouragingly to the farmer, and then drove the team in a trot to the Hemsterhus road with which the farm trail intersected through a broad dip in the forest.

The latter stretched in a wide arc from the Royal Arenberg forest of Querhoven across over the hills, sometimes pushing its boundary towards the tops, sometimes running in the dips on into the fields, and formed in the open fields of Hemsterhus the especial pride of the two estranged farms. For with this extended forest estate, the Brindeisener and Sintlinger families had been since time immemorial raised up somewhat above the remaining farmers. The Hemsterhus road did not form the boundary of the estranged farms' forests, but ran entirely in the Sintlinger zone, but so that the greater part of the forest gathered close next to the road right up to the Brederode farmers' forests.

Oaks, now in the May redness of young foliage, formed the main stock, here and there the wing-leaved crown of an aspen trembled, dull green pines clustered in various places, and now and again a birch placed its soaring branches high above the other foliage. The path thrust up unnecessarily wide over the hill under the widely protruding oak branches, with half-lapsed spurs and old lay-bys, sometimes a few sand patches, sometimes only a rocky edge. The wagon struck and thrust, but old Zenker lay with his elbows on his straddled knees, held the reins loosely in his left hand, the whip in his right, stared with wide eyes lost in the world through his deep heartache, now and then letting a careless "giddy-up" and "whoa" fall from his mouth, and only sometimes directing his grey eyes with their bushy eyebrows assuringly to the right side where unswerving grass paths led at wide intervals into the forest.

"Two", he said to himself when they again came to such an overgrown forest path.

"Three", the oxen boy responded and coughed.

"Two", Zenker maintained distractedly, and gauged the boy with such a menacing bewilderment that the adolescent climbed down, walked to the back wheel, and kicked the old muck from the rims. From this secure place, the oxen boy now continued to affirm and defend his assertion, which harvested him a few vigorous slanders, but the satisfaction that old Zenker, growling, turned the vehicle, went back along the road and turned into the second path. The further the team now advanced into the forest, the narrower the path became. The low hanging branches whipped the old man constantly in the face so that he finally climbed down, offered the reins to the boy and, his hand on the back post, walked after the wagon.

Suddenly the horses became restless, snorted, whirled their ears, whipped their tails left and right at their flanks, and did not want to continue.

A cloud of flies, shimmering green and blue, with the metallic buzzing of countless, tiny little gears, floated pruriently up and down above the shaded path. Sometimes the parasites vanished through the branches into the forest, but soon clustered again whirling over the path, and buzzed together in a self-contained cloud. The swarm sometimes moved deeper, other times it thrust around the horses' heads.

The old farmworker had surely been watching the boy's manoeuvres, but only carelessly, obliquely out of his whirling thoughts; but no shouts, no gentle pulling, no furious lashing through the cloud of flies set the team going forward. Now he grasped the matter, and commanded the boy to leave the driving seat and lead the horses slowly forward by their heads.

The oxen boy had received at birth a secret dram of the no-devil, forswore everything that Zenker said, and suggested that the flies only came from the nearby pond, and if he had been allowed, he would have progressed quite well. Nevertheless he followed promptly as ever, climbed from the wagon, stroked the horses' manes down, tapped them on the neck, and had soon overcome the animals' agitation so that he could draw them forward by the halter with a coaxing "hey, hey!" But they only proceeded for a few steps reluctantly. Then the swarm of flies was again sputtering through the branches across the path, the horses turned their eyes so that the whites appeared, snorted so that foam flew, and made an air, standing on their hind legs, to push the wagon back and fall back in their harnesses. The boy hung onto their heads, pulled up, and shouted constantly, almost crying with fury, "You satans, you satans!" Old Zenker finally intervened, and ironed everything out, led the animals back a few steps, and although no reason was present to him for playing the considered man, he acted as if he had just said that the proximity of the water could not be at fault for the swarming of the flies because the pond was over the hill, a good half an hour away, instead some carrion must lie in the forest hereabouts, a roe which a fox has killed, or something similar. And as he was still holding the shaking horses, the boy started the search. Just then the flies began oozing through the forest again, and the oxen boy, slapping about himself now and again, followed deeper into it the shimmering buzzing trail which was drawn in the air above him. Not long after, and he stood before a thickly enclosed, small clearing on which the sun shone, bent the branches apart, and lifted his body into it. But after one look he choked, leaping out, and ran back with the horrified cry, "A dead man! A dead man!" His face was fearfully pale, his lips were trembling. He tore around to the old man, swallowed, and stuttered just the same words all the time, adjured him to immediately turn around, and was only capable after a few steps back along the path of reporting that a naked corpse lay in the forest. And someone was still with it. He had seen two eerie eyes staring at him.

The old man slapped the horses a few times, shook his head, and examined the horrified messenger. When he had convinced himself that it was not playacting by the boy, he called him to take hold behind. They pushed the wagon back a stretch, and tied the horses to a tree. After that Zenker grabbed a stave, commanded the boy to also gather something up for defense, and started off on the way to the clearing.

When the grey head had thrown a glance through the branches, he would have liked most of all to have run away as well, if it were not for the boy. For not only did he find the boy's news confirmed — a mad horror smouldered about the dead man. He saw the corpse of a perhaps thirty-five year old man who, with sunken back, half crouching at the knees, lay on his chest so that his idiotic little head had sunk into the soft rotten ground.

The hands were clasping claw-like at the grass, the legs were thrown apart. It looked as if the unknown had been seized in the midst of a mad whirling dance by the imposture of death, and smashed to the ground. You could also think that the mysterious man had sprung down from one of the trees, and thus broken his neck. His body was as gaunt as the body of an abandoned, starved dog.

Obviously it was a matter of a vagrant. But why had the man been dancing before his death, why would he have climbed up a tree, and that completely naked? Only, could he not have fallen victim to a murderer?

Old Zenker was not capable of enduring the sight of the grotesque corpse for very long. He had let the branches close together again, and now stood there in horrified thought.

"Now it is striking again, overseer", the oxen boy whispered to him.

"What?" Zenker asked numbly, and listened at the same moment to the flies clattering over themselves with furious buzzing through the foliage.

"It is striking again. Just look, overseer!" the boy said, and squeezed himself through the branches.

Truly! A broad beech branch moved weightily down onto the corpse, rested a while, and was then slowly drawn back by someone hidden in the bushes opposite.

"Who is over there?"

Old Zenker had wanted to ask coolly, but it became a raw shout which almost tore his neck off. At the sound of his voice, calm reflection returned to him, he saw, heard and observed everything extremely clearly. The beech branch fell on the dead man as if he had torn the invisible hand away with his shout. Something grey rose up in the bushes opposite. Any moment it could burst forth straight at them. Then Zenker recognised, in the way that the dead man lay pressed lopsidedly on the ground and completely strewn flapping on the earth, that the unknown man was the man who had ridden the brown away from him the year before.

"It is the Nobody-incubus!" the old man said, and did not know why he felt a joy over it. He forgot entirely the invisible person opposite, pushed the branches completely to the side, and was about to approach the corpse. But hardly had he taken a step out of the bushes than he had to stop, for from the greenery opposite, a really frightful woman's face emerged; ash-white, mad with desperation, gaunt to the bone, with large blue eyes which blazed like steel studs under a high forehead through dishevelled, mousey blond hair, beautiful but bestially wild and horrifically desperate.

It was the mad person with whom the Nobody-in-cubus had vanished in the preceding year.

The old farmworker sensed that if he took another foot forward that the mad woman would spring out like a wild cat and bite through his throat.

He stepped back through the bushes, waved to the boy, took him by the hand, and walked back to the wagon. The boy had meanwhile gotten hold of himself so that old Zenker could calmly leave the supervision of the team to him. He was allowed to untie the horses from the tree, take a place on the seat,and had permission, if it became too monstrous for him, to take the Hemsterhus road. The old farmworker set off to fetch Sintlinger.

His cap in his right hand, he hurriedly walked the grassed, overhung way, and soon heard the oxen boy singing behind him and loudly cracking the whip.

11

With all sorts of thoughts thrown about disorderly like windblown mayflower seeds in old Zenker's head, he came out of the forest and through the dip in the farm trail. In climbing up toward the high butte, he was dissatisfied with himself that he had not in spite of that mad woman's hissing dragged the Nobody-incubus's corpse the few strides through the forest into the Brederode district, and thereby kept all the unpleasantness and all the idle chatter of people away from the Sintlinger farm.

When he had arrived at the high butte, he ducked, and looked cautiously down to the pear tree in the field. There he saw the farmer, Johanna, and blind Helene still there. The woman was no longer sitting, but stood next to Sintlinger who was pointing with raised arm in the direction of Querhoven, which had nothing to show but the pitiful smoke of its cottages above the Föhren forest in which its upper parts lay burrowed. While he was observing that, he deliberated how he was to deliver the news of the fatal crime in the forest to the farmer, for even if he came close through his surmising to the happy hope that the end of the Nobody-incubus could bring a return of the despondent farmwife to her old self, he did not yet dare to plunge straight down because he was too much afraid as an old bachelor of the unexpected oblique leaps to which every woman is subject to now and then. How good it is too, he pondered, that I did not send the boy. He would have knocked them both over the head with the news as though with a club.

When Zenker looked again, the farmwife was just then turning with Helene to go home, Sintlinger was still standing and continuing to stare into the forested distance. The old farmworker rose, and as soon as the slowly strolling Johanna began to sink behind the curve of the hill, he ran as quickly as his old legs could carry him down to the farmer.

His breath did not want to keep up. He arrived exhausted by Sintlinger, who had turned around at the din of the heavy boots, and Henker, overcome by the unaccustomed haste, delivered the tale of the dead fool in bursts and confusedly as if in great fear.

"If only it were also true", the farmer said with a light in his face, and turned around.

The farmer's wife must surely have also heard the loud cry of the old servant in the still air. She had turned back, and stood halfway up the hill in the middle of the path, and directed her pale face questioningly at the two men.

Sintlinger shouted to her that nothing more had occurred, that it only concerned the wagon, and she should go home in peace, he would be coming straight after.

Hesitantly, her head dipped down again, and the two climbed up to the forest.

When they had the high butte behind them, Sintlinger suddenly began running madly. The boy, who was still singing and cracking his whip from time to time, had come out of the forest on the Hemsterhus road. He called to the farmer that the woman had gone mad and was walking about furiously; but Sintlinger did not listen to him, instead running past. "He is in the clearing by the Brederode boundary!" the boy shouted after him, but heard nothing more than the scampering and slapping of the branches which struck together behind the rushing man.

Zenker followed with heaving breath at a long distance behind his master.

"Is he already through here?" he asked up at the youth more with his eyes than with the broken words, and thrust almost whirling past the vehicle, and encountered Sintlinger sitting on a tree stump before the wall of bushes behind which the dead man lay. When the breathless old man approached, the farmer turned a blanched, clouded face to him.

"Well, was I not right?" the servant asked in a whisper, thinking that Sintlinger had already convinced himself of the correctness of his assumption, and was recovering from the first shock. But the farmer did not answer, instead standing up silently, bending the bushes apart, and stepping up to the corpse. Zenker followed him, and examined once more the lifeless body.

"Are you quite certain", Sintlinger asked after a long look, "that it is the man who rode the brown away? Look at him well!"

Zenker smiled over the unnecessary question, and answered, "Oh, that you can see yourself, and that every Hemsterhus child must recognise."

"What?" the farmer asked.

"Well, that it is the Nobody-incubus, and can be no one else", Zenker replied.

"The Nobody-fool?" Sintlinger asked, stretching it out ironically, shaking his head, and stepped to the head of the corpse.

At this moment, the image of the incubus emerged from Sintlinger's memory as he had seen him from the yard gate a year before as the halfwit crouched by the boundary path and buried and dug up the red rags. It tallied — the fool had crouched down there just as grotesquely and confusedly as this corpse. It was the same long, thin neck which actually only consisted of two sinewy strands between which a groove ran down to his back. But where was the auburn shock of hair, and the scraggly little tail which he had seen flowing down the furrow in his neck so that the thought had come to the farmer at the time that this was no man, but an animal? This unknown man bore a dark-brown shock of hair which rose sharply like a peruke from the blueish white skin of his neck.

No, it was not the corpse of the Hemsterhus incubus.

Sintlinger, however, did not let his thoughts be noted, but searched the grass of the clearing with his eyes, and asked, "Did you not find any clothes?"

Zenker just shook his head.

"Perhaps they are with the woman. Where is she then?" the farmer asked.

"Over there behind the scarlet elder bush. But I advise you, farmer, she is the devil. Take care", Zenker said, and walked behind Sintlinger who stepped back through the bushes to come around to the place from the outside, for the clearing was narrow, and he would have had to step over the corpse. When they were making the small arc through the forest, the conversation of some people rang out from a distance, tearing quickly past, a higher and a deeper voice. It rammed into Sintlinger's head, he listened and started a little.

"Please go and see who it is", he said to the farmworker. "And if it has driven my wife here, hold her back."

Zenker hurried away as quickly as he could.

Far about Sintlinger's soul, there was a ghostily consuming dawning.

He knew that he actually should have gone towards his wife, and held her back. Nevertheless he was drawn onward like a sleepwalker by the falling moonlight.

"Now it must be fulfilled", he said with dry lips and, a moment later, stood before the mad woman who was holding this mad wake. But now all the wildness had vanished from her. The slender, emaciated body lay stretched out in anguish under the tree. Its proportions were still perceptible through the grey rags stiff with dirt which covered it. Her head, surrounded by the pale yellow flickering of dishevelled hair, leant back exhaustedly on the trunk. Her eyes stared desperately, as if nailed under her brow, through the leaves at the May sky, full of a burnt-out accusation.

The Blessed Farm

The cloud of flies thrust up, constantly hurtling away from the dead man and were drawn humming to him again. And each time, as the corpse seemed to awake from its paralysis and stir with a gentle groan, a bestially dull anguish darkened the mad woman's face, and tears ran from the wide eyes into her mouth, tears which she swallowed greedily like a refreshing drink.

In her lap, she held an old peaked cap, grasped tightly with both hands like it was her last treasure.

Sintlinger forgot his own life hardships before this distressing sight; he did not think of what this mad woman meant for him. Only a boundless sympathy filled him. "Hey", he said with a kindly voice, "woman, who had taken your man from you?"

The mad woman did not stir.

"You were fond of the Nobody, weren't you?" he asked with still greater love.

Although she obviously did not understand the words, she was touched by the sounds of kindness as if by physical caresses. A glow radiated over her features. Amidst soft, intimate whimpering, she lifted the cap to her breast, and kissed the empty air passionately.

Then Sintlinger heard the voice of the old labourer calling, "Mrs! — Mrs!! I beg you for God's sake! — Stay here! — Don't go there!"

The insistent cries swirled behind a rustling running which quickly approached.

The mad woman must also have been reached by the labourer's cries, for she lifted her head, stretched it like a protective animal before herself, and now noticed for the first time the farmer standing before her. Then a rabid ferocity suddenly passed through the mad woman. She settled on her arms, her eyes blazed again like blue steel studs. Amidst quiet growls, with bared teeth, she set off crawling towards him.

Sintlinger instinctively took a step back.

Then he was seen by his wife who in running up had come near the bushes.

She called his name shrilly, "Andreas!", and he saw her storming up, pale of face.

At once the strange whirl drained away from him, and he sprang at Johanna to hold her back at the last moment. But she slid past him, and wound through the bushes to the corpse.

After staring a bit, she sank to her knees there, and when he stepped up to her, he saw her with hands folded speaking in a low voice to the earth in endless joy as though saying a prayer of redemption.

"... Now you have helped me ... my dear father", she said in short breaths. "Now I know that it was well that you died. I thank you. You have torn the incubus from the world. Now everything will be good again as if was before."

Then the farmwife let herself be lifted up by her husband and led away.

When they came to the bushes where the mad woman was crouching, the place was empty.

They saw her hurrying through the forest like a grey ghost and vanishing behind the trees.

The old peaked cap lay in the grass. Johanna turned it around and around with a branch.

"The same cap", she murmured, "which he wore when he crept up to our child."

"What are you saying, Johanna?" the farmer asked her.

Then she flung her arms around his neck with a jubilant cry, "Andreas, the Nobody-incubus is dead!"

Sintlinger realised that he must not destroy her belief; for if he confessed his conviction to her that the corpse in the bush clearing behind them was not that of the halfwit from Hemsterhus, then it would be the worst thing for her spirit, if not also frightening for her life.

That is why he brushed her forehead, regaled her with all sorts of softly encouraging words, and held her in his arms until she had cried out her anguish and happiness.

12

In Hemsterhus, it was quickly agreed that the corpse from Sintlinger's forest was the gloomy remains of the Nobody-fool. With more precise examination, a few blue, longish running streaks were indeed discovered on the neck of the dead man in the region of the throat, streaks that were not dissimilar to the marks of strangling. But since only one voice dominated over the personality of the lifeless man, the cause of death played no role. In contrast, they breathed out in relief that the district was free of worrying about the fool. Sooner or later his accommodation in an institute for the handicapped or mad would have emerged as a necessity, and then this waste would have fallen heavily on the village funds. The corpse was also already in a state of advanced decomposition.

The District Court made up its mind quickly for these reasons, and already at twilight of the same day on which the dead man was found, he was buried by the wall of the Hemsterhus churchyard right next to the corner for suicides.

After a short time, the gravedigger had layered up a proper burial mound over the place and even placed at the head a sort of monument, a square sandstone which protruded perhaps a hand's length out of the ground and bore on the upper side a chiseled cross, like a boundary stone, on the back though, it bore the fool's initials, a J and an N.

At questions over the good soul who had in this truly Christian way closed the door to eternity behind the miserably departed fool, the gravedigger Wachsmann carried a secretive smile on his face for a long while, but then calmly named the farmer's wife from the blessed farm, and added steadily that it was now also time for the wicked tongues to begrudge the poor incubus his bit of blessedness.

It was certainly not discerned whether he was in-structed by Johanna to give this advice, but you would not go wrong in the assumption that it formed the most fervent wish of Sintlinger's wife to bring an end with this gravestone to the vague talk about the death of the bell-listener, and also perhaps to place the warning be-fore her own eyes to no longer entrust her life to the dark, subterranean waves which wander in the depths of every soul to who knows what end.

Certainly the farmwife did not thus achieve the one like the other without further ado.

For a long time, the defenders of nonsense in Hem-sterhus and the surrounding districts still passionately hunted for new stories about the mysterious death of the Nobody-fool, questioned whether the man buried absolutely was the incubus, sometimes encountered the genuine Nobody at the Querhoven sawmill, other times in the forest at Dingden, saw the mad woman, who had kept such a loyal wake by the corpse, crouching at night by the grave, had her captured by the court and indicted for the murder. Yes, they overheated their imaginations so that it was carried for a while like hot fly ash from house to house that Sintlinger, the blessed farm's owner, had strangled the fool, and then had the strange gravestone placed for the sin as a blood debt by his wife.

And always, when such a new cloud smouldered over the blessed farm, Johanna was again pushed back a bit into the darkness from which she had been torn, and it was not easy for Sintlinger to hold her to her new hope. He endeavoured to calm his wife not by confounding the gossips in the villages through fury and disparagement (he probably once called them lazy, cowardly vermin, because he saw that the still inwardly sore Johanna was suffering), but rather he advised her to close her ears and believe undisturbed in that confidence which grew by itself from her breast.

It thus also came about as he had wished.

One night he was shaken from his deep sleep. At coming to, he saw to his amazement that Johanna was standing fulling clothed next to him, mysteriously excited, with eyes as luminous as if they wanted to roll out of her head. She told him he should immediately get up and go out with her behind the yard, there he would see and hear something he would not have held possible.

Only half dressed, he soon after stood next to Johanna behind the barn where you had in particular an open view across the rolling hills of Brederode and Hemsterhus.

The late moon hung in the sky as though floating down uncertainly; a metal plate fastened carelessly with yielding nail to a slanting wall. The edges of its smoky, yellow disc were smeared and merging into a pale, hazy smoke which filled the entire sky and also reached to the ridges of the hills and to the clouds, which were so deeply encamped around the entire horizon that they continued the wavering of the hills into the endlessness of the heavens. Every gentle wave in this misty heap of hills ran as a weak pulse through the rolling hills on earth, and seemed to carry them out further with every dreamlike beat.

Sintlinger struggled violently against his drowsiness, and although he perceived all this, he held it to be just an effect of his dream-befogged mind, but was unable to ask his wife what was extraordinary in it, nor hurt her with a mocking remark.

She had also intentionally placed herself some distance from him, and he saw through the shades of the night the contours of her figure so that he could recognise how she, seemingly nestling into the air, was listening with all her senses into the expanse.

From the dark valleys, it swished like water drawing away. From the barn which lay as a black hulk immediately before him, that dull, monotonous sound ran out which is only visible with the eyes.

Suddenly he saw his wife make startled, defensive motions, and at the same time wave over to him; in between, she spoke excitedly and urgently in confusion, "Be quiet! — Come here! — Listen! — Don't you hear anything?" —

Now he was close by her side. Completely awake. But he saw nothing but the dreamlike sliding away of the hills into the dark-yellow haze of the moon.

"Just what is there then, Johanna?" he finally asked her. But she just turned her face quickly to him so that he saw her eyes shimmering damply, and instead of an answer seized his hand.

When the fingers of both of them had interlaced in each other, something strange happened. Sintlinger saw everything around about immersed in a more intensive glow. Seized by a more active vitality, the hills slid out quicker, and over and with them floated a quite gentle ringing in the high air, softer and softer, dying away more and more until it finally stood for a while in the trembling light of the most distant horizon and soundlessly expired. Then it was still, to the depths of the soul, completely still.

"Now she will never sound anymore, our bell. Now the good heaven has sucked out her chimes forever", Sintlinger's wife said, shaken. "Andreas, now we are really saved. Thank God! Thank God!"

Sintlinger looked up instinctively, and saw the bell truly hanging black and lifeless in the little tower over the roof ridge.

His wife scurried skipping into the house, and her "thank God" rang like quite youthful laughter.

He had to smile to himself in astonishment, and then followed her.

BOOK TWO

The Blessed Farm

1

Now the blessed farm stood as radiant on its hill as in the first days of the young Sintlinger marriage, saw with gleaming windows the forest about Querhoven darkening, gazed far out over Hemsterhus to the grey smoke of the distant heath, noticed more attentively in the evenings again the gentle wafting of the willows on the boundary path, and then it often roared from the crowns of the lime trees by the gate quite ungovernably over the waves of restively pilgrimaging countryside because it had to shout out the joy that the darkness which had flown for moons into its most secret corners had no power over it anymore. The farmer's wife was no longer startled as before by a blow against the chest in the morning; she was like in the good old days taken hold of by a gently confident hand from early in the morning. For a distant echo of the happy night shimmered constantly in her soul, that moonlit hour after midnight which had moved the land around about and sent with it the sounds of the bell of misfortune out of the world.

Nothing threatened her anymore. But before the light could blossom unchallenged over her, one more test was reserved for her and Sintlinger.

For sometimes a gentle shiver still brushed her. When she came to the place on the upper floor in the

Sintlinger's house where the shadow had wandered past her, it sometimes happened that the dreamlike contours of a man's figure emerged on the plaster of the wall and seemed to vaguely fade away. She was not able to state whether the man whose vaporous shadowy figure she saw had been large or small, nor what he had for other characteristics. She did not even know exactly immediately afterwards whether this man's figure had sunk back into the wall or slid into the darkness of the hall, or whether it instead had just been just a figment of her imagination. And while she instinctively smoothed her forehead with her hand as if to wipe away such cobwebs from the sweepings of her mind, she nevertheless listened with large eyes in the semi-darkness of the long hallway and the winding steps as if it were nonetheless possible to be put to fright by a mysterious sound. Then she smiled over her "imaginativeness", but distanced herself with measured evasions from the last shadowy circles which beset her mood in this place.

Such foaming shadows skimmed the blessed farm's mistress more often, and although she possessed the dauntlessness to not let it weigh heavier on her, like the sign perhaps of the solitary clouds in the summer sky left behind by a blustering storm, she did not however escape a gentle, though everlasting anxiety.

Amongst everyone, only old Zenker apparently noticed anything of this unease which surrounded the farmer's wife, and that because the old man needed to cope with a chestiness which had adhered to him actually since the running about over the dead incubus in the forest. He walked about with hurried breath, only managed half the work, and still had to sit down some of the time because the "going easy", as he perversely berated his work, made his heart choleric, struck him in the legs, and made his lips turn blue. This distaste with himself also sharpened his eyes for every fault and distressing sign in his environment, and so he had soon uncovered from the nooks and crannies in which he crawled to pause for breath that something was hounding his mistress. And since the dead incubus had from the grave as it were hung such a solid pack on his back, he guessed the holed-up fool had hewn some splinter into the farmer's wife before his final departure. But for that reason, actually only to beat around the bush, he pondered how to get behind the mystery which sometimes twisted the mouth of the farmer's wife. Not long and the opportunity for it ran between his fingers. Once when he was overcome for a moment by an insurmountable weakness when returning from the fields, as he stepped through the gate into the yard, he sat down on an upturned wheelbarrow, and coughed and tore his breath back into order. As he thus more crouched in a stoop than rested, the farmwife stepped out the house door, and started diagonally across the yard to the cow stalls. He called to her, waited with frightened hand gestures, and then went, as well as he was able just then, straight across the paved yard to the large dung heap, whereby he moved his lips as if praying, and made the sign of the cross to the earth with the fingers of his right hand as he if he were strewing salt next to himself. He did that to bring her to speak. The farmer's wife watched with a smile the strange manipulations of the old man, and when she learnt that he was supposedly addressing a fleeting shadow so that it would not be scary, she gave him a deferent tap on the shoulder, and said he should rather crawl into bed for a few days and not stir, then the worms would run out of his head by themselves. Then she continued on her way without minding the pernicious strip which Zenker had described as the tracks on which the dark shadow had weaseled across the yard. But nevertheless the old man had noticed the soft pallor which had scurried across his mistress's face, and now knew that his suspicions had led him correctly. Not two days had passed before Sint-linger's wife told him of the strange outlines which appeared and sank away again from the wall on the up-per floor. Zenker listened earnestly and sympathetically, and then lingered for a long time in head-shaking, meaningful silence so that Johanna also did not remain silent about the first terrible bedevilment from which the present shadowy images were probably no more than a residue in her memory which would fade away by itself.

Yes, yes, the old man answered, that is possible, in fact probable. But if it should show itself once more, you would do well to note whether the man who comes out from the wall is large or small. For many things had oc-curred to him in the thirty years he had been residing on the Sintlinger farm over which he must remain silent to strangers. But he did not hold it absolutely necessary "to keep his mouth shut" before the farmer's wife, above all because, as he saw it, she was also someone who had encountered such goings-on. She did not need to say anything about it to the master, for one knew that he would just have a laugh about it, only he had learnt that the wild Jakob Sintlinger, who had once gotten into the skirts of the Brindeisener wife, still showed his being from time to time. He indeed no longer did any harm to anyone if you left him to his ways, and if she were to see him come from the hall and vanish down the stairs to the front door, then it meant nothing more at all. Then it merely drove him over to the Brindeisener farmstead where as punishment he had to always make the at-tempt, whether he succeeded or not, to seduce someone in the other estranged farm for his old ardour.

The old farmworker would have shaken out a basket of ghost stories if Sintlinger had not then appeared in the vicinity.

So the grey head toddled off inconspicuously, and the farmer's wife talked to her Andreas about the stubborn cough of the kind old man. Sintlinger had obviously not noticed in the least that the two were both rummaging about in the ghost pot once more, and so Johanna had trouble sizing everything up and carefully turning old Zenker's tale back and forth. But since all such things are baked out of thin air, as is generally believed, the farmer's wife stirred with casual finger the old servant's new ghost dish round and round, not making it more palatable thereby, however, and also not more improbable, but, without wanting to, just becoming accustomed to taking a sharper look, which she let run coolly ahead of herself everywhere she went, especially when she had to enter the upper floor.

But the ghost of the mad Jakob Sintlinger seemed to have taken offense at the libel of the old farmworker. He was gone like a speck of dust blown out of your hand, and the farmer's wife began secretly laughing at herself and Zenker.

But perhaps anxiety is more pernicious when it has sunk from the consciousness deeper into the soul, into the region of our inner being where the evicted powers of the spirit still lead a mysterious life for a long time, possibly never vanishing either. In any case, Johanna had not disposed of her gentle apprehension after she had pushed it aside with a smile.

She would soon learn that.

She once heard the muffled murmur of men's voices seeming to hold secret counsel behind one of the doors of the upper floor. Her first thought was, admittedly not entirely fairly, that Andreas could well be in the study. She called her husband's name aloud and, at the same time, stepped up to the door behind which the muffled muttering was sounding.

But the sound of the peculiar voices did not just fall soundlessly before her feet. When she took the door handle in her hand to convince herself through an inspection, the murmuring sounded from the next room, and drew the woman thus, still emphatic about not giving in to superstition, from door to door, always deeper into the shadowy hall up to the loft stairs and, constantly enticed onward by the suppressed muttering of a menacing council of men, yes, befuddled, she was led up the steep steps, and finally stood before a door which she rattled in desperation. At this moment, the ghostly whirl shattered, and Johanna stepped to the dormer window to get a hold of herself, and looked outside. She stood on that gable side of the house which faced the Brindeiseners', and she could look into the other homestead as if into an open chest. Old Anton Brindeisener had just passed through the gate on a two-horse wagon, and was then turning onto the way which led out diagonally through the garden to the fields. He was holding the whip still between his knees, and his daughter sat wanly, sickly, and tucked in next to him. Now the wheels were passing inaudibly onto the grassed garden path, and Johanna heard exactly the farmer's rough, surly, muttering voice while, as if he could do no differently, he bickered grouching at the pale girl. At once, Brindeisener's voice was the same as that which the farmwife had covertly heard just then behind the doors of her own house, and she had to gather up the entire strength of her prudent will to not flee head over heels down the stairs.

This affair, which Johanna was incapable of bringing under control, prepared the ground in her a little for old Zenker's tale of the mad Jakob Sintlinger still having to, as punishment for his wild vices, make the attempt to seduce someone from the Brindeisener farmstead for his life's ardour. But an episode, small in itself, still had to intervene for her to seize on this belief as fact.

She was sitting one afternoon in the living room alone by the open window, and sewing. Everyone was in the fields getting the last cartloads of hay. Old Trine from Brederode was playing with Helene in the orchard whose treetops rose halfway up the windows. A quite pleasant wind stirred in the trees almost imperceptibly, and the light on the floor before the farmwife swayed weakly with it as if the sun were being rocked back and forth in the sky by gentle hands. Helene's laughter rang out from time to time, and it always sounded as if a handful of silver bells had been thrown up in the summer air. Johanna rose, smiling happily, to inquire over what game the nanny was unleashing the girl's joy ever anew with. Then she saw old Trine picking up the green, still tiny, autumn apples from the grass. They were little cows, and Helene was holding her hands in a vault to make their stalls. Amidst all sorts of teasing conversation and jesting difficulties, the little cows sprang into the finger stalls, and whenever a little calf came and also wanted in, it was so dumb and clumsy as to hop on the arm or chest of the child, making her laugh out loud in the most unruly way.

Thus the two played through the entire orchard, further and further from the window, and the girl's laughter rang out softer and softer. Now they had surely arrived at the low wall which separated the orchard from the fields. For Johanna heard how Trine sang the old meadow song of the shepherds, and took from it that the apple cows would now be driven over the wall into the field. When the old woman had finished singing, Helene tried to imitate the little tune, and because she was timid, it did not work out for the best at first. But when she finally mastered the old woman's simple tune, it suddenly seemed to have become a quite

different song. Almost no longer a human singing. —
Johanna let her sewing work fall and listened in her joy
quite particularly to figure out how the song actually
sounded. "Just as birds in the morning sometimes sing
quite high in the air so that men cannot see them and
think the light is making the music itself", the farmwife
said to herself, and whenever she wanted to continue
with her sewing, the child started anew with her little
song so that she had to listen again.

As the blessed farm's farmwife sat so enthralled and
forgot everything which was happening around her,
someone came cautiously with short scudding steps
from the hall. As soon as Helene's song fell silent, the
steps drew back; when the child began singing anew,
they gathered again, and penetrated further along the
hall towards the door. Already you could hear the sand
before the door crunching, and an agitated breath was
sniffing through the keyhole. All at once, however, the
door flew open so that it crashed against the clock case,
and little Peter Brindeisener stood in the doorway,
baffled and brash, seized in the most passionate way,
red with shame, and yet with eyes hot like darting
flames.

He did not see the farmwife at first, obviously looking for the singer of the song by which he had been
lured, held onto the doorposts firmly with both hands,
and flickered his eyes across the space instantly, leaning
timidly into the room.

Then he noticed Mrs Sintlinger who, startled by the
unexpected intrusion, was incapable of all but an astonished look. Seeing her, swivelling, stepping back so that
his blond shock of hair twitched like a little white flag,
and running away through the house was all one. When
Johanna reached the yard gate, running, he was already
rushing across the boundary path. He ran like a madman, as if catapulted, and when, looking back, he saw

Sintlinger's wife at the gate, he broke out into a strangled laughter which sounded vile to the farmer's wife, like nasty mockery. This cheeky sound of triumph and the entire incident took hold of Johanna's temper in a pernicious way. She immediately called Helene in from the orchard, and told old Trine gently to beware of the child. For even if the district did not abound with ragamuffins, she would do good to guard little Lena as if wickedness and malignity were constantly around in her vicinity.

Now the fact ate into her more and more steadily, the shadow of the upper floor was really, as per old Zenker's opinion, the residue of the wild spirit with which the mad Sintlinger roamed about behind his derelict grave and strove to fulfill the curse which his life could not quite fulfill. It seemed to her as if the shadow had flown out the dormer windows into the Brindeisener farmstead, and had agitated Peter there and driven him before it. Yes, when Johanna imagined the little boy's eyes, and heard his voice sound within her, it seemed to her as if something like a full-grown perfidy was stuck in the boy. Naturally the life on an isolated farmstead, and the vulnerability of a disposition recovering from having recently been shaken to its foundations contributed to experiencing the meshing of such ghostly possibilities as a simple fact. What she had so often heard told in her youth, that the farmers of the two estranged farms must continue after their deaths to struggle with each other as spirits in the air, she now thought she had experienced. In quiet moments, the blessed farm's farmwife even heard a soft-as-thought grinding in the air, and she pondered how to be rid of this new menace of fate, or whether it was not at least possible to belatedly rush to help the party of the Sintlinger's family spirits to give them an edge in the airborne struggle. There were not the rudiments of an angry fibre in her good will, and for that reason, she came to the idea of ridding the Sintlinger farmstead of all the shadows of the past by blessing the dead farmers belatedly, and thereby raising up their spirits into a salutary light.

2

That came about in no other way than that the farmer's wife proceeded in the way she had put a stop to the dead bell listener's ghostly game, by setting up a solid, consecrated memorial stone to mad Jakob and his ghostly clan, and thereby squeezing their dangerous unrest forever under the earth.

When Johanna spoke of this intention to old Zenker, the eyes in his grey head instantly gleamed like the polished panes of a lantern behind which a candle has been lit, and he was of the opinion that everything would thereby be done which the welfare of the farmstead had long demanded.

"And the stone must be put next to the lime tree, not far from the gate", the old man suggested. "If something evil wants to come up the hill, it will straightaway run into the cross and fall down the slope to the boundary path. And if the evil spirits want to come down out of the air by the lime tree, they can go no further. They will remain stuck in the crown and must hurtle out of there." Thus the labourer squeezed out the praises of the memorial stone right to the last drop. But in the end, he ran his fingers bashfully through his hair, scratched all through his grey mop, and suggested that what had been discussed was quite nice, only, it would not be able to be done as the farmer would not for all the world be brought to do such a thing. If it went exceedingly well, he would laugh himself silly, and hence they would from the outset have a rake with a broken handle in the hand, and the entire devilish inheritance of Sintlinger would just have to remain in the air.

The old man's misgivings did not come to anything.

Sintlinger had kept quietly on quite secluded paths during these weeks. Without intentionally hiding himself from Johanna, he tried to remain in the seclusion to which he had been impelled by his increased activity since the old farmworker had been required to remain aloof from all energetic labour because of his illness.

The farmer screwed himself to bursting in the tongs of industriousness — oversaw himself the particulars of the beet planting, drove the team over the potato field, crushed the overly rampant corn seed into the ground, and tore every leisurely breath from his mouth with impatient strides. During all that, a deeper and deeper peacefulness was to be seen gleaming in his face, and it often seemed to his wife that he was unreachable, although she sat at the table, walked through the fields, or worked in the yard side by side with him.

Even when Johanna spoke to him about the erection of the memorial stone, he did not drop down from the high expanses in which he was residing.

"Who would the stone be for?" he asked calmly, and looked at her so clearly that she became confused.

"Well, for all the Sintlingers", she answered blushing. He nodded contemplatively, and continued in thought, "... so that they remain below, you think, don't you? Yes, I understand. Such as you did with the incubus perhaps. Hm, hm."

With these words, he intimated that, despite his aloofness, the matter of the ghosts between her and the grey head had not remained concealed from him. And when Johanna began telling in her defence of the be-witchings, Andreas indeed let her unpack a part of it, but his face became ever more jovial, and he finally seized his wife by the arm.

"Dear Johanna", he said, "most people chase midges with their hands. You are hurling stones at them. If it helps, I don't mind. I am indeed a Sintlinger too. But I think, I have not yet driven it so far that you must be frightened of me, and such a stone could not disgrace me either."

After these words, the laughter which Zenker had prophesied sprang from the farmer's mouth, and it even sounded so mocking that the farmer's wife really did think everything had in this lighthearted way been in-differently knocked from her hand, and she turned away, and looked depressed into the distance. But for Sintlinger it had really only been a bit of fun. For that reason, he caressed her cheek lovingly, raised her face by the chin, and said, "No, no, Johanna, you must un-derstand a jest. You shall have your memorial stone ... What else do you want to say?"

But the farmer's wife had no urge to say any more. She squeezed his hand, and they parted, each to their own work.

***

The stonemason in the town, who was contracted with producing the Sintlinger stone, called himself a sculptor because in his youth he had undertaken a quickly failed attempt at artistic instruction. Since then he had been a blundering craftsman who needed twice the time to carry out every assignment because he had to knock about first with a wild wasps' swarm of rampant ideas before attacking a work. Perhaps he was only plunging himself into this inner seething swirl out of vanity in order to taste the hardship of "the true artist" and to convince the customers of the notability of his head. For the blessed farm, he at first came up with rotundas with globes, sitting and flying muses on a dome, porticoes with flights of steps in the open air, symbolic figures who sometimes carried extinguished torches, sometimes hourglasses, and were in every pose of deliberation and melancholy prophecy. With this colourful noise of plans, he revolved stubbornly before Sintlinger and his wife, although it had just been stated to him that it only concerned a simple pedestal with a cross. When he finally pulled himself out of his vain befuddlement and could understand the assignment, he was deeply disappointed, made a grey face and walked away hostilely as if he held this work to be below his dignity. However, his best work was always begun in this way, and it was to be expected that now in a short time the hope of Sintlinger's wife would be fulfilled. The farmer withdrew more and more from this affair, and ceded it to his wife and old Zenker to encourage the "sculptor" again and again. There was also nothing more than that mechanical impulse by which the work could be made of use, after the simple words of dedication had been determined by Sintlinger and the decision had prevailed with Johanna, not without great effort, to refrain from the ecclesiastical dedication of the memorial because of the libels of the people. After the endorsement of the sculptor, the work moved forwards at a gallop, and he was already giving the instruction to begin with the digging out of the surveyed foundation pit.

Only so close before the completion, a disturbance rolled into the stonemason's workplace for which he was not responsible. It not only hindered the erection of the memorial, it originated from events which also en-croached on Sintlinger's life in the most remarkable way.

At that time befell the frightful unrest in which all of Germany was placed by a terrible pit disaster in the Ruhr coal-mining region.

The casual handling of the spraying of the coal dust with water had caused a pit fire at the "God's Help" mine in Gelsenkirchen, which had spread with uncanny quickness and had filled a large part of the tunnels at the bottom of the mine with its billowing smoke so that more than a hundred mineworkers, cut off from the out-side world, seemed delivered to certain death. All of Germany shivered in numbing fear, and this incident pressed hard on the rural population, particularly on those who, like the inhabitants of Hemsterhus and its surrounds, were so close to the hearths of the misfortu-nate. The earth, the trusted, certain ground of all life, seemed to many a person now to be a deceptively treacherous cover under which unimaginable menaces massed together and storms ran through the depths, where noiseless graves were prepared which could yawn open at any moment and swallow humans whole. And because this commotion fell in the weeks before harvest, in which a more lively sensitivity for the welfare and woes of his life always seized the farmer at the sight of the ripening grain, every dark cloud which climbed up loading itself with greater danger, every wind screaming more eerily, every still heatwave weighing more sin-isterly than ever before. This fear, which each hid from the others and yet could not conceal, was increased still more when the news rushed through the villages like a grim reaper on horseback that with the rescue of the victims of the mine catastrophe not only did the relat-ives make wild scenes, but also the staff of other mines who drew the administration to the stingy neglect of safety measures. The despairing wives had raged like a screaming hurricane, bombarded doors and windows of the mine buildings with stones, and finally tore the mineworkers to commit outrages with them, they having been initially threatening and sombre, but now hindered and prudent having exhausted their attention and strength in the rescue of their poor comrades. Now, however, when the outburst of anguish from the widows and orphans had been suppressed unnecessarily by a strong police presence, and the rifles had even been let off at the first transgression of order, the dull paralysis of the men gave way to clear uproar. At the cries for help from the mine owners, the military had been called up from the nearest garrison, and had blown apart the rebellious mineworkers with a salvo, whereby three dead and a greater number of wounded were left in the square. These measures of stifling changed the mood for the worse. Like a forest fire, the uprising spread across all the mines of the Ruhr region as if all the blackened thousands only had one mouth to swear vengeance, one arm for striking, and one head for planning annihilation or humiliation of their enemies. The disorderly ramshackle nature into which all the obstructiveness of the rebellious workers usually soon petered out at the start, the ungovernable outbreaks of individual roughness and vandalism were suppressed by a deliberate will of unflinching circumspection and calm decisiveness, and transformed as if by itself into the unitary spirit of a well-disciplined army.

The man who had brought about the miracle of the pulling together of these wild masses belonged to no party and was committed to no programme. In the opinion of some, he was a mineworker who had hurried from the Belgian coal mines to the help of his oppressed German work comrades, others declared that he was a runaway primary school teacher from Silesia who had lost the exercise of his office because of faithlessness and obstructiveness. Everywhere that the fury of the mineworkers urged for open battle, he appeared and helped the men intoxicated with fury to regain their right minds and place proper trust in their demands. The beset transformed under the influence of his words into brave soldiers of adversity, the timid lived with a fire, and the purity of his dedication held the vicious in check.

"Mr de Favre, the uncrowned King of the miners", "the primary school teacher Faber, antipope and anti-emperor", those were the headlines of the newspapers which reported on the effects and personality of this un-common man. And like all men who deviate markedly from the accustomed forms of life, he was immediately an object of legends, so that it was impossible for those standing at a distance to form a proper idea of him. It was said he was small, cold, and demonic like Bona-parte, pale and unattractive like him, and nobody was able to withstand the inscrutability of his eyes and the stormy fire of his will. Others described him as a man of unusual size, gaunt as a Trappist, with a billowing beard and the kindly temper of a Franciscan. But no time re-mained for the image of the man to stick in people's minds, the man who had emerged out of the darkness implacably like a born military leader and dreamily rapt like a divine struggler for those without rights. For the events came in a rush. Faber or de Favre had called to-gether somewhere in the vicinity of Herne an assembly of mineworkers in the open air.

Here now the catastrophe overtook him. As with all explosions of a crowd of people, nobody knew after-wards to say rightly what the cause had been; and even over the order of events of the tumult, the most contra-dictory views prevailed. In the opinion of the police, de Favre or Faber was responsible for calling with impassioned urgings for resistance to the government's laws, according to a statement by the leader of the Social Democrats, he had only expressed himself as always in his well-known whimsical phrases. "Men, people", he was said to have cried, "you are all as eternal and divine as the heavens with all its wonders above you. You possess the power of irresistibility like it, if you establish internally the true justice of a guilt-free soul and join it in a united stream. Then you will overcome the antagonistic rich men, as true as my hand is attached to my arm. Nothing can withstand you. Kings will then be like the breath from your mouth which each of you blows, and God himself will be incapable of compelling you."

With these words arose a furious confused shout of "bravo", "insult to His Majesty", "blasphemy", "peace", "in the name of the law", "hound" and the like. The mob of men became a knotted ball which shot, stabbed, and punched itself. And when, after a while, the wildness had consumed itself in this way, it was as if Faber had been swallowed up by the earth. A large part of his audience made common cause with the police, and set off in pursuit of him amidst imprecations. In an instant, the enthusiasm for the mysterious man turned into hate of him. Rumours about all sorts of infamies, even criminal acts, darkened the air around the unknown trail of his flight.

Telephone and telegraph rang throughout the entire province, and the chasing gendarmes remained on their nags day and night. He was hounded like a murderer and robber.

Hemsterhus and all the villages in its neighbourhood and more distant surrounds fell into a violent unrest, for the rumour was spreading that the "hero of Herne" had taken, in his flight to his native Belgium's border, the way through the Westphalian plain and, encouraged by the many forests around Hemsterhus, it could not fail that the "enemy of King and God" would have to come with his tiny following through nowhere but here. Faber was imagined to be a bestial man in all whose pockets guns and daggers were to be seen, who blazed with wickedness, in whose proximity the farmsteads would catch fire by themselves. Hence people in all the villages during these two or three days after the Herne tumult were in a continuous excitement of fear. Any badly clothed stranger who would usually be allowed to tap calmly on the doors of the houses and farmsteads was immediately suspected. The youths shouted, the women ran for the gate, the men appeared with a short club in the background, and when the good-natured tramp or frightened dealer had identified himself and gone away as quickly as possible again, it was claimed after the event that it had indeed been the devilish miner, the "twenty-fold murderer", and they sniffed through every cornfield, omitting no narrow pass, and even shooting at bushes which seemed in the distance to be running ducking through the fields or crouching by the ditch like a man with a stooped back.

The air shook in all directions with the concussions of the shots, which were actually only let off for one's own reassurance; all the forests looked as if they abounded with rabble; every path carried traces of suspicious footprints; yes, even the shadow which lay outside next to a solitary tree was eerie to the overanxious, and the hidden corners of their own houses crouched menacingly in the darkness.

The Sintlinger homestead gazed with greater clarity into this general excitement, even if it often enough fluttered sinisterly through the heads of the women on the hill and stretched the necks of the labourers. To the farmer and his wife, it hardly seemed to scrape the soles of their boots. Though sometimes, especially during the last days when the entire district was excited by the hunt for the fleeing miner Faber and the rumours were prattled around all the villages, they stepped out before the yard, heard here the guns firing, there a whistle shrilling, and somewhere else a shout breathed into the air like a yawn. But for Sintlinger, merely a half mocking, half contemplative smile ran through his face at the tumult of general fear. "The people all act as if you could shoot the dead miners to life, or the people run around as if you could force the gravedigger with a thrashing to scrape the corpses out of the grave again warm. Oh God, and the poor beggar who addressed the miners, they should leave him in peace. He is frightened now most of all of himself, for otherwise he would not have run away", thus spoke Sintlinger after he had gazed around for a while, and then he strode into the yard again, and even in Johanna, the fright caught no deeper than the worry over the delay in the erection of the Sintlinger memorial.

The messengers who inquired after the progress of the work, and the carts which would bring the finished piece to the blessed farm returned empty-handed from the stonemason because the agitated master was not found at home. The news and the general excitement whirled him constantly around the district, and if you ever met him at home, his answer in the opinion of the servants was none other than "a market full of fools".

Nevertheless — how it had become possible, nobody comprehended — one day the dispatched wagon creaked with the finished memorial up the boundary path from Hemsterhus to the Sintlinger hill.

It was precisely the third day after the great tumult at Herne and the traceless escape of Faber. Sintlinger was sitting at the open window and reading the paper when a maid came in with the report that the wagon with the stone stood down below on the drive, and the sculptor had asked how the farmer had considered the setting up of the heavy piece of work, for the horse could not bring it up the hill in one go.

Andreas was just then reading the description of the Herne riot, and hardly heard a word of what the maid said. "What?" he asked absentmindedly when she had finished speaking, and then he had the report retold once more, but heard just as little of it, instead continuing actually to read Faber's talk which was reproduced at the end in summary. When he came to the words in which Faber had maintained that man had the power to compel God himself, he burst out into loud laughter, crumpled the newspaper angrily in his fists, and called out with hilarity, "The fool! The patent fool!"

Then he stepped by the side of the maid to the door, down the hall, and across the yard as if he intended to manage the approach of the memorial stone. At the yard gate, however, he hesitated, and said that old Zenker should direct the affair, turned around, and left the yard through the gate to the garden without worrying any further about the shouts with which his running wife pursued him soon afterwards. When Johanna ran behind the yard, she saw him disappearing far into the fields towards the beech stand with unusually quick steps.

3

So it remained. Even when Sintlinger had returned home, a self-absorption and reservedness prevailed over him, and did not even desert him when Johanna led him out before the yard gate and showed him the Sintlinger memorial next to the lime tree, with its polished base, the pleasant cross, and the tasteful iron grille. He nodded affirmatively, but absentmindedly, was pleased that Johanna's wish had finally been fulfilled, and then read the dedication on the front surface of the base, "In memory of the earlier owners of the farmstead", in a low voice, idly, and without thought; nodded momentously at it; looked wide-eyed into Helene's eyes, and drifted from her side, led away by a wind which had sprung up in his inner being and which did not let itself be governed. Perhaps he had been seized by the shock of a man who, living on a deathly lonesome island, suddenly hears fraternal human sounds ringing out next to himself, and in the first shock is doubtful — has the sound of a stranger's voice met his ear, or his own voice. In this region of the world in which he thought he lived alone with Helene, the horror of which had driven old Klim to his death and his wife hard up against the edge of going mad, there this mad Herne miner was breathing and speaking words which contradicted everything which his calamity had taught him up to now. The man spoke this madness before hundreds as if it were his surest truth. If he could speak thus from that place, then it was impossible that his own conviction of the nature of God and of men had the sole legitimation. That view, in particular, that the entire universe is ruled by unbreakable legitimacy. which must at the same time be just, possesses an absolute power opposite God too, and does not tolerate the tiniest divine power. This unknown man lived like Sintlinger in the same expanse, far from all orthodoxies of other men, and was able to express such obvious nonsense as that the soul of a man possesses power over God. How? Then *he* had made his little Lena as she now was! Then *he, Sintlinger*, was either a brute who did not deserve to live, or such a blessed man that he ought to be frightened of himself. The first, if, as everyone believed, Helene really was blind, the other, if she had according to his view moved back already in temporal life deeper into the extramundane power.

Sintlinger beat himself with these thoughts in the most passionate way, and did not become aware that the gate and memorial stone had been decorated the next day with garlands of fir branches, that a feast had been made of the midday meal, and the servants were sitting around in festive clothes.

Johanna probably sensed that her Andreas was wrangling with someone passionately in his soul, and suggested after some dithering that his incomprehensible behaviour was nothing but the dislike, not entirely quelled by his goodness, of the "plonking of the stone", as he had called the erection of the memorial stone. But when he bent to her ear during the meal, asked her to look straight at him for once, and then asked whether he truly looked like a fool, she forsook this worry. She reassured herself that he was ruled again by his peculiar nature, which was either a consequence of his earlier wildness or an inheritance of the Sintlinger blood, and she no longer disturbed him in his strange affectation. Sintlinger scuffed through the house and yard for some time yet, whereby he often paused or spoke excitedly with someone invisible, and then disappeared. Even when towards evening the servants began to celebrate in their way the dedication of the Sintlinger memorial, the farmer was not to be seen. In his unknown hideaway, he even tolerated a real tumult coming over the entire blessed farm, as if the pernicious power of the mad Sintlinger had not been broken with the memorial, but rather as if the wild estranged farmers had been enticed from their graves to rule anew. And strangely, old Zenker was the abettor and leader of the boisterous procession which swarmed about making a racket until deep in the night. From his pocket came the barrel of beer which appeared as if by itself on the sawhorse behind the barn. At his behest, his stepson from Querhoven had under protection of darkness smuggled himself with his accordion through the forest to the farmstead. At first a loud laughter skipped like the whip cracking of a wedding here and there. The giggling of girls gently tickled the air everywhere. Not long and it there was flicking, jesting, and cheering everywhere, from the stables, the milk cellar, the boiler room, under the lean-to, and in the hall.

And as the accordion quite unexpectedly whinnied melodically, labourers and maids hurried their evening work, and soon everyone swept singing and dancing over the level meadow behind the barn.

In vain, Johanna made the attempt a few times to stem the roars of pleasure. But instead of relenting to her satisfaction, they cheered her, encircled her with arms entwined, and skipped around her to the rhythm of the accordion so that the farmwife quickly extracted herself from the unshackled seething and carried herself away to the little bench out front. There she sat and gazed out into the darkening evening. The boundary path below could hardly be recognised anymore, and the Brindeisener farmstead looked in the shadows not like a house, but like a black-bellied billygoat which was swaying inaudibly on the hill. When a cry of joy from the Sintlinger farmstead crashed into it, it awoke with a weak, grumbling echo, and then sank anew into its dark turning inward to itself.

Someone must have been next to the house in the garden. And Johanna endeavoured to work out who it was; but she only saw blacker shadows moving in the shadows, formless, inaudible, like wild animals playing about the edge of the forest at night. Once she thought she heard the gentle crowing of Peter's voice, and behind it the rumbling of old Brindeisener's voice seemed to lumber in a muffled way. Only, the loud bustling pleasure of the servants then took hold of her attention again so that, without knowing it, she hummed along to the melody which the accordion player was stringing out endlessly. Soon the laughter, singing and music making was whirling out into the pale night as if it wanted to emigrate into the fields, then the jubilation arose again in the distance, and it was drawn heartier and heartier and freer and freer again to the yard. The farmwife abandoned herself to this swinging back and forth of the joyful racket, and after a while it seemed to her to be a happy promise of the future. This sinking away of the laughter and singing out into the field was like a harvest of happiness, as if high-laden carts of joy were constantly swaying from out in the world into her yard.

"Why could it not be true", the farmwife pondered, "that this stone over here has knocked through my wall of sorrow forever?"

When Johanna turned around, she saw to her astonishment that her husband was sitting next to her with Helene, whom he held by the shoulders between his straddled legs.

"Oh, is it you?" she asked finally, breathing out in relief. Sintlinger just nodded silently.

"Why have you not left Helene sleeping?" she asked after a pause.

Sintlinger bent his head to the side, and asked, "Did you hear it? They are still shooting."

Johanna tried to listen for something, but it was impossible. Only Helene explained that, yes, there was banging over all the hills, and you could also see men running if you set yourself quite calm within.

The farmwife said with teasing mockery, "No, such a thing, little Lena!" and caressed her cheek.

At this moment, a maid shrieked shrilly from the crowd of dancers behind the barn.

Sintlinger said, "I think it is time to call it a day. That was why I came outside."

Suddenly the blind girl cried, "There!" and stretched her hand out in the direction of the forest which stretched out from Querhoven.

"What is there, child?" Sintlinger asked the girl, and took her protectively in his arms.

"She is worn out", Johanna said, "we will go in". She stood up, and took Helene by the hand. But the child pulled herself away vigorously, and said with tearful stubbornness that she was not tired, but saw a man.

The farmer touched his wife's hand soothingly, and then said earnestly, "So the child sees a man."

"Yes", Helene answered very definitely, "there", and she pointed in the same direction as before.

It could not have been any different than if the perceptions of Helene's sense illusions were a result of overwrought nerves. But it turned out strangely; when Sintlinger and his wife made a survey with a show of attentiveness for the child's reassurance, old Zenker appeared, bent forward and uncertain from behind the corner of the shed. For an instant, he paused against the bench by the gate, then he stepped to the retaining wall opposite the Brindeisener farmstead, and looked down, straining.

"Look, little Lena is right. There is a man there!" Sintlinger said wittily to his wife. "But I think, now it really is bedtime, otherwise the old man will spill onto us."

He passed Helene into his wife's arms, and stood up. At this moment, Zenker cried out in senseless fury,

"Will you get down? Will you go straightaway, Brindeisener — Hey, you!"

Before the farmer could spring over, the farmworker had gathered a large stone, and tossed it down the slope.

Then the farmer was also with the raving man, "Has the devil got you, Zenker!" he cried, and shook him by the arm. The old man turned around, and goggled at him uncomprehendingly, and when the howl of pain now rang out shrilly with a boy's voice, he actually nodded contentedly, and a laugh covered his entire face.

"Zenker, you have hit the boy, hey!" the farmer said louder, and seized him firmer by the arm so that he came to his senses.

From below now, old Brindeisener roared up, dully crashing, as if someone was drumming on a large empty wooden chest. But you could only hear the individual words, "... devil ... band ... break in two ..."

Johanna took Helene in her arms, and hurried into the yard. The accordion playing broke apart mid-tune, and the servants hurriedly rushed out. When they heard what the "Brindeisener grumbles" were about, they all, labourers as well as maids, stepped to the side of old Zenker, and declared, "The brat", by which they meant Peter Brindeisener, "had got what he deserved, and they too would have smashed in his skull." For the entire evening, he had been "spying around" the farm, and whenever he had been chased away, his white mop of hair had the next minute been sitting watching elsewhere.

But the old farmworker now repulsed their approval. The drunken whirl had already blown completely out of him. He looked sheepishly down in front of himself, and said with aggrieved voice, "It is not right, you people, it *is not* right. No, *no!*"

Old Brindeisener had also poured himself out. You could hear him slamming one door crashing shut. But before he let the other thunder after it, he roared once more with the entire strength of his lungs through the night, "Cursed, cursed pack of Sintlingers." Then he smashed the other door shut, and the heavy bar rattled down. The Sintlinger servants broke out into loud mocking laughter, and the farmer had trouble quietening them, and stuffing them into the yard.

Old Zenker remained standing in the place from where he had hurled the stone. When Sintlinger approached him again, he seized his hand, and squeezed it excessively. "You are right, farmer", he said with dull doggedness, "quite right. It rules over me, I deny it no more — I have become an old ass", and after this prelude, he started on a long tale whose meaning consisted of that he, through the threshing about over the incubus, had turned "to clay, absolutely wrenched", the "blowers", the legs, the head, all were clay. And when he did not lie to the side for a while, and sit it out and bare his teeth, then it made him still and laid him on his back. Everything would now be in order on the farm, they had the Sintlinger memorial, and did not need him anymore. He wanted to go over to his sister in Querhoven for a few weeks, and his nephew could stand in for him meanwhile on the farm. The fellow handled the work as easily and as confidently as his accordion. He was of Zenker blood, and he would put no dishonour on his relatives.

Sintlinger held out steadily. But when he saw that the old man was reaching out anew to attempt a different question, he said that it could be better discussed tomorrow in daylight, now it was sensible to go to bed. With that he took the grey head by the hand, and pulled him into the yard. At the little gate though, the old man tore himself away from Sintlinger with the indication

that he still had something to do. Sintlinger vanished
into the house.

4

The farmer did not go straight to bed, but shut the
door of the bedroom, sat down on the bench along
the wall of the living room behind the table, and abandoned himself to his thoughts.

Not long, and he heard old Zenker taking himself to
bed; the gate rattled, the lock of the house door creaked,
cautious steps came from the hall, banged against the
first steps of the stairs, and trailed off up the stairs to
the loft. Then weariness also assaulted the farmer, and
he began discarding his clothes. He took his coat off and
laid it next to himself, unbuttoned his vest and placed it
on the coat. He pressed it down firmly once, twice, as if
something was in the piece of clothing which was defending itself against him. Yes, finally he pressed his
hands so vehemently onto the recalcitrant things that he
even bent his body forward over it.

But he had to straighten up unexpectedly; for a
strange thought was besetting him, as strange and irrational as if he did not have it in his head, but it had
climbed from his clothes into his soul.

"It's just nonsense!" Sintlinger said to himself, and
looked around the dark room.

"It's just ridiculous!" he repeated, but already
quieter, and he had to again think, despite his resistance
to this foolish idea, "Helene did not at all see old Zen-

ker. — She was looking at the Querhoven forest, and Zenker appeared from the opposite side behind the barn."

But Sintlinger paid no more attention to this absurdity of his inner being, completed undressing and went with a contemptuous smile quite preoccupied into the bedroom. In passing through the doorway, he even thought mockingly, "Perhaps he wants me still to make believe the child saw the Faber-fool running past, haha!"

But in the midst of this mocking it was as if a voice distinctly spoke, "Yes! Just go to Helene's bed, and if you can see her face in the darkness, then it is all true."

At the same time, the farmer felt the drawing in of the grey staggering in his head which tended to precede deep sleep. For that reason, he thought to himself that the dream was already breathing on him while he was awake, but still let himself be led to his child's bed, and strangely, as his hand pushed groping against the side of the bed, the shadowy cloud of his dreamy mood suddenly tore apart and gave way to a shrill clarity, almost a wideawakeness.

Sintlinger could still reason that this state was probably the consequence of the multitude of excitements during the day and the passionate struggle with his thoughts about the Herne rebel, but then he bent as if pushed over Helene's bed, and directed his eyes ceaselessly through the night in the direction from where the quiet breath of his child was coming. It remained dark. Not even the white pillow, let alone the contours of the child's head, could be seen.

"Well then!" Sintlinger said to himself disappointedly. "There we have it. Now we will go to sleep."

But at once he heard Helene's breaths become quicker and quicker, restive and irregular. Then she began to roll around, and emitted a yawning sigh.

And then the incomprehensible happened for him.

He in fact saw Helene's eyes below himself, not in their colour and the distinct curvature of the eyeballs. They floated with the unsteadily flickering light of quite distant stars in the darkness, moved as if seeking here and there, extinguished when the lids sank over them, and then again stood still for a long time in an enigmatically hazy luminosity.

Sintlinger knew nothing of the ability of many human eyes to radiate the brightness which they have sucked in during the day out again into the darkness, but took it as the visible proof of his child's mysterious power of sight which had just now been gifted to him as he had been secretly struggling doubtfully with the claims of the accursed rebel.

He felt an almost physical hand on his shoulder, which gently pushed him back and out through the door into the living room. And a shimmering haze of happy jubilation billowed around his head. With flying hands, he dressed himself again, and when he gently left the living room, it seemed to him as if the door opened by itself. The front door also opened noiselessly, and soon he stood outside under the lime tree by the gate in the growing starry brightness of the night. Just then the bell tolls of the Hemsterhus tower clock struck jadedly, but clearly through the air high above him and fell distantly to earth. They shot down racing quick, and shattered as if on stones, so that the farmer still heard swishing, or rather spraying, and for seconds afterward, their shards of sound ringing on all sides through the air.

With the most alert senses, Sintlinger found himself as if in the midst of the ghostly web of a dream. He slowly stepped to the edge of the hill, and looked straining down at the boundary path to work out where the sounds were actually striking. The bells had been silent for a long time, but he could not desist from staring down. It was completely still. He could only hear his blood ticking quietly. But no! They were steps! He stepped so close to the edge of the slope that he had to hold onto the trunk of a tree to not slide down. Without a doubt! Someone was coming in leaps along the boundary path from Hemsterhus, always a few whipped strides, then heavy steps of extreme exhaustion stumbling over each other.

"The man Helene saw!" it flashed through Sintlinger's soul, and he forced his brain with such force onto his ears and his sight that his eyeballs ached from the strain of looking. As if by a miracle, he could distinguish the pale, shadowy road, and soon afterward, he actually saw the shadow of a man disengage from the shadow of a tree and sway irresolutely for a moment in the middle of the way.

"Hey!" Sintlinger shouted down like a fool. Then the man shot away quickly like the shadow of a nightbird into the forest, and his springing steps rang weaker and weaker. Sintlinger quickly considered whether he would hurry down the slope to him, or cut off the large arc which he would have to make to the boundary path because of a projection of the hill, and run across the high butte. He drew back his feet which he had instinctively pushed forward to step off, and ran in long strides up the hill.

"And even if I should run as far as the pond", the farmer said, and in order to beat the fugitive, he plunged as if thrown diagonally across the meadow where the forest road joined with the boundary path. He was already at the crossroads and, his breath heaving, he peered sometimes towards the forest which he saw wavering as a dark cloud in the darkness of night, other times he directed his eyes searchingly along the boundary path which wound out from the narrowed little valley as if from a giant hole.

Nothing to see!

Everything as still as fallen leaves.

He waited a while yet, and then walked across the path into the meadow, but for no other reason than to sit down, and dispose of the excitement somewhat. For in the middle of the meadow was a spring which had made a little pool in the grass, where it stood for a while in the vicinity of a heap of bushes and looked shiny and black before running away. There Sintlinger wanted to lie in the grass, arrange his thoughts, and keep the road over there in sight in case someone came.

"That would be one for me!" he pondered in going there. "Wanting to compel God, and run day and night witlessly away from the gendarmes and the cudgels of the farmers." With a derisive laugh, he sat down under the bushes, reached for a branch with his hand, and began stripping the leaves from it as he continued deliberating. Only, it was not proper thinking, but a dreamy proliferation of falteringly connected thoughts which swayed here and there in his head. Without the least reason, he connected the Herne rebel, the man that little Lena claimed to have seen, and that vagrant whose steps he had heard on the boundary path into one person, and thereby felt himself to be in a significant linking of fates, as is peculiar to the facts which a dream places in our soul so that all the paths of its waning life run past that event and fetch from it the strength of a future direction. But in the midst of this deep sinking, doubt beset him as to whether he had not erred entirely with the running man on the boundary path, and whether it was not foolish to impute so much importance and this interpretation in particular to the remarks of his child. Sintlinger let the branch go from his hand so that it snapped back slapping into the foliage, and considered that perhaps all that which was fascinating his thought was just the consequence of that hallucinatory hypersensitivity by which he had been driven to nocturnal ramblings since before he could remember, and he decided to give up the futile chasing of a man who was probably merely imagined, and go home.

But before he rose, he listened once more to the little spring before him gently tinkling as if someone were cautiously unlatching a tiny subterranean door then swallowing at captured waves, and sometimes a small bubble even erupted from it, rustling through the grass. "Perhaps everything has the same life breath as we men", he pondered, "the stones, the plants, the ground, the water", and he sat down on his hands, bent down quite close to the spring, and listened.

But he had to jerk back in shock.

For a man lay there in the grass as if he were swooping down, his head by the pool from which he had probably wanted to drink. At this moment, he must have lost consciousness, for his face lay slackly sunken to the side, his arms languidly propped on the grass. He lay motionless, and his breath swept now and then gently, though audibly, through the grass.

"It is the Nobody-incubus", the thought jerked through the farmer in a garish flash, "what should that mean? Then my wife, my child, my farm, everything is lost, even myself." Sintlinger sat bolt upright in the first impact of an unrestrainable, futile fear, and was unable to stir. But already the next moment, he had pulled himself together.

"What do you want here?" he called out loudly.

The stranger did not stir.

"Hey! You! Stand up!" He seized him by the shoulder and shook him.

The stranger emitted a deep, long groan, but did not come to.

"It's just a drunkard!" Sintlinger finally laughed contemptuously, gave the man a rough blow on the back, and called encouragingly, "Ups-a-daisy! Off, old man!"

Then a slow, difficult pulling together went through the tall body of the man lying there. He rose, staggering and uncertain, sat up, and then remained with lowered head for a while as if to recover from the strain of straightening up.

Sintlinger could not recognised the features of his face in the starlight. He just saw an almost too high, powerful forehead like a pale, furrowed wall of bone, sunken cheeks, a long, unkempt, full beard, and buried in it a painfully clenched mouth.

Now the stranger lifted his head up, and stared searching to all sides into the darkness.

He did not notice the farmer sitting under the bush though, moved his head wearily, and said to himself almost inaudibly in the tones of a dialect unknown to Sintlinger, "No — no. — — It was nothing ... I will just sleep a little ... sleep ... sleep, just sleep ..." Then he let himself collapse again with an aching breath.

"Faber ..." Sintlinger said, gripped and uncertain.

The stranger moved his head in affirmation and said, "Yes, yes ... it's okay. I know you are there. But leave me now. Go sleep, sleep. You have need of it."

The farmer could from these puzzling words neither recognise whether the stranger really was Faber or some stranger whom a secret sorrow was driving through the night, nor whether his words had been directed at him or were the soliloquy of an exhausted man.

Without settling these possibilities clearly in himself, Sintlinger acted according to the impulse which had moved him since he had read the Herne miner's incomprehensible words about God, and he took on the fulfillment of the desire that he be able to argue over it with the strange man.

For that reason, the farmer said after a pause, "But you have run away."

The stranger answered half asleep, "You know indeed that I let you run out of human sympathy."

"You ran away out of weakness, out of cowardice", Sintlinger said, beginning to realise that the stranger was talking with himself as though with a different person in the manner of those half in dream.

"Quite right, quite right", the stranger responded, "because of the weakness of the others. For you are strong enough to bear external wrong. Be quiet now though, sleep, and don't constantly grieve."

Now Sintlinger was certain that the fugitive could be none other than Faber.

"Man", he thus said, "man, that is a lie on your own neck. You are afraid of your own death." At these words, the stranger started from his haze, sprang to his feet with a leap, and looked around, breathing hastily.

"That I cannot be", he said, murmuring to himself. Then he spoke louder, "If someone is there, show yourself."

His voice had been transformed, it was full of poignant confidence.

Sintlinger rose somewhat astonished, and took a step towards him out of the shadows of the bushes.

"Here I am", he said at the same time.

"So, so", Faber said calmly, and examined him through the darkness. "Who are you?"

"A farmer."

"From the district?"

"Yes, at home hereabouts. And you? — Are you not the miner from Herne who addressed the people, and then ran away?"

"And for that reason, you are chasing me, and lurking in ambush for me in the night?" Faber answered evasively with a gentle rebuke. "Not everyone who runs,

runs from himself. I have no fear. But I am sorry for those who pursue me, and I must preserve them from doing wrong to me."

"It did not occur to me at all that I would want to catch you", Sintlinger replied, shaken by something bottomless in the words, even more in the voice of Faber, and at the same time pushed aside hurtfully by the stranger's pride so that he defended himself against it with his old, cutting, almost contemptuous rebelliousness. But Faber ignored the farmer's abusive flaring up completely, and answered calmly, "So, if you don't want to do anything to me, then go, and leave me alone. I am tired from being chased, and want to sleep for a moment. — Leave me! When it is time, I will do what is necessary. Good night, man!"

During the last words, Faber had sat down again, and stretched himself out on the ground. He called the good night to the farmer as he was already lying down. Then he shoved his arm as a pillow under his head, and paid no more attention to Sintlinger.

"If you don't want anything more than to sleep the night in a meadow, then you did not need to agitate to thousands of people!" the blessed farmer called to him mockingly.

The stranger remained silent.

"Go! You!" he called grimly anew. "Yes, now you have outgrown your mouth! Where is the power, you braggart, the power with which you can compel God, when you get nothing in your need but — fancy trousers."

Faber made no reply to the bluster, and the farmer flew more and more into injustices. And the more he sensed that, the more vehemently his unrestrained temper overwhelmed him. But he achieved nothing with his attacks but making himself more and more disoriented and uncertain, whereas the other man's power grew.

Soon he found himself in a sort of self-defence because he felt that if the man stood up and walked away
without having spoken a cutting word to him, he would
be forced quite certainly to follow him, and to remain
until he had spoken to him.

Something like fear came over the farmer so that he
was no longer master over the clarity of his deliberation.
His words passed over his lips as if he were blowing on a
fire. He was already shedding the ties of his most secret
convictions, and exposing the glimmer and the air of
many hidden corners of his life.

Faber nevertheless did not show any tendency to
come out of his state of slumber, but exuded more and
more perceptibly a mysteriously high accompaniment
which led Sintlinger to ever new confessing.

With reluctance and in distress to nevertheless confound the "vagrant", the blessed farmer let fall husk
after husk from his life, and approached the deepest
transformation of his existence, the secret which had
come over him through his child.

But he did not want to have that snatched from him,
though he could not prevent skimming past this renewal
of his entire world as he spoke of a look which was able
to penetrate behind all being.

With these words, Faber unexpectedly leapt up
again, and encouraged Sintlinger at the same time in
the belief that he had only pretended to be sleeping the
entire time. The rising up of the tall man was so powerful, and he then looked in such a tremendous way at
him, that the blessed farmer, suddenly no longer finding
his way to his own words, fell silent.

"My dear man", Faber said gently after a little deliberation, "you have progressed a great deal. For sure. But
take care. For you have a nature such that you will end
up in a hardship and madness which is greater than that
you have come out of."

"Why?" Sintlinger asked with timorous irony. Faber rocked his prophet's head negatively, and when the blessed farmer pressed him to tell him calmly, for he was not a piece of thread which you could tear apart with two fingers, Faber gave him a reply which Sint-linger considered to be complete nonsense. He said something like that it could not fail that it would whirl him in the end into a terrible grinder, because he always took himself along everywhere his senses lead him, even to his God.

The sentences with which he ended in particular spoke with derision to all which Sintlinger had heard up till then. Faber said, "The knowledge about thinking has destroyed more souls than swords have ever slain men. Anyone who knows without thinking and feels without feeling, only thinks and feels what is eternally worthy of thought and feeling. The knowledge of thinking is like the look which sees a ball from the outside. The think-ing without consciousness experiences the movements of the universe, and the feeling which does not know it-self, the sensations of God."

This seemed to the farmer to be outright lunacy. This exchange in general was ending in such a grotesque way that everything heavy and profound from before was submerged by it in the improbability of a mere dream experience.

For the sound of Faber's voice yet rang in the still night air when the trotting of horses' hooves sounded quite weakly in the distance from the Sintlinger forest and quickly came nearer.

The noise tore the head of the still reflective com-peller of God around, and plunged him sharply back into the old fear. He began trembling, his breath whistled, in vain he struggled for steadfastness, as it ap-peared to the blessed farmer. Suddenly he stretched both hands out to him for help imploringly, and stuttered, "Farmer ... farmer ... brother ... do you hear ... they are coming again already ... farmer! ..."

Faced with this mournful breakdown, Sintlinger's old biting irony took possession. He tore his money pouch from his pocket, and pressed it into the fugitive's hand with the mocking words, "Yes, yes. Run while you can, poor beggar! And then take a shortcut to your God."

At this moment, the hoofbeats he had heard before came crashing loudly into the open just then. Faber sprang up with a grasshopper's leap, and ran ducking into the forest, in which quiet crunching soon wound away hurriedly and was extinguished.

Over on the road they clattered hastily stumbling past, paused at the crossroads for a moment, and then trotted quickly onwards.

The horse snorted; the misshapen balls of shadow which were its body surged past; a soft shimmer twitched a few times, presumably from the helmet of the gendarme. Then the hoofbeats tailed off into the dark tunnel of the valley to Hemsterhus, and had soon gone down behind the bulge of the Sintlinger hill into the silence of the night. The farmer, however, was suddenly beset by laughter over the Herne rebel who emerged like a giant out of the night, then ran away so feebly, and over the gendarmes who had so foolishly pursued him.

5

The next morning, Sintlinger met old Zenker, after some searching in vain, in the boiler room where he was sitting on the boiler box and looking with grey, lowered face at a heap of old plunder which lay on the floor before his feet — a pair of reddish, bone-hard tall boots, a disused stable jacket, a crumpled neckerchief, and a few straps.

On the master's entrance, the worker lifted his head, and nodded towards him in greeting with a mocking smile, "Yes, yes, just laugh, farmer! Life begins with rags, and with rags it ends. I came to the Sintlinger hill feeble, feebly will I climb down it again. Everything revolves. What begins grey must end grey. It cannot be any different for the likes of us! But in between it was sometimes nice and bright, wasn't it, farmer?"

"Then you will be leaving straightaway?" Sintlinger asked.

"Whether I want to or not, that springs from a different stone", Zenker answered. "It really puts me out."

With that he shifted along a bit on the boiler box, and Sintlinger sat next to him.

They then both talked over the old man's decision to go to his sister at Querhoven for a few weeks and, if it must be, spend some months recovering from his troubles with sitting and lying in warmth and calm; they skimmed this and that region of the past in their chatter, and the blessed farmer dispersed the clouds which made the distance from the farm appear to the loyal servant like a farewell forever, and said to him so much that was good and comforting that Zenker plucked up courage again.

"No, no!" the old man finally cried out. "I did not actually mean it so. You won't be rid of me the old rock breaker and grumbler completely. Don't cock your ears for that. Before winter comes, I will be roaring through the house again."

Then they negotiated over his sister's son, Gottlieb Meixner, and Zenker praised him with terse words as a diligent, sure and useful fellow to whom the only thing which adhered from his father and uncle, the braggart Meixner, was that he sometimes so-to-say got up a mad trilling. But then you just needed to pull the bridle between his teeth, with just a rough jerk, then the colourful Meixner rags would fall away and the Zenker blood would rise up to the top again.

Yes, it is strange, Sintlinger suggested, what fathers are able to play at with their children when they themselves do not know to lay out a table with their own meal. As they usually belch at those dishes on which their father and grandfather had once ruined their stomachs. Whether it will continue with the Meixner, Elis — he was named Elias — for very long? By that he meant the solitary estate owner at Querhoven.

Oh yes, Zenker answered, did the farmer not know then that it was going quite especially well again now for him, and all Querhoven stinks from the Meixner farm on Sunday and for a week after of roasts and wine, and the braggart Elis drove so that the horses caught their horseshoes in their tails. For in the previous year, the back-pained brother of his wife had died, the miserly invalid to whom the entire farm and everything had actually belonged as of right.

Now the money box stood constantly open, and if Meixner just bent over, money fell from his pockets.

The two talked about the turbid estate owner at Querhoven back and forth some more, and came thus by a detour again to the departure of the old farmworker, the circumstances of which they then determined quite precisely.

"Good, then everything is settled", Sintlinger said at the end, and rose. "Gottlieb will drive you over in the evening, and bring his things with him on the way back, and your wages will continue. Take note, Zenker, you belong to us!"

He gave the old man a hearty slap on the shoulder, and left him quickly, for he saw how the good grey head was overcome by emotion, stood there ashen and bit on his stump teeth in fury so as to not let the water out of his eyes.

"Gottlieb is in the back meadow", he called after Sintlinger in grim clenching. Then he seized the old tall boots, heaved them crashing to the floor by the boiler box, and said, "I will break the bones of those who want to confront our master."

When the blessed farmer arrived at the forest meadow, the greatest part had already been mown in swathes, and the fellow was still letting the scythe dance as if he had only just taken it in hand. Bad reapers stand stiffly, and pluck at the grass with the scythe like an old toothless cow. The good reaper actually concedes himself more to that cutting blade on the long handle. He does nothing more. After a short time, the scythe is seized by the swishing which lies within it. This swing merges into the reaper so that he flutters across the meadow more like a bird with outstretched wings. Sintlinger approached the fellow without being seen by him. Now, as he stood by him, he touched his shoulder from behind, and Meixner pulled the scythe out of its swing, and placed it smiling with its handle on the ground.

"Well, will it work out okay on the Sintlinger farm, Meixner?" the farmer asked.

"On my part, certainly", Gottlieb answered with a smile.

"But accordion playing makes things easier, well?"

"One after the other, as it comes."

"And if mother's ribbon is torn now?" Sintlinger asked with a smile, because Gottlieb had never gone out of Querhoven all his life until then.

"Well, then I think my trousers will stay dry", Gottlieb answered quick-wittedly.

After this cheerful introduction, the two reached an agreement over wages. The fellow received his initial payment,and was advised that he could start that day. Meixner was short, bright, with a tendency for mocking indirectness. Even when serious, a comical twitch flew through his very large, lumpy, irregular face. His eyes were especially strange. Somewhat squinty from birth, they lay in deep, spacious sockets, small, dark, full of dogged unease. He examined the blessed farmer with them, having heard so much about him, every time Sint-linger turned his inquiring eyes away from him. Then his eyes shot forward with stabbing grasps, and imme-diately sprang back, lapsing into timidity again, when the blessed farmer looked at him.

In general, the farmer was pleased with Meixner, and he explained this strange facial affectation to himself with the hidden whirling which old Zenker had spoken of. It will all give way, he thought, and if not, we are not married.

"Has anything else happened?" Sintlinger asked fi-nally, and surveyed with hidden astonishment the place where the experience with Faber had played out just hours before.

"Happened?" Gottlieb turned his face to him some-what perplexed.

"Well yes, I was just thinking", the farmer said with a smile, nodded in parting, and strode towards the road. There he walked a small stretch inconspicuously to-wards the forest, and looked for the tracks of the rider who had trotted past in the night. But in the ground up dust, so many vehicles had already embedded the wheel tracks and hoof marks of their horses this morning that nothing was to be found.

"Vanished from the earth", Sintlinger pondered, "thus it shall also remain." Then he turned around, and walked slowly up the Hemsterhus way to his farmstead. And as he belatedly progressed, he let his thoughts from the night return in leisurely recollection, and could not resist a bitter feeling towards himself suddenly, as if he had behaved ignobly towards Faber, even in the nasty harsh way of his earlier life.

From this lost state, he was awoken by the crack of a whip, and when he lifted his head, he saw himself standing in the middle of the boundary path right before two horse's mouths blowing their warm breath in his face. At the same time, a rumbling deep laugh, and mocking "Hey!" rang out.

Sintlinger sprang to the side, and recognised old Brindeisener crouching like a giant heap of logs on his wagon, and behind him could be seen little Peter.

Thinking quickly, he stepped with a smile up to the wagon to talk straightaway about the irksome affair which had been instigated by his servants the previous evening without his support. The men had curtly offered a hand to each other, and although the sneering drilling look did not fade from the eyes of the old estranged farmer for a moment, he reassured Sintlinger's worry with heedlessly indifferent words, but so as if it were not worth being cross about nor worth forgiving.

There was nothing more to say, he suggested, from a quarry even large boulders fall, and a hussy just stinks. It was never any different in the world.

With that he growled his mockingly good-natured laugh again, looked with contemptuousness down at the small Sintlinger, and did not endeavour in the least to

exclude his neighbour expressly from this offensive ex-
culpation. All he did to alleviate his words consisted in
the furious flaring up against his boy who alone actually
bore the blame for this recent quarrel of the farms. For
you could believe that he had not been sent by anyone
to do the spying. He was just always possessed by an
unnecessary rambling and looking about, carried on all
sorts of unnecessary behaviour, chattering, singing,
skipping, and whipping about, and did all but that
which he was instructed to do. And if he skived off once
more over to the farm, then the brat would be given legs
with the whip.

Little Peter had during this stern lecture from his
father inconspicuously pushed himself away further and
further on the board towards the back end of the wagon,
and was obviously waiting for the moment when the old
farmer would attempt to give his rancour a palpable
conclusion. One of the boy's feet already stood ready for
flight on the skids, and his hands sat with closed grip on
the edge of the side boards which he sat on, ready for
springing off. His large, pale blue eyes, made even more
gleaming by held back tears, went back and forth un-
cowered between his father and Sintlinger, and always
rested with bewildered surprise a little longer on the
deep, calm face of the blessed farmer. The boy had an
open, sympathetic being, even now when a fearful anticipation reigned over him.

When Brindeisener had thereby ended the angry
rumbling of his stern lecture, Sintlinger stepped up to
the boy, brushed his blond hair once, and consoled him
kindly, for it was probably not meant so badly at all by
his father.

The unexpected kindness which he was unused to
shook the boy so much that he grasped the hand of the
blessed farmer with both hands and squeezed it vigorously. But Brindeisener, seeing that, laughed roughly,

suddenly gave the horses a lash, and murmured to himself, travelling away quickly, all sorts of contemptuous things about "such Sintlinger flightiness".

The blessed farmer climbed up to his farmstead, shaking his head over such stupid, hard living.

***

On the afternoon of the same day, old Zenker was loading up his possessions, taking leave of everyone at the Sintlinger farmstead, and being driven by his nephew across to Querhoven. He had had to promise, if it worked out, to come over sometimes, and to take care of himself so that he could take up his old place again before winter set in.

That night Sintlinger pressed himself always in vain sometimes on one ear, sometimes the other, and could not sleep. Now he heard it quietly coming down the stairs from the loft. Now it stood out in the living room, and it seemed to him as if he were stuck behind the door and listening with restless ears himself to his own sleeplessness. He lit a candle, and looked at Johanna and at Helene, because he thought they were lying with alert eyes, and peering into the night. But around his wife's mouth, a half dreamt smile was playing, and the girl was sleeping raptly as if breathless.

He extinguished the light again, and buried his head deep in his pillow. It was no use. The incomprehensible listening did not let off from him. Finally he noticed how the wind was getting up, skimming sighing around the corners, and then sweeping with a gentle hum through the trees in the garden. Now he thought it would put him out gently. But suddenly he heard a rattle at the yard gate, and straight afterwards a sound like a fist banging against wood a few times. Noiselessly he rolled out of bed, dressed scantily, and walked through the front door and across the yard. The gate was shut. No sound stirred, and yet it seemed to him that someone was standing outside and waiting with shaking knees and trembling jaw for someone to open it and let him in. "Who is out there?" he asked in a muffled voice. There was no answer, and when he opened the little door, and groped in front of himself, he grasped at the empty night. It was so painful, that he carefully shut the little door again, and returned to the living room. There he sat down in the darkness behind the table, and was quite shaken.

At once, without knowing how it happened, he placed his hand before his face, bent over the seat, and said, "Everything is true. I need not have any worry. I am right. I alone ... not you, Faber, and you ... truly not ... truly not! ..."

For hours he struggled with the giant shadow of the Herne fugitive, until a light went up around him, a still, boundless brightness which his sleep tailed off into.

The next morning, Johanna found him, his arms placed on the table, in a deep dream.

When she woke him, he lifted his wide awake, pale face, and looked at her as if he were being forced to a confession. But when she asked him what it was, he stood up, and quickly dressed himself properly. Then he grasped her hands, and led her silently from the house across the yard, out deep into the fields.

When nothing more was around them but the quiet morning rustling of the ears next to them, and the pale bright sky above them, he stood still, and was about to start speaking.

But he brought nothing over his lips but the calling of her name jubilantly a few times, "Johanna, Johanna!" Then he had to fall silent, and enclose her shaking in his arms.

And after he had gotten hold of himself somewhat, he asked her to go back to the farmstead and not worry herself. He was nothing but happy, really happy, and *she* was also part of it, *her* and every Sintlinger.

For the first time in her life, Johanna saw something like the gleam of tears forcing their way out of his eyes, and she left him with surprise that the old, incomprehensibly passionate heart of her Andreas had been so quickly awoken again. On turning back, she saw his sunlit hair amidst the ears just as if a dark golden ball were floating above the pale expanse of grain.

How great his happiness was has emerged from a place in his diaries which can only have originated during this time of tense wrestling as he sought to bring back from the struggle with Faber into a sparkling level of life everything which the inaudible wheels of fate had ground down from the Sintlinger farm's wondrous life. Even those who did not possess the tiniest knowledge of the events of that chapter of his life would feel that the farmer had seized on a new, higher wave of his fate. For those, however, who kept their days by his pulse, a look opens up into that only dimly lit region where, directly behind the back of existence, the mundane powers of men are weighed against each other. Through the mere passing by of the enormous shadow of Faber, a new spirit had come over the blessed farmer, a spirit which drew him reluctantly into the power of the man whom he had called defeated. This entry also has a quite different effect in its wording.

The sentences read:

> When a man is born, at the same moment two bells begin to toll. One bell tolls below, one above; one as it were on earth, one, as the people say, in heaven. This doubled tolling does not stop as long as we live. And according to whether the man listens more to the bell above or to that below, he

is good or bad, big or small, and it goes uphill or downhill with him.

Some men, however, commit such a noise in the middle of their life with their business affairs or with their passions, yes, some even merely with their thoughts, that the sound of the two bells cannot reach them. Such men are stuck in the midst of the most extreme hardship which can befall a man here on earth. They have lost their way. When they look into the mirror, a strange face appears to them. For they no longer understand their own commerce when they do something, their own words when they say something, and their own thoughts when they are thinking. That is the field on which the fool grows as if he were wise. The lost then want to lead others, and those driven under the wheels hurry to give good advice to those foundering.

For there are truthfully people who through every labour for their happiness achieve nothing, as if constantly attacking and pillaging themselves like a robber in the darkness. They are also like mountain streams which must constantly plunge down if they want to remain living.

Little Lena, I am on the right path, I am on your path!

Little Lena, I hear it tolling! From the heights, I hear it tolling ...!

***

In this sunny air, the blessed farmer fetched in his harvest, and could not get enough toil. When the labourers and maids, numb with exhaustion, brought back the last cart in the evening, Sintlinger, on returning home, caught his child, and swung her and played with her through the garden.

He no longer heard the sound of the tower bells from Hemsterhus, and in the world, only the weather interested him. Thus it came that his eyes, which had misted over with light, also did not see to a side how a scene was playing out which could have at least torn his security badly if it had penetrated as far as the Sintlinger hill.

Perhaps three weeks after the blessed farmer's nocturnal adventure in the meadow, the news appeared in the papers that Faber, the leader of the Herne rebels who had vanished without trace, the wanted man, Faber, had given himself up to the court in Neustadt, a small town in Thuringia lying between Coburg and Sonneberg. Certainly every paper had put this notice in small print in the most inconspicuous, most hidden corner of their pages, because the entire raucous edifice of lies about Faber had collapsed in the meantime.

A month later, the news appeared only briefly that Faber had, taking into account his time in custody, been sentenced to three weeks in prison for incitement of a public disturbance.

Meanwhile the summer wind had finished its work in the fields. It did not need to sway the ears anymore, because the slow ripening was too monotonous for them. It did not need anymore to scare up the stalks when they wanted to lie down on the earth tired from carrying the ever heavier ears. It skimmed about idly, whistled softly to itself, and at most played heedlessly with the swinging of the last oat fields, or chased the birds through the air so that the first thoughts of migration came to them.

Around the many villages which could be seen from the blessed farm, a reddish blue haze floated; for the heather was blooming. It seemed as if a mild, reddish evening glow had fallen on the earth and struck roots there, the roads looked like golden ribbons which had fluttered down from the heavens. The forests were singing with still air, and the light played with clear astonishment over this late beauty about everything, and trees, houses, and people gleamed so that you would not think at all that they could have shadows.

Those were the days in which Faber left the prison of the small Thüringian town. The Superintendent handed over to him a pfennig for a meal, and at the same time made the demand that the freed prisoner no longer worry about the lives of others and the constitution of the state for whose care the authorities were appointed, but return on the straightest path to his home town to take up a useful occupation. "Above all", the prison overseer said, "if you are found in the course of the day by one of the police to be still in the area, then you cannot expect any less than to be seized and transported with a kick to Silesia."

Faber looked him rigidly in the face during this speech with his large, deep eyes so that the man could not endure the look in the end, and his clever, well meaning words felt foolish. He turned away confused, and Faber strolled out of the town smiling quietly. At the last of the houses, he met a poor girl who wanted to go to school. He just gifted her the pfennig from the prison, and then he abandoned himself to an unhurried, lazy strolling. After he had been walking a while along the main road under the yellowing maples, he came to from his deep contemplation, and looked in the direction which the shadow next to him laid on the earth. He stretched his right hand towards the ditch, and pointed to a meadow which turned between fields of stubble towards a little forest which stood bluish in the distance, and next to it in the distance, the tower boss of a village church flashed golden over the green of the fields.

Faber followed his shadow, leapt over the ditch, and strode with the long, solemn gait of his large feet into the meadow. For someone who is at home in his heart, every place on earth appears equally good.

6

Most parents are too unsuited for the education of their children because their memory of the early times of their own lives no longer contains the verve and scent of fables, nor the foreboding, angelically deep astonishment of the awakening spirit, but only the foolish and churlish derailments of that epoch, and they therefore see themselves hidden in the general current of thoughtless conviction, as if the young human being were only a foolish, irrational little animal which, abandoning its own instincts, must become enmeshed willy-nilly in wrong ways and end in aberrations. That is why the wisdom of most consists in that they bring the disappointments and bleak experiences of their lives into a system with whose help they tame the colourful rambling of youth. The fewest adults have an idea of the blessed breeding which the children practise on them, and that the world would long ago have choked in the narrowness of useful wisdom, precautionary fear, and anxious distrustfulness, if the souls of the under-age did not see again and again on earth the wealth of divine expanses and lead the people through all the barriers of the world into heavenly air.

The blessed farmer was preserved by his being and the events of his life from the danger of others reforming his little Lena through the abuses which the past had perpetrated on him.

For this child, who in the opinion of others had fallen too short in her fortunes, had brought to him straightaway the fulfillment of earlier, almost forgotten secret urges for being carried way from the existence of the great masses, the existence in which weakness, foolishness, and malignity formed the hidden foundations of human virtue. Now that her mysterious power of sight had at last drawn Faber's giant shadow into the conflict and, as he certainly believed, into victory in his life, the last cloud had vanished before the fulfillment of his deepest desire. He saw himself exalted on such a high, sunny plain that you could barely recognise the world of men below, and could hear none of their words.

For that reason, the care over the welfare of his child consisted of nothing other than avoiding everything which could drive her out from the region of her own, wondrous spirit. Also to be kept away from Helene according to Sintlinger's wish would be the knowledge of her "so-called outer blindness", as the farmer expressed it, and the knowledge of the death of humans and of any other creature. For the blessed farmer had learnt at base from old Klim and his wife what hardships human life could be led into by this double knowledge, and he intended to push it out to a time when it would be easier to deal with this double burden. They would in any case avoid having the child pushed crudely and early into a misery of life whose consequences would be hard to gauge.

With these considerations, he saw himself in harmony with his wife and with old Trine to whom the guidance of the child had by and large been left.

This old person originated like most good servants from the region around Querhoven; for the poor, little village hidden by forest possessed as it were the power of calling to life well-formed children in great quantities. But with that its power was also actually exhausted. With the bleak smoke from the many little cottages, with the gentle pastoral melodies of its countless tiny threads of water and the incessant hum of the forest which stood about the village, it also did not succeed in filling the children early with colourful, wondrous hazes. But to set the table nourishingly and to otherwise administer diligently to their bodies' needs was very badly done by the estate of the concealed village. For that reason too, the habits, or bad habits as you may want to call them, were pulled out of the children, to steal away after days, weeks and, at worst, a few years very quickly over the tree tops again into their home in the heavens. And for anyone whom life would not let go of at all, they had to just see that they found their way out of the village straight after their schooling if they did not want to chew straw with their teeth like a poor man's goat and cover themselves with air when it was freezing. Thus every year in spring, the boys and girls threw themselves out of Querhoven into the surrounding villages and towns, and did not take with themselves anything more than a little seed, a wreath of hope with which they fled, and the core of their being filled with resilience, human and divine faith, and a creed which was so deep and fuzzy that no Querhovener in his long life had ever completely gotten his bearings in it. To that, barb after barb were fixed in some place in their soul to everyone who had merely been incubated by the little, forest village, and anyone who had the desire to cultivate this region with a Querhovener had to soon give it up. For that reason, the saying went across the entire countryside that the Querhovener sipped with the blade, cut with the fork, and forked with the spoon. The first word which the children spoke was "*no*" and the second "*absolutely not*".

Nevertheless it was already recommendation enough for a servant if he originated from Querhoven, for it was said that the hen would pick its own head off before a Querhovener even stole an egg.

The other labourers and maids, however, for whom the diligence of the people from the forest village was a thorn in the eye, maintained that what even an ass would let fall, a Querhovener would still pick up.

Old Trine had possessed all these good qualities when, barely out of school, she was driven by hardship from her poor father's cottage into the service of others. Of recalcitrance though and of all sorts of bitter mixtures, there was not the slightest trace in her being. Whether it had once been different in her early youth, she herself did not know; for perhaps through the life and teaching of her parents, perhaps most of all through their ways, she had been brought to never see her own hopes and wishes as anything but powerlessly fluttering butterflies, which, when whirled up by the draught of the vehicle on which the life of her masters is drawn along, are carried along with it for a stretch and then fade away somewhere without coming close to her. The breath of long years had turned this selfless merging un-noticed into the requirements of others into the content and happiness of her being so that she gauged the world only by the detour over the wishes of those whom she served and she worried for their own welfare.

In this way, she had even come by her own name. As long as she had served in Brederode with the Parish Superintendent, she had been called the old Klim-Trine, and now that she had found herself a haven on the blessed farm, it did not occur to anybody to call her anything but the Sintlinger-Trine. This or that baker of jokes probably had a go sometimes at calling her by her own name of Katherine Wagner. But then the old woman would walk away as if it did not refer to her at all.

After a few steps, she turned around to the speaker, looked him in the face with a mocking smile, as if because of some stale joke, and called him a "dumb fool" or something still cruder.

For the sake of such qualities, she had been brought to the farm by Johanna for little Helene. It is possible that the blessed farmer's wife had also done it in order to have a last sound and breath of her own youth with her father and mother around herself and to let little Lena enjoy the hidden, sheltered enjoyments of a good and religiously enclosed life which she herself had been forced to push back into the inconceivable transitions of her fate. Johanna entrusted the child to the same hands by which she had been led through her youth, for after the early death of Klim's wife, old Trine had taken the place of her mother for her.

Nobody but old Trine would have been as suited to be playmate and guide to little Helene in the time of her mysterious, so enraptured childhood. For after the aged woman had recovered from her shock and pity over the affliction of the tender girl, she understood through the wisdom of her kindness and love how to move entirely in the air in which the child breathed, and to accomplish what Sintlinger wished, to keep away from her the bitter knowledge of her blindness.

She called all sensations through touch and feeling 'seeing', and transformed in that way all the fairy tales which she told Helene until deep in the night, from Snow White, the Wolf and the Seven Young Goats, Little Red Riding Hood, the Hazel Branch, and Tom Thumb. Thus the child did not become unhappy and discontented in her world, a world which was entirely filled by those quiet, inexpressible waves which seeing people also come close to, though only in rare elevated moments.

The Blessed Farm

In Sintlinger's records, a single short question is to be found which grasps at the wonder-worthy being of his child. They read:

> Who is capable of leading an angel? Only its own wings.

Nothing else, although the blessed farmer grasped directly the most secret, most hidden thing and was troubled for such a long time until he succeeded in also throwing a look at the unspeakable, at least as if through the crack in a closed door. Only by the shaking of his usually so steady writing, and by the foundering with which the awkward letters are somewhat pushed together, do you sense the emotion of the almost timidly delighted father over the inconceivable development of his blind little daughter.

We know that the senses are only the tools, not the masters of men, and yet when we listen to the opinions of most, the belief of almost all seems to consider it to be confirmed that the instrument plays the musician, the chisel governs the sculptor, and the plough steers the farmer. Only the works of the highest minds force these people by exception to consider conceivable the protruding of divine powers into the world of human existence. Only, anyone who looks attentively and un-flinchingly at his own life must be astonished a hundred times on the most ordinary day at the miracle which happens around him, and above all in him. Not thought of is the inexplicable puzzle of thinking in particular, the resurrection of the external world in our inner being, and the ordering of all existence which we only experi-ence through our soul. We are sometimes pursued by visions through which we experience ourselves only as windows from which the inexpressible power of sight of an alien being looks into this life. You sit or lie awake with closed eyes in a dark room. The door stands open, and we hear the wind sweeping through all the rooms of the house.

Then the front door is opened below. Someone comes up the stairs, along the hall to the room in which we keep ourselves. Its steps sound like restrained fury, like suppressed rage. And suddenly it stands in the doorway, ten, twelve steps from us, yet invisible. Only a clenching and squeezing emanates from it. It is in the darkness an even darker thing, and it acts like a pinching grip which clasps and compresses us. For of the art and essence of a man, we experience only a very incomplete idea through his visible gestures and his figure. The play of accidental movements perceptible to the eye must be transcribed in the depth of our being into a vision for which language possesses no words, the mind no images, and the world only the signals of the senses. On the strength of powers which will probably always remain a puzzle to us, we are capable of perceiving the loveliness of a landscape even at night. The horror of the wasteland seizes us even when we are unable to see anything. Rock faces roll anxieties onto us, abysses frighten us, and we sense in the floating high flight above us the endlessness of an expanse.

We can only sample the most secret sweetness of a flower's scent to its depths with our eyes closed. The unfathomable ocean exercises its strongest effects in darkness. Water sounds its most secret magic most clearly and affectingly to the soul in the deep shadows of the forest. The abyss-like clarities of a great mind first convince us completely when we have drawn the lids shut over our eyes' restive fervour for seeing, and only then are we capable of making the unspeakable annunciations of great music our own. Really, you could feel forced by these facts to the conviction that, though the eyes make this world visible, at the same time they deceive us about their deepest meaning by the whirl of colourful images. But certainly the world of the blind is no less many-sided than the earth of the sighted, only the people with benighted eyes conceive everything in a different, more inward way than the latter; for little Helene recognised the metals by the different taste which she felt on her tongue in their vicinity. Of iron she said that it tasted sour, copper was repugnant to her through a bitter sharpness, lead she recognised by its fat dullness, gold she loved because of its warm, flowerlike fullness, and silver she was devoted to above all because it possessed a clear, cool scent like fresh air or just poured water. She perceived the colour of flowers by the smell which they exhaled, and with a sense of touch by which the power of sight resided at certain distances in the fingertips themselves, she enjoyed the shape of plants. Once she was sitting with old Trine during spring in the beech stand between Brederode and Hemsterhus. It was sunny and still. The silver stemmed trees stood soundlessly as if bewitched, and held on their millions of little branches the golden red buds, swollen to bursting, to the light so that they would open fully. The aged woman told the child once again about Sleeping Beauty, who lay for years asleep in the forest of roses and could not awake at all. The old woman told everything in the properly grisly and nasty way Helene loved. But whereas little Lena usually got a fearfully pale, withdrawn face and overclouded eyes from it, this time she listened to all the oppressive things with bright cheerfulness, stroked the grass gently with her hands, and finally broke out into a delighted laugh, let herself fall backwards into the green, and giggled away ever anew and was unable to stop herself. But when Helene finally noticed that Trine was thinking that she was laughing because of the ineptitude of the telling, she said it would not be possible for her today to be properly scared because the trees were constantly smiling so hap-

pily above her and did not stop for as far as she could
see. Trine looked into the golden shimmer of the bud-
ding beech crowns, and now also felt the cheerfulness of
the trees storming into life, the cheerfulness which the
child had noticed in her deep soul, and she brushed her
hand caressingly and astonished through the child's
hair. At the same time, she said tenderly, "Just wait, you
dear, wicked little Sintlinger spirit, I will tell your father
that."

Just like little Lena was touched by the gentle soulful
laughter of the awakening beeches, she also felt the trail
of white, high little clouds wandering transported, far
above the earth to be a mischievous joy. The approach
of a storm had the effect of a frightfully oppressive de-
mon creeping up. The clear sky of day transported her
soul into a cheerful immensity, and the starry firmament of night was felt by her as an unfathomable mild
power keeping watch over her.

She recognised people from the sound of their voice,
the flow of talk, not only according to height, figure and
age, but received through the stronger development of a
secret sense, which is present in sighted people only
weakly as sympathy and antipathy, an unmistakably
clear knowledge of the nature of their character, that inner form of people, and surprised her purlieu often by
her awareness of the physiognomy of strangers.

Old Trine had been right. The Sintlinger girl strolled
like a little spirit through the blessed farm with strides
as if she were floating, carried about by invisible wings.
The noise of her movements did not seem to be produced by her, but hurried as it were behind her like the
audible shock of the earth which was touched by her
feet. It seemed as if she had already come into the world
before her birth, so little did her being fit the usual development of children, so distant and from the other
side of the life of others was her being, so unreal and

embracing did her voice sound, such an inconceivable shimmer floated about her figure, such an incomprehensible light radiated from her unearthly still, clear eyes.

7

The servants at the blessed farm wandered with dull astonishment and empty amazement around the unusual child, and always kept aloof from her somewhat, as if she were a being not entirely native to the earth. Incomprehensible developments, like those situated in the memory of forgotten dreams, beclouded and brightened alike the minds of the servants as soon as they tried to clarify whether Helene was really blind now, or not instead much more than seeing and thus not needing her eyes, like perhaps the dove is able to dispense with the horn of the goat because it possesses wings. And the life of this simple, earth-bound person acquired for itself an alien, strange taste out of this aura from the different world which oscillated around little Lena, enriched itself with foreboding possibilities, and sucked onto pertinent things around the entire Sintlinger farmstead, conferring on each of them an attachment to the strangely distinguished child. And for that reason, it became easy for them to eschew crude, intrusive curiosity, and to not disturb the conviction of the shadow-caught child that her life was not at all lacking what the others possessed. For with the painful adjudication of the defect, which she probably did not guess at though, the shimmer which they received from the dream and wonder of Helene herself would also have to evaporate. "How little Lena sees", became the description for touch amongst the servants, but this expression was also used for occasional incidents which jerked up ghost-like and inexplicable from their own being. Without anyone knowing it, everyone in the vicinity of the child was transformed and stepped through sides of their existence into a connection with her, sides which were hidden to them themselves and which never lit up in traffic with other people.

The only one apart from old Trine who acted without timidity around the child was the placeholder of the absent farmworker, his nephew, the Querhovener Gottlieb Meixner. She let herself be lifted onto his shoulders, swung in circles, and when she heard his step, her face immersed itself in joyfulness. And that was obviously just because he went to no trouble to muffle his loud laugh, did not trim his words especially, and did not put on silk gloves for her. He walked about with her as if with any other little farm girl.

Certainly he also carried a sunny corner in himself to which only the child had access. For a long time, he did not know it, until he discovered it one Sunday. He was sitting there, as was his habit, out beyond the yard on the grassy slope which stretched down next to the path from the beet field to the tree nursery. The servants, all the labourers and maids, had crowded about him, and he laboured tune after tune from his accordion. The sequences just jingled through the air; he made the songs whinny, brawled marches from the pleated case, and then pulled and squeezed it full of feeling again so that a beautiful folk dance wound forth. Thus it went on in colourful sequences, and when he lowered his instrument and made an air to stop, everyone urged him to just play one more.

Then little Lena stood there at once before the fellow on the grass, as if she had scurried soundlessly through the air, and followed with wide eyes, clenched mouth, and motionless face his playing music. When he had finished, the child lifted her little head, and looked with astonished eyes into the sky as if the sounds had not fallen silent in the accordion, but had flown into the heavens and were continuing to sing beautifully there still. It seemed as if Helene saw a shimmer drawing away, her face was so rapt. The servants were so seized by the wondrous emotion of the blind girl that they dared not look at each other, but stared at the girl as though at a miracle. The player himself, however, blanched a little with fright, and did not know how it had happened that he had done that to the child. And when he thought for reassurance, "I have merely grasped this and that chord", the accordion began to play again under his hands as if by itself. It sang notes which had never been in it, it ran a melody from Meixner's fingers which he did not know, and found an accompaniment to it as well which he had not heard in his life before. Thereupon Helene stood motionless, looked up for a while yet into the ether, looked about herself in astonishment as if looking at images which floated about her, and then began first to sway with the rhythm of the music as though in dream, then to turn, and finally she danced back and forth on the slope with her arms outstretched so that the labourers and maids held their breaths. For now she must fall over a mole-hill, trip on a rock, or fall over in a hollow. Only the child floated confidently as if she wore eyes on her feet. Finally she let herself sink down in the grass with a high exultant cheer of joy, and the fellow threw his instrument aside, sprang up, gathered her up, and swung her a few times through the air laughing. Since that day, the secret bond between the child and the accordion player

Meixner had been tied even shorter. A breath of the melodious sound by which Helene's entire being was filled had blown a little door open in the fellow's soul so that he could not arrive anymore by the usual whining of his music at his unhurried reverie, but rather, from that afternoon on, as soon as he was alone for only a moment, he grasped the clapboards of his squeezebox to set off on the trail of that miraculous song again which had passed over the Sintlinger girl like an enchantment and into himself like a rapture. Hence he hauled his accordion wherever he went, carried it with him into the fields at ploughing, rehearsed in the boiler room, harried the instrument for a few moments when grooming the horses, and sometimes in the middle of the night, he had a thought to pinpoint that melody which originated from the blind girl and which circled about him as a distant, enticing whirl. Certainly he did not then arrived any further in this attempt than pulling the accordion out from under the bed and being able to draw out a few timid notes from it. Then he had to give it up every time, because the labourers and maids brought an end to this "nocturnal foolery" quickly and often tangibly. But even despite this, a lasting trace prevailed over him, and often in the middle of ploughing, he reined in the horses and grasped his fingers about his thighs as if they were the clapboards of the accordion.

Even for little Lena it did not fare a hair better. She was always roaming about looking for Meixner, knew to find him in the stables, tracked him down in the barn, and stole out all alone into the fields to the labourer, and when she was searched for, the restrained playing of the fellow could be heard from a distance and the little girl seen dancing around him. She was entranced all of a sudden, no different than a little bee which stubbornly besets a flower from which it was once brought sweetness.

At the same time, some of the joylessness of the manner of the player skipped to her. Little obstructive-nesses spiked from her, passionate flushes flared up in her, she tore her head around quickly, and sometimes burst out with words which had been somewhat infected by the ribaldry of the labourer, so that the farmer and his wife fell into pondering how the swift darkening of the child was to be dealt with. Only they did not need to intervene. For little Lena was not long after brought back again into the enchanted angelic beauty of her old being by a wondrous incident without her parents' being involved. It went as follows.

Through Hemsterhus and the surrounding villages at that time, a female being was roaming about who, as they say, had once seen better days. For if she had also at the time already slogged along the same paths from village to village, from farm to farm, her restless life had fitted her yet more to the type, the way it forms all diligent people. She pulled a little barrel organ through the country as the diligent companion of her husband, carefully collected the pfennigs in the shrivelled little leather pouch under her apron, kept the wheels always greased, tolerated no dirt on the organ, polished the brass corners and the short series of yellow show pipes on the front so that they gleamed like gold, and was an ever zealous, cheerful helper for her husband. He walked, his hand on the draw bar of the organ, with measured, calm steps after his quick other half as soon as they travelled on, and pushed so strongly that the wife's effort actually consisted only in safely steering the little wagon. When they travelled into a village or stopped before a house, then before the man could take the crank in hand, the farmer's wife would appear in the doorway and call out affectionately, "Well, in the countryside again, Schwerdtner?" For that was the man's name. And everyone had a hearty sympathy for him, not only because his eyesight had been almost extinguished by a feverish illness, but because in his tall, well-built body resided an excep- tionally fine soul which properly gleamed forth from the cheerful calm of his face, the gentle art of his speaking, and the quite muted being of the blond, handsome man. Hence it occurred that the farmers considered Schwer- dtner's organ to be the most beautiful of all the wandering barrel organs, and rewarded the half-blind man highly when he endeavoured to bring something like feeling into the melodies through his cranking. After completing a full day's work, the couple then sat in cheerful harmony behind the table of the tavern where they intended to spend the night. The small, plump wo- man was at her husband's hand during the meal, and her leaping button eyes gleamed at the same time in proper happiness from her red, fresh face. She kept an active roguish tongue in her mouth, and almost always brought it about that the landlords deemed them by their faces and behaviour to have paid. When Schwer- dtner then pulled away the next morning with his Josefa, they thus went as if they were taking leave of good friends, and many a farmwife who was wedged into wealth and unease wished in all her bitter prosper- ity quietly for the reward of this happy nomad. Yes, sometimes, when the two drew across God's lonely fields or walked along in forests between high, green walls of trees, the Schwerdtner organ grinder's womanly draught horse fell before the little wagon into a strangely joyful oscillating mood, and she began singing with her thin, hard cricket's voice to the rhythm of their steps. The blond, beclouded man, however, then held himself still more upright than usual, and walked as slowly and leisurely after the little wagon as if he were wading knee-deep in a meadow of flowers.

Only, beautiful pieces, the craftsmen say, break the easiest.

The Blessed Farm

The feverish illness which years before had thrown a grey cloth over Thaddäus Schwerdtner's eyes had also, without his knowing it, penetrated into the clockwork of his heart. It had worked more quietly and more wearily since then, and after one such wandering singing, during which the little wagon always came into a quicker rolling by itself, the pounding in Schwerdtner's chest suddenly unhooked itself completely. Josefa heard only a gentle cooing behind her, like the startled sound of a stock pigeon flying up, and felt the wagon at once become as heavy as if the barrel organ were filled not with pipes, but with stones, and when she turned around, her husband was hanging with white knuckles onto the drawbar. His face was a bluish white, and the heart water, mixed with a little blood, was flowing from his open mouth onto his blond beard. When she sprang towards him, he could no longer talk. Only a weak stirring still passed through his clouded-over eyes. Then his fingers let go of the bar and he lay dead on the road.

Thus in an instant the glittering cords tore which had bound Josefa Schwerdtner to life, and she plunged into darknesses of which her mother could have presaged nothing when she had sat her as a child in her lap. After the poor woman had been somewhere for months, she again began pulling the organ through the villages alone. She turned from the organ the same pieces as her husband, and did not wipe the tears away which ran down over her face at the same time. But when she departed from a tavern, her eyes gleamed as happily as before, her cheeks glowed red, and finally a carter found her once lying in the street asleep next to the organ, the emptied schnaps bottle a bit further away. From now on, she drank away all her proceeds, and when the begged pfennigs did not suffice, she sold pipe after pipe of the organ to boys, and rattled on with the crank between the whining, shrilling, and hissing which was stuck in the organ like a swarm of beaten cats. It could not be helped that Josefa Schwerdtner quickly became a welcome target to all the pranksters for all sorts of mischievous tricks and hilarious antics. The maids adorned the always drunk woman with ancient hats, hung outrageous ribbons and decorations on her gifted Spencer, and the children laughed teasingly at the decorated scarecrow who tottered noisily through the village hewing about her with a stick.

It went on like that for a second year until she had also sold and drunk away the completely empty barrel organ and wagon. With a drunkenness which threw her as if dead in the forest litter for a day and a night, the delirious pain of her husband's death was released. She awoke from the desolate dream to her life's hardship, plucked the crass adornments from her clothes, and crept freezing into the next village like a person who has risen from a long illness. And as she strove across the fields to the houses, a colourful, ringing chiming must have surely flown from afar into her disturbed soul, for at the first farm which she entered, she set herself by the closed door, and sang timidly with her tuneless, crumpled voice one of the songs which her late husband had liked to hear when the two happy people had passed through God's lonely fields or between green, high walls of trees.

The farmers held it to be a new way in which the drunkenness was working through the woman. But a kindly man acted differently from all the others who had broken out into shrill laughter and mocked her from behind when she began to sing. For with the poor woman, a visible transformation had taken place so that she never stumbled anymore, but shuffled with helpless eyes, humbly and timidly through the world. The good man reached for his old guitar from the corner, strung the missing strings, and taught her with kindly patience the few skills in the handling of the instrument which he himself commanded from a previous age.

During the instruction, she slept in a warm little shed on his property, ate the offered food like a fearful dog, and walked away after the course of some time with new courage and the happiness that she now had something with which she could hide the sound of her shattered love.

This incident took place in the time when the first rumours of the wondrous being of the blind girl at the Sintlinger farmstead was penetrating into the villages.

Josefa Schwerdtner was struck by it in a quite special way, because the child of this usually so wild, raging farm was placed half unreal, half raptly by the imagination of the lonely woman into the region of an unimaginable world into which her dear Thaddäus had been taken. And the blessed farm's child lived in the same twilight which had surrounded her husband for a long stretch of his life. But that does not entirely explain by how many secret stirrings of her soul the helpless woman was lead through her inner being. She began not long afterwards to circle about the Sintlinger hill, at first from a distance, sometimes emerging from the forest and looking yearningly down at the farmer's stronghold, sometimes sitting on the Querhoven hills and staring across for hours, sometimes walking on the boundary path tirelessly back and forth and spying out all the entrances to the farmstead. When she met somebody during this vigil, her face blanched, she lowered her eyes as though caught and, when addressed, escaped saying what she was doing with a murmur and embarrassed smile entirely in the manner of a halfwit. Only one afternoon, when she had waited for hours in the shadow of an oak by the edge of the boundary path's ditch, luck was favourable to her. Old Trine stepped out with little Helene before the yard gate under the lime trees, and the two soon began plucking flowers on the slope. The widow Schwerdtner sat hidden, but near enough that she could now and then hear the voice of the child distinctly. It was to her then, as she later re-counted, at once as if she were hearing the sound of her own voice from the happiest time of her life, and suddenly she also knew why it lead her unceasingly around the Sintlinger farm and did not let go. When she came quite near to the child, the clouds of her years-long drunken confusion would draw away from the images of her beautiful past, and all that had been lost was given back to her. Hardly had this thought brightened her up than she held her guitar more firmly under her arm, and crept closer and closer to the drive up the farmstead's hill.

The two above had in the meantime collected a good load of flowers, were sitting next to each other halfway up the slope and deliberating whether they should play bride and bridegroom or entwine a wreath around the Sintlinger monument. They decided on the latter, and the old woman instructed the child not to leave the place where she was sitting, and began climbing up the hill to fetch some wool.

Now the poor Schwerdtner woman took heart. She forgot all her shyness, and hurried as quickly as she could up the hill. Even before Trine had disappeared through the yard gate, the Schwerdtner woman was sit-ting with pounding, heaving chest close to the child, and since in her excitement nothing occurred to her to say, she began to pass her trembling fingers over the strings of the guitar to entice the blind girl. Already after the first fluttering chords, Helene stopped playing with the flowers in her lap, and lifted her face listening.

"Are you a man or a bird?" the child asked.

"I am a woman", the Schwerdtner woman answered.

"But what were you singing with just then? You are speaking differently now."

"That was my harp. And if you want to hear it better, I will come to you. Yes, may I do that, little Sintlinger?"

And the blind girl quickly brushed all the flowers onto the grass, and sat upright and ready.

"Just come over", the child said. "I know already you are a poor woman, aren't you? Yes, come over."

The Schwerdtner woman moved quite close to the child, and seemed to devour the delicate, spritely beautiful being with her eyes.

"Let me see what you are singing with. It sounds much more beautiful than Gottlieb's accordion."

The woman offered her the guitar, and the blind girl groped over the instrument.

"Look, woman, you lied to me."

"How?"

"Because I see the farmer's grill in which the bird is caged."

And then the Schwerdtner woman had to think in astonishment that the child was right, because there really was stuck in the guitar a hidden ringing which she had not quite succeeded in enticing out, so she became confused, and began to tell all sorts of explanations of herself and the instrument in confusion. When she was finished with that, little Lena nodded dreamily, and asked to have the bird or whatever it was ring out once more. Then a door opened for the Schwerdtner woman, similar to that with Gottlieb Meixner, a door into her innermost soul, and to her own surprise, she plucked the most wondrous notes from the old harp, such beautiful sounds that the child listened enchanted. Then the girl dreamily took one of the fallen flowers, and moved it caressingly from one hand to the other. With that Helene began singing along to the soft playing of the guitar, so tenderly, in such sweetness, deeply, so unspeakably moving, like perhaps how the gestures of a blossoming branch ring in the soul when stirred by the first light of May. The Schwerdtner woman began crying, gathered all her strength though to allow none of her agitation to be noticed, and when it threatened to overwhelm her, she rose gently, and crept away as the child continued singing dreamily.

Up above, the yard gate creaked just then, and over on the Brindeisener hill, little Peter stood, and looked tensely at her.

Then the timid woman was seized by a fright, as if she had stolen something.

She began running madly, and heard suddenly behind her the boy's voice flare up, screaming after her slanderously and threatening. Then stones hailed after her, and she strained even more now to get out of range of the furious Brindeisener boy, who surely believed that she had done something to the girl.

Finally she was hidden. The pursuit and the stone throwing had stopped.

She staggered exhausted to the gutter of the road, let herself fall onto the grass, and began sobbing as if her heart wanted to spring from her breast. At the same time, she murmured constantly in great joy, "Now I have everything again ... everything ... everything ... oh, little Sintlinger ... everything ... everything ..."

From then on, when the widow sang before the doors of farmers, a different emotion arose in the farmsteads than before, yes, yet another, deeper one, like that which the Schwerdtner woman had brought before the houses earlier in those happy times with her husband's barrel organ.

Now she only had to rise to sing and the parlour maids placed the crockery in the cupboard and sat down on the threshold. There eyes first widened as if the world were opening up before them for the first time, and then lowered because something in the voice of the singer was divulging the most secret, most hidden things of their souls. The labourers stepped over to where they always paused; the mockery had been wiped from their faces, and they also listened in bashful emotion. Yes, even the farmer forgot his dignity, leant against the wall further back in the hall, and preserved only with effort the mastery which he believed he owed himself. And at the same time, the Schwerdtner woman did not perform any new songs, she sang like once before of "the little grass which trembles outside", of the sun which sinks over the dying soldier, the girl and the Hamburg merchant's servant, and the forester who waited for the return of his daughter. But her voice now no longer seemed to come from her, but came through from where the life's sorrow of all men rests, and was filled with a sound which placed every listener before a secret court and rescued them from the power of their fate into the current of an eternal destiny. The people were so strongly shaken by the poor widow's song that they looked astonished into her plump common face, paid attention to the movements of her lips, watched her pose and the play of her strumming fingers carefully so as to work out from where the force stirred which they were incapable of evading. But although they paid attention to everything, and believed for a while that the Schwerdtner woman was capable of the magical, that she shut her eyes while seeing as if she were blinded, yet everyone felt the explanation did not suffice to unveil the wondrous effect which emanated from the woman's singing. And when they pressured her to say from whom she had received the new art, she fended them off for a long time, and begged imploringly for them to stop asking, for she was afraid that by talking everything would be destroyed which had come alive in her, and she could then possibly fall back again into the old, terrible shadows of drunkenness. Only so much did she permit herself to say, that everything stemmed from a little girl on a hill farm who had eyes like her late husband. Then nobody tormented her anymore with insistent questions, for now it was known; and everywhere that the Schwerdtner woman had sung quietly like a cicada and furtively like swishing leaves, they said after her that she had received a new soul from the blessed farm's little Lena.

The Schwerdtner woman, however, never returned to the Sintlinger farm anymore, because she thought she would herself lose the courage to sing if she heard the blind child's voice just once more.

8

Thus in a short time, every house in Hemsterhus and surrounds learnt through the poignant songs of Josefa Schwerdtner something of the incident which she had had with little Lena Sintlinger. The residents of the blessed farm, especially the farmer and his wife, saw other consequences of this meeting emerge from their child. Helene had suddenly been rolled back by an inaudible jolt from the loud ribaldry of Meixner again into her still, gently spellbound state, and walked the old paths as before in cheerful abandonment with old Trine. When she met Gottlieb, her lips certainly curved into a smile, and she also answered his jesting calls and teasing, only she no longer fled as usual into the fellow's arms with a cheer, and when he asked her whether she would not like a beautiful song again soon, the blind child shook her head vigorously, and said, "No, never again, never, never again do I want to hear your accordion."

To start with, Gottlieb laughed at little Lena's rejection, and when he had tormented her teasingly for a while, he went away with the cry of rustic superiority, "Anyone who does not want, already has."

After a few days, however, when Meixner saw how Helene did not want anything more to do with his playing, not merely from playful stubbornness, but really started painfully and ran away hastily every time he came near her with his accordion playing, he decided to no longer think about the child's stupid quirks and to amuse himself again in solitary self-enjoyment alone with his instrument like at home in Querhoven. He thus went off to the edge of the forest in the twilight of evening, between secluded fields or in the beech stand, and after the accordion had cried out loudly almost against its will a few times as if in yearning, he endeavoured to steer its voice into a dreamy whirling, into the heavenly wandering which he loved so. Only he did not succeed; hardly had he sucked a few colourful transformations out of the box than he abruptly lapsed into the din of a timeworn dance piece, and only came out of it when he had, as though in an empty schnapps-driven frenzy, rattled down all the tavern reels which he knew. Then he went home ill-temperedly, lay awake in bed for a long time, and spat constantly in disgust. It seemed as if something had been stolen from the fellow's head or chest.

Nothing, but nothing at all even of the colourful, boundless wavering climbed from his instrument and carried him into that insecure place which appears to simple hearts as the highest happiness. He wanted to do what he wanted, to sit in the lonely, green darkness of the forest; to seek a bed in the high grass so that he saw, through the veil of stalks bending over him, the heavens with their white mirror of clouds in an unfamiliar way, transported, and doubly mysterious; to castigate himself amidst the servants with silence, or lash himself with a thousand somersaults of chattering thoughts — his accordion remained a clattering case. — If he only touched it, it made a racket like a wooden wagon. He held it over himself, lying on his back so that the play of the gentle sunny air would soothe it for a melody, he squeezed it between his straddled legs, raised it to his chest, shocked it with unexpected compressions the way you stamp right again limbs which have fallen asleep — no torments were of use, every taking by surprise rebounded, every tenderness was in vain. The instrument whined like a drunkard, or whinged endlessly like a talkative fool.

In addition, the most familiar handholds by and by became alien to him, and some were lost entirely to him. His diligence gave him trouble, and his work resisted him like an intractable horse. His large bumpy face became emaciated and turned a sandy yellow, his small black eyes did not stand still in their spacious sockets for a moment, and often they flickered up out of their depths as if they wanted to spring from his head.

Thus it reigned over Gottlieb all spring, and little Lena Sintlinger meanwhile became more and more distant from him, and it seemed as if she even smelt his shadow from a distance.

Finally the fellow could endure it no longer. At the loading of hay towards the beginning of summer, it came over him. The head labourer was standing on the cart and loading, Gottlieb was reaching up with a fork the hay pushed together by the maids.

When he was just about to offer up with the fork a carefully stuck together load of hay over the wagon sides, the wild flaming temper of the Querhoveners fell unstoppably into the tinder of his inner being. It fell so suddenly over the labourer that he was as if seized by paralysis as he held the enormous bush of hay on the long fork straight above himself and stared straight into the sky with discoloured face.

"Now let it go, it's already far enough over", the head labourer called to him from the cart and attempted to pull the hay off the fork. But Meixner made no effort to incline it to him. He stood wide-legged, pushed by the load he held, trembling all over his body, his arms shuddering, his face distorted, and seemingly scatterbrained.

"Dammit, it's fucked you, Gottlieb, hey!" the head labourer now shouted at the top of his lungs.

Then Meixner's eyes rolled back as if pricked by an awl into their sockets, the paralysis drained away from him, with an imprecation he smashed the bush of hay to the ground, tore the fork out, and began battering the innocent hay madly with it, as if it were a long hated enemy. At the same time, he shouted with clenched teeth, "Yes, everything is — I will prove it to you — am I then a — a — a ...? And that today still — now — straightaway —"

With his outburst, he became quieter and quieter. He said the last words softly, calmly, soberly, and looked at the same time at the faces of the servants, maids, and labourers who were thinking nothing else but that the accordion player Meixner had at once gone crazy, then he finally let fall the handle of the fork, and slowly set off in motion towards the blessed farmstead without speaking another word. Someone shouted after him, but he just shook his head, and continued walking without turning around.

Coincidence had it that he saw little Lena sitting before the flower garden's fate onto the fields. After a short, surprised pause, and a few instinctive steps towards the child, he stopped for a moment as though rooted to the spot, checked whether the child had noticed him, and then ran with long, noiseless strides into the yard, vanished into the boiler room, and went the next moment through the back gate into the flower garden with the accordion under his arm.

The blind girl continued still playing; she was holding a small summer beetle in her hand, felt from time to time with her fingertips the body and delicate movements of the little insect, spoke to it, and then lapsed into a deep, rapt mixture of feelings.

Then she heard Gottlieb's step approaching her in the flower garden. She felt that he was walking with shaking feet. A hot swishing emanated from his body which she perceived to be quite thinly drawn apart, and above rocked his face, flat and tensed unbearably in many humps. As he cautiously came nearer, she sensed how the expression of his face took possession of her own more and more as a painful grasp. Now he was with her, and sat down next to her. The girl shook in breath-pinching fright, "Why are you grasping me in the face, Gottlieb?" she asked stammering.

"Dear little Lena, let me play before you!" Meixner begged abjectly. "Just a single time! I cannot work anymore otherwise."

The child had closed her eyes out of fear, and did not stir, as if she were sleeping.

Then Gottlieb began begging anew and more insistently, "Dear little Lena, just open your eyes for God's sake, and look at me. Dear! Then I will play like the water flows, or like the bird sings — — you know that you can dance again, you ..."

Suddenly it seemed to the girl as if the labourer was lying on her like an incubus, and with a shrill voice she screamed, "No ...! No! Help! No! No ..."

The Blessed Farm

Meixner leapt back, and the accordion fell from his hands.

When he looked up, the blessed farmer was standing before him; his face was pale, and the labourer saw that he was moving his lips, but in his shock, he heard not a word. Sintlinger lifted the trembling child in his arms, and carried her into the farmstead.

There she was immediately put to bed because she desired it. Her body glowed as if in fever. She lay quite still with large eyes, and asked quietly again and again so that it was barely understandable, "Is Gottlieb still there?" With a few words, Sintlinger informed his wife of the incident, and then immediately set off to learn from Meixner what had actually happened.

When he came out in front of the flower garden, the labourer was still sitting in the same spot, but now bent forwards, propped on his fists, and staring rigidly at his instrument.

At Sintlinger's questioning of what it meant that he had not remained at work, had crept away, and scared the child here, he still did not stir, even let his head sink obdurately still lower, and swallowed a few times hesitantly. He should at least say "Ah" or "Bah", Sintlinger advised him kindly, and touched his shoulder.

Then Meixner shot up abruptly, and instantly stood opposite Sintlinger like a glowing white fire. Yes, he knew already that nobody could suffer him anymore at the farm, the farmer did not look at him anymore, the farmer's wife shied from him, the servants swept all the muck of the stables behind him, and they had also bewitched little Lena so that she ran from him like he was a robber. All that burst out of him confusedly. His entire face twitched, and tears were running over his cheeks.

"Aha", the blessed farmer said to that, "hm, hm, what you have brewed together there is foolishness. I know now. The best and only thing will just be that you abandon the accordion playing here at the farmstead completely."

And where else could he then play, the fellow asked mockingly.

"Wherever else you want", Sintlinger answered.

"Perhaps in the fields? Hey? — well? — or in the forest?" the labourer asked from his tense chest as if he were choking.

"Do it how you like", the blessed farmer responded, now very serious because of the untamed wildness of the fellow, "just no longer during the work or before the child."

"So it is best that I play *thus* with it", the labourer suddenly cried out, unnaturally tormented as if it were tearing apart his chest, then bent down, lifted up the accordion, but only in order to fling it down to the ground anew so that it burst apart, and then stamped the unhappy case into pieces with his feet.

At the same time, he was sniffing more than speaking, in fury and despair, in anguish and hate, constantly just the one word, "Thus ... thus ... thus ... thus ...", until only small splinters covered the ground.

"Yes certainly", the blessed farmer answered coolly when the labourer had finished the obliteration of his instrument and stood there pale and shaking, "that is admittedly the best for me and you, and here are your wages for the work on your accordion, and for your service on the farm. For that you have made the new year with that, you will realise well yourself." With that the blessed farmer threw ten marks in two five mark pieces onto the wreckage, and returned calmly to the farmstead.

9

Little Lena was again soon over the fever and fear in which the wild acting labourer had driven her. Gottlieb Meixner, however, vanished from the farmstead the same day under cover of the twilight of evening and appeared late at night before his mother's house in Querhoven. He thundered fiercely against the door with a stave, like a drunkard, and when his uncle — his mother for fear did not dare descend the loft stairs down into the house — had shoved back the bolt, upset and angry, the fellow plunged past the old man as silently as he had stood outside, fell groggily to the floor by the wall, and immediately fell asleep with a strange gurgling breath. Neither good nor bad words, nor shaking was able to bring him to his senses, and when the old man felt his face, it felt frail and cool, but by the light of a lamp, he ascertained that it was streaming tears soundlessly without break.

For that reason, Zenker took a hold of Gottlieb, and carried him into the living room to the wall bench, placed a bundle of old clothes under his head, and moved the table over hard so that the fellow, suffering in his sleep as though from an illness, did not fall down when he stirred.

When the next morning the two siblings came down in good time from their beds in the loft, Gottlieb was already sitting upright there, an elbow propped on the top of the table which he had pushed away, the other arm though driven stiffly with outspread hand against the bench seat like a stick which has been pushed into the earth. His face, pale and bitter, was lowered, his eyes stood motionless and lost. Thus he sat and did not stir. No questioning was of any use, no shaking helped, and when old Zenker seized him and pulled him up, he hung like a sack in his arms, but returned, when let go, back to his earlier pose of an exhausted, madly straying fugitive.

Until the cord became too short for the decent farm-worker and he declared with a furious blow of his fist on the table that, if he had not become ill or drunk from the farm at Hemsterhus, some dishonouring devilry had driven him down from the hill. But hardly had the old man time to get out the last word of this accusation than an almost mad fury came over Gottlieb. He sprang up, discoloured further into a more ashen tone, and made an air to leave. But his mother fell into his arms, and thus struggling constantly against her, he roared like a fatally wounded man, "They have stolen my soul! They have stolen my soul, the thrice-accursed, you will all see!" Then he superimposed, amidst ever new impreca-tions, Josefa Schwerdtner, the barrel organ woman, little Lena, the farmer, the farmer's wife, and the entire staff together so that nobody was able to know what to make of it. Wildest of all, however, was his fury over the blind child from the blessed farm.

He spoke her name quietly to himself for a while in anguished hate when he was back sitting motionless be-hind the table as before, and fell stubbornly silent to all persuasion.

Zenker and his sister were no more the wiser now than before, but their worrying had at least received a glimmer of an idea from the fury which the fellow had thrown at the blessed farm's little Lena. But what sort of relation she had to this fury was not to be obtained from the fellow with winding and twisting, so that nothing re-mained for the old man finally but to have a pure wine poured for the Sintlinger farmstead.

Meanwhile, hardly had Zenker taken the old slippers from his feet, climbed awkwardly into his tall boots, and taken his jacket from the corner next to the pot cupboard, than the raging broke out again from the sprawled fellow, and this time with such an unruliness that it really seemed as if all the screws in his head had burst at once. Not only did he again drag the inhabitants of the blessed farm through all the puddles of profanity, he swore never to go through that accursed gate ever again. But it was just as certain that his things must remain there for eternity where he had deposited them, in his room at the Sintlinger farmstead, and if ever an idea was had to take them away from there, to throw them behind the barn on the rubbish heap or send them here, something like that, then, he swore, the worst would happen. It was final with him, and he would have to burn the farmstead, the grain in the fields, or feed the cattle with nails.

"That I'd do!" he roared finally, powerless and hoarse. "That I'd do. For the child has killed my soul."

Only, the old man was not listening to him at all anymore, but strode darkly and palely over the threshold and out of the house, his sister behind him, pressing the corners of her apron with shaking hand to her eyes.

The house of Rosalie Zenker lay in a spacious garden of grass and trees, hardly two beds distant from Hornwasser over which the slab bridge led to the village lane. Just there, as Zenker had taken the first step on the rickety little bridge, Rosalie caught his hand and looked worriedly into his eyes.

Then he shook his head silently in answer, looked earnestly up and then down Querhoven's cottage lane, and the eyes of the poor man fell during his inspection. In this way, the eyes of both picked out a farmstead which lay on a rocky promontory almost vertically over the Hornwasser which formed a sort of pool before it found its way around the rocks.

This farmstead, rambling and dilapidated, proud and bristly at the same time, belonged to the only large farmer of Querhoven, Elias Meixner.

"He has it from him. Nothing else", Zenker said dully when they had looked at the farm for a while.

"Meixner madness! Sawdust, not Zenker blood, Rosalie, not a drop of Zenker blood! Adieu. I will see how I can impress the mother's influence on Sintlinger again."

He was already speaking the last words as he was going. Then the woman did not look at him anymore, but only heard from time to time his gentle cough sounding like mockingly amused laughter as if to say, "Let me be alone with the man!"

A t the Sintlinger farmstead, he found the farmer as composed and serene as ever, not a trace was to be noted of the air which his nephew had sucked in and which had implied nothing else than that for one, the blessed farm had again become the estranged farmstead, and that the devil was already riding all the witches in the early morning.

Only Johanna discoloured anxiously when she heard about Gottlieb's complete breakdown, then consoled herself for a moment in the thought that a whirl of nonsense had seized the fellow, but lapsed finally into earnest self-consciousness because of the particular hate which the perverse man threw straight at little Lena, and his outrageous threats against the entire farm.

Old Zenker, however, sat, turned his cap between his knees, and shook his head soothingly and disapprovingly to all that the farmwife said. And when she had finished with it, he suggested that, if Gottlieb really lost his head so that he came here to blow the red rooster over the farmstead, then he, his uncle, would still be there, and the boy would succeed only over his dead body in coming through the gate.

Sintlinger and his wife looked at the old man, moved, but from a different reason than Zenker thought.

"Naturally", he continued speaking with a smile, "do you think then, farmer, that I will go over to Querhoven once more? Since the boy is thus, Rosalie's house shakes all day like a mad shack. And there the pillow still makes a racket in bed. So, patched together, I am again ready for the roughest, and if you look at it from the same side as me, I am what was before, and will remain at the farmstead."

That pleased Sintlinger, even if he thought that the whole beat up with Gottlieb was nothing in itself, for nobody had pushed the fellow but the Querhoven buck and that on an especially crazy side, or, as the Cantor Pfeiffer from Hemsterhus would say, the anabaptist devil had him under its thumb.

Thus they smiled in the end over the entire business. Gottlieb's stuff remained in the room at the Sintlinger farmstead where he had deposited it, old Zenker ran around the farm as before, and the farmwife led her old gently firm regimen in the farmstead.

Sintlinger, however, was especially inspired by a surprised astonishment over the power of his only girl to arouse unusual, deep occurrences wherever she turned her face.

10

Nevertheless, a short time after those events, the weather in Sintlinger's soul was not the calmest. But he did not let himself be taken out of the region of the spirit into which his life and above all his blind child had led him.

Even when the entire district echoed with the accusations of the maddened Gottlieb, the blessed farmer did not stir to any countermeasures. The fellow, nevertheless, did nothing but rant against the child — the Sintlinger girl had stolen his soul, he maintained in wild uniformity, she was not a real person, but an incubus-like being created by all the subterranean foaming of the Sintlingers' mad blood, and anyone who lay by her, to remain themselves, they had to take care when coming into the light of her bewitched eyes or into the sphere of her much discussed voice.

Always given great difficulties by such badmouthing, he wandered from one tavern to another, harried anyone he could just catch in the middle of the road, rumpled lonely meadows with his aching unease, seared himself on sunny slopes until his eyes glimmered, glowing bestially, and finally sank into day-long wandering through almost impassable, dark forests in a sombre, silent pent-up mood which lasted all day as if it were the beginning of that dull stupefaction which the exaltations of mad men so often lead to.

Only, whenever his mother then began to hope that her son would find his way back through the door of silence to his old being, he upset everything again with the old blustering tour. Abruptly almost. A lost ray of sunlight which played over his eyes, the distant breath of a childish singing voice, once even the scurrying flight of a bird before the open window sufficed to tear his churning from all its secret bonds and to lead him again through the taverns, along the paths, through villages and remote places, and to fill the entire district with mad protestation that the blind child at the blessed farm had stolen his soul.

The braggart Meixner, his uncle, was secretly always behind him, bore him out in everything, refilled his money pouch which had been emptied very quickly with this restless wandering, and even took him to his own farm when Rosalie Meixner, his mother, lost all hope and referred him to the house. For the great Elis of Querhoven, as the farmers was now and then called, usually practised the bothersome raving and colourful enthusing in the district himself, and simply found it exceptionally convenient and sweet to see himself as it were as he whirled to and from the villages. Yes, Gottlieb was capable of the whining crackling in his voice, the endless noise which actually only consisted of insults and aspersions, even better than he himself. Gottlieb was lacking only the hard forehead with which the braggart Meixner let every insult to himself, which such a life of nuisance always reaps, bounce off. For as soon as a collected man cut calmly into the middle of the fellow's stream of grumbles, he could not draw himself out of the noose like his uncle with a gnarled wisecrack, but listened to the remonstrations of the gentleman, and crept away stooped, yes, sometimes he even got biting tears in his eyes, and then did not let himself be enticed from his forest hiding place for days.

If it were not completely absurd that his existential breakdown stemmed from a childish girl, then you would have to say that he behaved like a helpless man whose soul's love has ploughed into the ground for the first time. Only, people noticed in his fate a hidden shimmer of heavenly brilliance, for it only occurred to a

few of the thousands of involuntary listeners to take his
profanities seriously and to move the blessed farm with
all its inhabitants again into the shadow of its old, bad
reputation, but instead you heard from his fury only the
proclamation of miraculous powers with which the
blind child of Sintlinger had been equipped.

Gottlieb Meixner's fury had the same effect as the
gentle song of the Schwerdtner woman, only she maintained the opposite, of having received the gift of a new
life from the girl. Thus little Lena was lifted by them
both, by her slanderer and her admirer, into the light of
an almost other-worldly existence, and the name
'Blessed Farm', which at one time after the birth of the
girl had been bestowed more mockingly than seriously
on her father's property, now received a still more wondrous sound of deep significance.

11

Now and then someone stopped who, from Hemsterhus or from a village further into Westphalia,
had to go past the blessed farm to get through the big
forest to the Rhine; he stopped on the road where the
drive branched off, cast a furtive glance up at the Sintlinger memorial, scanned the gate with a hurried look,
or gazed from the edge of the forest down to the farmstead, and had to confess in wandering on alone that a
mysterious air truly stood about the farm on the hill,
and if you were not so sceptical, you could easily say
that something like a hidden gleam shimmered about

the lime trees by the gate and played along the ridge of
the house.

Many another climbed specifically from Brederode
up through the beech stand, and wandered past the
flower garden from behind the   farmstead, their eyes
round as trouser buttons with curiosity, their faces
readied for a pleasant smile, their mouths for a clever
word, in case they had the fortune to catch sight of blind
little Lena.

And thus it occurred that such excited people were
seemingly startled when the girl suddenly laughed in
their vicinity or even stood next to them, and in their
vanity and love of ostentation, they claimed afterwards
that their heart had been filled with a shiver at the sight
of the child, as if perhaps little Jesus had stood incarnate before them.

Foolish people leant straight over the gate, and
threatened insistently to enter the yard until they
caught sight of the girl or were finally shown the way
down the hill by someone. Then in leaving, they lifted
their caps, scratched their heads, and opined to their
feet, "Well, well, it could certainly be possible that
something extraordinary has hatched in the child. But
actually there is nothing more to see, and the blessed
farmer even has the soil on the *back* of his trousers."

Not long, and the reputation of the hill's blessed girl
had not only smouldered through those places which
had been prepared by the swirling tongue of Gottlieb
Meixner or the songs of the Schwerdtner woman, but
there were still moreover rumours of a miracle child
who had arrived somewhere on the Rhine.

That went against the blood of nobody more than
Andreas Sintlinger and his wife. Johanna was affected
joylessly by this jostling especially because of the ease
and simplicity of her nature; it pushed against the soul
of the blessed farmer because he was frightened that the

wonder-worthy being of his beloved child could be led by such premature blasts of praise into the wrong paths of vanity and self-satisfaction, encumbered by the breath of the crowd, brought to similar developments as those which befell the rebel Faber, who had also only fallen because he perched on the shoulders of everyone. But they were reasons which he kept entirely to himself; to his wife, he spoke of his most outward reluctance, of the anger that the barrel organ woman, Schwerdtner, was going from farm to farm, village to village, and filling her maw and apron as it were with their little Lena's voice. And because little Lena was entering her seventh year at the time, when other children were beginning to go to school, the blessed farmer decided to take on a governess at the farmstead so that nothing in the world to which she was born would disturb his only girl. Actually the thought originated more from the blessed farmer's wife and flowed with her from a consideration which aimed straight at the opposite goal to her husband's. The child would according to the hidden intention of the woman be pried from her own miraculously visible dream expanses for the earth of others in which she, in the opinion of the Münster doctor, would one day enter when her destiny was ripe.

The married couple, Sintlinger and his Johanna, found in it, even if by guessing a scent of this hidden estrangement should have befallen them, nothing but the action of unbreakable love which is proper to the faultless courage to concede entirely to the other half the freedom of existence, because each knows that different instruments play the same melody only a little differently.

Sintlinger did not now feel equal to the task of finding the right person from out of the grey distance who could be a companion and guide to his little Lena, and ceded it with a relieved sigh to his lawyer, the stepson of the remarkable notary who had mended old Klim's codicils, to deal with the scouting. Chance had it, men are accustomed to speak thus, that Professor Flöreck of Münster found in his local paper the notice which the lawyer had had inserted for the blessed farmer, and recommended the daughter of a small cooper for whose family he was from pitying love the medical help and energetic friend. This girl had passed the teacher's examinations, and had then started for domestic reasons on the teaching of the blind. Actually for the sake of her mother. Though she had no blind eyes, the grey hand had passed over them, and like with Schwerdtner, the organ grinder, all the objects of the external world since then had swayed as an indefinite cloud about her, and it had conferred on her something of the high-reaching step of the blind, though less of their peaceable, constantly wonder-seeing soul, instead she filled her life with sighing and displeasure so that her children sensed the preciousness of a mother actually more through a morose twilight which floated around her, and which pressed all the more strongly on the responsive nature of the children because the father worked his entire day in the large barrels and was constantly locked away by the thundering which he drummed out of the oaken belly with his wooden mallet. The sympathy with their joyless youth led them into the service of the blind.

Professor Flöreck had hardly read the notice than the name Sintlinger rang a bell in his memory so that he saw the dark eyes of a steely, small man like two whizzing bullets closing in on him, and suddenly recalled the puzzling case of little Lena's eyes. It had seemed to him in fact as if he were seeing the mirrored surface of a still pool hanging motionless before himself in the air.

For he knew and distinguished people only by their eyes, like the shoemaker judges by the shoes, the butcher by the fatness, and the tailor by the clothes, and he sensed a weak breath of the blessed farmer's rare un-usualness on himself across the series of years which had since elapsed.

His protege from the cooper's house had just then put the state teaching for the blind examinations behind her, and was thankful that the Professor wanted to help her on the way to an employment in which she could actively preserve what she had learnt, actively educate and progress through experience until the desired gap in the state's service would open for her.

The papers of Miss Elfriede Knille, as the cooper's daughter was called, were thus gathered; the Professor wrote a few lines of recommendation with them and sent it off.

When Johanna received this letter, she breathed out in relief. For the offers penetrating to the blessed farm from all parts of the world shimmered with the most colourful promises, rose here and there to threats with the most dismal fates in case of rejection, were filled with self-satisfaction and the side note of many other human weaknesses, so that it seemed to the farmwife that she stood with her only child in a public market, and was trying to sell her to a stranger from the bluster-ing crowd.

Andreas, however, when he had read on the first cer-tificate in large letters the words 'teacher of the blind', was pulled for a moment from the darkness, knitted his brows, and wanted from then on to have nothing more to do with everything. It concerned a female being, he suggested, and so a woman would always have a better sense than a man, for he would not choose the maids which were brought to the farm either. He did not care that what he said did not match up, he just remained in consistent stubbornness inwardly of the conviction that his child was not blind, and would have liked most of all to have sent back again without reply every letter which contained the word blind.

Johanna, however, read the Professor's few words again and again, and fell more and more deeply into the thought of a divine providence which attended on the Münster doctor so that everything happened systematically to prepare and where possible to quicken the entrance of that event of which Flöreck had spoken of as a certainty — thus she at least thought in self-willed hope — the time namely when the darkness over little Lena's eyes would be finished with and the veil drawn away from her sight. She definitely felt that not choosing this Miss Elfriede Knille would be tantamount to not wanting to lead the dear child into the light.

For that reason, the good woman of the blessed farm was somewhat disappointed when the governess arrived at the farmstead. For not only do the hopes of people carry the colour and the sound of their being, every image which strides from our hearts through the gates of wish and desire takes with it our pulse, is born from our body, and the shimmer of our soul smoulders from it. Elfriede Knille had none of the pious kindness, none of the self-consciousness in a thousand secrets. When she was received by Johanna down on the drive, she climbed from the wagon, shook her dress out, arranged her shoulders with a jerk, and only then offered Sintlinger's wife her hand, and that with a perceptible touch of benevolence, as if she were bolstering up a shy schoolgirl. She passed her hand through little Lena's blond locks, caressed them with her hand, spoke suddenly in a little falsetto of the dear, little person whom she would get to know better, and then got ready to take the child in her arm, to squeeze her to herself and kiss her or just to swing her in the air, nobody knew. She lifted her as high as her breast, of which a few correct intimations were present, and put her down again with the surprised exclamation, "Oh, how light! No, light as a feather!" She then said, somewhat taken aback, "Such a tender thing in the midst of this wholesome district", as if she felt she had upset the farmwife. "It is astonishing. Utterly astonishing. Is it not? Oh, so that is your farm-stead! Just like a castle. Really."

Then she stepped to the side to let the vehicle past. The horses pulled snorting in their harnesses, and had to strain a lot in her opinion. "That is at least a fifteen percent gradient. Perhaps the child is being overly strengthened by the constant overcoming of the sloping terrain, and inwardly induced, or rather affected. The first point though for a profitable intellectual labour is physical strength."

After she had greeted the "Squire Mr Sintlinger", and had been led through the farmstead, her measured, rhythmic step could still be heard for a long time ringing against the ceiling from the first storey where she had been housed.

Then little Lena said, sitting between mother and father listening to the striding above them with visible concern, into the middle of her parents' conversation, "You know, mother, I saw her exactly!"

"What's that then, little Lena?" Johanna asked.

"The Miss is straight like a tree. Quite tall. But without branches. Just a little above. And when she talks, a little door opens like with our clock, and the cuckoo calls."

"Yes, you know, little Lena, and who is the cuckoo with the Miss?" the blessed farmer asked.

"But of course", the girl answered, "her speech is."

"No, the being-clever, little Lena", Johanna said with gentle admonishment, "and you will also be that clever now."

Then the child made a quiet, aggrieved face, played with her fingers, taken aback, and asked after a long while with a deep breath of trepidation, "Yes — must I too?"

***

After the young woman Knille had finished moving in, Sintlinger let her existence stroll through his thoughts and realised that it would be good not to influence the governess's start with his concerns. Little Lena had betrayed with her words such a dreamily confident evaluation of the young woman that the tension filled the farmer even more with regard to what the outcome of the instruction would be. Hence he limited himself to having the young woman advised by Johanna that the consciousness of being blind forever and the knowledge of death had been kept away from little Lena for the time being. Elfriede Knille thereupon brushed with the straight fingers of her right hand from her nose over her mouth, looked at the farmer's wife with mocking merriment, began to intone pages about the demands of truthfulness, about the courage for self-knowledge, the worth of unflinching comprehension, and finally declared herself okay with it amidst shrugging shoulders and rocking head.

She had been too distinguished a schoolgirl and had thereby a pride in being an immaculate teacher, neglecting to remain a lively person. Through her studies, she had been welded onto the ship of unfamiliar knowledge, and now she travelled with unfamiliar oars, sailed in the breath of the knowledge of others, and saw the goal of all teaching in the transmission of a wealth of learning material which was transferred in good order to the student according to proven didactic rules.

If all teachers knew that the inner state of the instructor was the precondition of all learning, the number of mouth threshers would dwindle, and the schoolmasterly mobs would climb down remorsefully from the methodical wooden horse on which they smugly gallop up and down before the children. Each learning object requires a new adaption of the soul, each child has a different inner world with a different climate. Anyone who is not blinded by the miracles of his own God, is not capable of advancing into the divine depths of the child, which must be exploited if the student's head should become more than an intellectual work of craftsmanship, his heart more than a vulgar ruminant of emotions, and his life more than a useful noise.

Elfriede Knille had probably learnt this or similar views by rote. But now the preparation phase had been gladly overcome. Now she strode collectedly, surely directed, carefully engaged in the execution of her tasks. As soon as she began to teach, her voice became gramophone-like, her posture constrained, her movements practised impersonally, her laugh artificial, her face agonisingly serious, and her eyes stood like two drills under her forehead. For only rarely will a female being who has not yet given birth be able to exercise a teaching post, because only motherhood makes her sap ripe, sweet, and full for this divinely maternal matter.

What can such a being understand of the blessedly beautiful matter of how a person is liberated, how a person is birthed from the pure soul into the intellect. It is a quite weak bridge on which they are enticed by the miracle of the thing over onto this earth on which they shall take up residence until they wander again through the gates of death. How children are astonished by the images of this earth, how happy they are when they hear the divine mind tolling from it, still sounding to their ears from the eternal home. The hand must be absolutely selective and attentive which leads them from the surprise through the astonishment into the quiet disappointment of comprehension. Little Lena of the blessed

farm was walking this path like all children. But she had
to suffer through a preliminary phase, only more difficult, that of fear, which with other children does not last
longer than its scurrying past. Before each new object,
the Sintlinger child hesitated as if before an abyss and
had the feeling of having to plunge down helplessly
through a hole into the abyss if she did not succeed in
familiarising herself with the new unknown and in clas-
sifying it within the world of her inner being. For that
reason, she was often seen shaking before new things almost to the point of tears, and then touching them with
trembling, almost greedily fumbling fingers. The urge
for knowledge was more passionate with her because it
was not muffled and dispersed by the meddlesome nibbling of her eyes before it had been collected. Her thirst
for knowledge was a soundless maelstrom which was
slurping into its bottomless depths everything which
came near it. But, what had once strolled through the
mysterious gates of her senses stood hidden in her, and
was not so easily put into question by a new look as with
sighted people.

The young woman gave no consideration to all that
because it eluded her suppositions. This child, who was
till then accustomed to travelling in the surrounding
world through the wide-open gate of the souls of the
people with whom she lived, found herself, when the
governess's instruction had lasted barely half an hour,
opposite a windowless wall; everything was barred to
her; she was really "nailed down". Elfriede Knille almost
always said these words hotly and dismissively to herself when little Lena was released bowed, joyless, faint
from the restless cloud of the teaching hours.

It did not help at all that the governess also usurped
the child's free time to smuggle through the colourful
gate of play into the world of this wondrous, little being,
or at least take a look into these enchantments. As in-

curious as her instruction made the child, as dull did her irritations make her playtime. Little Lena's fine instinct scented correctly some intention of violation, and let the games glide over herself like the lessons, or swallowed them like a superfluous medicine; revolved unmoved, ran with pale face, sang soullessly and unhappily, and sank, becoming bored, into an indifference which was as fanciful as perhaps the gestures of a solitary flower in the field. Meanwhile, so as to entice the Sintlinger child from the enchantment, the young woman went for all sorts of playful antics, forced herself to comical portrayals, and even skipped teasingly about the little one who bore it all silently, or at most curved her lips into a smile which looked more like contempt.

"Do you like that?" Miss Knille then asked.

"Oh yes", was the answer.

"Why don't you play with me?"

"*You* play."

"But then do it with me too."

"No, it is *your* game."

"Won't you teach me *your* game?"

"You cannot understand it."

Thus ended all the efforts of the governess, who was beginning already to give credence to what had been the talk of the people in the district for some time, that this child was not real, but a supernatural being.

It was also no use when Miss Knille made cautious indications of her hardship to Sintlinger, and waved for his help from a distance. The blessed farmer listened very attentively, then nodded thoughtfully, and left her looking before herself with large eyes, without giving a reply. Only once did he say to her after a long silence, "I saw today a bird sitting in a mile-wide solitary field on the tip of a tree; by the beak, I noted that it was singing, but at the time I was walking next to a wooden wagon loaded with stones, could hear nothing, and when I got closer, it flew away in fright. Thus I know nothing of its song." Without adding anything further, he walked with a friendly goodbye from the room where this discussion had taken place, and soon after the young woman saw Sintlinger strolling off in the   distance hand in hand with Helene, with steps as quiet as if the two were float- ing through the flowers. The child's laughter sounded like the twittering of larks, and sometimes you could hear the child singing and the father calling with delight melodically in between.

"Is this not like a farm of maniacs?" the pedagogue asked herself, ran upset into another part of the fields, plucked on the way one daisy after another, said at the same time always "yes" and "no", and when relentlessly on the last petal of every flower a "yes" fell, she became furious, threw the last pillaged flower on the path, and thought, 'If I don't want to, nobody can hold me here.' Johanna, however, consoled the governess, she should just have patience, then the divinely solitary nature of her child will one day open unexpectedly and learn everything which it now rejected distrustfully, like a bird before the enticing food in the cage, little Lena will acquire everything as if at play.

Only this desired turnaround did not occur. For El- friede Knille was one of those people who always expect the transformation from outside, from others, was the sort who believed constantly they are doing everything conceivable, and meanwhile set their expectations on grumpiness, impatience, and disappointment. She had learnt a multiplication table and considered it perni- cious and perverse that there was so much in the world which was calculated by other operations.

But the blessed farm's little Lena did not let herself be enticed from the world of her inwardly turned look by any methodical trick, and the louder the zeal of the governess acted before the doors to her life, the deeper her spirit shut itself off with the thoughts whose bright shadows could be seen now and then floating across as dark patches on the pale blue mirrors of her irises.

With each day that the young woman drove her pedagogical siege work systematically closer and closer to the puzzle of this child's soul, the tension between the two increased. And when even Sintlinger had curtly said to the governess that if the learning was not working her way, then she should attempt it in little Lena's way, something like fury gripped the Westphalian cooper's daughter over this rustic irreverence, and she asked trembling whether that perhaps meant she should go to the school with the child?

Sintlinger, however, looked across at her pale flecked face, and just said that the farmer who occasionally learnt from his labourers was not the stupidest, and left her standing.

Since that day, it seemed to Elfriede Knille as if the entire blessed farm had sworn against her. The quiet industry of its servants sounded like secret undermining of her, in Sintlinger's open eyes she saw mocking arrogance. The parlour maid giggled derisively behind her, and old Zenker walked menacingly around her like an old, toothless wolf. Unawares she slipped out of the clothes of injured vanity into the pose of a defender of the treasures of humanity against rustic arrogance and apathy. "The louder a barrel booms, the harder you must strike" had been the maxim of her father, according to which she now wanted to act without deliberation, directly, even if it had to become still more difficult for the only person there was for her at the farmstead, the farmer's wife, that gentlest, kindest women she had ever seen. Elfriede also had the hope of coming into a public appointment in not too long a time. Thus for her sake, if it were not wanted any other way, it could kick off. It was the time of the high summer winds, that quiet swishing which you could hear skimming hard under the stars at night and sometimes see a short jolt of light twitch like the flashing of a polished knife blade through the darkness of the heavens. The farmers then said the Lord was swinging his scythe, and concluded thereby that the harvest was not far off anymore.

The governess lay for hours alone at night by the window, and lost herself with her secret fury over the tips of the trees in the orchard and into the hotly trembling darkness. But when God turned his scythe flashing, each time her breath was caught, she leapt back into her room, began walking back and forth heatedly, and now and then laughed derisively.

She broke off earlier than she had planned the exercises which were meant to make her student ripe for instruction, and began with the screwdrivers, crowbars, and the oxygen blowers of her actual system.

But if her patience had been strained to breaking point before, now every hour turned to desperation. Little Lena not only did not manage to add one and one, but she even resisted it with an unrelenting stubbornness which the governess did not understand for a long time and held for pure apathy. For the child in playing counted finger by finger, stick by stick, ball by ball; but no persuasion, no compulsion, no love could bring her to count up mushrooms and trees, the legs of animals and chairs, because she, divinely bound, could not be brought from the distinctiveness of the things into an abstract, lifeless play of forms.

And then, when she had gotten to know amidst difficulty the first point symbols of braille and should have been connecting them together for her first word!

She then pushed the book away in abject horror, straightened up her delicate body defensively, and stared with her pale face of deep unhappiness at nothing, with eyes which really looked like those of a blind person, for all the brilliance and shimmer had drained from them so that the pupils seemed embossed from dull horn. Then she shook her head so that her golden lock just flew.

"No, that is not true, Miss."

"Just what is it then, little Lena, you're trembling", Elfriede said, looking at the child shaking all over as if with a chill.

She should have been reading from braille the word "mild" and had felt on her sensitive fingertips the sharpness of the point symbols like the pricks of affixed grains of sand penetrating her inner being, and this encircled, lifeless hurting of her most excitable brain, which was meant to be "mild", that soft stroking over her face, the wondrous stirring of the roots of her hair on her scalp, the feel of still, delighted undulation which penetrated to her from the countryside, the floating toll of the evening bells in the air, the rapt hum of the distant forest, and the voice of her dear mother calling her and old Trine home, "Come home, it will not be *mild* much longer." It was impossible for her to separate herself from the living events of life, and compartmentalise the tangible and meaningful existence of her soul into a dead system of symbols.

Little Lena pushed back as if before a prison door, and defended herself in timidity and outrage as if before an injustice, clamped both hands tightly between her knees and burst out into pitiful tears with the cry, "It isn't true — I don't like it."

Only by this disappointment of knowledge, this shock, this true original sin of understanding, do all children succeed in being enticed from the blessedly needless heaven of their souls to the earth of drudgery, comparable to the scream of the newborn when it leaves its mother's lap.

The Blessed Farm

Miss Elfriede Knille was lacking the hand of true love which is alone capable of making the horror of this transition from one world to another more bearable for the child, she called it in her inner being making "a little dance", the "hysteria" of minors and the bellowing of a spoilt child; interrupted her instruction for a moment and waited by the window with strenuously hunched shoulders, her back turned to the room, inducing with each of the ever weakening sobs of the child a mocking chirrup.

Finally she turned around, "So. Are you now finished with crying? It is truly stupid if you burst out crying thus for nothing and again for nothing. Don't you think so, Helene?" The blessed child nodded painfully and thought, if only I don't have to read "mild" anymore.

This day she went to bed very early. When Sintlinger and his wife stepped into the dark room late so as to also go to rest, they heard little Lena start. Then she said, "Miss. Hey, Miss! Reading is quite, quite ugly. You cannot see anything at all anymore because everything turns black. Oh, I would like to sing!"

Then she sank back, shook herself with a sigh, and went back to sleep.

Only, Miss Knille was a dutiful, steadfast teacher, she had intended to last out come hell or high water. That was not easy. She was required now and then to increase the strength of her voice, to tap on the table so that there was the sound of a little bang. She seized the child hard by the shoulders and straightened her up roughly, or suddenly interrupted the teaching, ran into the forest, wrung her hands above herself, and called to heaven, "If news does not come soon about my application, I shall perish."

Little Lena, however, complained to nobody; she sat around like a bird with broken wings, did not play anymore, and did not sing anymore, but slept or lay quite alone with wide-open eyes somewhere in the fields. And then again a change came over her. The wildness broke forth from her which she had once been infected with by Gottlieb Meixner, and when the young woman wanted to bring the girl in such an emotional fever from her madness to her senses again, she suddenly bit her on the hand like a wildcat, and ran away laughing.

The blessed farmer's sanguine composure did not give way, even when his thoughtful eyes sometimes rested darkly on the governess. Instead Johanna lived through difficult days. Yes, the pious soul even took little Lena with her one Sunday to church as, you could not know of course, perhaps in this way God's blessing would make the child's learning easier. There something happened which the zealous Cantor of Hemsterhus, Liborius Pfeiffer, described later as the first spasm of the evil spirit in the Sintlinger girl.

Hardly had Pastor Ardelt in fact become aware from the pulpit of the presence of the blessed farmer's wife, who so rarely presented herself at church services, than his nature somersaulted, and the fanatic began working itself out of him with screams, incantations and blows.

Suddenly the thin, shrill scream of little Lena Sintlinger juddered through the rapt silence of the church. The preacher hesitated for a moment, the congregation started from their devout horror, the Cantor moved his glasses on his nose mockingly and looked from the choir over to the half grilled Sintlinger niche. Johanna was looking after the deathly pale, shaking child, but she was not to be consoled, instead insisting on leaving. Helpless and without hope, concerned in her soul, the mother had to comply in the end. After barely quarter of an hour, she left the house of God before which little Lena retained from that moment on a lifelong aversion, not to be overcome.

On the way home, as the superstitious folk related afterwards, the little girl from the blessed hill was suddenly transported away from the side of her mother, just the same as when a shadow or a heavy sigh passes away from us. When the carriage arrived at the driveway though, little Lena was running laughing and singing across the slope with whirling dress towards her deathly frightened mother.

Through this tale, the folk created the avenue for understanding the miraculous events which arrived shortly afterwards and which brought an end to the difficult hardship of the Sintlinger child at that time.

12

At the same time, the most glorious, one would like to say the sweetest act of the wondrous power of the blessed hill's child occurred. By that is meant a good deed which a poor mother from Querhoven received.

She was called Rütsch and lived in the upper part of Querhoven, called the Sweeps because the narrow village meadows widened there and spread into an arc. The ground was soured and shaded by the proximity of the forest. If the grain was to hold out as far as harvesting, it had to hold bravely to its hard clumps, and if it escaped the snowy decay of winter, the avenging frosts of spring, the summer's gorging by wild animals, and a thousand other perils, then certainly of ten stalks that together began the march to the harvest carts, six would be lost along the way, and the little pack of sweepings which the father of the house can fetch from the barn floor is always not much larger than the little pack of seeds which he carried out was. For that reason, only a few lived in the Querhoven Sweeps, and indeed such as those to whom fate had somehow turned its back, or those who made nothing from hardship on account of apathy, or finally those whose souls are as it were paved with gold so that they sit on a pfennig as if they were riding through life on a golden fox.

When you count the farms in the Sweeps, you have to begin with a poor devil and stop with one, and in between are four more hardscrabble farms, for there have never been more than six little farmlets in upper Querhoven.

There lived the poor mother who found such a miracle worthy salvation at the Blessed Farm.

Before she became Mrs Rütsch, she had been the child of the Ender family, where you wrote "loud" quite small, did not recognise "coarse", and heard "good" from every clock strike. At the same time, she had an industriousness like the restiveness in a clock, and was delicate and deft like a little partridge.

Her father was the one they called Vanlyßender, because his ancestry traced back into Holland, and he had nothing to do kinship-wise with the Ender people, whose head at the time was David Ender and who, born as woodcutters between rough blows, went through life with a racket, and smelt of schnaps even when dead. The property of Vanlyßender was situated in the actual village, and indeed at its lowest point between the mill and the farmstead of the braggart Meixner. When Ursula, whom this story concerns, left the school benches, the question arose of whether she would leave the village for the sake of service, like most Querhoven school-leavers, or whether she would crawl in with one of her neighbours, the big, curly Elis, or the miller. But his child could learn bellowing better from an ox and pushing better from a goat, her father suggested, and for that she did not need to move into the Meixner farmstead, and there was no profit to be made there anymore, and even if the stride of the miller was not straight for every day of the year, he was however closer. And hence Ursula moved into the mill, because she was a delicate being whom her mother had to attend to even after leaving school.

But hardly had she slept once under the roof, against which the rushing of water and the hum of the wheel passed without break, than the entire mill seemed to her not to be a house, but a ship which travelled on without standing still, and every time the girl looked out the window or stepped to the door, it seemed to her that she had been moved a step further away from her father's house so that it again lay further and smaller up in the meadow, and a world much more beautiful and brighter than that of the previous day spread out around her. And she could not walk without singing, and could not work without making a happy face. The miller and his wife for the first time felt quite strange in their house, and nobody could think how it had been before Ursula Ender served in the mill.

The farmers thought that the farmer had secretly had a porcelain path built into the works, for Ursula merely scurried over with loading up or helped with fetching out the sacks, as the flour suddenly came out lighter than usual to the growling crackle of the farmer. Admittedly Ursula was already a full grown girl, full and supple, hearty, and yet with a rapt charm in her face like the shimmering melancholy of still water.

The hearts of the young men, however, were smitten, and many wanted to do absolutely nothing more than drive grain to the Querhoven mill, once they had seen Ursula.

The mill only pulled its earnings in from ten villages, the miller dowsed his walk with tavern water more often than usual so that it fell into disorder, his wife endured the "settling with the bakers" easier than normal, and Ursula was easily coping with the young menfolk who swarmed around her day and night. For a proper girl never thinks of marrying, and the one with whom she had already silently tied her fate, Anselm Rütsch from the Querhoven Sweeps, walked so quietly about the house, looked so much from a distance at the mill, that she always had reason to laugh about the fooling about of the fellows, of whom many dressed themselves up as if they were maypoles and not men.

Anselm Rütsch, however, walked on another path whenever he should meet her, cast his face down if she unexpectedly came into his vicinity, left the room in which the mill's Ursula was spoken of, and all that because he found the thought too fanciful that some girl, and Ursula from the mill at that, could see something in him. Meanwhile a love consumed the gentle fellow, filling his head constantly like a light drunkenness during the day, and troubling him in the night as if his bed were filled with buckthorn and not feathers.

Only, he never confided in her, and the girl had to be touched first by death before he found the courage to talk out loud about what filled the stillness of his heart. This happened after a hard winter's night when the frost had hung the mill wheel from top to bottom with ice so that it could not stir anymore. Because the grain filled the entire hall hard up to the beams of the ceiling and all the customers, not just those who sat in the room, but also those who were walking past or asked in from outside, behaved as if half the district would undoubtedly die out if the mill stood still for only half a day, the mill's lad climbed into the wheel with the axe, the properly fattened miller followed after him, and even Ursula tied her skirts up and began working about with an ice pick at the spokes.

In their haste, it had been neglected to raise the wheel out of its bed. Whilst the three now hacked and pounded in the gear assembly so that it sparked, the en-tire burden of ice released itself as if by a devilish magic from the spokes at once and fell with a crash into the wheel sump. The next moment, the wheel also began quick and ever quicker to set itself in motion. The men just succeeded in springing from the spokes with a leap. But as they shouted to Ursula, they saw the girl drop from spoke to spoke and vanish into the water.

When she was finally able to be fished from her grave underneath the mill, her body seemed dead ten times over and only something for the graveyard.

But her limbs gathered themselves together of their own accord, almost without a doctor, and when the veil of fever about her broke, the first glance of her eyes, de-livered from death, fell on Anselm Rütsch, who was sitting stubbornly and pale as a ghost by her bed, and had wrestled day and night as desperately as her own heart for her life. Ursula Ender was actually looking at the fellow for the first time in her life, but in such a way that the fate of both was decided forever.

She became almost as straight and flawless as before, and quite healthy, but no more for the mill, and not even for the house of her parents, but for the farm in the Sweeps.

Her first excursion was the walk to her wedding in the church, and the first proper stroke of work, she did for Anselm Rütsch who, now as her husband, was with happiness even gentler and quieter than before.

A shadow must certainly first also be overcome be-fore the happiness of the two could properly begin to sing. That was the man's mother, a narrow, miserly wo-man who took a kick at the poverty of Ursula and the hidden sectarianism of her parents, a kick which she could not get over. Hence, after the first three weeks of the young marriage, she moved from the house in the Sweeps to a daughter who had married somewhere in the Rhineland's coal mining region. But Ursula had to promise her with a handshake to spare her husband, and all life that descended from the couple, all the ana-baptist mischief. Querhoven was deemed to be a colony of the Münster anabaptists who had been attracted by a scattered, swooning heap of enthusiasts into these once immeasurable forests. The bloody tribunal of the Bishop in June 1535 drove them in flight from the vanquished new Zion to the wasteland here. Ostracised, hidden, from fear and anxiety for their life, concealing the ar-dency of their passionate fear of God in secret, this laid the foundation for the spasmodic, extraordinary exist-ence of the Querhoven people, and for a secret religious service of which outsiders never learnt anything tan-gible, but which which was constantly practised and was not to be wiped out by anything.

The residents of the Sweeps by contrast were the off-spring of the forest workers whom the Royal House of Arenberg had first settled there perhaps a hundred years before, and hence stuck as firmly to Catholicism as the spokes of a wheel to the hub.

Old Mrs Rütsch thus moved from her house in the Sweeps because she could not bear for even her elbows to smell heretical, and threatened Ursula with her ven-geance if she should perhaps attempt to secretly baptise a child or harm it with some other heretical hocus po-cus. She would be constantly on her guard with prayers and masses, and if she should lapse, then, so swore Mrs Rütsch, the child would come into the world as an ape or grow up to have goitre. So as to stop the thundering mouth of the old woman, and out of love for her husband, Ursula promised everything, and her mother-in-law rumbled away.

As the children now began to march Ursula into bed, you could see how their mother had kept the promise given, for one was dearer and prettier than the next. They gave the mother as little worry as if they had already been set up perfectly for living before heaven had let them fall in Ursula's lap. And the harder the mother had to aim by her thumbnail when she measured off slices of bread, the happier the Rütsch house in the Sweeps jostled, as if frugality and austerity were the single true clapper with which the bell of happiness could be tolled.

Only, when the fourth came, it really seemed to the mother that God had carried the child into the house with his own hands, it was so extraordinarily beautiful.

The little boy had pupils as deep as if their blue had been fetched from out of a well, and hair grew on his head, hair pale yellow as overripe oats and soft as virgin silk. Yes, although little Rütsch was from head to foot without flaws, everyone who saw him thought his hair was the most beautiful thing on him, and he was simply called Snowy.

Everywhere he arrived, the door opened before he knocked, he was given before he asked, they nodded before he spoke, and his mother was played most raptly of all by him. It seemed to her that she had first come into the world with his birth and first knew since then how fond she was of her husband and how beautiful life was, a true gift of God. She did not neglect her three other children in any way, and she was as fond of them as before. But she loved them only like the past Sunday. The fourth little Rütsch, however, Snowy, was her everlasting feast day.

In this way, five years passed like the single swaying of a blossoming branch through the blue heavenly air.

On the morning of an Easter Saturday, Anselm Rütsch, the father, was walking with the wood and palms to Hemsterhus for consecration, and Snowy was permitted to accompany him as far as the bridge over the Hornwasser, behind which the strip of forest dividing the Sweeps from Querhoven stretched over the valley. There they said goodbye to one another. Snowy did not let go until his father placed the wood and palms on the planks of the bridge, lifted the boy up and kissed him. But the child did not get enough. When Rütsch tried to place him back on his feet, he asked for yet another kiss and yet another. He clustered about his father as if he wanted most of all to crawl into him. Finally Rütsch said that if he gave all his goodness to him, there would be nothing left for his mother. Then Snowy let his father go, remained standing on the bridge, and called after him for a long time until he could no longer see him in the trees of the little forest.

He took the way back over the meadows so as to bring his mother a beautiful bouquet of flowers in case he had given his father a kiss which actually belonged to her. But when he had gathered a handful of primroses and buttercups, he saw even more beautiful ones standing in the meadow, threw them all away, and began plucking new ones. In between he floated sticks in the Hornwasser, held his hand to his mouth and made cuckoo calls. But it never answered because it was not there, and so Snowy could not figure out whether he would become rich and live a long time.

When the little boy was tired, he saw a tall birch tree in the meadow, standing in the spring sunshine, moving its long branches so that the golden blossom buds barely trembled, and humming as furtively to itself as if if were telling a story which nobody in all the world was permitted to hear. Snowy listened for a while, and then thought he would try to figure out what the old birch tree was humming to itself so softly, so he walked over, sat down under the tree, and looked up into its crown. There bees were flying back and forth so that it was dusted with gold, the shiny switches glittered, and the sun lay in Snowy's eyes so that he could not help himself anymore. He closed them and fell asleep. In time he slid down the trunk, sank into the grass, and continued dreaming. A smile curved about his mouth, he sighed deliriously, but whatever beautiful stories he head heard from the tree, nobody has ever learnt anything of them.

When the mother missed her Snowy, it was already about midday, and he lay pale and with fallen face in the grass; for the spirits of the earth, which are at their most dangerous in the month of March, had taken command over the child in his sleep. Now his mother was waking him, he opened his eyes, smiled confusedly, did not know where he was, staggered, and if his mother had not carried him home in her arms, he would have fallen over his own feet and certainly not moved from the spot.

At home, his mother sat Snowy on the bench behind the table, laughed that he was acting so scatterbrained, placed a piece of fresh cake next to him, and went about her work, for she nursed a habit, which she had been practised at her father's home, of cleaning the entire house on Easter Saturday from cellar to chimney so as to ease the glitter of the new sun into every last corner. She washed soapy water from the loft down the stairs, through the hall into all the rooms, and when she undid the ties in the late afternoon and let down her skirt, Snowy was still sleeping on the table and had not touched the cake lying next to him.

Then Ursula became afraid and called her husband from the shed where he was chopping kindling, and the siblings so that they could talk to him and tease him. Snowy, however, just leant back and made eyes as if everyone, father, mother, and siblings, all clustered exuberantly around the table, were not before him, but far, far away, perhaps on the edge of the forest; he smiled lovingly, indulgently, and said after quarter of an hour, could they now go again. They should not be angry, but he could not help being sleepy. His mother should place the bed deep into the corner, and when Ursula Rütsch had done that, Snowy moved as if seeking shelter, pressed hard up against the wall, and lay for a long time there as if in secret anticipation with half-open eyes, and then said in an inexplicable context, "Now it is enough." Then he asked to turn the bed so that he could comfortably see the blessed Maria and the little angels which stood on the corner shelf behind the little lamp.

His mother did for the little boy all he wished, and he thanked her barely audibly, but so sweetly and full of love that a painful tearing went through the middle of Ursula's heart.

Then Snowy lay still and slept without breath. The entire night, he did not stir, and the next day as well. He ate a single little crumb of cake, and drank one gulp. That was his entire feast day's eating. Then he gave the little mug and the cake back, smiled to everyone in the room, and let his eyes close again.

In the afternoon, he asked for the neighbour's children. They came and played all those games which had always pleased little Rütsch the best: horseshoe tossing, blind man's buff, and chicken walking and others. In between, they told all the droll stories, bent over with laughter, and did not rest until a happy glow also rose in Snowy's face. Finally he opened his eyes, looked clearly at everyone, stretched his little hand over the edge of the bed, and waved weakly with it. Then the children knew that their dear Snowy had had enough, and they left.

But every time he spoke, little Rütsch's voice sounded more unreal, and every time he opened his eyes, his look came from further out of the world, and the foreboding fell in his mother's breast that it was a sleep which led out of life. But she could and could not consider it possible, and as soon as he even opened his eyes, she bent over his bed, and asked her dearest boy whether he was not a little better already. Snowy smiled each time, infinitely poignant, stroked his hand gently over his mother's cheek, and said his dear mother should not worry, it was becoming easier for him. Not long, and it would all be good.

Thus it went the entire Easter, from Easter Sunday until Tuesday.

On the Wednesday morning, when his three siblings were packing their canvas satchels on the bench to go to school, Snowy abruptly straightened up, quite taken and still, and followed every hand movement with astonished, attentive eyes. Then, when his mother had left the room for a moment, he said farewell to them all, and wished them all the best for school and the world. The three little Rütschs noted well a strange solemnity in their little brother. Only it was high time they went to school. For that reason, they stormed off, and called from the garden to their mother in the stalls that Snowy had just spoken as if he wanted to die. The ladle which their mother was just then wanting to pour from into the can fell from her hand, and when she came flying into the room, Snowy was still sitting upright in the little bed, and he looked with such an expression of divine happiness into his mother's desperate face, and such a thousand year old seriousness was in his eyes at the same time, that the scream which she had wanted to emit remained in Ursula Rütsch's throat from astonishment and fear, and she could do nothing but follow the eyes of the child which were now directed again at the

image of the Mother of God with the two angels on the
shelf in the corner of the room. Thus this rapture remained quite a while in the little boy. When it faded
from him, his head sank, and he gathered up the bedcovers with his little hands into a small heap. Then he
raised his face, and asked his mother if she would like to
fetch the playthings which he had received for Christmas.

His mother was compelled, sobbing, to pull him into
her arms, and ask crying what in all God's world it
meant, but the broad depths in Snowy's eyes were so
vast that she walked, quite still as if in a difficult dream,
and sought out everything which belonged to the child
— both the little pilgrimage pictures, the little wooden
horse, the little turned board on which a sheep had once
stood, and a few other things. All that she placed before
the child on his bedcovers.

After Snowy had pondered for a little bit, he made
from his playthings as many piles as he had siblings.
The little horse, however, would go to his dearest friend
Hieronymus, the neighbour's boy.

"Don't you want to play anymore at all, Snowy?" his
mother asked, and held back her tears.

The boy shook his head calmly, and simply said no,
for he had to go away, and straightaway at that. Just before, when his mother had entered, the little angel had
trembled, and that more than the night before. Only, he
knew it exactly, when such a little angel did not tremble
more often than twice, then quite certainly what you
think must have happened has happened. Hieronymus
also said that.

"But for God and Maria's sake, my child!" Ursula
now cried, unable to hold herself any longer, and
plunged to her knees before the bed. But Snowy smiled
happily, stroked the glass pane, and whispered raptly,
"The little meadow ... the beautiful little meadow ..."

And as he said the same word softly and ever more softly, he leant his head on his mother's neck as if overcome with joy. Ursula Rütsch, however stood like a post, and did not move a muscle. For she thought her Snowy had fallen asleep, and she did not want to disturb him.

But when she finally looked into his eyes, he had already died.

Then the hammers of despair began beating against her body and her soul from all sides so that she quite lost her mind, let the dead child fall onto the bed, screamed like a whipped animal, and ran across the Sweeps straight into the forest. At the same time, she cried constantly, "I won't give my child away! No, my Snowy must not die!"

The entire forest echoed from her laments until her husband, deep in the tall wood, heard her screaming. He went with another woodcutter after the voice, and they finally found the despairing woman back at the Hornwasser's source where she was cowering by an old fox's den, scraping the ground with her fingers, and saying constantly, "I won't give my child away! No, my Snowy must not die!" But her voice was already quite hoarse, almost extinguished, from all the crying and calling out.

From then on, Ursula Rütsch was transformed as if pushed out before the door of the world which had slammed shut — she always sat in the same place, and looked without turning her eyes at the bed of her dead child. The funeral passed by, people came wanting to console her, stood helpless before her motionless, anguished maternal face, shook their heads as if they hoped nothing more for the poor woman, and set off again from there silently. Ursula noticed none of all that. She remained lost, though her husband asked her to pull together, her three other children were crying around her, the cows in the stalls were bellowing in hunger, and yet she did not stir.

Thus she was driven into the world in which Gottlieb Meixner had been driven by incomprehensible vortices from the blessed farm to Querhoven. He gave through his bluster the first push that diminished somewhat the numbing anguish of poor Ursula.

The people say that exactly three lots of three weeks after the Easter Sunday on which Snowy was hummed to his fatal sleep by the old birch tree, the crushed Meixner was drawn after days of brooding through the Sweeps into the Hornwasser forest, again jeering and whining at the entire world. He made a racket along the road of which not everything could be understood. But what could be heard was that he was warning the entire Sweeps to be on their guard.

It even raised Ursula from her seat, and led her to the window. Just then Gottlieb directed his shouting at the Rütsch house, "... cleared out, everyone is lost in the Sweeps, I say", he roared. Only, when Ursula appeared at the window, deathly pale, agitated, motionless, the raving was choked in Gottlieb as if by a hand. He sat down on a milestone, and looked silently into the poor mother's face. Then he groped on the road next to him-self, grabbed a stone, tossed it in the dust, and spat at it.

After this encouragement, he sprang up, and shouted in a strangely mournful way, "Yes, Ursula, what I tell you, the witch little Lena has stolen your child, your Snowy, too. As true as I live, says the gentleman. Haha! All around cursed, all around cursed, yes, stolen."

Embarrassed, Ursula listened to the whining singing of the misfortunate man, which, sounding ever weaker, vanished towards Querhoven. Then she returned to her place, looked at the floor for a while, shook her head in astonishment, and then smiled for the first time since the death of her child.

After this encounter, she found her way back as it were into her work again.

Only she had a strange way of walking, a bit like after the fall through the spokes of the mill wheel, as if she was not moving on firm ground, but on a swaying foot-bridge which lay over an abyss. A fearful fumbling preceded the grasping of her hands, and she talked more from up above, like someone for whom, startled out of their sleep, the dispelled dream haunts all their talk against their will, and when good Anselm Rütsch was not constantly about her, she fell back again and again into the old sitting and staring in which she con-stantly spoke to herself in a low voice, requests for forgiveness from her Snowy, reproaches over her hu-man fear, hatred of her mother-in-law, and endless self-accusations that she had driven her child to death be-cause she had deprived him of the life's bath of baptism.

She could see her entire life only through the shroud of her irredeemable sorrow, and succumbed thus more and more to the fate of hollowed out people who see the self-created shadow of their constantly oppressed spirit as real existence.

But at the return home of her husband on an early autumn day of this sombre year, she told of the visit which two angels had made to her that afternoon. One had remained standing by the stove after their entrance into the room and had begun playing with the little horse which Snowy had gifted to his neighbour Hieronymus, the other meanwhile walked to the bed of the dead boy, and wrote all sorts of indecipherable, mysterious signs in the air over the bedposts. And to her inward amazement, what this signified had become the answer for her, he did what he wanted. After that the angel again strode to the door, and the other angel fol-lowed without hesitation. But when they arrived at the threshold, the angel became smaller and smaller. Its wings shrank until a little, blond-haired girl stood in the doorway.

She turned around, looked lovingly at the troubled mother, waved to her, and pattered hurriedly away. Ursula ran after the child straightaway, but saw nothing more than a splendour which hung in the treetops in the garden and then slowly pulled away up high as a haze of light towards the estranged farmsteads of Hemsterhus.

Now it seemed constantly to her as if she must yet succeed in scraping Snowy out of eternity.

Poor Rütsch was so taken aback by his wife's tale that he did not emit a word. This shock to the depths of his soul did not leave him for the greater part of the night. For either his wife had now really gone mad, or God himself had given her a wondrous sign as to how she should find her way out of the darkness. After he had argued it that far, he pulled himself together for an impassioned prayer, left it all up to God, and fell asleep.

In the morning, his spirit had really clarified itself, and he said to Ursula that if the epiphany were really true which she had spoken of, then in his opinion it meant nothing else than an invitation that they should go over to the blessed farm to the wondrous child of the farmer Sintlinger. Who knows, the ways of providence can never be fathomed, what she must have thought after the disappearance of the angel could yet come about, namely that, as she said, heaven was no longer keeping Snowy completely to itself.

Thus the couple dressed in their Sunday best, and set off on the path, climbing along the long ridge of hills which separated Querhoven from the district of the estranged farms, and soon stepped out of the edge of the forest, which ran along two or three trees deep as a dark green beard of firs on the high border as far as the forests of the arid mountains themselves. There they saw the estranged farmsteads now lying before them, the undulating rising hills behind them, the forest enclosing the two properties in the first, wistfully colourful foliage of autumn floating from the treetops, and on the furthest horizon above it, a still, transfigured light in the air, that gleaming road through the heights, of which the opinion was that it was the reflection of the Rhine current, which flowed along, hours distant, still further behind the forest.

Anselm Rütsch and his Ursula stood, looked across to the prosperous farmsteads, and the poor woman especially was so taken by the still light in the heavens that she began snatching at the seams of her apron with the twitching fingers of her right hand. But her husband, whose understanding had been opened deeper by love and anguish, realised what his wife had been touched by it, and comforted her that what she saw in the sky was by no means a ghost train through the air even if it looked that way. What she should have a mind for at this moment was plucking up her courage for the walk to the blessed farm. For the angel which had appeared to her had dissipated as a splendour in the treetops. For that reason, it was his opinion, they would also see the shimmer of the Rhine today as clearly in the high air as it had ever looked his life long.

After these words of comfort, Ursula directed, as was her habit, her large, dark-blue eyes in a sort of sombre searching at Anselm. But he just nodded quietly after his words, and Ursula then offered him her hand in farewell, and said he should just return again in God's name. For since her own hardship led her to the blessed farm, she also wanted to accomplish it alone, entirely alone.

It was at the highest time of the second hay harvest, and the blessed farm lay soundless, almost abandoned by all the residents, in the late morning, autumn sun. With pounding heart, Ursula ascended the steep driveway. With each step that brought her nearer to the large gate, it seemed to her more and more sharply what a woman dumbed-by-misfortune she was making a walk which she herself did not know the aim of. When she thus arrived under the transparent shade of the lime tree, she knelt down by the Sintlinger memorial, and said an impassioned Lord's Prayer. Towards the end, as she breathed out the words "But deliver us from evil" imploringly from her soul, the certainty unexpectedly beset her that she would see her dead Snowy again. At that she was intoxicated with shock and happiness. When, arriving at the gate, she once more looked back at the Sintlinger memorial, it seemed to her that the black iron railing around the cross was interwoven with garlands of red roses. The inner yard, wide as a market square, the tall hall which appeared to her like the entrance to a church, it all heightened her discomposure. She headed for the Sintlingers' house and soon came to the back part of the lower hall, where left and right from the stairs to the second storey the door to the kitchen lay opposite the door to the room in which little Lena was taught.

When she helplessly, irresolutely looked from one door to the other, not knowing where she should turn, the clatter of dishes rang from the kitchen. If only nobody came, for God's sake, Ursula thought. But hardly had she finished thinking this cry than she heard steps seeming to approach from behind the door, and without actually really knowing what she was doing, she fled to the door of the teaching room, seized the handle, and in the next moment stood, not as if she had walked, but as if she had been pushed, timid and ashamed, into the classroom.

Her heart was pounding audibly, and she turned in a circle, thinking now, now she must collapse. In this clamour before her ears, she heard a hard female voice ask, "Why did it occur to you to upset my teaching? Who are you?"

Then Ursula finally raised her lowered eyes, and looked at the governess who had spoken, so as to excuse herself. But just as she looked into the face of Miss Knille, who stood tall in angry fear by the table, the poor mother's hope for the best faded. She swallowed the request to be excused, and looked full of desperation into the room. The governess did not understand the unfamiliar woman's strange behaviour, and thought she was dealing with a madwoman who must not be upset by severity. For that reason, she immediately altered her tone, and said, "Please, will you not take a seat?"

Then she pushed her own chair over to Ursula, and retired to the door.

Ursula Rütsch had meanwhile seen little Lena who, still oppressed by the teaching, was sitting on her chair behind the large table. Her face was pale, her blond locks stood like an aura of transfiguration around her forehead, she kept her eyes still in searching reverie turned towards the area where Ursula stood.

This mysterious sinking into one another of the pair did not last long, then the governess saw the just then still fallen figure of Ursula rise, her careworn face blossomed into a sort of radiance, and then the surprising thing happened, she lifted her arms yearningly towards little Lena, and cried with rapt, tear-choked voice, "My Snowy!"

After this cry, her strength seemed exhausted. She sank into the chair, and her arms fell loosely into her lap.

The child of the blessed farm smiled now across her entire face, and said with her unreal singingly beautiful voice, "You see, now you have brightened up." With these words, she approached Ursula, who did not know what was happening to her, huddled up against her, and said, "But I am not called Snowy. I am little Lena Sintlinger, and you must not cry anymore."

Ursula Rütsch, however, now timidly took the girl's head between her hands like a precious object, and pressed her face into the blond locks as if they were holy water.

But as soon as the governess saw Ursula grasp Helene's head, she thought, now the madness of the strange woman will break out, and she fled from the room to fetch help. But she had hardly stood shaking outside in the hall than it occurred to her that she had just left the child in the woman's power. She was frightened of Sintlinger's reproaches ,and ran and ran from the yard, behind the barn into the fields, all the way to the beech stand, and when she had lost her breath, she merely said, "I am not staying a moment longer at the witches' farm", then she again had the strength to continue her flight.

While the governess was thus hounded from the farm, little Lena found herself and poor Rütsch becoming more and more intimately entwined. It seemed to the woman from the Sweeps as if she were not with a human child at the Sintlinger farmstead, but was sitting in the chamber of an unearthly house, and the girl's eyes shimmered in the enchanted, worlds-wide light with which her dead child had looked at her during the nights and in the dreams of her sleep, but entirely without the tremors of separation, without the pain of the irretrievable loss that, without knowing it, she had added to everything from the anguish of her soul and the wounds of her heart. In the eyes of the hill's blessed child, she saw her dead child in heavenly blissful rapture, and they were also like two peepholes through which her foreboding was met by an unnameable breath of the heavenly hereafter to which her dearest little boy had been transported. Whilst little Lena asked for her name, where she was from, whether she also had children, what they were called, and much more, which the blind girl talked happily about because she no longer sensed the governess, her little hand carelessly played in Rütsch's hand, and the pair went from the room, down the hall, and left the yard through the gate. And more and more often, the poor woman had to bend down, and peer into the eyes of little Lena Sintlinger for the transfigured look of her Snowy, whose voice she heard ringing in the words of the girl, but freed, unearthly, heavenly. When the pair had then strolled outside along the level part of the driveway to the place where it turned in a steep drop to the boundary way, Rütsch overcame her mysterious fear of the child, grasped her under the arms, lifted her towards the blue sky, hugged her, and said in joyful rashness, she would never forget what she had given her, for she had got back her dead Snowy directly from heaven, and even more beautiful that he had been in life.

Then she ran primly down the slope.

Only when she had already ascended the top of the hill on the other side which separated Querhoven from the district of the estranged farmsteads did she turn around and look at the blessed hill's child sitting in her pink dress in the greenery next to the gate's lime tree so that she looked more like a large flower blooming in the shade of the massive tree in heavenly stillness.

Her husband was still waiting faithfully where she had left him, in the quite shade of the row of trees which ran from the forest of the arid mountain to the top of the crest of hills, and had already had all sorts of confused misgivings as to why his wife remained so long at the Sintlinger's farmstead. Now he saw her hastening up the hill, and the closer she got to the trees, the more she quickened her pace. Then he finally emerged from the shade of the trees, took a few steps hesitantly along the path towards her, and looked inquiringly into her face. Ursula Rütsch, however, when she stood opposite her husband, suddenly recalled once more all the torment and gloom which had lain on her for many weeks, and was seized by the miracle which the blind girl had effected in her more than ever in the depths of her soul. Hence her face was quite shaken with joy. Slow tears ran over her cheeks. She said exhaustedly, "Anselm, come, come!", took his hand, squeezed it heartily, and in that way they silently descended towards Querhoven.

13

This experience of the blessed farm's little Lena with a mother almost riven apart by the pain over her dead child was, for both participants, the immediate district, and in more outlying areas, an incident which entailed the weightiest consequences.

The blessed farmer came in from the fields, in the late morning of the day in which the incident occurred, right at the time when Anselm Rütsch and his redeemed Ursula were on the hill opposite disappearing behind the strip of forest towards the Querhoven Sweeps.

Little Lena was still sitting in the same spot where she had been left by the highly delighted mother, and was playing in deep rapture with a butterfly, a brown, modestly adorned butterfly which the folk call a cow's eye butterfly. Now the little creature probably did not belong to the noble, especially clever butterflies. But what the farmer then saw was for all that strange, even wondrous. Covetous, with a certain delighted zest, the butterfly hovered about the child's little blond head, almost intoxicated with the light, and as soon as little Lena stretched out her hand, the sylph settled down on it, sat at first quietly entranced, and then began a heaving spreading and closing of its wings as if in extreme ecstasy, strolling up and down her rosy fingers. Little Lena, however, said to it something which Sintlinger, because of the distance, could not understand. But he noted by the sound of her voice that she was sometimes unhappy like a first-time mother, sometimes whispered lovingly, sometimes enticed, and the modest butterfly followed her in all that — it flew, begged with stubborn insistence, nestled trembling in her hand, and seemingly then sucked tight with its feet to her skin. When the blessed farmer approached, the butterfly was just dispelled of its intoxication, and flew falling, tumbling, uncertainly away, just a butterfly again. Little Lena, however, turned her face in the direction of its flight, reflected with a smile, then stretched out her hand, let her fingers play enticingly, and said, "Come. You will come straightaway!"

"Here I am already!" Sintlinger answered as if he had been the one meant.

At that the child was startled in the way you are just startled from sleep, when you have the feeling of falling down deeply with a jolt. She let her arm fall powerlessly, and tilted her head with a timid sigh.

"Where did you learn how to do that with the butterfly?" the blessed farmer asked.

"From the woman", the child answered, quickly pulling herself together.

"From which woman then?"

"Well, the one who was just here, who came in the door quite dark, and then became quite bright. You know, father, through a quite wide, tall gate. At first she cried, and her child has died. Think, she thought at first I was called Snowy, hahaha."

Now she laughed her silvery-ringing laugh again.

Thus the blessed farmer learnt of the wondrous events.

In the evening, the governess arrived, and attempted at first to explain her long absence with a letter for whose receipt she had been called to the postal agency in Hemsterhus. But when the appearance of Mrs Rütsch was mentioned, she discoloured, looked hostilely at the farmer, then looked from one to the other confusedly and derisively, and said gruffly that, yes, if it comes to that, then she must declare that this would be her last day at the farm. Tomorrow she must depart with the first train to Dingden. She had received a notice of employment from the government, and must report within two days.

Sintlinger nodded confidently and, without asking a word, let her depart the next morning in the first grey of the awakening day. Little Lena had not been reachable for a last word from Elfriede Knille, not the entire evening, and the next morning more than ever not. And now, when the governess was travelling between baskets and suitcases through sleeping Hemsterhus, with a light in which everything hovered in dissolution and uncertainty in the forest behind, through which the mist was driven into long strips by a constant wind so that it looked as if the trees were caught grimly, darkly, silently in a futile wandering; now it suddenly seemed to her that she was not travelling towards the daylight, but towards the darkness, that she was like a person who flees their fortune, and it was no use that she laughed derisively, slandered the mad farm, and finally began singing quite lustily in defiance.

When she bought the ticket in Dingden, her hands were trembling, and she could barely say the words. In

the carriage, however, she did not look out the windows
into the pleasant morning, but had a feeling like that
once when as a small girl she had been disrespectful at
mass in the house of God and had to think all her blessings had been taken from her then and she would
succeed at nothing. In changing trains at Bocholt, in the
midst of the muddle, she was suddenly gripped by the
angelic, wondrous being of the blessed farm's little Lena
as if by an otherworldly light, and burst out into loud
crying.

***

To Ursula Rütsch from the Sweeps, her dead Snowy
had been gifted to the depths of her soul by little Lena
Sintlinger, and the life of this poor woman had thus won
a new, large expanse for her old existence, that province
of wonder, in fact, that other worldly land in which she
had always been at home through the deepest powers of
her anabaptist origin. There her beautiful child now
resided in the sunless light, and when he yearned for
her, the stream of her soul then stepped over the earthly
banks and trembled a while happily in the reflection of
eternal rapture.

At this time, her firm connection to the concealed
rites of her anabaptist forebears was with necessity fulfilled. She took her three other boys from bed one night,
wandered with them deep into the tall wood by the hidden forest pool behind the Sweeps, and baptised them
there, fervently following in the footsteps of old ceremonies again. When the three boys, intimidated and
seized by the ardent belief of their mother in her white
shirt with folded hands, strode to the softly glistening
mirror of the pool, they were really more like the light
shadows of blessed spirits than living people, and when
Ursula Rütsch now perceived before the immersion that
a star standing directly above the pool altered its light

so that its uneasy, smouldering flickering suddenly passed into a peaceful, white radiance, the good soul believed the sins which she had committed by the forced dropping of the secret desire of her forebears would now be made good again.

Her return and reawakening remained hidden like only such a thing can remain hidden. Her husband, Anselm, acted as if he had slept especially deeply during that night, the Rütsch boys remained silent partly from joy in possessing a great secret, partly from fear of their teacher, the Hemsterhus Cantor. They remained properly silent, without any winking, curling of the mouth, twinkling of the eye, or pridefulness. Thus Querhoven for the time being learnt nothing of the reinitiating of the sectarian spirit by which it would be so deeply gripped in a few years.

It was only seen that Ursula Rütsch came alive to a hidden splendour, that she seemed moved into the happiness of the best time of her life, that and a deepened, mysterious veil was seen over her face, even over her entire being. But that was all considered to be the effect of the blessed hill's girl, little Lena Sintlinger alone, and the magic of that rare child ran again vividly through all the folk of the villages and small towns in the areas surrounding Hemsterhus. That Ursula Rütsch, everywhere she came into conversation with people, spoke of the hidden blessing and miraculous powers of the blind girl is clear. In her words something was also caught always of the religious fire of her reawakening, and she called Helene none other than the "little spirit of grace", "a real child of heaven", and thus through her experience indulged in her secret beliefs which she could chat about in this way. All her praise shook with religious ardency, and as she spread the fame of the blind girl, all sorts of awe and joy over the hidden aspects of mankind, nature, and God ignited. The experience of Josefa

Schwerdtner, who had been rescued from drunkenness by the Sintlinger child and had received another affecting voice, now emerged anew in the memories of all the people.

When it then became known that the governess had at the train station in Bocholt suddenly broken out into distraught, loud weeping in yearning for the blessed farm's child, the opinion arose in all seriousness that little Lena Sintlinger was in possession of powers which were capable of working across three flowing rivers, across all living things, yes, even beyond the shadow of the grave.

Always, when the people are touched by the foreboding of their spiritual boundlessness, their cheerfulness and faith in life is usurped, and of all the villages, Querhoven encountered the magic of the blind child most embracingly, for that the miracle of such a bright turn of fate had been afforded to a woman from its midst, the village residents experienced as justice for the Querhoveners oblique and eccentric nature which had been mocked so often by everyone. The skewer planes now travelled swishing through the fastened wood in all the cottages, the woodturner's blade cut the pegs and cream spigots from the wood with a more joyful screaming, and the boys and girls stuck together the matchstick boxes with more cheerful, more momentous diligence than usual. All these zealous, narrow people, burdened with an ancient stigma, seemingly still pushed aside on the path of life as the offspring of cast out heretics, were reliant for their existence only on expecting, by miracles and extraordinary upheavals, a fulfillment of those hopes which hung in their souls just like a tousled, drunken lock of hair hangs in the face.

That is why they heard in the voice of the Schwerdtner woman and the new life which Ursula Rütsch had been gifted by the blessed hill's girl the auspice of the approach of a better, more elevated time, yes, the miller, who admittedly that year mixed up his legs more often than usual when he came out of the tavern, even talked of a "call from Zion", and recalled in especially excited moments the place in the Bible, "Out of the mouths of babes and sucklings thou hast perfected praise."[*]

***

There in that gentle world, which even here and there, and especially in Querhoven, was occasionally overlaid with a burst of sparks, an incident — actually, if you consider it properly, two — burst so that it vaguely startled even those who already began to see in the Blessed Farm's little Lena something like the eyes of the Mother of God and in the Sintlinger farmstead a future site of grace.

The time had moved into a new spring, already quite far into it, about Ascension Day[†]. As the farmer liked to have it, the crows could already hide themselves in the grain, and even the grass in the meadows stood thick as felt. By the warm running water especially, quite broad stripes lay one upon the other, for the stalks were no longer capable of holding the many fat leaves upright. And Ursula Rütsch, as a prudent farmworker, began like other housewives to already make use here and there of such overgrowth for tending the cattle. For the winter hay was very meagre, the cows had already been having to bite into the straw for a long time, and the butter churn certainly produced whey, but little butter, which still tasted lumpily bitter anyway.

Hence, when all the work in the house was done, already deep in the darkness of the hours when the evening dew began to fall, she set off on the path into her back-most little meadow. It stretched along a side

---

[*]   Matthew 21:16.
[†]   Fortieth day after Easter.

shoot of the Hornwasser down a warm slope. Sometimes Anselm went with her. When he came too late from the forest, however, she absolutely would not tolerate his assistance, but secretly crept with grass tote and sickle out the backdoor. And when she returned, it was sometimes already moonlit, so late that good Rütsch saw her humping along from a distance like a broad-leafed tree; it was that dark already, and Ursula had loaded grass that high up over her head. Then he did not stand with his hands in his pockets, but ran towards her, took the load from her back and scolded her strenuously over her lack of consideration for the child which she was expecting again. But Ursula just laughed at her husband, and because of the child she comforted him that it would grow as it were in the shadow of the Blessed Farm, and she sensed how it would prosper; for she had never been as happy as this time in all her pregnancies, not even when Snowy was on the way.

Only once, when she was again out in the forest meadow so late, something confounded her which certainly neither her husband's concern nor the suspicions of any other person in the entire district could have guessed at. She was finished, had the load already on her back, and was seeking with her feet the old slab which lay as a bridge over the little ditch of water, found it, and began straightaway to stride along intrepidly when she heard the slab crack behind her from a hurried leap. But no time remained for her to think what it could be. Behind her the breath of an exhausted man wheezed, seized the load, tore it off her with such wild violence that she staggered, and as she gathered herself with a shrill scream so as not to fall, it sprung onto her back, struck its legs firmly over hips, and began at the same time to strangle her about the throat with its hands so that her senses lapsed, hurting her like claws or wooden clamps, squeezing, tormenting and riding her as if she were not a person but a horse.

Rütsch, who was standing behind the house had hurried immediately at the shrill scream, found her lying as if lifeless some distance from the load, and after he had brought her again to her senses with a few handfuls of water from the ditch, he learnt of the mysterious attack, immediately sprang here and there in fury, shouted oaths into the night, but saw and heard not the slightest, not even the quiet stealing away of muffled steps.

Only, before anyone could find their way to the first conjectures, only two days later, Josefa Schwerdtner, who was moving with her songs from village to village, was preyed on in exactly the same way.

When, in the depths of evening on the way to Brederode, she tried to go past the stone quarry lying a quarter of an hour from the village, it sprang at her, making the stones roll, and before the fearful widow had made a few steps in flight, a hail of fist blows fell on her back, head, and neck. Disheveled and badly mauled, the savaged woman finally pulled herself together from her stupefaction. The guitar had been trodden into small pieces, but her bundle of belongings was intact. Thus she shuffled trembling in fear and anxiety to the first Brederode farmstead.

The excitement over these two attacks was great, yes, it assumed such a degree within a short time that no female being dared leave the house after light. But the more insistently people engaged in solving it, the closer people came to the incomprehensibility of these two attacks, which had obviously been committed by one and the same person, and indeed someone from the immediately surrounding area. After the police and the public had put a long series of abusive arrests and the most perverse suspicions behind themselves, the gravedigger Wachsmann of Hemsterhus made the claim amongst his most intimate confidantes that it concerned the grave of the dead Nobody-incubus, he did not say it out-right, but that it was at least a bit fishy. He had once heard the door of death opening in the fool's burial mound, and another time the twit's corpse chuckled. What that was about, he admittedly did not reveal, but he just implied that he himself believed very much in the roaming of the Nobody-incubus beyond the grave, because a man who did not sufficiently enter life could not die completely either. That sufficed for the spread-ing of the belief that the Nobody-incubus had squatted on the two woman.

Only, after the incident had veered into the realm of the grisly, many old, almost forgotten ghost stories were awoken. Unkindly house spirits began to recall their du-ties everywhere, pounded on the windows in the middle of the night, fell with the whimpering of little children into wells, and walked up and down the distant fringes of the forest wringing their hands in despair. There were people who swore they had seen the Nobody-incubus incarnate as he usually had been, tall, gaunt and stooped like a giant framed crow, and heard his idiotic throaty laugh. Yes, before the affair had petered out into the vague mists of wonder which the folk always needed for their lives, the figure of the Herne rebel Faber had ghosted into the general whirl for a moment. He had ap-parently been encountered sitting by the edge of a secluded path, emaciated, diabolic, with eyes like sharpened knives, and when the person to whom this incident had happened squeezed by timidly and full of fear, he had laughed contemptuously after him, and called out something which had sounded like mockery and devilish threats.

And yet, if a single man had had eyes where they be-longed, in his head, and not, like everyone, on his

wonder-addicted tongue, then he would have discovered the malefactor at one glance.

Hardly in fact had the wondrous resurrection of Ursula Rütsch from the Sweeps occurred at the Blessed
Farm than Gottlieb Meixner's restless roaming about
came to a standstill. He appeared in the house of his
mother, sat around helplessly and pale, spent the day
absently, and lay at night with open eyes. Finally he declared that he had to go to Echternach for the Virgin
Mary, otherwise he would die. He departed emaciated
and turned away from the world like a penitent. The
first attack happened perhaps eight days after his going
away, and when he returned again, it had all already
subsided into the general cloud of wonder. He was
asked only in mocking whether the Echternach Mother
had twisted his neck over it all, or whether he had fallen
into the hands of the wild miner, the rebel Faber, along
the way, for he really looked as if strangled and beaten
up, not like someone who had received blessing.

"If your nose isn't dripping, you don't need to wipe
it", he answered calmly and with an indulgent smile,
nodded at those who needled him thus, and went, to his
mother's astonishment, even shock, into such a quiet,
solitary life that it was as if a divine hand had really put
the drawbar of his wagon to rights.

14

The waves of this rumour, which took its beginning
from the Blessed Farm, did not rebound all the

same to this secluded farmer's stronghold, at least not to the extent that it lifted the life of its people off the rails.

Here the going away of the governess had formed the more momentous event for most. The maids and labourers were joyful that the eyes of the wooden goat, as they called Elfriede Knille, no longer beset them as silent sermons. Old Zenker made three large crosses in the air whenever she was spoken of, Trine came out with a deep sigh of relief from the angles and corners where she had for months subjected to a precise scrutiny all the rubbish which had been washed there by the broad current of Sintlinger's prosperity.

Now that she was again little Lena's protector, she saw that as a triumph of her educational methods over "the newfangled incomprehensible stuff of this strange aunt from Münster". Only little Lena was seized after the departure of the governess by a passionate inclination towards solitude. Thus, as if the everlasting educational noise with which she had been surrounded for six months had put her life in confinement, the child fled into silence. In the middle of the chatter of others, yes, in the middle of her own talking, her pale mirror eyes suddenly became large and motionless, her fingers played about each other, she fell silent, and looked as if she were in another world, with a humming song between her lips. Or she stood for a long time all alone in the field, let her hair and her dress wave in the wind, knelt in the meadow, and carefully held favourite flowers in her cupped hands as if in prisons; yes, once Johanna encountered her behind the barn at the gable end where she was obviously playing with nothing but the light and shadows. Sometimes she stepped entirely into the sunlight, sometimes she took the side of the shadows, then she again gave only her arm, head, or half body to the light or darkness. And Johanna, to

whom these dreamy movements were incomprehensible, noticed though in the girl's changing facial
expression what multifarious experiences she was enjoying. When asked, the blind girl answered that she
was letting the song of the light and the shadows sing in
herself.

When Sintlinger experienced such a thing with his
child, you could see in the bright deepening of his face
how great the joy was which he felt over it.

But Johanna was the only one on the entire farm
who was led by all these events to worry and concern.
For a long time, she admittedly did not carry this dark
burden around with herself. For from her earlier experiences, since the whirl after the death of her father which
had almost flushed her out of the world, since that time,
she knew how dangerous it was to lock up fears unexpressed in her nature — because they then lost their
shape, penetrated through all the parts of her spirit like
mildew, and did not rest before her mind looked surrounded on all sides by insurmountable dark walls
which closed together more and more threateningly, so
narrowly that in the end her heart in her own breast did
not find space enough to beat. That is why, when Johanna had seen for a few weeks how Sintlinger
refrained from everything which held little Lena to reg-
ulated, purposeful activity, as if he were keeping himself
and his child seemingly hidden in the rising tumult
which the incident with Ursula Rütsch led all the time to
the hill of the Blessed Farm, yes, as if he were support-
ing the child's inclination to detach herself with every
fibre from the accustomed life foundations of others and
to be more and more nothing other than the playmate of
wind, light, water, shadows, flowers, and animals; when
she noticed this, she found her dear Andreas beset in
the bright light of day by the whirl of his night wander-
ings, and she took him one evening at that time curtly

and decisively by the hand, because, as she answered to his astonished gaze, important things had to be discussed.

Andreas knew very well the vigorous abruptness in which the angelic goodness of his wife clothed both sides of itself, and knew too well that it was always seized by his wife on occasions which she did not feel entirely up to.

Hence when, after a meaningful silence in the evening, she brought forth nothing more than astonishment over the glimmering, restive brightness of the night, and talked about the harder sound which the grain emitted with its ripe ears in the stirring of the wind, he smiled smugly occupied at first by her shy tenderness for him, and then took the insecurity from her by teasingly saying that was enough beating about the bush, now she could go on for his sake, and perhaps he was not wrong in the feeling that the conversation was heading for little Lena.

Then everything came out quite hastily, everything her hidden gravity had amassed during the weeks — that it could not remain so with little Lena, since she must not grow up like a tree, and the two weeks of instruction must in any case not be the sole schooling she underwent.

"And as true as I am standing here next to you, dear Andreas", she concluded with a voice strained by constricted sobbing, "if she just grows up and knows nothing, absolutely nothing, nothing of anything, then she will reproach herself and us, and that rightly so."

Sintlinger stroked the heated brow of his wife reassuringly and led her, without answering, to the bench which ran along the back wall of the arbour.

There he sat silently next to her for quite a while, and she sensed that, sitting upright, he was looking into the night.

And while the blessed farmer thus remained silent, Johanna's deepest fear passed through her again, that the dislodgement of the governess sent by Professor Flöreck had postponed the path to the child becoming sighted, and the fear that little Lena must now remain trapped all her life long in the ghostly night of her eyes beset her with such an aching, passionately sudden blow that she hastily grasped her husband and shook him fiercely.

"Dear, Andreas, wake up, misfortune is starting to grow about our child", she cried at the same time.

The blessed farmer emerged from his rapt thoughts, took his wife's right hand in both his hands, and said with an astonished smile, "On, my dear Johanna, if you consider it quite properly, we are both being foolish; and the longer we deliberate, the worse it will be. You are searching for a light to ignite a glowing star, aren't you?"

Johanna answered softly, "I don't know."

"Or it is also so", Sintlinger continued his thinking aloud, "that you think a stream must overflow, dry up, in one word, decline, if you do not hang a mill wheel in it."

The poor farmwife became more and more despondent at this talk from her husband, and said timidly, "I don't understand you."

"Oh my dear wife, *I*, even *I* am like someone who at first *knocks* on the door behind which our child resides. But over the weeks, sometimes it has seemed to me rightly that the butcher escapes himself in that he is a butcher, and the king with his kingship, and the judge in that he has made the jurisdiction his trade. They all hide themselves away in their profession, from something which is the most important thing for everyone though, namely to be human!"

"My dear Andreas!" the farmwife now cried in shock and almost crying. "What does all that mean? I don't understand."

"Let it be, Johanna", he answered earnestly. I want to think it over and tell you when I have figured it out. But becoming someone, such as little Lena, is like a singing without moving the mouth, which all the world hears. Don't you think so too, Johanna?"

Only the farmer's wife stood up, dried away her tears furtively, and went away more aggrieved because of her husband's words than when she had come out.

The blessed farmer, however, restlessly traced the forces which threw a shimmer about the life of his child, a child who felt everything that entered her sphere as an unearthly happiness.

Only half a year later did he receive a surprising clue through a black hen. During the period when the beets were being split, Sintlinger had the hens caged behind the yard in a wire netting enclosure so that they would not run around in the fields and scrape up the small, delicate plants in their chase for cockchafer grubs and earthworms. That same thing also had to happen around the grain harvest. For the sitting hens then drove the young hens out into the fields. There they not only trod proper lanes deep into the plough strips, they also pulled down the ears, picked them for their little ones, and ran, scratching and raking proper pools in the best grain.

To make the escape from the fenced garden completely impossible now for the hens, the farmer had had the wire netting bent inwards at about a man's height. The efforts of the hens to get out were now entirely in vain. For if a desperate flight also only carried them as high as the fence, they there ran up against the inwardly bent netting, and fell down again.

A black, long-legged hen succeeded, however, after many unsuccessful attempts to fly over, by making a run-up from the middle.

When it had now filled its crop to bursting, it wanted to return again to the prison and its companions who were crouching puffed up in cosy balls in a corner next to each other, sometimes blinking with head aslant, and rattling their voices sleepily through their closed beaks whenever a bird flew over them. For its life, the black hen would like to be in the midst of the comfort of the others. Only the way in which it had succeeded that morning in flying over the fence had vanished from its memory. It ran up and down without stopping, constantly stuck its head through the mesh and propped its strong legs against its body to push it through. For it probably thought that if it could stroll in so easily to the others with its eyes, then the body must slide after it by itself.

It continued in this striving for hours, and was still running helplessly back and forth when it was already darkening and the people were returning from the fields. One or two of the maids and labourers probably saw the incessant running of the creature and laughed over the "stupid bird". But when the blessed farmer walked by as the last person, and perceived the hen and its futile attempts, he immediately left the path to put an end to the creature's torment.

Only, as he strode over, his gait became slower and slower, his cheerful face more serious, his eyes more thoughtful, and finally he stood quite still.

He forgot the supper, ignored the calling out to him, and had not yet stirred when it had already turned dark and the restive hen was still running to and fro like a shadowy wisp.

Finally Johanna came out to search for him, and found her husband in the midst of the beet field like someone whose spirit is lost in the world. He neither heard her approach, nor looked up at his name, yes, he barely sensed the way Johanna seized him with violence by the shoulders and turned him around.

And even then it took some effort to wrest him from the spell of complete detachment from the world. With a deep, almost anguished sounding sigh, as if he were shaking off a difficult dream, he came to himself and answered her question of what it was about, at first only with a gesture, grasping her hand with his right hand and caressing her forehead with his left, quite gently as if he were clearing away cobwebs. At last the words came to him, and he said in the quiet, almost timid way of the deeply enraptured, "See, Johanna, half a year ago you asked me what would become of our little Lena if she did not learn like normal people. At the time, I gave you an answer; but it was not yet the right one, because I myself did not know it. I had to let you cry and go away aggrieved, and yet could not help. But now that hen there taught me how it actually is around our child."

Johanna let her hand fall from her husband's right hand.

"Don't you want to hear it, wife, or perhaps another time?" Sintlinger asked.

"Oh, Andreas ... no, just speak ...", Johanna said with weary affection.

"So, little wife, note, people, you and I with them, are like that creature. It was gated in and wanted out. Between the place where it was and the wide field which it longed for, the wire netting was strung, transparent, but impenetrable. It allowed the creature to be there where it wanted to go but hindered it alike from achieving that. You see, the wire netting is like a person's senses, their eyes, their ears, touch, etc. They enable us from the garden of our own life to know about the lives of plants, animals, water, and the stars, and yet hinder us also from reaching them.

For the same arrangement whereby the senses are windows, also makes them into impenetrable walls. But behind our senses is the true world, what our fathers called the other side. Only those who can reach there may truly call themselves human. Such a man possesses more than all riches and all the knowledge from books, for he is with God. What else does he need here?

Our little Lena is there every day of her life. So what is there for her still to learn? With that she can only become less than she is."

After these words from the blessed farmer, his wife was seized by fear. She gave not a word in response, groped in the darkness across the furrows of the beet field where they had been standing to the edge of the path, sat down there, and gazed despondently with wide, dry eyes into the darkness.

Her heart shook, and she wrestled constantly with the cry, "God in heaven, blessed Lord, do not abandon my Andreas and my child."

Sintlinger had come to her, and was sitting by her side without saying a word, for he did not want to hinder his wife from entering the world which he had opened for her.

The gentle waving of the willows by the boundary path sounded in the darkness like invisible things walking in long vestments through the air. Now and then the distant forest rustled in dream. At the Brindeisener farmstead, a chain sometimes rattled from the stalls as if shackled creatures were walking up and down restlessly in their cells.

After a long time, Johanna rose soundlessly, and walked towards the yard. Sintlinger followed, as silently as her.

The Blessed Farm

It is surely possible that the blessed farmer's wife spoke to old Zenker about the events of this evening, and that the Querhoven farmworker made his sister privy to this secret.

After some time, the rumour sprang up in the circle which the Cantor Liborius Pfeiffer gathered around himself that the blessed farmer had spoken to the devil in the shape of a black hen.

Sintlinger, however, followed the path further into the stillness which had closed around him on this evening, for in his notes, we encounter the following passage:

> When we work and strive, enjoy ourselves and are distressed; in one word, when men live, they are perhaps also like the king in his castle who sees himself at the same time as a child playing before its locked door. And the king only knows himself through the child before the door of its house, and the child learns the meaning of its play only through the invisible eyes of the invisible king who watches its play.

BOOK THREE

The Blessed Farm

1

From the day on which Sintlinger had been led by the incident with the black hen inescapably into the other-sidedness of the life of his child and the world, the path of Johanna, his wife, quietly, imperceptibly uncoupled itself from the train in which the blessed farmer and Helene were heading into the unknown. Not that the farmwife set herself in open opposition against the essence of the two people most beloved by her — her simple, good-natured soul was not only incapable in the lustrous clouds of the earth of losing itself in infinite worlds like her husband and her child, but took the floating away of the two as an ordeal from God, and she bound herself firmer to the thousand duties of house-wifely activity so as to counteract the breakup which she anticipated, and to preserve a secure ground for the two to which they could save themselves at the bitter end from the unrealistically colourful throng. Hardly had her serious, unshrouded eyes even met those of Andreas with a reproachful question, hardly had she once again placed her hand admonishingly on his arm, than the thronging of all kinds of curious and wonder-addicted people to the blessed farm began anew even stronger, almost as strong as the time when the news of the in-comprehensible blindness of Helene had first excited the entire district. And, as in those weeks, next to many needless things, some honestly stricken hearts had been driven to the hill by the urge to help and to console, now many people also arrived at the Sintlinger's farmer's stronghold, people who, burdened by the hardships of the body or the soul, really saw an otherworldly light playing over the roof under which Helene resided. But precisely those who came through the gate of the blessed farm with "great burning eyes" or the visible passion for the frisson of a miracle healing were fended off in a gently way while it was signalled to them that here it was no more a place of pilgrimage than a doctor's residence. The servants made short shrift with such physically impaired people, the farmer's wife told them decisively to go away again, and even Sintlinger gently showed the way down the hill to all who presented themselves with a secret request that, perhaps, Helene might like to take the little bottle in hand which they had filled with their water, touch their diseased leg, or at least let the light of her wondrous eyes rest on them a while. For the farmer and his wife were united in that through such a throng their child must certainly be lost in an increasing vanity, if not something worse. But everyone to whom only a piece of bread, a small bowl of soup, or a pfennig for a meal was given did not knock in vain on the door of the blessed farmstead. So as to more easily ignore them, and to shut out those who had only been looking for the wondrous power of the blessed hill's girl, the space opposite the kitchen on the lower floor, and which had formerly served as Helene's classroom, was furnished as a dining area for the poor. There a long table was placed before a bench for all the vagrants and tramps who were drawn to the Sintlinger farmstead by hunger, hardship and surely also curiosity.

There it often occurred that two or three at once enjoyed the hospitality of the blessed farmer and, a safe roof over their heads, clean windows before their eyes, a solid meal in their stomachs, felt saved by the spirit of this strange farmstead, and began telling of their past lives.

It can also not be missed that Sintlinger himself listened to many of these confessions. But now it was done for a different reason than before when he had reached, for his own reassurance as father of a blind child, longingly after the hardship of others to seek comfort in their suffering. Now he was led entirely from his existential anguish, and sat in an elevated way, a brother of these earthly rejects, amongst the men who experienced their going off the rails, their wild delinquency, or their dull indebtedness in a deeper, more significant manner as soon as they could tell it to the blessed farmer, and often their life felt almost like a dignified affair of divine providence. Yes, many a one of these foundering men, when he was again sensible of his past as a disgrace in the darkness of the people down there's general contempt, saw after weeks and months the blessed farm in his memory like a bright miracle lying on its solitary hill, and endeavoured in vain to figure out in what way the precious and wondrous things had been gifted to him by Sintlinger, since the farmer had done nothing but listen.

In such a way, the reputation of Sintlinger and his child grew in ever widening circles, and that just through an arrangement which had dammed up this wondrous current.

The strange, often anguished sound of so many stranded, broken lives did not pass by the blessed farmer himself without trace. Not, as hostile mockers maintained, that he appeased a concealed voracity in listening to such wild debaucheries, and had to refresh in the alcoholic haze of drinkers his disgust of his old vices again and again so as to allow an innocuous appeasement of the addiction for intoxication and bluster which he had only arduously suppressed. Oh no! But these game hunters of good repute also stalked close, certainly without guessing it, to the basis of his being as it blossomed in the blessed farmer at that time. For in reality, as something new never comes into the life of men, instead only new forms emerge as much as may occur, Sintlinger's mind rambled during those long months in the regions through which his intoxication had once driven him.

It had probably also always seemed to him at the time that the whirling about him was outside the life between heaven and earth, and now, as he looked from the soulful stillness in which he lived with Helene to the incomprehensible existence of these lost men, it sometimes seemed to him as if he were seeing in their lapses his own helpless attempts of that time, not only to escape all the swirling of madness, but to thereby get at the same time over the general dullness and into the life of extraordinary beauty and power. Barely one of these men who perhaps bleated like a goat had been born as a goat. There had been in each of these derailed lives a time when they had passionately wrestled like only the sainted can for the highest transfiguration of existence, and if the blessed farmer saw it correctly, he had been preserved from that hopeless foundering only by his inherited wealth. For where would he have landed if to the fever of his passions suddenly one day hardship, hunger, and contempt had been added; and, in contrast, what sounds, what light would many of these tramps have finally risen to if the meanest hardship had not completely smashed them into the midst of suffering!

Poverty must be controlled, and the struggle of the possessionless to get by must be relieved, the blessed farmer said to himself when, shaken by the fate of such a vagrant, he stood up, and walked pondering out of the room for the poor and around the yard. And he said it so often that he not only began to believe it, but began to act on it with the energy peculiar to him. Certainly he did not run, as is the way of most bringers of happiness to the folk, with his Jew's harp before him, and on paths which would still have to be built first. He worked at first thoughtfully into an area which was actually repugnant to his innermost being, which he himself must have sensed, for in his notes from time to time could be found a series of observations about the aid to oppressed people, of which the most remarkable read:

> The man who combines aid with disrespect is like the man who slams the bread in the starving man's mouth with his fist so that his teeth wiggle.

But he did not content himself with this mere intellectual exercise. Sintlinger began at the time a restive rambling through all the places of the surrounding district, naturally without betraying any of his intentions. Soon he was sitting in the field margins with a poor little farmer at Hiesfeld, and discussed with him the best way in which the small farmers, the smallholders, and the crofters could be helped without strengthening the power of the magnates and directing the main profit into the pockets of the large property owners. Then he appeared in Dinslaken and Walsum among the carters. He also sojourned often in Holthausen and Vörde, began to renew old acquaintances, even if not in the same way, took an interest where it was not expected, showed friendliness without deviousness, and offered assurance, even if no open-mindedness was returned.

Most of all, his proximate neighbourhood, Brederode and Hemsterhus, certainly occupied him, but above all Querhoven. His sympathy for the poor devils of this forest village was aroused most actively of all, and from calculations and dispositions which were found in his papers afterwards, it can be seen that he was seriously engaged with pursuing the supply of electricity to that area, above all to help the squalid life of the many spigot turners and skewer makers of this secret nest of heretics by the installation of small motors, and thereby pointing the way for them to do more profitable work. The fine nose which is peculiar to the oppressed as soon as they feel the work of a helping power around them soon foreshadowed the blessed farmer's intentions to the Querhoveners before anyone else. Whereas the others saw in his busyness only a new quirk of the wondrous man, they obtained from his multifarious inquiries about their production and living conditions the right to definite expectations, and because this waving into a beautiful future came from him, the man who had given their religious fervour new stimulus through his miraculous child, their otherworldly and worldly hopes ran together into a current so that they considered the boldest things for possible and the most improbable for natural. Not long, and everywhere the rumour spread that Prince Arenberg wanted to settle carvers from Thuringia so as to bring about a better use of the wood from the forests; the installation of a cablecar was disputed like an affair of the next day; in farming circles, the rumour arose of the foundation of a buying cooperative and of the communal production of agricultural machinery.

The mockers, however, of which there were in this district more than anywhere else, quickly appended funny little tails to these projects sailing in the clouds, and spread the news that it was understood cows would be milked with machines, and that in a while artificial legs would be purchased for the servants so as to be able to control the tempo of their industry at will.

But the folk likes to divest of the serious all of its greatest expectations, probably to safeguard themselves in advance from the painful reverses of disappointment. Enough that a colourful, fuzzy whirl foamed about the beautiful approaches of Sintlinger to be a friend of the people, even before any of his ideas had assumed firm shape. This ridiculous bustle did not particularly disturb the blessed farmer — he wrote in his pages the sentence, "Anyone who has not sat on a horse in his dreams before shall certainly fall under the hooves with his first ride awake" — and, next to his daily work, he indulged himself steadfastly and bravely in the thought of how people, especially the poor, could be helped. It then followed by itself that from the thoughts of the alteration and upgrading of the Querhoveners' gainful employment, considerations arose over a direct and better connection of the entire district with the next place on the Rhine. This project also offered itself too easily and insistently for the simple reason that, for as far back as Sintlinger could actually remember, all the men of the district had never once let come to rest the thought of creating a shorter connection with the nearby current. Now the blessed farmer planned first to pursue energetically the building of this road, to keep all his other plans though in the background, and to offer their realisation as it were only as a necessary consequence of the changes which must be initiated by themselves through the achievement of that aim. While he was approaching ever closer to this thought, he realised that it would be good if possible to use old paths in the establishment of a new connection, so as to save costs and reconcile folk more quickly with the new road. Now two connections to the Rhine already existed — the main road through Brederode, and the boundary path which led past the estranged farmsteads and then lead into the forest road. The blessed farmer felt surely that the general public would certainly be more in favour initially of the branching off of the Brederode main road, although an entire series of considerations spoke against it, and he himself, if even more by nature, felt a proper dislike for these plans. But he planned nevertheless to suggest this path himself, and to discern subsequently as many difficulties and adverse things about it so that the choice would fall by itself to the forest path. For farmers put themselves out for nothing except a plan which they can bring about differently out of pure obstructiveness to what others wish.

Thus Sintlinger then ran up and down the old, potholed forest road, either early before the traffic stepped up, or towards evening after the finish of the day's work. For there were two places which could endanger the realisation of the project — the curve which was necessary to lift the new road to the level of the forest road in avoidance of the current excessive gradient, and the steep descent deep in the forest on the Silber slope, at that place where you could see across low, scraggly spruce stands to the calm, dark mirror of the beech pond. In both places, the necessary curve had to be placed for the most part on the Brindeisener property. And when Sintlinger stood under the high butte on his property at that point on the boundary path from where the new main road would have to cut in an arc through one of Brindeisener's most beautiful acres in order to be led at a moderate gradient by the edge of the Sintlinger forest across the Faber meadow to the forest road, he admitted that this line would provoke the fury of his mistrustful neighbour straightaway. For it could be easily attributed by the dismal farmer to intentional, malicious damage. But exactly the prospect of such obstacles enticed the blessed farmer deeper and deeper into the firm intent of pursuing with all means this and only this plan.

Just one thing was odd, that his considerations hurrying ahead, when they had overcome and settled wave after wave of opposing combinations, fell into an empty, lightless setting which indeed lay quite far ahead, but for that reason it was afflicted all the more because those considerations all resided nearest those matters of our soul which lie a long way off from our life and are as delicate and unreal as if they stood in the light of stars which were unreachable to our eyes. The blessed farmer, after he had trailed off in thought a few times in this way, imposed the belief on himself that if the plan led him thus beyond life, people at whom it was aimed would not be able to linger either in the old, narrow existence as soon as they settled into the enjoyment of the realisation of his endeavours.

But it was strange that this comforting explanation did not satisfy him either, and that, to escape a deep inward divisiveness, he finally brushed aside all the brooding and burrowing, and, when it was in the morning, watched the mist as it climbed up from the forest path into a thousand wonderful shapes in the early light in the treetops, or, in the evening wolfing down such intractable knots, listened to the dreamily soft wingbeats with which the forest readied itself for sleep. That then always went on for a good while entirely as wished until some unforeseen incident startled him — the shrill, whinnying laughter of the woodpecker, the starting of a roe deer, or even just the laborious coming to perch of a large bird. All such incidents acted on Sintlinger in this frame of mind as if someone were physically touching him, and speaking a warning, 'be on your guard!' or 'watch out!' And always when such unexpected incidents abruptly tore him from his rapture, he looked around, or remained standing and looked with concern into the depths of the forest as if somebody were sitting there with plans for him. Yes, sometimes it seemed to him as if a face emerged out of the darkness, whose features he could not recognise, not even its outline, he just felt a constant, large gaze directed at him from out of the darkness. And every time it happened, he caught himself either falling into deliberations as if he had just received profound advice, or nodding his head encouragingly as he strode on.

One evening when he had once again been eyeballed by the unimaginable face — and in striding on drifted into a rapt contemplation of what it could be that always emerged before him in such mysterious ways, he came on the road to one of the deeply rutted spots. He came unawares upon a pothole so that he had to violently pull himself back to avoid falling into it, and as is the way of all men who stumble or founder, after he had escaped the small mishap, he looked around to see if anyone had noticed his clumsiness. The evening was still young, all the colours were barely thriving as they lost their lustre, and the blue of the sky had the fadedness and weariness of overworked eyes. The shadows of the forest were smouldering as a grey breath across the road whose indistinct parts went downhill just then and seemed to break off into vagueness in the distance, rising half into the treetops. Three to four hundred metres in front of him, an unusually tall man was striding, clothed simply like a pedlar with very short trousers which hardly reached to his ankles, and with a long, solemn gait. In his left hand he carried a bundle which he sometimes threw over the one shoulder, sometimes over the other, so as to afterwards carry it again for a long time in his left hand. And every time, before he swung his bundle to a different place, an unease came over the dignity of his gait, a sort of grotesque spring or just a change of step which Sintlinger could not exactly see, and when he then decided to pay close attention, the stranger suddenly stood still, looked into the forest, deliberating, and then just as the twitch again passed through his body, he sprang with a convulsive leap over the ditch,

and vanished into the thicket as if it were not happening
entirely according to his will, but as if he were torn by a
spasm into the darkness.

The blessed farmer smiled gently at this comical behaviour of the unfamiliar man, but soon thought again
of the mysterious divisiveness of his inner being and
this still inexplicable gaze of an unimaginable face. Perhaps it is the countenance of the master in me, and I
have already come quite close to the gate from the world
to the other side, which is why I see what my senses are
unable to grasp, the blessed farmer thought.

And not long after, his senses were again situated in
the shimmering grinding step of otherworldly considerations. Then he came out of his forest, and saw behind
the hump of the high butte the enormous, greyed with
age quadrangle of his farmstead looming up, immersed
in the blind shimmer of the almost sunken sun.

He strode down the slope of the forest road as far as
the place where it changed into the boundary way and
where his farm road branched off as well. Before he
turned into his fields, however, he took a look at the
edge of the forest across the Faber meadow. There he
caught sight of the same stranger who had skipped so
convulsively into the forest. He was moving about stiff-
leggedly in the high grass of the meadow, peering peculiarly into the green as if he had tubes before his eyes,
groping now and then carefully amongst the blades, and
looking for a long time at what he had found. Sintlinger
could not see if it was a mushroom, a flower, or a beetle.
For that reason, he walked leisurely down a bit, placed
himself by the edge of the ditch, and peered across.
There he soon realised that the stranger, a deeply
greyed man incidentally, was collecting flowers, probably for tea, and though he had abstained from picking
the red meadow flowers which were called redheads by
the country people of that district, because of their

tuberose raised receptacles. The man was completely devoted to his activity which he pursued in an unusual way. For he did not find every flower worthy of collecting; but as soon as he had discovered one agreeable to him, he lifted it close to his eyes, then held it up towards the sky, and it seemed to Sintlinger as if he then spoke each time to something in the air, as if he were talking it over as people say. The blessed farmer sprang across the ditch, and approached the strange man who sent now and then a disapproving, screening look at the farmer strolling over, apart from which, however, he continued undisturbed in his wondrous work. Suddenly, when Sintlinger was still perhaps three or four steps from him, he made an air to flee into the forest, but pulled himself together, walked directly towards the blessed farmer, planted himself in menacing anxiety before him, and observed him in a sort of idiotic concern for a long time without saying a word.

"What are you looking for here?" Sintlinger finally asked and looked up at the tall old man, from the large feet stuck in cutoff tall boots, over the ten times patched trousers, the vest which was held together with only the top and bottom buttons, to his grey stubbled face which, fashioned from little sacks and deep wrinkles, had the effect of something which looked like a deep and passionate, though pointless ruination. His large grey eyes still shone, even if like the forgotten light in a lonely house, though calmly, coolly, full of a penetrating, if also impersonal power.

"Where are you from?" Sintlinger asked again, because he had received no answer to the first question.

The questioned man pressed his lips still firmer together, continued holding the flower which he had plucked motionless in his hand, then looked up high, shook his head, and let it fall disappointedly.

The Blessed Farm

"You — sir — man —", he then said with a quiet voice, observed the blessed farmer still more sharply, and then burst out into an almost soundless laughter. Thereupon he turned around, swung his sack of flowers onto his shoulder, and set off, without saying anything else, towards the forest.

Sintlinger was certain that he was dealing at a minimum with someone of confused mind, and followed the poor man with his gaze.

But the man turned back unexpectedly, and after he had again planted himself with the same menacing anxiety, he began, "You — sir — man — I know already. What were you seeking in my meadow? Trampling the grass and tearing up the flowers! — If I know everything, nobody needs to speak first, for I have eyes and ears. Thank God, and God thanks me. For what use to God is being God when there are no proper men. Hey. Is that right: sir — man — you?" And again the almost soundless, mocking laughter followed.

Then Sintlinger noticed that the man had a very high forehead, and an almost sawed-in mouth, and was taken aback by it in an incomprehensible way.

"Is this your first time in this meadow?" he asked.

The stranger examined him with his penetrating, impersonal eyes, took his chin in his hand, deliberating, but in the end shook his head dismissively, and then continued talking as if nobody had interrupted him.

"Yes, by the forest the flowers are especially calmer, stiller, I mean, in their soul. For they don't have a need to try to shoot up high, because they always have the trees nearby. And I need just that, for she is lying in a screaming fever, has a temperature like a steam boiler. Oh, she is young, young and stupid, and she would like the man who almost spits on her. Do you know the farmer Kinast in Schmalenbach? No? Then good. You see, for that reason I am taking the flowers from the forest here, in the evening, from the shadows, from a wind-still meadow. It will come over her like a mild, gentle hand.

But the flowers from the sunlit meadows out there, they are almost purely mad from the quest for high air and hence flower as wildly as when men scream something in passion. Ha, and if I take the tea from there, it will break the poor, young, stupid thing completely, for that she is.

I am here for that reason, do you understand me? Sir — you — man! Hahahaha."

"What is your name then actually?" the blessed farmer asked when the soundless mocking laughter had faded away.

The madman shook his head and said, "That is of no matter. Or do you — man — sir think, if you say his name, you then know who he is? — Good night!"

Laughing and in great leaps, the flower collector then vanished into the forest.

While Sintlinger was then walking home, the evening already darkening deeper, and he thought about the experience he had just had, all the comical, grotesque oddities of this man vanished, yes even the unattractiveness of his soft voice and the bleating of his laugh, and he felt the painful, hidden beauty of this remarkable stranger, and now, as he recalled his words, "For what use to God is being God when there are no proper men?", he even heard him speaking next to him, but now with a deep, melodious bass, and he saw distinctly his face before him in the darkness, and noticed even how he passed his hand over his chin, and that done in a gesture as if an extensive full beard had been there previously.

And when the blessed farmer saw this, it immediately connected with the thoughts of his unconscious question as to whether the stranger was in the meadow for the first time, and like a lightning bolt, it tore through him that finally this mad collector of flowers had been the rebel Faber, who, foundered in his life, quickly made a mistake, and driven by a confused spirit was led back as a distorted shadow of his former being to the roads of his past. And as he put together these combinations which sailed over all the mountains, he had to also smile over his thoughts, though he could not hinder the deep bass from speaking constantly around him in a calm, collected rhythm just like the wind whispers whether I hear it or not.

Yes, the melody of this sonorous, confident voice was still around him, even when he had already started walking again. The beat of its sound gradually even adjusted to the rhythm of his step. And suddenly it said quite distinctly, "You are in the black mill ..."

And then it continued talking in the same way, "The thinking without consciousness experiences the motions of the universe, and the feeling which does not know itself, the perceptions of God."

Thus it spoke exactly to the sound, words which the Faber rebel had spoken to him two years before on that night in the meadow, and which had also been lost to Sintlinger because he had not understood them except in their approximate sense.

The blessed farmer strode as with avidly listening legs, and when the talk about him broke off, he emerged as if from a whirl, and thought the incident could not be explained unless the stranger really had been the quickly decayed rebel Faber.

When he arrived home, he went into his study, and looked for the page on which the meditations were with which he had refuted Faber's words at the time. It was the contemplation of the tolling. It now appeared to him to be insignificant, false, unreal, contrived. Such an agitation seized him that he crumpled the paper in his hand into a ball, and threw it in the corner.

After coming down, he found the large living room already dark, the entire farmstead deathly still. Only the rustling of the trees waved muffled about the house, and outside, out in the distance, he sensed the inaudible clamour with which the stars moved through the blue endlessness.

Perhaps, the blessed farmer pondered, Faber is right, and I am going astray with my helping my fellow men, just as he has gone to the dogs by worrying about people who knew nothing and wanted to know nothing about him.

Then he stepped into the bedroom, and remarkably found Helene still awake, quiet, with wide eyes, lying in bed. Johanna was already fast asleep.

The blessed farmer bent over his child, and after he had kissed her, he said, "Little Lena, are you still awake?"

"Yes, daddy, I'm still awake", the blind girl answered.

"Can you also still see quite well?"

Helene waited a little and then said, "Yes."

"Well", the blessed farmer said, "look now at the forest meadow behind the high butte."

"What shall I see there, daddy?"

"Do you not see anyone there?"

"No, just flowers and forest."

"Good night, little Lena", the blessed farmer said.

The next day, Sintlinger accidentally learnt some more details about the person of the flower collector whom he had encountered. From time to time, namely, the former attorney Knöttner presented himself at the Blessed Farm and, as in the days of his courtly dignity, still journeyed through the world with the blue folder under his arm, on legs constantly placed meaningfully, as if everywhere he were heading straight for the broad open steps of a town hall. And yet he had been for perhaps fifteen years spooling in a score of villages the thread of enmities, nursing suspicions, and searching everywhere for unfavourable stories so as to increase the confusion with his legal help.

From this almost all-knowing malicious man, the blessed farmer learnt that the strange flower collector had been Tea-Jörg, whose real name was Georg Hunatay from Schmalenbach, formerly a rich, unusually clever, farmer's son whose head had even found its way deep into Latin. His only failing, a too delicate, timid disposition, a heart sensitive as an egg without its shell, had been his misfortune. It always heads that way in this world unfortunately. For when he fell in love after a long time trembling and selectively, and that just like a lamb in the moonlight, his little fiancee had been made properly drunk and finally unfaithful by a bold daredevil. Before she could awake from her stupefaction, she was already the wife of this wasteful madman, a true farming rogue. Jörg became so gaunt that the clothes almost fell from his body, and his eyes crept as deeply into his head as if they wanted to be buried there. And yet the couple torn apart did not stop loving each other in the old distant way. Then, when the misery of the unfaithful woman had become more and more apparent through her husband's squandering, the betrayed Jörg even moved as a labourer to the farm of his rival so as to preserve the farm from complete ruin, and the farmer's wife from her husband's mistreatment. He served thus for probably twenty years, filled by a hope about which he had spoken to nobody, not even with his eyes. The sudden shameful death of the farmer finally led him from this dark corner and brought a timid shimmer into his life, for now the way was free to his old hopes. But hardly had he taken the first steps to his beloved than the aged farmwife was again snatched from him by an ardent whirl. This time she was caught right in the net of her youngest labourer. With that poor Jörg's head was as if nailed forever with a hammer blow to the night of a ghostly pensiveness detached from the world.

He vanished into the little room at his father's house as if he were withdrawing with living body into his coffin, and brooded from then on over books which he let nobody see.

Only from time to time, he fell into the restiveness of a months long roaming about, but which was not a nuisance to anyone. Then he collected tea in a mysterious way, and strangely, always for people who were at the time still healthy and freshly walking around. Whether it was true, he did not know, but people maintained that everyone at whom Tea-Jörg aimed his witchlike efforts at healing died a short time after, and it thereby provoked a horror every time he left his room for a new wander, because then nobody knew for certain whether it did not mean this time *their* death.

This was the tale told by the attorney Knöttner, and when he had left with a gift, the blessed farmer sat for a long time sunken in deep thought and looked from time to time attentively at the spot where the narrator had sat. Then he went into his study, and searched for the crumpled, discarded meditation. He found the ball of paper still lying in the same corner where he had tossed it on the evening of the previous day, picked it up, smoothed the paper out carefully, and wrote after some consideration the following sentence:

> For a man who is on the correct path, mistakes also have their deep sense. There are familiar things which pass one by with strange faces.

After this occurrence, the plans for bringing happiness to the folk faded away completely from the blessed farmer's life.

2

Thus the Sintlinger hill grew like a mountain up into the air, receiving from the twenty or thirty villages the foreboding of a mysterious light on the world, a light which burns in men, gleaming from the one gloriously, remaining hidden in the other behind filth and rubble, a light which all the same nobody does without.

And while the Blessed Farm blossomed ever higher into this shimmer, the Brindeisener farmstead was led deeper and deeper into an arid darkness. The old farmer sank entirely into the bitter, menacing taciturnity, the inheritance of his breed, and he often sat there like a pile of forgotten wood standing deep in the forest, rotted by damp, brittle, covered in lichen, with loosened bark. And when he saw the incomprehensible life on the Blessed Farm going in and out, he laughed abruptly in delighted contempt, full of a marinating feeling of pleasure, for this pilgrimage of drifters back and forth, this crying of mad women about the walls, this extravagant simpering about the girl who had been given nothing more by God than blind eyes and a face as white as a cabbage butterfly, truly, it was a particular delight for old Brindeisener, this quite colourful, extraordinary haze which stood all about the Sintlinger farm like the air of a madhouse. Now, when someone reigned up there who sometimes really talked as if mad, who had only raised one child, pale and blind, a half corpse, now was probably the time that this raucous weed of the Sintlinger clan was to die out. And it had the appearance that the old farmer would still live to see the collapse which his family had secretly wished for since time immemorial. Thus the inherited swarm of shadows swelled in this sombre farmer with an almost missing

soul, and gave his old age the power to live past the
soundless dissolution of his own house, seemingly
without a deeper agitation than the accustomed bitterness of his everyday life. The farmstead was rotten in
every beam, the roofs caving in here and there, the
equipment rattly and outdated, the industriousness dull
and worn out in joylessness. The servants carried out
the work unhappily and irritably, the farmer's wife bore
her approaching old age gruffly, and the oldest son,
Jakob, already heading for forty, made no arrangements
to marry and thus bring the life of the farm onto a
brighter course again. He shunned with a mocking
smile every girl, let no dance or skip come near him,
avoided all sociability, even that of work, and only now
and then did he rest with a maid whom he unexpectedly
ambushed in the darkness of the loft, or drank alone
and malevolently in the forest until he started a discord-
ant singing which then sounded as if the wind had
caught itself in an empty wooden tub, monotonous,
dull, tuneless.

Only little Peter floated about this withering place,
like a belated butterfly tumbling in the cool, chalky sun
of autumn. In the imperceptible foundering around
him, he only ever experienced the magic of his childhood.

Nobody thus sensed at the Brindeisener farmstead
that the rot had nestled into every corner of the rambling property, which for the time being certainly
resembled more a carelessly tended affluence, tended by
surly old people, becoming insignificant, yes, even
bleak.

A single person amongst them all felt the descent,
felt how the air of quiet goodness and gentle love hid itself away ever deeper in the Brindeisener earth. That
was the daughter Amalie, behind whom, since the illness in the month of Sintlinger's wedding, a dwindling

walked, at first distant, then nearer and nearer. And every jolt which pulled life at the farmstead deeper into the shadows squeezed off a piece of the pale girl's existence, so that she finally had to wrench for her breaths as if they were stuck in a deep well.

One day now, she was sitting with her mother at the table in the large living room, and stripping feathers. It was late autumn, a morning whose mist lay heavy and still silvery from the night's frost on the ground, and only rose with a few soft strips of cloud towards the sun beaming down from white veils, also invisible. Amalie sat before her little pile of feathers, which quivered constantly from the short, demanding breath of her illness, and, whenever she had stripped three feathers, looked out the window for a glance through the tree nursery to the fields.

There Jakob was driving a team with the plough across the potato field. The old man was standing lurking on the edge of the field, goading on, and labourers and maids were bending down busily in the field with small baskets in their hands. You could not see what they were doing. They were all stuck to their knees in the silvery mist, and you would think they were not on the ground, but ploughing the clouds, scraping in them, picking flakes, and collecting them in baskets, just like you could probably imagine the dead flying over up high in the clouds. Amalie saw all this still deepened by a fear of living which she did not believe herself, and in a frailness which made everything still more blessed and rapturous. But her mother had finally had enough of "this stupid fuss", admonished the girl to rather stick to her work, and imperceptibly skimmed with a glance the emaciated face of the invalid, in which a gleam was working like a reflection of the white misty light.

Then the consumptive cried desperately, "Open the window!" But before that could happen, it threw her backwards across the back of the chair, her right hand clutching in the feathers, and from her blue mouth a pitiful thread of blood dribbled and slowly flowed down her gaunt neck.

After a short paralysis, brusque wrenching, and loud calls to stop "fooling around", the old farmwife realised that her daughter was dead, took her feather-light body from the chair, pushed the door to the adjoining room open with her foot, and laid her there on the bed. Then she returned to the living room, knelt before the cooking stove, and hooked ashes through the grate. At the same time, her tears ran silently and slowly from her eyes. She paid them no attention, but prepared precisely and steadily the firing for the midday meal. When she was finished with that, she stepped into the yard, called the parlour maid, and sent her to her husband with the news that "just then Amalie's light had gone out".

Death, who had lived for a long time with the girl in the company of everyone at the Brindeisener farmstead, and had dwelt hidden, at first small, then larger and larger in her, had now stepped out of her. He had unlatched the door, and walked diagonally across the yard and down the hill to somewhere else in the world where a heart was longing for him without knowing it. All the stones on which he trod still rang from his mysterious steps, the air was filled by the shadows of his eyes, and the leaves on the trees in the garden trembled from his breath gliding past.

When little Peter came out of school, this shimmer of death was still present in all the corners of the farm, on the entire hill to the meadows of the boundary path, and out across into the world, and the boy, taken aback when he received the news of his sister's expiration, let his knapsack fall in the yard under the windows of the living room, and noticed that everything around had suddenly become different. He went to the dead girl, and looked at her, so as to detect in her appearance how she had induced the transformation, and what sort of state being dead was. But her face had the expression of blessed peacefulness, and there was also nothing else remarkable about her, only perhaps that her lips were blue, and a breath of this colour also lay on the lids of her eyes. Peter thought how strange it must be if when nibbling blueberries, in addition to his mouth, the skin around his eyes were to turn blue. But as if he had hurt his sister with this idea, he stole away, even before any-one at the farm could notice anything, back across the fields, up the Querhoven slope, and walked and walked until he suddenly heard the Hornwasser rustling below him behind the Sweeps in the forest. There he sat down by the banks of the stream and, after he had watched the gliding past of the little ripples for a long time, he threw leaves, stalks of grass, and pieces of wood in the water, and noticed how everything was carried past. In the end, he threw a small stone into a stiller depth. It disappeared into the water without appearing again, but then from the bottom mysterious circles swelled up and ran across the water as if an invisible being were breath-ing from the bottom towards the mirrored surface, and the boy was seized in his chest as if by a painful stabbing, and it seemed to him that he had now seen what death was.

He left the banks of the forest stream in flight, and when he saw the paternal farmstead from the Quer-hoven heights, he broke out into wailing tears.

At home, he met his mother and father already in the first preparations for the burial of the dead girl, and helped in a childish way, constantly dazed by a distant whirl so that he now and then threw away what he held in his hands, and ran out in front of the gate to see whether Hemsterhus, the mountains, and the paths still stood in the accustomed places or were gliding away in this grey undulating which he felt around himself.

Brindeisener and his wife walked around even more sombrely and reserved. They behaved no differently, especially the estate owner, than as if Amalie, by this miserable death, this long inglorious end after an illness proper to poor people, had brought indelible disgrace on the family. What sort of faces the bearers would make with the light coffin, for this pitiful, emaciated corpse which was surely suitable for a tailor's house, but not for the Brindeisener farmstead. The farmer sent such and similar thoughts after his daughter's shadow, and even brought it as far as reckoning this pitiful death of Amalie's to be a malevolence, derisive thanks for all the inconveniences which he had had with her.

The days up to the funeral passed by in such a perverse gloom, and nothing changed then either, although the burial took place in all the solemnity which befitted the Brindeisener's position as an estate owner. Almost constant tolling of bells clanged to no avail; to no avail did Liborius Pfeiffer let the famous hymn "Eternal Grace", with its call and response between the soprano and alto voices, waft across the churchyard during the lowering of the coffin; the bass tuba boomed, and the Pastor did his best with the funeral sermon. Anton Brindeisener, however, was looking with knitted brows and downcast eyes only at his folded hands, because he believed the funeral cortege was hiding behind the mask of sorrow nothing but mockery and schadenfreude.

Even on the way home from the funeral, he remained bitterly wrapped up in himself, and barely brought himself to nod at the word of comfort and regret of the few who had accompanied him to the farmstead to be hosted there by him. "I know you already, you little friends", he thought behind those asseverations of sympathy, and he spat furiously. Then he again abruptly swung his giant legs into a gait as if he wanted to run away. At the boundary path, there where you turned off to his farmstead, he was beset by wondering whether Sintlinger and his wife would perhaps also come along to his house. Already across the little bridge, having hurried ahead of the others, he turned around, and saw the blessed farmer just then in conversation with two others turning into his own driveway. "It's okay, neighbour!" he called to him with a mordant laugh. "Keep coming, keep coming!" and he concluded to himself stomping onward in an attack of senseless hostility, "I will beat your hemp for you!"

It was only a small little crowd who found themselves together at the farmstead — the brother-in-law Kirchner from Dinslaken, brother of the wife, a scrawny, outwardly humble, dignified farmer who talked more by gestures and the restiveness of his large, brown eyes than his mouth. The son of Brindeisener's brother, from the poor, other side of the family, mercurial, round, brisk in all his thoughts and movements and filled by a cheerful, devious irony. The blond bearded wood dealer Riedel from Dingden with a damaged left eye, which lent his good-natured face almost some of the affect of a wild baring of teeth. The sawmiller Wiehr from alongside the Hornwasser, a long-bearded sentimental drinker who agreed to everyone and left nothing at all for himself. Then there were also a few farmers from Brederode and Hemsterhus, childhood friends of Brindeisener, who had through life been long estranged from him, and almost all were already leaning out the gable end of their lives, grey headed, half or entirely supplanted by their grown sons. They were joined together through their love for their own youth with the surly hill farmer, and called this intertwining friendship.

To these men, a quite respectable swarm of women were coupled, mostly their wives, only a few isolated strands, widows or old spinsters. Young girls were entirely absent, because Amalie, cast out and shy, was probably filled by a burning desire for devotion, but had gone through life friendless. The party sat at the long table of a large room on the upper storey, actually more a hall, low, oppressed by the beamed ceiling, restive through the windows on all sides, and yet half shaded in by the wide overhanging roof.

The men occupied the upper half of the long table, the end towards the gable; the woman sat towards the door. A clammy air hung over the entire party, that of the disability and awkwardness of solitary men and un-accustomed ceremony, the awe of lyricism and the secret urge towards obligatory expression of permissible sentiments. The customary, quite brief meal actually weighed everyone down more than the girl's death.

Like a murder of crows throws itself from field to field in untoward, clattering flight, the conversation rose, fell silent with each new disappointment through a half missed dish, and then overran with all the greater noise a thing which was actually terribly incidental to everyone. They ate with cautious forks, attentively directed knives, and balanced half-filled spoons back and forth economically. The woman sat there with screwed up noses, the men often broke out from nowhere into mocking laughter.

Brindeisener's eyes smouldered just so from hidden fury. His challenging appetite for food looked almost like gorging.

He sat obliquely opposite Sintlinger, and when, heated by the work of chewing and concealed irritation, and red in his furrowed brow, he straightened up and pulled down his vest with an unhurried snuffle, his look encountered the delicate, steely-mild blessed farmer, who was leaning back in his chair, strange and benign, and had soon become with all the restraint the natural centre of the men. Then Brindeisener plunged each time all the more wildly like an annihilating force on the meat bowl, or rampaged in the cabbage, and the growling during his eating, which was meant to have sounded like contentment, was nothing but spiteful snatches, "pompous dog ... prattling stallion ..." and other things. Old Brindeisener was secretly seasoning his mealtime with such exclamations coined for Sintlinger.

But still, after the concluded meal, the party joined together more easily. The women exchanged the delights and disappointments of house and work, of children and servants. One rippled through the shallows of gossip, another stirred entirely in the sorrow of her marriage, though they all yielded to the nature of their gender to see the fates of life as divine providence and to refuse responsibility by attributing events to the twilight of miraculous forces. Old Mrs Brindeisener told again and ever again anew about Amalie's foreboding of death on the morning of her passing away, and that everything had been as eerie outside as in a churchyard. Thus nothing, absolutely nothing would have helped just then, and if "a doctor from Münster had quickly been in the room", "he" would still have managed it and squeezed off the heart of the girl in her chair. By that she meant death. Truly, Amalie had all along been like a picture hung on a thin cord between heaven and earth. And she always complained in the end about the fate that so much money, sorrow and worries should be thrown over the hill like ashes to all the winds. Then her eyes overflowed, and she had to come to the help of her nose which was creating a noise as if the drips from an overfilled bottle were smacking down.

Always when this hissing on the part of the women sounded, old Brindeisener started from his drowsy listening, could not suppress a contemptuous twitch in his face, and placed his balled right hand like a colossal pendulum before himself on the table.

Jakob jogged in occasionally to ply the men with drink.

Peter appeared now and then in the doorway, looked at the party with clever, astonished eyes, and vanished when he had counted up everyone, as if someone were missing whom he must hasten at a quick run to meet before the yard gate. Then he placed himself every time on the little apron roof of the flowing spring to the right of the driveway, and behaved with his glances as if someone could still come on any of the many paths which were to be seen.

In truth, however, he was concealing therewith only a dreamily burning other expectation. For when the boy had run down with his eyes ten incidental paths, roads, and field margins in the surrounding area, his glance fell on the drive to the Sintlinger farmstead, trotted up it, and then trembled before the closed gate of the blessed farmstead for a long time until a magical light began playing under the lime tree, such a blossoming right into his soul that he had to begin turning in a dance on the little roof. With it, he sang ardently the meadow song of the shepherds, a melancholy, short verse, and for as long as the entire world circled around him like a ringing merry-go-round.

After that, the boy was driven again and again up to the door of the gathering. He counted the people up with a tense look, but what he yearned for was not there, so he leant for a while on the door, disappointed, and then plunged again in great leaps to his game of en-ticement before the yard gate.

Meanwhile the men were also strolling in leisurely chatter through various regions of their farming lives. The outlook for the winter sowing after the plague of mice during the dry summer was spoken of, and the modest yield of the beet harvest was lamented.

Brindeisener still absented himself from all that, sometimes brushed his hand over his long, gauntly wrinkled face, gave a nod to himself over *this* opinion, shook off *that one* with a vigorous gesture, and was thus also here in his own house what he was known for being outside — a tall, dry, meadow tree leaning sunken in the corner.

Abruptly, seemingly coming out of his empty brooding, he suddenly placed his head listening on his hand, and asked Sintlinger across the table how it was actually going with his road building. He asked it as though he were seizing the blessed farmer rapaciously around the throat. The others immediately ceased their conversations, and listened to the two. Sintlinger sensed very well the derision in his neighbour's words, but because he had abandoned the welfare work, and thus did not himself stand on his own side anymore, he could with a smile give old Anton a mischievous answer which mocked both himself and the questioner ingratiatingly. But the old bag of sorrow of a hill farmer had not intended merely to push the conversation in a cheerful way onto a new track, it was for him about pouring a decent bucket of bitterness abruptly over Sintlinger's head. That is why he did not stop finding fault with those "scatterbrained plans", and because the blessed farmer amiably reassured him that it was surely not yet the time for building the road, and if the matter were ripe, it would fix itself one fine day, because Brindeisener felt thus more and more inferior through Sintlinger's self-effacement, he passed over into teasing the blessed farmer directly as a pure "maker of smoke" and "fabulist". Now he, old Brindeisener, would get his teeth into the matter, for with "mere running around forest roads" you surely send the skewer makers of Querhoven mad in the head, but a clear, worldly sophisticated man like he was would only laugh over it.

The blessed farmer listened with undivided attention. With these words from the old farmer, a flickering light passed over Sintlinger's face, like a belch from his madcap years, and he recalled his plan of working on the inherited contradictoriness of farmers so that they had to bite firmly onto the opposite of their intent. And he decided on the spot to make a beginning with the chief opposition. It was pure delight for Sintlinger, for the entire road business had come to an end for him.

Since the blessed farmer was thus a little while in considering how he would sling this hidden cord around Brindeisener's legs, the old estranged farmer thought his neighbour had already been driven into deep embarrassment, and so he thought to completely overrun him. Thus he banged on the table, and asked "that the cow be milked out", that is, that it be decided which of the two ways to the Rhine should now be constructed, the one through Brederode or the one along the forest road.

To that the blessed farmer responded with a gentle smile that it would naturally be the one through Brederode, the direct opposite of what he wished, and began clearly and insistently to lay out all the advantages for the selection of this connection. He brought forth every favourable reason in such a bright light that the majority of the funeral party leant more and more animatedly towards this project alone. Only the dignified Kirchner from Dinslaken, and the Hornwasser sawmiller did not go along. The one rolled his eyes disapprovingly, the other snorted through his nose contrarily, and harnessed the blessed farmer here and there with adroitly strewn "as one assumes" and "if there is no other way". Brindeisener, however, sat dead quiet, grew ever straighter by the wall, and swelled vis-

ibly in the delight of a fatal derision. Hardly had Sintlinger "let his calves out", than Brindeisener expressed
himself as if he had already thoroughly rebutted him.
Everything happened just as the blessed farmer had
thought, and as his opponent with a roar kicked all the
spokes from the wheels of the Brederode plan, Sintlinger could not hold himself anymore, and laughed so
heartily in the midst of all the disparagement of his ingenuity that old Anton pulled back and suddenly cried
aloud with an angry bulging of his forehead, "Never,
never, so long as I live, will I take part in this Brederode
nonsense!" Then it became still as dust in the room.

And in the midst of the silence, the blessed farmer
said with bated tongue, and an apparently uncertain air,
"Yes, it is all no use. We will have to do it. Keep me in
mind, Brindeisener!"

"We! Who is we? What sort of we is there?" Brindeisener asked mockingly.

At that, Sintlinger tapped him with his foot under the
table, and made a sign to him inconspicuously with his
eyes. Out loud he said, "Yes, yes, so it is! But I must go
outside now", stood up, and started for the door. The
old estranged farmer thought Sintlinger was check-
mated and wanted to evade in this way the mockery he
deserved. For that reason, he quickly grasped the man
by the arm across the table as he was hustling away, and
called out , "Stay here, I say! What you perhaps have to
say to me quietly outside, you can comfortably say aloud
in this room. I can stand it, that is certain."

"No", Sintlinger replied, "it is also for my sake. But
that would be a minor matter, I pity you. So come!"
Now a general cheering broke forth over the wedged in
blessed farmer.

When it had died away, Sintlinger bent down over
the table, and said quietly into Brindeisener's ear that
he should desist from that foolish forest road. For even

if the others would all profit, they would both be the only mourners, and probably have to bleed their nicest fields. But the old farmer was so blinded by the near-ness of the triumph over Sintlinger, and felt in that confident prediction, to his disadvantage, so little of his own loss that he stated Sintlinger's misgivings aloud to the entire circle, and assured solemnly, and even if it cost him half his property, he would not rest before the white stones of a main road gleamed through his forest.

Now, it was so ordered, the blessed farmer said, then he would stand by Brindeisener's side, and as a sign of unity wanted them to shake hands before everyone that they would support the construction in every way. Like it or not, old Anton had to shake on it.

But Sintlinger endured his defeat with such conten-ted cheerfulness that everyone became suspicious and pondered in secret in what way perhaps it was possible that the blessed farmer had set up everyone on the bench, especially Brindeisener though, for a hidden fall perhaps.

That produced a relapse into disconcerted taciturnity from which nobody was as taken aback as the grieving father. Whereas he also recovered first, and indeed in a loud rumbling talk which was whipped ever more vehe-ment by secret doubts.

Thus everyone, except Sintlinger and his Johanna, ignored the racket unworthy of a house in mourning produced by the singing of the little blond head, Peter, down below on the spring's roof before the yard gate. It had become more and more impassioned over the hours, and sometimes climbed to a genuine, high screaming. For as the boy thus sent his voice over to the Sintlinger farmstead, so that it elicited what he dared not hope for, and desired to bursting, he had to think of the night when, as a little tot, he had also sent his singing from the dormer window over to this magical farmstead, and this memory awoke the shimmer, the wavering, the boundless and adventurous thing which had penetrated to him from there ever since he could remember, and which he had tried to capture with so many unsuccessful attempts. It seized him like a spring-ing in the air, and so he sang for the hundredth time, "Hey — hey, hey — hey! I am here!" loud and blaring in the most various embellishments of simple note com-binations, and he added every time entirely for himself with a soft humming, "Little Lena! Little Lena Sint-linger!", as mysteriously as he had once heard a birdcall from the source of the Hornwasser in the forest on the Dürrenberg; Peter imitated such a ringing as if it were tapped with a little silver hammer out of the shimmer-ing bell of the clearest sky. The ten year old sang to himself so that his throat hurt from loudly making his voice sound high and fine. But the water in the spring under the little roof rumbled away calmly, and if Peter also thought it was beautiful and just like that time at the source of the Hornwasser, then he also thought about what would really happen to the water if he went and shut off the wooden pipe so that it would have to spray in fear to all sides. But then he thought of his new Sunday best, of his mother's face and his father's large hand, and decided, if the water constantly drowned out entirely his quiet singing, at a later time he would stop its wooden mouth up, and not a little. For the time be-ing, he stalked away like a wild animal, once or twice around the entire yard, dived up the steps and, standing in the doorway, surveyed the party again, especially Sintlinger, of whom he had once heard his brother Jakob say to the labourers that he could eat more than bread, and then Johanna, the blessed farmer's wife, but soon noted with his disposition turning heavy that it was wrong to stand here and gape so long when "someone" was missing. Peter did not want at all to

think the name "little Lena" here, for God's sake not before so many people! Everyone would have immediately
seen it in his face. For that reason, he quickly hurried
off again to his little roof over the spring, and called his
blaring song to the lime tree by Sintlinger's gate. For his
main verse though, he walked this time from the spring
away across the drive to under an old apple tree in
whose crown a few solitary golden yellow leaves still
hung. And the Brindeisener boy thought, if his Hornwasser birdcall worked as finely for him now as the
leaves of the apple tree trembled in the sun above him,
little Lena Sintlinger could not do anything but come
over.

So he pulled his head back and sang so heartbreak-
ingly fine that he became fairly giddy. When he set his
head straight on his shoulders again, the entire world
floundered and jerked for a while yet behind a blazing,
red veil. That is why Peter thought, still a little dizzy,
now it should certainly have helped, and really! Hardly
had the whirl faded from his eyes, than he saw, still uncertainly though, more like travelling through the air,
little Lena Sintlinger step out the gate, and float down
the hill to the boundary path. There she remained
standing in the middle of the way, and turned her face
back and forth helplessly. Peter immediately ran down
as if called, placed himself opposite little Lena on the
other side of the road, stared with fitful breath at her,
but did not say a word. The girl, however, having perceived him running, waited a bit, and then said a little
irritably, "You, Brindeisener boy, why are you standing
there and saying nothing? Hey! Else I cannot find the
way to my mother and father who are at your farm!"

Then the boy plucked up his courage, went, took
little Lena cautiously by the hand, and showed her the
way. But he could not speak. In his chest it was beating
loudly, hardly bearable, and he was feeling quite weak

because he was holding, as all the people said, "a little angel" by the hand.

But little Lena Sintlinger let her silvery little voice run on long threads, and as the two children merely walked those few steps up the hill, she managed, as they say among farmers, to talk about the Lord's nose and the Virgin Mary's apron ties. But Peter's tongue lay askew in his mouth with astonishment. He did not bring forth a single word because he was still astounded over the girl's magical eyes.

Little Lena abruptly broke off her chatter, worked her hand free, turned to him, and asked whether it was true that he was called Peter, and when the boy could unfortunately not deny that, she had to laugh terribly over such a funny name. Then she asked to see his face. Peter did not grasp straightaway what she was stretching her hands out to him for. Finally he understood, tilted his head, and tolerated her hands feeling his face. Never before in his life had hot sun touched him so, never had a flower brushed him so softly. He went hot and cold down his back when he had to stand there thus, his face close to the breath of another. Her hands seemingly breathed over his skin. "You are quite handsome, you know, Peter", she said finally, finished with the examination. "Your mouth is quite cheerful, your cheeks too, only your forehead. Look please, mine does not have such knots either."

Peter had to feel, and then she said, "Right? Yes, but you also walk quite differently to me. And you also sing more roughly — sing again like before, please — hey hey! No, don't you want to?"

Peter was ashamed to sing into little Lena's eyes everything he had felt with those words, and told her he knew something much better. She should just see how he could run. And he began to bolt like a hare, gallop like a horse, leap like a deer, whinny, blow, snort; flew

around her and stormed away. Little Lena was trans-
fixed by this wild springing dance, and before she could
stop herself, she was also running. Peter, who was just
then rushing around the corner of the barn, saw her
already hastening down the hill with outstretched arms
amidst high laughter, straight towards a large stone
which she must fall over. "Little Lena!" he cried with all
his bodily strength. But she already lay with her face in
the grass, and when he hurried to her to lift her up, he
saw that her face was streaming with blood. He was for
a moment senseless with grief, love, shock, and worry,
lifted the girl up, and because he had nothing with
which to still little Lena's crying, he pressed his mouth
to her own, sucked, without wanting to, her blood in
with his breath, and ran, silently sobbing within, to the
farmstead and up the stairs. At the same time, he
clenched his teeth, and thought it would be quite right if
they struck him dead on the spot.

Thus he appeared in the doorway of the room — his
face white, his eyes desperately wide, his mouth dripping blood as if he had drunken her blood. He looked
terrible, and when the blessed farmer's wife caught sight
of him, she screamed so shrilly that Peter laid the girl on
the threshold, and took flight down the stairs and out of
the farmstead.

It soon turned out that nothing more had happened
to little Lena that that she had received an insignificant
wound to her forehead, but the blessed farmer's wife
could not stop recalling all the ghostly bewitchings during her haunted period when she had felt proper fear
and loathing for the Brindeisener boy, his running
around and his spying, and had even considered him to
be a delegate of wild Jakob Sintlinger.

She pondered that as, carrying little Lena in her
arms, she strode back to the Sintlinger farmstead. The

blessed farmer was walking behind her, and humming softly to himself.

"I don't know how you can be singing, Andreas?" she asked.

"Why shouldn't I?" he replied, and kept humming.

"Yes, but think though, what could have happened?"

"To little Lena? — Our little Lena?" he asked incredulously.

"Well yes, she could have easily smashed her head completely on the stone!" she answered, persevering in her fear.

The blessed farmer made no response to that. She soon heard him afterward humming to himself all the more cheerfully, and when she turned around, he was walking behind her, his face turned to the sinking sun, then he caught her glance with a smile, and finally said with affectionate reproof, "Johanna! Nothing bad can befall our little Lena, keep that in mind."

It would soon have passed from the mouth of the blessed farmer's wife at this moment that Peter, when he had appeared on the threshold with little Lena in his arms, had looked precisely like a murderer. But she feared Sintlinger's laughter, and kept it to herself.

On the same day, they had to search for a long time on the Brindeisener farm until Peter was found in the straw of a barn. He was still deathly pale in his face, and from time to time a shiver went through his body, for he believed that little Lena Sintlinger had received a fatal injury through him. Still shaken by the death of his sister, he had wished passionately in the darkness of his hiding place to also die.

Hence when he was led before his father for sentencing, he was seemingly begging with his eyes for a good deal of pain and reproach. The old farmer was also still filled by hidden seething over the tangle with Sintlinger, and was sitting in the middle of the room, his giant hands placed on his knees, rubbing thumb and fore-finger together, and clearing his throat, an extremely irritated human animal.

Hardly had the white head of the poor sinner ap-peared before him than the lurking storm of his temper broke forth, and he hewed the boy with a terrible blow diagonally across the room. But then the actual punish-ment began, and because Peter took all the torments without a sound, the fury of the grey-haired wild bull climbed still more. And if his wife had not finally stepped in-between, wresting the half unconscious Peter away, the short-tempered farmer would have struck the boy dead.

After a short time, the cracks, boils and bruises had vanished from his body. He was roaming about as ever.

And yet — in his depths, something in the Brin-deisener boy must have been unhinged forever by this incident. For not only his still more decisive aversion to-wards all farming employment, but even that towards all farming types actually emerged from that experience with the blessed hill's girl and its painful consequences. He became even more rambling and adventurous, but also more solitary, and actually held himself together only through the pressure of school and an uninhibited ambition in his exceptionally competent mind.

It went so far that, at the age of thirteen, he curtly and boldly gave his father the choice of either letting him go to an elite secondary school, "the higher school" as he expressed it, or he would run away. Liborius Pfeif-fer, the Hemsterhus Cantor, supported Peter's efforts so emphatically, through effusive praise of "this excess of head", and knew above all to stroke the fur of the es-tranged farmer's vanity so that the boy's wish was complied with. That the schoolmaster also did not begrudge his pietistic fanaticism a crumb is self-evident. The teacher drove Peter, before the farmer, through all the Gospels and prophecies of the Holy Writ, purred up and down the ladder of dates, calculating that a proper horror befell the old man before enormous numbers, and the man finally defended himself against "hearing still more of such devilry". But when he was alone in the room again with the Cantor, he struck him on the shoulder, and laughed with wild merriment that he had himself actually thrashed the boy from the farm between the "book slabs", and had taken the last farmer from the Brindeisener hill. For Jakob was anything but, maybe a proper coal shovel, but no farmer.

Later the thought crept up behind this quite proper judgement by the ageing hill farmer that Sintlinger with his blind "songbird" of a girl was actually guilty of the conversion of the old Brindeisener blood in his boy. Certainly this thought presented itself only later, quietly, incidentally, seemingly already innocuous when it occurred. For the farmer's boy from the Hemsterhus estranged farm raced like a runner, playful and scintillating, through the classes.

3

As it is common to the female nature in fact that all experiences awaken in the woman only fears or hopes, Johanna was not only lit up by garish fright straight off at the launching of the old hostility of the estranged farmers between Brindeisener and her husband, and the matter of their children, but she also walked about for a space of time afterwards in the darkness of uncertain anxieties.

For in those weeks, an echo of the musically rhapsodic period which the girl had experienced with Gottlieb and his accordion flew through the life and being of little Lena. In the feverish nights which followed the injury at the Brindeisener farm, she sometimes leapt up in her sleep and, without properly awakening, she looked about as if searching, to then slowly fall back again wearily and to sing softly in her dreams a medley of all Gottlieb's popular songs. Once Johanna even noted that her child was placing her arm across the covers as if she were holding her dress gathered up for dancing, and was performing with her entire sleep-bound body the movements of a person who was abandoning themselves to the waves of rhythmic airs.

Even in a waking state, she lapsed more often again during that time into wild and confused obstructiveness, was caught in hot abrupt moods, was amongst the servants a lot, and sometimes walked around with such brash, vehement steps that everyone who saw it was thrown into fear that the accident could be repeated with a worse outcome than that the child had just overcome. Even if not clearly, more vaguely, the feeling came over the farmer's wife that little Lena was like a bush in the darkness which suddenly lights up fierily in the light of a distant glow.

And all that was not easy for her to bear, because she could not speak to anyone about it. For on the one hand, it meant keeping little Lena's disposition free from those shadows which it could not understand, on the other hand Johanna had to strive to hide every utterance of hidden concern from the eyes of her husband. He went about bright-eyed, more confident and lucid than ever. And yet the distant echo of the funeral of Brindeisener's daughter also affected him deeply and for a long time, even though he talked to no one about it other than his concealed papers. The entry about it is the longest of them all and distinguishes itself from the other notes also by such a degree of darkness, yes, downright confused ambiguity, that only a proper translation can create clarity.

Obviously the urge for clear knowledge of the soul of old Brindeisener and his clan had driven the blessed farmer to sentences which also touched on the secret of the essence of all human inspiration. They read in our manner of speaking:

> The water of the spring is lively and participates in the damming and streaming of the subterranean sea which makes its hidden ways between the rocky roots of mountains.
>
> But the confined surface is also attracted by the paths of the stars. It quivers towards the light of the moon, and trembles in desirous happiness when it is met by a stray reflection of the sun.
>
> But there are enough such secret human wellsprings that are only capable of ringing on deep moonless and starless nights. Anyone who has alert ears, hears again in the gurgling and sobbing from their darkness sounds which once arose from birdsong in the sunlight. Such constricted waters suffer hardest of all in the depths during storms, and yet not amidst storms which exhaust themselves completely in rage. They are tortured most of all by those storms which lie in still, dry fervour, sombre and dull, for hours above the mountains, searing themselves with their fervour, and bringing forth only blue smouldering lightning and unrestrained thunder ... The fury which cannot be mastered, only

suppressed, must necessarily in the end destroy the man and his entire life.

In this reflective manner, the blessed farmer made use of a last relapse into the cheerful mockery of his earlier times, and received at the same time through being together with so many common men a push which never again summoned him to an active intervention for the welfare and advancement of others. For following the funeral of Amalie Brindeisener, there began the almost miraculous, most elevated time ever granted to the blessed farmer during his life. They were the long years, perhaps eight or ten, in which Sintlinger achieved what most, even distinguished men can only acquire through the images of their longing. His fate assaulted him from all sides as a dazzling thing. If his life before was sharp and pernicious like a rifle bullet flying to its target, now it glided forwards like circles spreading outward in a pool, yes, his being was in these years like the clangour which wanders everywhere in striding forward.

For the people, the life of the blessed farmer and his child tailed off into the unimaginable, because it deviated so completely from the usual and strove towards a goal which even the cleverest amongst them were incapable of finding. To that was added the crowd's addiction to wonders, its love of inordinate exaggerations, and the direction and spirit of the times which, sceptical and superstitious at the same time, found itself once more on the way to toppling venerable truths, exposing certainties as paper monuments; in general, as calm people said, meeting a great turning point in the world, or as the timid suggested, rushing towards an outrageous collapse.

Almost countless legends and anecdotes exist which deal with the wondrous life of the blessed farmer in these years of light, and they show him, according to the state of the observer, as a wise man who strives for a new religion; as a confused dreamer; a clever friend of mankind, yes, even as a sorcerer.

For really, the tale was told that once upon a time a poor man arrived at the blessed farm whose cow was meant to be calving, and it was in danger of dying because of insurmountable difficulties. In the deep dark of evening, the crofter stormed up the steep drive, and arrived breathlessly at the Blessed Farm. They had trouble understanding the stammering of the discouraged, foundering man, and when they finally succeeded, he learnt from the farmer's wife that her husband was wandering in the fields towards the beech stand. If he absolutely wanted to meet him this evening, he would have to take a chance at catching him in the little patch of bush where he sometimes waited for the fall of night. But she could not give him any further guidance, and it was uncertain in any case. The poor farmer had already been scratched enough by the witch's claw which in the people's opinion grew on Sintlinger's big toes. For that reason, he was frightened immediately by the farm-wife's ambiguous information, but set off all the same on the path to the beech stand, for when it concerns a cow, then the farmer freezes even in hell. Thus our farmer also ran with all his strength through the fields, and thought to himself constantly along the way, 'And should I have to deal with the devil himself, it would be all the same to me, if only my "Whitey" does not go to the knackers.' Then he suddenly noticed that the path was beginning to sink under his feet, and as he looked up in horror, he was already standing quite close to the beech forest, and yet could not go in. His legs were as if bound together, the earth before him looked like a deep abyss into which a rushing water was shooting, and between the grey trunks, a rolling began to get louder and louder, and the exuberant talking and laughing of two men's voices sounded in-between, quite as if two men were playing bowls passionately in the air. First one called "eight", then the other "five". The first, when he listened closely, was the blessed farmer's voice, but the other sounded burnt out and hissing, terrible, so that a chill ran through the farmer's bones. Nevertheless, he plucked up his courage and called into the horror and the raving, "Blessed farmer, my cow is sick."

"Thick", it mimicked back at him mockingly from the forest, and broke out into such a devilishly mocking laughter that the farmer crossed himself and turned around trembling.

When he finally found his house, half-dead after hours of running astray, everything had turned out happily, and his "Whitey" was standing there and licking the most beautiful black and white calf in the world.

After that evening, nobody doubted anymore in earnest that the blessed farmer was on good terms with the devil, and Sintlinger's incredible discourse with the black hen received a new affirmation subsequently with this new incident. By such stories which the folk simply borrowed from the treasury of their forebears' legends, and polished anew, they tried to explain Sintlinger's behaviour as it became more and more enigmatic and incomprehensible.

Sintlinger was found standing before trees and being reverent and gripped like others are before the sanctum in the church. He listened to the wind like a schoolboy on whom an unfathomable teaching was being bestowed. But he was particularly taken with the mirrored surface of still water, and the Hornwasser miller once saw him sitting by a secluded pool, and actually talking to the water as if it were a human and not a thing.

Yes, the same miller claimed to have seen a ripple run across the pool at the rapt words of the blessed farmer, as if the water understood Sintlinger's human words and was giving him an answer.

That would probably have been the time in which Sintlinger recorded the following words in his papers:

> The image of the trees, the sky and a bird flying past on the still mirror of a pool is not something that arises from the being of the pool. Whenever the image vanishes or appears, nothing essential is taken away from or added to the pool; it is no less and no more a pool. So it is with the soul and all earthly images of the senses on its still mirror. It is more prolific at base than the earth, and does not need the world. But the world without soul would be like a heap of rubbish.

Sintlinger was strolling at a great distance, quite beyond the borders of his class, yes, beyond most men, and he enjoyed at the same time the advantage over quite solitary spirits that, at least for the time being, he was never beset by fear and helplessness resulting from his almost complete break with the ideas of his neighbourhood. For actually, seen rightly, the dreamily beautiful wondrous being of his little Lena was leading him, as he had intended it would, into this new world. Sintlinger thus always felt he was creating nothing, but only absorbing what was offered to him.

The unease which the full moon brings over the spirits of men, the clarifying urge of its waxing perfection, and the faltering and hesitating during the decline in its shining light, that and much else, the blessed farmer obtained from the soul of his child. He felt more deeply and indescribably the formation of storms long before they occurred, and gathered from overlooked signs, perhaps the sound which the horned flight of the beetle produces, the echo caused by the cry of a bird in the forest, yes, he read from the gestures of trees and field crops with certainty the changes in the atmosphere so that he seldom missed the right time for sowing and harvesting.

His wealth grew not only with the heaped carts which the fields sent into his barns, but also with the thriving of the cattle for whose welfare Johanna sacrificed all the quiet attentiveness of which she was so easily capable.

This calm, confident swelling of Sintlinger's wealth lent his unusual life a power of persuasion over other people so that soon the thought emerged here and there of, if possible, experiencing the tangible usefulness of such a being, but with the old faith and without devilry. Especially amongst those becoming impoverished, from hardship or debt, this party of adherents stirred in ever increasing numbers, and wherever two or three farmers with patched overalls came together, surprise was expressed over Sintlinger's wealth.

In the end, a few decided to ask the blessed farmer directly. For the sake of certainty, because two pairs of ears always hear more than one pair, several such broken farmers acted together, and they selected Elis Meixner from Querhoven as their spokesman. He had fallen deep into debt again owing to his mad rages of pleasure, and simply believed that through knowledge of a certain trick he could in an easy way come into a measureless heap of talers again. In addition, he was stabbed by a secret envy and hostility towards Sintlinger which had its base more in the wide-ranging nature of both men than in the displeasure over the injustice of the blessed farmer towards his nephew, the accordion playing Meixner. But he made everyone believe that he would actually be fond of Sintlinger if he could only forget one thing about him, that he had sent Gottlieb to ruin. For, since his raving had stopped, he had roamed about like a chicken that had caught a cold, without pluck or sense.

Meixner was also threshing in this old fury on the day when he went with the others to the blessed farm, and said that they could leave it to him — if Sintlinger had a hidden trump, he would get his hand on it, and even if the little hill sorcerer wanted to quickly sit on it.

The men were led in error by the maid into the room for the vagrants. A few were sad over this disrespect, others were angry, above all Elis Meixner. His red-bearded face discoloured. He sat down derisively on the vagrants' bench, sprang up again, and paced the room with large, enraged strides.

Then the blessed farmer entered, apologised over the ineptitude of the maid, greeted everyone in the most amiable way, and asked them to come with him into his room. There they could say what they wished from him. The others all immediately forgot their displeasure before the dignity and gentle force of Sintlinger. Elis Meixner, however, fell into his usual schnapps-rumbling and asked him, and that almost as if he were leading a grievance, how he arranged it that his life, business, the peace of his farm, his marriage, yes, even his misfortune was knocked so into bright fortune, although he did not believe more than that a pound of beef made a good soup.

He said these words with the mocking laugh and bitterness of a genuinely bankrupt farmer.

Sintlinger looked at him attentively and calmly, sat down on the bench, nodding his head to the others, and said nothing at all for a while. But when the others began to reproach the Querhovener for his impropriety, Sintlinger stood by the beset man and excused his behaviour. For anyone who naturally has large feet needs tough boots and is then not capable of treading softly.

"That with the pound of beef is also not so simple, Meixner", he then said in cheerful seriousness, turning to the sheepish man. "For it is strange that this pound of beef acts so differently with different men — with some a chasing after whores, idleness, deceit, fury, and hypo- crisy; with others love, meekness, consistency, and clever economy. My dear man, that lies not in the flesh, but in the strength of our inner being. Someone who has died in his soul can probably digest the nourishment, but not transform it — and the meal acts in such a one only according to its nature. Concerning fortune, there it would be to say, you must listen to the furthest and finest, if you want to do for your neighbour what is right."

Yes, good, thought the poor farmers now, having re- covered from their embarrassment. But how was that to be done, that they would like to know.

"There you should proceed with your soul like someone who seeks a space in his house where he will be least disturbed. For the soul can endure everything except a racket. It is still and mysterious like the sound- less thing from which grows the stalks of grain and the clover flowers. Someone who runs thundering like a horse will never, never ever come to it."

The farmers did not understand him, looked at each other helplessly, and dared not ask.

Elis Meixner, however, had meanwhile collected himself again, and asked whether Sintlinger meant the Church's soul or the one which all men had without dis- tinction.

"All men without distinction", Sintlinger answered. "Anyone who is capable acts like me. I sit perhaps on a chair in front of the farmstead and rule everything from here. Then the messengers come, five or six with all sorts of requests. I let them wait, and do not stir. Finally the white, distant, radiant thing comes which you hardly see, and it beckons in me. Then I rise and command. Thus everything I do, and everything which happens to me turns out happily. And someone who is thus like me, he will understand me and act like that."

The farmers, however, went away more confused than they had arrived.

Behind the hill, on the boundary path, the braggart Meixner began cursing his head off, and none of the men took him to task anymore, for each thought either the blessed farmer just wanted to tease them, or his truth was so whimsical that another person would never be able to make use of it.

Nevertheless it did not stop that people constantly came to the Blessed Farm with all sorts of requests for the farmer's advice. One wanted to know the sympathetic means which Sintlinger must have given his wife for the care of the cattle. Another asked him again what he had used that every fury had been choked in him forever, whilst he himself only had to move his tongue in his closed mouth for his molars to swear and blasphemy by themselves so that his ears grated.

To each he gave an answer, to none a straight one, for most did not actually come to better themselves, but out of vanity to have also asked. Only, when they were at home again, they did many things differently, and from being together with the blessed farmer, some even brought a different spirit into their lives.

Once Sintlinger received a new labourer who was so industrious that the sun never rose early enough and the day was always to short. Where the others walked, he ran, and yet he never had a delighted face at the finish of work. Even in dreaming, he was threshing or ploughing, in short, he strove for work with which he could never be finished during the day because he undertook too much.

When the farmer had watched him for a time, and had warned him in vain to take some leisure and not long with his leg's first step already for the second, he sent him one day away from the field.

For, he said, the profligacy of exaggerated industry was all the more dangerous because it was generally considered to be a great virtue. The proper work was surely a good path to heaven. But only the sober find it, those who stay back each a day a bit behind the racer, but at the end of their lives have gone a thousand times further than he has. And the beetle which is always turning a large ball of dung behind it is no more distinguished than the one that does not do that. The wealth of men, however, ranks before our real fortunes no more than as a pile of muck.

It went so far that hardly anyone did anything important without Sintlinger's advice, and everything successful or profitable within ten miles happened as if by his prompting, even if he knew nothing at all about it. But the blessed farmer remained faithful to his principles. He walked alone as per normal, never collected followers or kindred spirits, only gave out advice that was asked for, never intervened in another's life, and held himself apart from every office.

At first they wanted to make him District Councillor of Hemsterhus, after that Superintendent, and in the end he was offered the dignity of being deputed to the County Council. He shook his head with a smile to everything, and continued to stroll hands entwined with his little Lena through her distant, wondrous life. Meanwhile, when the efforts to win his uncommon powers and his renown to the service of charitable societies and establishments did not stop, he had to give a gruff answer, contrary to his acquired goodness.

"If I pull my wagon correctly, it will happen that all men move on. But those men whom I must load up with force so that they move forward are like stones which I carry to a high mountain in the expectation that they will begin to flower there. If the bird itself does not want it to, then its song does not change."

And when it came to his ears that many took offense because he and his little Lena avoided all church activity, he said, "When the springs run dry, the fish cluster together and bring their mouths close to each other so as to give each other moisture. But this state is for a long time not as good as them forgetting one another in the streams and lakes. What applies to the fish, applies still much more to men, of whom each has a sea within himself which is without time and without end, and where the sun never sets. Leave me alone with the proselytising. Your physical brothers are the killers."

So completely did Sintlinger sink in his devotion to this intangible, unimaginable world that even the foundation walls of his nature dislocated.

The years were approaching in particular when Helene could no longer sleep in the same bedroom with her parents. She settled in one of the rooms of the upper floor, next to Sintlinger's study, and it followed of its own accord that not her mother, but the blessed farmer now slept on the other side of the wall from his child so as to be at hand as needed.

Johanna found this solution quite in accordance with the devoted relationship in which the two stood to one another, and pushed for it herself. But when she lay alone for the first time in the bedroom next to the servants' room, having extinguished the light, and was already half in dream feeling once more for the bed of her husband, her hand grasped in the emptiness, and when she straightened up in fright and called her husband's name, the echo of her voice against the walls of the half emptied room resounded as if it were coming from an extinct world.

The blessed farmer's wife smiled surely at her emotionalism, but could set nothing against the deep shock to her inner being, bent down, and gathered together the covers with both hands into a ball which she pressed tightly against her face. Thus she abandoned herself with hunched up body to the flood of tears which would not stop.

Now, she felt, her husband, to whose unachievable wisdom she never found her way, had moved even further along. And so it also occurred. The blessed farmer had been led so far away from her that, though he still shared caresses, cordialities, sympathy, and all the understanding of loyal goodness, he no longer shared with her that stream of passion by which women are endowed anew by their men with the power of their being.

Amongst the mysterious embraces which his spirit followed on the way which his blind child was leading him, the delight in melting into an ardent blossoming with his wife's embrace finally stopped completely. And when Johanna felt the yearning, she balked though out of chasteness from answering it rightly, made herself doubly numb through work, dulled through possessing herself twice-over with worry, and could not avert constantly seeking for something lost, feeling something menacing over herself, and seeing danger approaching.

For this reason, she also walked right at the end of the procession in which enthusiastic, miracle-seeking, and earnest seekers streamed together from all sides behind her husband and her child.

4

Meanwhile, Ursula Rütsch from the Sweeps had given birth to the child which she had been taken with in the whirl through which the blessed hill's little Lena had taken the sorrow over the dead Snowy from her forever. Only the new child had, with the evening at-tack which Ursula had suffered from an unknown man in the forest meadow, incurred some damage. For she brought into the world on the due date a girl who pos-sessed, next to the beauty of Snowy, the blessed little Lena's angelic tenderness, but only lived a few days, and that without even touching the breast of her mother. Then she died quickly and without convulsion, without wincing, just as if she had never even been in the world.

And poor Ursula Rütsch seemed herself to have per-ceived it thus, not as if it had been a real child, her child which she had given birth to and barely possessed prop-erly, having to again give her away already, but as if it, half a shadow of Snowy and half a reflection of blessed little Lena, had flitted just for that reason from her body into the world, to point her mother on the right path which had been prepared for her from the beginning.

She had already suffered after her beloved son's death a passionate relapse into the anabaptist faith which still haunted most of the Querhoven houses as an ancient shadow, to the extent that she rendered a new, higher life for her remaining three boys at night through the waters of the forest pool. But now after the blanch-ing of her last child, she let the force of the new spirit break from the guarded secrecy more and more openly into her life, sat for some time over the old Bible every evening before going to bed, and also began her day with solitary reading of some passages which, whenever the work allowed it, became a lasting meditation, and she turned within to that higher region of her being in which she did not discount ever exalting her waking and sleeping through the power of the holy words.

In the midst of the consequences of her "awakening", neither the progress of the domestic matters, nor her relationship to her husband and children suffered, nor did her being suffer in the least any alteration for the worse. For that reason, her husband, the good man Rütsch, not only did not stop her, no, after he had undergone a concealed darkening of his soul on account of the harming of his loyalty towards the Catholic faith of his fathers, he even adopted this and that breath of the spirit which his Ursula, beloved above all else, had made at home in his house in the Sweeps.

But he was not the only one grasped by the force which settled ever deeper into the life of his wife. All of Querhoven, so far as it did not consist of families which had immigrated later, betook themselves soundlessly, wandering like in the pictures of an ancient dream, onto the path which the beautiful Ursula had been led. Sounds dating from centuries ago, which had long since lost their audible magic and turned into restless circling of blood, capricious moods, or persistent quirks, in short, into an exuberant and querulous existence, began to waft with quiet, magical melodies through the deepest soul. The astonishment, as if over an approaching time of reawakening, which had been gifted to this nest of poor skewer makers and spigot turners, had received by Sintlinger's plans, from which various improvements in their conditions of life were to be hoped for, a real basis, visible goals, and conceivable paths. The old subterranean stream of intoxicating wonder in Querhoven had been lifted into the light. Now the maternally deep, touching life of Ursula Rütsch poured a shimmer over these forefathers' faith which nobody had ever properly known or practised, a faith before which they had had to bow to in forgotten corners of their breasts sometimes like shadows before a shadowy thing.

Perhaps for an individual person something similar happened to that which, in the twilight of old age, suddenly roars his first love through his heart ardently, although it has preserved no features anymore of that image which he can point to, no death he can grasp, no gesture he can be enraptured by. He just becomes happily besotted.

As sensually as these simple people experienced their souls, as sensually did they also experience the visitation of the new spirit. At the crofter property of the Vanlyßenders from whom Ursula Rütsch descended, the wall of the house which shimmered on many a dark evening in an indescribably wavering light was that which had never before been touched by anything but the last beam of the sun. The miller heard the outcast feminine demons of that district again for the first time in half a century conversing in a murmur at daybreak from one hole in the banks of the millrace to the other and wandering away with a sob which, however, became more and more cheerful in the distance and finally tailed off in a quiet, glorious singing. By the forest pool, woodcutters returning home saw the white figure of Katharina Tauche wandering, and on approaching she vanished again with arms extended and happy laughter into the water in which she had drowned herself a long time ago out of religious melancholy.

To the silent conversation of two intimates over new, remarkable events, the hearty friend of the one and the loyal brother of the other joined. Those moved by it ignited each other mutually, the awe of themselves and of the unusual tales disappeared more and more, the lonely fervour which slackened so easily longed for the ardour of another heart, and so, rising above its own strength, it soon swelled out of the frisson of concealed visions into the ardent fire of loud proclamation before everyone. The "talking in tongues" in secret religious circles was there, making a centre in which the whirling of the individual could enliven itself anew and penetrate deeper and deeper.

Nobody knew to say how it had come about, but after the course of barely two years the religious life of the Querhoveners arrived at an imaginative but firm order which barely excluded anyone who had from their fore-fathers an anabaptist fibre in their body.

In that time, the hearings over the building of the new road to the Rhine had progressed so far that, in the parish councils of the three represented villages of Hemsterhus, Brederode, and Querhoven, the final resolution turned out in favour of the forest road which led through the forest of the two estranged farmers, as Sint-linger and Brindeisener were still called when they were named together.

The plan which Sintlinger had put aside a long time before and had only advanced in a flippant jest against Brindeisener began to near fruition. At the same time, the blessed farmer assented to the surrender of certain strips of his field and forest possessions, and also en-joyed just a little the pleasure in the firmly concealed fury of old Brindeisener over the butchering of his best strips of plough land by the new course of the road.

The latter surely cursed, but only with thumping strides in his gait, and lamented too, but merely with his eyes, and cast abuse in the barking tone of his cough.

Apart from that, he did not allow the displeasure of being entangled through his hostility to the blessed farmer in a business which he would otherwise have battled to the last breath of his obstructive brutality to be noticed. And then he was hindered by thoughts of his status from breaking his word and upsetting the apple-cart, contenting himself, as it always went, with trying to hound Sintlinger with mocking over the losses from the road building into the fury and wildness which he himself arduously concealed. But the blessed farmer was not to be brought out of his distant indifference and comforted Brindeisener with the consideration of the advantage to everyone, as if this old bitter farmer had not been mocking him, but rather himself. It went so far that old Brindeisener, after long, dull persistence, confessed one evening the painful realisation to his wife that he seemed to have been deceived into the road building by the little hill sorcerer over there so that he had actually acted by God no differently than if he had held out his own trousers to Sintlinger. With angry glimmering eyes, he received the officials from the Land Registry for the surveying of his property, and if it had gone his way, he would have torn the red and white posts from the earth and broken them to pieces over their heads. The most annoying thing of all, however, in the entire affair was the fact that the blessed farmer, without effort, had also here again soon become the midpoint by which all measures received their meaning — try as much as old Anton might to also win space and prestige with his counsels.

The remaining residents of Hemsterhus, after they had raved for long months in empty faultfinding about the project, turned, because it was taking too long, back to their domestic business, this one at his sawhorse, that one behind his plough, some to the eternal conflict with their wives, and others to games and drinking.

Only the Querhoveners did not stop following with the liveliest sympathy all the turns and transformations in the execution of the construction plans. Not only for the reason that the road led through a part of the place and they, always pushed aside, were now integrated significantly into the cogwheels of the world, no, above all because in their passionate state the opinion had arisen that this new road which headed out from them must be conceived entirely as "a compelling auspice of divine providence" that would begin a new time, the great new age of humanity where, as always, "the empty and sinful might also face a challenger, and the heavenly Zion will come on all paths amongst the people".

And because this undertaking which brought such a significant light to their outer and inner lives had taken its origins from the blessed farm, their faith took great pains to divine behind this profane matter an enigmatic divine providence. In their secret nocturnal meetings, which were held in turn at the homes of the most distin- guished fanatics, they sought in the Holy Writ passages which bore out the delusion that from its corner the re- newal of Christianity would have its beginning when the measure of the sins of faith was full. And thus it happened that they became more and more full of the pride of all sectarians, of looking with concealed disesteem at all men who let their souls rot in the dead breath of priests, in that they believed you could reach God on a paper bridge and with the feet of others. Al- though their religious practices slowly adjusted to the fixed forms of certain ceremonies, the spirit by which they were driven assumed, according to the nature of the leading proponents, a more and more diverse exist- ence. This polymorphism in the appearance of the new spirit was one of the main reasons for its powers of dis- semination. The circle of its disciples grew constantly because everyone felt struck at once by the mouthing of a revivalist with the sound of their own nature in their innermost being.

In the end, only two people in all of Querhoven kept themselves apart from the current which carried the people of this poor village towards the shimmer of an indescribable, far-off expectation — namely, Gottlieb, the nephew of old Zenker, who had left the blessed farm in such an adventurous way a long time ago, and his uncle, the braggart Meixner, who lived on the only large estate above the mill.

It was said that the great Elis, in this period when both stood outside the movement, had attempted by obliquely placed, sneering words, as was just his way, to awaken the old blustering state in Gottlieb and steer him towards the secret bustling of the fanatics. Only, the young man since his Echternach pilgrimage had fundamentally changed so that nothing could bring him to the loud excessiveness of his earlier hostility to the blessed farm. But even the carefree cheerfulness of his innate being and his accordion playing seemed to have left him forever.

He had set up a woodworker's bench in his mother's living room, and cut skewers from dawn till dusk with his various chisels from pegged pieces of wood, without looking up or around, indifferent to his aggrieved mother, to the world, yes, he even gave the appearance of being indifferent to himself. His bumpy, large face was pale and emaciated, his small eyes had forfeited their abrupt attacks of unease and lay lost and motionless in the bottom of their spacious hollows, and if something in this quickly extinguished life was still to be distinctly recognised, it consisted in an inescapable, almost painless sorrow. Except he more often and for longer periods clasped his hands between his knees or propped his head on them, and sat by the window that looked out on the slope which separated Querhoven from the district of the estranged farmsteads, so that you might have thought the circling of his hidden dreams still swept towards the blessed farm where his life had been dealt a blow which nobody understood. But when his mother asked him once bluntly about that, he did not answer, no, he did not even look around, but stood up, went out, and avoided from that day onwards keeping watch from that place again. He now spent the hours of his leisure outside the house, most preferably in the darkest spots of the forest. There he lay on his back and stared motionless into the darkness of the treetops above himself, or threw himself on his face and pressed his forehead into the moss as if he wanted most of all to bury his head in the earth. Because of this complete aversion to life, his mother finally came to the shocking presumption that her son had burdened himself with a concealed misdeed which was now consuming him from within.

In this extreme hardship, an alteration occurred in his life. It happened on an evening when the believers of Querhoven had gathered in the house of Vanlyßender. In accordance with the nature of this gentle family, all the quietly spiritual, deep-souled, silently moved people arrived who were accustomed in hysterical devotion to lifting themselves over great mountainous dream clouds closer to God. After the eighth hour of evening on that early autumn day, the spacious room began to fill with believers who entered with the quiet greeting, "God let us prosper!", and were received by the father of the house, and his wife. When at a quarter past eight, the stream of arrivals swelled for a short time, Rütsch and his wife, who had arrived in the meantime, also participated in the ordering of the crowd of humanity, in particular they brought this and that old person who had remained standing modestly by the door closer to the table and assigned them a place on a chair or the bench lining the wall. Soon the large, low room was full of visitors who, silent or exchanging terse words in muffled voices, looked forward in the most various ways to the beginning of the hour of edification — some sat in collected humility as if sucking down into themselves; others, hands entwined firmly on slack arms, stood erect, their heads raised listening; *these* leant raptly by the wall, *these* cowered in corners; most sat kneeling until right up close to the table over which the small shaded lamp hung in a dully reddish ball of light. The places around the table were all possessed bar one. Ursula Rütsch had taken a seat next to her mother on the bench by the stove. When nobody else was coming, the expectation of the believers flowed together into a wordless demand. Ursula raised her head, looked into the faces of her brothers and sisters who had turned towards the table, looked to them questioningly, and all returned in answer a nod of assent. At that, Ursula rose and fetched her father, old Vanlyßender, from behind the stove where he had hidden himself, and led the sheepishly smiling, old man to the place of honour under the lamp, thereby assigning the chairmanship to him for the evening. After the old man had sat down and, holding his crossed hands on the Bible, had waited for a while, he succeeded in lapsing into the greater nature which everyone expected. The sheepishness vanished from his countenance. He folded his hands, rose and spoke with sunken eyes and deep fervour the prayer of awakening:

> "Your eyes, oh God, are above the mountains and and do not sleep. Your feet wander with the wind, travel with the water over the earth, and do not rest. Your dreams grow as flowers in every field. You talk in the hum of the forest and fill the song of the birds with your voice."

And when he now came to the place which concerned the indifference of men to the thousandfold call of God, his voice climbed to grieved emotion. But he spoke the closing, "the request for release from the shackles of self-seeking hearts and the captivity of possessive wills", convulsively.

His high, child-like pure old man's voice was choked many times by the tremors of the prayer. He brought the call for awakening forth like a shout, and then had to sit down, quickly dropping. Here and there could be heard suppressed sighs, groans, yes, even sobs from the assembly. But when the hymn had been sung, "Oh sinners, come and let your heart be stirred. Your saviour stands with you, wants to cover you with grace", the anguished excitement of the believers had relaxed into a quiet, raised excitement of the soul.

After that, old Ender, as had become the custom, called, "for an innocent, simple heart to point the assembly today the way to the godly heights." After a few hesitations, a tender girl, just having outgrown childhood, stepped timidly up to the table, closed her eyes and fumbled with her hands for the Bible which had been pushed towards her. When she had grasped it, she pressed a kiss on it and then opened it. All those present followed with suspense the outcome of "the choice". Vanlyßender drew the opened book to himself and read, "The Book of Ruth, chapter one, verse sixteen."

A happily astonished brightening passed over the faces of the believers that the child, led by her innocent soul, had fallen on this loveliest region of the garden of God. Old Ender used approximately these words to express the religious amazement of everyone at how the Lord was working visibly through the child in the spirit of this hour. But then he began to read:

> "And Ruth said, Intreat me not to leave thee, or to return from following after thee: for whither thou goest, I will go; and where thou lodgest, I will lodge: thy people shall be my people, and thy God my God."

Vanlyßender read the words slowly, with a solemn voice, and when he had reached about the middle of the verse, the door opened as if by itself. The soft hum of the distant forest flowed into the room and accompanied the singing voice of the old man like a heavenly organ.

Everyone felt that that was a sign from above and, after a concerned look at the door, directed their gleaming eyes and pale faces at the lit table. Ursula from the Sweeps was seized most of all. The mien of her beautiful face dissolved into a sleepwalker's reverie, and so, with rejoicing, rigid eyes, she rose, gently took the book from her father's hand, and read onward:

> "Where thou diest, will I die, and there will I be buried."

Soon after the first words, the tone of her feminine voice was already transformed into the swinging, high sweetness of a child-like way of speaking. Then she broke off her reading. It had seized her. She directed her enraptured eyes at the open door, and listened for a while to the gentle hum of the distant forest. And now she began, "And when God has imposed the death of a loved one on us, we are by no means separated from those who are taken from us. The dead enter transfigured through the gates of the heart into our life. And when we eat, they sit next to us, reach into the bowl with us and sate themselves with the meal which feeds us. My sleep is filled by their image, I meet them on the path." Thus Ursula Rütsch indulged for a while yet in the sorrow over her dead children. It seemed to everyone who had known Snowy as if the dead child were speaking from her mouth. But towards the end, the sound of her voice changed again — she spoke softly, like with the chiming of a little silver bell, gentle as a breath. And hardly had she spoken a couple of sentences thus, than the audience whispered, "Now the blessed farm's little Lena is speaking through her."

The enraptured woman must have heard the quiet remarks, for after a hesitation, she said, talked directly to the audience, "You are right, you brothers and sisters, the time approaches fulfillment. The Zion, the new Zion on the mountain is near. Grace comes to us again through a child, and the blessed girl whom God sends is already in our midst. Whoever believes in her will be elevated in their heart; but whoever defies her will be cast out into the dark and wander in the darkness. Woe to the blinded! Woe to them!"

In the deathly silence which followed this exclamation, a noise suddenly arose from the door, as if a man were sinking down, and suppressed sobs could be heard. The kneeling people turned around, the circle opened, and Gottlieb Meixner was seen still half in the vestibule, his face buried in his hands, lying in the doorway. He was stammering constantly to himself in anguish. By the sound of his voice, they were self-accusations. And when he had been lifted up, he stood there palely with downcast eyes and dared not look at anyone. Everybody was delighted over the awakening of the fellow who had kept away for so long, the ranks of people moved up to him, squeezed his limp hand, and went home uplifted. The accordion player Meixner did not stir from the place in the vestibule to which he had retreated. But when Anselm Rütsch and his wife departed as the last, he too stepped out of the house and followed them from a distance as far as the Sweeps. And then they saw him in the light of the late half moon standing for a long time yet like a pillar and looking at the Rütsch house.

But those who only saw in Gottlieb Meixner's agitation his awakening into the existence of the chosen were deceiving themselves. His mother too. He neither asked for baptism, nor did he give anything but a forestalling answer to the urging to finally climb into the bath of life.

Yes, when one day the white baptism shirt was sent to him by someone with a reminder note in rough letters, he soon sent it back through a distinguished member of the secret congregation. And because he continued all the same, even if he only stood in the doorway, in his attending the assemblies which Ursula Rütsch presented herself at, and never stopped exalting the beautiful woman through shy, sorrowful veneration, it had to be recognised that the fellow had been occupied by a different spirit to the holy one. But the presumptions that Gottlieb was burning with love for the beautiful Ursula did not stand up either, for he never emerged from the distant awe in which he watched her, listened to her, and followed her from a distance whenever she went home in the darkness. But a few months after the beginning of his ministration over Ursula Rütsch, in May of the following spring, the Schwerdtner woman found a new guitar lying on the threshold of her little cottage in Hemsterhus, and she took it with delighted astonishment as the secret gift to her of that unknown person who had destroyed the old instrument during the attack in the vicinity of the stone bridge at Brederode.

Nobody conceived of the idea that the rueful transgressor of the poor street singer and the shy venerator of Ursula Rütsch could be one and the same person. The Schwerdtner woman again moved with the sound of the voice of the blessed farm's little Lena in her softly sung songs from village to village, from house to house, and the people soon attributed the stirring beauty of this late requital to the other wondrous characteristics of the little widow. In addition, restless times broke out not long afterwards over that district and hindered the following up of the hidden errors of a passionate nature.

5

Querhoven's heretical Christians were of course not well spoken of around about in the villages, and the mild expression for their secret churchgoing and acts of grace, "penury for heaven", was very descriptive though for their distressingly brusque shutting off towards all contamination by sectarian wind-borne seed from outside. They preserved a complete silence over their inner organisation and teaching, pursued no capture of souls, and let all the mockery turn ineffectual in forbearing kindness. But when all those standing without still believed that the deepest peace reigned amongst them, misunderstandings and inner frictions were preparing themselves. The unconquerable stubbornness of Gottlieb Meixner, despite all enticements, in not giving up his place in the vestibule at the door of the enthusiasts' church, but constantly observing the acts of grace from outside, half eavesdropper and half listener, at first had a disquieting effect and then led to proper discord. For the spokesman of the exorcist-leaning party reproached that party grouped around Vanlyßender with great indeterminacy, with soft indulgence of feeling, for which reason enraptured souls were so to speak only touched at the hems, were not beneficially daunted and agitated to their depths, won in the storm of faith, but rather were only tepidly rocked back and forth. One man even placed a wooden blade on the table before Vanlyßender in an assembly of "the soft" and asked with loud, reproachful voice all those present, "Do you not know that our Lord Jesus brought the struggle? The Lord also said, 'I am come to send fire on the earth'*."

---

*   Luke 12:49.

And with that, he vanished from the circle. For inwardly possessed people with constant fervour for their high intent neglect too easily the form of their outward actions, and, you could say, blow the trombone on a blade of grass. And so not only did this bellicose exorcist play the wrong note amongst the Querhoven faithful, but also the others of both parties raised far too often comical justifications for their special ways. Posters appeared on the fences with the great question, "Am I a lukewarm one?" And whenever a soft one came into the vicinity of an ardent enthusiast's house, the entire family inside began singing the battle hymn, "Spring up, my heart, and arm yourself." The dispute over the pace unexpectedly turned into a dispute over the leg, they drew apart in the interpretation of basic truths, and, from the honest endeavours to unite, they were inflamed even more. For nothing enraged as much as the repudiation of a trifling matter. In this seething, the calm ones fell on the idea of entrusting the office of adjudicator to the blessed farmer. For even though he kept himself to one side, he was by way of his nature one of them, and the awakening of the entire village had actually received its beginning from his farm.

Vanlyßender was thus sent to Sintlinger with the question of whether you should use force in the soul for the sake of faith or leave everything to the actions of God.

The blessed farmer listened to the long arguments of the distressed old man, deliberated for a while, smiling, and then said that with whistling, it is not about the pursing of the lip, but the song. But the right song arranges the lips by itself. They should deliberate that among themselves. In addition, he asked that he not be bothered with such questions anymore. But the Querhoveners did not stop communicating with him for assessment of every item of belief which their unease had badly concocted. And when Sintlinger had deployed a few consoling evasions, he became displeased, and according to the opinion of one, he would now give as an answer the parable of the fish, according to others, however, they were shown heatedly from the farm with the following words, "I am not your pope, and if you still want to know something, then pay attention to the water when it rolls together into drops in your hand and thus becomes a reflection of the whole world. If you hear it bring forth a sound at the same time, you are right to make chase with shouts and controversy after God and your soul. Otherwise, place a blade of grass in your mouth and breath through your nose, if you will become of your own or another's mind."

This reply from the blessed farmer ensured the spirit of quiet fervour in Querhoven was again victorious, and everyone returned to the path of soft, enraptured service. The Sintlinger memorial under the lime tree at the blessed farm's gate was one morning covered all over with red dog roses. Ursula Rütsch, to whom this homage was attributed, again sang the praises of the "divinely-sighted" little Lena more often; and Gottlieb Meixner arrived unmolested as an aloof participant in the assemblies again. And thus the secret pilgrimage of the poor Querhoveners would perhaps have slowly exhausted itself for the sake of the shimmer of a distant, new faith in this enraptured indulgence.

Only, when people have abandoned a house, they at first avoid it properly, and burning words do not stop smouldering if they have not been wiped so thoroughly from the ear. In any case, as deeply as many believed, the devout rising above this world of the Querhoveners had not taken root again, otherwise the braggart Meixner would not have been able to achieve such ill-fated importance among them.

The Blessed Farm

At the time, this dissipated large property owner was plunging again into serious financial difficulties. Because of a thousand marks which he had not been able to pay at the promised time, his last four cows had been mortgaged. His wife had, as daughter of the only large property owner in Querhoven, once been a proud and beautiful girl. Now fate had dashed all her hopes, she sat around despondently at this event which had already occurred to her often, and was startled by every unfamiliar voice which sounded in the yard, ran into her bedroom, and buried her head in the pillows. For she always thought the bailiff was there and fetching their last cows, and if that happened then she would definitely not survive it. She had withstood the beams being sawn from the roof trusses and used up in the fire, her only child, little Mathinka, having to be taken from the girl's school, but now she would suffocate herself if that was not spared her. Big Elis, her husband, laughed at her, whistled, and comforted her. Because of these few Bohemian rogues, he only needed to hold his hand up on the first good path, and it would fly between his fingers doubly and triply. With steadfastly acted cheerfulness, he set off everyday for another friend who had allegedly asked him not to pass up an emerging opportunity. For money was always in his house, and the more the great Meixner needed, the better it was for the backer.

But the wealthy helpers only haunted his head, and when he had happily put the next hill behind him, he turned into the best village tavern, instantly began slandering all the world, as was his wild way, drank without interruption, and went home every evening with empty hands and in a state where he could barely bring forth the lies with which he thought he could comfort his poor wife. But she had after a short time given up all hope, and was roaming about like a sick hen on a rainy day. Mathinka, her fourteen year old daughter, was always around her with love and words of comfort. But what can a child apprehend of the hardship of her seniors? In the midst of the solace, in the middle of the crying around her and the misfortune of the house, the girl was suddenly assaulted by the whirl of her youth and said, laughing cheerfully, it would be best if she and her mother went from this detestable farm out into the world. And every time she said that to her poor mother and placed her hand on her heart in promise, she felt her germinating bosom. Then it blazed like a fire through her, how beautiful she was. Yes, it sometimes became so wild in her that she went out quickly, imprisoned herself in a secluded room of the large, dreary house, and then began singing and dancing loudly until she collapsed exhausted in a corner and cried softly to herself. Her mother, however, when her daughter was thus drawn away from her by the whirling addiction, watched behind her, nodded with dead eyes at her, and then said, "Yes, yes, child, the best thing, you are right, is to go away from here — but not into the world, rather out of the world." This grey owl's flight fluttered more and more often through her soul so that in the end she knew no way out other than seeking calm in the general, hidden pious enthusiasm of the entire village. On a pretext, she attached herself to Gottlieb, stood silently with him by the door, and sucked herself full of an enraptured, peaceful reverie from their pious indulgence. Only, hardly had she drawn the crooked, disintegrating side door of the farmstead closed behind her on returning home than she was already hanging again on the cross of her old despair.

In this way, the appointment for the public forced sale of the cows moved ever closer. The woman still had no ground under her feet, and her husband had still not found any money or helpers. Then the farmer finally decided to grasp for a salvation which he had always rejected before out of shame and fury with himself. He set off on the day before the auction on the path to Hemsterhus to the blessed farmer. If he does not help, he thought to himself as he was walking, then the world shall experience something for once. But yet, as he thus threatened in dull fury, he had to laugh again mockingly. For if he let his proper pipes play and smeared the business with the Querhoveners properly around Sintlinger's mouth, the little man will, without knowing what is happening to him, dance not only into the first, but perhaps into the second thousand.

At the foot of the Sintlinger hill, Meixner was already rid of the bankrupt's hangover, and when he entered the blessed farmstead, he had the broad, weighty step of the great Elis, and almost bowled over in the doorway a pale, timid vagrant who apologised and hurried away with tears in his eyes.

He found the blessed farmer in the room for the poor, holding little Lena half embraced with his arm, and when Sintlinger rose to take a step towards Meixner, the serious fervour of heavy deliberation lay over his entire face to the depths of his eyes. For he had just then heard the confession of a misled life. The door handle was still warm from the hand of the departing man, and the loud, anguished memory of a hearty, though astray human striving still quivered in the air. And, as was his way, he greeted the weatherbeaten bankrupt farmer more heartily for that reason, and offered him in memory of a previous incident another room for their discussion. Meixner was taken aback by the distant, strange coherence of Sintlinger so that he forgot in an instant all the smart archness, and broke out into a cordial abashed laughter. "It, my dear man, is just the right room for me", he roared in perpetual laughter, and slapped Sintlinger humorously on the shoulder at the same time. "Isn't that the vagrants' bench?" he asked and let himself fall heavily onto the bench. "Yes! And so it is thus the fighter's room?" he asked again after a sharp pause and looked around the large, bare room with haggard cheerfulness. He almost blurted out, "Just good for me." But he could still hold back the words, and Sintlinger saw under the twitching of his reddish beard only the quiver of his chin and the tremor of his mouth.

The blessed farmer thought for a second that Meixner was already drunk that morning, but recalled the appointment the next day, and now knew that anguished shame and desperate pride had thus bested the poor man.

For that reason, he spoke to him with cautiously kind words. But instead of now divesting himself without further ado of his request for a loan, for he saw that the blessed farmer was ready for it all, Meixner took hold of his cunning plan, sprang up, ran about the room, fending off with his hands, and then said, thoughtfully buried in his beard, "Not yet, brother, not yet."

Little Lena moved anxiously over to the blessed farmer who made a half turn on the bench, and thus screened her with his back. Meanwhile the braggart Meixner had again returned to the bench, and began with a jesting kick towards Sintlinger's leg a confused chatter over the "crouching", "whining", and "dopiness" of the Querhoveners, over the secret bickering and their annoying embassies to the Sintlinger farm. And everything he said was full of crowing about his high regard and loathsome praise for the good characteristics of the blessed farmer, and the more the braggart Meixner entered into this sickly sweet sloppiness, the more furious he became at himself, his position, and Sintlinger, and he praised ever more thickly from growing hate, his face took on pale splotches, he laughed hoarsely, and finally sprang up with a leap as though stabbed, close to choking in misery.

Little Lena was startled by that so that she cringed by the blessed farmer, and cried out, "Chase the man out, daddy! Don't you see, he has a dog's face!" At the same time, her entire body was shaking, and she began crying loudly.

Sintlinger comforted the child, spoke a few words of apology to Meixner, and led the weeping child away. The bankrupt gave a constrained laugh, and stroked the child's head caressingly. But his hand shook, and when the door had closed behind them both, such a fury seized him that he turned white as chalk and stiff as a rod, and since he was not allowed to rage, the tears shot into his eyes. Thus the reentering blessed farmer met him like a pillar of hate, standing almost out of his mind in the middle of the room, and was taken aback at the sight of this wild disarray.

"Don't be offended by the child, Meixner", he said reassuringly, took him by his slack hand, and led him back to the bench. "You know, the mouths of children are dovecotes. But you aren't taking it well either concerning tomorrow, are you?" Sintlinger thus spoke kindly, and the pale man, stiff with fury, seemingly received a cramp from the touch of a true human hand, his face twitched, his teeth ground, his tears fell just so, and finally he sobbed with a rattling that shook his enormous body to bursting.

"Stop, Meixner", the blessed farmer said, "it will all come right again. How much are you missing then?"

Meixner pulled himself together violently, and shook his head.

"Is a thousand marks enough?" Sintlinger asked again.

The bankrupt shook his head wordlessly.

"Here you have two thousand. I sold three oxen yesterday. Take it, and when you can, return it." With these words, the blessed farmer pushed two thousand mark notes deep into the side pocket of his coat, then grasped Meixner's hand, and said, "Now go, and give my regards to your wife. Let it come right within yourself, then what is outside will run okay by itself behind."

As if in a dream, the braggart Meixner went down the blessed hill and walked in an indescribably elevated air halfway along the boundary path. A song unexpectedly occurred to him, which he had not sung since his boyhood. And with loud voice, he began singing, "I walk through a grassy green forest, and hear the little birds a-singing." But the pure blossoming of his soul was foundering in him already after a few seconds. He grasped for the notes in his pocket, drew them out, took a look, felt them and, when he had convinced himself that it was really, truly, precisely "two thousand marks", he broke out into a loud, wild laughter. Then he swung his legs in a dancing gait. Thus he shot into the Hemsterhus tavern, settled down at a table, slammed his fist down, and asked for a bottle of wine, but "Meixner wine, of the best, not that accursed toad piss."

He drank through the middle of the day, and when the landlord, a distant relative of his wife, had finally induced him to go home, he stumbled away, but not to Querhoven, instead over to Brederode and there collected all sorts of rogues about himself with which he made a racket until deep in the night.

But this day he did not drink himself out of hardship into ever bolder confidence. He tumbled deeper and deeper into remorse, into self-accusations, into the cursing of his wealthy marriage, and when he strode to his farmstead in the darkness, his fury had reached such a height that the curses just whistled from his lips. "My wife is at fault with her smart ways for my getting the face of a dog."

He entered the farmstead in a rage, tore his wife and daughter from their beds, began beating them, which he had never done before, and chased them through all the rooms whilst roaring without stopping, "I have a dog's face, and you are to blame for everything!" In the end, he saw nobody before himself anymore, he ran into something, became deathly tired, collapsed and fell asleep.

The miller down by the Hornwasser, having stepped out of his mill, heard him raging, and said to himself, "Well then, certainly, tomorrow is the deadline, or rather today. For it is already turning grey over the Vördner hills." The drunk's raving and the screams of of female voices suddenly broke off.

"Well, now sleep", the miller said contentedly. "You can have a drink; but such behaviour is filth." Before he walked back into his mill, he looked once more at the Meixner farmstead which now lay soundless in the grey up on its pile of rock.

Then a white figure slid from one of the buildings, hesitated, scurried ducking through the garden, came to the dilapidated picket fence, and bent it apart.

"What's that then?" the miller asked apprehensively, but before he could finish saying the words, a scream shrilled out. Like a white streak, it flew through the grey air, and fell into the Hornwasser so that white spray splattered up.

Then it was deathly still ...

In the morning, the Querhovener farmwife was found battered, bloody, and drowned in the Hornwasser. The Police took her into the mortuary at the church-

yard, and the gravedigger buried her the following evening in the corner for suicides. Mathinka sought shelter
with her relative, the Hemsterhus tavern owner, who
wanted to adopt the beautiful, wildly passionate girl.
The braggart Meixner stood at the kitchen window of
his farmstead, and gazed with boring eyes through the
garden at the hole in the fence which his wife had
broken on her last walk. He stood there thus day and
night and night and day until he had found what he was
seeking. Then he burnt all the clothes down to the shirt
which he had worn on his body that unfortunate night,
ceded the farm to his creditors, and started a new life
with the blessed farmer's money in a small house where
he returned to the skewer maker's bench from which
the fury of love for the estate owner's daughter had once
tempted him away and killed his happiness and honour.
He did not drink anymore. Instead a sinister smouldering had ignited in his dormant eyes, and when, after
finishing his work for the evening, he sat on the little
bench in his humble cottage, alone and menacing, as if
half in a sleep from which he started now and then, he
had something of the look of a bursting, ravenous predator occasionally sniffing the air for prey from its lair.

The blessed farmer was deeply shaken by the terrible
fate at the Meixner farmstead, because the crushing
stone had been set in motion by his little Lena. Nobody
figured out the reason why the wild braggart Meixner
had felt himself tainted by a "dog's face" just on that ill-
fated day, whereas he usually always tended to mock his
"beauty" with others. The wildness of that night was
considered to be entirely an outgrowth of the drunken
madness, and the braggart Meixner began, the longer
the more so, to be esteemed again, because of this
wrenchingly decisive leap by which he had rescued himself from the whirl of debauchery onto firm land again.
And Sintlinger did not want to disturb this beautiful

pulling together, hence he kept to himself what had happened with Meixner at the blessed farm, and also did not insist on the repayment of the loaned money.

6

Thus the current could rise further unhindered. — After the course of a few weeks, the braggart Meixner emerged from his aloof, exigent silence somewhat, and joined in now and then, with weary, downcast mood, such that it seized everyone who observed him, in the secret hours of edification of the "wayward Christians", as the sectarians of the village were also dubbed in the surrounding area. Like a runaway animal, timid and stooped, he emerged, kept his hands buried in his pockets as if freezing, and lingered impassively, leaning collapsed in a corner, his head pressed on his chest, during the long prayers, and said farewell to nobody on leaving in the same way as he tended to speak to nobody on arriving.

The impending disintegration of a man shows itself through the immediate break with the old being and all its habits. The person loses his step, as they tended to say. So, in the complete transformation of the braggart Meixner, they also saw the beginning of his approaching end, in addition to which, he established himself with his silence in that party with whom his wife had found solace and at the same time the courage for her last agony. It was thought justifiable to recognise in it the silent expression of a confession of guilt, timid remorse, and awkward piety. How much truth was to be found in all these conjectures is difficult to say. On one such "evening", which was held this time in the Sweeps in the Rütsch house, the braggart Meixner had again spent half the ceremony slumped as per his custom, terribly menacing, with hidden face in a corner, when he suddenly started sharply at Ursula's speaking.

Ursula Rütsch had again fallen completely into her old "hereafter-rapture" and was singing the praise of the blessed death, and the deeper she fell into the light of the visions of her dead children, the more unreal her voice became.

The braggart Meixner twitched as if jabbed from his rapture, grew up stiffly to his full height, took on a martyr's face, and had to swallow louder and louder as if almost crying. Suddenly he emitted the death cry of a giant tormented animal, swept aside with his arms and legs everyone who stood in his way, and plunged out the door into the open.

People also counted this incident amongst the many wondrous awakenings, saw it as fulfilling all the conjectures over the spiritual state of the unhappy bankrupt farmer, and waited with reverent awe to see which track his fate would lead him on — the path of the "black" or of the "white" retribution, that is, the path of the voluntary death or the path to bright exaltation of life. But they waited in vain for one or the other. As similar as the conditions of his awakening were to his nephew's, the accordion player Meixner, the braggart Meixner climbed to his heights quite divergently from the accustomed path of grace.

Assailed as a rascal suddenly by God and distressingly overcome, the great Elis submitted immediately afterwards into an unsociable, wild piety. His daily work became a breathless struggle. No place was found for rest in his house anymore, and when he sat downcast with closed eyes, a tremor constantly passed through the creases of his face — a face which looked like the face of a gorilla whose being swayed between sleep and raving madness, eerie, stricken, filled by subterranean fires. In the middle of the night, by darkened windows, he began singing pious songs from out of some corner with his wild bestial voice, roaring so that the cottage shook.

He sang terribly, formlessly, in the end like the captured roar of a gorge, so that those who had listened for a time were beset by a chill and had to walk away shaken.

And other times, only screams were heard being uttered, dull and long like blasts of a trombone, and then it laboured groaning with whirring, slapping, splintering wooden rods like in a torture chamber.

It was observed that he lived only on bread and water, and did not sleep in a bed, but right where he stood, sinking for a short rest into the wood shavings.

When he appeared, emaciated, bowed over, like a ghost of his former self, then anyone who was standing before their door stepped inside, frightened faces pulled back from the window, and children were pulled away. Only the old and some young women were so shaken painfully by this figure of weather beaten, wrecked, religious contrition, that they greeted him with humbly faltering voice, "God flowers for us, Meixner."

"He flowers", the self-tortured man thanked them hollowly, and at the same time with a flickering look which they felt like the licking of a flame hotly over their entire body, and often so deep within themselves that a whirling giddiness came over them.

Not long after Meixner began appearing again in public, an old, solitary woman called Mechtildis Tautz, but known only as old Mechtel to everyone, died in Querhoven. She did not bear by chance the same name

377

as that unfortunate young woman who had ended her life more than half a century before in the forest pond out of religious fear, and who still had to haunt that place as a ghost — no, she was descended from the same family, and, as her life progressed ever further, she was shaken deeper and deeper over this misdeed so that she had actually devoted the last twenty years of her existence to the atonement for this crime. But she applied herself to this sad business not with gloom, but with a childishly trusting soul. Presenting active eyes, a cheerful face, and a kind heart of eternal goodness, she sat in her little room, and let the beads of the rosary glide through her hands, or read long prayers from her many books. And next to her own concerns, she also administered to the hardships of strangers who, because of too much work, found no time and collectedness for prayers to prevent threatening evils. For a few pfennigs, she prayed Our Fathers, litanies, and rosaries in any confession, fulfilled faithfully with complete devotion the penance and vows of others, and spent her existence in this pious business. She was so caught up in this heavenly rummaging that, hobnobbing with her kind Lord as it were, she had kept aloof from the church in Hemsterhus for half a lifetime and missed the use of the means of grace. Yes, in the end, she had even, enticed by the gentle spirit, now and then taken part in the prayer meetings of the quiet souls at the Vanlyßender and Rütsch houses.

One day she was found sitting lifeless in her chair, holding the rosary in her hands, her head lowered onto her chest, her face glowing with such a cheerful peace as if she were still indulging in the happy dreams during which she had been surprised by death. Since she possessed no next-of-kin, the pious of the circle to whom she was loosely attached threw the means together to pay their last respects to the old wizened shell. But the

Pastor of Hemsterhus refused her a church burial because she had kept aloof from the church for so long,
and designated that she should probably be buried in
hallowed earth, but close to the field for the suicides,
not far from the turfed mound of the unfortunate Katharina, that lost relative for whom she had wrestled her
whole life long. The entire anabaptist place was certainly shocked, and seethed in displeasure over this
unpitying hardness, because everyone noted that the
blow was directed mostly against themselves. But
Vanlyßender succeeded in dampening the agitation, and
they took heart under sufferance in the words of the Saviour to not resist evil.

In silence one evening, for it had still been ordered
that the dead woman be lowered just after dusk, the funeral cortege made its way through the sole lane of
Querhoven. Quiet, mournful singing alternated with
muffled prayers. Almost a participant from every house
hurried to the last celebration for the outcast woman,
and already in the middle of the village, the escort had
grown to a considerable procession. In the vicinity of
the mill, the path cut across the Hornwasser and ran
along its left bank. Before the little wooden bridge, the
bearers set the coffin down to swap shoulders. During
this short pause, Gottlieb Meixner stepped from his
mother's house, and merged into the procession. Soon
after, the coffin was again hovering up high, and the
men's feet were clattering over the planks of the bridge.

Then, when the bearers had just reached the other
side, the braggart Meixner suddenly sprang from the
millrace bushes where he had been lurking, rushed in
long strides across the narrow meadow strips, planted
himself in his wild bulk before the bearers, flung his
arms up, and shouted, "Stop, go no further! Set the
coffin down, I tell you!"

His arrival happened so unexpectedly and his appearance was so terrible that the bearers placed the coffin on the ground in confusion.

And now the man exhaled the sombre blaze which had taken residence in him during the weeks of silence, solitude, and castigation. His ugly face was chalk white, his mouth was foaming, his words seethed and boiled from his trembling lips, and then his voice roared again like the bellowing of a bull.

"Cursed is anyone who leaves this poor woman to the shame of the damned servant of the devil", he cried in conclusion. "You have hearts of mush and a faith trembling like dry grass. I tell you, God is with you! He has punished my sins; but I arose from terrible night. No flesh on me has not been castigated. For that reason, I tell you, our earth is holier than the churchyard of the Pastor. That I know. Turn around, shun the godless Christian-in-name, defy! Fight! Fight!"

Old Vanlyßender sought to calm him. It was in vain. His nephew stepped up to him. He tossed him aside, laughing derisively.

Many had been numbed by his words as if by a hailstorm. And when the procession could again set in motion towards Hemsterhus, it had melted down by a half. The others withdrew to their cottages with the new prophet.

It could be that despite this obstructive flare up of the Querhoven spirit, everything would have found its way back again into calmer ways. For immediately after this evening holdup, the braggart Meixner ducked again into his long practised taciturn solitude, a mortifying disillusionment for those whom he had diverted to himself in the hand waving, a triumph for his enemies. That was not so much the piously quiet ones of Querhoven as the churchly pious ones of Hemsterhus. A little heap of faith snoopers and virtue sniffers had in fact existed forever in this parish village, and they maintained the moral standards of Hemsterhus and surrounds for the greater glory of God through a secret network of spies. According to perpetually exercised custom, they also kept watch over the purity of faith, and especially spied on Querhoven and its heretical mood with a spirit motivated by outrage and indignity. Many, many years before, a soldierly farmer had been the leader of this voluntary clerical listening post. The village smith had followed him, but then the dignity had again found its way back again to the church father, its old traditional place, where it remained until the Cantor Liborius Pfeiffer took up his position in Hemsterhus. Despite him being the son of the resident cobbler, he succeeded in attaining a significant authority at a comparatively young age. He soon kept watch over the slime trails on which the illegitimate children were smuggled into the world, had a fabulous sense for all the faults and defects of others, and never diminished in Christian patience with this persecution.

At the same time, nature had treated this man quite badly. He was thin, ordinary, red-headed, and tainted with the most curious gait in the world. When he was thus strolling along, it looked as if he were constantly alternating his left and right feet, withdrawing a step, half executed, and correcting the error by a new and greater misstep. For that reason, his legs found themselves in a constantly futile whirling, and no person could explain the expediency of such locomotion. Incredulous people maintained that he had a machinery of gears under his coattails. To this quaint leg rolling, his face stood in glaring contrast — sagging long cheeks, eyes always watering and shaking in sore lids as if they were struggling against a bite stuck in his neck. For immediately after this evening holdup, the braggart Meixner ducked again into his long practised taciturn solitude, a mortifying disillusionment for those whom he had diverted to himself in the hand waving, a triumph for his enemies. All these dreary inhibitions were certainly the impulse for his beginning early in full seriousness the deepening and enrichment of his inner being. But from his spiritual progress came only too soon a passionate spiritual whirl. Liborius Pfeiffer fell deeper and deeper under the influence of the Catholic ecstatics, Katharina Emmerich, Angela of Foligno and Heinrich Seuses, Anna Vetters and Hemme Heyens. The preoccupation with the confessions of such half or wholly disengaged spirits robbed him early of his joyful Christianity, and in the place of a straight, unaffected faith, a thousand secret wounds from the burning desire for rapture and martyrdom had arisen in his inner being, a fanatical frenzy for the persecution of his own errors in the weaknesses of others. This smouldering faith hawk constantly heard in his inner being calls which shook the sleeping man awake, scourged the tardy, and, bitter over betrayal, pulled the Christian to Jesus.

From the start, he had given his attention to the reawakening of the sectarian spirit in Querhoven, and had after long urging and sinister reports finally gotten through to the Pastor of Hemsterhus so that this priest, mellowed by age, decided to make an exemplary retribution with the dead prayer-woman Mechtel. But now, since the denial of a church burial for the old woman had induced a wild rebellion of the heretic spirit, he felt pushed more than ever to get after the faith sinners with firebrands. He peppered the Sunday litany of devotions with new calls for mercy towards the sins against the faith; he smuggled into the school prayers the request to God for annihilation of the enemies of the Church. He especially put the screws on all the Querhoven children during instruction, and by and by they saw his means of correcting of bad habits as not dissimilar to torture.

This spiritual fire-raiser thus brought it about after a short time that the Querhoveners were able to quickly recover from the disarray over the taking sides for an open insurrection and their new prophet was able to perceive with surprise the deep effect of his first appearance. He took faith in the new office which was nothing but the different exertion of his old being, translating the raving, ranting, and disputation of his inner being into his environment.

These two men, who each looked so alike, were already soon standing militantly opposite each other, and like with a proper rustic brawl, figuratively speaking, cowpats, posts and broom handles, ploughs and harrows flew back and forth.

Pastor Ardelt of Hemsterhus saw the fertile spiritual weather of his church parish endangered by this constant rumbling storm, and noted how badly he had acted in decreeing at the Cantor's urging the refusal of the church burial. For that reason, and because the disputing over faith never kept far from the usual bad behaviour of hostile men, he avoided entering into the religious controversy, and tried to settle the excitement through external means. The grave of the old prayer woman Mechtel was subsequently blessed by him, and, in his role as District Schools Inspector, he put a stop to the Cantor's behaviour as a schoolmasterly suppressor of heretics. To the braggart Meixner, he dedicated a kindly dismissive Sunday sermon whose love looked like mockery and which stroked with hidden talons — in a word, it made the bankrupt farmer out to be a bankrupt founder of faith because it buried him amidst ridiculousness.

And in order to then do one last and remaining thing, he asked the offended Cantor over one day, packed a small cartload of goodwill on his back, and made it clear to him finally that it was acting wrongly to place the measure of a straying thinker on the braggart Meixner and to make the Querhoveners responsible for their folkish beliefs. The former was nothing but a boozing bigmouth, whilst with the latter, it was about the dreams and dislocations of their forefathers, and with both, you orient yourself most of all with lenient alertness. Furthermore, if an urge for conscious spiritual disobedience and a temper for clerical subversion is present in everyone, then you must turn towards that from which it alone arises, namely towards Sintlinger, whom, alas God, all the world calls none other than the blessed farmer. During all the Pastor's placations, the Cantor had restrained his feelings in his cloud of bitter surliness because his hustling, which he described as divine fortitude, had not been applauded. Now, with the naming of Sintlinger, he breathed out, for he suddenly saw a broad field open up for new clerically religious head-bashing. Filled with enthusiasm, he immediately sprang for this way out, placed all his powers at the Pastor's disposal and left happier than he had arrived, with the promise "to enter into the study of this new task", because this blessed farmer had a head which was not made of mush. It was of little use to good Ardelt that he advised calm and prudence to the Cantor again, and implied insistently to him that he was implementing his own measures for the blessed farmer, and conspicuous jumping in could impair things more than otherwise. The little cold shower before leaving did not aid the zealous Pfeiffer in achieving temperance in the least. His long sagging cheeks twitched with fervour, he swallowed vigorously his zealot's food, and nullified the Pastor's admonition with energetic gesticulations.

The gears under his coattails purred away, and his legs whirled him down the stairs and out of the parson-age.

The Blessed Farm

The Hemsterhus Pastor had meant simply to pull out from the schoolmaster his opinion. Now he must have had the unpleasant experience that the violin can play the musician and the dog can hound the master. For Pfeiffer's hustle and bustle brought it about in a short time that the Pastor was squeezed into ever new fiery corners and constantly placed before an escalating agitation A great part of the village and surrounds was infected by the intolerant ardour of the Cantor, and the church committee was entirely transformed into the organ with which Pfeiffer drove the Pastor into a corner.

In addition, all of Germany, even the entire world, found itself at the time as though at the conjunction of an excited hustle to find for humanity a new, more lively relationship to the eternal power. Pope Leo XIII, the wise, calm disciple of Peter, had died, and the Jesuits had managed to achieve the election of Pius X. The scholastic religious fervour of this rustically simple nature proved suitable for ruthlessly bearing down on all tolerance. And thus soon a vigorous combative mood towards the dilution of the Roman confession through too friendly a relationship to other confessions and against every tiny weakness in deviating from the core discipline of salvation spread itself through the entire Catholic world.

Thus Pastor Ardelt was stuck in an unholy pincer. Ever more insistent decrees pressed down from above to pursue the purification of faith with all means. In his own parish, he was caught in an ever narrower confinement by men whose feet itched to run fervently in pursuit of the Church's enemies.

Now many intelligent Catholic priests, as soon as they were getting on in years, considered the teachings and dogma of their Church in itself more from the standpoint of social and human usefulness, and, from wisdom which they called humility, did not insist on the base of confusion from which the necessity of dogma arose as a violent way out from unholy contradictions. In their consciousness of the enormous world power of the Catholic priests' state, they carried their life more calmly past the house of a heretic than the members of other Christian sects who sought with the doggedness of upstarts the right to their existence in purely intellectual battles of words.

It stood inwardly exactly so with Pastor Ardelt, in part because he was a farmer's son, in part because the years and human experience had moved him from the passionate zealous whirl of his time as a chaplain. Only now and then did he still tail off into the religious raving and thumping on the pulpit with which he had once scared little Lena from the church. Usually he was content in himself that every Catholic possessed their own particular Christianity, every person relayed the colour of their existence to their God, and the world was filled with as many confessions as their were people. The Church's orders of teaching and dogma were there for the goal of being able to move everyone undisturbed and unmolested as though in a large, well arranged house, and the external compulsion to confession was actually the silent prerequisite for freedom of thought. But then every resident must be seen to adhere to the main points of the house rules, the respective inventory of dogma. Apart from that, you should refer to the particularities of everyone's nature and the weaknesses of their life. That he was moving with such thoughts entirely on the tracks of the old liberal theology made the snorting at the Querhoven fanatics and the blessed farmer so impossible.

Nevertheless, the old Pastor realised that something, and indeed something radical, had to happen which would free him, if possible in one blow, from the senseless religious seething of the Querhoveners as well as the addiction to persecution of the strict Christians of Hemsterhus, and shove a bolt over the blessed farmer's mouth.

He made the decision to push the blessed farmer to enter the church committee, and strove thereby towards the goal of perhaps emulating the estate owners and the way they make the worst wood thieves into forest super-intendents to put an end to their thefts in the forests.

When, after long pondering of the church fathers, he presented this suggestion for consideration, he evoked from everyone an expression of flustered bewilderment, and Liborius Pfeiffer even asked whether it would not be better straightaway to commit the care of God's house to Satan himself. But the clergyman did not let himself be dissuaded. He pointed to the Christian duty of counselling his straying brother in what is right, and if no other way worked in leading the blessed farmer from the agitation of wholesome vanity and ambition unnoticed back onto the path of his childhood faith, and if that was also not achievable straightaway, at least the hidden feuding with the Church and the fermenting of unrest in souls would be complicated.

"The paths of divine grace", the priest also said, "move only too often for our weak understanding in wondrous, not always easily overlooked arcs, and if Sintlinger absolutely declines the acceptance of this God-blessed honorary post, then he will be obligated to provide reasons for it, and when I have the so-called blessed farmer just so far, you can rely on it that I will elicit the additions to God's gracious inventory from his fortifications, and bring the fragility of his faith to a clear confession so that the visible right is given to me to take sharper measures against all his undermining."

The outlook for the final beginning of a fresh, joyous little religious war convinced the hesitant, and the Pastor set off to capture Sintlinger. But so many priests flee

before the fiendishness of life and fall into the fiendishness of their own heart. Each of their thoughts then has
two faces, and each plan two intentions. Thus it had also
been ordered with the Hemsterhus Pastor. While he was
walking to the blessed farm, he ran his large powdery
hands, actively malingering, along his walking stick
from the handle to the ferrule and back again. He only
actually sought the blessed farmer on the face of it as
the leader of the zealots of his parish. In his innermost
soul, he was striving with his plans for the capture of
Sintlinger towards the prospect of holding the zealous
Cantor and his following in check more easily through
Sintlinger. And as the new office would by and by bring
the blessed farmer from his clever reserve to respect
and finally veneration of the old faith and Church, in the
same measure must his eminence as a free power outside every confession dwindle in the eyes of the
multitude. His wife was coated all over in a particular
and distinguishing way with the gentle salve of wonder
which the priests had always known to make clever use
of, and so the Pastor could hope to bring his parish back
into a peaceful calm again, and indeed do so without the
tumultuous assistance of his Hemsterhus religious sen-
tinels and to the surprise of the ecclesiastical authorities
who were less and less at peace with his clever means.

Pastor Ardelt thought through all that once more as
he strode in the warm, clear autumn afternoon on the
newly constructed road which went through the lower
part of Querhoven and then strove in an arc through the
valley between the two estranged farms. The high,
cheerful heavens were full of silently drifting white
clouds, and resounded in the entire dome with soft,
timid birdsong again. The old tall willows next to the
path were already turning yellow in the breath of their
last transfiguration, and the aged soul of the man of
God took this special beauty of the world for a consoling

auspice from the Lord that the success which he hoped for would blossom from his walk. That is why, when he was coming ever nearer to the blessed hill, he pushed with trusting spirit from himself all the unease which tried to steal up on him, and climbed the steep driveway. He surely felt a gentle affront when he saw the unconsecrated Sintlinger's cross under the lime tree by the gate, but, not long, he thought, and this dead stone will be redeemed through the consecration of the Holy Church to a proper divinely blessed life.

The wide yard lay empty. And after he had stood and unhurriedly observed the exemplary order of the wealthy property, he caught sight of old Therese through an open door in the barn as she bound all sorts of shortly chopped roots into bundles with baling yarn. There he learnt that everybody was out harvesting the second hay, the farmer's wife beyond the high butte, the farmer at the beech stand. Without paying any further attention to the old woman, for she had also become one of the eschewers of church at the farmstead, and was also of Querhoven blood, the Pastor squeezed through the back side door out into the yard. But as soon as he was outside and his eyes could sweep about over the sunlit undulating hills, the joyful trust in the good outcome of his beginning overcame him again. It did not last long before he also caught sight of the blessed farmer next to Helene sitting in a field margin on the slope of the hill which sank down towards the beech stand. Above them, the maids were binding the second hay in the meadow.

Ardelt approached the pair as if only strolling for his own enjoyment. He saw that Sintlinger, after he had come into view, whispered something with lowered head to Helene, and they both rose and walked towards him. But he gave the appearance of being entirely sunk in the view of the beech stand which stood soundlessly in the depression as if it were a colourful pond overflowing with light.

The pair's steps came ever closer to him, then it suddenly shot through the Pastor's head that he had once been shown out of the house years before by this man. That is why, when he now turned in astonishment to the pair, despite all the forced friendliness, a quiet exasperation lay in his face. But he succeeded in greeting Sintlinger with open-minded politeness, and he also obliged Helene with loving words. Thus the two men came into conversation, in which the farmer soon noticed a deeper intention of the Pastor's which the latter concealed less and less whilst he soundly steered his way out of the casual to and fro over the weather and farming. But the blessed farmer turned every intensification into trifling cheerfulness, until the Pastor gave a jerk and with an almost challenging voice asked, "Why, Sintlinger, haven't you actually attempted felling for your profit the beech stand from your father-in-law's, good old Klim's, farm?"

The blessed farmer smiled, pondering, then said quickly that he would answer in a minute, called a maid over, and sent little Lena home with her.

"So, now we can talk undisturbed, Pastor", he said full of cheerful force, and straightened his shoulders, "for I sense well that your walking past is a coming here. Isn't it?"

In this way, the blessed farmer instantly flipped the furtive cleverness of the clergyman on its head so that the man of God had something of the rigid helplessness of a carp's eye in his look.

In order to come to his help, Sintlinger slowly set his feet in motion along the path, and continued, "But, to come to the beech stand, a branch more on a tree is always a branch too many for it if it does not have to sprout it. That you know yourself and would certainly not also want Dingden in play next to Brederode and Querhoven."

"Above all not Querhoven. For they are surely good people, but bad Christians. Faith, however, Sintlinger, is both horse and wagon at once."

Ardelt smiled contentedly. That was at once where he had wanted to go, before the most hidden door of this small, unassailable monster next to him, and he set off outright for his goal. He counted it as a reproach on Sintlinger to segregate himself from everyone. For anyone who believes they have acquired a treasure must also share it. It would then turn out whether it was a proper one or only a moth-eaten thing. The blessed farmers rejection of all honorary posts was also touched on, and finally the Pastor came to the farmer's neglect of religious and church duties.

Thus far Sintlinger had let the clergyman go on unchallenged. But now he straightened up towards him, and asked, "Why should I go to your church? Someone who always has a table laid in his own house need not look for a meal in a stranger's house."

"Sintlinger, Sintlinger", the Pastor answered after a short hesitation, "that is spiritual arrogance."

"Certainly", the blessed farmer interrupted him, "that I know, and it was meant that way too. Someone who wants to reach high needs high courage, Pastor."

"Wonderful, and someone who evades the leadership of the Church in these matters sinks unavoidably into madness. Unavoidably! Let that be said, Sintlinger, by a man who has not become older than you are in vain."

With these words, the clergyman expressed an honest conviction which always took hold. And even the blessed farmer became hesitant as to whether he would not be better to appease the old man and let him leave in peace. For he noticed how his stick trembled from the shaking in his hand.

For that reason, he walked a few steps in silence and hesitation next to him.

Ardelt, however, thought he had already placed his knee on the blessed farmer's chest, and called out in rash triumph, "You see, Sintlinger, so it is. Already you are stricken in your heart. How shall it further develop though, if you leave it longer and longer, if the Saviour must knock for you always in vain through the hand of his servant. Have you already considered that?"

"Look at your hand, Pastor — it is empty", the blessed farmer answered softly and in earnest.

Ardelt spun around in shock.

"Yes, I meant it so", Sintlinger said and nodded to him. "If you really want it then it is so. Now answer *my* question. Just tell me from which the sound originates, the drumstick or the drum?"

"From neither alone", the Pastor answered, and thought to himself, just strike one hook, fox, and I will seize you.

"So the drum remains mute as a stone when it is not struck?" Sintlinger asked steadfastly.

"Well, what of that? Certainly it is so", the Pastor uttered his reply.

"Like the drumstick and drum, don't you think, is the relationship between the Church and the faithful who also hear the sound of divine truth tolling through the efficacy of the Church?"

Ardelt wrinkled his brow and hesitated to make a decision. But the blessed farmer waited only for a moment and continued with raised voice, "The drummer could spare himself the work of drumming if he knew that his instrument creates the whirl much better alone if he will just hang it on a tree and lie in a field under the sky as it brings its sound forth. — My dear man of the pulpit, go and work calmly on skins which were silenced long ago. I and my child are drums who play by themselves."

Ardelt saw that he was on the point of ruining everything. For that reason, he relented, and said, "But the bad example, Sintlinger!"

But the passionateness of his old nature had seized the blessed farmer. He abandoned himself to it, and talked blazingly in a way he had not done for years, "The bad eye makes the world bad. How does that concern *me*! Do I and my child look like godless people? Or does my farm operate too much like a devil's house? So, don't worry. Must then all of Christianity be demonised? Oh no, man, I feel you yourself do not believe your words."

Ardelt forced himself to continue, and said gently, "Dear Sintlinger, you misunderstand me. I am nothing, purely nothing at all. I am only the representative of Christ, and *his* words are eternal and enclose the world and everything in it."

At that the blessed farmer broke out into loud mocking laughter so that the Pastor was appalled.

When Sintlinger had again gotten hold of himself, he said, "Good, we are at an end! Answer me just one more question. And if you can say yes, then you shall be right in everything, and I will be a fool and remain so until the end. Is there in the world, on earth or in heaven, a wagon which has a seat on its hub, or a gate which contains the entire city to which it leads?"

"No, that is certainly impossible", was the Pastor's answer. "But what is that all about?"

"Or will a man succeed in possessing his body in *one* grasp of the hand? And as truly as that will remain impossible for all eternity, as certainly are there no eternal words. For the word of man is nothing more than the hub on the wagon, the gate to the city, and the hand on the human body. But the soul of man is deeper than the entire world and more than Christ with all his words and miracles.

Even you, little man, are merely a hammer in the hands of others. And when the smith strikes with the hammer off target, what can the hammer do about it? I am not angry with you. Go in your God's name from me as you came to me."

Then the Pastor looked at the blessed farmer with a face full of horror and fear, tried to say something more, but shook in abhorrence and walked quietly away.

Sintlinger perceived none of all that. He had put a straw between his lips, and was looking raptly through the dusk at the beech stand.

Then he heard the Pastor calling once more.

As he turned his face, the Pastor just then threw his arms up beseechingly, and called out, "Woe to you, Sintlinger, Sintlinger! You and your child, you are accursed, accursed!"

Then he vanished hurriedly into the darkness.

The blessed farmer smiled sadly, and returned to his solitary deliberations.

After a long time, it was already night, he started and saw in the darkness the giant figure of the rebel Faber standing next to him.

Then he was frightened so that his heart turned cold.

But the figure nodded to him full of satisfaction so that the blessed farmer became afraid and fled hastily.

During this same night, he roamed about without finding peace, like in the earlier times when the intoxication had driven him, and on returning home, his face was pale and bitter like it had formerly been.

7

The above depiction of the argument which the blessed farmer had fought in the field during the autumn afternoon until evening with the Hemsterhus Pastor has been reconstructed from quite comprehensive notes which can be found in his papers over that incident.

At the close of the notes stands the following sentence:

> Anyone who embroils himself in the struggle over the pecking order of virtues is just as sinful as that person who loses himself on the stepladder of vices.

If these words of the blessed farmer's are held together with his victorious belligerence of that afternoon, and if at the same time the tales from his surroundings are observed, you will note that the remarkable man had counted not the battle of words with the Pastor, but that with himself as a lapse against his arduously obtained knowledge.

For it was reported that Sintlinger was for a long time after that shrouded by the old passionate shadows, was roaming about, stopped to look around on paths and in forests, in villages and in secluded fields, as if he had to scout out the concealed hiding place of a man from whom he was threatened. He spoke to nobody about his unrest or the person whom he believed was following him, nevertheless, he often revealed his secret himself almost completely by asking on his return home whether somebody had not been there in his absence or been seen in the vicinity of the farm, though he would start in the midst of the conversation, listen tensely, and then leave the house hurriedly to peer all around whilst standing before the farmstead.

Thus no other interpretation of this state of his soul is possible than that he still could not detach himself from the mysterious Franz Faber with whom he had had a discussion many, many years before on the night of the dedication of the Sintlinger memorial. And that it was so is proven by the final denouement of his life, but an explanation is also found in an entry in his papers which otherwise remains obscure. Immediately below the last mentioned record stands the exclamation:

> He was with me again! When will I be rid of him! His eyes were directed at mine, and he spoke words to me which I did not understand.

In this inner unease and uncertainty, he held even closer than ever with almost sickly fervour to his blind little daughter. He hardly let her out of his hand. Where he went, she had to be with him, and often in the night, Helene still noticed that he stood for a long time next to her bed and hurried passionately to her.

While Sintlinger was thus again, yes, almost as if in flight before a power which he did not feel up to, submerged more deeply in the nameless gleaming waters which streamed from his child's soul, and even more than ever insulated from the hustle of the world, the confusions of the time and the struggle in the neighbouring surrounds swelled higher and higher around the blessed hill.

Pastor Ardelt had left the farmer as a chastised man, injured in his dignity as a servant of God, defeated by a stronger spirit, compromised by his vain expectation, wounded deeply in his peaceable old man's heart, pushed thus into an ungovernable whirl so that he had mistaken the path on the way home that evening and only reached the parsonage in Hemsterhus late at night.

The housekeeper heard him finally coming along the road, recognised his hand as well in the unlatching of the little gate in the fence, but was startled when she straight afterward heard the gate slammed so that the entire yard whirred. She quickly raised the waiting meal from the hot stovetop, and hurried to the door to oppose herself manly if, instead of the theologian, perhaps some stranger was forcing his way into the house. But she hardly made it with the candle halfway down the corridor which led from the kitchen to the main hallway when the door was already flying open, and she saw the old master rushing down the hall with agitated, long strides, the stick like a rapier in his hand, his hat on his neck, and storming up the stairs without listening to her call and subsequent cry of fright.

But up above in his room, the upset man of God placed his stick with exaggerated care in its accustomed place, hung his hat precisely on the nail, then walked with cautious steps, without lighting a candle, into the middle of the dark room, pondered the floor for a while, and then said, "Good, if you want fire, you shall have it. Liborius Pfeiffer is right, such spawn deserves no mercy. — Lord, am I not your servant?"

And now began in Hemsterhus, at first quietly, then ever louder and more tempestuously, the struggle against stray teachings, sinfulness, and nefariousness of the undisciplined spirit.

Ardelt submitted more and more to the fanatical ardency of his time as a chaplain — for someone who has only been pushed aside mechanically by the years from the confusions of youth submits only more defencelessly and fiercely to the riots of his old temperament when the protective wall of dust and life's inactivity is suddenly blown away. Though the Pastor avoided speaking of the outcome of his conversion walk to the Sintlinger farmstead, he immediately swelled into long sermons of

damnation and rage whenever someone even mentioned the name of the blessed farmer. But his measures
were not directed against this "arch-heretic", as he now
called Sintlinger, but against the colourful, fervent rummaging for salvation of the Querhoveners. He described
that place as the body of Sintlingerian faithlessness, and
swore to hack limb after limb from them, then the sacri-
legious soul on the hill would perish by himself.

He engaged unhesitatingly with the "eradication of
the devilish smouldering". Every confession of a Querhovener became a distressing court of inquisition and
often ended after tumultuous explosions by the clergyman with the refusal or averting of the absolution. He
pointed Communion goers away from the Communion
table. He subjected the baptised Querhoveners to a
shaming driving out of the devil before the granting of
the sacrament. The Sunday sermons dealt with nothing
except crimes of faith, the lot of sinners on earth, and
their damnation in hell. The windows of God's house
were rattling again, the pulpit was trembling. Ardelt
raged like in his wildest years of zeal.

The zealous Cantor Liborius Pfeiffer was thereby
helped more than ever onto the horse for which he was
made, and he paid every honour to his nickname during
this period. The torments of the Querhoven children at
school began again. His public prayers seethed with the
fervour of persecution. Where he walked and stood, a
shadow of hidden darkness lay around him. He could
not speak without after three or four sentences already
lapsing into his religious concerns. His lips quivered
constantly as if from silent sermons of defending and
damning, his restless eyes rubbed their lids still rawer.
A trembling often ran through the bags under his eyes
like that which precedes an outburst of tears.

But whereas the Pastor deployed his entire force
against the Querhoveners, the Cantor also turned his

weapons against the blessed farmer. Be it that he was ruled unconsciously by memories of the reading of his ecstatic confessionals, be it that he really was gripped by the delusion that the hardships of the time had again returned the power of violent persecution of dissenters, in short, he took measures as if the sequence of events must necessarily lead to a painful religious trial. There exists by his hand a "List of all the calumnious stray teachings and life sins of the dangerous heresiarch Andreas Sintlinger, known as the blessed farmer of Hemsterhus, and his blind child Helene, known as the blessed little Lena."

In Pfeiffer's "mandate" are to be found unbelievable accusations and absurd tales, like the story of the conversation of the blessed farmer with the devil in the shape of a black hen, and his playing bowls with the devil in the beech stand. It contained the many sayings of Sintlinger's, in part of course twisted, which were passed around amongst the folk. Aside from that, this modern file of heresies also delivered a few new sentences, however, which completely bore the stamp of Sintlinger's spirit, although the circumstances were not stated in which they had been expounded. They read:

> Do not care so much for God, otherwise you will soon become like whores who talk only of reputability so that they overstrain their own.

It states further:

> Is it not a fool who throws midges up into the sky and strews sand in clear water so as to learn thereby how high is the one and how deep the other? — But those who want to reveal to others with their talk and words the secret of God and their own soul act like such a fool.

The most vehement indignation, however, was excited by the last saying:

> What the horse was before it became a horse is the same as that which the man was before he entered the shaped figure of his body. For if we were not in everything and if this all-oneness did not also flow in us, then we would not be able to recognise anything.

The bill of indictment never left the side pocket of the Cantor's coat. In every company, Pfeiffer invaded and kindled a horror of the dangerousness of the blessed farmer, whose deviancy he put down to the vices of his ancestors and the debauchery of his own youth; he recalled the story of the vanished Nobody-incubus, and swore that everything would turn out exactly as everybody in the district had known about the father's house, and what this half-witted man had at one time witnessed to many faces, namely, that the destruction of the farm would have its beginning with a child, and this being was none other than Helen whom God had already struck with blindness before her birth. "But don't you know", he tended to say after this wild prophesising, "don't you know which forest the Nobody-incubus lost his life in, and who found him and buried him? The poor fool was in the way of nobody except the one whose terrible end he had foreseen. I must shout with Moses to you: 'Depart, I pray you, from the tents of these wicked men, and touch nothing of theirs, lest ye be consumed in all their sins.'*"

Thus he spread through the entire district a dull trembling, a hidden fear.

In this charged air, an ecclesiastical event took place which not only took effect in the narrow world of Hem-

---

*   Numbers 16:26.

sterhus like a lightning bolt, but excited the world, and it not only where it was subject to the Roman Catholic faith.

In that same autumn, the then Pope Pius X issued his encyclical *Pascendi Dominici Gregis*.

This epistle acted as a damning of all free science and as an attempt to monastically cloister the entirety of Roman Catholic Christianity, including the world's clergy, provocatively, even disturbingly.

Pastor Ardelt received the encyclical and the attached letter from the episcopal office as he had just sat himself in his armchair after his midday nap. Hardly had he read the introductory chapter of the papal breviary than the aged priest was so stirred that his eyes were moistened.

"Finally", he cried with relief when it spoke of the way in which modernism should be combatted. It seemed to the Pastor as if the Holy Father had sensed his poor position in the struggle against the desire for renewal of the Church, and had rushed to help him at the right moment with his entire might. Now Ardelt was secure and strengthened in all the measures for the annihilation of this lunacy of the heretic Querhoveners, but also immunised against the frail goodness of his own heart and the liberal moods of his poorly guarded thought.

"Yes, annihilation", the Pastor said menacingly to himself. "And when I have stilled this brood, the rooster on the blessed hill will stop crowing by itself."

Then he stood for a long time sunken in deep thought by the window, and looked down at the grassed forecourt in whose middle an exceptionally beautifully crowned tall maple kept watch over the little garden gate. Ardelt fell into brooding in ever deeper ardency, so that he finally had to start drumming rhythmically on the windowpane with the fingers of his right hand. Suddenly the entire window trembled under his hand as if under a powerful blow. A jerk just then went through the old man's entire body so that he had to step back in shock and work a bit to catch his breath. But soon his heart was again wandering the old path with a steady beat, and the man of God looked down curiously into the yard as if the disturbance which he had unknowingly afforded himself had come from there. The sun was filling the silent forecourt, the brownish yellow autumn leaves were stirring by themselves as if in the last quiet convulsions of escaping life.

"Yes, what was that then, that thunder before?" the priest said to himself, being superstitious like many Catholic clergymen and believing firmly in forebodings and signs. "I know already that it will cost effort and make a racket. But for that reason, I will not be unfaithful to my duty." Only, he had to stop speaking. For the shadow of a man was approaching the little gate, automatically ran along the path, straightened up from the ground at the little gate, swayed for a moment as a long thin shroud in the air and then sank slowly into the yard. And at the same time, nowhere was a being to be seen to which it belonged to. "Is all the world suddenly burdened with ghosts?" he asked himself apprehensively, closed his eyes, walked to his armchair, seized the arms tightly with his hands, and murmured fervently, "Lord, abide by me! Joseph and Maria, don't abandon me!" While he thus struggled, there was a knocking on his door, louder and louder. Then the Hemsterhus Pastor came to himself again, lifted up the papal missive, called with strong voice, "Come in!", and when Liborius Pfeiffer appeared in the doorway, he brandished the pages like a flag in his hand, took a step towards the Cantor, and cried, "God be with you, Cantor! Here I hold our victory in my hands."

Both men began with determining the church's work plan for the week. But then they lost themselves in the exchange of new intelligence from that corner of heresy, and, bolstered by the combative spirit of the papal words, swung together more and more inflamed in their resolve for a ruthless struggle against every abstaining from confession, and finally discussed new actions by which the gravity of their spiritual errors could be made physically palpable to the Querhoveners. Though the Pastor resisted this type of struggle, and was certain of making a lasting impression the following day on the straying dispositions through the act of the solemn reading of his sermon, and the subsequent procession and walk of penance and prayer around the church. But Liborius Pfeiffer adhered to his view that, if it worked no other way, the soul must be chastised through the body. And here, the Cantor was also well versed in the ways of the world, here it would not work any other way. Being kicked can only be healed through stepping back, and having caught a blow from a fist, there is no return blow for a long time.

In this blazing with words, the gears under Pfeiffer's coattails unexpectedly began working again. He saw the evening loading more and more shadows on his back, sprang up, and was whirled out of the Pastor's room by his legs even before he could take a proper leave.

Not long after, Ardelt heard the entire Pfeiffer family singing songs of the Stations of the Cross. In-between sounded long murmured prayers, for the school stood quite close to the parsonage. The light went out, and then flared up again, and each time, a new song of penitence rose, only more and more inflamed.

However, when the encyclical had been read the next day in the mass after the Gospel, when the Pastor's sermon had clattered like a hailstorm from the pulpit, and after that the song of penitence had gone with droning music around the church, neither Ardelt nor Liborius Pfeiffer nor even the other members of the religious fraternity could ascertain any especially deep impression on the Querhoveners who had been constantly watched for a blanching, blushing, elbowing, or nodding of the head. In contrast, everyone who had gathered in one of the school's classrooms after the ceremony of atonement had ascertained that the Querhoveners had kept themselves hidden as always behind the mask of deep devotion and humble prayer, except for a few of the Meixner Christians, from whose eyes sometimes even something like intractable derision had travelled. And because an effect was needed, they liked to believe in the hidden rebelliousness, although the man who had wanted most of all to catch sight of this concealed religious hate was only the village baker, a weeping prayer whose eyes became wet with every devoted stirring of his mood. But he maintained steadfastly that he had distinctly felt how the scapular cloth on his chest stirred at the sight of this heretical obduracy as if it had been moved back and forth by the appalled hands of a saint. Then everyone finally all took heart again firmly in the pious abhorrence of such religious apostates who along with the gestures of devotion followed the devilish music of their malevolent hearts before God and humanity.

Certainly those who had seen no impression of the papal words on the Querhoveners had been as correct as those who had wanted to have noticed a secret rebelliousness lurking in them; for, in fact, most of them behaved as if the uproar of outrage over faithlessness did not refer to their failures. They returned that very Sunday to their poor village quite unconcerned and as calmly as usual, not balled in counselling clumps, sombrely persistent, with sharply bitter eyes in their faces, but in twos and threes in which ever way peaceful affinity and accident had brought them together. And yet each of them, man or woman, bore a knowledge in themselves of the oppression which would after this day be burdened still more heavily on them. But they all had in silence, even as the rumbling of accusations filled the vaults of the church, placed their worries with God to deal with them entirely according to his will and to preserve them always from the wrong of replying to hate with fury, disparagement with bluster, and invective with slander — for they knew that only a pure heart could mediate between God and men, and that this life in all its guises only then had a deep, precious meaning if it was acted out in the light of our eternal soul.

And all their sorrow reached no further than to touch sufferingly on their countenance for a moment, or to lead their gaze for a while to the side, questioningly across the hills out into the emptiness. The calm chatter lay across the churchgoers like the humming song of the wings of busy bees, until right at the end, there where Vanlyßender walked in the company of two other grey heads, an old evangelical song rang out from a little mob of women, at first timidly, then more and more heartily and freely. And like a little spark, raised up by the wind and led away, here and there flames ignited until the path which it had taken, lit up like a single strip of fire, propagated the melody of blessed faith from group to group so that after a short time the procession was moving in the roar of a pious hymn. Here and there a group separated from the procession and strolled singing to their homes, until the song, only kept up still by a few throats, died away behind the Sweeps' strip of forest ever quieter like an echo, and finally fell silent in the trees.

And if you want to say so, these inwardly turned souls had the joy that right in those excited days, an ancient, half crumpled "little document" was found amidst ancient junk in the loft of the Vanlyßender house, which

secured them in steadfast serenity opposite all the oppression from their adversaries. It was one of the
eighteenth century editions of the little book "Of the
True Love", which that learned friend of God Hans
Denk had first had published in 1527. In it was found
formulated almost word for word the confession which
the Querhoveners had been led to solely from the impulse of half-forgotten tradition by a rapt surmising,
and they felt bound in joyful tremors across the long
centuries with the fraternal community of that time, "no
longer just an impotent voice in the storm, not a little
branch without a tree, or a song which no bird on this
earth has ever sung".

These were the words through which, after a week,
old Vanlyßender made the quiet community familiar
with this blessed book. Everyone had gathered for the
evening at the Rütsch house in the Sweeps, and the old
man explained here and there from his own pondering
the opinion of the long blown away seeker of God.

The blessed Christmas week reigned in the world,
and as the pious people listened to the simple and clear
words of their beloved "father", they heard through the
closed windows the night wind burrowing softly in the
snow and now and then passing with louder blasts into
the loaded crowns of the trees so that a woman burst
out in the middle of the devotion with the exclamation,
"Be quiet, there are people walking around outside the
house!"

Vanlyßender let the little book fall with his right
hand, shifted his glasses up above his eyebrows onto his
forehead, and listened like everyone to the murmured
rumbling with which the weather was labouring about
the house. Nobody, however, heard any sound but the
muffled whispering of the wind, and now and then the
falling of snow loads. For that reason, the old man
pulled the glasses over his eyes again with a smile and

continued talking, because he had just reached the place which required his interpretation, "Faith is thus neither an affair of the Church nor of the State. Religion goes only from the pure soul of the individual to God and back again from God. Anyone who wants to practise it differently must inevitably resort to violence in the end and arrive at bloody hands. Or as the blessed farmer has said, 'The real brother of the proselytiser is the killer.' Nobody overstrains themselves because of their belief, for we can point with the finger to countless paths to heaven ..."

With these words, the woman's voice from before cried out again, but this time fearfully, and before Vanlyßender could admonish her to be calm, a great tumult rushed up to the Rütsch house, a window was pushed in and smashed, and many disguised voices called inside, "You dreamers, stop chanting. Make a stand, otherwise you will be chased from house and home."

Then it fled away in all directions.

When the assembly had recovered from the shock, and hurried outside the house, they had all already vanished like a ghost into the night. No cracking of branches ran through the nearby forest, no crunching steps in the fields of snow.

Though everyone knew that the wild intrusion had been prosecuted by none other than the Meixner followers, they had not recognised anyone so as to be able to bring them to account. For that reason, voices of fair-minded outrage arose in the general excitement which now occurred. However, Vanlyßender called everyone once more into the room, instilled tolerance and vigilance in them, and released them with the old hearty wish, "God let us blossom!"

8

But nobody can stem the course of a river if he parries its waves with flowers, even if it were a mighty large bouquet. The Christians, however, as the "quiet" Querhoveners still called themselves, aimed with their gentle steadfastness nothing at the Hemsterhus campaigners against heresy, and above all nothing at their own wild religious brothers. Actually they did not want to at all. They just felt bound by their pure souls and by God, as they understood him, and declined to be hammer or anvil.

But all around them the mad merry-go-round was continuing.

For the wild Meixner following had not really been wrong with their reckless wake-up call through the smashed window. The Pastor of Hemsterhus had decided in favour of the urgings of the Cantor to intervene against the religious rebelliousness of the Querhoveners with violent means, if the hitherto utilised mild castigation by the Church came to nothing against their obduracy. The commons of Querhoven was, with the exception of the former Meixner estate, in part of the estate of Prince Arenberg. The other part belonged as a gift to the respective Pastor of Hemsterhus. Most of the Querhoven farmworkers only fully owned their house plot, a little garden, and their cottage. The strips of field, whose yield made up half of their livelihood, they had leased since time immemorial from the lord and the parsonage in Hemsterhus. Nobody knew that it had ever been different — the possibility that a change could happen one day occurred to no one. For what necessity forges finds in use its own explanation. Thus the Querhoven spigot turners and skewer makers had forever harvested their cabbages, potatoes, some twenty sheaves of corn, and a few bundles of oats from the little field, and faithfully carried the lease shilling on John the Baptist's feast day and New Year's Eve to the Hemsterhus parsonage or to the Head Forester Wiesner at Dingden, the way others take the interest to the creditor, and some hair-splitter may have counted up all the lease amounts from father, grandfather, and so on, and found that the little field was already more than paid for long ago, and if he were introduced one fine day with a princely and spiritual nod of the head to the sovereign lord of the field, then not a hair would have needed to move in the whole world. It ran so much according to the line of the law that it would hardly be worthwhile grasping his cap in thanks.

When the Meixner followers thus emitted in the night the cry of warning about house and home, most of the quiet friends of God considered the notion to be just smoke from excited brains. However, in the days up to New Year, all sorts of things clustered in from all sides. Elis Meixner bustled back and forth, and, amongst the people of his following, there was a constant secret running around so that the calm part of the anabaptists were also gripped inwardly in their own way for an unpleasant surprise.

Up to the second day after New Year, everyone had been as one as to in which direction the menace was to be met. And really, after the one had placed the lease groschen on the counting board at the Head Forester's office, the other at the parsonage in Hemsterhus, it was revealed to them here as there that a withdrawal of the leased fields was quite well possible at some time, and that the people would do well to look around for a new lease, perhaps from the Meixner estate. The same process in both places had an effect like a talked about play, and there could be no doubt over whom had arranged the little piece, because the Pastor had waved with the religious cudgel more vehemently at the one than the other as he spoke of the authority for temporal punishment for transgression against God and his Holy Church.

Only, neither the quiet nor the wild ones were lifted from their hinges by it.

"The Lord Jesus will mediate it in you, as is right", the former answered, smiling kindly, and walking quietly and well-mannered through the door. The others let their faces blaze, broke out abruptly into an insubordinate mocking laughter, and even probably said that, without an axe, no healthy tree has yet fallen, then threw their caps on their heads, and rumbled out of the house.

The Head Forester Wiesner in Dingden was an upright spirit, and on his wholesome chest, no injustice or spider's venom could settle down so easily. Thus when he noticed the complete failure of the threat, he recoiled from continuing to help the Church to bring hardship and misery on the poor people for the sake of their faith. He thus let the Pastor know that the royal stewardship did not plan on pushing further along the purported path, because the forests would lose sufficient manpower through the probable moving away of so many families, which with the shortage of people could not be replaced as easily and especially not as well. He warned about over-stretching and severity, because it was also to be feared that the social-democratic pestilence would come in addition to the religious scab.

But nothing is harder to rein in than an old man who has been forced out from the cover of his life experience. Ardelt thus gave the upright, fair-minded man an unctuous reply which was spiced in addition with all his spiritual pride.

The Blessed Farm

To make things worse, at this time one of the most industrious amongst the fervent fanatics fell dead. It had been one of those who had tipped his nose at the Pastor on the New Year's lease day with a derisive answer. The consumptive, emaciated man had been seized at his woodworker's bench and thrown into the shavings so that he was taken away without a last confession or communion, which he had avoided for years anyway.

When Ardelt now refused him a church burial, and the gravedigger burrowed a proper sinner's hole in the earth for him next to the hanged, his friends reached an agreement this time to go wherever it took them, to meet hardness with hardness.

Vanlyßender certainly warned them off all acts of violence, and when they did not want to let go, he got the better of himself and even sought out Elis Meixner to call to his attention with an emotional appeal how dangerous such a beginning was for the entire community of the friends of God, and anyone who had not taken the decision to be crushed, should not also stick his fingers between the gears of a machine. Only, he was unable to arrange anything with the sinister man. Someone who always wants to extinguish the fire with tinder, Meixner said, must also experience once what the flames do to his own body.

The worked-up fanatics adhered to their will, and dug for their part a grave for the dead man at a bushy place on the slope between Querhoven and the area of the estranged farms, a place at which they had often gathered, and brought over several hundredweight of heavy stones.

On the evening now when the body should have been lowered in the Hemsterhus churchyard, the fanatics carried the coffin with their dead friend out amongst the trees. It was an eerie funeral procession. Silent, with lowered heads, next to each other in twos and threes, with tightly clasped hands, they walked along. Many of the men carried a mattock or a shovel on their shoulder. In the dark of the spring evening, which made everything both starker and more shadowy, they themselves looked like shadows following their own broken lives. At the head of the procession, a cross was borne, as if broken just then from the bushes, the crosspiece bound together with cords. Only now and then did a sob from the widow interrupt the eerie silence which followed like a powerless echo the woeful whimpering of the fatherless children. The end of the funeral party was formed by Elis Meixner who, quite emaciated, just skin and bones, followed at a distance deeply bowed with the help of a stick. Fire-red strands of hair hung down on his sunken temples, he seemed deathly sad and weary of life to the point of collapsing. When the procession reached the edge of the wood, the crying of the widow and children increased so that a shiver rippled over everyone's skin. The braggart Meixner, however, raised his head, paused for a moment in helplessness, looked around dully, and then emitted a sound of pain like the bellowing of a dying bull. Here by the forest grave, he now held his first great sermon. It was an expressed storm, a fervent blast, a wild flash, more a simple stringing together of exclamations, protests, and invocations. Everyone looked timidly at him, and it would perhaps have not surprised them if he had died on the spot from the fanatical eruptions of his fervour.

"Brothers! Sisters! Firebrands of God!" he called at the end. "From today on, this place where we are burying our friend shall be called Gethsemane. For from here, our new suffering begins. But I will sacrifice myself, if it must be, for our good thing, for you, for the true faith. I will sacrifice myself in a different way from that nice blowhard of a blessed farmer who is silent now and cowers in his wealthy life when fate shines our hair with steely combs. And now lower our brother into the earth and roll the stone onto his coffin so that nobody but Jesus Christ alone can disturb his rest. As an ostra-cised man, you go there, brother, as a pure light, you will awake before God, the Lord, as we will soon awake like a rested flame and a consuming fire. The morning nears, the storm! Amen!"

So shaken was everyone by his words, that the hands shook of the men who rolled the heavy stone onto the coffin and then towered a hill of earth over it, on which they stuck the cross they had brought with them. After that everyone scattered in all directions into the deep darkness. For a quick step was approaching from the village, which could well be that of a gendarme. The wo-men pulled their overcoats over their heads, the men also shed their coats, took them over their left arm, swung the shovel or the mattock onto their shoulder, and each walked in a different field margin, from all dir-ections to the village, like workers coming from the field and out of the forest.

Soon after, they received the request from the Pastor and the police to dig up the dead man and inter him in the churchyard at Hemsterhus. They remained stub-born, and answered that the body had been buried honestly in peace. Anyone who wanted a disgraceful and dishonourable burial should hold it in a way that he would be able to answer to God for. They would cer-tainly not stir a finger.

The agitation grew.

Meixner held sermon after sermon, each wilder and more inflamed than the previous. They seemingly smoked from his mouth. Like formerly when he still drank, he was in a constant intoxication.

One day, he vanished entirely from the village and the district, and left behind the notice that if his house went up in flames, the Lord would have lit it himself. Then the time would have come.

"Not before a blood debt is committed on us and is atoned for will you see me anymore again." These were the last words which the prophet spread about before his mysterious departure.

Now the events followed on like the hoofbeats of a galloping horse.

Liborius Pfeiffer segregated the Querhoven children at school entirely from the others, and called the benches on which they sat Satan's benches. Pastor Ardelt communicated to his twenty leaseholders on the first of April the announcement that they would on the first of October be returning the leased fields to the office of the Church. At the same time, the entire holding was being transferred to a generally hated Querhoven tattler for cultivation. This quick rise of an ignoble soul increased the bitterness and pain of those who stood before ruin if a way out did not shortly offer itself. A few turned to the Royal Administration for the granting of a lease, but received an adverse reply, even when their position as forest workers was taken into consideration. Others began familiarising themselves with the thought of selling house and garden to the government if nothing else came up, so as to move to the mining district and become miners there. It could not be worse for them in any case, and though they would have less sun and freedom, they would be doubly lifted up by the high earnings.

But everyone was depressed. Wherever they went, it was like saying goodbye; whatever they saw bore the melancholy colour of a pang of separation; whatever they heard grasped them like a last farewell. Even the dead in the graves were worked up. From one house, the grandmother who passed away two years before was seen one evening coming in from the field. She had raised her apron, and was collecting handfuls of the field, sometimes from the right, sometimes from the left. And the more the load grew in her apron and the more the old woman was drawn to the earth, the more fervent the gestures of her anguish became. She struck at her breast, wrung her hands, and then threw her arms up again in accusation. At the same time, she cried more and more vehemently so that it was in the end as if the whole world were sobbing with her. Trees, hills, clouds; everything shook in the twilight before her great anguish. In this woeful agitation, the reminder was suddenly extinguished, and everyone who had seen it embraced each other, and burst out into tears as well.

Eight days after that, the Hemsterhus sexton collected during the High Mass his pfennigs as always with the collection bag. But whenever a Querhovener that day just stretched out an arm to contribute his copper too, the fanatical man pulled the bag away, his look turned fierce, and his mouth pursed.

Thus many heretics' pfennigs fell under the bench, and when one rolled on the ground before the sexton, he kicked it away with his foot so that it clattered down the entire aisle. There at the end, a poor, pale Querhoven boy stood with his little prayer book next to a bench close by his mother who sat in the lowest place. When the boy saw the kicked pfennig running along the floor, he bent down, caught it quickly with his fingers, and rejoiced to be able now for once to throw something in the red bag like an adult. For he had not yet noticed what the sexton was doing, because he had been reading too devoutly from his book. The Brederode and Hemsterhus people though, when they saw that, laughed to themselves, sharpened their eyes to see what would now happen, or nodded encouragingly to the sexton.

When, after a while, the sexton now arrived at the bench of the boy, the latter tried to properly dispatch the caught pfennig, but did not manage it because, in the same moment, the collection bag swerved with a jerk and moved away. But the little boy wanted absolutely to feel like a giver for once, picked the pfennig up again, and thus tried his luck for a second time with the collection bag. But not only did it leap away furiously again, the boy soon after received by accident a terrible blow in the face from the thick end of the long stick. Blood sprang from a wound to his forehead, the boy turned pale, staggered, and fell with a loud groan on the flagstones.

Not much was missing and the Querhoveners would have broken out into a single cry at the sight of this brutality. But they controlled themselves. Most of them stood up calmly, and left God's house on the spot. The Pastor interrupted his ceremonies in vain, and commanded them from the altar to remain there. Nobody bothered with him, they walked silently away from there.

In the same night, the small wooden house of Elis Meixner went up in flames. The fire raged and howled as if stirred up by a subterranean blower. It was a single giant sheaf of red and yellow flames. They stood straight in the still air and high into the darkness, and sparks like fiery seeds were thrown down at the sides now and then.

A signal from God!

Nobody stirred a finger to extinguish it, and anyone who perhaps wanted to deal with it was held back by the fanatics. They stood around in an eerie paralysis of expectation, the way trees tower up from the earth in the stillness before the storm, with weary branches, quietly tired leaves, with a rustling which sounds like an inner rippling thrill. And when they had borne for a while the burden of their inexpressible tension with face turned silently to the ground, they passed their uncertain hands over their hot brows, looked out longingly in every direction into the night, nodded to one another full of anguish, and said wearily, "He will not come", or, "Pay attention, brother, we are being held for fools."

Then the roof rafters of the burning house suddenly collapsed, and a rain of sparks was thrown tempestuously to all sides so that the onlookers had to step back so as not be singed. In the moment of apprehension which followed this last eruption of fire, many heard from the Dingden slope the precipitate clatter of a heavy booted running on the stony path. It came closer and closer.

A giant shadow could already be perceived. At the same time, the noise of approaching fire engines, the crack of whips, and wagoners' cries sounded from Hemsterhus and Brederode stronger and stronger. But the attention of the fanatics was directed entirely at the slope.

It was him!

Wheezing, like an overheated machine, he raced up.

"Meixner, dear brother, Meixner!"

The fanatics clustered towards him. But he rushed through them and sprang, lit up red for a moment by the glow, like an upright predatory animal in long, hulking leaps over to his burning house; without looking around or pausing in the whirling of his course, he ran diagonally through the village, his followers behind him.

He could not be overtaken, he was still running so fast. Already out of the village and halfway up the slope on the other side, he shouted, "To Gethsemane!" and began at the same time to slow down. But when his followers tried to come near him, he fended them off while he called menacingly, "Nobody may come near me!"

A few curious people from the quiet Ender's people and even the Catholics of the village followed the hurtling procession of fanatics at a distance, and waited from afar to experience what was going to happen.

To start with, everything was deathly still. After a long time, a stirring and cautious walking back and forth arose, and then a soft, monotonous murmur like the dull sound of the waves of a distant river arose, died out, rose, broke off, and then rolled on again endlessly monotonous in the tepid, still spring night in whose clear sky the stars flickered luridly and restively like red, green, and white balls of fire.

Thus it went until about midnight.

Then the wind began rising in the trees and drowned out the endless prayer of the fanatics.

Tired from long futile eavesdropping, the curious tailed off and returned, shaking their heads, one after the other to the village.

But when the last light in the cottages of the village had been extinguished, a roaring singing began to break forth from Gethsemane, and climbed to such a wild power that from time to time the roaring of the wind in the tree tops was drowned out.

Vanlyßender, whose farm lay next to the devotional space of the fanatics, could not sleep this night, rose, and went out towards the din, and stood nearby in the cover of the trunk of a pear tree.

Hardly had the song of the men fallen silent than the braggart Meixner raised his voice. The initial words were already terrible. "Therefore I will be unto them as a lion: as a leopard by the way will I observe them", he cried. "I will meet them as a bear that is bereaved of her whelps, and will rend the caul of their heart, and there will I devour them like a lion[*], thus said Hosea in the thirteenth chapter."

---

[*]   Hosea 13:7-8.

Then he continued with calmer voice, "The people say, nobody can split wood with light, and if the butcher does not have the courage to kill the steer, he will be run through by its horns, and the people must starve because they have no nourishment anymore. By that they want to say that even the wheels of God's chariot are smeared with grease, and nobody becomes full if he makes himself a meal in which every second bite is an injustice. Be vigilant against such thoughts and feelings, my brothers. They are silent guests at the table of your soul who squander the good of your life. They stem from the accursed one on the blessed hill. But I will be a different guide for you, a different prophet. I will trample that dwarf together with his blind girl into the muck if he confronts me. I will smash the houses of the godless, and cast their doors onto the path. Rise, brothers, the great day is here! We have the dice in our hand, and will strew like chaff in all the winds those who have shed the blood of our children and want to drive us as beggars into the world. — I have been during the last two weeks far in the empire, and have fetched advice from the Herne rebel who once travelled like a storm through our land."

Vanlyßender could not listen any longer. A shiver of fear seized him. He crept away, went to the houses of his friends, woke them up, and advised them to hold themselves ready in the morning for the wild Meixner preaching insurrection.

9

In the clear morning which followed on from this night, Sintlinger, his wife, and little Lena were sitting after the customary breakfast at the table in the large living room.

"I heard it too", little Lena said.

"What?" Johanna asked.

"Well, especially towards morning. It was a shouting as if a hundred wild men quarreled", Helene answered.

"No", the farmer's wife said again, "after the fire I soon fell asleep, and did not awake anymore. Until this morning."

The blessed farmer said nothing, just looked out the window again and again into the treetops of the orchard, and nodded every now and again thoughtfully, but obviously only at the progress of his own concealed meditations.

"Andreas! — Dear!! —", Johanna said, and placed her hand in reminder on his arm.

"Yes. — Now, what were you saying, dear wife?" he asked after an almost imperceptible start.

"The milkmaid has already been in the yard today. She said that in Hemsterhus the opinion is that the prophet Meixner set his house on fire himself. What do you think?"

The farmer did not answer, but just looked into his wife eyes in steady thought.

"Yes, Andreas", Johanna said with a laugh, "you have known that for a long time. I don't have that way of hearing speech through the eyes."

"Children! Children!" the blessed farmer said finally. "It is a misery with the people. The men get beards and remain children. With them it is about the reins of horses, which they no longer or not yet have. Meanwhile the mare on which they sit races away with them wherever it wants. But each scolds the other over the breakneck speed. Yes — and that Meixner himself lit it, why should that not be possible?"

Then a silence followed.

"Old Zenker says", Helene began again, "our Gottlieb was certainly not at the night bluster."

"Why do you say 'our Gottlieb', little Lena?" Sintlinger asked his child. But she suddenly turned pale.

"Be still please", she asked quickly. "Quite still. — Now! — Do you hear it too?"

But before the blessed farmer and his wife could decide, the front door was kicked in, heavy booted steps rumbled in the hall, and then the youngest labourer seemingly plunged into the room. He was almost out of his mind with excitement.

"Tear the window open, farmer! — Tear it open, I tell you! — Tear — it — open!" he shouted.

"What is it, Wendel?" the blessed farmer asked calmly.

But everything in the fellow came out in a rush.

"There is roaring ... they are raging, they are raging like wild animals. The Querhoveners have gone mad. The bells are howling more than tolling. Do you not hear it? — Ha! Now it's even going off in Brederode!"

The weak droning of bells penetrated through the door. Sintlinger sprang up, shook the labourer by the shoulders as if he had to tear him from his sleep, and cried with a smile, "Wendel! Hey! Boy!"

Then the boy awoke from his whirling, looked around sheepishly, and wiped his hands embarrassedly on his knees. At the same time, he said as if in apology, "The rebel from that time, the people say, is in behind them all. They have taken over the parsonage."

Only, suddenly he was startled again, "Dammit! Now its going off even more."

With this exclamation, he stormed out again. You could hear the servants running together into the yard and vanishing through the gate.

Johanna had torn a window wide open.

You could hear bells screaming up from the valley, short and shill between the howling of a crowd of folk turning mad, and through everything pious singing.

The blessed farmer still stood in the middle of the room where the labourer had run away from him after he had made the remark about the rebel.

"Then we will meet each other. We two. And perhaps yet today", he said, so softly that nobody heard it. But when the din of the uproar now rang even more distinctly through the window, the blessed farmer turned pale.

"I am going down there", he said calmly, but eerily abrupt, "and little Lena must come with me. Dress her, Johanna. But quickly!"

The farmer's wife knew that opposition was unthinkable, and fulfilled her husband's wish with flying hands.

In barely five minutes, the horse stood before the carriage, and, in the next moment, Sintlinger and little Lena were racing down the hill in the vehicle so that it looked as if the carriage lay on the nag's back.

At the boundary path, the blessed farmer whipped the horse even more, and loosened the reins so that it shot like an arrow.

The bellowing and singing was now already close to Hemsterhus.

"Are you afraid, little Lena?" he asked without taking his eyes off the horse and carriage, but received no answer, and when he looked at his daughter, he saw her reclining in the carriage, her pure eyes directed into the boundless sky, full of expectation, and the light garment over her breast was heaving stormily.

Then he noticed for the first time that Helene was not a child anymore. A deep despondency befell him then, as if she were no longer in possession of those powers in whose shelter he was permitted to dare to confront the danger of the rioters and perhaps even the eerie Faber rebel. But his hands holding the reins barely twitched in this doubt. He smiled, but full of a blessedly suffering astonishment. The horse raced onwards.

Now it had already left behind the ridge of hills between Querhoven and the estranged farmsteads, and Sintlinger looked over the meadowed lowlands towards Hemsterhus.

The bells had stopped storming. The roar of men had fallen silent, only the pious singing continued in a muffled way.

The vault of the heavens lay in radiant blue repose over the young earth, and, up on the tips of a willow, he saw a finch singing, bending back and trembling.

Then he moderated the horse's gait.

But it still continued at a gallop to the old boundary path, as he saw over on the new main road the Querhoveners' procession just disappearing between the first houses of Hemsterhus. An enormous, rough cross was being borne at the head of the mob.

The blessed farmer's deep calm, his peaceful oneness had full power over him again.

At the tavern where the paths crossed, it was as still as if everything had died. Only a tall, young man dressed in town clothes stood in the doorway, he and stepped back into the house when the blessed farmer travelled past, continuing towards the village, to the church and parsonage where countless voices were roaring.

But before he could reach there, the wild, ear-numb-ing roar broke out anew. The bells howled, and the pious singing rang with beseeching fervour into it.

As he appeared in the square before the parsonage, he just then heard Meixner's voice call, "Beat everything up which is set against you, brothers. Smash the fence! We want the Pastor!"

A hundred-voiced shout of consternation sounded, the people streamed back, dull axe blows crunched, and wood splintered. But at the same time, the first onlook-ers who recognised him called out, "The blessed farmer! The blessed little Lena! To the side!"

It sounded relieved and jubilant at the same time.

Sintlinger climbed pale and serious from the car-riage, lifted little Lena out, handed over the reins to a labourer, and strode hand in hand with his child through the lane which led up to the parsonage.

The "quiet divines" of Querhoven, who had tacked themselves to the heels of their rampant friends, had crowded around the hewn down fence so as to not be mistaken by the public for the others, and, as a reproach and admonition of the Lord to always be close to them.

Their song broke off immediately when the blessed farmer and little Lena walked through them. Frisson and delighted gleaming came into their faces, and the call was heard from within their midst, "Thank God."

Within the courtyard, however, the wild mob had gathered around their prophet, the braggart Meixner. They each wore a halter made of golden willow switches slung about their body, in which most of them hung an axe, with a few a long knife. They were all pale from the night-long exaltation, overwrought, their eyes wide and nervous with the lewd, timorous look of flagellants — pitiful, unattractive men who only salvaged their embar-rassment through wildness. But now the twenty to twenty five men stood gathered in an impenetrable clump behind the braggart Meixner, who like a mad anchorite shouted their demands at the windows of the parsonage, and thundered from time to time with his fists against the locked door. But nobody showed except the cook, whose pale face appeared now and then behind the barred kitchen window, and then immediately vanished.

But from the windows of the schoolhouse, Liborius Pfeiffer leant out, and shouted into Meixner's ravings his imprecations, "Satan! — Damned son of hell! — Devil's soul!" The rest was lost in the din.

Suddenly a stone flew at his chest.

He threw his hands up in the air, and vanished. The whinnying laughter of the "baptists" followed. The braggart Meixner took up the Cantor's last insult, and called it into the silence which arose, "Yes, like devils, you have treated us. Now don't incriminate yourself so that we act like devils against you. — Come out, Pastor! None of your hairs shall be pulled. But we don't want to be banished like beggars, we want to keep our faith, our dead should not be treated like the hung, and our children not like young convicts. We want peace! — Come out, Ardelt, or we will bash the door in."

Meixner ripped the axe from its willow strap, the others did the same.

At this critical moment, the blessed farmer stepped out from the crowd of quiet divines with little Lena. Then he sensed that someone was pushing towards him. When he turned around, he recognised the accordion-playing Meixner. His eyes were full of such an imploring devotion that he put little Lena in his care, and quickly sprang across the space through the raging men to the topmost step by the parsonage door.

The braggart Meixner, who had just raised his axe to smash the door in, gave a jerk when the blessed farmer unexpectedly appeared next to him, and instinctively took a step back.

"Good morning, Meixner!" Sintlinger said ingenuously with winning sincerity. "Forgive me, I have come to help you." With that he turned to the others.

"You men, you too. You want to keep your fields. If you need fields, come to me, and you shall receive as much as you want. On that I give my word before everyone on Meixner's hand."

He did it.

Then he continued, "You want to keep your faith. You can take the morsel from a man's teeth, but never, with no power, can you tear the faith from his soul. That can only be done by someone through committing their own wrongs. Acts of violence though are always wrong. So hang your axes and knives in your willow straps. And now I want to talk with the Pastor for you. Just have a few moments patience, and everything will be okay." He grasped Meixner's hand once more, squeezed it heartily, and said, "We will do it, won't we, dear man."

Then he went, knocked softly on the kitchen window, and called in reassuringly. When he returned to the door, the old housekeeper opened it, let him in, and locked the door behind Sintlinger again.

Ever new cries of astonishment over Sintlinger ran through the crowd, and everyone was in suspense over the outcome. Meixner had stepped right into the yard, had grasped the cross from the grave of the anabaptist friend at Gethsemane, could not keep himself together for shock, broke out now and then into mocking laughter, and fired up his following to not be led astray by anything if the windbag came out with empty hands, but to be ready to go. Now the iron was hot, now it must be forged.

But nobody answered him, everyone shunned him with their eyes.

Then a woman's voice screamed out shrilly in the interior of the parsonage full of desperate anguish, and then burst out into loud crying. The lamenting slowly approached the door.

Then the door opened, and the blessed farmer stepped out, deathly pale, distraught, let his moist shimmering eyes rest sadly on everyone, and could not speak for a while. Finally he pulled himself together.

"The Pastor has just died of a stroke. He asks everyone for forgiveness. So God has decided everything. And now do not disturb the rest of the dead man, go home. I will worry about the rest."

Everybody was shaken.

Little Lena hurried on Gottlieb Meixner's hand to her father. The "quiet divines" clustered full of joy, happiness and thanks. The incendiaries began dispersing, and went without farewell from their leader.

But the latter stood ashen, with eyes aghast, stone rigid, his hands knotted desperately about the upright of his cross.

He saw Sintlinger by the side of little Lena a few steps in front of him on the point of going away, speaking with old Vanlyßender.

Everyone was looking only at the two men.

Nobody was paying any attention to the dethroned prince, even less to the change which was taking place in him. His eyes were directed burning at the blessed farmer. Suddenly they flickered like a wolf's, his face twisted into a grimace. He seized the cross, and raised it for a terrible blow against Sintlinger.

But little Lena screamed out, and pulled her father towards herself. Thus the cross smashed on the ground, and broke shattered.

The attack was so unexpected, carried out with such ferocity, that those standing around were thrown apart full of fright, and looked without clearly comprehending from the blanched Sintlinger to Meixner, who was standing there with bent-over body, spread legs, wheezing breath, and wide-open eyes in bestial bewilderment.

Everyone saw that a hellish storm was working in him. He tried to scream, but he emitted no sound. Then he let go of the anabaptist cross, raised his arms, and opened his hands like rigid claws. Then he began staggeringly, shaking through his entire grotesque body, to attack Sintlinger, and was already emitting with the first step a sound like the growl of a tiger.

It was a sight of paralysing horror.

Even the blessed farmer backed away from this terribly distorted face.

But Gottlieb Meixner had quickly stepped from little Lena's side and arrived soundlessly behind him. Now as this obviously mad human animal set off in motion towards Sintlinger with an abysmal groan in his chest, the fellow sprang with such force onto his back from behind that the giant fell from the unexpected impact to the ground like a knocked-over stake.

And now Gottlieb laboured and struck at the man lying there until he was completely exhausted.

Nobody stirred to part the maddened fellow from his victim, yes, the braggart Meixner himself was letting it all happen to himself defencelessly as if he had suddenly become a penitent on whom a just sentence was being carried out. Yes, he did not once gnash or groan, although he was already bleeding from many wounds.

When his nephew finally desisted from it, he rose and went away silently from the village, without looking at anyone, with lowered head, across the fields, without paying any mind to paths or roads, always straight ahead to the forest.

Nobody dared hold him back.

Full of inexplicable horror, they followed him with their eyes, and saw how he vanished bowed into the thickets. After quarter of an hour, a gendarme appeared in Hemsterhus to arrest the leader of the Querhoven breachers of the peace, and lead him away to the prison. Only, he had already withdrawn himself from earthly justice. The official found him in the spruce stand where he had hung himself kneeling.

Beautiful little Mathinka, the deranged farmer's daughter and only child, was out of her mind with anguish from the shame which her father had brought upon her.

In that same night, she fled Hemsterhus, and Peter Brindeisener, who had gone quite early to the Hemsterhus tavern for a long celebratory drink to his brilliantly passed final school exams, and had watched with her from there the walk of the mob of rebellious men, let thirst and delight wait, and accompanied the unfortunate, beautiful girl through the forest to the railway station at Bocholt.

Some time later, Johanna encountered her husband sitting disconsolate and despondent by the edge of the forest.

He lamented to his wife that he was by himself incapable of anything, that he was both inwardly and outwardly defenceless.

"What shall happen then", he cried after a sombre pause, "if little Lena is taken from us — if from me — from me? Then it will be for me like a river whose source has dried up, like a wind which loses its grounding, like a house which extinguishes its only light at night-time — I am running dry, losing my way and darkening."

Johanna passed a gentle hand over her husband's hair, and encouraged him.

The blessed farmer shook his head, and answered that, yes, everything would certainly have to be borne, that he already knew, but it was nevertheless odd that when he sat here in the darkness by the forest and gazed over the meadows, such a horror always sprung up in him.

It was the Faber meadow which lay before them, with the heap of bushes and the spring pond in the middle.

"Andreas, that's your imagination", Johanna said to her husband, drew him forcibly by the arm up to her, and asked in leaving, with a happy mocking laugh, "What is this meadow meant to have done just now that you must become so terribly disheartened. Do you know, Andreas? I don't."

The blessed farmer answered after a while ambiguously, "Yes, dear wife, who could know that! Think please of that strange thing, Johanna, that in recent times it often seemed more certain to me that our own mistakes are the reason why others can hurt us. For where there is no door, then there is also no entrance."

Amidst such conversation, the blessed farmer and his wife returned to the farmstead in which everyone already lay in sleep.

BOOK FOUR

1

After these violent events, everything happened which calmed again the stirred up population of the district around the blessed farm. The ecclesiastical authorities sent in Ardelt's place a sophisticated, prudent successor called Spiller, a former assessor and Doctor of Laws. He communicated and united with the peaceable spirit of the Royal Arenberg Head Forester, Wiesner. The notice of withdrawal of the Querhoveners' leased fields was not only withdrawn, but the interest reduced, even if only modestly, because of the poor state of agriculture at that time. Yes, to those who aspired to an expansion of their farm, the prospect was held out of new land, and when not long after the former Meixner estate in Querhoven passed into the possession of the government, many of the poor skewer makers of the forest village could add another little field on the slope to their narrow leased strips. The body of the mutinous fanatic was lifted out from under the stone on the forest slope, and bedded in the hallowed earth of the Hemsterhus churchyard, even if the church's presence at the ceremony remained limited to a casual blessing. The zealous Cantor Liborius Pfeiffer was moved far away in the interests of the office to a parish of the Catholic diaspora, and slowly but painfully broke the habit there of his wild zeal for conversion and suspicion, although he continued to passionately lament with close friends the Babel-like confusion of Christianity, and to hold out the near prospect of a terrible divine judgment over a sinful Europe. But with exception of a letter to the Hemsterhus church father, the superintendent of the faith fraternity situated there, he never again reached out to that period of his life which ended with a shattering of his holiest intentions. A little while later, the daily papers also got hold of the Hemsterhus revolt. For the first time, the names of the blessed farmer and his blind daughter also rang out into the wider world. Certainly skewed, nobody could construct a picture of these two people whom in the willed solitude of their life had become the reason and impulse for a movement which itself is spreading more than ever in our days further and further. The "friends of God" from Querhoven, or "men of Christ" as they were finally called, fell, after the favourable conclusion of the wild vortex in which their fanatical brothers had plunged them, neither into the vain boastfulness of successful novices, nor even into an extravagant proselytising, no, they still adhere to the simple beliefs they had won. The former fanatics had been pushed back by the terrible death of their leader quickly onto the prudent paths from which they had been shooed by Meixner's divine raving, and such a deep change took place in them that these people who had been led astray were soon distinguished by a special inwardness. In a few weeks, the Querhoveners again formed a unanimous congregation. They continued to seek the way to God not through an intermediary, nor through the power of a church, but only with the piousness of their elevated hearts, and in active love for one another. They asked, "Does the tree or the flower need someone or something to provide them with the air, the rain, the sun, the sky, as the only powers and properties which their being detects? Well, and is it not said that man is more than a plant in the field? Why does man demean himself thus? Nobody who can eat bread returns to the pap of the infant. Your own hunger is better than the chewed morsel from another's mouth."

They believed with fervour in that which the monk Eckhart, the deepest Christian of all time, called the divine base in every human being, and accordingly saw good not as something foreign to the soul, by command of an externally originating power, but as a human life's necessity, and being bad was something they held to be as much a mad lunacy as perhaps drinking poison to quench your thirst. Hence, they also treated every bad man like a brother who had fallen ill, with love and never tiring sympathy.

Thus the Querhoven lived as "men of Christ", like it was perhaps reported of the Christians of the first century before the Church had lapsed into the idolatry of external power.

They declined to engage with opponents in a religious dispute. "Anyone who proves with words can be rebutted with words", they said, and "Two men who come into conflict for the sake of their faith are like two storms which collide. They do not stop their lightning and thunder until both have destroyed themselves." And thus they taught only through their transformation.

At the same time, however, they emulated nature's power of persuasion, which educated through nothing but the mysterious beauty of its life patterns, and the number of those who affiliated with the Querhoveners grew constantly.

The Roman Catholic Church was most taken aback by the success of this stray teaching, having believed it could strip off with tolerant kindness the sectarian opposition, and lead the new force slowly into the tracks of its old forms. The new Pastor, Dr Spiller, worked with this in mind incessantly on them, in that he sought to convince them that their views were nothing new, but rather the old fundamental teachings of Christianity, and consequently of the Church, and that its effect would be far more sustainable if they submitted entirely to the wisdom of the Church's discipline. But everyone defied him — most insistently, however, the old sweet-tempered Vanlyßender, and he also proved to the clergyman why it was impossible.

"For the reason, namely, Reverend, that we are not like that", the venerable old man said, "because we Querhoveners, from the first to the last, do not consider Christ to be a god, but a divine man, a son of man, as he is always described by Mark. The list of ancestors in Mark and Luke is just as much the work of priests as the teachings of Paul and the Gospel of John which cannot be from the disciple of Jesus. This higher man, namely the Lord Jesus Christ, had never wanted to found a church, and he had also not introduced any sacraments, not a single one. We are the new, young heart in the old body which calls itself after the name of Jesus Christ. That is why we do not separate ourselves, because we do not want to tear the heart from the body, but renew it, that is the body, with new blood."

When the old man had thus spoken to the Pastor, he apologised that he, an uneducated man, spoke thus. But in his soul, he knew and believed that man was a being who bore God and heaven within himself from the beginning. That is why whoever seeks the path to God, to the highest blissfulness, must only seek into his deepest inner being. And heaven will one day be on earth when everyone will have the courage to live after the laws of their deepest inner being.

The Pastor of Hemsterhus was himself gripped by the simple words of the possessed, pure old man against his will so that he could not master his emotion.

He emitted no word and lowered his eyes with a pale face. At the same time, his breathing became heavy for a few moments so that it even attracted Vanlyßender's attention. For that reason, he took heart and also said to Doctor Spiller the final thing he knew.

"Pastor", the old man cried out enthusiastically, "I know it, and will die by it if it must be. When someone becomes an emperor, or a pope, or a poet, or a great scholar and industrialist merely for the reason namely to be more than a great, pure man, then he descends every time and becomes less than he was."

At the same time, the skewer maker reassuringly touched the clergyman on the shoulder with his hand.

Suddenly the emotion fell away from Doctor Spiller; he shook the old man's hand off, looked at the old man with a reproving face because of his irreverence, and walked once about the room of the parsonage in which this remarkable discussion was taking place.

Then he stopped before Vanlyßender, and measured the withered, pitiful little old man amusedly from head to toe.

"Yes, Vanlyßender, so there was no original sin?" he asked cuttingly.

"No", the old man answered calmly.

"And no salvation either?"

"No."

"And all men are angels?"

"When they have the will, yes."

"And a murderer, an adulterer, child abuser ... Man, is such a man also of God?"

"In his deepest soul, yes. For no wave reaches to the bottom of the sea, not even from the most terrible storm. Or can there be a wind so strong that it would be able to extinguish the stars?"

Dr Spiller backed away more and more with the calm, confident answers of old Vanlyßender as if in growing horror.

The old man, however, had lapsed into a sort of dreaming rapture, and gazed distractedly with his clear eyes into emptiness.

Then the first beam of the red of evening fell into the Pastor's darkening room. Like a shimmering, red wall, it placed itself between the two men and separated them from each other. The old man was startled from his distractedness, riveted his eyes onto the shimmer, and a blissful smile thereupon came over his entire face.

Then he said with quiet, loving voice into the long silence, "Look, Pastor, at my hand! Now I hold it in the sunshine, and it blossoms red. In this way have we Querhoveners stepped into the sun. And God lets us continue blossoming."

At the same time, he bowed before the clergyman, and walked away without a sound.

Dr Spiller looked for a long time in astonishment at the closed door, and then began striding about his room agitatedly again.

Nevertheless he also did not neglect subsequently to discourage the Querhoveners from their errors with every means. Yes, when it quickly went downhill not long after with Vanlyßender, towards the grave, he even increased his solicitation of souls. He insisted with the bowed relatives on access to the dying man, and drove his conversion attempt with a vigour which honestly spoke derision for these solemn, final moments. Vanlyßender gave no answer, but lay there still and mild. Then, all of a sudden, the expiring sight of the pious old man smouldered in a scowl, and he said with a clear voice, "I do not want to know anything about your sacrament. To someone who is of impure heart, it is of no use, and the good man does not need it", he nodded to the priest kindly, turned away towards the wall, and died smiling.

In the night which followed the death of the good old man, but already towards morning, the weaver Staupitz, the best friend of the recently departed, stood up, since he could not sleep for sadness, and strolled out into the forest in which wild Meixner had preached revolt over the grave of the fanatic. There the aggrieved man sat under a tree, and recalled the deep metamorphosis which had happened in him and the whole village during those years. Then the darkness and sorrow overcame the man more deeply again, and he asked himself what would probably become of the new spirit after Vanlyßender, who had been a father to everyone, had died. And he gazed up full of anguish through the branches of the tree into the heavens. The first wind of spring was stirring the treetops there. The blue of the night had turned paler, and the stars were already burning more ashenly. Just as the Querhovener, filled entirely by his sorrow, wanted to ask the Lord himself whether in the future perhaps still stronger visitations would be awarded than those which had once had their beginning here from this forest, the light raking of the morning wind became stronger and stronger. It swung the treetops back and forth like bells being moved by enthusiastic hands, and the rustling of the leaves suddenly changed into a thousand-voiced, jubilant tolling which rang over the hills, forests, and villages all around and into the depths of all the world. This mysterious answer confused the Querhoven man so that he sank as though into the real whirl of a dream. When he awoke from it again, the brightest of days stood over the earth, and he walked down into the village, and reported to everybody what he had just experienced.

The Querhoveners took it as a good omen and a solace. And although the Pastor did without the religious service at the burial, because Vanlyßender had died in hostility with the Church, everyone who felt of one spirit with him embedded him in the earth with a sort of elevated, joyful anguish.

Here by the open grave was also the first time the prayer was spoken which is generally ascribed to Vanlyßender. According to the tale, when the coffin had been lowered into the grave, beautiful Ursula Rütsch from the Sweeps, his only daughter, stepped with her four blossoming boys to the edge of the grave. Like all the participants, the five each held a small bunch of field flowers in their hands. And after the pale, blond woman had stood there a while thinking with lowered brow, she lifted her head a little, and then said the prayer with her beautiful, poignant voice:

"Not on the mountain Gerizim, nor in Jerusalem is God alone to be found, nor in Rome, nor in Wittenberg. You build the temple from stone, and do not capture him. You erect churches, and no hand can bind him. That is why towers which reach up into heaven have been built for us in our own breast, a house with the golden roof of the truthfulness of the heart, with walls made out of our good will, and a love which never ends. For from the beginning of existence until his downfall, God is in the man, either to his pain or to his blessing.

Oh, Lord of the world, you soul of our soul, make that we are yours in joy, in happiness, and in the peace of the good. We implore you, let us not fall back into your womb through the torment and darkness of evil. The light is yours, and the shadow. The day comes from your hand, as does night. Let us reside every day in that depth of our being where we are not parted from you, where there are no words, nor thoughts, nor goals, but fulfilment. There let us be at home where we were before our earthly beginning, and where we will be after our earthly end in eternity. Amen."

When Ursula Rütsch had prayed this legacy of her father's, a silence reigned in the churchyard so that you could hear the humming of summer flies in the sun. Beautiful Ursula Rütsch from the Sweeps was herself gripped most deeply. To preserve herself from collapsing, she knelt down and bent over the grave, so that many thought she was having trouble in her anguish restraining herself from climbing into the grave after her father. Only she was just struggling to say something, and could not pull herself together. Finally, from this difficult struggle of her burdened heart, she spoke into the silent stillness with a loud voice that thing which moved every Querhovener, the entire funeral party.

"My father", she cried after the dead man in the grave, "you blossomed to the end. So let us all blossom, God, until we die."

Then she rose, and let her little bouquet of flowers fall on the coffin. The four Rütsch boys followed the example of their mother, and everyone else also stepped up and threw their flowers as a last farewell into the grave of the revered man so that the coffin was then completely covered in petals.

On the way home though, once out of Hemsterhus, the Querhoveners sang pious hymns again.

Since this burial, it became a custom among Querhoveners and their followers to throw flowers on the coffin instead of three shovels of earth as a last farewell to the dead. At the death of a man, they stressed the victoriousness, the transfiguration, rather than the anguish of parting. But, that desolate orgies were celebrated, drunk and danced, and that loud processions with masquerades and screaming concluded the obsequies, is a legend invented by all the ecclesiastical and religious enemies of the Querhoveners, and was thoroughly refuted straightaway the first time it appeared in the public notice by Pastor Dr Spiller of Hemsterhus over the calumniation of religious institutions, public disturbance of the peace, and the carrying out of forbidden processions committed at the burial of Vanlyßender.

The famous lawyer Dr Weißpfleger from Würzburg, who took on the defence of the oppressed forest villagers voluntarily and for no payment, invalidated all the ridiculous accusations in the sensational case which contributed so much to the spread of the new men of Christ. Weißpfleger, eloquent in spoken and written word, also then became the first representative of the new movement which aimed at a complete transformation of the Catholic Church, perhaps after the pattern of the old evangelical congregations, those purest and most passionate of Christians who were persecuted through centuries by the Roman Popes with the most stubborn gruesomeness, with fire and wheel; Christians whom Eckhart and Tauler associated with, whose sprig St Francis of Assisi actually is, and who then celebrated in Protestantism a stunted victory.

2

All this struggle by the Querhoveners for the assertion of the faith they had won was kept aloof from by the man from whose being and life the new world of the poor forest villagers had received so much, the blessed farmer, Sintlinger. Through the clever complaisance and placability of the new Hemsterhus Pastor in leaving the leased fields to the sectarians, Sintlinger's promised help had been pushed aside so as to prepare for the disturbance of internal influence by the hindering of external obligation. The blessed farmer thus did not end up assigning leased fields from his estate to the Querhoveners.

But just as Dr Spiller was mistaken over the effects of his sober measures on the spirit of the Querhoveners, he soon also had to experience the futility of this indirect combat with the blessed farmer. For Sintlinger was not merely not taken aback by the resolution to the dispute over the leased fields, but even expressed his overt satisfaction that the hardship of the oppressed skewer makers was so judiciously relieved.

And yet Sintlinger was pushed by the struggle of the Querhoveners still further into the aloofness of his secluded soul than his being had ever previously sent him. But someone other than the Hemsterhus Pastor was at fault for that. For it is vouched for that the blessed farmer had intended to take part in the burial of Vanlyßender, whom he had also revered. The carriage with harnessed horse already stood in the yard that day. The labourer Wendel was sitting in the driving seat, and old Zenker was once more walking around the vehicle with his stick checking whether everything was in order, striking the upholstery in search of missed dust, stroking the horse's flanks, running his hand through its mane, checking the buckles of the straps, and finally discovering that the bit was placed too firmly in the nag's mouth. While he was now falling into a dispute with the quick-witted labourer over it, Sintlinger stepped out the door, in his black coat, the tall hat on his head, and approached the carriage, a gentle smile on his serious face. Lower the bit just one link further, Zenker", he said. "As, if I have to wait until Wendel lets you have the last word, Judgment Day will be here and my good Vanlyßender will in the meantime have risen from the grave." His face deepened a shade more in calm earnest. He stretched his hand out for the carriage door, and raised his foot to climb in. But before he could get properly in his seat, the Hemsterhus postman stepped through the little side door into the yard, lifted his cap in greeting from his sweat-soaked head, and, since he saw the farmer was so close to leaving, tried to go past him with his delivery into the house. "Nothing for me?" Sintlinger called after him, and bent down from the carriage. "Certainly, a letter", the postman answered back over his shoulder. "Well then, why should I not also *receive* it?" the blessed farmer said cheerily, took it, and while he quickly ripped it open, at the same time he gave Wendel the sign to depart. Zenker stood directly in front of the horse's head, and it took a while before he hobbled to the side and could make the path clear. Meanwhile Sintlinger had read the name of the writer and the first words of the letter. That sufficed, already after a few steps by the horse, to restrain the labourer from continuing the journey. The old farmworker saw his master suddenly transformed, bent passionately over the letter, becoming ever paler, and turning page after page in complete absorption. Minutes stretched into minutes. Sintlinger shook his head here, nodded thoughtfully there, then, coming to the end, he let the letter sink down onto his knee, and gazed for a long time, as if seeking counsel, up into the summer sky. "So, so ..." he finally said with a deep sigh, climbed out, gave the order to unharness, and walked back into the house with large, motionless eyes staring into thin air.

The old man, when he saw Sintlinger gesturing so strangely to him, roared after the farmer, "Yes, yes, go inside all the time! The diving headfirst doesn't stop with you, and even if you lay the saints on top of each other seven times inside you." But he cut off all baffled, curious Wendel's questions by the teeth, and lay all the blame on his "mucking about" having put the master off his journey. The blessed farmer came down the stairs after a short while in his work clothes, called to his astonished wife through the half-open door into the kitchen that he could not go down to Hemsterhus owing to a letter, but had to go into the forest where he was expected. And before Johanna could ask anything else, he was up and away.

The farmwife hurried as quickly as the maids allowed her after her husband, but achieved nothing more than seeing him from the yard gate disappear just then over the high butte towards the forest with great strides. Sintlinger walked without stopping along the forest road. The deeper he penetrated into his forest, the clearer the certainty became in him that he could only succeed in properly reading and understanding the letter he had just received if he was in that place in the forest where years before he had set eyes on that mad flower collector whom he had held to be the wandering rebel Faber. For the writing stemmed from this man who had skimmed his life like a ghost in the night after the dedication of the Sintlinger memorial, and kept him entangled since then with tentacles that would not let him go.

"Am I not foolish myself to let myself be constantly driven by this man like an incubus?" he asked himself over and over again, and yet did not manage to take the letter from his side pocket, to tear it up and scatter the shreds in the forest, but ran further and further until he came to about the place from where the forest road rose in turning halfway into the treetops in the distance.

There Sintlinger walked to the left so deep into the stand that he could not be seen from the road, then sat

down on an old, moss covered stump, and read the letter which bore neither place, nor date, nor salutation,
but began immediately:

> Recently I have read your name in various news-
> papers, and learnt therein what great influence
> you have attained in the district there. I congratu-
> late you from the depths of my heart for the great
> transformation which has been carried out in
> your views. For the night is still unforgettable to
> my memory in which I, a restless earthly fugitive,
> a hunted man, met with you for the first and only
> time. Is it not twelve or even thirteen years? But
> there is no time to our souls, and the spirit of man
> knows no separation. You were right with the
> truth which you taught the Querhoveners — the
> unbounded love of men for one another is the sole
> revelation of God in us and of the world of God
> which is one and the same. For that you need no
> church, no priests, and no sacraments. How I
> would like to hurry to you and squeeze your hand
> which, despite the difficult lot of your child, has
> found the strength to struggle free from the en-
> tanglements of possessiveness and impassioned
> pride to the bright expanse of boundless love for
> thy neighbour. Although you mocked me in that
> night, and laughed after me derisively when I fled
> into the forest before the gendarme riding past, I
> was sure of the effect of that hour and my being
> on your life. Believe me, there is no man who can
> be happier over this outcome than I am. Would
> you believe me that there has been in the course
> of the years often moments where I felt myself
> physically walking next to you?
>
> I beg, do not knock yourself at the unrest and the
> somewhat heated rambling of my words. It is in

part a gift of my nature, but today an outlet for my joy, and probably also somewhat more the consequence of my state. I have not yet recovered from the sabre blow of the constable, which I received during the demonstration of the Berlin unemployed in Moabit. My forehead, which was almost split, has certainly healed, but in excitement, weakness still overcomes me time after time. As soon as I am completely fixed, I will come by you, for in the Rhineland-Westphalia coal-mining area, something is again being raked together, and I must go there to restrain the workers from foolishness and irrationality, even if what befell me here should also be bestowed on me there a second time.

In any case, I will visit you during my sojourn in the locale there. Hoping then to yet spend time with you.

Yours,
Franz Faber.

Sintlinger read the letter over and over again. The deeper he penetrated, however, into Faber's line of thought and world of ideas, the more and the deeper he found himself again in conflict with it. Especially the place in which it spoke of Sintlinger's change, his turning from the "possessiveness" and "pride" to the boundless love for thy neighbour. What did this man know of him and of the way of people generally! Again and again, he, Sintlinger, had learnt that the teaching of the mistaken is of no use since a man of another opinion constantly understands according to his own way, not that of the speaker, and thus falsely. The thinking of your own head is already a confusion of the truth which taps on the inner walls of your skull, how much more the word, that new degeneration of thought. When men speak with one another, they place two bits of wood next to one another, one never yielding to the other.

And love? God, yes, love! Does it not exist according to its nature in the boundless willingness to make the state of the other your own? And is that in all eternity not a futile, useless beginning? An oak is never capable of transforming into a beech tree, one drop of water never into another. How can one person exchange their inner guise for that of their neighbour? We men must eternally remain alone, alone like hills and mountains which only concur in the depths of their roots of stone where they are not yet hills and mountains. The blessed farmer had even had to learn that in relation to his wife, not to speak of old Klim and the braggart Meixner, the Pastor and all the Querhoveners. Now, and even the de-lusion of help by which this foolish man was hounded out of one hardship into another, one defeat and disap-pointment into the next! Man is set against himself in the lunacy if he believes that with thinking he can be helped from the failures which life inflicts on him. For thoughts only ever come after, when everything is over, like messages which report a misfortune, or a piece of luck, it all depends. And it is precisely so with our help-ing our neighbours, men, and society. We only ever arrive there afterwards, always too late. Children are educated according to principles which no longer apply when they are grown up. We are the cartwrights who build wagons for people pining away, and when we are finished with that, death has already fetched those whom we should have helped along. Yes, even our own experiences are of no use to us. The teenager can learn nothing from his childhood, and the man nothing from the teenager. Even less can it be transferred. Horses are always being brought to a market which is already over. All endeavours to teach, to love, and to help are therefore pointless, they only cause us to be hindered in achieving our own perfection. Instead of being radiant as stars in the sky, and consoling everyone who wanders in the darkness or in the night, we demean ourselves into weak flickers which whir about lighting the darkness in the corners without be able to drive away the misery and hardship. Thus if Faber likes to always act and think as he wants about the world and about him, Sintlinger himself, that should not divert him. There is for him only the one commandment: he wanted to continue to fulfill, without looking to the left or to the right, his duty to himself, to his deepest needs, and to be like the storm which does not care for whether men think it is coming exclusively on their account. It purifies the air even there where the sound of its thunder no longer reaches. When air flows back and forth somewhere, the air layers of the entire world conform to it in the end. Everything, the innermost part of the soul too, is subject to laws which are not to be shaken off, are inescapable, which God himself cannot strike off. For these laws are the statesmen of his power.

Or had he, Andreas Sintlinger, the farmer sitting here on the moss covered stump in his own forest, who was called hereabouts the blessed farmer, perhaps come to this knowledge by his own power? It had led him to it certainly against his will, and by inescapable necessity. And now came this turbid somebody, this Faber, and spoke of the condition of his little Lena and all his being as well as a malign fate. The blessed farmer broke out into loud laughter which echoed through the entire forest. He was himself thereby torn from the whirl of his passionate questioning. He stood up, and looked around anxiously to see whether an eavesdropper was not perhaps somewhere nearby unnoticed; for the forest has as many ears as there are leaves hanging on the trees and needles on the branches. Actually, over there on the forest road, a man stood and looked attentively towards the area where Sintlinger found himself, shook his head, stabbed a few times at the road with his stick, deliberating, and then set himself cautiously in motion to find out from whom this loud laughter in the forest originated.

The blessed farmer saw the stranger coming ever closer, ducked, and ran soundlessly into the forest until he had a thick stand of saplings behind himself. Then he stood still, and listened again. There was no more sound to be heard except the seething of light in the treetops.

The quick run had taken his breath away somewhat. Hence he laid himself in the moistly warm moss, took his cap off, and pressed his hands into the soft, green cushion. Thus he gradually calmed himself down, and when he now thought over his flight from the unfamiliar man, he smiled indulgently and leisurely over his comical haste. But, thank God, he had ironed things out with himself, and again felt himself sitting on the old, safe horse.

He abandoned himself to a dreamlike lapse of mood, and followed with curiosity a tiny little, cicada-like creature which, probably shaken by his hand from the tip of a little tree of moss, was making efforts to get up through the green tangle again. To alleviate the insect's endeavours, he let off some of the pressure from his hand. The little tree of moss rose, and in a short time, the creature was freed from its prison and running up his forefinger. There it stood still for a long time in the perfect rigidity proper only to insects. Only its tiny antennae trembled constantly as if from the after-effects of fear. Thus the blessed farmer had the leisure of observing the creature, and of becoming extremely amazed at its indescribable beauty. Its body, perhaps a quarter centimetre long, in the form of a tiny torpedo, only with stronger tapering at the back and head, was clothed in a metallic pale green over which lay a powdery white mark. The same colour too were both the half wings, frizzily curled little fans in whose hollows the suggestion of a red shimmer hovered. The rings of the abdomen were relieved with deep black crescents, becoming fainter and fainter towards the middle so that you could barely define the place where they stopped. The greatest wonder, however, were the black, fierily smouldering eyes on the pointed head and the two tenuous, black antennae which ended in dark green tufts, like in magical electric flames. The little creature stood on pink little legs, and now, as it began to run, it looked as if it were rushing on a pink little haze.

And this wonder was seen by scarcely one in twenty million men. Perfectly hidden, it blossomed in the magic of its splendour, and withered again, perhaps after hours or days, without having known its beauty itself ever any differently than in the beauty of its inner harmony of which the outer shape was the expression.

So divinely alone, even unknowing, is how men too should carry their perfection. Like his little Lena carried it, and as he endeavoured to live by her example. And the blessed farmer recalled with delight the knowledge which had come to him years before at the sight of the black hen before the wire mesh. All the shapes of life are always symbols of the same truth. In everything there resided the inexpressible king who watches the play of life's gestures, but most distinctly in man.

Now, and had he, Sintlinger, more and more purely over the years, had he not also become more mindful in living? Like this animal, even if also not unknowingly, and even if not by intent.

Yes, yes, more and more purely, for himself, of course.

But how? What consequences had it had for those with whom he had come into contact?

And for the first time, he saw his life as he had never seen it before. It came like a raid, an intrusion, a heaving off of the hinges. Whether he wanted it to or not, a soundless stormy wind tore him away — his father-in-law, old Klim, had died of it. It had pushed the Pastor Ardelt into the grave, hung the braggart Meixner from a tree, disturbed the peace of the entire district, sundered men, even alienated himself from his wife, inflamed the old hate of the Brindeiseners anew, driven Gottlieb from the farm.

And what had actually remained to him himself of all that?

A few scanty written sheets in a locked drawer.

The dark consciousness of guilt at the uprising of the district had driven him to Hemsterhus to make good what originated from him. And had he not in cowardly fear of the responsibility pulled along little Lena as protection into the turmoil, and had his girl not been as though transformed since then?

A strange power was operating in his life, and had confused everything, despite the master, the invisible king within him, so that, now after decades of struggle, he saw himself entangled in injustice just like before when he had sinned against life through the heavy derailments of drinking.

The blessed farmer was shattered and shaking all over. He looked at his hand, and noticed that he had crushed the beautiful cicada between his fingers.

That unsettled him even more deeply.

"Am I then a monster in that I must annihilate everything which I touch?" he said disconsolately, with faltering chest.

"Why does it all happen to me? — Why?" he asked further in horror.

Then the answer came quite distinctly, "Because you think your thoughts, and feel your emotions, and because the love is thus missing from you which sacrifices itself without weighing up and without asking."

It was spoken quite clearly, only Sintlinger could not discern whether it came from within himself or from outside of himself.

With constricted heart, he waited for the talking to continue.

And while he listened, a place in Faber's letter occurred to him, that place in which he wrote to him that, over the years, he often felt physically near him, and at the same time, he thought of how often the image of this man had appeared really incarnate before him in that time.

Full of a dreamlike horror, he finally raised his eyes, and looked around. Had the stranger on the road perhaps even been Faber?

But the entire forest was empty and deathly still. The trees stood unmoving in the sinking evening light.

As if shattered, the blessed farmer rose, and walked away in the forest, heedless of as to where.

In the depths of night, the blessed farmer's wife felt in her sleep that someone was seizing her hand.

She awoke, and saw that her husband was sitting on the edge of the bed next to her.

His fingers were cold and clutching her hand like a vice.

He did not answer any questions, and, after he had sat there for a while, he went from the room again without saying anything.

3

Amongst the folk, nothing was known of this hidden visitation but the legend that the blessed farmer had once again left the devil laughing deep in the forest.

Sintlinger listened to that with his accustomed smile, without attempting to clear up this foolish misunderstanding. Even towards Johanna, he did not come out of his silence, except insofar as he spoke of the bothersome claim of a man who had once associated with him in his wild period. For the sake of her peace and impartiality, he asked not to be asked for his name. The commotions which his unexpected appearance gave him, and a taste of which she had not been spared from on that night, were now completely past.

He brushed his hand gently over his wife's forehead after this disguised truth, and Johanna saw him in the accustomed way leave her again in the light of his mysterious reclusiveness, probably calmed, but also a little disappointed that the darkness had so quickly discharged from Sintlinger again, that darkness through which he would eventually have to be led back to her and the society of men one day. For it had become a fixed idea in the dear woman that little Lena could not come into possession of the light of her eyes before Sintlinger had been chased out of his desolation.

Only, as she also inconspicuously observed her husband, she could not perceive *one* secret darkening, not *one* slip of irritability in him by which she could have borne out the fearful yearning in herself.

The blessed farmer thought he had recovered completely from his breakdown in the forest. He no longer placed the fate of old Klim, the Pastor, and the braggart Meixner alone on his register of guilt, but saw in their unfortunate denouements the consequences of their own errors, and the effect of the forces which have defined the life and death of every man since eternity. Contained in his papers is also the justification of the state he had won for himself, not a word of the self-accusation which had overcome him in the forest. Only quite quietly did something of the pain he bore echo in the phrase which is found at the end of the series of thoughts with which he dismissed the influence of Faber's letter.

"At first, the music made the instrument", the enigmatic words read. "Since then, the instrument makes the music, and every great song must degenerate. For nobody can play the music of heaven purely except in their own heart."

You don't go astray in seeing in these sentences the confession of hopelessness towards all human striving for the last perfection. But a particular brusqueness of the blessed farmer's flared up immediately after these events so as to insulate his life entirely from that of others, as if to at least affirm the heights he had won. He declined earnestly and decisively to take sides in the business which took place after Vanlyßender's burial between the Hemsterhus Pastor and the Querhoveners, and was also able to evade being a witness in the subsequent court case.

Branching further into the endeavours of these sectarians simply meant for him returning again to the labyrinths of former times of folly, to the bitterness over the trivialities of common people, and finally to the old mocking laughter. Everything he attempted, they imitated like the shadow repeats the existence of the tree, without colour, without scent, without depth.

Thus, in these decisive hours of destiny, Sintlinger went out over the bounds of self-preservation. For in every man's life, a moment occurs when our powers have experienced their highest possible increase. Then we must turn from master to servant of our works, and, if it concerns ideas, endure the changes which are now already bound inexorably with every realisation.

But the entire world continued burning Sintlinger only with his own anguish.

One day he took Helene with himself out into the field, and when they were both completely alone, he asked the girl whether she saw a man in the distance approaching the farm. He meant by that the rebel Faber who had signalled a visit to the blessed farm in his letter. Sintlinger, who was firmly convinced of Helene's power of seeing into the distance, and had experienced already wondrous proof of this ability, suffered a complete disappointment for the first time. Already the changed way in which Helene accepted his question that day made him suspicious. The closedness of her poise did not relax as usual, her face took on a suggestion of distressed, earnest contemplation, and the clear bottomlessness of her sightless eyes deepened still more inwardly. She raised her head for only a moment, as if peering out, then shrugged her shoulders indifferently and dismissively, bent down, brushed the palm of her hand across the grass, and answered at the same time that, no, she saw nothing. What should she see? It was not like before with her anymore at all. But when the blessed farmer now insisted with chagrin on her explaining to him what had changed, how it had become different in her, the girl gave no answer for the time being, walked next to her father, plucked, sometimes with her left hand, sometimes with her right hand, flowers, stalks, blades of grass, all of which she caught precisely, and threw them far away with a passionate gesture. But as Sintlinger did not slacken in inquiring with all the worries of love about the changes in her mood, she said a few times louder and louder, and finally almost shouting, "Nothing — nothing — nothing!", and suddenly began running straight across the field into the middle of a strip of corn as if fleeing from her father. The startled blessed farmer followed immediately behind his child. But as soon as Helene saw she was being followed, she flew straight through the rustling rye, and only stopped in the field margin on the other side with flying breast, flushed face, and still eyes which smiled and at the same time played sparklingly and yet over-flowing with tears. Thus she let herself be clasped in her father's arms, and asked, sobbing more and more vehemently, not to be questioned anymore like before. The servants also did not know to talk to her of anything else, and all the people neither, and with one word, she did not like it anymore. With all the impassioned and turbid talk, the silver tinkling peculiar only to her was sometimes lost from her voice, the words muted into a completely foreign sound, and even Sintlinger was a little struck by the hot trepidation which had seized his daughter, and so he let her go in a sort of fright, and asked her to defend herself with all her powers if such a moody whirl tried to attack her again.

During the walk home through the completely still summer light, amidst the waves of larks' jubilation in the air, and amidst the widely spaced silence of the tall stemmed, sown fields, Helene sure enough came again completely into the distance enchantment of her being. She seized her father's hand, and the blessed farmer enjoyed the gentle, wondrous play of her floating gait. Not only that, the entire boundlessness of childish impressionability came over her again, and she began chatting apparently without connection about what she had experienced on the trip to the Hemsterhus uproar. Then it had seemed to her as if she were being borne away to never, ever return, not to the blessed hill, not to her mother, to nobody, not even to him, to her father who was guiding the horse and was sitting next to her. But the strangest thing of all had been that her dear father had remained there during the trip, where he always was; only she, she alone had felt torn away, racing quick with each hoofbeat into the unknown. And that it had not actually properly stopped anymore since then. And even this afternoon, when her father had asked her about the man in the distance, it had been so. Sometimes it was not nice at all, and sometimes it was even downright scary, and at the same time beautiful in a way that cannot be said.

As Helene twittered that all out fuzzily and in a rush, she flung her arms around her father's neck, kissed him stormily, and promised to compose herself and not to be naughty anymore. He should just not say anything to mother.

Sintlinger stroked her hair from her forehead, and the worries from his soul. Hands entwined, looking as joyful as ever, they strode through the back little gate and across the yard. But as Helene climbed up the few steps before her father, and vanished through the door, the blessed farmer felt a darkening fall so abruptly over his eyes that he passed his hand over his face as if this shadow over his soul were a shroud to be swept away.

For it may well be that the anguish befell him which is imposed on parents who are darkened by the transition of their child into a different stage of life, confused as if seeing the child vanish around a corner on the world's path, tempted back with no call of love, with no cry of yearning; he could also have been gripped by the sorrow over the tailing off of little Lena's mysterious power to look with the far-sighted eyes of her soul at the emergence of fateful people on the horizon of his life, and perhaps you would not go astray in the assumption that for that reason a feeling of defencelessness took hold of him, similar to the feeling of the soldier who has lost his weapon.

One afternoon, Sintlinger, Johanna, and little Lena sat at the dining table in the large living room.

The girl had propped her head in her left hand, and was listening in the quiet absentmindedness of her sixteen years to her parents' conversation.

The clear, still sunlight of the late summer, the song of the birds already restless to migrate, and the dry scent of approaching autumnal fullness were streaming through the open window. At once, Helene leant back passionately in her chair, folded her hands together, and sank into such a delighted listening to the song of the birds that her face was dipped in the shimmer of a fervent transfiguration, and quiet tears entered her sightless heavenly eyes.

"Little Lena, what is it?" the blessed farmer asked, and placed his hand concernedly on her lower arm.

"I don't know", she said struggling and smiling at the same time, "I don't know. The singing, the singing! Just listen though when the birds sing lustily down so, you know, then it is just as if you were falling into emptiness. God, like in a dream of a tall house, you are falling and don't know to where."

Johanna, being of a sober nature, reproached her for this aimless wallowing into which the girl was tempted more and more.

"You know, child", the farmer's wife said, "my father could not suffer such talk at all. A woman who sews without knots, sews emptily. And then he always thought that every man was both a herder and herd of cows all at once, and if the herder does not coerce the herd, then the herd will rule the herder."

"Yes, yes, dear mother", the girl replied and laughed delightedly. "It is exactly so with me. Inwardly it taps like a thousand goats' feet. No, it is not to be said how."

And yet as she spoke this, she stood up, transported again into dreaminess, as if she were looking down at herself, and then asked the blessed farmer quietly as if with the curiosity of someone half asleep, "Did I not dance once, father? As a quite, quite little girl. Well? Up and down the field margin it went, la, la, la, laaa! Lalala, laaa. Lalala, laaa! La, la, la. Laaa!"

And she began twirling and singing in the room.

But the blessed farmer caught her in his arms after a few turns.

"Come, dear Lena, come here, and sit down", he said, and led her back to the chair. "The Hemsterhus uproar excited you a lot." But Helene was not to be dislodged from her memories. She sat there, constantly still and listening in astonishment to herself.

"No — no — such a thing!" she said, taken aback. "It is becoming more and more different. Besides, when I was seeing and hearing, everything came from the expanse within me. Now everything comes into me. Quite, quite different. I just don't know what it is meant to mean! Before the accordion playing was quite far ... quite far away."

"Accordion playing?" Johanna asked almost harshly. "Silly girl! From where in all the world now would accordion playing be coming from?"

"Yes, accordion playing", Helene replied fervently. "Gottlieb played for me that time. I hear it quite distinctly. — Oh! — And now it comes nearer and nearer ... and it is ... as if ... now it goes quite soft up over our house ..."

While she was speaking so disjointedly, she had again stood up, penetrating with all her senses into the distance, and then walked from the room as if carried away hypnotically.

Helene was so confident in the house, yard, and fields despite her blindness that Sintlinger and his wife also let her go now, in the opinion that she was only stepping out the front door.

"I don't know what that was meant to be about", the farmer's wife said, watching after her with a worried shaking of her head. "The girl is not at all the same any-more."

"You think too that it is since she went with me to Hemsterhus. Perhaps from the fear of the braggart Meixner", Sintlinger said.

"Yes, Andreas, you could say that, certainly", Johanna answered. "Or it all comes about because she is now coming into her nature ..." But the blessed farmer's wife interrupted herself, listening sharply to the house.

"Oh God", she then said in a rush. "Can't you hear? She is walking up the stairs! Andreas, it would be better if you went after her. The steps have such a nasty turn."

Sintlinger ran out instantly. He found the hallway empty, saw nobody on the first flight of stairs, heard no more steps, but heard little Lena's insistent voice, and in answer, the awkward words of a man sounded all around.

He could not perceive what was being said. And now he arrived on the loft floor, stepped along the narrow passage, and arrived before the open door of a room.

There an astonishing sight greeted him. Gottlieb was kneeling or cowering before Helene (he could not see exactly, because the girl obscured him in part) and hold-ing one of her hands in his large, rectangular mitts. Everything was drowned in the dark haze of the loft, an accursed, dreamlike image which the blessed farmer en-joyed in astonishment for a little while.

But now Helene sensed Sintlinger standing behind her, and called, turning around, with delighted voice, "You see, father, the accordion playing was in the loft! But, Gottlieb, now stand up. He wants to come to us again, think, and is afraid that we are all still angry at him. That isn't true though! Come, father, you tell him. He won't believe me."

Thus little Lena babbled in confusion, and then stepped to the side.

Now Gottlieb sprang up, and went towards Sint-linger, who was stepping completely into the room. His lumpy face was bone white, his eyes lay in quiet ardour in their spacious sockets. Thus he stood before Sint-linger, and said haltingly and shaking everything which his burdened heart had carried so mazily for years. The result was that he had to return to the blessed farm again, otherwise he would truly perish. The wicked and stupid things he had committed should be all forgiven. He had atoned enough, and thought that he had now completely "un-Meixnered" himself. The blessed farmer did not let him entirely finish speaking. He was gripped by the fidelity of the fellow, even if the new attachment to the Querhovener "men of Christ", to whom Gottlieb adhered, did not please him. He was moved deepest of all by the wondrous circumstances under which his little Lena had perceived Gottlieb's secret creeping in to the farmstead. For now he noticed that the mysterious power had not been entirely lost from his daughter in her adolescent body, and he drew the hope of being able to also lead his life again further and further into isol-ated heights. Hence he took the fellow by the hand, and led him through the house to his wife. She received him with fresh benevolence, and when she had heard everything, she was also seized by amazement, and asked Gottlieb impishly where he had left the accordion now for whose playing little Lena had hurried out of the room. For it would be nice if he now played a right cheerful little piece.

But the fellow answered disconcertedly that he did not understand the revered farmwife at all. He had come to the farmstead just as he was now standing.

There was not so much as a damper key from an accordion in his pocket. Oh, and playing! He had not played anymore for years. That is all over forever. Or he would not know what would have to happen for him to have the desire for it once more.

"I did not play, Mrs Sintlinger. On my soul not!" he protested once more in closing, because Johanna was looking from one to the other with raptly smiling distrust, as if before a mischievous surprise.

"Yes, but what does all that mean", she now called out loudly. "Then something deceived little Lena just then."

Then the blessed farmer whispered something in his wife's ear so that she looked at her girl now with even greater astonishment. So strong was the urging of her look that little Lena, red all over, threw her arms around her mother's neck, and said fervently, "He did play though, mother. Oh, and *how* beautifully he played."

4

Gottlieb felt just like a bird battered by a storm for a long time into inhospitable, unknown regions, which finally finds its way back again under homely, maternal rooves. Full of keen cheerfulness, he worked on the blessed farm like before, but without the springing of his old mazy whimsicality, instead quiet, sunny, prudent. And his uncle, old Zenker, liked to cede to him more and more the outward management of the manifold farming operation, which his aged hands had held in the end more and more weakly and falteringly. He just hobbled unobtrusively behind his nephew to immediately sort out possible derailings, and prevent errors of judgment. For of his pride that the steady Zenker blood had won through in the fellow now, he let little show in his gruff, gnarled way. Even Johanna felt benevolently the intervention of Gottlieb Meixner, if she also awaited in vain evening after evening for the sound of his cheerful ballads. She also incited the servants, and urged the strange fellow in vain to take up the old playing again. "What is destroyed remains destroyed", he answered to all demands with calm earnesty, and turned away, as it seemed to the farmwife, often with a wistful smile.

Even little Lena tempted and coaxed Gottlieb in vain. She went out like in her childhood to the labourers and maids in the fields, and sat in the midst of them. But the cheerful laugh and teasing springing up and down of the conversation, like she carried from that distant time in her memory, had drained away from these people. Everyone was frozen in the pose of a timid veneration towards her, immediately broke off their activity when she appeared amongst them, stopped their chatter, and stood or sat as if in tense expectation of a new wonder, like tableaus in ecstatic delight around her. She never encountered a fresh word like those for which she yearned. They whispered cautiously, as if from a distance, their mazy, whimsical stuff so that she never succeeded in seeing these people clearly before her with her mysterious, inner sight.

One time the blind girl sat again in this solitude amongst them, and endeavoured in vain to be with them. The people's words were only an indistinct mumbling which did not appear to be proper to her, but penetrated through her from somewhere like a wind which moves the stems in the field or skims through the treetops. And when it was no longer possible for Helene to separate it distinctly from the quiet, monotonous music which the summer air along with the blades of grass, the breathy rustling of the broad fields of grain, the humming of countless insect wings, and the deep tones of the distant forest infused more and more deeply into this sunny song of the earth, something remarkable happened to her. Though at first still behind this eternal melody, a different, transfigured, human singing sounded, inconceivably gripping, and it came out of the unending spacelessness closer and closer to her so that she also felt powerless in the depths of her soul, like a field of quivering wheat and trembling grass. Without knowing what was happening to her, she rose from the field margin in which she was sitting as if by an irresistible call. The servants, when they saw it, fell silent at once, and everyone directed their attention to Helene, who stared for a moment into the broad sky.

Her body stood and trembled so stormily that it seemed to simple people that right now a miracle must happen, and the blessed hill's girl would rise up in the air and be carried floating away. Instead of which, she began to sing at first softly in dreamy tones a melody never heard before, which quickly climbed into abrupt, trilling wooing; she began turning, at first on the spot where she stood, raising her arms longingly, and then began to get carried away in a hovering dance. But she was already stumbling after a few steps, composed herself though, boosted her singing, forced herself to more impassioned movements, and threatened the next moment to fall with nervously wide eyes and pale face. Then Gottlieb Meixner sprang to her, like that time in her childhood, and caught her in his arms. But hardly had she felt the embrace of the fellow than she cried sensually gasping, "Gottlieb, man, swing me up!"

Only, the labourer answered sheepishly, abjectly, "No, no, that won't work", and held the trembling girl until she stood safely. Helene felt the way he released his hands from her cautiously, and lingered motionless with closed eyes. When Gottlieb withdrew his last hand from her arm, it passed like a fearful awakening through her. She raised her hands, and groped over his face, but she soon drew back, turned away disappointedly with a shudder, and began seeking out with timid, groping steps the path over the meadow to the farmstead.

Someone offered to accompany her, but she declined with a pained smile. After a short hesitation, she walked diagonally across the sloping meadow, with the hovering gait peculiar to her, and the servants saw her heading for the path which led to the blessed farm from the high butte. For the whirling, the differentness of the world, had attacked her today more vigorously than ever before.

The girl asked herself in vain what it must mean, and yet found no answer for it other than that she had been seized by a similar state to the one when she had in her parents' room first been pulled into the world by the birdsong, and then been led by a magical accordion playing to the loft. To figure out what it meant, she had pursued Gottlieb with the stubborn request to play again like that time in her childhood. But today she had experienced that the music after which she yearned did not come from Gottlieb, and was not a memory of the accordion playing of her childhood, but the beguiling song of an unknown thing which had been sung to her from somewhere outside her, so passionately that she had had to stand up as though intoxicated and dance because she would otherwise have collapsed in a faint. And as she considered that, she skimmed her hand through the blades of the long meadow grass next to her whilst she walked, as was her habit. But she had to draw back her fingers in shock, for grass, rye, and leaves were not gliding coolly through her hands, but instead she was feeling human eye sockets and saw with her finger-tips the hump of a strange, broad forehead so that the same hot shudder went stormily, almost fearfully through her breath again. All this bustle, all these multi-farious enchantments under which Helene suffered had begun on the day in which she had experienced with her father the uprising of the Querhoven fanatics at the Hemsterhus parsonage. Then something had burst in her through the shock she had received from the wild braggart Meixner, and, in addition, it seemed to the blind girl sometimes as if since then a mysterious wall had been drawn about her usually borderless world, from where, in moments of high excitement, incomprehensible, not yet experienced things edged towards her, and even from without, whilst everything else had been given to her by entering a secret gate in her own inner being.

Helene did not know, being denied the divine sense of the external face, that she lived in a heaven whose boundlessness did not shine in the reflection of the earthly light, as with sighted people, but in a shimmer which came up in an unearthly way, dreamily from her own soul. Destiny was beginning to lead her out from this paradise, like an angel which it is calling to the land of men. But always, when the Sintlinger girl was filled by the passion of seeking for her new existence like today, she experienced in the end a double pain, finding the access to her new longing shut off, and also being homeless in her old world.

Usually Helene had sensed from the high butte that the surrounding countryside was like the circling deluge of waves. Today it was rigid and empty up there, an op-pressive, chest constricting expanse. A monotonous, razor sharp breeze also sang in the high air, and when she went down the slope on the other side, she did not encounter anymore the magical stillness of the depression in which the land here sunk towards the forest, and in which Helene had always experienced the dreamy happiness of a girl's room. The ground under her feet behaved abruptly and aimlessly. The forest did not stand in the same place as usual, and exhaled strangely, reservedly a humming she had never heard before. In the song of the larks, she heard only the high shrilling. From everywhere, the actions of people penetrated to her. The bellowing of the cows in the fields sounded menacingly. The more Helene composed herself, the further she went astray, like in a completely unknown land. And after she had wandered about for hours, criss-crossing the path ten times, walking up and down the field margin again and again, recoiling from trees and ending up in fields, she heard the calm purring of a shrub next to her, crept under its down-hanging branches, sank down exhausted, and began crying help-lessly and softly. At the same time, she said over and over, "I will not find my way home anymore to the farm-stead and to my father and mother."

Finally Helene fell asleep exhausted. Thus the blessed farmer found her, having set off to search for his child.

Helene opened her eyes, heard with astonishment the voice of her father, listened all around, and thereby acquired an astonishingly enigmatic smile in her face, like children have who are guarding a secret which they do not comprehend. Of the experience that she had just had, Sintlinger learnt nothing. She gave confused an-swers to every question, so uncertain and hesitant, and also so extraneous that he could not explain the shiver which gently shook her from time to time, and nor the garish redness which inflamed her face now and then. At the same time, she walked unsteadily and joltingly next to her father, like she was drowsy, so the blessed farmer seized her hand so that she did not fall over. But Helene withdrew it from him with vigour, and then said apologetically that he should not trouble himself, she would pull herself together now by herself.

After a few steps, Sintlinger noticed how Helene raised her hand to her eyes, examining it as if she was sighted like other people, and when the blessed farmer asked her what she was doing with her hands, a blissful shimmer scurried as an answer across her face, which transformed abruptly into such a deeply rapt astonishment that it almost looked like anguish.

But the blessed farmer sought an answer always in vain. Nothing was to be prised from the servants either, other than that Helene had performed a "sacred dance", and had thereby almost fallen over, had Gottlieb not caught her.

Thus the blessed farmer's world suffered through the whirl that spun Helene out of her world.

At this time, the almost entirely acquitting judgment occurred in the case of the Hemsterhus Pastor against the Querhoven men of Christ. The small fine with which the villagers were condemned for a minor breach of the peace only heightened the lustre of the acquittal. And even if the Querhoveners had never considered any other outcome than this one to be possible, everyone breathed out in relief anyway, since the unease which each had secretly carried within had been taken from them. They took the judgment by the court for a judgment by the world over the rightness and purity of their religious beliefs, and were full of joyful thankfulness towards God for imparting victory on them in the struggle against so many and mighty adversaries.

The day of the judgment's announcement fell in the vicinity of that day in which Ursula Rütsch of the Sweeps had once been saved by the blessed farm's little

Lena in a wondrous way from the anguish over the death of her Snowy, and by which all the Querhoveners had been gifted for the first time the will to a new Christian life. In the devout souls of the forest villagers, both widely separated events now dovetailed in a single act of divine providence, and produced the desire in everyone to festively celebrate the memory which the Querhoveners in fact declared festive. On the Sunday in September which is dedicated in the Catholic Church to the celebration of Mary's birth, the Querhoveners organised a sort of procession of thanks to the Sintlinger memorial under the lime trees at the gate of the great hill farm. For from the blessed hill, they had received the best part of the spirit which beatified all those who submitted without thought to it, though the blessed farmer also held himself aloof from their common life, and he had also made the final victory difficult for them in that he had eschewed being a witness in the court case. In the eyes of the Querhoveners, certainly only after some contemplative pauses, that did not contain an expression of deliberate hostility by Sintlinger towards them and their endeavours, but only the proof of the hill farmer's unrelenting urge for seclusion and to not have the earthly circles drawn around him and his girl disturbed. And those who had undertaken to teach the few opposed Querhoveners something better recalled in finishing the expression of Vanlyßender when he had in a matter of belief once been quite roughly dismissed by the blessed farmer. At the time, the old man had said to those who had flared up scathingly and been resentful of him, that he was not to be torn away by fury as well, "The higher and more mysteriously a cloud goes in the heavens, the deeper it grips the human soul. And does that soul not act foolishly which resents it that the cloud does not worry about men? It gives and asks for no thanks. Is that not divine?"

In this way, the Querhoveners came in the proper festively elevated mood for their procession of thanks to the blessed hill.

Without trumpets and drums, without flags and pageantry, in a simple upliftedness, festively dressed, they wandered towards mid afternoon not along the new road, but along the old field path over the high ridge which separated the district of the estranged farms from the Querhoveners' area. And while, clustered in informal groups or ordered unintentionally into pairs behind one another, they were not actually walking, but swirling; they discussed the many changes and dangers by which, through the course of the years, their faith had become ever simpler and purer, and their life clearer and richer; stood still in the view of the beautiful region here and there; and, in walking onward, identified to the left and right in the meadows the few flowers with which the autumn was adorned.

The blessed farmer was just then sitting on the little bench under the lime tree by the gate, and, in an endeavour to calm his mood, was letting his eyes rest in the quite sunny brilliance of the afternoon. When he raised them after being lowered for a long time, and said to himself in thought, "Many a time being still is simply made difficult for us", he caught sight on the ridge on the other side the festive swarm of Querhoven men of Christ, but did not know what it signified. They stood quite still, and also gazed across to the blessed farm, and the gaze of Sintlinger here and the Querhoveners there met without recognising each other. But Vanlyßender's friend, the weaver Staupitz, who had received the leadership after the death of the good old man, without any doing on his part, when he saw the miracle farm before him, the goal of their pious starting out, he walked to the head of the swirling mass, and managed to order the Querhoveners behind him into a proper procession. Thus the column moved down the leisurely slope to the boundary path. Now the blessed farmer recognised them, and was immediately forced out of his more composed mood again. In addition, the entire staff over on the Brindeisener hill had all stepped out before their gate, and looked at first in astonished silence at the unaccustomed parade. But soon the labourers were starting all sorts of silly teasing, and the maids accompanied each shout with screeching laughter in which soon the merriment of old Brindeisener joined in with loud booming.

The displeasure over this "mischief" seethed in the blessed farmer, and he was determined that if the Querhoveners wanted to come up to him, he would confront them, and turn them away. Only, then the good people, on turning in to the driveway, began singing, and it did not succeed all to well in the excitement, and someone from the Brindeisener hill shouted, "The old wench is out of tune!", Sintlinger's agitation increased to furious bitterness. He went quickly to the house, shooed his own emerging servants back into the yard, had the gate and side door closed, and forbade anyone with immediate loss of service from taking a step out or answering any question. His face was pale, and his eyes blazed like a drawn iron, and as he then stepped abruptly into the house, he murmured, "I have enough whirling around me. I could do without this nonsense right now!"

When the Querhoveners heard the gate of the blessed farm fly shut, and the mocking derision from the Brindeisener hill still increasing, the pious hymn came to a stop in everyone's throats, and many suggested it would be better to turn around than to burden themselves for the sake of goodwill with still more shame. But Staupitz refreshed the lowered fortitude of the timid by reminding them that they had undertaken this walk not because of some man, but alone out of thankfulness towards God, and hence had the duty of allowing nobody and nothing to put them off it. Least of all, however, should they take umbrage at the behaviour of the blessed farmer. For the entire district had often enough experienced that this strange, elevated man fled honour more than any illness, and if he were the enemy of the Querhoveners, then for what reason had he stood by them in adversity in Hemsterhus, and why in all honesty had Gottlieb Meixner been taken in by him again, and now held as firmly as anyone to him?

These words from the weaver ignited the pious fortitude of the Querhoveners again. The interrupted hymn was started anew, and now almost in defiant joy, so that the mockers on the other estranged farm's hill forgot their silly shouts, and watched almost with fear as the column of Querhoveners clambered up the blessed hill, because nobody knew whether these mutinous Christians were not up to a hidden devilry again, like the Hemsterhus axe procession under the leadership of the braggart Meixner.

Meanwhile Sintlinger had hurried through his spacious house to look for Helene, and to keep her away from any involvement with the Querhoveners. He was not acting according to a clear idea, but in the urging of a blind worry. But the girl was nowhere to be found, and when the hymn of the approaching men of Christ suddenly started anew and now tempestuously, the thought seized the blessed farmer that the fanatics could be coming up the hill to take their revenge on him for declining to be a witness in their court case. This sprang at his throat, and immediately he let searching be searching, hurried down to the vagrants' room, whose window looked out on the lime tree by the gate, and established himself there so that he could observe everything that happened outside unseen. He saw the undulating column slowly climbing the hill. These people were devout, as if flags rustled above them, their eyes full of collected light, and even the withered old woman who, breathless from climbing and singing, made a face as though choking, was in a secret way gripping and awe-inspiring, so that Sintlinger no longer understood his suspicion that these people could have been driven up the hill by a desire for revenge against him. When the Querhoveners had finally arrived up top, each stuck his little bunch of field flowers in the mesh of the iron grill which surrounded the Sintlinger memorial enthroned with its cross. Then they knelt down in a half circle on the grass. The weaver Staupitz and the beautiful Ursula Rütsch from the Sweeps, as those revered by all the men of Christ, received the place directly before the cross. And after everyone had spent a while in quiet meditation, the old weaver, a tall, thin man with an expressive, beardless face under an abundance of youthfully tousled white hair, rose and spoke a few words about the meaning of the day's walk and the day which he called a celebration of the manifold birth of the pure faith. Then he commanded "the entire world of men" to the eternal peace of their eternal soul, and admonished those present to free themselves of all anger, all wicked appendages of their hearts, ill-wishes, and revenge, even when their neighbour acted differently to what they would have expected. "Nevertheless, anyone who strikes in his thoughts the man who is his enemy inflicts a wound on his own spirit for which no doctor on earth is to be found." In concluding, he demanded Ursula Rütsch, as a promise never to deviate from the hard-won faith, to say in everyone's name the prayer which her blessed father, Vanlyßender, had bequeathed to the world. And the beautiful Ursula, in the memory of the wondrous uplifting which had once been bestowed on her in this very place by the blessed farm's little Lena, came in praying to such emotion that everyone prayed the ending aloud with her rapturously.

From her own, full heart, Ursula Rütsch added still inspired, "And blessed is this farm, and everyone who resides on it!"

Then the Querhoveners walked down the hill again to their poor little village.

The blessed farmer, however, leant as though in a dream against the wall of the vagrants' room. His face was painfully sunken, pale, and his eyes stared in dry burning at a stain. He seemed to himself to be like an apostate of the elevated world on the other side into which, wandering after his child, he had penetrated during many years of struggle. Full of bitter shame, he finally straightened up, and hurried soundlessly up the stairs to his room, the door of which he locked behind himself.

Little Lena had also experienced, from the window of the room above the vagrants' room, hidden from everyone's sight by the thick crown of the lime tree, the thanksgiving of the Querhoveners. But the girl was seized in a quite different manner to her father. The dreamily still, accursed expanse of her childhood land unhinged its mysterious gate and let her spirit enter, no longer tormented by the yearning which she did not understand, by unease whose meaning was hidden from her, and a craving that could detect nothing and whose incomprehensible fervour grew the more firmly she caged it inside herself. She enjoyed again the sound of the undulating land around herself, the day surrounded her in an almightily peaceful embrace, the great depth of the clear autumn sky lay as an unchanging blessedness in her heart. The pilgrims' song was full of the magic of all the songs which she had ever sung. All the wonders of her past life stood around her, but at first not yet different from the way perhaps the world of a

glorious region appears to us sighted people behind silver mist. And she saw the crowd of Querhoveners
kneeling below her with her inner sight in a transfiguration inexpressible in our language.

But when the voice of the beautiful Ursula from the
Sweeps then rang out, it seemed to the blessed hill's girl
as if she were addressed from her own breast with a
trusted and yet unfamiliar voice. Helene was gripped so
much by this melodious speech, which she had anyway
already heard once before, that she paid no attention at
all to the meaning of the words, but penetrated deeper
and deeper into her memory with ever growing ardency
for the feminine, soft sounds, until finally the veil before
her past tore, and the experience stood tangibly and distinctly before her, the experience which she had had an
unthinkably long time ago with Ursula Rütsch from the
Sweeps. She saw the woman suddenly appear again in
the torturous hour with Miss Knille, sank into her lap,
was led by her hand under the lime trees, and finally felt
herself lifted up and kissed full of a sweetness so that it
seemed to her as if her entire childhood had been nothing but a single cuddle. She sank into this feeling as
though into a sun-shower, and did not know at all anymore what was happening around her. Ursula Rütsch's
prayer fell silent. The pilgrims tailed off over the hill
into the distance. It was quite still around her. "I was
kissed, oh, and how I was kissed!" little Lena whispered
in the intoxication of her heart, and clutched dreamily
at the air with both hands yearning. And when she felt
the leaves of the lime tree's crown around herself, the
spell of rapture only faded from her enough that she
could stand up and move. Still filled by the magic of that
time as if by a ghostly intoxication. She went out of the
room, down the stairs, and stepped under the lime tree
with an expectation as if she must still encounter all the
people whose celebration she had just witnessed. But

the place was empty. She felt the grill with her hands to "see" whether someone was still there and only keeping themselves hidden. Everywhere she found little bunches of flowers: honeysuckle, bleeding-heart, autumn crocus. Then she sat down on the little bench, folded her hands in her lap, and let herself sink back into dreamy thoughts. The images of her memory moved further along, and she saw herself sitting after Ursula Rütsch's departure in the meadow in the full light of the sun. A butterfly, the little sylph, played about her, caught itself in her hair, ran over her hand, teetered and rocked on her finger, flew away and let itself be enticed back again. Yes, little Lena felt immediately the breath-like delicate movements of the butterfly's feet and the silky soft touch of its wings on her hands, and instinctively loosened the grip of her fingers so as not to hurt the dream sylph.

But when she wanted to close her fingers in each other again, she no longer felt the butterfly, instead she held the head in her hands, the man's head, which she had grasped when, after the unfortunate dance in the meadow, she had felt Gottlieb Meixner's face, and she had recognised it with a knowing without understanding as the head of a completely different person, a lover. In shock, she raised her hands to bury her face in them, but had to desist from that, for it seemed to her as if she were raising the mysterious head with them up to her mouth, and suddenly all the sweetness of the caresses, all the ardency of the kisses were also around the head which she had just dreamt. And as this unfamiliar experience rushed through her, a feeling awoke in her lap like she had never felt before.

Full of fatal helplessness and fear, Helene burst out into loud crying.

Sintlinger, sitting in his room over his papers to find the way back in the records of his deep discoveries again to that elevated world he had attained, heard her loud crying first. He hurried out to her, and was shaken to find his blessed sunny child in such bewilderment. In secret, he was also frightened that his little Lena had seen with her wondrous power of sight the decline and infidelity of his own soul from which he had again wanted to free himself, and he bombarded her with questions about whether she was crying because of him, what he had done to her, or what had otherwise happened to her. With reluctance, she allowed herself to straighten up, but answered with nothing to his concerned, affectionate urging. Even Johanna rushing along was powerless towards this stream of tears breaking forth again and again. Finally Helene answered stammering and intermittently sobbing and faltering, "No, please, don't ask! No! No! Nobody! Carry my bed out of father's room into the room over the vagrant's room looking out on the lime tree. Yes, please, please! Father, don't be cross with me! But I must now sleep alone, and please, please, don't ask why."

The farmer's wife looked Sintlinger in the eyes with a deep look. Then they soothed Helene and did everything according to her wish.

The blessed hill's girl was transformed by nature and life amidst anguish and beatitude into a new state. For we humans are incapable of remaining overly long in the same form of our existence. Only for the child are many years sufficient, but only as long as until it has discovered itself through its surroundings. Then that constant confusion of its existence begins which only stops in the quiet lucidity of great age. We escape ourselves through friendship, it drives the inspired into the enchanted circle of the hero so that he places himself as servant in the possession of higher willpower, even before he has achieved the steely hardness of heroism. This insufficiency and suffering is negotiated by lesser people through all sorts of coarser pleasures, and even troubles the spirits of the select so that they never stop in the attempt to spread out their life over the last expanse into the immensity of the divine being. With all their intentions, plans and hopes, the people find themselves in a constant wandering which according to their character is sometimes like a crawling in the darkness, a begging at strange doors, the raids of the greedy, and sometimes like the dauntless incursion of a conqueror.

The yearning for the deepest transformation and renewal, however, which is bestowed to men on earth, drives the young man and woman into the embraces of love. Someone receives through a theft of God their holiest spirit, and goes away with it. And now they must make a pilgrimage to them until they have gotten back their lost spirit more richly by being restlessly devoted to it.

Only, as seldom as sleep falls suddenly, within a heartbeat, from our eyes, as seldom does the great upheaval through love transpire in an instant. The alienation from ourselves often occurs even before we know by name the passion to whose power we have become a slave. On a thousand dream paths, this divine peacelessness approaches people, and they have visions, even before they know those whom they see.

5

One night of that same September of 1909, when the whirl again passed stronger through the blessed farm, four students from the Silesian Corps entered the Café Royal in Breslau, which was known amongst the academic youth of the Silesian capital simply as Café Rabble.

Konrad Kaden, known simply as Kaka in the Corps, pushed the red portiere back first and held it to the side with his right hand. As he waited for a moment, he scanned the fully occupied room with one look. "Come on", he called to his fellow students who were hesitating a bit on the outer threshold. "You can't table yourselves outside."

"God forbid", a jarring voice answered, "for that we need your little head Kaka."

Amidst general laughter, so that the couples at all the tables looked up, the Silesians strode completely inside. In the left, back corner, a large table was still vacant. The waiter pointed it out to the young gentlemen, and hurried, respectfully and officiously, in front of them, slapped the white tablecloth quickly with the serviette, adjusted it, and then placed the salt and pepper, ashtray and bell in correct order.

Meanwhile the students slowly approached.

They were Spiegel, student of law, a tall, militarily sturdy fellow with an almost upset-looking feudal restraint; Jungmann, the son of a Namslau pharmacist, blond, sinewy, with cheerful laugh; Rupprecht, medicine student in his third semester, the son of a late head teacher from Strehlen, who had a fat, round face, hanging cheeks, and such a nervous scrofulous nose that his pince-nez continually fell down; and the small square-built Konrad Kaden, son of a manorial estate owner from County Grünberg, who possessed in addition to his unusually thick head the special peculiarity that he ground somewhat sideways with his tongue as he spoke and was an outright rascal. All wore suits of good cut, had well tended hands, and endeavoured to show unforced excellent manners.

They had ordered a glass of lager each, clinked glasses, and drank a deep swallow as if in a general at-tack of exhaustion, then they stared at each other for a joke, and broke out into loud laughter.

"A humid box", Rupprecht said into the silence which followed, and caught his pince-nez with his hand.

"Well, and what did you say outside? And now it should suddenly be humid! I don't understand you", thus Jungmann joined him cheerfully in the parade.

"Well, listen now, please, Jungmann! Do you want to provoke me perhaps?" the medicine student asked.

"Help, bagpipes and sawdust! No, Rups, never", Jungmann interrupted him, "but look please, along the way, and even outside the tavern, you said all sorts of beautiful things about him. He is a serious fellow, only just with the errors of an almost genial talent ..."

"And ditto knowledge", Kaka threw in.

"... for all I care also knowledge. I know nothing of all that, am called Curly, and ask for mitigating circum-stances."

They laughed cheerfully, and drank again.

Then Jungmann continued on, as he saw Spiegel was preparing to speak, "Silence! The mad things which are said about him, they do not bother me either. For I am, God knows, no coward. And if he had in two years whizzed about in fifty universities, instead of five! Each is indeed a paradise with food for snakes ..."

"Pardon, Jungmann, it cannot continue in this way", Spiegel now interrupted, "I note by your words that un-fortunately almost all of Breslau is infected by the Grabbe-like ways of this splendid Brindeisener. So it won't continue! In half an hour, Vollberg will report here with him, and the matter is not yet clearer. I for my part agree with Rupprecht that we have arrived a bit, shall we say timidly, at recruiting him for the Corps. That he is from a good family, may be. He throws the money about freely. Not stupidly, that I did not say. But also not always with taste."

Then he narrated an episode which he, as someone uninvolved, had witnessed in the "King of Saxony" on Albrechtsstraße, where Brindeisener, presiding over a long table of thrown-together students, had without any reason plied the entire circle with champagne to the point of vomiting, and concluded, "'The King of Saxony' is indeed a good local, even if not first class. But taste, at least in our Corps' sense, was not betrayed by it."

"Well, he cannot be a Silesian before he is a Silesian, otherwise he need not first become a Silesian", Rupprecht responded.

"Again a Brindeisener paradox", Spiegel replied after some hesitation, and leant back dismissively in his chair. "The matter with the pregnant Bolzen in Jena, my gentlemen, is fact. Or does someone know otherwise? You see. In addition, he is meant to be a phenomenal fencer. I have spoken with a Heidelberg Swabian. You know him, Weibrecht. He was last semester in a Corps tavern. Yes, a splendid, bright fellow, don't you think, whose eyes never so much as flickered. He had some matter in Greifswald with that very same Peter Brindeisener, and with it caught a cut that almost split his face. Frightful! As if hewn by a reverse cut. Yes, this elegant fencer Brindeisener is nothing more than a wild natural slasher. Shall we say a whirling drunk."

"*Ergo: Facit! Ex est!*" Jungmann finished mockingly. "So we won't recruit him! And then I must append yet, I have seldom yet seen an underdog who would not have comforted himself that he merely received a thrashing because he was the better fencer. I say nothing against the Swabian."

"By the way, where is the ... the ...", Spiegel began again.

"Penitent", Kaka patched in mockingly.

"... not in a bad way either", the interrupted student continued somewhat irritatedly, but suddenly did not know anymore what he had wanted to say, and thus closed with the repeated question, "Yes, where is he from actually? That must at least be clear."

Finally the moment came for Kaden too to give a longer talk. But he immediately became a little self-conscious, and ground his tongue so that, in the low voice in which the discussion was being held, he was difficult to understand. The four thus tilted their heads close together, and Kaka spoke.

"That I know precisely. He comes from the region between Emmerich and Wesel. So from where the Rhineland is more Friesian or Westphalian. For me, he is the model of a Westphalian. But that is by the by. His father possesses there a large estate which has been in the same family for centuries. I believe the place is called Hemsterhus. He has told me all sorts of things about the region which is still haunted by Münsterish anabaptism. I tell you, the fellow can tell a tale! Simply mad!"

"That is interesting, but is besides the point, Kaka", Spiegel said coldly, and when Kaden hence looked at him in reproof, he continued soothingly, "Naturally for the moment, dear friend. I thought, in particular, that you wanted to tell the story now of how our Magnifica was charmed into having a daughter by Brindeisener's conversation. So, please, continue, Kaka."

"Two estates lie opposite each other there in the hilly region. Both the same size and called in the surrounding area the estranged farmsteads."

At this moment, Vollberg and Peter Brindeisener entered, the latter in front. With one look, he had

scanned the four eager heads of the Silesians put together, recognised the situation, and when the students
now started as if on command, and looked at the two in
greeting, they met a mocking smile on Brindeisener's
face. He had developed to the full height which was normal for his family. His lankiness seemed angular
because of his markedly heavy-boned limbs, and yet, as
he now moved to the table, seemingly laboriously, the
arduously controlled twitching for a swift leap lay in a
hidden way in every step. His face was also quite as contradictory: the bold high forehead bore two humps over
the eyebrows, like the nubs of a sprouting horn; at the
same time, his face ran out straight into a fine nose with
the noblest nostrils. The lips thin and burning red, a
chalk-white, strong set of teeth, as though glowing with
blood; altogether a cheerful gruesomeness. Two deep
creases burrowed from between the thick, almost white
brows up into his forehead, and two creases slipping
from his nostrils to the corners of his mouth added to
his tanned face a touch of sarcastic melancholy. The
most beautiful part of him was his large, implacably
still, light blue eyes, full of a steely fire; both slow in
their movements, and of an alert depth like the eyes of
the hard of hearing. About this face, in which cheeki-
ness and kindness, ingenuity and temper contended,
blond hair blazed like a pale yellow, ungovernable fire.

Vollberg introduced him, "Brindeisener, student of
philosophy."

The arrival bowed gently, smiled strangely, greeted
Kaden in a friendlier way, and said, sitting down, "Yes,
for a change, I am building castles in the air with Professor Stern."

Then he let out a soft, nervous whistle, looked at
Vollberg, who had taken a seat opposite him, and stuck
both forefingers in his ears for a moment, for he was a
little drunk.

Spiegel had begun recounting a duel which he had contested with a Markoman. Everyone listened with half an ear, a little irritated by Brindeisener, who stared with scarcely controlled boredom into the bustle which tailed off into all the blind alleys of the duelling code, and found no end. Suddenly his patience was up. He leant a little over to Vollberg, and said, "You don't believe it, Vollberg, but how should someone write music, if music could only be perceived with the ears."

To Spiegel, who had flared up briskly because of the interruption, and was now looking inquiringly at Brindeisener, he said with a gentle smile, "Pardon me, Mr Spiegel." Then he continued without turning back to him, "Oh no, if we did not also know scientifically that the keyboard of the cortex's organ was inadequate for sensing the highest and deepest notes, just as little as the eyes are able to perceive all colours ..."

"Forgive me", Vollberg said, interrupting him, "on the way here, we in fact had a very interesting dispute about music following a performance of Carmen."

Brindeisener paid not the least attention to the disapproving astonishment with which everyone looked at him, drank his beer in one gulp, handed the glass to the waiter, and continued talking, "... able to perceive all colours ... please, let me first complete the sentence I began ... every unaffected man with a fine, sound nature knows intuitively that he hears with his entire body more unspeakable, in a word, more wondrous things than with the crude eardrum."

"That I don't believe", Kaden said, "why would we have ears then?"

"Well, for hearing naturally", Brindeisener replied calmly. "I am also not saying that we *don't* hear with them; but for comprehending the most sublime music, they are too blunt. It is incidentally established that we only perceive the highest notes with the temples. For we can distinguish between hearing internally and hearing externally."

Vollberg leant back, and gave him a sign to stop.

But Brindeisener's face twitched unwillingly, and he continued to pontificate, for he wanted "to smoke out the boring gang".

"The external music whose waves tremble through the air is only a pitiful attempt to express the indescribable thing that is played by an invisible instrument of our inner being", he continued.

But in looking up, he caught one of Spiegel's contemptuous looks so that he faltered.

A momentary silence occurred, which Spiegel used by speaking with a contemptuous sneer, "So, haha, to come to my Markoman, hahaha ..."

"Oh, please, let the dolls be now", Brindeisener cut into the beginning laughter.

"Explain yourself, my gentleman, better. I surely heard wrongly", Spiegel flared up jarringly. "You said dolls."

"Naturally, does it sound wrong to you? You don't seem to know yet that dolls sounds just like vegetables, cabbage, and Leipzig-style mixed-veg, all nonsense. As you will", Brindeisener responded with belting voice, the love of a fight awoken in him, and calmly leant back provocatively. "Of course, those present are excluded. That is, *if* they want to be."

In this nasty moment, the portiere flew apart, and a ravishingly beautiful girl, her expensive hat askew on her black hair, seemingly sprang in from the street, smouldering, and as if in flight from a swarm of young gentlemen who were following her raucously like a hungry mob. Peter Brindeisener, catching sight of her, immediately forgot everything, straightened up in astonishment, and changed colour.

The beautiful girl, who saw that, called over, "Well, grumpy, what's happening?"

She rushed through the local, and vanished up the stairs to the upstairs room, the entire swarm behind her.

An uproar arose at all the tables. Someone called out, "The egg shop's on a journey." At that a right whinnying broke out. The Silesians also sprang up energised, happy to get out of the embroilment in which they had fallen. "A fantastic woman!" Rupprecht cried admiringly and with twitching nose. "The pure shirt of fire!" With laughter, they grabbed their things, and, after their flip- pant farewell to Brindeisener, squeezed through the whirl with which students were saying goodbye to their drunken fellows. Only Spiegel still made a few provocat- ive remarks, but let himself be calmly drawn out the door because he saw endorsed the view of his Corps brothers that Brindeisener "had doused his nose, and that completely like a drake".

Thus the Silesians left the café.

Brindeisener sat sunken down as if a cloth had been unexpectedly thrown over his head. When he looked up after a while, he saw himself alone at the table, stood up, stepped to the bar, and asked the barman whether he knew the girl here "who had just fallen in from the street with such a racket". Yes, certainly, came the an- swer, that would be the daughter of a Saxon high official, who had escaped from her Dresden pension and immediately registered as a prostitute here in Breslau. But she had not let anyone have their way with her up to now.

Peter Brindeisener sighed with relief, and said with a smile, "Beautiful! Thank you. Consequently, bring me a bottle of Mattheus Müller."

When he had drunk the first glass of champagne, he sank again into a brooding from which he could not be enticed by any of the skirts which either approached from behind to press up against him, or even pinched his leg and whispered all sorts of risqué temptations to him.

He said to each the same thing, "Nothing happening, Eulalia!" and fended them off with a wave of his hand as if he were driving away persistent flies.

This silly society, these Silesians who thought that he with his four semesters should perhaps fawn upon them! Yes, and why had this thing with the music of his soul attacked him suddenly today amidst these future pillars of the state, and then immediately afterwards this dark-haired, wild, fiery girl had to storm in — Brindeisener felt a hand on his shoulder again, heard amidst his brooding someone speaking to him, waved them away with his hand, and murmured, without look- ing up, his accustomed, "Nothing happening, Eulalia."

To that an exuberant man's laugh answered. When Brindeisener hence spun around in shock, Vollberg was standing before him.

"I had to go past the Rabble here again on the way home", he said, and pulled up a chair, "for want of a beer, and because I suspected you would still be here, I decided to come in once more."

Vollberg was pushing his words out, and was embar- rassed because he noted of Brindeisener that he sensed he meant something other than what he said.

"*Summa summarum*, dear Mr Vollberg, do not trouble yourself any further. It was all very obliging of you. You are splendid. But I slaughtered the hens with one jerk. This Silesian thing doesn't work with me. Un- derstand me right — but I distinguish sharply between men and people. God, they are all individual turnips, without roots except, of course, those from Adam for which they can do nothing, and which they don't always make the best use of either."

Brindeisener now overwhelmed the mutinous Silesian with kindliness, invited him to drink wine with him, and poured out his witty thoughts as quickly, but at the same time he took on an ever more anxious, even sorrowful face, so that Vollberg thought now that he would fall stiff as a poker, drunk from his chair, and he would then have to "get him home".

Only, what frightened Vollberg did not happen. Peter Brindeisener only approached the state of the first sobriety in drinking which he called the "glassy time". Then he and his life became transparent to his understanding. Usually he stood up then and went home. In the face of this good fellow, this Vollberg here, who was attached to him in such a stirring, almost adoring way, he could not manage to leave today.

"Pardon, Brindeisener", Vollberg said, "what was it actually that you lost the thread of so with that girl before, that we all thought you were suddenly drunk?"

Brindeisener pondered for a moment to himself and then answered, "Imagine, Vollberg, you go as a young mule in the night alone into the forest with a girl who must flee her home town because her father has hung himself in the forest that very afternoon and she can't bear the shame. Imagine, the beautiful girl, what she gives, I mean *in puncto* sensual beauty. This girl, almost mad with shame and injured pride, close to dying, on the arm of the mule suddenly falls into a seeming fury of love, shakes all over, sobs, throws her arms around his neck, and sucks him firmly to herself with kisses which burn like molten lead ... Look, Vollberg, that is the air at home with *us*! ... Certainly, it overflows the boy surely too. But in him, in his innermost being, the mysterious instrument plays a sound like that only the heavenly spirits know for certain. And as the mule touches just then with trembling fingers the naked body of the girl, it turns white in him, and the internal angel sings so loud that he pulls his hand back and lets the girl slide from his embrace. For, Vollberg, you may believe it or not, there truly are angels in the world. True angels ..."

Brindeisener fell silent, and sat for a long time in rapture.

Then he pulled himself together again and continued, "And now it heads here in Café Rabble towards midnight, a hundred miles from there, in Silesia, and the door opens, and the same girl, to a hair the same girl, steps before you. Is that not something to make you go rigid? The devil once more! And for that, to escape all that haunting, you move over the years further and further away from your home. So that everything does not constantly get all mixed up, day and night, heaven and hell. — But that was not Mathinka at all, it was the Saxon high official's daughter, who has run away from her parents, has registered as a prostitute, and now does not dare do it. Nota bene, if it is true."

Brindeisener had fallen entirely into a soliloquy, and now fell silent again into his brooding.

"Did you say Mathinka, Brindeisener?" Vollberg asked timidly.

"Yes, that is what the girl from my home village was called. Actually Martha Kathinka Meixner. Her father was the wildest fellow I have ever known on earth."

Brindeisener straightened up stiffly, and looked searchingly around the entire local.

"You know, Vollberg", he then said softly, but again as if he were sitting alone and speaking to the student as if to himself, "it may be silly, but what is *not* silly in life? You lift the dress of a willing girl, and withdraw your hand again, from shame, from pride, from pity, from fear of her love, what do I know. But hardly is this attack of chastity over than you are annoyed by the dereliction. Go home, my dear friend. I beg you, and don't be cross with me."

Vollberg stood up, unsettled, and murmured something about thanks, showing an interest, and being ready for any service. Brindeisener's face was very earnest, no trace of drunkenness in it except for a dark, feverish glow in his eyes. He shook his head with an indulgently ironic smile at Vollberg's words, offered him his hand in silence, and watched after the departing man thoughtfully.

At the same time, he murmured without moving his lips, "You are half asleep, half awake. But both so overheated that you dream and live in a fever and don't know whether you are living or dreaming."

In the upper room of the café, a mad racket suddenly occurred. Men laughed menacingly, women screeched, hands were clapped again and again, and calls of bravo could be heard. Two waiters came plunging down the stairs laughing, and ordered champagne urgently at the bar. "That is a mad party today", the barman said.

"Yes, God knows! But quick, quick!" one of the waiters answered.

Brindeisener turned his head slowly to the group, half listening to their words, half listening to the racket above. And if it indeed were Mathinka from Querhoven, he pondered, then I could fetch today what I once neglected to take. For nothing probably remains but to drink up the poison which fate has gifted us, so that the water can finally be pure again. "So up, toreador!" He paid, and, smiling mockingly at himself, climbed slowly up the broad stairs to the upper floor. The space was cut here by the stair landing into two unequal parts. Brindeisener turned to the smaller, lefthand room, for the racket was sounding from there. Through a short corridor three steps long, he approached the portiere which gaped apart by a hand width. In the usually cosy room, everything had fallen into disorder. The table had been pushed against the wall, and the chairs placed in front in two rows facing each other to create an open space, somewhat like a lengthy racetrack. At the narrow end by the door sat the sought-after girl, by her side a pretty, though already older prostitute. On the chairs to the left and right sat the gentlemen of this lecherous house, young playboys of the better classes, small town runaways, professional fornicators, wilted goat-faces in every pose of arousal — springing up, pinned back, thrown forward, huddled in heat. But the attention of all was directed at the dark-haired, beautiful girl who was obviously the focus of this madness. In what manner, Brindeisener could not immediately figure out. Had she been dancing, singing, miming, you could not tell. All the men were aroused by extreme astonishment. The girl's entire body rippled, a single deluge like the swirl of a seething brook. At the same time, her face smouldered in the most contradictory emotions: in desire and contempt, shame and wantonness, disgust and heat. The prostitutes coaxed her soothingly, but she shook her head energetically to everything. Obviously she did not want to dance or mime, or whatever she had just done, anymore. Then Brindeisener saw that a prostitute was gently lifting her dress higher up her right leg as if paying no heed, so that almost the entire lower leg could be seen with its divinely formed, elegant calf. When the men saw this, they broke out into whinnying bravos, and a quite young little fellow, an officer in civil or a student, immediately sprang up from his seat in a sort of bacchanalian whirl, gulped down a flute of champagne, and approached the middle of the empty space. He was blond, stocky, well-built, and very well dressed.

Brindeisener could still not comprehend what it was all meant to be about; for until now it looked almost as if the youth were challenging the girl to a contest. Arriving in the middle, he bowed before the beautiful girl, who again nodded and immediately assumed a defensive pose. Her eyes blazed in fierce wantonness. She blanched, pursed her lips, and her bosom began leaping yearningly. But she gathered her dress still higher, and placed the leg forward still more provocatively.

The youth had stood still until now, in lustful greed as though paralysed. Now, when still more allure was being unveiled before his eyes, he bowed where he stood, and lifted up with shaking hand a blue silk garter. Leading it to his lips, he approached the girl, who did not bat an eyelid and looked at him burningly.

So the thing was conducted that way! The garter had been slid from the girl's leg, and it was now about who could put it on her and take her with him. The young man had approached the girl in four or five steps. "Kneel!" everyone commanded in excitement. Reluctantly, he went down, and pushed himself towards the girl. He was already lifting the hand with the garter to put it on her. Then he unexpectedly received a foot in the chest so that he flew into the middle of the open space. At that a real clamour broke out, there was shouting, clapping, stomping, orders for more champagne, and toasts to the girl. The rebuffed youth smiled wanly, his lips set between his teeth, the entire fellow a wild, wanton oath. You could see that he was preparing for a second attempt, and could note in his movements that he was intent on everything. He quickly drank two glasses of wine in succession, and passed his fingers between his collar and neck to make air for his heavy breathing.

Brindeisener noted that the girl was now uneasy with concern, probably because she feared the refused fellow could use violence on a repeated attempt, and she riveted her eyes on the portiere as if pondering flight.

"Now go!" Brindeisener thought to himself, stepped into the room, and immediately fastened on the girl's helpless look with his eyes. He saw how she seemingly

recoiled at first on seeing him, and then willingly fell towards him. This inner embrace lasted a second. Then
Brindeisener asked with a motion of the head, and she
affirmed with her eyes. On a stand hung her silk-mix
coat, her hat, and her umbrella. Brindeisener grasped
everything, placed it over his arm, stepped into the
circle, lifted the garter up, and when he approached the
girl, she stretched her beautiful leg towards him.

The men flared up in a short jerk like a cheated mob.
Brindeisener, who towered over everyone by more than
a head, straightened up still more, looked around himself with his cool, wild eyes, and said loudly to the girl in
the moment of silence which occurred, "I have been
somewhat tardy, forgive me!" Then he helped her with
putting on her things, and led her away after a few moments through the gaping swarm.

At the square-like expanse where many roads
crossed, the couple stopped in the glaring, sombre pale
green of the gas lanterns' light. Brindeisener looked
around at the café in which the racket had now broken
out into the lower room, and was immediately raging by
the door as if it were about throwing unruly drinkers out
violently in the air. Suddenly the door flew open as if off
its hinges, and like hungry dogs, a rabble of young men
plunged out, "Where is that ass?" — "I'll slap him like a
fly!" — "I'll tan his hide properly!" they shouted in confusion.

"For God's sake!" the girl whispered, pulled Brindeisener into a perfectly dark, narrow lane, and tried to
start running quickly. The estranged farmstead's student was pulled with her for a few steps against his will,
but brought the frightened girl to a stop with a jerk in
the middle of the lane, and said with a smile, "Run just
one street at this pace, and it could happen that we are
chased as burglars and put inside. So, girl, put the
cream onto your little feet." Then he listened to the run-

ning and shouting of the pursuers in the neighbouring lanes. It tailed off in various directions, and soon nothing could be heard but the shapeless, quiet hum which hangs in the air over the houses of a sleeping city. Here and there an electric tram tinkled.

Brindeisener slowly stepped out, and sensed from the soft, steady step of the girl that she had not grown up in the city. She clung to him rapturously, and pressed his arm to her breast passionately again and again. "Terrible", she whispered suddenly.

"What?" Brindeisener asked, and stopped.

"Terrible, I mean", she said in hot indignation.

"Why?" he asked again calmly.

"Well simply, you should kiss me, kiss me. It is so indecent! I will run away from you on the spot."

Brindeisener took the wildly smouldering girl to himself, and they kissed each other in such an intoxicating way that the girl staggered when he finally let her go.

"Why don't you call me Peter?" he asked her softly now.

"Why?" she asked teasingly back, and laughed deliriously. "Truly, there you have the right name. But not anymore now, not now, and then I believe not later either. You silly Peter!" She pushed longingly up against him again. "And how shall I be called then, dear?" she asked in passionate tenderness.

"Mathinka", Brindeisener answered.

"No, ugh! I don't like that! It sounds too kitsch. No, no", she responded with the purest teenage disgust. "Call me Wally."

"Wally, the doubter", Brindeisener said mockingly. "Good, so Wally."

And as he led her further through a confusion of narrow, windy lanes leading to smelly butcheries, across squares and little plazas, then through already half unlit streets closer and closer to the Oder, she began in connection to the irony of his last words to narrate the circumstances which had led her to the cobbles here. She was really the daughter of a Saxon estate owner in the vicinity of Meißen, and had surrendered as a thirteen year old girl to her uncle, the brother of her own father, who had surprised and used her once in a secluded room on the sofa.

The eternally-the-same whore's story, Brindeisener thought to himself. Sometimes it is the brother, sometimes the cousin, sometimes the coachman, sometimes even their own father. And as always with such tales, a wanton aversion seized him, a lustful darkness.

The girl chattered away constantly, and the thoughts burrowed mechanically in him, "So I will shut my eyes again, and sate my soul with beautiful flesh."

Finally they came to the university square, walked past the Swordsman, and arrived under the passage to the university bridge.

The crescent of the moon hung like a white, falling shard of a plate in the autumnally clear night sky.

In Brindeisener, a sentimental desire for stimulus had formed from the disengaging swathes of intoxication, from the disappointment of having mistaken the person of the girl, and the constant displeasure with life. He stepped with the girl to the parapet of the bridge, leant over, and looked raptly at the softly gleaming current which escaped their sight far out in a curve under the black heaps of the overhanging treetops.

"Is it not", he asked more to himself, "as if the gleaming river came from out of those dark trees over there? And perhaps everything is absolutely dark, I mean even further above. Entirely above, you know. And man makes light merely artificially with church lamps, gas lanterns, and so on. And everyone steals softly past by themselves like the water down below. Tell me please, girl, have you never itched to end your 'life's happiness' in such a great puddle?"

"What are you meaning?" the girl asked in shock, and let go of his arm.

"Meaning, haha? — Well now, good, meaning!" he answered in mocking stubbornness. Then he began searching the mirrored surface again with his eyes, until he saw lying up by the bushes on the shore a slab, a long piece of wood which barely stirred on the soundless water, and a yellow point of light glittering from the tiny cottage of the boatman. At the sight of this pinhead-sized shimmering button in the broad night over the mouse-quiet, great water, the feeling of a boundless loneliness in the world overcame the student, climbing to a seeming horror when he now heard quite, quite softly from over there the singing of a high-pitched woman's voice, probably the boatman's wife lulling her baby to sleep.

And suddenly it seemed clear to Brindeisener that he was on the point of sinning with this girl against the only light of his life, against the blessed farm's little Lena, with this so-called "Wally" who looked so similar to the Querhovener Mathinka Meixner. This thought seized him so starkly that in a flickering the face of the girl from the blessed hill appeared from the water — pale, divinely transfigured, but bleeding from a wound to the forehead just as he had seen her as a boy in his father's garden on the most terrible day of his life, when she had fallen over a rock in the grass, and he had thought he was guilty of her death. All that raged for a moment in him as though he were being ridden by an incubus.

Then the girl prodded him impatiently, and asked, "Where do you live then? I'm cold, and I thought we were going, because with the light you would trouble yourself to no avail to see some fish."

Brindeisener straightened up, shaken to his depths, and answered, completely transformed, with mute trepidation, "Yes, forgive me. Come!" With that he turned around, and led her back into the confusion of lanes.

Wally resisted, and showered him with reproaches, whined, and scolded him.

Brindeisener did not say a word, but walked along incessantly with long strides.

Finally they came to Holteistraße, where Wally lived. At the front door, he shook the contents of his wallet so hastily into the distraught girl's hand that a portion of the coins fell onto the cobbles.

He did not bother about that, but set off silently and hurriedly towards home.

When he crossed the university bridge again, he stopped at the same place as before, and stared at the current which now ran past invisibly under him, for the moon's shard had vanished again already, and thick darkness reigned. And again his youth and childhood began chasing him — he heard the high-pitched scream fall through the night when little Lena Sintlinger was born; Sintlinger's wagon rattling down the hill and plunging into the darkness.

Then standing before him was the blessed farmer's wife, of whom he had long believed that she was at times a bird who could fly through the air. The angelic voice of Helene sang ballads through the colourful trees of autumn; she sat with the Schwerdtner woman on the sunny grass; and he felt again in himself the fear of that time that the drunken guitar woman could perhaps bewitch the beautiful child. It seemed to him as if he had been young only for that reason, to drift constantly about the blessed hill in search of miracles, the hill being a miracle to the entire district, but he had been fascinated with it forever because of this quiet, unearthly delicate, blind girl, because he himself had had to suffer so much under the brutality of his father and the dull gloom of his family. After brooding for a long time, he straightened up on the bridge's parapet, and said to himself that actually the entire stupid, wild bustle of his current life was nothing but a continuation of the suffering in the bitter shadow of his father's house, and that it was now time to make an attempt to arrive at the heights in which the blessed hill's little Lena lived. He smiled with aching happiness over himself, and continued on his way home, shaking his head, and surprised over the visions of his being.

Arriving in his room — he lived on Mathiasplatz — he laid himself half undressed on his bed, and immediately lapsed into confused dreams. And as he was driven by the changing images of sleep through all the heavens and hells of his life, he lay immediately in such a high blissfulness of mood like he had never felt before. Although he felt it coming from a depth within himself which he was not dreaming, it also came from soft, beautiful hands which felt his cheeks without stopping, and placed themselves tenderly on his forehead. He could not see the being to whom they belonged, only the joy over it was almost painfully strong, and filled him, even after awakening, like a supernatural light.

6

In this way, Peter Brindeisener and little Lena Sintlinger, without knowing anything of each other but the wild dreams of their own hearts, were led to each

other from the same region of their life through the twilight to a new day. The blessed hill's girl now lived alone
in the room overlooking the lime tree, and the massive
rustling of the ancient tree was always around her. Because the constantly changing world of her being now
no longer collided as often with the existence of other
people and their conceptions, which to little Lena herself assumed forms that seemed strange and frightful,
she was no longer so startled over everything new, but
experienced the changes anew avidly as if a fairy tale
was happening to her. Sometimes the powerful sound of
the lime tree fluttered quite distantly from her, sometimes the hum in the night stood over her dreamily
quiet as if it were someone leaning over her and talking
to her purringly. The spaces of the house and yard, usually only regions within herself, slid out of her and
placed themselves in the reality around her. Everything
sounded different, right up to the call of the rooster and
the creaking of the wagon. Everything which had usually been so inseparable to her own being, like the
dreaming of your soul which your own will can one way
or another reshape and weave together, assumed sharp
contours and fixed shapes which formed around her in
an immovably definite, though alien way. In this way,
the world became narrower around her, for the world of
the blind has no horizon. But now it placed itself like a
girdle around everything, she felt like everything was
caught more orderly, more collectedly, even according
to a goal which she did not comprehend, like a
dammed-up river, and waves of heat chased through
her, preparations for a leap. — Once, when it was again
seizing her like that, it happened that her mother
opened the kitchen door below, and listened up above
herself, for it had seemed to her just then as if her Andreas had been walking across the hall upstairs with fast
impassioned steps. And yet she knew precisely that

Sintlinger had gone into the forest with the wagon team. Only, that abrupt walk across the hall upstairs had entirely the gait of her husband, and indeed from the time when he still roamed all over the place. "What is it then?" she pondered to herself when the steps did not fade away. "Is the Sintlinger farmstead really haunted? The step cannot be stolen away from a man, and carry out a walk alone wherever it pleases." And when she had overcome this short eruption of fright, she ran resolutely up the stairs to see what sort of relationship it had with the meditative stride of her Andreas.

But she saw no one there but Helene. The girl was cradling her reclined head on her clasped hands, and running passionately up and down the hall with lunging strides, as if she were climbing up over the clouds. "Little Lena", Johanna called to her, taken aback over the child's behaviour, and at the same time smiling at it, and when the blessed hill's girl not only did not hear, but even began to hum along to her impassioned walk, and to rock her head, the farmwife repeated her call a little crankily. "Little Lena, dear, little Lena", she said, "now listen. You will frighten someone with your wild running about alone." But Helene, who was just about to chase down the hallway to the loft stairs, threw her head excitedly and abruptly over her shoulder, and answered gruffly, almost cheekily, "Go, leave me! — What are you asking me? — I want to be alone." But hardly had her words flown from her mouth like a cracking whip than she turned around and plunged down the hall, down the half flight onto her mother's breast, and apologised amidst tears for the sharpness.

"But girl", Johanna said reprovingly, and brushed her hair from her hot forehead, "what were you thinking then to be running like that? You could make yourself unhappy!"

Then little Lena embraced her mother's neck again passionately, and said, "Yes, mother, happy or unhappy! — it is the same! — I love you, mother ... I love you! ... oh, *how* I love you!!"

With that she found no end with caresses and kisses.

These occasional leaps into exaltation were felt by Helene to be like a break from the quiet mining of her inner being, which was leading her through ever new experiences, each more wondrous, more unusual than the previous. At times, little Lena perceived the shape of things anew, quite different contours which wavered like an ardent fantasy of her own, and also as if they were moved back and forth by a breeze, a breeze which nevertheless could not be sensed, neither heard with the ears, nor seen with the fingers, not even with the eyes. Despite this, Helene grasped at the things, and even at the shapes which were familiar to her through her life up to then and which stood firmly behind the wavering of the new contours, dull and powerless like a useless remnant. So it came that she unexpectedly bumped into edges, wounded herself on sharp points, and was then as frightened to her soul as a sighted person who unexpectedly falls over a step on a level, firm path. Each time she stood before this new experience in rigid fright. For she recalled from one of old Theresa's stories that there had once been a man who had been content with nothing, not even with anything at all, and as punishment for him, everything he grasped at was immediately transformed. It was happening just like that for her too, but she could not think of anything by which she had misdemeaned, and was also incapable of imagining who would play such a prank so that she constantly saw everything doubled, as dream and reality, as day and night. She lived right to the movements of the finest capillaries of her nature in a constant state of confusion. All the changes were connected up with her dance in the meadow, and the sensation and puzzling experience of the man's head, the only certainty in her which, vanishing, renewed itself again and again. But just for that reason, the blessed hill's girl shied from asking someone for advice about what it actually meant. For then she would have had to tell them also that she was sometimes torn from her sleep in the middle of the night by a violent embrace, with such a wild clutching that she felt the grasp of the hands still painfully on her arms, sensed it for such a long time until she had often kissed the place ardently and for a long time. Such a thing could not possibly be said. But to not be allowed to do something is at the same time the most dangerous urge to do it.

And really, not long after — the winter was abating, and the first warm March days were strolling with tepid breath over the undulating hills — when little Lena was leaning on the fence of the flower garden behind the yard, holding her face to the friendly breeze, and thinking about how strange it was, that thing people called wind. When you paid proper attention to it, it seemed no different than if people were running past all around you, a long, soft-soled, unending procession of whose steps only the rustling of the clothes could be heard. Nobody knows where this airy being comes from and to where it goes, and it is as if you only understand it when you place yourself opposite it; for then it happens that it sings a song into your ears without stopping, always the same and yet always eternally different. You listen in on all the world, and in the voice of the wind, all the voices of near and far awaken. The broad forest hums to itself, the bushes in the field margins purr, the solitary trees in the fields swish softly, and even houses whistle with their roof ridges and gutters. Thus the entire earth goes past us like an airy being, and happy that we are listening to what can never be understood, it brushes our hair with gentle hands from our foreheads, and cuddles up around us so that we feel more distinctly than ever squeezed in the air. The blessed hill's girl gave in to this daydreaming as she leant on the fence and listened to the sound of the March wind. She was carried quite far from herself, quite far out by her fine hearing, and in the end it seemed to her really as if the soft footsteps of many men were coming towards her. Then little Lena knew that it would not last much longer, and the walk of many would turn into the walk of a single one, and the unknown male being with whom she was enmeshed would again stand with her.

But before that could happen, her father came, who, returning from the fields, had already seen from a distance her unmoving, white face, and approached her in the garden. What made her so still, he asked, and she, in an inner whirl, paying no attention to her imposed silence, answered that it was not still at all, for far out there the steps of many men were constantly walking. What did that actually mean? — It was perhaps the walking and travelling of people who were working out in the forest on the last part of the new main road. — She asked whether someone somewhere was coming on the new road. Oh yes, the blessed farmer answered, and, because of the fervour in her voice, he looked sharply into little Lena's face. But it was all the same wherever you walk, you never get further than if you sat under the best tree in your fields, and paid attention to what it said with its leaves. For the new thing under the feet is nothing new to the soul.

When Sintlinger had said that, he noted that his girl's face suddenly took on a strange, remote trait. Then she turned around, and strode the little path down to the arbour. There she sat down on the bench, her hands in her lap. For she had wanted to ask her father whether it could be that for once someone from that distant world was coming here to the blessed farm. But since Sintlinger had said such an extravagant thing, she did not want to talk further, but sat there disappointed and sunken in an empty, but blissful numbness from which her father was unable to dispel her as much as he kept on talking. She lowered her head, and did not listen to him at all. Finally she stood up abruptly, and said cuttingly that she knew better. With that she walked away, and it did not stir her at all that her father remained behind, taken aback and wordless over the ever further progress of the change in his child.

In this same time of spring, when the first swarms of birds were skimming over the blessed farm, old Theresa sensed that she was coming to an end, and like the aged wild animal, when it can barely continue anymore, just crawls deeper into the forest from which it was born, thus the unstoppable desire entered the frail servant for the place of her childhood, for Querhoven. What else was there to keep her at the farmstead where she was no longer useful for anything, but just hindered with her clucking rummaging, or at a minimum got in the way. She had devoted her entire life to others. Now she wanted to at least die her own death. And because her being had never been accustomed to enclosing the necessary things with colourful silk cloths, but grasped everything to be done with a vigorous hand, she did not sit long in a half whirl in a corner with this last business, and did not cook it up with secret tears, but had in less than three days cut free from everything which kept her at the blessed farm. Certainly, when she stood before Sintlinger and his wife to say farewell, her tear ducts overflowed, because Johanna was the only person on whom a reflection still lay of the time in which she had also been young. But she did not wail here either, but let the silent drops tail off silently in her wrinkled face, and her hands kneaded her handkerchief shaking and convulsing while, aside from that, she spoke the brave, even amusing words about old hens whom you must let have time for brooding their last egg. "And now farewell, farmer and Johanna", she said in conclusion, and rose, "you have both risen well with the farm. There I have no worries. Do not take it wrong that I threw you all in my pot. Yes, and with little Lena, trust me, it will not merely get better again, no, it will once more turn out well far beyond all understanding. And just because of the girl, I am ensuring that I get quickly down the hill. For some people are taken away slowly, others are made ready for the coffin over dinner. And if little Lena should run into a dead person, now when she is stumbling over everything in the world, then she could, who knows, perhaps get the giddiness even worse. One day she will certainly have to learn well what death is. But I at least want the door closed so quietly behind me that she shall think I went straight out into the green meadows. Now I am starting to bleat, old nanny goat that I am. So once more, farewell and no harm meant. She is up above, is she, in the room looking onto the lime tree?"

Somewhat longwindedly, she climbed up to little Lena, who, her hands propped up, was sitting at the open window, and daydreaming.

"Hello, little Lena", old Therese said. The girl did not stir. "Hello, little Lena", the old woman repeated after a little while. Dreamily, she finally turned around, and her sightless, large eyes looked into the room for a long time.

"Oh, it's you, Therese", she finally said with a deep breath, detaching herself from her rapture. "I should probably have to come down again? Say I don't want to. No, no." With that she stood up, and began, her hands clasped stiffly behind her, wandering up and down the room excitedly, but with soft, long, almost inaudible steps. And as the blessed hill's girl floated restlessly back and forth, more a moth carried through the air than a person, the old woman said what she had to say, that she would not be there for a few weeks because she had to go over to Querhoven to her brother's daughter who had a heap of children and sometimes did not know where her head was. She had come there to say adieu and such like.

But little Lena did not stop striding, said nothing to any of it, and remained silent for a long time even after the old woman had stopped speaking.

Finally she stopped before the old woman, and asked her, "Tell me please, Therese, am I very wicked?"

"No, little Lena."

"But I don't want to be like father."

"Oh, little Lena, dear girl!"

"You should not say dear girl! For I don't like that anymore either."

Then she began striding again in a floating way, and lapsed again immediately into brooding dreaming. "I wouldn't like that. I wouldn't like that", she said thereby a few times happily and fervently to herself.

"What wouldn't you like, little Lena?" Therese asked. Then the girl stopped, and said passionately, "You know, in your place, I would not go to Querhoven, I would go further, much, much further! I would walk and walk constantly, I would walk without stopping."

And when the old woman laughed joyously over that, the blessed hill's girl became almost furious, and cried out, "Yes, that I can tell you! And I know for certain, if it lasts any longer, then I will scream at once, and run away."

"Yes, little Lena, where do you want to go then?"

"Where there are paths, I will go. Simple. Where there are people."

"Oh, little Lena, you will come to life anywhere, no need to go further. You shouldn't either."

"Right! You think I don't know. There is a city which is so large that it does not stop, and more people than trees in the forest. Everyone in a heap alongside each other. Yes, yes!"

At that, the blessed hill's girl went to the window again, took her head in her hands, and became sad.

Therese watched her for a long time compassionately. Then she stood up, placed her hand on her shoulder, and said lovingly, "Little Lena, will you listen to me?" The girl nodded her head in silence. "You know, I am an old woman. I know it too. It is the old story with the world's little door. It has merely to be opened from without. By the Lord himself. People must go through the door whether they want to stay amidst the living or whether they want to go out again. But everything which the person wishes in the depths of their heart comes from there. And if what you want is quite correct, then a beautiful day will arrive for you. Then rely on me, on old Therese. Now adieu, little Lena, and may it go well for you. Now I must, I must however see that I get over to Querhoven." The blessed hill's girl had calmed down under the old woman's words, as if sleeping. She did not stir either when the old woman hesitantly left the room and closed the door behind her.

But after a long time, she sprang up, spread her arms out jubilantly, and cried, "It will come about! It will come about!"

In this way, her mysterious expectation grew more and more. The red light from the centre of her maidenly being spread over all the regions of her life so that soon her entire world was aflame.

In this soulfully fervent, most decisive spring of her life, an event occurred paradoxically which brought the entire scent of the unearthly time of her childhood once more over little Lena and the blessed farm, and showed the entire district's image of her father once more in a deep, wonderful shimmer.

It is the stirring story of the scissor grinder Liebeneiner from the village of Old Lessig in the Essen coal region.

He lived there with his numerous family in a large block of flats which was like all the other smoky, dismal, giant boxes, and only distinguished by it standing somewhat to the side on a little hill. But thus Liebeneiner's children could at least play in a little yard, which was always better than the street, and in winter they slid day in, day out on pieces of board or frozen-over stones, sometimes even on a loaned-out, proper sled, down the short slope, and made a racket out of loud merriment like other children, sometimes certainly out of hunger too, for it became more and more difficult from year to year for Liebeneiner to fill them up. If he still liked to grind other people's knives and scissors sharp, for himself he found no cutting tool which would have been able to slash his hardship and poverty asunder. And at the same time, his wife was still childbearing and, in addition, unfortunately still such that she blossomed more and more with each child. But finally, his grinding stone could not turn any more than it was, and it was unable to bring about for him in all eternity so that with each reversal a piece of bread departed from him. The room became narrower with each year, and his wife was already working with two cradles. When the fifth child was born, there was no more talk from the scissor grinder of a christening spread. They named the little Liebeneiner Silvester, so as to thereby give the Lord a wink that it might be the last, because it was already getting too hard to manage. Father and mother, however, gave each other the promise to forgo their love until the scissor grinder Liebeneiner's door had been forgotten by the stork, and they immediately acted seriously about it in that the husband was already moving that evening with his few items for sleeping into the room under the roof. Thus the firmness of will actually stood more on Liebeneiner's side.

He noticed certainly after a short time that, with all his resolve behind him, it went on worse than before. But he held out bravely for an entire week in his voluntary night imprisonment, and when the yearning for his wife took too much from him, he began singing in the middle of the night, and so that the people in the house did not hear, he crawled with his head under the bed, and kept singing to himself. That certainly helped for a day or two. But then it got worse rather than better. The songs beat in his blood, and finally one night, the boards of his shelter even began to glow fierily. For that reason, he resolutely set up his travelling workshop the next day, and went away with a rush. He travelled without stopping, as if there were someone behind him who wanted to arrest him, and did not rest before he had arrived at a distant village where nobody had heard tell of Old Lessig. There he poured water into the grinding box, and began purring away. But when evening arrived, his little grinding wagon was unexpectedly coupled to his heart. He turned the draw bar around, and began pushing the vehicle homewards in a laughing dream. But in the middle of the fields, his guardian angel stirred, and tore asunder the rosy veil which was sinking thicker and thicker over his eyes, so that he recalled his promise, and saw his beloved wife who would then have to walk about again for nine months heavy and despairing. That is why he let the wagon stand on the divinely lonesome road, sat at his stone, and began counting his week's proceeds. With that he realised now certainly quite quickly the foolishness which he had been on the point of committing. He might count back and forth, it remained as it had always been: he must split every pfennig seven ways, and if a new mouth arrived, then it hardly sufficed to stuff each little head with air. Thus he stood up, turned his workshop again, and travelled out even further into the countryside.

Thus it came that he often travelled around for six weeks, and when he arrived home, his beard had grown as far as the last button on his vest, and his children did not recognise him as their father until he took the bread rolls from his little money box, and stuffed one in each of their mouths. But his blossoming wife, for whom he had brought the best and largest piece of white bread, first flung her arms lustily around his neck, sobbed a little bit that he had been away so long, and cursed their poverty which did not allow her to have her husband there where he belonged, next to her. Only then did she reach for the gift, and consume it slowly.

But once, in departing, she pressed herself to him as fervently as if she wanted to pass out of the world through her husband's body, and it had almost come over the scissor grinder that he should lead her aside and play on her an ardent little song. The air in the room was already beginning to flicker like a flaming stove. However, Liebeneiner composed himself, stepped to the door, made his hand into a fist, and travelled down with it in an energetic wrench against the panel so that the blood sprang from his knuckles. "So, that's it", he said relieved, and stepped back.

"What did you do then?" his wife asked him, standing next to him, and still making nothing but heaving breaths.

"I have extinguished the flame", he answered with a smile, went out quickly, seized the draw bar of his little wagon, and rattled at a run down the little hill. Had Liebeneiner known how it had gone with his wife, he would have acted differently this time. But he thus remained away still for a full eight weeks, and came so close to Holland that he could hear the wooden clogs of the Flemings clattering. His wife sat at home in the meantime, and every moment in which she was not hounded by the work, she spent at the window, and looked down the falling pathway to the street on which her husband had gone from her, and if a man appeared who approached the house, she was startled, and turned scarlet with joy, because she thought it was her Kon-stantin whom love had unexpectedly seized and driven homeward. This blanching and flushing of the young woman had not happened three or four times when it was felt here and there amongst the men of the house in which the Liebeneiners sat and waited that there a fire was burning on which something could be forged. And the landlord came, sat demurely in the room, talked of many things, and inquired in closing whether anything needed doing. The milkman poured one and a half in-stead of one litre into her jug. The young miners combed their hair still more boldly on their foreheads, laughed happily in her room, and where they could, grasped for her full arms.

Not long, and the entire world was turning before the young wife like a colourful, sputtering wheel. She walked about in a blissful whirl, and the fervent circling finally became so strong in her that one amongst the swarming vermin succeeded in relieving himself of the teasing honey with her.

Konstantin Liebeneiner travelled restlessly from vil-lage to village, from town to town, and his pouch swallowed such an abundance of nickel and silver pieces that it was close to bursting. Then he thought it was now the time finally to see how it stood at home in Old Lessig. And as he travelled home, he considered that if it took him this time and led him on over both the little mountains, he would not be able to stop anymore. This prospect made him so cheerful that he ran like a boy with his little grinding wagon, and as soon as he was in the open fields, he sang in competition with the birds.

When he then finally turned in Old Lessig from the street onto the path which led up the little hill to the house in which he lived, he encountered everything as he carried it in his memory, and saw his wife sitting at the window, her head leaning yearningly on the panes. Only, when she caught sight of him, she blanched, started as if stabbed, and it seemed to him right away as if she were throwing her arms up in the air and tying them together over her head. Thus he saw her falling back into the darkness of the room.

Liebeneiner held this shock and flaring up to be an expression of female delight which almost climbed to despair, moved his wagon hurriedly askew so that it would not rush down the hill by itself, quickly gathered up his little pouch of money and gifts, and hurried into the house with the happy thought that today an especially joyful business waited for him; for to make a mournful person happy is the most blessed of human affairs, the more so when it is your own wife. But as he stormed into the room with a laughing greeting, he saw his wife sitting in the darkness, on a chair, in the darkest corner, turned to the wall, her head tilted on her breast as if condemned to death, and she gave no sound, and did not stir.

Then the scissor grinder thought, aha, if my wife has got her back up while I was away, I will make it right for her so that she not only springs up in laughter, no, into pure jubilation.

So he threw the money and bread on the table, grasped her about her torso, wheeled her in the air, and as he shook her lustily through and through, he cried again and again, "Hello, Christy, wake up!" But soon he sensed that he was then holding in his hands a person, and not his wife, and not a person, but a stone, turned

white to the retina of his eyes and cold down to his toe-
nails, let her slide carefully down onto the chair, and,
for a long time, emitted no sound out of fear. When he
then pulled himself together and started talking, it became somewhat easier for him. But his wife remained as
he had found her — turned to the wall, crumpled,
soundless. Finally he was discouraged from his cheerful
rumbling and jesting glee, and felt that now the right,
lovingly affectionate talk was coming into his mouth.
But hardly had his first loving words taken wing than
his wife screamed out, threw herself on the floor before
his feet, and confided to him amidst sobs all that had
happened with her in his absence.

Liebeneiner stood for a long time as if hit by lightning, and did not stir. But when his knees began to
tremble, he made himself strong with superhuman
power, said quietly that he would return, left the fallen
woman lying there, the bread and the money on the
table, and set off with his little wagon as cautiously as if
he were merely stuck in a nightmare, and not within a
terrible world.

He travelled that same afternoon and the entire
night without looking up or around, without thinking,
almost without a heartbeat, and when, towards morning, he sank down by the edge of the ditch before a
village, he had just as much strength still to see the
world rush away with a whistle. Then he lapsed into a
sleep as if he were dying.

On awakening, he found himself in a bed, and a
crowd of people were standing around him, and watching him with startled and compassionate faces. So as to
bolster them and himself, he began laughing from the
depths of his lungs so that the people ran away in horror
apart from an old woman, who only endured it though
by keeping her ears covered and by looking away.
Liebeneiner was himself not entirely okay with his

laughter. He had the feeling that his face was frozen, and when he was finally able to stop, the tears were running over his cheeks and the old woman's.

But with that, the cramp had also broken, and he stood up, walked into the yard, and looked around for his little wagon. When he finally found it, it seemed to him, since he had had to leave it standing on the road before the village because the entire world had passed away from him like a whistle, ten years had passed, and not three days as the people assured him who stood nearby and shook their heads over the scissor grinder, who just a few hours before had lain in a screaming fever, and was now emphatic about going away, although he still dangled like the tether hanging on the wagon. But when he made a few remarks over his hardship, they believed entirely that the fate of his trade had come over him prematurely, drew back from him, and let him depart. For according to the people, all scissor grinders were contorted with as much certainty in old age as all chimney sweeps die as drunkards.

They saw poor Liebeneiner staggering down the road as if he would at each step stumble and fall, were deeply gripped, and sighed in relief when they had finally lost sight of him.

Then Liebeneiner was alone in the world again with himself, his hardship and his Lord, and did not know where to begin, whether he should throttle his heart with his left hand or throw it away with his right, or whether there was no help for him but to let it be, and let his life turn to sludge like washing water over gravel heaps, and putrefy in the mildewy puddle of a roadside ditch.

Anyone he might ask from afar for advice chewed their tongue on their hollow tooth, shrugged their shoulders, and skipped self-consciously around the first corner, and what they left behind as an answer was, looked at carefully, worth as much as an otter's egg, without shell, without white, and without yolk, and the living thing within it smelling like poison. Thus Liebeneiner ground from village to village, and paid no attention to where he got to in the world.

And when he arrived in Hiesfeld, four or five hours distance from Hemsterhus, many days' journey from home, the scissor grinder was in a state that he no longer asked anyone on earth for advice, but wanted to be content if he met somewhere a heart which still chimed exactly as it had once been hung by the Lord at birth, or if he looked into two eyes which had never been encumbered by a terrible shadow. For he had the indescribable feeling that during his weeks of roaming, everything had come right in himself by itself. He trusted only the pure hand, the fine feeling, and the bold thought to raise this finished newness from the deepest concealment of his soul uninjured into his life.

With such thoughts, he sat on the first evening in the Hiesfeld tavern, and consumed his sparse meal at the hindmost table. It was already shimmering deeply in the twilight, and except for him, only a little old woman was there, looking more like a ball in the darkness, she was so fat. She clattered carefully like him with her eating utensils, as is the way of people humbled by misfortune, did not talk, and he hardly heard her breathe. Then Liebeneiner thought, aha, it is probably also someone for whom life has buried everything. And because he soon afterwards saw a guitar which belonged to her, he was strengthened in this view, for those who sing for money and in front of people cry all the time as soon as they are alone. And when after a few moments the land-lady came, sat down by the little woman, and began talking intimately with her, the scissor grinder pricked up his ears to figure out what secret losses the guitar woman actually suffered from. The fat little woman was

none other than the Schwerdtner woman; but Liebeneiner did not know her yet.

Thus, it did not last long, and the old street singer
talked of the great miracle which she had experienced
when she had been healed of her drunkenness and her
despair by the blessed hill's little Lena Sintlinger, and
had received in particular a voice, a supernatural voice
which still sounded as young today as ten years ago, and
which she would surely not lose, and even if all her hair
should fall out from old age. For what the Lord sends
through an angel never changes, and that little Lena
Sintlinger on the hill by Hemsterhus was no human, but
an angel, that was known for a hundred miles around.
And to solidify the miracle which had happened to her,
she told even more miracle-worthy tales of salvation by
the blessed hill's little Lena — the story of Gottlieb
Meixner, beautiful Ursula of the Sweeps, and the stories
of many others.

Liebeneiner did not hear the tales of the Schwerdtner
woman to the end, but stood up, and crept out of the
room in the dark to his little wagon under the shed roof.
For it had passed into his soul with a bubble of light that
if anyone could bring help into his life then it was only
little Lena Sintlinger about whom he had just heard the
unknown woman speaking. And before it had entirely
become morning, he was clattering with his workshop
out of the little yard of the tavern at Hiesfeld. The bell at
Hemsterhus was just tolling midday when the scissor
grinder turned onto the new road into the little valley
which drew between the hills on which the estranged
farmsteads lay, on the left the Brindeiseners' and on the
right the Sintlingers' farmstead. And he did not know
which of the two was the blessed farm. But he had not
sat for long undecided on his wagon's little money box
at the place on the road where the driveways went, one
leading here, the other there, when the doubt was

settled in him, for the farmstead to the left, dark and half decayed, more a gigantic heap of mould, with half blind, surly windows, skewed gates, and gnarled trees in the garden, could never ever be the place where a heart was capable of growing undisturbed into the Lord's peace.

He waited only until the little bell at the blessed farm would raise its midday voice, because he thought as a childlike man that if something elevated were to happen to him at the farmstead up above, then he must also be called up high. But the little bell hung and remained silent, and remained silent and hung, until he saw that it had no rope for tolling. Then he laughed at himself, how dumb he was to not know that someone needed no bell who was inwardly full of blessed voices. With that he rose in a good mood, and pulled his little wagon up the hill. When he was passing through the gate into the yard, the servants were just then coming out the door of the house from their meal, and the labourers and maids were soon around him, asking jestingly where he had the steam for his machine, and whether he scorched the knives like all grinders so that they would never get sharp again and he would always have something to do. Liebeneiner returned the jokes in a cheerful way, and meanwhile examined the faces of everyone, especially the maids, in case one of them was perhaps the being to which he had directed his hidden hopes. But although none had a dissolute face, furtive eyes, and an unfavourable manner, his heart did not go out to any of them either. Finally the blessed farmer's wife appeared, greeted him amiably, asked after his home town, how it came that he was roaming so far out into the world, and several other things. And Liebeneiner answered each question in his simple way, but could not prevent the words about his home town making him somewhat depressed, and a sad blanching crossing his face. About his wife, he said she suffered heavily, and nobody knew what was actually wrong with her. And if he should have the honour of putting in order all the cutting tools at the farmstead, then he would ask to be allowed to grind outside under the lime tree, because he would only stand in the way here, but outside in the shade of the tree everything would work much better.

Out of embarrassment, Liebeneiner overdid himself somewhat with his talking, and Johanna Sintlinger smiled kindly at his curious ways, especially over the florid kindness with which he assured her in closing that he would "sharpen the sewing scissors of the dear lady and her daughter as an extra for nothing, and do so especially well", let him pull his workshop under the lime tree, and sent out to him through a maid a solid pack of work and a pot of food so that he could fortify himself beforehand.

Not long and Liebeneiner's grinding stone was swishing and whistling so that the water flew and the sparks sprayed, but it darkened more and more around the scissor grinder because the crown of the lime tree let fall such soft light through its young, spring leaves, and because every look which he lifted up from his work gifted him a colourful, broad undulating landscape of sunlit earth; for before this kind farmwife who worked so freshly and steadily in the wealthy farmstead, he felt the misstep of his wife again more bitterly than before, and was frightened of probably never breaking free from poverty and hardship. And that increased constantly as the sun dropped lower and lower, because the girl for whom he had come so far to the farmstead did not let herself be seen. And so nothing remained for him but to travel away again in the evening with his old burden of anguish and hopelessness.

But if it is so, Liebeneiner thought wearily, then everything I bear now already lay with me in the cradle.

This thought seized him so that in panic he could not go on anymore. His mind stood still, and Liebeneiner straightened up with difficulty to look into the heavens to see if that was really his fate.

But when he lifted his eyes, he saw the blessed hill's little Lena standing before him. She had a blue dress on, was sitting on the little bench next to the cross, held a golden yellow flower in her hands, and was looking at him fixedly with sightless, large, heavenly eyes. This gaze, which did not come from earth and nor from a human, went right through the poor man.

Only, it almost made him stumble when little Lena now spoke to him.

"Hey, scissor grinder", she said with a soft voice, "why is it dark around you?"

Liebeneiner could not answer because of the surging in his chest.

Little Lena lowered her face, and stroked the flower with her hand, and waited.

"Miss ...", Liebeneiner finally broke forth in a stutter; but could not say anymore. Only a reverent, struggling breath passed from him to her.

But little Lena shook her head because of the tone in which he had spoken.

"No, let it be", she said. "I already know everything about you. Mother told me, and I also say, let it be. You will travel away, and everything will turn out okay again. I know it, everything nice seeks out the man. And even if it takes a long time."

The blessed hill's little Lena said that, for she was still trembling in the blessed expectation in which old Therese's words of comfort had lifted her.

Then she stood up, let the golden flower fall, raised her arm a little, and said in passionate fervour, "It will be fulfilled!"

The Blessed Farm

Liebeneiner, who did not know how things were with little Lena, believed no less than that the blessed hill's girl was conjuring his misfortune away, and he felt at once the wall crumbling in his chest. It hurt so much that he began turning his stone quicker and quicker, and when he looked at Helene, who had sat down on the little bench again, he was neither unhappy nor poor, had no hungry children at home, was not a betrayed husband, and his wife was stained by no more than a desolate dream which had overcome her uncalled, as if in sleep.

At this moment, the sunny newness, which he had not dared to dislodge from his soul's secrecy, stepped truly into his life. All the dark burdens of anguish and sorrow which he had borne for weeks had vanished, and he began singing the song which closed the door of youth forever and which at the same time blessed his life forever with all the past, but unfaded blessedness:

> Beautiful is life in happy times,
> Beautiful is youth, it comes no more.
> That's why I say once more:
> Beautiful are the years of youth,
> Beautiful is youth, it comes no more.

Liebeneiner had an unpractised voice, as for many years he had only gotten round to making his grinding stone sing. He sang as if he had a ball of cotton wool in his mouth, so that the notes blurred as if behind a forest, sounding from a far-off distance. But that itself, next to the beauty of the melody, moved the blessed hill's girl as if she were not listening to the scissor grinder singing, but as if all the splendour of her incredible anticipation was beginning to blossom resoundingly out from the wide world around her.

She was especially gripped by the words, "And from the vines pours noble wine."

That is why, when Liebeneiner had finished, Helene asked him to sing the song once more.

At the end, the scissor grinder had to tell her about his many criss-crossings through the world, and Liebeneiner sensed before the beautiful girl's eyes what an exceptionally glorious trade had been given to him. His villages became prospering cities, and the civic nests in which he had been placed were like paradises in the world. And when he finally parted, he was the happiest man on earth. He travelled into the twilight as though into a new morning. The clattering of his wagon had the appearance for him of a continuous song, and he marvelled without break at the miracle through which he had been reborn internally and externally.

Little Lena Sintlinger, however, sat for a while yet in the blessing which she had gifted the scissor grinder and received back as a richer gift, and in her dreams, Liebeneiner's visit turned into a fairy-tale-like embassy from the new world in which she was being driven by her yearning.

The blessed farmer encountered his little daughter in this happy abandonment under the lime tree, and for the first time again after such a long, confused, dark time, her soul blossomed towards him in the old, unreal magic. But she did not talk anymore of accursed skimming through the fields, of mysterious, profound enchantments which she had experienced from flowers and creeks, from the lonely sky and from the enigmas in people, but indulged in the wonders which waited for her when she was one day led down from the farm and out into the big wide world.

Sintlinger did not disturb her with his doubts, but let her enthuse in all the colourful conceits, and even promised her that he would journey away with her one day so far out into the world that you would be unable to think about returning to the farm. Helene laughed happily like a child over this prospect, and covered her father's face with fervent kisses. But when the blessed farmer had led her into the living room, he returned to the place at which he had spoken with Helene. And there he sat on the little bench alone for a few moments, sounded his own words to Helene more deeply from his soul, "Then we will both journey so far into the world that we would not even think of ever finding our way back here to this farm."

But now they sounded to him like an ill-fated threat.

Have we not gone far enough already, my dear little Lena, he pondered to himself. Then he felt himself pulled up from the bench, and began rushing down the hill after the scissor grinder in order to look at the man who had enticed his child a piece away from him again. He wandered about in the meadows between Quer-hoven and Hemsterhus, even crept around the tavern there, but met the man nowhere, and returned again to his farmstead in the darkness.

In his room, he lit a candle, and read for a long time from the journals of his life. But it did not work today in helping him find his way back into his elevated world. His deepest attainments appeared to him in part inconsequential, in part alien, in part incomprehensible. 'When it goes on like this, in my living body, my brain is being taken from my head and my soul from my chest', he thought.

Then he stood up, crept quietly to Helene's door, and listened for a long time to at least hear her breath.

But he heard nothing but the creaking and cracking of the great sleeping house, went back, and sank dazed into heavy sleep.

The wandering in the twilight which had driven the blessed farmer that evening across the meadows between Querhoven and Hemsterhus in search of the departing scissor grinder became the grounds for the rumour that the Herne rebel Franz Faber had been at the blessed farm.

It came about thus. In the time which is spoken of here, the merchant Stenzel from Dingden found himself on a ramble through the villages of the district in order to collect the money due from the small traders who obtained their small draperies from him. On the same evening, he left Querhoven after dark on the meadow path which runs almost dead straight to Hemsterhus. When he thus, calculating to himself, walked through the green, he heard on the not too distant secluded road a man running behind him, whom he might have thought was trying to catch him if he had been hurrying after him on the meadow path. But he paid no further attention to the hurried running of the stranger and also cared not in the least when he heard that he was being called after incessantly with broken voice.

"Hey, hello, hey!" it sounded, and then again it seemed to Stenzel as if the other cried, "Mr Faber, hey!", the name which at the time was again carried by all the papers, and when he had thought he heard it the first time, he then really heard it. And no less irritated over the disturbance than over being confused with a rebel, he said to himself, "Eh what! I don't see why Stenzel should stop when Faber was called for. Burst your collar for all I care!" And without turning around, he added something more to his long strides. But finally, because the calls of the man hurrying after the merchant were preventing him from working out his mental computations, he stopped, and turned to the stranger who was just then on the point of leaping over the ditch, and coming to him diagonally across the meadow. Only, hardly had the rushing man surveyed the merchant for a brief moment than he waved and called in apology, doffed his cap in greeting, spun around and went away, as it appeared to Stenzel, towards the estranged farmsteads. When the Dingden merchant arrived soon after at the Hemsterhus tavern, he told the tale of this incident, and described the man who had pursued him so stubbornly as being a small, sinewy man with a beardless face. And as he was still speaking, someone stepped in, and said he had just seen the blessed farmer walking past the tavern like someone who was looking for somebody. Everyone was immediately in agreement that the man who had shouted after the merchant could have been no one but the blessed farmer. They ran out, and looked around for him, but could not discover him anywhere anymore. Those, however, who hear the grass grow thought that if Sintlinger had expected the rebel Faber then he must have dropped in on him previously, and if that had happened then he will also certainly have come even if not on that particular evening when Stenzel from Dingden had been called to by the blessed farmer. That a rat's ball of adventurous conjectures was made speaks for itself, the more so as at that time somebody had also claimed to have seen the Nobody-incubus who had lain buried for years in the Hemsterhus churchyard. But after this colourful, turbid froth had settled, the conviction remained in the heads of everybody that the blessed farmer had been in cahoots all along with the rebel Faber, and all the wisdom of his head and of his life, he had only obtained from this sinister, toppler of everything, whose commands he had to obey unquestioningly, because he was smeared with the same devil's salve. As strangely as the mysterious power of the people manifested itself in getting on the track of that idea of hidden connections, as certainly was the rumour of Faber's visit to the blessed farmer at that time mistaken. For this man, whom his followers called the new saviour, but the masses called the rebel, sat at the time in a Berlin jail behind lock and key, because he had borne favourable witness for a poor woman whose old, ailing husband, in striding over the carriageway during the great Moabit riot, had been knocked down by the constables' sabres so that he died soon after. Faber, who had looked after the old man in the face of the ferocious security squad, had at the same time himself had his forehead wounded quite seriously, and now sat in custody because the court was attempting to stamp him as the main instigator of this vexatious uproar.

This near and distant seething foaming about the blessed farmer disturbed him little, at most it furrowed a darkening of ill-tempered, even disparaging indifference into his face when a new story was conveyed to him again which interweaved his life with this man whom he rejected inwardly as a pernicious power.

But when he received one day bound in a ribbon an issue of the newspaper the *Vossischen Zeitung*, which, marked in blue, contained the trial of the widow Hermann (as the woman was called whose rights Faber had stood up for), Sintlinger at first examined the address reluctantly because it came from a female hand, then scanned half distractedly the article, and finally broke out into mocking laughter when the reporter, in order to characterise Faber, mentioned a piece from one of his talks. Full of grim, almost furious merriment, he read the words, which were:

> In every moment that they live, with every word which men speak, they can provoke the revision and revolution of the state to which they belong, and indeed simply through them selflessly advancing their interests, proudly without vanity, modestly without lack of dignity, truthfully

without deviousness, kindly without calculation, regally like a child, and simply like a sovereign whose undeniable might precludes their parading it. When someone truly wants a revolution, that is, a transformation for the better, here he must start on it, and indeed within himself. For the conditions of the soul must lead the ordering of the state, not the other way around. Anyone who wants to achieve freedom only through the ordering of institutions, and thinks the inner freedom of the individual is thereby created, acts like somebody who builds a house for a man who is not yet born, who fries a fish that has not been caught, and who celebrates the victory of a battle not yet won.

When the blessed farmer had read that, such an agitation seized him that he tore the page up into little shreds, and threw them before the stove with the words, "Windbag, miserable windbag! Just hold your mouth and live."

Then he spat furiously on the little heap of paper, and when Johanna asked after the reasons for his unrestrained outburst, he answered with pale face and shaking words, "It is nothing, wife! I am spitting on the court of a fool. That is all."

With that he left the room, and slammed the door behind him.

7

In the meantime, the road, for whose construction Sintlinger had once, half seriously, half playfully dissimulating, given the last impetus, had been completely finished, and because the blessed farmer, despite all his aloofness, was deemed not only by the folk, but also by the authorities to be the actual father of this undertaking, it followed with necessity that an especially honourable role was intended for him with the ceremonial official opening. One day he received from the County Commissioner, a Baron von Zwinin, an extremely flattering letter in the man's own hand in which he was entreated, "not to deny the ceremonial opening of this economically so important highway his cooperation or at least his attendance". Then a short outline of the ceremony followed, which was meant to begin at the blessed farmer's property. There, "at the source of the fruitful idea", the County Commissioner wanted to make a speech, after which the ceremonial procession of carriages would move through the forest up to the heights opposite the pond. Here, at the boundary with the district of Hemsterhus, the farewell of the parish council and honoured guests would take place. "I personally would be eminently delighted", the letter concluded, "if I could approach you at this opportunity, good gentleman, and receive an insight into such an exemplary enterprise of yours."

The date of the planned ceremony had been set for fourteen days later, on the seventeenth of May, and Sintlinger was asked, if it appeared expedient to him, to suggest alterations.

If Sintlinger had still been sitting as firmly as before on his unearthly sun-horse by little Lena's side, the answer to the County Commissioner's letter would not have been difficult for him. He would have just pushed all the colourful commotion aside with a laugh. Though he surely laughed mockingly after reading the letter and tucking it away; after a few strides, he pulled the letter out again, scanned now this, then that place, sighed heavily, shook his head, and felt a helpless darkness crashing over him. By the afternoon, it had gone so far that his entire life seemed to him to be like a river which was breaking its banks, and was streaming wildly and away across country in all directions. "What concern of mine is your road and your flags?" he pondered upset. "If you have taken seriously one of my fads, then that is your affair. Wash yourselves with whining and fussing wherever it itches you. But leave me out of the game!"

But while he was flaring up so furiously, he felt in the darkness around his being a ghostly light, unbreakable threads drawing closer and closer, threads which he had woven himself under the force of fate with all his striving for the highest human freedom. He shook this off happily in the next moment as a ghostly deception of his excited imagination, but sensed soon that he was again stuck in these mysterious conspiracies.

In addition, he received on the afternoon of the same day with the second postman a letter from a Cologne Association for Land Improvement with the query as to whether he was inclined to welcome in the near future a gentleman possessing the instructions and authority to enter into discussions with him over the sale of his property. This new urging was from the point of view of city speculators not so astonishing, because latterly the plan for a branch line to the Rhine had been broached louder and more and more seriously; and because industry seizes every opportunity to relocate their enterprises to the countryside, because of the cheaper workforce, the farsighted business people calculated probably on the building of factories which, being on the railway, in the midst of the vast forest, and not too far from the Rhine with its small ports, would have to become foundations for a brilliant future.

'Certainly', the blessed farmer continued deliberating, 'and so it should really amount to that I once, when I was driven to the road construction, raised the hand myself which now encounters arrangements to push me complete with the farm from the hill.' And at the same time, his own words occurred to him, which he had spoken to little Lena a few days before, "Then we will both journey so far into the world that we would not even think of ever finding our way back here to this farm."

And when he indulged in these thoughts still further under the lime tree by the gate, he recalled suddenly with glaring clarity the deep impression which he had received many years before in his quiet time on a wood gathering trip into the forest at a weed infested, small spring. Although it had been perfectly still, the delicate blades of the grass overhanging the spring had constantly trembled purely under the cool breath of the sparse thread of water, as if they were not moved, but stirred from their own, inner emotion.

And just as distinctly, he remembered the thought which had shot through his brain like lightning at the time, "Perhaps it conducts itself with all beings, even people, like with this blade of grass — it moves us, and we believe we move ourselves."

'But if that is so', he continued deliberating despondently, 'if it indicates a different path for my life, down the hill into the world, as little Lena says, why should I stiffen against it?' Really, in the end nothing remained for him but to depart with his wife and child from the district with the people who stood in part friendly, in part hostile opposite him, overestimated him coarsely, or, what touched him the worst, translated his thoughts erroneously into life, imitating his being askew.

Yes, away! That would be best, for then little Lena would emerge from all the colourful whirling haze again back entirely into the existence of her heavenly sighted eyes, I would no longer run around as the fool of my wisdom or, as every farm dog has been barking lately, as a mere poor imitation of this Faber fellow.

"If it moves me, why should I not move myself?" he asked himself aloud.

At this moment, his wife stepped from the yard, heard the sound of his words, but avoided all appearance of concern, and sat down by her husband as if she was also weary of the day and wanted to let the unease die away into the May darkness. In truth, her alert disposition sensed an air around Andreas, whirling down from all sides, and driven off erratically again, like the time when it had once chased him through a drunken frenzy. What had passed in the past weeks from him to her was often in any case consuming her heart with helplessness, and the seeking of fingers strove after that which she would have liked burrowed in her hand.

"Was Brindeisener's dog here again?" she asked after some thought on the way you are best to begin, and moved somewhat closer on the bench to test whether her husband was ready for discussion. But Sintlinger did not stand up, instead making room for Johanna. At the same time, he answered her query, "You mean because I spoke so loud. No, Brindeisener's dog was not here, but others were, also hounds, if you want to say so. For there is enough barking here, and barking from the mouths of men is harder to endure than dogs yelping." And so, one word pulling itself after the other, the blessed farmer talked about his distress like in earlier years when he had sunk staggering to his wife. He probably hesitated over his blathering, but was led, in order to dull it as an injustice, from this bitter feeling to ever greater open-mindedness. He talked about everything which had oppressed him, not only during these days, but for a long time, how it was steaming from the farms and houses all around once more vapidly and fuzzily and stupidly towards the hill; he spoke about the irritating masquerade of the road opening, and that it seized him with horror to be misused as a poster which others fastened themselves to; he touched on the incomprehensible change in Helene, even for the first time on the interweaving with Faber, and came finally to the Cologne Land Association's offer. Yes, he was tempted by the lust for an almost complete evacuation so far as to speak more decisively of his migration from the land than he had previously thought to, and framed the enticing image of a house, transported so completely into God's lonely mountains that they would have no other neighbours than the forest and no other playmates than the stream, light, and wind.

Johanna probably did not dare anymore to draw his fervent head to herself with gentle hands, but though it seemed to her as if her husband were fleeing down the hill like in earlier times, and seeking protection in nocturnal wandering, today he was running away in spirit in all directions at once. And so the simple woman, in accordance with the maturity of her years, and in all her kindness and cleverness, placed against the rambling mood of the blessed farmer the terse clarity of healthy human understanding. About the behaviour of people, she said it must be accepted that the cattle in every stall are coloured differently, so why would you desire that people be all coated in the same colours. If he wanted to remain entirely out of the way of people, then he was also allowed to no longer be seen on his own farm, and if that was against his honour, then he would have to first lose his mind. Thus the County Commissioner should just arrive calmly at the farm. She was not frightened, and there was a long time yet in which Sintlinger could hide himself away. With little Lena, it was not turning for the worse, as he feared, but for the better. Up until now *Andreas* had had her, now *she*, the farmwife, wanted to school the girl, and give to her as a woman what a woman needs. The thoughts of migrating from the land, however, she called, without holding back, a cricket's fiddling and a midge's dance, and when Sintlinger furtively seized her hand, and squeezed it affectionately, she immediately became joyful, took his head, kissed him smiling on the mouth, and said exuberantly, "It must no longer be only about doing things correctly, if a man called the blessed farmer by people should not finally become a fool."

Arms entwined, they stood up, and went into the house.

The next morning, Sintlinger wrote letters to the County Commissioner and to the Cologne Association in the terms suggested by his wife, and sent them immediately with Wendel to the post office in Hemsterhus. And that was good, otherwise the execution would probably have remained undone again. For when Sintlinger had seen the labourer, who had other errands to deal with in the village, driving away on the wooden wagon, a feeling came over the farmer like those which seize someone who, unacquainted with swimming, is pushed by another into deep water. 'All events are uncertain, and all acts as well', he pondered in going back into the yard. 'That I know anyway. It only comes down to necessity.' Thus, standing thoughtfully in the middle of the yard, he heard his wife singing through the house as she cleaned. Now her voice was ringing on the lower floor, then it was trilling up the stairs to the upper floor, finally it seemed to him even as if she were rejoicing out into the world from a dormer window, and then

Helene's song was added to it so that the entire large Sintlinger house overflowed from happy singing. He turned away, half bad-temperedly, half displeased; dawdled out the gate again, stepped to the edge of the hill, looked thoughtlessly down at the new road, and murmured again and again quite emptily, quite absent-mindedly, "It only comes down to necessity. Absolutely ... absolutely ... it only comes down to necessity ... absolutely ... absolutely ..."

As a result, the blessed farmer was left in a daze, and wandered about for a few days, and he stepped to the hill's edge again and again, and looked and listened down to the new road as if the unconscious belief was moving him that the exact contemplation of the road could rescue him from this futile pendular swinging of his spirit. Thus he sat completely dulled in a brew of thoughts of annoyance, self-mockery, indifference, hope, and horror, so that he paid no attention at all to the effect which his frequent, incomprehensible stepping out before the gate exercised on the Brindeisener farmstead.

Over there, however, the news of the honoured role the blessed farmer was meant to play at the ceremonial opening must have been revealed through Sintlinger's servants or from the village. It had sent old Brindeisener's fury again to a seething boil, and he read into Sintlinger's noticeable stepping outside and his strange behaviour over several days only an act of showing off and of a mocking of his person, he who had actually only been assigned a place amongst the supporters at the public celebration. Although he had sacrificed more in fields, and had influenced the construction more decisively even than Sintlinger, he, the great estranged farmer, was meant to only trot along behind with the swarm of dust swallowers, while this sweetly poisonous, blessed little skulker had managed once again to feed his cows full on another's meadow. The old farmer stomped his massive limbs grimly up the rotten stairs, sat brooding at the window, and roared about thunder-ously. But when the blessed farmer stepped again and again to the edge of the hill, swallowed the new, his honoured road with his eyes delightedly, and blinked across mockingly, the violence in Brindeisener tore all its tethers. He stepped out before his gate, laughed mockingly, as if someone was banging on a hollow board, and when that made no difference, he called over a derisive greeting, swung his arms, more a threat than a wave, and finally let his fury snap by roaring with all his lungs across the boundary path that Sintlinger might like to sharpen his eyes, for on the path lay not only or-ders and honours, but "droppings and other rubbish". Yes, irritated still more by the gentle waving away and hurried stepping back of the blessed farmer, he would have given it everything, and collapsed from the piled up filth of hate, if he had not been rescued from further riotous behaviour by the intermediation of his Peter, the student. By blandishments and amicable urging, he fi-nally let himself be moved, although with reluctance, to return into the farmstead. Arriving in the living room, his fury turned against Peter, and he reproached him for always being secretly in cahoots with that blessed mob over there, and if he had an honourable bone in his body, then he would have long come to an end with his accursed studies, which had no other aim than lazing about in all the towns, losing all his money, and beggar-ing him, the farmer, his wife, and everyone at the Brindeisener farmstead. What was he wanting here then? Right now! Why must he remember his parents then during *these* holidays of all times? He had other-wise barely come home in two years, but had hung about with relatives and side kicks. If he had only ap-peared to hinder him from pressing his thumbs for once firmly into the eyes of this Sintlinger rabble, then he should simply run off again, preferably today rather than tomorrow. For he knew that the duty remained on his old shoulders alone to hold the honour of the Brindeiseners high and exalted.

And after the old man had cleaned out his liver so thoroughly, he propped his head in his hands by the window, and sank into a taciturn brooding for hours.

Peter had, erectly, without a word of response, without batting an eyelid, listened with pale face and rigid eyes to the in-part justifiable reproaches of his father. He also did not attempt to put himself in the right inwardly, waited a while in silence for whether the old man still had something to say, and then spoke quietly with arduous control and emotion, "Father." And because Brindeisener did not stir from his self-absorption, he repeated still more insistently the same call, "Father!" The farmer remained like a rock, and did not feel his son nestling against his feet. For that reason, Peter pressed what he had wanted to say aloud convulsively and fervently into his soul. "Let it be, father", he said quietly to himself, "it shall happen regardless." Then he stole inaudibly with long tip-toeing strides out of the room, went up to the edge of the forest, and looked down at the blessed farm until his eyes filled with water.

For what had overcome him like a ghost in the autumn of the previous year, on the university bridge in Breslau after that mad night, had remained alive in him, and had brought about a complete transformation in his life. He had moved to Münster and had enrolled with the law faculty in order to aim at the state exams, making use of the two semesters which he had studied, one in Greifswald, the other in Jena. The dreamlike hope, which he had always carried within as a whirling in blessedness, had turned into a clear light. He believed certainly and steadily that he possessed the right to the belief in rising up from all the falling and straying, from the dark destruction of his family to the heights in which Helene, the blessed Sintlinger girl, lived, because this wondrous being, through an incomprehensible fate, and despite all the hostility of their families, had often been moved so soulfully close to him, and every contact with her had released an almost painful happiness. So strongly and passionately had he been moved by it that he not only believed that he was now ripe for the highest epoch of his life, but he even grasped with the shaking hand of a blissful, almost drunken anticipation into a future which would perhaps even lead little Lena into his arms. Then, then everything was okay. Then his falling had turned into climbing, his straying was only holy searching, and every plunge into the abyss an abrupt leap in the air. For there was no misfortune, no misdeed in itself; what use man made of it, that alone decides good and evil, fortune and misfortune.

Wendel, the labourer who had taken both the letters to the post office for the blessed farmer on his errands trip into the village, had returned inordinately late in the day to the farm, only towards evening, and also with fully run-out horses. Taken to task by old Zenker, he thought he could come away easily over the responsibility through cheeky flippancy, and confused the insistent inquiry over the reasons for the delay with general arguing, and thus had it lead nowhere. Only, the condition of the righthand horse in particular turned worse in the night, its body running down quickly, now being in a dripping sweat, and then feeling ice-cold again. No infusion, no rubbing down helped, sometimes it steamed in fever, sometimes it trembled like an aspen leaf. The obdurate labourer was beset in fury and kindness with whether he had given it young clover, over thrashed it, or had left it standing sweating in its harness. Wendel sometimes said this, sometimes that, sprang from one story to another, steeled himself against the discovery of his inconsistencies with menacing anger, or laughed with mocking amusement when a new lie was struck from his hand. Then he sat on the boiler box, dangled his legs indifferently, and conceded the waiting on the sick animal entirely to old Zenker and his nephew Gottlieb. Towards morning the horse died. Then Wendel climbed down from his box, lolled about lazily, and, over-comfortably, said yawning, "Thank God, it is over with the nag", left the stall, and threw the door shut behind him. Gottlieb was so infuriated by this un-feeling rawness that he seized a cowpat, and threw it after the departing fellow. The latter did not turn around, and his mocking laughter tailed off across the yard. The fellow, who had been ridden well by the spirit of contradiction since his days as an oxen boy, had been casual and lazy for weeks, and seemed to have become completely mad. What had caused this complete re-versal in his being had eluded until now every insight, and so his misconduct was endured, in the firm belief in the proven good nature of Wendel, and according to the kindly laid-back spirit of the farm, as disparities which everyone, especially young men, are beset by now and then, and grow out of again by themselves after some time.

But now that old Zenker and his nephew felt that all the quarter given to the labourer had to be stopped, they went before the blessed farmer, and reported to him everything without a breath of extenuation or excuse, but rather indignantly, seething; and, paradoxically, the old farm worker was now even more fervent than his nephew, Gottlieb, so that the latter tore his head around a few times as if listening angrily. Sintlinger listened in silence, looked calmly at the floor, placed his hands clasped together sometimes one way, sometimes another way, and sighed heavily now and then. "Good", he said at the end, leaving the vagrants' room with both of them, it having become over the course of years something like the discussion room of the farmstead. At this moment, the youngest maid plunged into the room, a happy, pretty girl from Walsum who had only been serving at the farmstead since New Year, and, loved by all because of her cheerful friendliness, was not called by her actual name, Meiwald, but just called teasingly little Meier*.

As stated, she plunged into the room with pale face, heaving breast, and trembling lips. Now it was enough, now she could not endure it anymore, she cried as if at the end of her tether, but then looked at Zenker and Gottlieb, turned red all over, and asked to have both men leave, for what she had to say should be for the blessed farmer alone to know. Hardly had the two both left the room, than little Meier burst out into tears of despair, and told Sintlinger of her hardship, with the request that he not think badly of her. Wendel had been following her since her first day, at first with importunities, then with proposals which were not to be denied, became with every day crazier, even often coarse, and had been showering her with presents in the past weeks which he had been secretly smuggling into her things since she had rejected everything. With that she emptied her pockets, and heaped a quantity of jewellery, necklaces, rings, earrings, spangles, and the like onto the table, which, bought randomly, gaudy plunder and valuable pieces, exceeded by far the poor labourer's wealth.

And where he had got the money from, she knew as well, for she had seen on many evenings Olbrich from Hemsterhus sneaking about the farmstead, who was

---

* Meier = estate administrator.

known as a grafter and receiver of stolen goods from disloyal labourers.

Little Meier asked for immediate release from the farmstead, and bemoaned anew her pitiful fate to be embroiled without being able to help it into the life of such a bad fellow.

When the blessed farmer had heard her out, his face had turned pale, he smiled coldly, comforted the nervous girl, and then stepped to the window for a short deliberation. When he had returned, his lower lip sat between his teeth so that little Meier was frightened by the unaccustomed sight. He waved his hand reassuringly, pressed a ten mark note in her hand as a reward for her loyalty, raised her wages by half, and suggested that now she had moved to the farmstead properly and hopefully forever.

With that she was let go, and sprang out joyfully. The blessed farmer measured out the room with quick steps a few times, and fought a short fight. But he decided to cauterise the boil to bring the farm and himself at once thoroughly into a healthy air, since otherwise the roof on his house and his own head between his shoulders would get mouldy.

His entire being transformed into a tangle of steel wire strained to breaking point. When he thus went out, Wendel was just then walking across the yard, staggering from secretly obtained schnaps, gesticulating wildly with his arms, and making a racket. At the sight of the blessed farmer, the drunk was startled, and looked uncertainly with his chalk-white face full of despair and derision for a moment, then he suddenly shouted tormentedly, "What do you want from me then? You, blessed farmer! I'm having nothing more to do with you. Leave me in peace, that I advise you. I'm having nothing more to do with you!" Then he staggered onward, turning around from time to time, and shouting over his shoulder with garish laughter so that the entire staff ran out from the stalls and sheds, house and barn.

"Keep listening to the devil, Sintlinger", the possessed fellow cried out again; "you stole the oats from Satan, and I sold them", he roared again. "Use Gottlieb, the Christian swine! For all I care, he can lie sleeping in little Meier's shirt as much as he wants, haha! All mad, like the nag in the stall." Sintlinger stood silently, and grasped with two fingers carefully for the uppermost button of his jacket. But his hand trembled so that he always went past it. Suddenly it went all red around him. With three steps, he was by the raving fellow, who was just then trying to disappear into the boiler room, pulled him back, threw him like a ball into the air, lifted him up, carried him at a run through the gate, and threw him like a bundle of rubbish with a wide swing down the hill.

The drunk raged for a while yet on the boundary path. Then he began singing, and reeled away. The blessed farmer went up to his room without looking at anyone, and locked himself away.

In the evening, Johanna found her husband sitting on the bench under the lime tree. Quite alone, in the deep May twilight. He had propped his elbows on his knees, his hands clasped together tightly, and his head hung down low. He sat there quite so, demoralised, sunken like in the swirling years after a drunken defeat.

The good soul sat down next to him, placed her arm around his neck, and said softly, shaking him, "Dear, Andreas, dear!"

The blessed farmer did not stir.

Then she began lovingly and insistently to reproach him for this unseemly sadness and despondency, for he had treated this roguish Wendel as he deserved, and she spread out all the fellow's thefts and lapses in detail before him, and concluded with the reinforced assurance that he had done absolutely right not to cover up everything again with a gentle, kindly cloth. For a man is yet no fool.

Finally Sintlinger straightened up as if he were entirely alone, and looked for a long time with anguished face up into the crown of the lime tree, "It is roaring in the trees, Johanna", he then said softly. The farmwife, not understanding him straightaway, indicated to him that everything was quiet as a church, not a breath of wind stirring.

"And even if", he said dully, "it roars, oh, an ill wind roars in the trees."

Then he collapsed again, folded his hands, and fell silent.

As Johanna kept watch over her sorrowful husband, Helene began singing in the flower garden behind the barn, "Beautiful is life in happy times", the song which she had learnt from the scissor grinder Liebeneiner, and the entire yearning, joyous fervour of her maidenly heart lived in the girl's silvery light voice.

Then the blessed farmer started, and said with a struggle, "Go, Johanna, fetch me my child! Go quick, my little Lena!!"

The farmwife hurried away. But Helene was as if bewitched, did not understand her mother who called out disjointedly and from a distance, and she continued singing.

When Johanna returned to the little bench, it was empty, and Sintlinger called to her from halfway down the hill something comforting which she could not understand though. Then she saw him, striding lustily, vanish into the darkness.

Little Lena, however, let her soul climb with her songs into the heavens for a long time. She walked back and forth along the short path before the arbour, and sang sometimes loud, sometimes only with the colourful dreaming of her inner being.

When she had gotten carried away to the point of weariness and wanted to return to the house, she heard steps on the path which led past the beech stand to the flower garden, and a deep, young man's voice greeted her from the fence, "Good evening, Miss Helene! Why don't you continue singing?"

Then a blissful shiver blazed through the girl, as if she were having an epiphany. It took away her breath, and she remained standing on the path, her hand pressed to her heart, without sound.

The unfamiliar man whose voice had sounded far above her, as if from a tree, waited in vain for an answer. Then he slowly and hesitantly went away. The grass rustled softly as if blissful wingbeats were carrying him carefully away. Helene stepped to the fence, leant over, and held her face listening out into the world for a long, long time. Then she sent a farewell furtively again in the direction in which the steps had faded away. "Good night, my beloved, sleep well."

And without knowing what she was doing, overwhelmed by the unsteady fire of her heart, she kissed her hands, and stretched them out after him.

With the passionate movement, however, she came to herself, blushed with shame, and quickly returned startled into the house.

On the last day before the celebration of the road's opening, Johanna was walking towards evening once more in the Sintlinger house's grandest room, where already in the afternoon the table had been set for a light meal which would be offered to the County Commissioner. She wanted to see whether anything was still missing, and whether everything was in the precise order which the blessed farmer's wife kept the entire household.

There she met little Lena to her speechless astonishment in her new festive clothes sitting alone and motionless at the table, her white hands clasped on the white tablecloth, her golden blond, abundant hair curling over her delicate shoulders, dreaming to herself with enraptured distractedness. And when her mother reproached her for "this foolish fussing", the blind girl half awoke from her rapture, but did not reply with a single word, instead standing up blushing, inclined her head as if she were looking at the floor, and then said softly, "And if the County Commissioner lifts me into his carriage, and takes me with him into the world, then don't be sad, dear mother."

Then she walked soundlessly up to her room.

There she sat adorned by the open window, and when the crown of the lime tree began to cautiously rustle, she also again began singing yearningly and softly, and did not stop until her eyelids became heavy. And with each piece which she laid aside in getting undressed, she said raptly, "Tomorrow. — Tomorrow."

8

Thus the morning of the seventeenth of May came along and unfolded after a short misty hesitation into a spring day of the clearest beauty. The hills undulated like a colourful sea in the shimmering of their young fields around the blessed farm. It looked like an enormous merchant vessel, greyed with age, which, overloaded with goods, was furrowing its way broadly and steadily; and the many little bushes which stood here and there on the knoll, swarmed gently around it like laughing pleasure yachts under fluttering pennants. Like a thousand ringing fountains, the lark song climbed into the blue sky and drizzled back again into the grass, frittering away gently. Every leaf of the trees had a delighted voice, every change in the wind a resounding breath, every blade of grass a rapt whispering, and when the little bell of the Hemsterhus church tower tolled the morning mass, it all rang out with an unholy joyfulness, not like a call to piety, but like the whirling tinkling of a cheerful organist.

Not long after the fading away of the tolling, Sintlinger was already on his feet. In festive clothes, only instead of the long black coat, he was still in a comfortable house jacket, the blessed farmer walked through the entire house to see what preparations for the County Commissioner's visit had been made everywhere under the guidance of his wife. For he himself had kept almost completely aloof from the preparations for the festive day, at most he had hindered through a mocking demeanour or derisive compliments here and there the overstepping into too garish an exaggerated desire for adornment, a desire for which everyone on the farm rushed — labourers, maids, farmworkers, all the way down to oxen boys — as if this day of ceremony meant a new period for the blessed farm, the beginning of a cheerful, easier life for everyone at the farmstead.

Everything sparkled, everything was in an almost oppressive order and cleanliness. The mangers in the stalls had been scrubbed white, as if the feed troughs were not for cattle, but for men. The tails of the cows had been combed, their horns washed as if with soap. The horses stood with wiped hooves in the fresh straw, the work wagons stretched out their drawbars like a well-fitted company under the shed. The cobbles had been cleaned almost white with water, and even the giant manure heap lay there almost appetisingly, not a tuft of straw stood out over the neatly layered pile.

Sintlinger shook his head over so much unnecessary work, and when old Zenker stumbled just then stooped out of the horses' stalls towards the tack room, he called to him, laughing loudly, "You have all caught a bug off each other, Zenker! It is more a pastry shop than a farmyard."

The old man shook his head in silence, raised his stick, pointed over towards the house, and vanished grumbling into the tack room. When the farmer looked over to his house, his wife was leaning there out the window with a reddened, happy face, had probably been watching him for a while, smiled at him, and he inquired of her whether the rafters of the loft had been scrubbed too, and why in all the world colourful ribbons had not been placed on all the chimneys. Johanna said something funny about a jealous mocker, and withdrew in a teasing pique. The blessed farmer continued his round, full of cheerful mocking, full of gentle derision towards all this exaggerated pomposity, and made himself smile over his bitterness, whose seriousness, however, he felt boring too deeply for it all to be able to be called simply silly.

The yard gate had been entwined with wreaths in which colourful paper flags were stuck; on the driveway, a large green triumphal arch had been erected.

Then he became annoyed, and called out angrily, "That is pure fairground fussing, and you should take part in such a thing as a festive joke? — Dammit!"

He almost envied old Brindeisener over there, who had excluded himself from the fuss in aggrieved pride. His farmstead was as if nailed up all around, it had seemed empty of people for years, no team in the fields, not even a hen in the garden. Only the windowpanes looked blackly down in the slime-green light from the bitter faces of people who observed secretly full of sneering malice the cheerful life which spread itself on the road.

"If everything were not so dire at that rotten farmstead", Sintlinger pondered, "then you would almost like to wish to be permitted to at least be able to sit for today undisturbed up there."

When he turned around, he saw through the young foliage of the old lime tree Helene standing at the window in her pink tulle dress. She stood erect and motionless as if in a pink cloud. Her face bore an expression of unearthly, rapt solemnity, and the blue of her eyes seemed almost black to the blessed farmer. He looked at her apprehensively for a while, but then opened himself up, and tried to shake her with mocking laughter from this ridiculous dreaminess; but he emitted neither a loud laugh nor any mockery, instead hearing himself say to his shock quietly and timidly merely, "My dear little Lena." He was so seized by it against his will that he had to turn away and think of why Helene had not noticed him, and how it should come about that even she attached such importance "to this entire nonsense".

He stepped to the edge of the hill, pulled out his pocket watch, saw that it was not long before eight o'clock, the arrival time of the County Commissioner, looked along the road, listened towards the forest from where the carriage would have to come, and said, to conclude his interrupted contemplation, "My God, the entire district is having a ride on the merry-go-round today. Then it merely remains for the blessed farmer at least to carry his head coolly on his shoulders."

Thus he strode strongly back to the farmstead, ordered the harnessing of the carriage for nine o'clock, dressed, and went, annoyed by the tall hat, slowly and

hesitantly again to his waiting place before the farmstead.

Little Lena had meanwhile gone into the flower
garden, and was bending down here and there. Little
Meier stood behind her, and received the plucked
flowers. The hands of the blind girl were reaching in
such a tenderness for the flowers as if she were grasping
for floating notes and breaking them from the air, and
once she even spread her arms as if she wanted to embrace the plants, and press her face fervently into the
blooming shrub. Then the last line of the music occurred to Sintlinger that he had written in his notes, and
he thought that perhaps just then God was playing his
music in Helene. But this afterglow from his former
world was only quiet and quickly fading, and unable to
change anything anymore on the path on which every
fate was running, besides, the rolling of a carriage could
be heard just then in the still morning distance. Thus
Sintlinger lifted his gaze away from the beautiful image
of the two flower-picking girls, and turned it to the
forest where a landau with cover pulled back emerged
from the trees on the new road at a leisurely pace and
paused for a while. Sintlinger could distinguish exactly
three men, and the coachman up front who just then
raised the whip and pointed with it at the blessed farm.
Then the vehicle set off again in quick motion. The
farmer called over to the flower garden, "They are coming!", and then descended very slowly, setting his hat
right with a smile, down the hill.

He was just arriving at the opening of the driveway
when the carriage stopped before the green triumphal
arch. The tall gentleman sitting in the back, with the
pale face and short-cropped moustache which sat under
his large nose like a black splodge, was surely the
County Commissioner. He waved over at Sintlinger's
greeting, called out, "Pardon, one moment!", and then

spoke quickly in a somewhat jerking way to the two men seated opposite him, the County Engineer, Leipelt, with his gleaming red, beery face, and the County Secretary, Kölbing, an exceedingly tall, exceedingly blond, mildew soft man who accepted the Baron's information with constant submissive nodding of his head. Then the County Commissioner looked up at the sky to the weather, threw his light coat in the carriage, and, with the words, "Thus right on nine o'clock! Isn't it!", he stepped down to the road, and touched the rim of his hat as an acknowledgement in parting, while the carriage slowly drove away to Hemsterhus. "I surely have the honour of seeing Mr Sintlinger before me? County Commissioner von Zwinin", he said, approaching the blessed farmer.

The latter replied that in this instance the honour was just as much travelling in his, Sintlinger's, carriage, and as the County Commissioner overwhelmed the meaningfully spoken courtesy of the farmer with assurances of his high regard and an explanation that he had sent his carriage with the gentlemen to Hemsterhus, his brown, incisive eyes played over the taciturn, small man, astonished that this should be the famous blessed farmer after whom the entire district danced, even when he was not whistling. Thus they climbed slowly up the hill.

Von Zwinin also behaved towards Sintlinger, as they climbed the hill, in the way of a man whose inner fabric was close to expiring. Sometimes he plunged into obligingness, other times he stepped back painfully from himself, and measured the man striding next to him with a smile. He talked of the gentle swelling of the hills, of the castle-like position of the farmstead, inquired after old Brindeisener, stopped again, looked around, gnawed his lip, and flicked a stone out of the way with his foot. But each time, he gathered himself again from the jerking away of his disordered being into the situation by placing his hand patronisingly on the blessed farmer's shoulder and assuring him of what joy it provided him to finally make his acquaintance. Thus nothing was left for Sintlinger but the ingratiating defence of the praise, and a smiling silence which did not reveal the mocking cheerfulness it originated from. "Not worth the talk, Commissioner" or "When such a thing is initiated, it runs by itself", and in such and similar ways, the blessed farmer pushed away from himself the strong expressions of esteem with which the County Commissioner glinted at him again and ever again. Thus it came about that the two only progressed gradually, and needed almost a quarter of an hour for the small climb which was usually accomplished in one and a half minutes. When they had finally arrived above, Helene stepped out the gate with the bouquet of flowers which she had collected with the help of little Meier in the garden, and the maid squeezed herself to the side bashfully.

"This is my daughter Helene", Sintlinger said softly, moved by the charm which floated about his child-like little daughter. The gently gliding, confident step of the blind girl, the elevated excitement of her mood carried the delicate, beautiful girl over like an unreal phantom in the air, so that an astonished exclamation erupted from the County Commissioner. But then he stopped in silence, and enjoyed with pleasure the hesitant approach of this being which everywhere in the district stood in an aura partly of holiness, partly of angelic bewitchment. Her face was even paler than usual. On approaching, it became more and more beautiful. The bound eyes, which usually had the breath of the dull gleam of a pool which was about to freeze, now overflowed from of the depths of the irises with an apprehensive fire so that the heavenly blue around the edges of the pupils was darkened by shadows which had the gleam of old polished bronze. The breaking forth of these passionate flames elevated the irreality of her being somewhat, and the child-like delicateness of her body seemed like a precious flower blooming unsuspectingly in an abyss.

"Good morning, Commissioner! A beautiful welcome to our hill", she said in great excitement, almost stammering, and offered him the small bouquet. Her delicate bust surged as if it wanted to flutter from the captivity of the sheer tulle, and her delicate, white hand shook.

"A thousand good mornings, Miss Sintlinger! That is precious, really precious. You make me indescribably happy", the County Commissioner said with the accustomed exaggeration of his caste, but at the same time in a fervour which grew with each word and transformed him completely. The blood drained from his face, his eyes turned completely into greedy suction cups, his delight became brash. Thus, as if he were in one of the houses of Brussels where he did his studies, he devoured the charming girl's figure with his eyes.

"You are yourself the most glorious of blossoms", he said almost without control, and covered her hand as far as her wrist with kisses. Then he picked a flower from the bouquet he had received, and stuck it on her breast with the words, "Allow me, Miss Helene, that I put the flower in the only place worthy of it." With that he pressed, as if by accident, his fingers deep into her bust.

The blind girl emitted a shocked, soft cry at this shameless touching, staggered back, and would have collapsed if little Meier had not sprung across and caught her.

It all happened so quickly that Sintlinger did not comprehend the scene. With a leap, he was also with his child, who leant with chalk-white, painfully despairing face in the arms of the young maid, and he persuaded her soothingly to not let herself be overwhelmed by her excitement, and to rest herself in her room or in the garden for a bit. But when the Baron, torn from his paralysis, now wanted to participate in calming her down, the blind girl pulled herself up wildly, and rushed little Meier, who was meant to be leading her, into the house, almost pulling her with her.

The men remained behind, taken aback, and the County Commissioner stood, his darkened, twitching face lowered, and murmured something to his feet. The blessed farmer comforted him, and attributed the attack entirely to the delicateness and overexcitement of his daughter.

"Yes, yes, women!" the Baron said with a deep sigh, and smiled dully and bitterly. "Hopefully the poor girl has not come to any harm."

Then Sintlinger began leading the County Commissioner around his farm, and made himself more animated and interested, in order to shoo away the shadow of this incident, than he would have considered possible, and the Baron needed the strongest expressions of praise due to the wondrous order, exemplary discretion, and the entire glorious undertaking, and to thereby run off his concealed anguish. Inside the house, Johanna dispelled her concerns when she was told Helene was sitting quietly and cheerfully by the window and it was all okay with her. That is why a cheerful mood arose during the hurried meal which was admittedly dealt with by Baron von Zwinin almost alone, and indeed for all that somewhat violently.

When the three left the grand room, and headed to the exit down the darkened corridor and the winding steps, the County Commissioner assured them that this hour belonged amongst the most momentous events in his life. Then he tried to also kiss the hand of the blessed farmer's wife in farewell. The woman, however, withdrew it from him, and suggested with a smile that such coinage was, as he had seen, not appropriate in the countryside.

At that the Baron looked around once more at the yard, and cried out quite helplessly, "A wonder of an estate, really a wonder!"

Then he led the way out the gate.

Down below, the new road was teeming black with people. The band began playing a fanfare when he became visible at the edge. The Baron recovered his poise entirely. Magisterially erect, with momentous creases above his nose, and a benevolence about his lips, he climbed solemnly down the hill, as he thought to himself, "My blood will not throw me once more. Horrible, horrible! But a terrific girl, the blind one, the devil too!"

Then he began his speech immediately, standing under the triumphal arch, "Honoured guests! It gives me honour and joy to open today a new road, probably the most significant piece of our County's roads, to public traffic ..."

The brass instruments of the musicians flashed in the light. The farmers stood motionless. Here and there in the long row of carriages, a horse snorted. The County Commissioner's words rang out loudly in the people's silence and in the sun.

Nobody noticed that with the ringing out of the speaker's voice a white figure had abruptly started in a window of the Sintlinger house and stepped back so appalled it looked as if she were falling to the floor.

It was Helene, who had bravely concealed from her mother the state of her inner being, and had lamented with a weary smile the faintness in her limbs and her headache, and begged that nobody make a fuss for her sake. She wanted most of all to be left entirely alone. Then she had buried her face in her hands, propped her arms on the windowsill, and little Meier, who refused to move a step away from her, could do nothing to free her face and at least let her see her eyes. For the incident with the County Commissioner was incomprehensible to the maid, especially its consequences, and she could not explain Helene's sudden reversion from radiant cheerfulness to this deaf, dull desolation except as the result of this distinguished gentleman being in secret an evil man, and having blown on her poisonously with his breath. And when now, as the County Commissioner's voice rang out from the road, Helene, as if stabbed, started abruptly and plunged away fleeing from the window with the cry, "Ugh", the maid saw herself confirmed in her opinion, caught her lovingly in her arms, and asked her to say what the County Commissioner had done to her, and told her she would not repeat it to anyone, not to anyone, and if she wanted, not even to God Himself. But then Helene freed herself with a fervent jerk, and rebuked her in outrage for daring that. She shouted the last words in agony, and then gazed straight ahead for a long time helplessly. But because a loud cheering and blaring of music sounded up from the road just then, she went and closed the window, took her face in her hands again, and listened seemingly straining to the ever weakening noise of the carriages departing.

When every sound had faded away, she said softly to herself, "Now they are all gone." Then she sat there again almost collapsed, impassive, weary to the point of falling over. Inwardly, however, she was constantly distressed to the point of screaming, for from the hideous ring of the County Commissioner's voice, from his vicinity, she felt it all over her body like the running of a horrible beetle, smelt an unbearable stink around herself, and sensed the grasp of the baronial hand on her bosom like the gorging of a fervid mouth.

It was barely possible anymore to maintain her mask of calmness. With her last strength, and seemingly deathly pale,, she asked the maid to leave her alone now, for she had to lie down in bed. Little Meier was de-ceived, readied the bed, and left calmly because she noted how the blessed hill's girl had suddenly livened up soothingly.

Standing erect in the middle of the room, Helene listened for the maid's departure. When the kitchen door below had snapped shut, she bolted the door, and then she abandoned herself in a sort of fury of violated shame. She shook all over, cried, turned, spat, and be-cause above all the disgust and stink had not drained away from her, she also lost the last bit of control. Already almost out of her mind, she literally tore the clothes from her body, and, wheezing more and ever more quietly her "Ugh!", she approached the bed, and, when the "purification and deliverance" had finished, threw herself on it, grabbed the bedcover with her last strength to draw it over herself, but then lost conscious-ness completely, and sank, naked, thrown down, into the deepest faint.

While this was happening on the blessed farm, the long ceremonial procession of carriages turned up the new road through the forest, the carriage of the County Commissioner in front, and Sintlinger in his best coach behind him. Here and there the procession paused, cheerful chatter and laughter stirred in the vehicles, teasing calls went from carriage to carriage, the forest hummed in the sunny wind with its young foliage, and the thousand treetops dusted a hundred thousand bird-songs over the cheerful festive company.

At the forest mill, the procession finally stopped, and here, on the boundary with the Hemsterhus parish, Baron von Zwinin took leave of the festive participants with a formal speech, thanked everyone once more for their loyal assistance in helping this work of civilisation, and hailed with words of almost effusive commendation the spirit of the blessed farmer, "who does everything for others, wants nothing for himself, forges the crowns, and is happy if others would wear them". But today he had to presume to strictly tell the truth to this stubborn enemy of honour. The child must not be violently separated from its father, and "the beautiful road on which we stand is your work, Mr Sintlinger!" Thus he spoke directly to him in concluding. "That is why I believe I am acting of a mind with everyone when I invite you to give voice with me in the cry, 'Three cheers for Mr Andreas Sintlinger of Hemsterhus, hip, hip, hooray!'"

With that the official ceremony was over, and in the spacious garden of the forest mill, that beautiful excursion destination where the last wheel had rotten away long before, even decades ago, a joyful throng began to develop.

The blessed farmer, smoked out by everyone, probably also against his will, came somewhat out of his secret bitterness into a certain cheerfulness, even if all the joy possessed a mocking undertone, and every smile ran like a mask over his rigid face. From his eyes, an unyielding spark even broke now and again, and when the County Commissioner had left for a while to socialise with a party of civic dignitaries at another table, he also stood up inconspicuously, gave his lad the instruction to drive away in half an hour noiselessly without him, and then walked as if on a whim down the tended path which led in beautiful curves to the pond, the highlight of that area, a metallically dark, fathomless basin of water which lay motionless and menacingly deep in the forest, and of which the legends went that it never released again men whom it had once swallowed up, because its unexplored depths were connected to the other side.

Hardly had he made his way at a leisurely stride past the second curve than it occurred to him, as if tempted by the idea of the distant dark water, that his suppressed gloominess was like a strong robber. He heard distinctly the voice of the County Commissioner next to him, "A thousand good mornings, Miss Sintlinger!", and saw his child pale at the sound of these words, tremble and, her hands held over her face, collapse. Actually he had only walked off to the side so as, with a Polish holiday as they say, to get away from the empty comedy, but now that he was assaulted by this image, he took off his tall hat, tucked it away, and began running home more and more quickly diagonally through the forest without following any paths. From the forest mill, he heard, sometimes high, sometimes deep, once even with the Baron's voice, his name being called, "Sintlinger, Mr Sintlinger", finally even in mournful plaintiveness, "Blessed farmer!", followed by general laughter. He paid no attention, felt something like fear almost growing in him, and hurried away across the roots and sticks.

Exhausted and flustered, he finally arrived at the blessed farm, and was astonished over the cheerful carelessness which occupied everyone. A number of the servants had gone to the village for a dance with which the smallholders and servants were celebrating the day, as was their way, in the Hemsterhus tavern, the others were dawdling about idly and laughing. Nobody gave any look which indicated to Sintlinger that he should ask after how Helene was getting on. Yes, when he took his wife aside, and asked her palely not to deceive him with such presumed cheerfulness, but to reveal to him for God's sake everything as it stood with Helene, Johanna laughed vivaciously in his face at first, and then reproached him properly over this shadowy talk of his on the brightest of days. It was nothing other than that little Lena had been overburdening her heart to bursting for a long time with expectations and childish hopes, and was now sleeping off in her bed all the excitement.

She had bolted the door, and could not be awoken. This reassurance naturally increased the farmer's worrying instead of lessening it. He tapped his wife's forehead with his forefinger, smiling bitterly, sprang softly up the stairs, listened tensely into the locked room, knocked timidly a few times, called her name lovingly and insistently, but received no answer, and heard not a sound. For that reason, he was inclined to accept his wife's lack of concern, the more so as, with repeated listening, he heard a long comfortable sound like a deeply sleeping person tends to emit when stretching unhurriedly. But now that it was moving towards evening and Helene still had not appeared, his worrying seized him even more strongly. Everyone was occupied with milking and feeding out, the singing of the maids was ringing out from the open door to the stalls. He secretly fetched a ladder, climbed up to Helene's window under the shelter of the lime tree, and looked into her room. But just then the light of the sinking sun broke with such fury through the young foliage of the lime tree that he could not see anything distinctly for the garish red gleaming, flickering, and playing of the light. That is why he pushed the window entirely open, and was in the next moment inside the room.

The deep faint of the blessed hill's girl had in the meantime merged into sleep. Agitated by restive dreams, breathed over by the reflection of the twilight, her beautiful uncovered body lay, as if shimmering from a fervour of the senses, in such a passionate pose that Sintlinger's brain danced first from a hot jolt, and then from an icy blow. For his child was blossoming sorrowfully and blissfully like a fallen angel. With trembling hand, he grasped at the clothes strewn all over the floor, because he buoyantly thought it would be better that nobody, not even little Lena, saw them. But he did not move them, and straightened up again. Then he carefully covered her so that she did not awake, went to the window, knocked the ladder over, unbolted the door, and left the room noiselessly. During all that he had become so calm that he felt a coldness towards freezing in himself, and a strangling in his throat so that it seemed to him any moment that he would scream and choke at the same time.

Sintlinger's wife recoiled at the first sight of the face of her Andreas, and was really frightened that something terribly irreversible had happened to little Lena, because the blessed farmer simply looked as if he had come from a mortuary. But when he had composed himself enough that he could explain that little Lena was lying stark naked, as if she had been overpowered, and her clothes were torn to shreds and strewn across the entire room so that it could only be thought that a sudden madness of spirit had taken power over her ... no, he would not bring himself to say the other thing. That would be terrible.

But the farmwife did not collapse. After an abrupt cry through her full chest, something like a mocking play twitched about her lips. Thus she turned, and climbed hurriedly up the stairs to Helene.

After quarter of an hour, she entered again, and found her husband restlessly drumming his fingers on the window sill, his eyes directed into the tops of the trees in the garden. On turning around, the exclamatory question was written all across his face, "Well, isn't it terrible?!"

Certainly it was terrible, Johanna answered this expressive look, and indeed terrible because little Lena was her husband's daughter, and had once attempted, like had previously been the norm at the Sintlinger farmstead, to cut the roll of thread to pieces in order to find the start of the thread. She said all that with a happy mocking air, but then turned serious. The girl had promised herself fourteen colourful villages from the County Commissioner von Zwinin, and because he had not led her away in his carriage like a princess, the disappointed blood had passed through her, and she had torn her dress to shreds with all her vain hopes. That was surely the old Sintlinger way, but not a good humanly one, above all not feminine, and Johanna had washed her head properly so that she confessed everything shamefully, and if he wanted to convince himself, she was coming straight down, or he could also go up to her, for she would surely soon be finished with getting dressed.

Despite this clear conciliation, Sintlinger stood up with wide eyes, and placed his hand on his wife's shoulder protestingly as if in preparation for a moment-ous objection, but changed his mind, shook his head, and went, without having spoken a word, out through the hall, behind the yard, placed his hands behind his back, and looked raptly at the forest darkening in the evening.

He stood motionless until it had gone dark. Then he sighed as if from a raw abyss, and murmured, "So, so! My blessed little Lena is thus a woman." —

Laughing at himself in despairing mockery, he swayed back to the farmstead as if into a strange house.

9

When he entered the room, little Lena had just gone out, and his wife, made thoughtful by the curtness and jittery appearance of the dear girl, was sitting in a corner, and looking tensely at her clasped hands as if they really held in her lap the tangled roll of thread she had spoken of before, and which she was unable to disentangle either.

It seemed to the blessed farmer as if he were living not in his house, but residing in an inflated egg. Only, he forced himself not to beset his wife with the cry which was growing stronger and stronger in him, namely, 'Dear, Johanna, if our little Lena is a girl like any other, then in the end everything I have pondered so frequently was a delusion.' He walked back and forth in the room, churned within himself everything he wanted to say, and listened up now and then to hear whether a wavering, unreal sound was not to be caught through the ceiling from Helene's room, a sound which would blow all this gnawing out of his head like foolish froth.

The next morning as well, when he stepped into the yard still before daybreak, everything was as empty around him as the evening before, only today the entire world stood around him like an inflated egg. He looked wordlessly at how the labourers were loading three high box wagons with grain, grain whose delivery to the little county seat on the Rhine had been ordered by him. On the carrying over of the last sack, it occurred to him that he would rather take over himself the guiding of the vehicles and the delivery of the valuable freight, for old Zenker was becoming more and more mentally frail. So he inquired, since everything was ready for departure, jestingly of the old farmworker whether a little place was also free for him to travel along, and, in the forest when the slope had been overcome, he clambered up onto the wagon's seat by Zenker. Only, the creaking, groaning, and jolting of the wagon, and the grumpy talkativeness of the geriatric servant did not bring him what he had hoped for — the tearing up of the numb, all-shattering ring in which his thinking sat — no, it just shook him more firmly into it, it lowered him deeper and deeper.

That is why, when the business was dealt with towards evening, he had the farmworker drive home alone with the labourers, and although the paling of evening was already perceptible in the sky, he strode lustily out of the town into the forest in the happy prospect of putting his head in order again with his legs. Among the trees, the quick march certainly turned into a tardy wandering, and, being startled again and again from a disintegration of his mood and being surrounded by his intertwined inner state over whether it would soon start resolving itself, he only progressed slowly, and was surprised by nightfall in the middle of the forest.

And strangely, now it was getting darker and darker around him, this humble life of his inner being also stopped, and it seemed to him as if he were locked with his entire soul in a dark room from which neither windows nor doors led out. Soon the dance of his thoughts slackened entirely, his disposition lay like a misty boggy meadow around his closed, dark-as-night soul, and when he forcibly pulled himself together, and tried to place in all this inner darkness the sunny and radiant figure of his little Lena from her most blissful time, he did not succeed with this either. Her being surely appeared about him, but only like one who always walked invisibly next to him. But just as the blessed farmer sent his look out sharply in the direction in which little Lena hovered darkly in the darkness, it seemed as if even this last residue of her being would be swallowed by the dead darkness. And when that had happened a few times, he only heard in the stillness of the nocturnal forest a mysterious creeping following his steps, sometimes deep in the forest, sometimes quite close behind him, and not long and it was no longer even the soft, floating gait of Helene accompanying him, but an ailing, dreamily unsteady staggering, as if sounding out of the earth below the path, which spookily imitated every sound that his feet emitted in walking.

He had so often experienced that people, interwoven into his life, were around him, even before his eyes and ears, yes, even before his thinking could have perceived them, and it had long become a fearfully blissful custom for him, knowing himself to be in the company of the invisible, that protectively around him stood Helene's power which they had to obey.

But now that in the nocturnal forest her sunny image could not be forced into being with any power of his will, this accompaniment by the unthinkable oppressed him more and more strongly. The blessed farmer sat down on a stone, took his hat off, laughing mockingly, and passed his hand up over his forehead into his hair. When he drew his hand back, he felt that it was damp from sweat. That increased his self-mocking cheerfulness even more, and laughing at the top of his lungs into the forest, he dried his hand on his thigh, "Hahaha!"

He was sitting just then opposite one of the many grassed side paths which drove deep into the forest from the road like narrow tubes, and so he heard his own laughter, muffled and ghostily transformed, echoing in the distant darkness. Yes, as he watched, the echo quivered past as a visible shadow, and faded away between the trees.

Then Sintlinger thought that this night had purely intended for his own delusion to bewitch him, stood up, and said loudly, "I am not a woman that I am frightened of the shadow of a shadow." Then he followed the hallucination deep into the forest until he came upon a clearing. The darkness around him was starting to whirl with his agitation. In this veil-like confused circling of the night, he saw in the air before him the outline of a large tree with broad branches. He lowered his head instinctively, and tried to go towards it. Then he kicked unexpectedly with his foot against something soft, and when he bent down, there lay in the spring's short grass a grotesquely tall man, as if covered by the drooling light of the shadowy tree, and surrounded by the sour haze of clothes never shed. Sintlinger became nauseous. In disgust and revulsion, he hewed with his stick at the being's torso and chest, not knowing whether it was his imagination or reality. But the figure gave no sound, and did not stir. That flung Sintlinger completely into the whirl of his overwroughtness so that he, seized by horror, threw his stick away, and ran through the forest in the senseless fear which is peculiar only to dreaming.

The entire world stood as an irrational, distorted, transparent image before him, set ablaze by the constant stark grimaces, and extinguished as garish scraps of light in the darkness. When, on arriving home, he stood breathlessly before his wife's bed, he stammered in extreme distress, "Johanna, save me!" Then he quickly tore off his clothes, and plunged seething in such an intoxication of lust at his wife that Johanna thought she would have to perish.

On the evening of that day, when the dam wall before Sintlinger's lake was bursting apart right to its base so that the unfettered waves plunged over the land of his hard-won earth, perhaps at the time when night befell him in the forest, Helene stood up from her chair in her room, where she had sat almost the entire day alone and in a state of complete fluster, like perhaps how the wind rests over us as a shapeless air under the sky over the earth when the roaring is over which gave it its shape.

Desecrated in an indescribable way by the coarse spirit of the County Commissioner to the depths of her girl's nature, she was locked out from the colourful stream of all her hopes and expectations; and through the concealment of an endured violation which she did not understand, she never ever thought of being able to return to the state of old confidence in her parents anymore.

In the stillness which had entered the entire house, she recognised that night had fallen.

She stepped to the window, opened it, listened to the peaceful rustling in the foliage of the sleeping lime tree, and thought of how she had crept that time straying among the bushes behind the high butte, "I will never find my way back to my father and mother."

Even before she had properly finished thinking that, she heard her mother's steps coming up the stairs, and quickly threw herself dressed into bed, pulled her dress in everywhere, covered herself as far as her lips, closed her eyes, and pretended to be deeply asleep. Johanna entered noiselessly, remained a while standing by the bed, then touched her forehead in an airy kiss, and said straightening up, "Thank God! Poor, dear girl."

Then she went for a short while to think to the window which little Lena had just left open, closed it, looked around the entire room once more — the blind girl heard the turning of her body, and felt her gaze in the air — and then walked noiselessly away as she had come, but calmer than on her entrance.

Her steps faded away on the creaking stairs. The kitchen door snapped shut. The door to her bedroom also creaked softly shut. Then there was nothing but the soft whispering of the large, nocturnally still house around her.

The blessed hill's girl remained lying for a while quietly, but realised that there could be no thought of sleeping, and recalled that she had been stuck the entire day between the walls of her room. If she went and took pleasure in the open, high hovering of the heavens over herself, it would certainly do her good. With no more noise than if someone brushed their hand over a polished tabletop, little Lena stole down the stairs, through the hall, and soon stood in the middle of the yard.

No drawing was to be felt in the air, no prickling on her forehead. She felt only a divinely weighted play passing through the high heavens and stirring peacefully in the depths of her soul — the moon did not appear either; the stars alone chimed in the world.

'I want to walk up and down the path in the flower garden. Perhaps I will hear the beautiful man's voice again which delighted me so on the evening before the road ceremony', she thought, and set off towards the side gate at the back. She already sensed the force of the long wall of the stalls on her right hand acting against her, to the left it pressed lighter and disordered. There lay the shed. So it was alright, and she strode vigorously to the side gate. But, what was the meaning of that sud-denly? The steadiness of her steps left her. She did not rightly know anymore where the ground was — some-times her foot fell into emptiness, sometimes it kicked before setting down. What was it then? With a futile spring she pulled herself to the side and a block of wood fortuitously came to hand. Her heart was hammering, and in her temples, the blood was rushing heatedly. But she recognised that she had ended up in the shed. And as she stood, and waited for her chest to calm down and the roaring in her ears to completely stop, she turned her forehead sometimes here, sometimes there to get to know the locality precisely. Opposite her were all sorts of equipment, she felt it stretching freely into the dis-tance before her. But behind her was something strange which she had never encountered before. A joyful being interwoven with rapt struggle, and now she heard it breathing doubly like a glowing flickering and in confident draughts. A seething fervour struck towards her from it, and shrouded her completely.

"Who is sitting back there?" she wanted to ask, but was unable to emit a sound for excitement, instead experiencing something similar to that in the nights of the dream bewitched by the unknown man. She felt indescribably surrounded, and her chest clenched to the point of bursting. Made frantic by rising sobs and anguished bliss, she opened her mouth to scream out shrilly, come what may. Then she felt someone approaching her, and heard through a veil of gently stirring humming Gottlieb Meixner's voice talking to her. He was talking of the love which little Meier had thrown at him since her first day. The road ceremony had loosened all the bolts between them, and today, just now, as she stepped into the yard, they had come together completely with each other in a good love. Then, he opined, and would not be led astray, that her spirit had led her straight down for that reason. He had actually never ever intended to tie his life to the apron strings of a woman. But with little Meier it was just something different, and if little Lena would be so good as to lay her hand in theirs, then there would certainly be a holy blessing over them, and he would perhaps again take up his harmonica, and finally arrive at the songs which only she alone, little Lena, knew.

Then he called the ashamed little Meier over, and little Lena complied with him, and placed her hands in both of theirs.

But it was not her that actually did that, but a stranger, someone else who swished up and down during the incident, in flood or storm, to what place, whether in heaven or on earth, she did not know. She also found herself soon afterwards in an incomprehensible way alone in her room standing before her bed, threw herself on her face in it, gathered the pillows with her arms, and shook all over, since she thought the great Sintlinger house was in flames, and she breathed numbly with fearful astonishment to herself, "... the people! ... the love! ... heavens, oh heavens!!" ...

Her words became softer and softer.

Before sleep tore her from the whirl, she was greeted softly quite from high above by the beautiful man's voice, and pushed forwards, already transformed, to a sound in the dream which faded away into a blossoming wilderness like someone's step in young grass.

That night, the entire blessed farm thus stood in an invisible fervour of passion, and on the morning of the next day, all the rooms were filled by a dead, shattered air.

Little Lena lay still for a long time after awakening, and was sunk in a brooding to figure out what had actually happened with her, and how things actually were in this world. What she also pondered, was that she and life and all people remained accursed mysteries to her, which became more terrible, the deeper they tailed off into confusion. For she did not know that everything on earth is veiled in secrets, the most wondrous incomprehensibility, however, lay in the time in which she had just lived. When she could no longer think any further, she found the solution to her struggle — everything and everyone was alien to her. With little Meier and with Gottlieb, something had happened which drove the red of shame into her face at the idea of meeting them. Between her parents and her stood the unutterably loathsome thing that the County Commissioner had done to her, and which had at the same time killed all her hopes of going out into a world of happily delighted people. "What is it then, is it love?" she asked herself again and again. "And why did little Meier and Gottlieb embrace each other so that I myself became breathless to the point of screaming?"

Shaking her head, she stood up. Her hands were ice-cold. "Just what is love then?" she asked, stepped to the window, and leant her face against the panes. "Gottlieb said, he got it from the festivities", she continued pondering, "and I? Why did I have to tear my dress from my body? That was certainly not love. Gottlieb spoke to me about it — but if I should talk to someone about it, I would quite certainly have to run away screaming. — Oh my God, just what is it then!"

With this exclamation, she turned away from the window, buried her face in her hands, and walked helplessly about the room.

Her cold fingers dug into her cheeks. Just what should she do? Why were her hands so cold, so dry, and why was her face glowing?

She flung the door open, and shouted into the house, "Mother!", and once more loudly, almost desperately, "Mother!"

Her voice yelled back so shrilly from every corner that she was startled, and, with both arms propped stiffly in the doorway, listened for an answer. But nothing stirred in the entire house towards her, no door, no step, no sound.

She had surely been forgotten. Disappointed, she withdrew into her room, listened once more through the closed door with her face turned to the floor, then threw her loose, forward hanging hair with an abrupt movement of her head back over her neck, and walked about the room again. A strange whistling in the air immediately surrounded her, like the swishing of thin, whipping hazel switches. "Good ... good ... good ...", she said in a vengeful indignation which she did not understand; "... good, then I will go ...", she repeated, opened the wardrobe, pressed her face now in this, now in that dress, and finally chose a light blue, airy dress which she liked to wear most of all her dresses. She had dressed as if in flight.

Without the least secrecy, she left the room. It will show whether a single person in the house likes me still, she thought, and intentionally trod loudly.

Her mother, who had just come in from the dairy, and was working away about the stove in the kitchen, heard loud, heavy steps coming down the stairs, and though it was the little maid, but decided not to go out and reprimand her, because she just wanted after the unexpectedly wild night to work fervently by herself so that she did not feel the feeble and sore distractedness in herself.

Thus little Lena came down the stairs and through the hall, without her mother even having seen her, nevertheless all the world must have known, the unhinged girl thought, that nothing more remained for her than to leave the farm. At the front door's threshold, her forlornness overcame her like such a shame and despair that she shot rapidly across the yard. She felt it twitching about her, plunged through the side gate at the back, and heard little Meier's voice call her name. She still misses me, Helene thought, then sensed that she had the path to the beech stand under her feet, and ran straight for a long time until all the sounds of her father's house had fallen away behind her. Then she changed direction, and walked in a broad field margin up a gentle depression towards the new road.

But, the quiet fanning of the young sowing at her feet, the dreamily weak hum of the forest above her was still around her. Now and then, the humming of a besotted fly shot past, and in the air, pure as the burning of a tolling sea, the song of thousands of larks billowed, blaring as if to burst the vaults of heaven with melodious sound.

Who knows, it could have been that little Lena would have been borne down in the end by the peaceful jubilation of this May morning again into the blissfulness of her unearthly soul; but as it is said, chance decided that the heart of a lark in the blue sky above her was torn in the immensity of its happiness from its own song. The bird plunged through the air, and fell straight at the feet of the fleeing girl. Now the blessed farmer's command that little Lena be guarded from any knowledge of death had slowly fallen into oblivion. But she used the word dying without knowing what it actually was, because we essentially only become acquainted with death through our eyes. When little Lena Sintlinger now bent down to the bird, felt the last twitches of life in it, held it in her hands, breathed on it, listened for a heartbeat, carried it in her hand for a long while without slowing her walk, and finally opened her fingers to return it to freedom. But as often as she gave it a little swing into the air, it always fell like a stone back into her hand. Then she finally threw it away from herself in horror and doubled her haste, because she thought death was also behind her, and if she were fetched, she would also have to die. With the aid of her hands, she clambered up over the embankment of the new road, and flew along the firm path.

Nobody met her, no vehicle came towards her or overtook her.

In her opinion, she had been walking for an hour and more already. She was certainly deep in the forest, and must already be close to the Rhine.

That is why she stopped, to get a little air, and turned her face upwards at the same time — for it occurred to her that people said that a mysterious glimmer in the air accompanies the great current, and whoever feels it achieves an immaculate blessing for what they just then intend to do. And so she turned her face to the sky to, if possible, be privy to this heavenly auspice.

Yes, she was lifting herself with the entire passion of her frightened, yearning life into the infinitude, but could not, despite all her straining, notice any of the sunlike enchantment which moved up above. Instead she had the feeling as if shackles were falling from the depths of her being. In her inner being it seemed as if a door were opening, and a freed deluge poured from her like she had never felt in any moment of happiness. And now the glimmer she had longed for also approached, but not from above. It came towards her so that even its blissful striding could be heard. In the greatest intoxication, she spread her arms out, and thus, swaying with delight, she neared the indescribable thing, of which she felt it was the same thing of which she had once, behind old Therese, had a certain foreboding.

Then a shock tore right through her so that a ringing sprang through her spine and into her brain, for she saw a man standing before her, physically saw him, and this seeing was completely different from any she had ever experienced.

"Oh God!" she breathed in extreme fright.

But as she thought that now death was really there, and embracing her with its arms, she heard the same beautiful voice talking to her, which had greeted her in the evening before the road ceremony by the fence of the flower garden, "What is it with you, Miss Helene? For heaven's sake, just open your eyes for once. It's me, Peter Brindeisener."

But the more kindly the youth spoke to her, the more stricken she became, felt his face with trembling fingers, and then burst out into wailing tears. Fervour crashed over her, and she hung unconscious in Peter's arms.

The student thought no less than that the beloved girl was dying. That is why he took her in his arms, and carried her running through the forest, and while he hurried with his precious burden to the Sintlinger farmstead, his heart exulted despite all the fear over the providence which had burdened him with the news of the abrupt illness of Helene's at the road ceremony with such worry that he had crept day and night about the farmstead, and had finally sought that morning for salvation from his helplessness in a long walk through the forest.

Now he was carrying in his arms the one for whom all the waves of his being had been seeking for as long as he could remember.

With disturbed, sweat covered face, his blond hair sticking to his forehead, he arrived at the farmstead, and placed Helene in the arms of the startled farmwife with the explanation that he had found her unconscious in the forest.

She looked at him in horror, scarcely thanked him, and said mutely, "So then."

Then she climbed the stairs laboriously with Helene, and left him standing.

For Peter Brindeisener's face looked just as wildly excited as that time when he had in his youth boldly penetrated into Johanna's room to catch the sweet voice of the blessed hill's girl.

Peter stood for a moment stiffly before the Sintlinger farmstead, listened to the soft crying and lamenting of the farmwife coming from Helene's room, and then walked numbly down the hill to his father's farmstead.

Johanna immediately sent messengers in all directions to find her husband, who had flared up days before from the madness of his fury of love, and gone away. But even before the first messenger had returned, she thought otherwise, helped old Zenker harness the carriage, and told him, whatever it took, to hunt for a doctor in the city.

The carriage rattled down the hill, and roared away towards the forest.

The blessed farm lay in the sun as if with held breath. Johanna stood again before Helene's bed, and saw her lying waxen and motionless with her face in the pillows, dreamy-eyed and peaceful in the way only death brings to people. If a soft twitching had not run from time to time under the skin of her forehead, the farmwife would have made the three signs of the cross over her in eternal farewell, and abandoned herself to the anguish which crouched like an animal before the door.

"So my foreboding did not betray me, that misfortune would come to my little Lena from this accursed Peter Brindeisener", she thought for the hundredth time. She had unconsciously spoken it aloud. Then the girl opened her eyes, looked up in astonishment, looked at her mother, shut them in shock, and then said softly, "Draw the curtains."

When the doctor appeared in the darkened room, he found no signs of illness with Helene except for a quickened pulse, she willingly completed all the movements which the doctor desired of her. Only her eyes were held firmly shut, and she could not be brought by all the means of kindness and loving insistence to do anything more than open the eyelids a crack, and then close them in horror. When that had happened a few times, the doctor looked at the farmwife momentously, excused himself from Helene consolingly, and revealed to Johanna outside that, if everything was not deceiving him, a miracle had happened with her daughter. He definitely believed she had received sight again, to what extent was admittedly not established yet.

The Blessed Farm

When the doctor had gone down the stairs, the blessed farmer's wife knelt down in the same place where she stood, and kissed the floor.

Then she went in to Helene, bent over her, carefully enclosed her in her arms, but was unexpectedly seized by such a storm of happiness that she burst into tears, and, at the same time, as if out of her mind with bliss, only emitted the one thing louder and louder, "My dear, dear little Lena, thank God!"

She probably felt how her daughter was making weak attempts to detach from the almost painful embrace. But the farmwife burst out ever anew into more cries, and asseverations of happiness. Finally she noticed though that Helene wanted to say something, and when she got a hold of herself, and was still, Helene whispered into her ear, "I love Peter Brindeisener, mother, I love him ... I have always loved him ... always ... always ..." The girl was so seized by this first confession that, after all the excitement, she could not hold out anymore the breaking forth of the fervour, speaking quietly and ever more quietly, and raptly falling asleep.

Johanna walked away on tiptoes, and took back in her heart all the aspersions which she had made on Peter Brindeisener. For he could not be a bad man if he had helped God to work such an extraordinary miracle.

So what Professor Flöreck in Münster had foretold had thus happened, nature would one day draw away the veil from these eyes in just as mysterious a way as it had mysteriously spread it over them.

Soon the entire Sintlinger farmstead was exulting, and when a messenger who had been sent out after Sintlinger returned again without having found him, the happy excitement of the others revived him in his joy to a new enthusiasm. There was roaring, laughing, and calling from every door and window, and the entire district was instantly seized by it.

The blessed farmer came to the farmstead in the dark of evening from Querhoven. His face was pale and sorrowful, and when he heard that everyone was in jubilation because little Lena had been freed from her blindness, he staggered, and would soon have fallen over backwards to the floor, had he not gotten hold of himself and trudged into the house.

The labourers and maids thought that the happiness had clouded the blessed farmer's mind. But as they were still talking about how it was possible that somebody could make such a despairing face from pure joy, the bell in the little tower began tolling so shrilly, so strongly that everyone started in fright.

The farmwife did not yet know anything about Sintlinger's return. At the sound of the little bell which had been silent for decades, she came running out the door, and asked the crowd of servants what sort of nonsense that was meant to be.

They fell silent in embarrassment, and then finally answered that Sintlinger had just then come home.

The little bell was still whimpering and twitching. Johanna was up the stairs as if chased. Truly, there her husband stood, wedged tightly in the beams of the little tower, holding himself firmly wedged with his left hand, and constantly striking at the bell with a bar. Sometimes he hit it, sometimes he missed.

Finally he heard the begging, the screaming, and the banging of Johanna, let the bar fall, bent down, and said mutely, with a rigid expression on his face, "Yes, yes, Johanna, scream, scream! The stones will fly into the air straightaway, and the Lord will be gone for dust."

Then he burst out into laughter, and climbed down laboriously from the narrow beam.

10

O n the morning of the following day, the Hemsterhus gravedigger Wachsmann was walking across
the churchyard after the morning bellringing to make a
quick appraisal of the what order the graves were to be
laid out in during the following months. First he strode
the broad line of trees between the graves of the wealthy
and, at the sight of the large, splendid memorial stones,
vividly enjoyed once more the income from the betting
that he enjoyed, as the great bundle of keys struck
against his leg, and it seemed to him that the money
earned tinkled again fresh and young in his pouch. And
when he then with the bend in the path came from this
distinguished area of his garden of corpses to the region
first of the morally suspect, and then of the impoverished, he paused and looked quite glumly over the
broad flight of simple wooden crosses, and the sunken,
often completely overgrown mounds as far as the grey
sandstone wall of the churchyard enclosure, and
thought to himself, if he had lived by the Christian love
which he saw manifested so often in this region, then
he, his wife, and his children would have long ago
starved in God's name. Only, that was not the worst that
was to be thought here. Among those who had made off
with a silent mass and a paltry sprinkle of holy water, he
saw here and there the grave of a miser who had turned
cold for his secret sack of gold, and, as meanly as he had
lived, had now also smuggled himself out of the world
without honour and shamefully among the rabble and
vermin, only to withhold from him, the gravedigger, the
due reward.

Thus he came into an ever bitterer meditation, and
saw that the sense of honour in the world was almost at

an absolute end, and perhaps, if the police did not intervene, each of his dead would be burnt up in their own
ovens, fertilise their cabbages with the ashes, and the
gravediggers could meanwhile hang their stomachs on
the fence so that they would be filled by the wind.

But it was not to be mistaken. Anyone who toddles
off under the earth as a rogue will also be treated as a
hound at heaven's door. For God, and the pope know as
much as Wachsmann in Hemsterhus that the fear of
death must be maintained if you want to preserve men's
religion.

Shaking his head, and laughing to himself mockingly, he now walked quicker through this bleak part of
his garden of mounds to the gate, and threw a last gruff
look over the graves of the poor as if it would be pleas-
ing for him to discover some mischief by which he could
elide his inner gloom. And actually, back in the last
corner of the wall of nameless dead, a grey, cowering
figure was stirring.

Wachsmann stopped and shouted across a rousing
"hello". But the sunken little heap of a human did not
stir. That is why, already fired up with fury, he asked
who was loitering there this divine morning. For it
surely sometimes happened that a drunken vagrant
tottered along in the summer night, arrived at the
churchyard, and slept off his drunkenness between the
graves. And because the strange, wrapped-up breed
there made no reply to his second call, Wachsmann set
off angrily over the graves, and soon stood wildly gesticulating and blustering before the reprobate, who despite
all the racket cowered there calmly, his head lowered
between his knees, just a heap of holed, stinking clothes.

Finally he lifted his little head, pushed his filthy cap
back, and stared at him from red, watery eyes with a
stupid, crafty dullness.

It was an old vagrant with a sorrowful, withered face. Pale yellow hair hung mazily down by his ears like oakum, and, from the corners of his wrinkled, old lizard's mouth, the slobber of his deep sleep was still flowing.

This misery alone was not at fault that the words of indignation came from the gravedigger; around the old vagrant lay a mysterious horror. His nose snuffled; his horny mouth chirruped; from his extinguished eyes, a flash of mad bestial lust sometimes flashed.

Wachsmann made his retreat step-by-step, and said at a confident distance, but already very pityingly, that the churchyard was not a bedroom.

At that the drifter grasped about in the air a few times with outspread fingers, felt the ground, shook his head, and then said to the gravedigger, "You, you! What is there, cannot be lost, but you must find it again. For when one dies, it cracks, and it cracks so you hear it. It is clear though. It must be found though. — You know, I am not totally mad even if they also fed me for years with madhouse apes so that I lost my mind. Haha, haha! Celery is good against madness, and so I have kept my head together. You understand, until one evening the red bird flew past my window. Then it was time, and in the same night, I am off, pst, pst, widewitt, witt, witt! Do you understand me? It surely threw me head over heels in the forest, haha, and not too close. A bit much!"

Then he grasped about again on the ground, and murmured at the same time, "It must be found though ... I am in fact ... am in fact ..."

Finally he shot upright, and cried with a discoloured face, "Ha, you think, my fingers are like yours? No, no, little friend! They are witches' string. Pay attention there!"

He caught the fingertips of his left hand with his right, and distanced his hands from each other slowly, as if he were stretching out an object made of rubber.

A horror now really seized the gravedigger, and he stepped back even more.

"But wait!" the obviously mad vagrant called to him, "I am not finished with my tale. You probably don't believe it, hahaha? The dancer in the forest did not consider it possible either, and tormented my little brown pigeon until I wrapped the witches' splits around his throat."

He abruptly sank from the wild sparks as if shattered in despair, and sang:

> My pretty bird in the black forest,
> Where did you stay? Will I find you soon?
> I will search among the birds and red clover
> And find merely winter and white snow.

He wrung his hands in lament, and the tears ran in streams down from his old watery eyes over his haggard face.

Thus sunken in himself, constantly crying, and softly singing, he walked past the gravedigger, and vanished from the churchyard.

Wachsmann stood numbed, and stared as if at a ghost. When the vagrant had sauntered around the corner of the wall, the gravedigger came to, and it was immediately certain to him that this monstrous man had been a ghost, and indeed none other than the Nobody-incubus.

To the first person he met, an old retired farmer going to early mass, he told of how the dead Nobody-incubus had just then been at his grave, and he had seen with his own eyes how he had ridden away in the field on an elder bush. The entire air still smelt of sulphur.

The old farmer raised his nose in the air, and said that, yes, he smelt it too, and yesterday the blessed little Lena had gained her sight. There was something not right about the world. For it had also tolled at the blessed farm. He nodded to the gravedigger, vexed, and clucked on over to the church.

The news spread amongst the folk that the Nobody-incubus had come again the following night, had lifted his own gravestone from the earth, pressed it together with his hands like a soft gingerbread biscuit, and stuck it in his pocket. The next morning, the memorial had really vanished from the mound of the man who had been buried many years before as the Nobody-incubus.

The gravedigger, who was interrogated because of this, shrugged his shoulders, and said he had always maintained many years ago that it was the Nobody-incubus roaming about at the time who rode Ursula Rütsch in the Sweeps at night and assaulted Josefa Schwerdtner on the stone bridge in Brederode, and it would be no different now either, and, in particular, things happened of which you would be best to remain silent. But as much was certain, that even the other side was having a difficult, uneasy time now, and it impinged sometimes on the graves as if it wanted at all events for the dead to be out and brought back to earth. But the graves which had been closed by a proper burial, struck down well with the great bell, not merely tinkled with the little ringer, beautifully fumigated with incense, sung blessedly, if possible trumpeted, there he would lay his hand in the fire, they were safe, for the good faith helps everywhere.

It could not be missed that the folk connected the appearance of the Nobody-incubus with the gaining of little Lena Sintlinger's sight, and especially with the fates of both the estranged farmsteads, and thought the red bird of which the Nobody-incubus had spoke was only properly to be understood if you thought of the red rags which the fool had during his lifetime once torn up over the cradle of the sleeping blessed little Lena amidst sorrowful sobbing.

These interweavings into daring and often absurd conjectures did not stop even when the police were asked by one of the mental asylums to search for ... an escaped inmate, who had up to then refused to reveal his name and place of birth, but as per the description was none other than the vagrant whom the gravedigger Wachsmann had met at the Hemsterhus churchyard on the morning after Helene's gaining her sight. However, the clever tender of corpses knew to refrain from any testimony so as not to lessen the weight of his ghost story, and so as to let the usefulness of the substantially refreshed awe of death work undisturbed. The Hemster- hus parish had also placed more value on the ghostily wandering Nobody-incubus than on the living, and so the vigilance of the authorities with respect to the es- caped fool slowly dropped off. The likeness of the two beings did not come into question anymore, and the folk enjoyed the freedom in general to tell of ever newer mysterious deeds of the haunted Nobody-ghost, the more so as he really did appear in villages from time to time, arrived suddenly in mysterious ways next to lonely wanderers on secluded paths, yelled out in a shrill voice in the silence of the fields, and committed all sorts of fiendishness at night. Seeking berries and mushrooms, he looked out from the trunk of an old oak with a con- torted face, finally whinnying like a young horse, and if you looked closer, his grimace transformed into a knot- ted branch. At the farm of a Brederode farmer, all the motley red cows miscarried, and he had hovered before blessed little Lena's newly received sight as a wondrous bird, it was told, and had then departed as a splendid heavenly music with an incredibly melodious sound.

These stories were so adventurous, and the inferences drawn from the rumour were just as strange — the angelic nature of little Lena, her unearthly being; the years of Sintlinger's wavering in a high, widely influential life after an unfettered youth; the gentle spirit which had lent the shimmer of holiness to the mad estranged farmstead over one and a half decades, all that was declared to be nothing but an evil bewitchment. Established by impure, malicious spirits as a deception which separated the true from the false Christians, and which inspected all the good for the firmness of their belief. The Church helped the heavily laden wagon, full of fancy ideas and superstition, somewhat further along in this direction, and also found it very beneficial for the strengthening of its shaken power by darkening and diminishing the authority of the blessed farmer. It even went so far as to see the salvation of little Lena Sintlinger from the horrid wonder of her blindness to the full delight of her liberated eyes as just the beginning of the decline of Sintlinger's blessed path. In this way, the worst was constantly said about the blessed farm, which was not left veiled in shadows though by the trumpeting of all these malicious mouths. Except perhaps for a silly maid or a foolish oxen boy, nobody took any of the many disapproving little folk tales at face value.

Yes, even the farmwife had laughed loudest over the stories which were unloaded on the farmstead, although she had usually liked to stand in the fluttering light of superstition.

But she had obviously been healed forever from this aberration of human worry over life after she had landed, despite the long foreboding and dark, menacing signs, in such a gloriously incomprehensible way at the fulfillment of her fervent hopes.

Hermann Stehr

The liberated Helene certainly proved to be like someone who unexpectedly steps out of deep darkness into the glaring midday sun. Her nature staggered back into its depths at first before the completely new, unfamiliar world, and would have liked most of all to remain there in the society of the resounding shadows by which she had been surrounded for as long as she could remember. For that reason, she lay there during the first days for the longest time yet with closed eyes, and indeed most of the time even in the presence of people. As soon as the door shut, and she was left alone, she lifted her eyelids hesitantly, in fearful curiosity, and roamed about everywhere with her eyes. Everything was colourful, fixed, strange, shimmering, stood nearby, and yet thrust through the sharpness of its contours full of a menacing hostility. Oh, and how people were transformed, and the yard, the garden, the paths, the hill, forest, and sky! Everyone who appeared before her, labourers, maids, and farmworkers, were observed by her for a moment, then she let her eyelids fall, and compared the visible figure with her sightless conceptions from before. And almost nobody came before her whom she would not examine in astonishment again and again, fingering them suspiciously. With old Zenker, she was astonished by his wrinkled face and his stooped figure, because the old man had lived in the appearance of her eyeless sight upright, with a gentle child's face. Faced with Gottlieb Meixner's grotesquely square build, she broke out into laughter; she measured her mother with a quiet smile, in which you noted a slight disappointment; and when the blessed farmer's own pale, furrowed face appeared before her with the set back, overly large, dark eyes, she was immediately frightened, cried out in anguish, "That is my father?", buried her head in her pillow, sobbed, and then threw herself at Sintlinger's chest. She flung her arms around his neck, and softly cried amidst tears constantly, "My father ... my dear father ..." Nobody could decide exactly whether, in the agitation of Helene's first sight of Sintlinger, disappointment or joy, happy surprise or shock was principally to the fore. And the blessed farmer himself was overwhelmed by the most conflicting feelings when he held his now-seeing, little Lena in his arms for the first time. The throwing up of his hands could just as well have meant horror as astonishment, his blanching and the lowering of his eyes, the highest happiness or sorrow.

When he was finally released by Helene, he stood opposite her, looked at her wide-eyed, and said in disbelief with an anguished emotion in his face and voice, "So, so! So, my little Lena, you have now really become a person like us others. Now, how is it then for you here, child?"

The girl was frightened for a moment, let her eyelids fall in contemplation, and answered, "Oh, just think, father, I am happy of course."

At that the woe in the blessed farmer's joy only deepened. He answered with an inner turning away, "So, so. So, so." And walked out shaking his head.

For little Lena Sintlinger it turned out with everyone like it did with her father, even if not so crass. She saw her most intimate things confounded, her closest things alienated, familiar things transported. What had already begun months before was now complete — her entire world, which she had usually carried within herself like a gentle lunar landscape, now lay as a glaringly colourful, ungovernable tumult around her. Her soul, which had days before perceived the ringing of the night stars in the depths of her own breast, had been flushed out like a peace-loving king from the old capital, and now lay at the outermost borders of its empire in endless struggle with hundreds of thousands of invaders.

When for the first time from the yard, she caught sight of the undulating hills of the broad countryside, she had to hold onto Peter Brindeisener, who wanted to show the earth to her, as he thought her eyes were closed. Helene saw lying around her there nothing fixed, no movement stiffened for centuries. Instead, she saw a living, foaming dance of churned up waves surging towards the blessed hill so that she became dizzy and laughed out in a shrill voice like a child who has ridden a merry-go-round for the first time. "Wow!" she cried at the same time in exuberant awe. "That is a mad whirling around, Peter. Look, and everything plunges into the sun. Oh my! Dear, but look, what a fire it is."

Then she shut her eyes, and leaning back in the arms of her beloved, she collected this new, great image of beautiful earthly peace with the stillness of her other-worldly, sightless seeing, whilst the fervour of the evening blossomed over her face. Until Peter kissed her on her closed eyes, more and more ardently so that she finally raised her eyelids, and looked at him wide-eyed and in astonishment, almost like that first time in the forest out there when the night tore apart around her and she had found herself in the world, physically opposite a lover to whom she had been making a pilgrimage for months in her dreams like an unfamiliar shadow.

The blessed farmer's wife, however, bravely suppressed the eruptions of her simple nature at the sight of the fuzzy silence in which her little Lena came into joy over the newly gifted world and her love. Yes, she even supported inconspicuously the couple's trysts. For she had not only apologised to Peter Brindeisener for the hostile way with which she had received the unconscious little Lena from his hands, but she had to make good again if possible to herself for all the bad things which she had inwardly attributed to his nature for as

long as she could remember. When she saw the powerful youth with the untameable eyes serving so tenderly,
almost timidly around her delicate, elfin little Lena, she
could not grasp how she could have seen the same person previously only with averse, directly hostile feelings
so that he had once even seemed to her at the funeral of
Amalie Brindeisener to be a murderer. Now she felt joyous pride when she saw the student, with a heavy calm,
in which yet a feathery wrenching twitched in each step
like a secret creaking under the soles, coming and going
thus in fluttering dignity.

However, the madness of his laughter sometimes
still infused her with fear, almost with something like
horror. When his narrow, blood-red lips were raised
over his white teeth, it looked as if he were grinning
with his massive, chalk-white, predator's jaws.

But when she heard his boyishly innocent chattering
and joking around with Helene on the little bench under
the lime tree, this impression also seemed to her to only
be a last, stubborn residue of her old hostility, and she
reproached herself that she had at base a quite bad
heart.

Never, as long as the Sintlinger farmstead had stood,
had the blackbirds piped from the tips of the lime tree
so fervently, so passionately in the evening as on those
few days in May when the children of the two estranged
farmsteads sat on the little bench next to the gate, and
mutually unlocked the wonder of their love and their
life. The lovers bore the treasures of their life together,
wove their memories into a wreath, and were astounded
over their choice of love, which Peter Brindeisener explained to the raptly listening Helene as the working of
a primordial decision of the universe. He claimed to
have heard the first cry with which she had entered the
world, and that he almost believed he had heard her
singing in a dream which he had himself dreamt even

before her birth. For whenever just the sound of her voice came to his ear, then it had, as he effusively put it, "each time gripped his soul to its primordial depths".

Peter's academic holiday quickly came to an end in this way, and he returned to old, sombre Münster in a feeling of elation, in a jubilation of life like he had never experienced in his life before.

11

It is told that in the few, perhaps fourteen days which elapsed between Helene gaining her sight and Peter Brindeisener's departure to the university town, they sat yet again next to each other like lovers thrown together by an explosion, and marvelled at the mysterious, momentous interaction of their past life paths, seized by a new amazement whenever they discovered again a new shimmer with which their joint fate had as it were itself illuminated the track to their union. In the arbour of the little flower garden behind the barn, it would have happened, during the evening, in the period when the shadows of all things deliquesce. There they both sat hand in hand, and spoke about the sweet enticing play which they had plied as children on the day of Amalie Brindeisener's funeral, and that they would not have obtained each other in the end, if little Lena had at the time been not too rapt to see Peter's face exactly with her fingers so that his head had never left her since and had caused her directionless love so much torment during that time; that she had however never known in the clouds of her unconscious passion which man this mysterious head belonged to, which she had felt in her fingers for months with every awakening, until the lightning strike in the forest had shown her the culprit. And now she also believed the stories that men roam about without heads, because she had learnt that heads without men can wreck so much mischief. Thus the blessed hill's girl twittered away, and teasingly asked at the end whether Peter had also lived the entire time without a head since his head had gone after her.

At that Peter Brindeisener suddenly became very thoughtful, nodded his head, and then answered with a dark voice that it was always possible. — And after some thought, he added whimsically that it was all the same and now sorted out forever. He had opened her eyes, and she had given him back his head. Thus each had become whole, even if neither knew exactly where the one began and the other stopped. During this light-hearted skirmish of love, the blessed farmer was said to have stepped into the arbour unnoticed in the dark, and settled down soundlessly next to Peter on the bench. Squeezed into the corner, Sintlinger had listened to the couple's conversation, which soon continued again, after this jesting effervescence, in the search for providence in their past. Peter now maintained that fate had even been helped by their fathers in that they had, half in hostility, half in a struggle for predominance, without knowing it, even built them the road on which love had then brought them together. Was that not the ultimate? It was without precedence!

At these words, the blessed farmer had, with a sudden, cold grasp, unexpectedly seized Peter's hot hand, pushed his pale, anguished face close before his eyes, and then asked with strained voice, "Do you really believe that, Peter?"

Then he had walked away, before the shocked couple
had recovered from their start, without any explanation,
impassioned with a certain indignation, and had then,
though already out of the garden and deep in the dark
fields, suddenly laughed loudly in shrill mockery. People
say that it sounded despairing of hell, and if not entirely
that, then certainly demonic, almost like the laughter
which the blessed farmer had once elicited from the
devil in playing bowls in the beech stand.

After Peter's departure, it had also seemed to the
blessed farmer that, wherever he walked or stood, a
three-legged auburn mouse ran after him at a distance
of ten to twenty metres, did not disappear from him all
day, and crouched all night on the threshold of his bedroom. With that, the pious people thought, it was
proven that the black one was drawing his circle more
and ever more narrowly around the enemy of the
Church and God, and was not letting him out of the invisible thread for even a minute. Nevertheless Sintlinger
had also not been abandoned in this most difficult time
by his innate dauntlessness, had struggled with Satan
through entire nights for weeks, torn up the contract
with him a thousand times, and scattered the shreds
into the storm. But each morning, the paper on which
Sintlinger had committed his soul to the devil lay intact
in his writing desk in the old place. Until the tormented
blessed farmer began begging the three-legged devil's
mouse constantly to desist from it. But even that could
no longer save the poor man, this standing and talking
loudly to the earth out in the deserted fields, often for
hours. The events in the destiny of the blessed farm
began being drawn into the vortex of their last fall. The
actors were driven forward from their fieriest centre,
each by a different blazing flame, so wrenchingly that
the dumbfounded populace of the surrounding district,
certainly with the exclusion of the Querhoveners, knew

no better than, through the collecting of superstitious, ghostly features, to confuse the lives of these people with the demonic, because it was incomprehensible to them otherwise.

Nevertheless these schemes of superstitious haze also proliferated in the vicinity of actual hardships which the blessed farmer struggled against at the time. Johanna actually heard night after night the pondering strides of her husband above her in his study sounding endlessly back and forth, sometimes excited, sometimes swift, and then breaking off again in the middle of the room for a long time when he remained standing as if nailed to the spot or paralysed. And when she crept up the stairs noiselessly in bare feet and looked through the keyhole, she saw light still, and thought she saw her husband standing motionless by his desk. A few times, it also seemed to her as if he flung the window open passionately, and slammed it shut again straight afterwards so that the panes rattled. But then it was always towards morning, already in the grey of early morning, and startled from dozing, she thought that it had perhaps been the morning wind which rattled the doors and windows. But she did not thereby calm herself down, instead, after each of these animated nights, searching through the room of her Andreas, right to the smallest corner, to find something to stop what was not letting her husband sleep, even if she guessed that it was connected somehow with Helene's gaining her sight.

Finally one day, she opened on an off-chance the little door to the stove in Sintlinger's room, and found the entire firebox filled with little scraps of paper which had been torn up. Every shred was thickly written on by Sintlinger's hand, she was capable of deciphering a little, and what she read, she could not understand at all. The word God occurred often; in other places, she read of eternal omnipotence and kindness, of the idea of the world, of the foolishness of life, of the inner desolation of the human spirit and its existence, of building roads; he had even written of the Brindeisener farm, of Helene, Peter, of her, the Querhoveners, the Pastor and old Klim, her father. From all that, she could see though finally that her Andreas was wrangling and struggling anew with God, and was divided with him and with his own entire life. Startled, she stuffed the mountain of his shredded papers back in the stove, lit it all up until it had burnt down to ashes, and left the little door open so that her husband could see from it that she knew about his restless nocturnal struggles. For a few days, this invisible intermediation by Johanna helped too. But only for a very short time. Then the blessed farmer was again beset by the same torments. Often, as if by an abrupt stab through his inner being, he placed his knife and fork on the table during the meal, and looked with such a consuming interest at Helene, as though she were a complete stranger who resembled from afar a beloved person whom he could not picture in his mind anymore. Then it sometimes happened that he stood up with the loud exclamation, "No, it is not possible!", and went out, or that he sprang up, embraced his girl, and kissed her fervently on the mouth and eyes, at the same time whispering softly in a sort of beseeching ardency, "Dear, dearest little Lena! My little Lena! My little Lena! Mine!", as if he were thinking of the possibility of being able to melt back into the old world again through his fervour. But Helene was depressed by this strange behaviour of her father's, scared off, and finally fearful, avoiding being alone with him, or running away when she saw him coming towards her in the fields. Then Sintlinger began his endless nocturnal wandering in his room again so that the blessed farmer's wife could not endure it anymore, for it pained her as if he were striding about with heavy, iron-shod boots on her raw chest.

For that reason, when she saw him creeping once more behind Helene in the fields, she immediately left the farmstead on the opposite side, and surprised him as he stood in the field margin of the godforsaken rearmost field, and — it almost looked this way — battled agitatedly with a molehill. She approached him there, and reproofed him in a loving, but earnest way for that hustling and pondering with which he was sinning against God, against his nearest, and most of all against himself. And if he did not control himself, but continued to reproach little Lena for gaining her sight as a misfortune, and the Lord for this as a mistake, then it could really still go as far as the people now already maintained about him, that his old soul would leave him, and he would fall into a pool of madness from which he would no longer be able to be rescued. And when she had said that, her briskness was gone, she embraced and kissed him crying so that her hot tears ran down the farmer's neck. At the same time, she whispered, "My husband! My dearest, dearest Andreas!"

But what now followed, words from the deepest misery of his heart and of a spirit attacked from all sides, went past the simple soul like the roaring of a distant storm, and the more bitterly and more cutting the blessed farmer tore at the torment of his destruction, sometimes at the whole world, sometimes undercutting himself, the more Johanna saw his fervour approach the moody raving of his long since overcome period of drunkenness and madness, the more her inner fears vanished before the hopeless disintegration of her beloved husband, and she obtained the certainty that it was at base nothing for him but the happiness over the glorious transformation of Helene's fate, which he could not confess upfront, because he had previously always maintained that his child was not blind at all and thus also did not need to become seeing.

When Sintlinger hence came to the end of his long explanation, she was almost rid of all her worries, and calmly listened to his last words, which were, "Thus it is Johanna. You must understand me. As long as little Lena was blind, I saw, and indeed deeper than thousands of men. Now my child has obtained external sight, I am blinded in spirit, and do not understand my previous understanding. So, either the fact of little Lena's soul's divine eyes was an illusion, in which case all the wisdom was also an illusion which my mind discovered in that region of the world. All the happiness during the time of the blessed farm was a delusion. Your father, the Pastor, and Meixner died in vain because of me, and all the Querhoveners are children who have run after a madman. Or, I have fallen into the deepest night of existence. Oh God, and my dearest little Lena has succumbed with her sight to the blindness of others. But how shall we find our way out of a night in which light is a darkness?!! Wife, dear wife!" He flailed his arms about dismissively, shook his head in despair, and left his wife standing there. With long strides, he hurried diagonally across the field with its sparse white clover, went between the small spruce trees at the edge of the forest, and vanished into the green without once looking back. Johanna watched after him with anguished pity, and said to herself after him, "Yes, dear, you certainly have it bad. That I like to believe. But, everything will work out, and then it will be better than if all had not been. For after the maddest weather, the sun shines brightest."

Sighing, and looking back again and again, she walked back to the farmstead.

But Sintlinger, who had wandered so far from the world of men, had again tangled himself so deeply in the earth-bound turbidness of his thought that he could not tear himself free anymore with the simple bravado of which his wife had been thinking. It even went so far with the blessed farmer that he again began going into taverns. He certainly lost none of his dignity. With the grim disarray of a fleeing king, he entered the bar in a way that shocked the landlord and patrons, and ordered a large schnaps. Then he sat sunken before it, his emaciated hands lying stretched out on his thighs, and did not touch the drink. Nobody dared talk to him, and he himself brought no word over his lips. And when everybody had then crept on tiptoe from the vicinity of the creepy man, and the room was empty, because even the landlord could not endure being with him, those who were secretly looking through the window at his behaviour noticed that he smelt the schnaps again and again, and then flashed his eyes around the room as if he hoped he could succeed by the scent of his old period of intoxication in stealing himself into the middle of the dance of those colourful years of madness. He drank with his nose, as folk say. But, what he yearned for, he probably never succeeded in obtaining. — After he had been sitting for a shorter or longer time, he placed a mark note on the table, and went away silently, distant, lost within himself. And once the Hemsterhus baker, Hoffmann, the tearful prayer, indeed his antagonist, followed him from a distance after he had observed his incomprehensible behaviour through the window. And as he thus walked along behind the solitary Sintlinger, and paid exact attention to him so as to be able to properly belittle him at home, it happened that the malicious man was overcome against his will by an emotion, a fear, as if it were not a devil's accomplice walking there before him, but a most venerable, really a blessed man. This wave of compassionate veneration grew so quickly in him that he cried out from behind to Sintlinger, "Blessed farmer! Blessed farmer!", began running, and soon stood short of breath next to the man. But when he looked into Sintlinger's unfathomably sad eyes, all the words of comfort which he had wanted to say were lost, and he managed nothing but an embarrassed stammer.

But Sintlinger touched his shoulder gently with his hand, and said calmly, with loving reproach in his voice, "Did I call you an ass, baker, a fool or scoundrel?"

The person concerned was so taken aback that he could only shake his head. "Well then", Sintlinger spoke firmly, "let me go my way, and do not berate *me* anymore."

Old Anton Brindeisener resigned himself remarkably easily to the new relationship into which the hostile estranged farms had been brought by the miraculous love of the two young people. His Peter was to him at once no longer the son turned bad, the dream of death in his heart, but a hellishly clever, lettered fellow who in an instant had done what the most famous doctors had not achieved, namely giving little Lena Sintlinger her sight and showing the mad pack up there that a Brindeisener had more sense than such a nonsense cackler as that Sintlinger.

In addition, he still knew the Brindeisener way thoroughly, now that his Peter was on course. Not a year and he would have his fill of flurrying in books in his room, chuck all that rubbish on the heap, become a farmer, and marry the blind girl, as he still called the, now sighted, little Lena to himself. Thus the possession of both families would be unified in one hand. The name of Brindeisener would rise from all its farming existence into the brilliance of a real, lordly power, and the Sintlingers would vanish forever, swallowed, devoured.

Whenever old Brindeisener caught sight of Sintlinger over on the other hill, he called in joyful cordiality, "Good day, neighbour! A beautiful day, isn't it?"

12

After Johanna had been carried away a bit by the new whirlwind which had seized her Andreas, she got a hold of herself with a firm grip, mindful of earlier failures, and headed back entirely into the joy over her girl's happiness. And she did that with the unbreakable intent of not letting anything or anybody discourage her from it anymore, except for God. Johanna did not return fumbling and half disjointed from the weeks when she had been shaded in the sorrow of the deep worrying of her husband, no, with a jolt as it were, she leapt next to her newly reborn child, and was astonished at what changes had meanwhile happened with Helene right in front of her. From the delicate as moonlight, little elf, if not yet a steadfast young woman, then a little stalk standing with the best sap had emerged. Usually she had floated when walking, just like leaves being driven across the ground, now she skipped away with steely decisive steps. Before her hands had pulled whatever she wished for towards herself softly and magically, now her fingers grasped boldly and undeniably. Usually her quiet voice had convulsed to the depths of the soul, now the air just resounded from her joyful voice and a laugh which hardly broke off. Her eyes had recovered from the frozen pale blue of her sightless period into a blazing depth and into abrupt, almost rapaciously grasping looks. Her hips began to sway. The delicate oval of her angelic face vanished amidst strapping healthy cheeks. She attacked her work like a zealot who had sat lame for years, and attacked delight and joy like a starved man attacks a set table. Often she sprang up in the middle of her work, threw her work exultantly towards the heavens, and cried, "Children, children! You do not know at all how beautiful the world is."

She hardly needed to learn anything. While she had been sitting around enchanted in the otherworldly experience of her blind eyes and wandering through aimless heavenly dreaming, she had learnt all the skills as mysteriously as a child can learn the speech of adults even before it is capable of speaking a word. Each grasp lay ready in her hands, and only waited for the call. What she had only once skimmed with the hem of her dress, she achieved like others can after years of effort. If she had been a miraculous child from another world before, now she made the day's handiwork into a sort of magic, not just through the puzzling manner of genesis in her, but much more still through the fact that she was not using up her industry and her powers, but rather increasing them so that she was like a miracle lamp which produces oil through its consumption. She resembled in that way entirely her father in his youthful days of madness when the delight in work had always surged from his body like a rested storm from the mountain which releases it and loses nothing thereby. Many more of Sintlinger's characteristics also experienced in Helene a transformed new existence. The blue of her eyes not only deepened, it overran with an ever gentle, bronze tint, like a shadowy reflection of her father's black-as-night eyes. The abruptness flared up from her like a kick always withdrawn, and her intoxication, her insatiable hunger for life found no satisfaction in the excitements of work, resulting in it overflowing in all sorts of noisy delight, unconcerned by the commands of careful decorum. If Johanna had not forcibly prevented her, she would most of all liked to have been swept across the yards in the arms of the maids to the music of some barrel-organ. Thus she raced to and fro along the upper floor's hallway until all her partners sat out of breath in the doorways. She thronged to every not too far-flung garden concert, and she did not want to miss any celebration, any festive parade. As if overnight, she stood in thousands of flames. She was like a sea which wants to toss all its waves in the blow of a single fountain into the air, like an earth which knows nothing but the intoxication of a single spring. And if just *one* planned delight was taken away from her, she lapsed into a lament as if she had lost an irretrievable treasure from her life. Then she sat down, and wrote with unpractised script, learnt in days, and in an orthography which obeyed only the commands of sincerity, moving outpourings of grief to Peter Brindeisener, "dat yu mus spen da lub in shadoz az you pland", and adjured him to come to her on the Sintlinger hill in eight days, "an no longe goe awae in al aterniti". One of these letters closed, "For yu ar my as-senshun, yu ar da aternil world awaknin yor Helene."

Seldom was the blessed farmer's wife skimmed by the shadow of a fear when she saw Helene with gasping chest attacking life. Mostly the boundless whirl of the awakened girl tore at her with too loud a delight and joyfulness, or her eyes became moist with emotion at the thought of how much the dear child must have been tormented in the long night of her eyes if she now had to bear such possessive hunger. The blessed farmer, however, embraced the heated girl fearfully, or stood with pale, twitching face to the side, or eluded her entirely, as if this buxom, loud farmgirl were not his girl, exposed to the other side and transported to earth, but her flat, empty ghost. Yet when he came home, and did not find his child straightaway, fear would overcome him immediately. He ran about the farm, out into all the margins of the fields, and called after her with a shaking, fearfully falling voice.

However, in this fiery seething of awoken hunger for the world, little Lena Sintlinger never entirely lost the connection with the shadowless light of her blissfully blessed period. When she enthused with breathless rapture over the new sweetness of the earth, it always happened that she let her eyelids fall over her eyes as if she had to sink back into the maternal space of her old, otherworldly dream gaze for a moment, because what delighted her in the summer glow was only to be understood in the soundless light of her soul. From there, she then looked with her, deep-down still unearthly face as if through colourful panes at this life.

Whilst little Lena Sintlinger was still enmeshing herself deeper and deeper in her new existence so that every path she saw only existed in order to stroll down convivially, all the houses only possessed windows in order to be able to brandish colourful cloths from them, a sky over the rooves in order to exult at it, and the days always fell too short to come to an end with all the jesting and laughing, Peter Brindeisener was meanwhile floating with his deepest dreams in the unreal, transfigured heights from which the blessed hill's girl had been gifted to him like a heavenly being. He felt everything had recovered in him. He no longer needed the diligence to wrestle away arduously the plunder of a thousand inane distractions, his collectedness no longer arose from the remorse over wasted time and strength, his pride no longer tasted of the vanity of the half-broken. The iron, cool tenacity of his centuries old breeding had grasped him purely from the depths so that he steadfastly ordered his studies devotedly day by day like his forefathers did with their fields, but without their sombreness, without the silent doggedness, for his mood had recovered, been placed in the brightest of sunlight as if it had not once been battered irremediably by the brutality of his father. With his ample gifts, he was the most distinguished student of the law faculty. Through the coolness of innate ingenuity, the fullness of his experiences, and the familiarity with the tricks of an often precarious existence, he found his way in the most convoluted legal conflicts as if he were not the half inattentive, most griped at, having twice abandoned his studies, student of law in his third semester, but a young scholar, even if finding the law lay closer to his being than interpreting the law.

It probably seemed that Peter Brindeisener felt that the eager steps to or from the lecture were like a strangeness in his body, and laughed quietly, but delightedly at himself. But in the subsequent hours of work, he was entire dedication, without needing to have the incentive of a goal. The earnest activity and the sense of duty sufficed to gift him a joyful, pure elatedness, and he was even surprised in astonishment that the world of men did not invent as the ideal of its deliverance and transfiguration a female being, because everything which accounted for its greatness originated from women. In such a way, he also through working circled about little Lena, whom he liked to alienate himself from out of pious timidity as if placing her heaven, and therefore he spurned to compare this delicate as a breath, hazy figure with the obtrusive, adorned beauties which he encountered on the street or in society. Like a hermit carries the picture of the Virgin Mary, so did Peter carry the image of his blessed beloved silently within himself, and awkwardly avoided letting some confidant even guess at his happiness from a distance. And when it occurred now and again that those sitting around him noticed that this cool, powerful man's face filled with blood in the midst of a lecture, sitting there with enraptured eyes, as if spellbound, then some suggested that he was succumbing to the aftereffect of too vigorous an evening in the tavern. For nobody guessed that Brindeisener still suffered under proper schoolboy attacks of his love, that he felt the cheeks of little Lena on his, her lips on his mouth, and her breath as a hot wave skimming over him. That is why he was also freed entirely from the torment which his eyes had previously always prepared him in which he saw every woman, every girl only as a human source of enjoyment without clothes, if possible with a horizontal denouement. He had usually called that the "dauntlessness and penetrating power of his look", and been proud of it in many ways. Now he had been thrown up into such constant wallowing that he even heard the name of his beloved in the rhythm and tone of the tolling of every bell.

He, the hundred times fallen in action, behaved like a beginner in love, and let his passion be cooked up in himself to an ideal which would have been suitable for the being of a sixteen year old, but which did not befit a man who had so often carved his life, and the existence of men in general, into atoms through the scepticism of his razor sharp mind.

That is why it could also not be kept at bay that already after a short time then a shock to his elevated condition, if not also a retrograde movement, would have to occur from a quite inconsequential incident.

On a Sunday, he undertook an outing in the surrounding area of Münster, entirely alone, quite in solitude, only in the company of his dream vision which never left him. Thus he went off down Roxelor Street, past Koesfelder Crossing, into the countryside. On returning, he turned around often towards the area he was sashaying through to impress the places on himself from which he had again received all sorts of wondrous delights through his smitten heart. It was already passing deep into evening, the mist was beginning to climb from the fields in the distance, and hung in the light of the sinking sun like a reddened gauze before the area so that the hills of the distant horizon were drawn in cloud-like curves into the still fiery glimmer of the ether. There he saw after some lingering the delicate elven figure of Helene, as she strove in the incorporeal, not to a goal, but was just carried along in the enjoyment of her existence in rapt purposelessness, and finally faded away in the direction to which Hemsterhus must lie in his opinion.

This joyous shock to his inner being was so hefty that he thought on entering his room as if he were walking high in the air, and realised light could not be endured in this state of his soul. For that reason, he sat down quietly at his desk in the dark room, and when the pale reflection of the streetlights in the window disturbed him, he even turned away, and turned his face to the wall. When he had spent a while like that, the apparition did not repeat over the twilit red fields outside, but he found instead how all the sounds around him, the travel of the electric tram, the movement on the stairs, human voices, and the rattling of wagons sounded weaker and ever weaker so that a perfect, unreal stillness soon surrounded him. And when he penetrated into this precipitous world of silence with the most rapt attentiveness, so as to catch a sound, he heard a clear, bright, high note trembling, soft as a breath, like moonlight skimming over the trees, and after some seconds, the same note at the same pitch, but fuller, more insistent.

Peter Brindeisener listened with the most devoted attentiveness, his lips a little open, as if to breath in the magical sound. And then a second, third, fourth, a long series of notes rang out, which softly like the first, but skimming past as clearly and calmly as if each had only the sense of its own beauty and clarity, not the sense of a melody. And yet it was a song which sang itself, but an indescribable song like perhaps the movement of a procession of birds in the blue sky brings forth, or the reed on the pond when its stalk quivers in the sun.

The listener was led by the mysterious notes deeper and deeper, and with each soft ringing, he was pushed a vertiginous step further into an abyss of incomprehensibility, which he sensed was nothing but his existence.

And the notes themselves, that was the song of the soul of the blessed farm's little Lena. And gradually, Brindeisener did not understand how, images arose from his past life. He travelled home in his Greifswald period early in the morning with noisy fellow students from a rural festivity. One wanted with the stubbornness of a drunk to go along the beach, and at once the sea shone towards them, still, gleaming from the light of the last stars. Then he was walking as a youth through a spring storm. The tepid drops drizzled down on him. In an oak on the boundary path, a cuckoo called, and his father grumbled down at him from the hill ... They were quite different things which he saw, as if they had not the tiniest thing in common with the deeply inspired sounds which he was meanwhile constantly hearing. And yet a hidden incomprehensible consistency was there, as if he were perceiving through the sounds, which originated for him from little Lena's soul, the meaning of his entire past, making his life deep and also his sky wide.

He felt at the same time as if a wondrous light were radiating onto his back, only he dared not turn around, so as not to tear himself from his daydream.

And as Peter Brindeisener sat thus in bewitched rapture in the pitch-black room, a good friend of his came up the stairs, inquired from the landlady whether the student was at home, knocked gently, and stepped soundlessly into the room. He saw the silhouette of the motionless student sitting there outlined on the window, snapped the light on finally, and broke out into a

genuine Red Indian war-cry. Brindeisener spun around
in bewilderment, but the visitor, a stocky, jovial fellow,
looked about everywhere to see if he did not detect
something hidden which would clarify for him the
meaning of this "stupid existence", and discovered on
the table a letter which had arrived in Brindeisener's absence. It was the first of Helene's letters. Before Peter
could pocket it, the student had seized it, saw that it was
written in a female hand, and danced around the table
before Brindeisener's pursuit, amidst mad mocking
laughter, deciphering the awkward writing and the
dreadful orthography with a clamour, and did not sense
the increasing irritability of the lover. In an instant, an
ungovernable wildness broke over Brindeisener. He
seized him as if he wanted to throttle him, tore the letter
from him, and threw the speechlessly shocked fellow
out of the room, seething all over, silent, all his limbs
shaking, like a large predator in a rage. Following this
incident, Peter Brindeisener changed rooms, and withdrew from traffic with the student body as if by a violent
jolt.

He rented a room in an inconspicuous house in the
tangle of little lanes around Romburger Hof, its windows looking out on a forgotten courtyard. There, in the
vicinity of the little hotel in which Helene had slept a
night as a child, he led an almost hermit-like life during
the last four weeks before the long vacation, wedged
into a studious diligence which assumed almost fierce
forms, as if it were possible to keep something inwardly
violent from touching ground through this constant,
murderous tension.

But in the twilight, at the time of the evening bells,
the astonished landlords saw the well-built, secretive
student leaning out the window and listening, as deeply
seized by the notes of the bells as if he were praying.

In the last week before the start of the long holiday, Peter Brindeisener had delivered a quite comprehensive dissertation over the right of primogeniture. He already itched so strongly sometimes to get out from the bridle of his industry, that he feared that the wild, genial skittishness of his spirit, resisting every urge, was beginning to break forth from the depths of his being, that same skittishness which had already destroyed so many honest attempts at a purposefully restrained life. And he tied the bands of his will still tighter, and did not allow himself the smallest pause for beer. He sat bravely and unswervingly to the very end so that it would in his opinion have had to have become his most successful dissertation ever.

Only, when, to obtain a complete overview, he went through the entire dissertation once more, he straightaway received a blow. Already towards the end, at the end of an intricate, but very precisely led conclusion, he had, and indeed had written it thus, as if it formed the necessary zenith of the logic's arc, "In general, no drowning man senses the water which covers him, and thus you do not feel anymore the death which you die. However, through pity, compassion, fear, angst, and shock at the death of others, you die futilely and in torment a thousand times during your life. You fools! What frightens you when faced with death? Every breath is a dying." Beyond that everything was in agreement again.

Horrified, Brindeisener put the pages aside. How? Was the tearing up of his unity intervening again already? In vain, he underwent the keenest inquisition to discover the coupling by which these words had smuggled in, these words which, in themselves were not stupid, but were glaring nonsense in the midst of a legal dissertation, and signified a disturbance, no, a proper spiritual blow. Brindeisener worked himself up to find the most shameful, shattering expression for it, sprang up, and ran about the town aimlessly for a few hours as if possessed, until he had calmed down so far as to consider the incident to be an "interruption of the logical functions" resulting from overwork. Though there was something concealed within him that was not at peace with it, Brindeisener decided to look on the case thus, rewrote the section with the omission of the derailment, and when everything was finished, it occurred to him that he had dealt with this question like a formal legal process against himself, and he fell into an almost frolicsome cheerfulness over it.

In an elevated mood, the semester passed him by, and he happily travelled back to his home, looking forward in silence to the surprise which his unexpected appearance would have to give Helene, for he had left the day of his arrival uncertain. He wanted to approach the yard gate in the depth of evening, and to sing the "serenade" by Strachwitz in Mendelssohn's composition through the darkness over the boundary path across to the lime tree by her window, that romantically passionate song which begins with the words, "How I would like to sing at your feet my deepest song."

He hummed the melody during the entire journey, and was thereby only the hungrier for loud, intoxicating singing, so that, during the changeover in Haltern, he could not control himself anymore at the sight of a pretty young girl, but loudly exulted, "Your beau—tiful head ro—ocks in ste—ep, your heart listens quietly." It spun people's heads to the massive man, who, blaring over everyone, sang so that the wooden hall hummed, and he fell into dancing steps at the same time. A few thought he was crazy, others that he was mad with drink, most rejoiced over the gigantic blond enthusiast. In alighting at Bocholt, his cheerful exultation certainly was in danger of being upset like a popped cork. For there he met his brother Jakob with the carriage which had come to fetch him and his things. The forty year old was crouching like a weathered old man on the seat of the half-covered carriage, and turned to him his dulled, red stubbled face as he stepped up to the carriage with his luggage. From the mumbled welcome and the bash-ful smile, Peter realised that he was already somewhat drunk again. God, and how the carriage, horse, and har-ness looked! The undercarriage covered in muck, here and there the seagrass of the upholstery was spurting out of the torn seat, the little steed was as thin and un-groomed as a long-haired farm dog, tethers instead of reins, the harness tied together here and there. The stu-dent thanked heaven that it was already dark, for, as slowly as the journey went, they could thus go through Hemsterhus unrecognised by night. With a loud cry, Jakob started from his dozing, shouted at the horse, lashed his whip along its back, and then the cart lurched and rattled away to the forest which stood veiled and black behind the level fields.

Peter leant back in his seat with his eyes shut, as if he could thereby escape the dismal images of the decline of his family, and gathered every force to not succumb to these unpromising, bitter feelings. "Whereas the golden twilight looks through the arched window", he hummed to himself from the song which had just inspired him so. But the intoxicating words had no power anymore, and when he opened his eyes, he saw the pines of the forest to the left and right moving past like an endless funeral cortege in the mist.

Thus it continued for three quarters of an hour. The forest must have soon come to an end. Then Jakob stopped, clambered circuitously and uncertainly from the carriage, toddled about, and, after futile searching, slapped off the water on the front wheel of the carriage. Then he laughed out cheerfully, approached his brother, shook him by the arm, and began complaining about his misery, life on the farm, and above all about old Brindeisener, his father. He talked growling, doggedly, and with mocking derision, broke off, walked around the horse to his seat as if he wanted to climb up and drive away, but turned back each time, and began anew. Peter saw that he was in a state in which any brusque word would have to make him wild. Hence, he laughed obligingly between the snatches of his endless litany so as to keep him in a good mood, and reminded him in addition wittily, but sparingly, now and again, to think of driving on. But he thereby achieved only the one thing, that Jakob became firstly quite high-spirited, and now began babbling away in colourful confusion about the Sintlinger farm, the blessed farmer, and little Lena — and that Peter had made a fortune in opening her eyes, for there was money at the Sintlinger farm like manure, and the blind girl, since she was seeing, was no longer recognisable, cheerful, plump, healthy, laughing in spades, dancing to every barrel-organ, in short, a girl of whom it was no longer believed that she had once been a saint and had bewitched people. Certainly, the pure quiet nonsense was riding Sintlinger. But she, the farmwife, was a splendid woman, like they are in books.

"And now, my dear Peter", he said finally, "I think, we will sign off. No? Now, do you know something? Now we are driving straight to the Hemsterhus tavern. There you will plonk down for me a tidy one in thanks that I have told you how it is. For we must celebrate seeing each other again. Yes. Pst! And there you shall see who is still there. Hey, I tell you. Dammit! The landlady died. Now little Mathinka Meixner is there, and runs the business ... runs the business ..." He broke out into such a mocking laughter that he could no longer speak.

"Good", Peter said drily, "understood. So onward! But I will drive the last bit. Sit yourself down in the back, and play the gentleman."

Laughing and delightedly slapping his brother on the shoulder, Jakob assented, and as the exchange of places was completed, he continued babbling constantly about what a bust Mathinka had, how she appeared in such a way that the men were right mad on her, the tavern was never empty because of her, not perhaps of farmers, but of fine townsfolk, even the County Commissioner ...

Then Peter drove off with a passionate jolt. It tore the words right out of Jakob's mouth. He leant back, and had fallen asleep after a few minutes.

When he awoke, Peter was driving straight up the hill to the Brindeisener farmstead.

Jakob roared, "Stop!", and because that did not work, he sprang out of the carriage, and ran back to Hemsterhus. But Peter was detained by his father until deep in the night. In the light of the unshaded lamp with the soft red light, he sat opposite the ancient man, who had taken it into his head to disclose to his son everything that had depressed him for a long time, and that he had been pondering for weeks. And thus he talked, without looking once at Peter, monotonously, querulously, as was his way, his head inclined to the tabletop, as if he were mumbling to himself all alone prior to dozing off all the displeasure of his joyless existence. And when he had thus spoken for a long time and in-depth, as though half asleep in high senility, he straightened up with a groan, pushed the lamp on the table away from himself, and sniffed in pain so that Peter thought his father was succumbing to a stroke. But as he looked up, he looked into a face disfigured by despair, ashen, and the half extinguished eyes were smouldering with dismay. That is why he seized his arm, and shook him fearfully.

The old man pushed him away with his hand, and smiled derisively. "You must know, Peter", he then said softly, and looked around the room cautiously, "must know. Yes. Hm. How long will your studies continue until you are finished and no longer need any money?"

"Two years, I think, that is ...", Peter answered.

"Two years? Hm. Yes. Haha! It will actually take everything of ours, you understand. It is consuming us. Scandalous. It is everything. I cannot give anymore."

He forced it out torturously, lumbered up apprehensively, and stepped across the room, away from the table, into the dark. There he blew his breath a few times noisily at the floorboards, as if wheezing himself out of an excessive effort. Then he said softly, without looking at his son, "Then it is simply the only salvation, that you — ah — ah — put the books aside, study half a year to become a farmer, marry the Sintlinger girl, and throw the two properties together. That way we would all be free of the burden." Then he squinted over to see what impression it had made on Peter. He had propped his head in his hands, was staring at the tabletop, and could not stir himself.

Old Brindeisener waited a while yet. But when Peter still did not answer, he interpreted that as silent obstructiveness, struck his right hand on his thigh, and then said, smiling mockingly, "Haha! That is my opinion. Do now what you will." At that, he left the room, and toddled to his bedroom.

After a long time, Peter started as if waking from a desolate sleep, looked around worried to see whether anyone was still in the room, extinguished the lamp, and walked slowly and softly out before the farmstead to the place from where he had wanted to sing the song to Helene.

The Sintlinger farmstead lay soundless and peaceful in the darkness near midnight. The sky was hazy. Only a solitary star sometimes shimmered through. It seemed to Peter to be directly over the large lime tree before Helene's window. Then such an aching violence of love overwhelmed him that he thought he could now sing out loudly anyway. But he succeeded only in whispering timidly, "How I would like to sing at your feet my deepest song." The song itself lay in his chest like a dead knot.

He went up to his room, lay down on his bed, and looked numbly out into the night. Then he felt that the tears were about to run soundlessly down his cheeks. He clenched his teeth to secure himself against that. In this fending off of weakness, the thought pushed itself into his consciousness against his will that if little Mathinka Meixner had come back, as his brother had said, the girl in Breslau that time had perhaps been none other than she herself. He refused to accept this absurd idea. Only, it returned a few more times in varied images. During all this, he continued crying silently and unrelentingly.

13

If men knew the mysterious manner by which their lives must obey from within the laws of the universe, just like a tree, a river, or an animal, and that they were interwoven in exactly the same way with the existence of other men, then they would not look on it anymore so reluctantly that the true, decisive events are not those external, noisy incidents of earthly fate, those victories and defeats which fall to mind with jubilation and tears, but movements of our inner being, noiseless as the flight of light and shadow, and inexorable like affinity

and gravity; that a fate is decided long ago when it
manifests itself, just as blossom and rot can manifest
themselves first as a result of ripeness and decay, and as
no echo can arise without a preceding sound. But, since
men hold the forms of their sensual perceptions to be
the essence of experienced facts, from there stirs every
pain, every disappointment, every despair on earth. For
when the bells of external fate ring, most men do not
know anymore that they tolled them, or when.

When Peter Brindeisener arose the next morning, a
change had taken place within him which he did not
comprehend. He felt physically battered, as if he had
wandered through abysses in his sleep to the last drop
of his strength, and though his mood was not sombre, it
was completely empty and powerless. He pushed his
breakfast away after a few bites, and walked across the
deteriorating yard, through the unkempt fields into the
Royal Arenberg forest to the place by the Hornwasser
where he had once been driven as a boy by the fear over
his sister Amalie's death. There he threw himself down
in the soft grass of the forest, and stared at the little
stream driving its waves soundlessly, like liquid glass,
over the stones. And he had not lain for long when, in
looking at the noiseless streaming past of the little water
course, the memory came to him that the knowledge of
death had attacked him as a choking in the chest at the
time when he had seen the circles which had been created over the still, mirrored surface after the sinking of
the stone he had thrown in. The memory of it was so
distinct that he felt the same knotting of suppressed
sobs in his throat as he had at the time. And while he
was astonished over this play of his inner being, he
spoke, as though in explanation of those events over
which he possessed no power, the words which had
thrust themselves into his last legal dissertation, "In
general, no drowning man senses the water which cov-

ers him, and thus you do not feel anymore the death which you die." In fear, he stood up, leant against a tree and thought of how the evening before he had had to cry unrelentingly against his will. At the same time, that conversation with his father occurred to him, of the impending collapse of their existence, the corruption of his brother, and the advice of his father to rescue everyone from destruction through marrying little Lena. And now he realised the reason for his unearthly sadness. He stared numbly into this darkness.

Finally he awoke from the sinking, gazed through the tops of the forest trees at the sky, seeking help, and looked sorrowful after he had delved for a long time into the blue specks of ether. "Of course", he said dully, "everything is thereby finally shattered. Everything. Everything. Everything." He slowly set himself in motion, and whilst the crying was again choking in his throat, he hummed softly, "How I would like to sing at your feet my deepest song." With that, cold shivers ran over his body so that he had to break off the despairing singing.

Without knowing where he was wandering, he came out of the Hornwasser's hollow and up over a hill, and arrived on a forest path which he knew led back to the farmstead and opened shortly before the end of the forest onto the newly constructed road. He walked back along it, and soon stood under the last trees, below him the Sintlinger farm and his father's property. The blessed farmer's fields lay in the light of the high morning sun. A gentle breeze was driving the almost harvest-ready expanses of grain up and down in fertile waves. The field margins lay like green boards in between. It was a peaceful, efficiently managed, lovingly fostered prosperity, and the Sintlinger farm, with the aged brown wood of the massive side of its barn, the long row of stalls, and the towering house, stood proud and certain on its hilltop, and the flickering of the full light gave the scent of a heavenly shimmer about its heavy, high thatched rooves.

He hardly dared look at his father's fields, for the blessing sun which had brought the abundance to full development over here, had passed there like searing vermin grub through the furrows so that the crops wasted away towards the harvest, meagre, emaciated, as if overcome by disease. His brother was mowing grass in a forest meadow, and a little maid was scraping to-gether the scarce whiskers of green fodder. And as he took in with one look all the neglect about his father's farmstead, that giant, collapsing, brown puffball, the bitter knowledge came to him that his years of un-bridled enjoyment of learning were at fault for this irretrievable decline. However, if he yielded to his father's foolish thoughts, and really misused his heav-enly love for Helene to marry her, then he felt he would not raise his decaying relatives from the current of their foundering, but would pull himself and the wondrous girl with him into the morose dissolution. Just as he pondered this, he heard a shrill, laughing cry from the forest meadow, and saw how his brother, who was prob-ably still half drunk from the night-long drinking session, threw aside the scythe, and sprang at the maid, who let the load of grass fall from her arms, and fled into the forest, Jakob in avid leaps behind her.

Although he knew that there was no sense in it, be-cause the distance was too great, he shouted a curse indignantly at him, and then listened with held breath in the stillness of the sunlit peace. No sound could be heard, and after a while, he saw the maid plunge out of the forest at another place, and rush at a hurried run to the Brindeisener farmstead. If a spark of hope had still glimmered of rescuing himself and his love in the sunny light of his soul, then it was all extinguished in him by this incident. He sat down where he stood under the tree, and lapsed into brooding about what would happen now if he went straight down to the farmstead of his parents, and, without having seen Helene, went away, or if he begrudged himself one last wistfully beautiful get-together with her so as to possess forever a blissful shimmer over the difficult, hard life which now arose for him, a shimmer in which he could walk erect.

The sun climbed higher and higher, the midday bells of the villages all around hummed sleepily in the humidity, from the Hemsterhus tower it struck one — Peter Brindeisener sat and pondered, and could not come to a decision in himself. Then, when he had once again whirled to a resolution, and lifted his face for a blinking, shaded gaze over the undulating hills below him, he saw Helene arm in arm with her mother, probably after the midday meal, stepping out from the yard for a short walk in the fields. She had a flower-patterned housecoat on, a green embroidered apron tied in front, and wore around her neck a broad, white collar. Her blond hair blossomed like a pale golden crown about her head. Now and then, she released her arm from her mother's in leisurely wandering, and bent down for a flower on the edge of the path which she showed to her mother for appreciating. At the pear tree below the high butte, he heard her laughing loudly, and saw how she endeavoured to embrace her mother. When the farm-wife, however, cheerfully fended her off, she began throwing her arms about, dancing down the path alone amidst jubilant singing, so that her skirts flew until she sat, with a high-pitched whoop of happy exhaustion, falling almost onto the grass of the slope.

Peter Brindeisener devoured with thirsty eyes that picture of youthful intoxication with life. His gloom vanished as if melted away by a glowing, darting flame.

When the two had returned to the farmstead, he still sat with hammering pulse, and the entire world hung as a flickering veil before his eyes. Finally he composed himself, and sprang to his feet amidst mockingly exuberant laughter. These weeks of holiday should pass over him as a blessing on the arm of his angel. Then come what may, come what must. Thank God, he was still called Peter Brindeisener and not Peter Cadaver.

Waving his hat in the air, he sang defiantly, "today is today", and strode straight up the new road to his father's farmstead.

And thus began weeks of love for the children of both the estranged farmsteads, weeks which resembled entirely the harvests of that year in which they fell. An intoxication of abundance with fervour and high sun, days full of flickering light, and nights of dreamily blue starry reverie.

During the day, each, Peter as well as little Lena, worked together in the fields with the harvest, the student keen and devoted, as if it were really a case of him taking the first steps from the books into the farmer's existence according to his father's advice; little Lena full of happiness and delight, as if it were all not work, but just a game that offered her the opportunity to sing from the fields over the boundary path to her beloved, or to wave down from the high harvest carts with her colourful headscarf like a flag of joy, or to sit still for moments and watch him going to and fro over in the flickering sun by the forest like a dreamlike, unreal being. In the evening, they then sat joking and laughing either next to each other on the little bench by the gate under the lime tree, or in the arbour, or they walked up and down the short little path of the flower garden, or lost themselves out in the fields as far as the forest where they stood and looked at the deeply darkening wall of trees, beyond which a happiness had unexpectedly come over them that had begun long before. But, wherever they sat, Sintlinger crouched somewhere, motionless like a stone, furtive as a shadow, averting his gaze and paying no attention; wherever they walked, they caught sight of him on a distant field margin striding aimlessly and pointlessly in deep brooding, unable to be fetched by a call or to be enticed by anything out of his distractedness. And when it happened that Peter Brindeisener sat by the light of the lamp in the living room of Sintlinger's house, the increasingly odd blessed farmer also lingered there self-absorbed to the side, almost without speaking a word. Only when Peter told this and that anecdote from his travels as a student so lustily and floridly that Johanna's full breast just shook in delighted laughter, and little Lena listened with consuming luminous eyes, or let herself sink back with falling eyelids into her previous world, did such an ungovernable stream of sorrowful darkness well up from his deep eyes that everyone became sheepish because nobody knew what was happening in the mysterious man. Little Lena alone always composed herself from this passing depression first, and always in the same way. She sprang up, and fell into childish, precipitous laughter, skipped trilling through the room, and went in exuberant cheerfulness to the door and out of the farmstead; and once, when she had come to the edge of the slope, where she stood and looked out into the tepid night, Helene abruptly let herself fall to the ground, and rolled down the hill in an eruption of madness to Peter's shock. As if seized by inexplicably demonic whirlpools, she vanished amidst singing snorts of laughter into the dark at his feet, and when he sprang after her in consternation, she was coming towards him again from halfway down the slope, running past him as if blind, but turning around after two steps, throwing herself from above onto his chest, and vanishing in a rush and amidst blissful laughter into the farmstead as if led away by the night.

But as the days passed, the fields emptied, the fervour crackled in the still air, and the nights still brewed heat, this blaze came over Helene more and more often. And Peter Brindeisener sacrificed himself willingly to the intoxication filling her. They often strolled all day through the forests, for Johanna, Sintlinger's wife, had lost all worry over her daughter being by the side of the student, so that she never thought of imposing herself or another person on the couple as a chaperone, probably from the instinct that little Lena was protected enough in the blessed child-like state of her being.

Thus they could both dance to their hearts' content until deep in the night, wherever in the surrounding areas a worthy opportunity offered itself. On the second Sunday of the holidays, they drove to a garden concert which a military band was giving at the forest mill, and revelled with the group they were attached to until close to midnight through the large, brightly lit hall. In the third week, they enjoyed themselves at the festival of St Rochus in Dingden. They visited the county seat, and travelled by ship for a bit on the Rhine. And Helene, who was seeing, experiencing, and enjoying all that for the first time, did not emerge at all from her delight and elevated happiness. Sometimes she was entirely a brilliant white fire, full of ungovernable delight, sometimes she acted airily colourful and fussing like a little bird around Peter, and then quiet hours came over her again, as if she were still strolling in the light of her otherworldly eyes, and Brindeisener trembled in a love which made him ache as if in despair.

Then it happened that, in the middle of laughter and the play of joyfulness, he was beset by a dark spirit. In particular, when they returned from a pleasure trip or a drive, before parting, his being often changed so that he let her arm drop in shock, or even stepped back from her, looked at her achingly, and struggled with himself, as if he were battling to conceal something hard and bitter from her that could not be spared her in the end. "Little Lena", he said towards the end of the period once, "little Lena, I don't understand you. You must see it, though. I don't believe it." And when the dear child urged him in fright to tell her what it was, that she did not know what he meant, Peter shouted out her name in aching happiness, and lifted her up as if he had to throw her back into the heaven from whence she came. On this day, it also happened that Helene, after she had come back to earth again, was walking numbly and swaying next to Peter, with eyes closed as if she had become blind again. Timidly, uncertainly, on shaking feet, she strolled by herself as if she were entirely alone. At Peter's question about what she was thinking, she began talking with a completely altered voice, so quietly that he could not understand a word and yet was seized by it in a frightfully deep manner.

And when he strode into his father's farmstead, and then lay in bed with the window open, this sylph-like talk of little Lena's was in the sound of the night breeze skimming over the roof, in the purring of the trees, yes even in the pale haze of the moon which fell through the window onto the floor. It was so deep and entirely within that he could not withstand his listening anymore, stood up, half dressed, leant out the window for a while, and then strode up and down his room soundlessly in bare feet. He had to disentangle himself from her. He could not bear it anymore. It was tearing him up. It seemed as if he were rising and falling at the same time. What use was it to him to hold forcibly onto this unreal dream any longer? But when he just imagined that he was leaving, he felt the breath draining from his chest and his heart standing still. The entire world was

extinguished. His existence lay there like forgotten rubbish to which he was returning in order to sustain
himself again from it.

Thus he struggled until the grey of morning. Then he
sat tired and shivering on the edge of his bed, looked at
his feet, spread his toes apart, and said dully, "God is
destroying me. God is destroying me."

When it had become quite light, he rose stiffly,
sighed heavily, and stretched his arms with closed fists
behind him. At the same time, he said slowly, "Then I
must just go away through the dark door ... go away ...
into my night."

At that he threw himself, as he was, onto his bed,
burrowed into it, and fell asleep like after a punch to the
head.

But strangely, after this argument with himself, a
fierce, wild fire broke out with Peter. His cheerfulness
was like a volcanic eruption, he walked along as if he
were devouring the earth with his steps, danced as if he
wanted to destroy little Lena, laughed a rattling laugh,
and his pale blue eyes flashed. On excursions, he began
to feast, and comforted his father over the frequent
spending that it would not take much longer until he
held Helene in every way. But as long as he did not yet
have certainty, money could be no object to him. Little
Lena Sintlinger was often fearful, and sat despondently
with her eyes closed during the seething of his delight.
Sintlinger shunned him when he could, and did not let
himself be seen in the house anymore whenever Peter
lingered for a visit in his living room. The farmwife, who
had usually allowed all the pair's colourful pleasure
trips with a happy smile, just held out bravely, at most
so that sometimes a dark astonishment appeared in her
face, and a thoughtful crease even appeared here and
there on her forehead. She heard with satisfaction of
how Peter's holiday would only last another fortnight,

and thought thus that her child should have her longingly awaited delight in peace until the end. The more
so as she noted in Helene's being that the "eternal
sweetness" did not tickle her palate anymore anyway.
Not that the girl betrayed it with her countenance, or
even spoke about it. But she worked more soberly, often
walked through the house again quietly and in contemplation, straightened up in the fields, and sank with
lifeless eyes dreaming into the sky, and once she found
Helene in the garden, enraptured and devoutly kneeling
before a flower on which a butterfly was sunning itself
motionlessly. And when she finally noticed her mother
approaching soundlessly behind her, she looked around
after the flying away of the butterfly with shimmering
eyes, and said softly and sweetly, like in her enchanted
period, "You know, mother, once when I was a still a
little child, I could quite surely talk with the butterflies.
Yes, yes, quite surely." Then she stood up, shaking her
head in amazement, brushed her apron down thoughtfully, walked away from her mother to the place by the
fence where she had been struck to the heart by the first
loving greeting of Peter Brindeisener, and gazed out
into the world. She also began, as she forfeited the delight in her affected behaviour, to lose her pleasure in
garishly colourful dresses, and if it had been down to
her, she would have removed all the flowery, radiantly
ruffled, over-adorned dresses from her wardrobe, and
shrouded herself again in the soft, dull, light colours
and materials for which she had had such a mysterious
affinity during her sightless period. Undoubtedly, the
mocking looks and remarks of Peter had also exercised
an effect with this return of Helene's to the preferences
of a past time. For he had not been able to contain entirely his mockery at the sight of his all too often
garishly colourful and rustically adorned Helene, which
was stirred not only by the injuries to his taste, but

more from the bitterness over himself and his entire life. But the blessed hill's girl, to whom the power of her inner vision was returning again more and more, had certainly taken a hit through these small displeasures with her of her beloved, not just to her feminine vanity, but much deeper in the region of her soul where we perceive the darkening of a person's being before we distinctly understand it. Some sorrow smouldered about her Peter, a jarring note shrilled from him, a clenching and balling ran out from him, and often drew like a shadowy mist behind his radiantly loud cheerfulness. She was experiencing it in the visionary power of her all-seeing soul, and was unable to bring herself from fear and apprehension to ask him or her mother about it. She was often beset in the solitude of her quiet moments by a helplessness so that she looked down inquiringly into herself to figure out what was happening within herself, or, in the middle of her sleepless nights, she grasped her left hand with her right, placed her head on her bare arm, and, at the same time fervently and imploringly, said his name quietly to herself, "Peter! — Peter!!" During that time, the County Commissioner Zwinin vanished from his post because of serious lapses from want of moral discipline, and even if his secret flight had occurred previously and already been discussed in the district, the first news of it now caught the ear of the Sintlinger girl, who was certainly beset again by the memory of the taint which the contact with this degenerate man had inflicted on her on the day of the road's official opening. Moreover, after the disappearance of the desperate man, as if it were possible in no other way, a cloud of rumours arose about people of the district who indulged in secret in the same want of moral discipline as this monster. That the name of Jakob Brindeisener, Peter's brother, was also tattled and with good reason, did not excite any wonder, and when one day the little maid left the Brindeisener farmstead after an angry scene, it was said that she had been overpowered by the dull, unsociable blockhead, Jakob, and was going away to send the authorities for his neck because of it.

All this, which only brewed vaguely and distantly around the blessed hill's girl, weighed down the air of helplessness, uncertain apprehension, and dark foreboding by which she felt herself enclosed even without this. And when she was once again struggling against the shadowy shroud which was sinking over her soul wherever she liked to look, she heard the anxious buzzing of a fly next to her scurrying through the air, and was so startled by it that she felt her legs go weak, and had to sit down on a chair. It happened in her room. The deep evening penetrated as a grey seething through the open window. Except for a few birds, which were seeking with quiet, high peeps for a place to sleep in the crown of the lime tree, not a sound stirred in nature. Helene looked around herself, and then sat there motionless with her eyes closed in an inexplicably avid fear and listened, almost with skipping heart, for whether the buzzing would repeat. It not only remained still, but slowly the room, the crown of the lime tree, the entire farmstead, yes even the world outside was seized by a burdensome faltering. And when this expiration around her had reached its highest degree, the blessed hill's girl saw with lowered eyelids herself fleeing across the fields to the forest on the morning of that day in which her lover and the light of her eyes had been gifted to her. She saw herself holding in her hand in shock the lark which had fallen dead out of the air, and heard, just like now, the anxiously fervent buzzing of a fly by her ear, enraptured. Helene experienced all that glaringly right down to every detail, and then saw herself stumbling further in a rush across the fields until she crested the road embankment on hands and knees. At this point, the inner series of pictures was extinguished. Helene opened her eyes and looked around herself in her room which was almost dark as night. Then she stood up from her chair, and walked in a sort of dream-like directness diagonally across the room to the wardrobe. Then it occurred to her that mayflies have in people's opinion an especially fervent buzz to themselves. But now the dismay had entirely vanished from her. She opened the wardrobe, and as she felt her dresses in order precisely with her hands, she remembered yet having worn that decisive day a delicately light, especially soft muslin dress. At that, she left the wardrobe standing open, returned to her chair, and lapsed into a contemplation which was more like deep acceptance. When she awoke from it, it had become quite deep in the night. "Who knows?", she said softly to herself, stepped to the window, and clutched at the moist, smooth leaves of the lime tree. "Who knows?", she said at the same time softly to herself. "Peter goes to Münster again in eight days. I just want to have made exactly such a delicate light-blue, simple dress as I wore that time when he gave me the gift of vision in the forest. With that, I will surprise him in parting.

I also want to have my hair combed exactly the same. Everything shall be like that time. Then perhaps his cheerfulness will become more active again when he sees that I want to be entirely like I was before. And everything that has turned dark since then in the world, in my father, in Peter, and also in me, everything, everything, everything will then lapse back again."

She closed her eyes, and did not open them anymore during all that was still to be done. As if she were the blind girl again, she pulled the covers down on the bed, undressed, walked through the room, bolted the door, and lay with lowered eyelids until sleep had led her from the world.

Hardly had the grey dissolved into the first light the next morning than Helene went, in short skirt and dressing gown, quietly shivering from the cold, to the bed of her mother, to her great surprise, and after she had wished her a good morning with an infinitely soft kiss, she began without any rationale, as is the way of children, to speak about things which had intruded on her the previous evening in such a strange way. She talked so emotionally, so delicately of the necessity of instantly, no, today at least, possessing a new dress be-fore the week just beginning came to an end, so that the farmwife, who had been listening until now whilst lying down, half sat up with smiling astonishment, brushed her hair from her forehead with her free hand, and said in kindly reproach, "Oh go, little Lena, because such a thing does not get someone out of bed at the first cock's crow. I think you have not finished your night's sleep yet." For really, the eyes of the blessed hill's girl had an exhausted shimmer, and they filled with moisture at her mother's partial refusal. Thus the two lingered a while in wordless opposition, the farmwife still shaking her head with astonishment, little Lena with lowered face, helplessly plucking at her fingers. All of a sudden, how-ever, the girl was torn from her stooped pose, embraced her mother fervently, and, her head buried in her breast, she repeated amidst sobs the request for a delic-ate light-blue, simple dress like she had once owned. During all that loving back and forth, Helene let slip against her will a series of remarks, by which Johanna figured out who had given the impetus for little Lena's fervent commotion and foolish plan. But she did not let anything of this insight be noticed, instead asking the girl amidst caresses to calm down. It would be followed up in all respects according to her wishes, and if a horse was free, she could herself travel this morning to the dressmaker in Bocholt, and see to everything as she wished. She only tied one condition to it, to not think on this trip of meeting with Peter Brindeisener, because in the past few days so many irksome incidents had happened at that farm, with the maid and Jakob, rows and all sorts of conflict, that it would also be good for the people's sake to exercise a certain restraint. Yes, she thought, it would have to be painful for Peter himself to confront her under these circumstances. For it had attracted her attention as well that he had not been seen for a few days.

The blessed hill's girl had, plucking at her fingers again, listened attentively to her mother, and when she now fell silent, Helene stood up from the edge of the bed where she had been sitting, nodded her head in agreement, with large, thoughtful eyes and a distant earnesty, and then quietly said nothing except, "Thank you, mother dear", kissed her fleetingly on the mouth, and vanished noiselessly like an apparition from the room so that Johanna had to gaze after her for a long time. But the workday at the Sintlinger farmstead had already been divided up, no team could be dispensed with in the early hours, and so little Lena had to be patient until after midday, when the horses were fed. Then she would be driven by Gottlieb over to Bocholt — Johanna had thought up this accompaniment for Helene because the secret antipathy of Meixner towards Peter Brindeisener would guarantee her safety from something which she could not name.

Helene proceeded with the sorting out of the entire affair with a gentle, implacable stubbornness, and found in her father, Sintlinger, a tangible support against all the hindrances which the farmwife knew how to apply inconspicuously. At the same time, the blessed farmer did not step out from the darkness and taciturnity which was burdening him, just sat listening at the table, let his large, dark eyes slowly go from wife to daughter and back again, pressed his emaciated hands together, and then propped his head up contemplatively again. In the end, he reached across the table, seized little Lena's hand, and cried in an outburst of love, "Child, dear child, okay! You may go at one o'clock then." At the same time, his careworn face beamed for the first time in many months so brightly that little Lena's shyness before her increasingly oddly behaving father instantly vanished completely. She sprang up, embraced him, and kissed him on the eyes, forehead, and mouth. In a storm of tenderness, she asked her "dearest father", "the best in all the world", for forgiveness for everything which she had done to him, in short, she was so flustered and gripped that the blessed farmer became quite taken aback and bewildered. Then she went, already dressed for departure, with him into the fields, and the two spent an unforgettable hour under the high sun of the cloudless late summer sky in a unity which ran together from their depths like the way it had been for them only in the most beautiful moments of their enchantedly blessed past. Helene was entirely the rapturous, blessed hill's girl from before, and did not let her hand leave his the entire time.

In the hallway of the house, she parted from him, and went to her room to deal with a few things before her departure. As she slowly climbed the stairs, what her mother had said about the unpleasant events on the Brindeisener farm occurred to her, and that Peter would certainly be suffering a lot amidst these nasty incidents. It was not enough though to wait until the day of departure to help him, and to set his hopes and joyful confidence right again. By then something, perhaps something even darker, could happen, and she would then bear the guilt, because she, cowardly and faint-heartedly, only because of other people, had left him alone with his anguish. What did she care about the gossip of people when it involved Peter's happiness and their love! And even mother would not in truth be angry if she did not keep her promise, when to hold it meant something worse than to break it. Thus, arriving in her room, she wrote a short letter in which Peter was asked to step by chance from the forest onto the road at four o'clock in the afternoon between Bocholt and Hemsterhus by the split pine — a tree well known across the entire district. Someone would be travelling past at this time who needed to speak with him.

She sent this letter with a dairymaid, on whom she had impressed attentiveness and silence, across to the Brindeisener farmstead. Then she carried on actively and with relief the preparations for her departure, and accepted from her mother a series of orders for procurement in Hemsterhus. At one o'clock, Gottlieb drove her in a light half-seater down the hill. The Brindeisener farmstead lay dilapidated and morose in the still midday sun, secluded, as if all life had long since been extinguished in it. Its rotten gate was shut, no face showed at the windows. Helene felt a fear climbing in her, and when they turned from the drive onto the new road, she asked Gottlieb to drive quickly, for it seemed to her as if she would arrive too late. But soon she had to smile over her attack, for overhasty rushing would only have to lead to her coming past the mooted place before the given time, and thereby missing Peter. When they had thus passed through Hemsterhus, and were approaching the forest, she had the gait of the horses moderated, and devoted herself to the magic of the midday stillness of the forest, whose trees moved barely perceptibly in slumbering dream. At the split pine, an anguished jolt went through her, and she had to look back to see if Peter was perhaps already lurking behind the trunk for her. But the place was empty, and Helene leant back in a quiet disappointment, felt herself tiring, closed her eyes, and through a dreamy unease, she constantly heard the great, steady hum of the forest reaching out to her and sounding like the distant swishing of a massive ocean.

She did not find the dressmaker at home, and had to have the dressmaker's elderly mother take the measurements. Disappointed, she again descended the narrow wooden steps. Her heart was aching so much that she had not been able to look into the still, white face of the old woman, and nor could she utter her name. Already on the street, she turned around, hurried hastily back up the steps, opened the door, and said, "Please, Mrs Seiler, tell me, when is Miss Babette coming home?" But she paid no attention to the old woman's explanations, instead standing with heaving breast, and sucking in the rapturous stillness of the overly clean room. Then she walked away hesitantly, and reproached herself for not having sat down for a moment in a chair to enjoy the quiet magic of the dressmaker's room for longer. Even the walk to the draper's was to no avail. They certainly had some muslin in store which was as soft and fine as what she desired. But such a delicate light blue was an odd colour which nobody in the area desired, and hence it could not be obtained. At best, the merchant Stenzel in Dingden might perhaps have such a thing in his store.

The tears entered Helene's eyes as she strode down to the tavern in which Gottlieb had stopped off. She weighed up whether it was not practicable to travel over to Dingden right now, but heard from Meixner that they would have to go back via Hemsterhus, and then barely arrive in Dingden before evening, even if the horse were allowed to step out and not be reined in. Helene passed her hand sorrowfully over her eyes, and strained to find a way around it. But nothing resulted thereby, other than that she only ever saw Peter walking before her, despondent and sorrowful because she could not show him how she really was. And saying everything to him, speaking of all the worries which she carried on his account, no, she could have managed that even a week ago, but now it was no longer possible for her. She rose as if from a paralysis, and saw that the clock had already moved past the third hour. Just a quarter of an hour more, and she must miss Peter in the forest. Gottlieb was startled by the rushing haste with which Helene was seized after her sitting there raptly for so long, pulled the horse from the stable, and barely five minutes later, the vehicle was shooting away with the two of them. The heart of the blessed farm's little Lena was as if filled by hot fly ash thrown up by a burning torch. She saw everything through a grey cloud of dust, Gottlieb, propped back holding the galloping horse's reins firmly, and driving it with cries and cracking whip, the trees drawn up jerking into the sky, rushing past, and she just waited tensely for when the massive, parted crown of the split pine was to be detected over the forest. Meixner must have become suspicious that this tree was connected in some way with the suddenly altered being of Helene. For when the greyish green tip of the pine rose in the distance, he let the steaming horse slow down. But as soon as they came close to it, he rose, shouted, and whipped the animal on so that the dust whirled up again, and the carriage rattled on at a hellish pace. Helene saw how a man suddenly sprang from behind the tree, and ran gesticulating towards the vehicle, she shouted Peter and Gottlieb's names shrilly, and when the latter drove the horse on even more, she made to spring out of the racing vehicle. Then Meixner pulled the animal back with a jerk, and examined, bitter and pale, little Lena who was reproaching him for his senseless driving with a self-conscious voice, and, at the same time, tears in her eyes, a happy smile about her mouth, waving to Peter who was approaching slowly with long strides.

"A mad drive", he said, as he smiled mockingly and approached the carriage, "you could've killed someone. Gottlieb, what came over you then? That was an utter driving into the ground! Hahaha! Hello, little Lena! Yes, yes, pale too, well? Haha!" He offered her his hand, took his hat off, and wiped away the sweat streaming down his face.

Helene looked dismayed at his restive, twitching eyes, his nervous mouth, saw him gnawing his lips with his teeth amidst the mockingly creaking words, and placed her hand distressed on his left hand with which he was holding onto the carriage.

"Won't you step up?" she asked anxiously. He just shook his head. "Or shall we walk together on foot, if you are too hot? Gottlieb can drive ahead slowly, and wait at the Hemsterhus tavern. I still have errands to make in the village."

"Hemsterhus tavern will be good with me", Peter Brindeisener murmured bitterly.

"What did you say, Peter?" Helene asked timidly.

"Oh, it isn't necessary. My dear, just no inconveniencing yourself. It isn't necessary. If we just keep it as it always was. You ride in the carriage, I will walk on foot alongside. That's best. Hence, Gottlieb, forward slowly."

Meixner twitched the horse into motion, and Peter, hand reaching out to the carriage, strode alongside with his body erect.

Helene glanced furtively sometimes at the disturbed man walking darkly next to the carriage without a word, his eyes directed into the distance.

Suddenly he let his hand fall from the carriage, brandished his arm in the air. and began singing with his beautiful voice a student song:

> I'm a journeyman on his way,
> Not having any sorrow,
> A spring refreshes me today,
> Hock does it tomorrow.

"Do you like that, dear little Lena?", he asked after the first verse.

The blessed hill's girl looked at him anxiously.

"Not cheerful, my child? So, so. Well, then, a wistful disc."

And he sang:

> The song is forgotten,
> The wine has gone flat,
> I wander silently and bleakly about ...

But little Lena could not bear the melancholy melody. She cried out distressfully, "For God's sake, Peter, stop! I'll have to die otherwise."

In the house that was Brindeisener life, the windows and doors were already smashed in, but at little Lena's outcry, the dark, wild frenzy with which he was made senseless tore. He looked around in shock, stepped up to the girl who had sunk back, caressed her cheek with his hand, and said shaking, "Poor, dearest little Lena. I cannot help it."

Then he stepped back again, and walked hunched, brooding to himself, next to the carriage until they emerged from the forest and the first rooves of Hemsterhus were to be seen. As they slowly travelled around the corner at which Bocholter Street opened onto the new road, Peter saw through the trees of the garden strip Mathinka Meixner stepping back from the window of the tavern. Then his face was distorted by a bitter spasm. "That too! Now, then closure", shot through his head. He stepped up to the carriage to say goodbye and hurry away. But when he saw that little Lena, reclining in the carriage, pale, distracted, had been startled by his sudden approach, and had smiled at him pitifully, the hardening of his mood left him for a moment, and he could not bring himself to give the wounds another blow with his brusque departure. "Come, dear little Lena", he said softly, "you are quite upset by the excitement. Dear, dear child! Don't be angry with me. However, life is not working out well with me."

They had now arrived before the tavern. But the blessed hill's girl did not stir; she sat motionless as if she did not want to stand up anymore, and just smiled bravely. "Come, we will go in for a moment. Then you can drink a coffee, we can chat as usual, you can relax, and Gottlieb can meanwhile run your errands for you."

"Yes, yes, Peter", she finally answered submissively, "if you think so. It is probably the best."

She rose slowly, and walked to the tavern as if asleep, after having committed her errands to Gottlieb. When she arrived at the door, she said softly, "Dear, Peter, wasn't that little Mathinka, daughter of Elis Meixner from Querhoven?", and at his affirmation, she shook her head sorrowfully. "I feel sorry for the poor girl. She should be so beautiful, and people say so many bad things about her. Don't be hard on her, dear Peter. But come now, I am quite alright again. already" Then Brindeisener opened the door for her, and thought at the same time, "I'm a hound, I'm a hound, an evil one."

The large barroom was completely empty. On several tables, which were assigned for the better visitors, lay clean, red checked cloths. On the walls hung colourful posters — "Drink old Dessauer" — "Dortmund Union" — "Salem Aleikum Gold. Something for Connoisseurs". Peter had grazed little Mathinka with one look on entering, as she stood tall, adorned, and fulsomely behind the bar. But he turned away immediately, said something trivial to little Lena, and read the touts on the walls at the same time. Then he directed her to a rear table. Mathinka Meixner followed with a contemptuous smile the sheepish, timid way in which the blessed hill's girl walked between the tables to her place. After both had taken a seat, she stepped with a provocative, fresh pertness to the table, pushing her abundant, dark hair back with a light motion of her hand, and asked, after an ingratiating preamble with the most winning of smiles, "for the esteemed guests' wishes", quite as if she were lead designer for a large dressmaking business.

Little Lena did not dare to look up at her, but busied herself with her handbag. A red wave passed over Peter Brindeisener's face, and with a fleeting glance, he ordered for Helene a cup of coffee, and for himself a glass of beer and a dozen cigarettes. When the beer stood before him, he grasped the glass, poured half of it down his throat, lit a cigarette, leant back with a weak laugh, and when little Lena, startled by this new outburst, looked up at him, he said loudly, as if in the continuation of an interrupted conversation, "It is indeed all nonsense!" The blessed hill's girl discoloured, grasped his hand, and whispered imploringly, "Be good, dear Peter, be good." But he leant close to her, and began talking passionately and quietly to her, "Look please, little Lena, it is no different, what use is it? Yes, if you do not see the brutal life of the fixed eyes in the visage, I wanted to say face, the fixed eyes without any overlay of feeling, then nothing is of any use, nothing at all. If you want to insist, nothing remains in the end but, like King Solomon, to laughingly call everything utter nonsense."

"And me", little Lena wanted to ask with cramped heart, "and our love?"

But Mathinka Meixner was bringing the coffee, and little Lena grasped the spoon with trembling hand, stirred the black, bitter drink numbly, and drank it in silence. For she had forgotten in her bewilderment to add sugar and cream.

Peter Brindeisener caught a mocking look from little Mathinka, saw her full bust, her slender waist, the beautiful neck, and the passionate eyes, then blanched for a breath, and began talking to Helene again, half irritated and in a rush. He was torn back deeper and deeper into his inner strife, and tore up mockingly, derisively, blithely, like a madman smashes himself bloody, all that was beautiful, blessed, and elevated in his life with an ungovernable voracity. At the same time, he drank intemperately.

Little Mathinka observed the growing agitation of the wild, blond, sinewy man, and the collapsing, inconspicuous little Lena, who sat there helpless and dull, and what had only overshadowed her on the couple's entrance was now seizing her searingly in her breast. That Sintlinger had driven her father to his shameful death, and that this cheesy-pale, stupid girl, little Lena, was at fault for the failure of her first commitment of love to Peter Brindeisener, in that night of flight after the Hemsterhus uproar which had cost her father his life.

An untameable passion, hate and vengeance against the blessed hill's girl seized her, and she burst out into ungovernable mocking laughter.

Then the blessed hill's girl straightened up, closed her eyes for a moment, and then said affectionately and calmly to Peter, "Now I must go, however, and run the errands. Farewell, Peter." She took her handbag, and walked quietly and coolly away.

Rigidly upright, with large, almost horrified eyes, Peter gazed after her, then he propped his head in both his hands, and fell into dark brooding. Now he had wandered out through the dark gate, and the world had slammed shut.

"So, now I can go", he murmured dully. At a sound from the bar, he raised his head heavily, and saw that little Mathinka was smouldering at him with a bewitching ardency and willingness.

"Don't make eyes, little Mathinka", he said in weather-beaten grief, "she is not one like us two. Do you understand? Here we are just two tattered vegetables. Yes, yes!"

Then he turned away, sank into brooding, and continued drinking; but he did not get drunk. In the night, he finally left.

There was a bright moonlight. When he saw the Sintlinger farmstead lying in the cool shimmer on its hill, he sprang over the ditch, and climbed through the orchard towards it.

"Just once I can still act as if I were alive", he pondered, "and sit under the windows of the blessed."

He turned the corner, and sat down on the little bench under the lime tree, in the deep shadows, in a state of complete emptiness.

It blew weakly now and then in the lime tree as if a sleeper were softly emitting a breath. Out in the moonlight, it trembled and flickered as if with soundless insect wings.

Then the window above him was opened, and little Lena leant out. She lingered there without moving, for perhaps half an hour as it seemed to him.

Then she sang softly, almost to herself:

Beautiful is life in happy times,
Beautiful is youth, it comes no more.
That's why I say once more:
Beautiful are the years of youth,
Beautiful is youth, it comes no more.

She sang the entire song as if the moonlight was re-sounding over the world, clearly, blissfully, without anguish, and without shadows.

Then she drew back, and calmly closed the window.

Peter Brindeisener, however, ran away as if chased.

The next morning, forest workers saw a red-silk shawl floating on the pond.

They fished it out, and by that evening, the entire district knew that little Lena Sintlinger had found her death in the water.

14

The pond in which the blessed farm's little Lena sought and found her death was a large, gloomy mirrored surface with brownish water, not far from the boundary of the two estranged farms in the direction of the Rhine, reachable from the forest mill in barely half an hour. It was the receptacle for a strong stream which, without finding a visible discharge, poured into it. In the middle of the water, a weak, funneling circling had always quivered here and there, from which it was ascertained that the stream discharged into the interior of the earth there, losing itself in subterranean hollows

and gorges, or, as a few suggested, wandering mysteriously, deep under the earth, in enigmatic ways to join
the great current of the Rhine.

Amidst the common folk, the legend went that the
pond never gave up again what it had once grasped in
its quiet, uncanny whirlpool. And so it happened in fact
with Helene Sintlinger, who had fled into it from this
earth's inextricable puzzles.

That same day on which the misfortune happened,
the Querhoveners hurried over with rods, nets, and long
hooks, and began, supported by the labourers from
Sintlinger's farm, to search through every corner, every
crevice of the dark water, to turn every stone, and to
rake under every tree root, in order to yet provide the
blessed farm's little Lena a dry grave.

However, it was in vain, and when they were keeping
vigil on the evening of the third day, standing with pale
faces by the bank, and discussing whether to risk the
last possibility and venture into the middle, into the
deadly whirl of the vortex, or to desist entirely, because
it looked as if it were God's will that the girl's body had
been withdrawn from everyone's sight, when the Querhoven men stood in the light of the sinking sun and
looked with helpless wistfulness into the water, the
weaver Staupitz, who was leading them, had a vision.
He gazed through the clear water to the bottom of the
pond, and there he at once saw little Lena physically lying there, not chalky, bloated, and corpse-like, but in a
living, blissful peace, as if she had not died at all, but
were just sleeping. The reflection of the radiant blue of
the sky was spread like a bulging bed under her. The
blessed farm's little Lena lay down there thus, and yet
also up above, torn away by the vortex, and yet hidden
in a blessedness which seemed more glorious than the
beauty of the earthly heavens above them. The men
marveled with almost skipping breath at the trans-

figured little Lena, until the wondrous image became paler and paler, and finally vanished into the depths of the pond.

The Querhoveners went that same evening to the blessed farm, and told of the circumstances under which they had seen little Lena again. Then they returned to Querhoven, declared that puzzling apparition before their religious eyes to be a sign from God, and stopped looking for the vanished girl. Soon the conviction also spread from the village of poor skewer makers and spigot turners that little Lena Sintlinger had been been transported through the water directly to heaven without having to taste death, and whoever had a pure heart could see her lying in a heavenly cloud at the bottom of the pond.

Although the Hemsterhus Pastor, Dr Spiller, campaigned with all his means against this glorification of suicide, considering it a devilish trace of heretical superstition, more and more people saw little Lena Sintlinger lying transfigured in the water, and on some nights, a pale radiance was seen in the place where the red silk shawl had been found, like a shimmer of otherworldly stars hovering over the dark pond in such a way that people really began to consider Helene to be a saint.

The entire district was very gripped by the fate which had passed over the Sintlingers' farm, and everyone felt both shaken and raised up from the depths of their souls.

Even the farsighted flower collector, Georg Hunatay from Schmalenbach, appeared by the pond, despite his old age, arduously walking on two sticks. For this martyr to the purest love wanted, before his end, which he felt to be close, to see at least once the transfigured, unearthly apparition of a being who had been failed by love in this life like he had, but yet had been raised into a blessedness after death, which his pilgrimages on earth had sought for in vain. Thus he sat for hour after hour by the banks of the dark, eerie water, and invoked the image of the transported blessed girl with quiet singing and sorrowful words of fuzzy profundity. He called out incessantly to her, and threw flowers into the water at the same time, until the surface of the pond looked like a single flowering meadow. It was all in vain. Little Lena Sintlinger did not appear to him, neither as a shimmering image during the day, nor as an other-worldly radiance in the dark of night. And thus he returned to Schmalenbach, sobbing to himself sorrow-fully, locked up his house behind himself, and from then on did not let himself be seen by anyone anymore.

The Sintlinger farm, however, was veiled in impenet-rable night by the fate which had befallen it. The farmwife was like a bush which had been constantly torn apart by a storm, had been shattered, and yet could not die away, had lost all its leaves and yet did not die. But, when the horrid death of her only child was raised by the pious faith of the Querhoveners and the emotion of the entire district to a blessed miracle in heaven, the anguish was also transformed in her soul. One day she emerged from the self-absorption of sorrow as if from a graceful touch by God, and it was given to her that Helene's existence, as if placed between the most dis-tant stars in the universe, really began to look like a holy affair of heaven's. For she recognised more and more clearly in Helene's life and death the guidance of divine will, and that the early, horrid end of her child signified the only salvation from the life full of misfortune which would have been bestowed on her alongside Peter Brindeisener.

Only, that would perhaps have not yet sufficed for her to escape the destruction of the horror. But when she had first wrestled her eyes from the night, she saw the state of her beloved Andreas, whom everyone still

called the blessed farmer. She would never tolerate anguish and sorrow overwhelming her anymore then. No
words came from his lips, no look from his eyes. When
he lay down, he did not sleep, and when he moved, he
was like someone dead. His farm, his life, the world, and
all men, nothing was there for him anymore.

Soon after getting up, he took himself to the edge of
the Sintlinger hill. There he stood, lay, or crouched until
night, and looked with unmoving eyes and clenched
mouth over the boundary path at the Brindeisener
farmstead in which the ancient farmer still lived alone.

Why he stared at the estranged farmstead day in, day
out was not to be wrestled out of him. But it will surely
have been a hate which was so boundless that it impelled Sintlinger in constant numbness to view this
presence, from which he assumed, in the constitution of
his being at the time, that all the misfortune of his family and the disintegration of his own life stirred from
that giant hovel of rubbish which the Brindeisener
farmstead had become.

One evening, Sintlinger stood again before his gate
and waited for what he had already experienced and
suffered a thousand times to happen. Then he saw old
Brindeisener creep from the farmstead looking exactly
like a monstrous, rotten, enormous heap. The geriatric
estranged farmer, now already far past ninety years of
age, walked in a stoop so that his long, down-hanging
arms almost touched the ground with their fingertips,
and he looked more like an ancient large animal than a
man. Sometimes he paused, sniffed the air suspiciously,
like a flushed piece of game, and then sank into the pot-
tering which had always led him around the farmstead
at nightfall since he lived all alone, because his oldest
son Jakob sat in prison, Peter had gone away somewhere with Mathinka Meixner, and his wife had been

lost to him in death many, many years before, he did not know when, like a forgotten dog.

Here he grasped at a half-rotten cart, there he tried to stick a weathered wheel on a collapsed wagon. He pressed dangling fence battens against nail stumps so that they could pass for fixed until the next gust of wind. With a half-handled pitchfork, he began to push about a heap of rubbish, rattled piles of junk, laughed mockingly, fell into a rage, began swearing with a squeaky tearful voice, and then moderated it again into a monotonous, deep grumbling, as if it were only an endless passage in which a caught wind was fretfully seeking a way out. And like every evening, he finally started, saw Sintlinger over there in the darkness standing on the hill and staring, walked to a bowed apple tree, drew his hunched body up arduously, laughed shrilly, and then shouted, "Good evening, Andreas! Andreas, where are you? Hahaha!"

And when Sintlinger as always remained silent, he continued in his mockery, "Aha, the Holy Ghost got into your head again! Hey, you booze sniffer! Accursed breeder of whores! Corpse father!"

Thus the blustering continued, and became more and more ghastly, until Sintlinger could not tolerate it anymore, broke away violently, and hurried into the farmstead.

The old estranged farmer raged for a while yet, and finally crept somewhere through a gap into his house. But his fury had not played out yet with that. Returning to the living room, he leant out the window, and sang his mocking song with a wild, improvised melody over to the blessed farm.

The hate of old Brindeisener was more infernal than usual, and Sintlinger, who had heard everything from his room, struggled with all his might against his fury, threw himself into bed, and wrapped the covers around his head. But the old man's words shrilled constantly in his ears so that finally the fury overwhelmed him like a frenzy. "Good", he said to himself, "if the rage is over me, then it can just have me. And if I let the old, growl-ing animal perish in the fire, then that signifies no more than that I am burning out Schwabians with the pine."

He sprang from his bed, dressed scantily, sought in the dark for matchsticks, and stepped, having decided on everything, quietly into the dark hallway. But he was so agitated that his teeth chattered, and his entire body was shaken by a great shivering. He hardly knew where he was. Everywhere he fumbled to, he banged against a wall, and, after he had groped about like a drunkard for a long time, he gave up on finding the top of the stairs, paused, and listened in the nocturnally silent, large house for whether someone was still awake and had heard him. Then he heard steps walking across the yard, and then the latch of the little side gate quietly clinked.

The cramp in him slowly faded away, and he stepped back into his room.

The next morning, the body of old Zenker was found next to the barn at the Brindeisener farm. A torn-open box of matches lay strewn on the ground next to him; his hands were stretched out still knotted to the straw which spurted from a hole in the wall, his dead eyes were wide-open and rigid, his toothless mouth was firmly clenched; he lay there, a little heap of paralysed, wild revenge.

After this incident, the blessed farmer kept himself hidden from everyone for days, and when he finally let his wife into his room, he was completely transformed, and disclosed to her the decision that he did not want to remain on the farm of his fathers any longer, he did not want to incur the danger, after all the misfortune, of bringing still more badmouthing and shame over him-self and those who associated with him. Furthermore, his life was finished, and nothing more remained to him to do but to serve his soul, or rather, what perhaps still remained of it.

He said all this with a calm voice, relaxed face, and unmoving eyes. The farmwife attempted in vain to penetrate deeper into his thought. To everything she said, he shook his head, and finally, when she fell helplessly silent, he smiled in poignant affection, brushed his hand gently over her forehead, and asked her not to abandon him in the new life which was now beginning.

Because of the service which Gottlieb Meixner had shown him and his little Lena, and also as thanks for old Zenker, Sintlinger presented him with the blessed farm, at first by way of lease. He kept for himself only the meadow by the new boundary path, a few adjacent expanses of field, and the forest behind it. There he constructed a simple, comfortable house which looked similar to the homestead on the blessed hill. Only, here the front projection culminated in a little domed tower, whereas on the blessed farm, the tower protruded from the top of the roof ridge.

Apart from the necessary furniture, Sintlinger took nothing but the bell from the old farmstead. When the thought of the house building had become insistent in him, after that evening in which the thirst for revenge had ambushed him, and after the days of complete seclusion, he had lapsed exhausted into a dream as sharp and distinct as an encounter in life. He saw little Lena in a light blue, long billowing dress with her high, floating, blind steps walking across the meadow in which, sparsely strewn, large, blue bellflowers grew here and there. The girl walked up to every flower, spoke with it, and tolled it, and when Sintlinger awoke, he still heard distinctly the sound of the flowers in his ear.

For that reason, he was emphatic about taking the bell with him, although his wife thought that in this way misfortune would never leave her. Sintlinger overcame her resistance, and then also tolled the bell at all three hours of the day like his forefather, that mad Jakob Sintlinger with whose life, his manner and his fate had such a similarity.

It probably lay in the different surroundings — the nearby forest, the long slope descending on three sides from the house — that the sound of the bell now soun-ded different, softer, more cautious, almost like a feminine singing voice. And the people of Hemsterhus, Brederode, and Querhoven, after they had heard the tolling for a few days, said that the bell had taken on a human voice since the move, and not long afterward, the legend arose that whenever the blessed farmer tolled it, his dead, transfigured little Lena sang with it in heaven, and finally it happened that Sintlinger himself believed it, because he remembered his dream.

After that, he shut his eyes every time he tolled it, and the sound of the little bell led him up and out into the world. Everything all around, heaven and earth, was a mysterious melody, all immersed in sound, in the sound of his child's voice, who had led him in life so deeply into all that was otherworldly, into the heavenly things of earth and of men, so that he no longer under-stood today what he had pondered at the time. But as long as his little Lena sang to him through the voice of the bell, everything was like it was at that time, and he had the old feeling of the blessedness of the entire uni-verse through his soul.

But difficult days came often enough, even whole weeks in which it seemed to him as if he were locked out of himself. Then his ears were blocked, his eyes dull, his head like a bony nut, and his heart was as empty as empty chatter.

Mostly this feeling of exclusion from himself and the entire world, this enormous deathly loneliness befell the blessed farmer in the hours of late afternoon. Then he pulled as usual gently and tenderly on the bell rope, grasped with pining ear for the sound in the air, and let the resounding of the bell's swing tremble through his arms and into his chest. But the sunlit dust did not awaken in his soul. Everything in him remained dead like in a ruined house.

When he felt this paralysis in himself, the pain seized him every time so deeply that he pulled on the rope like someone calling to the entire world for help, and the bell shrilled from the blessed corner like a despairing cry which finally breaks off abruptly.

In Hemsterhus, Brederode, and Querhoven, when the people heard the bell raging madly like that, the mothers blanched, pulled their children away from their play into the living room, closed windows and doors to the tormented sound in the air, and said in fright, "Come, be quiet! The blessed farmer is screaming."

It occurred to Sintlinger at such times that he no longer comprehended the world which he himself had given birth to from his own depths, actively and creatively. And yet he sat in the middle of it, but confused as if he were in the irreality of an immeasurable forest from which he saw no way out. Not a living sound came to him, neither stirring from his past, nor anything stirring from his present. Johanna often saw him sitting for hours on the verandah of the house with lowered eyes, and speaking, but without a sound, his lips moving in the way passionate men think excitedly, and when she asked him what he must be grappling with again, he either paid no attention to her, or just curled his lips bitterly, or even said something incomprehensible like, "If shadows were shadows, then you would also know that things really exist. But then, when the forest rustles, I don't know if it is me or the forest. Oh, my dear wife, a hen, a house, a man, a God, me and you! What is all that?" — With disturbed eyes, he looked helplessly about himself, let his eyes fall again, and sank into his self-absorption.

Towards the end of one such darkness, when it had jerked him once again through thousands of invisible gorges and hollows so that his body was frail and his face quite wasted, he unexpectedly seized Johanna's hand in passing with a pained grip, and said arduously, desperately, like someone who has come to the end of their resistance, "You know, Johanna, it is coming to an end with me, entirely to an end. And now I have only one more wish. That Faber might come and talk with me once more. That is the only thing which can still help me."

But the farmwife knew nothing of the decades long struggle of her husband with this great man. She knew him only, like all the people of the district, from the almost forgotten Herne rebellion, as a wild, murderous vagrant and scarer of people. Hence the good woman became discoloured, and asked, with tears of fear in her eyes, how he could submit to these terrible thoughts, for this monster had been sitting in prison for years or was perhaps already buried in some criminal's grave.

Then Sintlinger broke for the first time his carefully guarded silence over the concealed, mysterious struggle in which his spirit had been involved with the spirit of this rebel, from the first and only conversation on the night after the dedication of the Sintlinger memorial, in the meadow where their house now stood, and he went through all the secret hardships and bewitchments which he had experienced with it, mentioning also the letter which he had received on the day of Vanlyßender's funeral, and reassured her that actually only this man was to blame for the failure of his wisdom and the complete disintegration of his world. This information about such an enigmatic relationship between the men seemed to the farmwife to be like the delusion of a sick nature, sailing on all the clouds, and she knew no other counsel than to embrace her dear Andreas with his shattered heart, and to say to him that if it were as he thought, which she did not understand though, and did not want to understand, then everything would certainly turn out well, for a man like him could not end in such a hole of sorrow like he was now stuck in. That she quite firmly believed.

After that, she went away, and kept to herself the concern which nevertheless sat in her heart.

In that very year now, the relationship between the workers and the employers in the Rhenish-Westphalian industrial region had heated up to an unbearable tension. All the companies were seized by it, and they feared the outbreak of a strike of the largest sort. Amongst those who worked most actively at the avoidance of this struggle, the name Franz Faber was also treated in the syndicated press with respect as a man of great insight, wise moderation, and purest, highest love of man. And when the calm was finally reestablished, it seemed inevitably certain to Sintlinger that Faber must follow up his old promise and seek him out, although the blessed farmer made no other arrangements than to increase his painful yearning for it from day to day.

And his heart, which desired it, did not betray him.

Johanna was furtively keeping an eye on her husband through the living room window one afternoon, as he again sat motionless and slouched on the verandah, and even if he did not stop moving his lips soundlessly in eternally erratic thought, she noticed that the dark work of a peaceless spirit was still in him. For from time to time, he lifted his head, passed his hand over his forehead in a sort of calming invocation, and then looked peculiarly and exactly into the distance, to the place, behind the gentle low cleft of the valley between the two estranged farms, already turning blue somewhat in the distance, the softly moving wall of hills separating the district of the estranged farms from Querhoven closed off the horizon. But she could not work out what was drawing the attention of her Andreas, as she thought, always right there. For there was nothing remarkable there. The small beard of spruces which ran down from the forest of the Dürrenberg stood like a breached, dark shroud, and the light of the already sinking sun was flashing in golden sparkling stripes and points through the branches. But towards evening, when the play of the sunny shimmering was already beginning to glow red, she saw an unusually tall man descending the footpath over the Querhoven hill towards the new road, the former boundary path, and approach them slowly and dignified like a king. Between the estranged farms, in the middle of the valley's cleft, he paused, and looked sometimes at the Sintlinger, sometimes at the Brin-deisener hill, with an attentive gaze as if he were not sure of which farmstead he should be climbing up to. He carried his hat in his hand, and his light, grey coat wafted in the gentle breeze which sometimes also drove his enormous full beard over his shoulder like a thick whitish cloud. After some thought, he continued on the path, but now with lowered head, lifted his face at the place where the path to the estranged farm's forest made a turn, examined the Sintlingers' house of refuge for a moment, and then strode decisively over the ditch's small bridge to the entrance to the garden which stretched out almost as far as the road.

As soon as he set his first foot on the ditch's little bridge, steering energetically towards her house, the blessed farmer's wife saw her husband abruptly spring up, breathing out heavily, with both hands seizing the railing of the verandah, and then hurried precipitately down the steps and through the garden to the stranger.

The Blessed Farm

The two men met at the garden gate. Johanna saw her Andreas open the little gate, and stretch out his hand to the tall arrival. But even before the other man could grasp it, the blessed farmer began to stagger, and the stranger had to catch him in his arms to prevent him from collapsing.

Johanna emitted a cry, and sprang down the steps of the verandah, through the garden, towards the two, for she thought a misfortune had befallen her husband as a consequence of the long period of grief. And in fact, when she approached the two at a run, she saw Sintlinger approaching palely, half faint, with closed eyes, but yet smiling happily, hanging on the arm of the stranger.

Franz Faber, for that is who the stranger in fact was, waved to her not to fret, greeted her with winning kindness, and gave her to understand through gestures that she should abstain from all loud words.

Arriving at the verandah, he asked her just as silently to leave him alone with Sintlinger. Then he sat for a long time silently with the shattered man, and held his hand in his own. But the blessed farmer looked down constantly before himself, and was incapable of looking at the man whom he had struggled with. Only now and then did a twitch pass over the face of her Andreas, a trace which was a mix of bitterness and blessedness, and also looked like the blissful smile of the defeated.

And every time, when such an attack of broken pride came over Sintlinger, the farmwife, watching the two from behind the window, noticed that Faber placed his hand comfortingly on her husband's shoulder, and she recognised in the movement of his great beard that he was speaking kindly to him.

No, that was no fool, like Sintlinger had so often scolded him with being, and even less an evil traducer and enemy of all, as she had thought with the masses for a long time; he sat there, in contrast, like a tall kindly father of men, and the terrible sabre scar, which was hewn diagonally across his forehead, increased his venerableness still more into the almost unsettling. And the simple, pure woman felt that her helpless, rushed-about husband was now saved. She moved away from the window, and went into the kitchen to prepare the evening supper.

Not long afterwards, she heard the pair talking to each other softly at first, then in a more and more lively way.

That same evening, Sintlinger spread out his entire life before Faber — how he had been awoken in the midst of the inherited wildness of his blood to a new existence by the birth of the angelic little Lena, and been led by her to indescribably bright heights; how darkness and shadows had then come over him after she received her sight, above all such a deep night of the spirit had embraced him after Helene's death that he now stood there confused and shattered, and really did not know anymore where there was to go. The blessed farmer lost his last timidity, and spoke of his deepest secrets.

When he had finished, and looked at Faber full of the tensest expectation, he noticed surely his deep agitation. The massive man leant there with lowered head and closed eyes. Then he nodded heavily, looked deeply at Sintlinger, grasped his hand, and pressed it with kindly force.

But he ignored the life confession of Sintlinger and told of how he had already been because of him over for a day with the Querhoveners who regarded themselves as his disciples. There he had already learnt many things about him and his fate. The rounding off and proper insight had come to him, however, only now through he himself. He thanked him heartily for his trust, asked though to let him have that night so that he could consider everything once more for himself. He was also worn-out that day.

Sintlinger sat there disappointedly after this answer, lowered his face, and gnawed his lip, but then overcame himself, stood up, and handed over to Faber his journal pages with the remark that still more was contained in them than he could tell, most of it, or rather much of it, was what he had experienced within. If he wanted to read them, then it would be even easier to find what must have broken him.

Franz Faber accepted the pages with a meaningful thank you. After that the men separated, and Faber climbed up to the little room where his bed had been prepared for him.

The next day, Faber remained almost entirely in his room. During meal times, he sat at the table as if lost in a great distance, and the blessed farmer and his wife were often gripped by a mysterious shiver when he let his eyes, with their gaze reaching over the earth, rest on them for a long time in a fathoming way.

On the evening of this second day, the blessed farmer and Faber walked, at his suggestion, around all the places which had become peculiar to them on their first encounter twenty years before, from the heap of bushes to the still pond next to which Faber had been found by Sintlinger collapsed in a faint from his flight; they strode over the ditches, strolled in the moonlight along the little valley, climbed up to the blessed farm, sat below the lime tree by the Sintlinger memorial, gazed over at the decaying Brindeisener farmstead, looked up at the windows behind which Helene had lived the last years of her life, and lost themselves in the forest past the high butte for a bit.

Sintlinger talked still more about the struggles and entanglements of his existence, and how he had actually constantly, below the surface as it were, had to wrestle with Faber up to then, until everything had crumbled like dust in him.

Faber had until then walked almost silently next to him, and his share in the conversation had actually only consisted of the spurs to lead on the flow of Sintlinger's tale and to imperceptibly guide it.

When Sintlinger had spoken the last words over his dissolution, Faber paused, and asked, "And do you know, Sintlinger, why it could not happen but that you disappeared before yourself? Do you know that?"

Sintlinger shook his head.

For that reason, Faber continued speaking, "You are my brother, Sintlinger. That I learnt from the Quer-hoveners, who claim that they received the new path to God and their entire altered life from you. Most of all, deeper still, it became known to me through your notes that you are my brother in the Holy Spirit, which only now begins to achieve a dominion within men, without the covering of dogma, without allegory, and after it has roamed about guiding them in disguise for all these cen-turies. Once more, let it be said, you are more deeply my brother than any other man on earth.

And that is why we had to wrestle with each other, even before we really knew each other. For men directed in the same way are close to each other, even if they don't see each other, and if there are oceans or centuries between them — the pulling together of one becomes the victory of the other, and through the fall of one, many others who are living in uncertainty stumble and fall. For that reason, I also know about your inner being.

Shall I continue talking, or do you know yourself now too, why you confused yourself?"

"I beg you, keep talking, Faber", the blessed farmer said softly.

"Well, since you want me too, listen. The bell which you toll every day does not sound to you its ring, your own voice, or your spirit, but the voice and the spirit of your dead daughter Helene. But just like that now is, so too it was when she still lived, as I have read, from the first day of her existence. Even at the time, you actually lived only her life, pondered with her spirit, and felt with her heart.

Your life, however, your spirit, and your heart remain in the place where they had been even before the child was born. You found wisdom, and did not become wise, lived the virtue of another's heart, fancied yourself free, and was caught.

That is why, when a change came over the child, when she obtained external sight through the commotions of love, and then even vanished from you into death, everything before you had to be transformed and disappear, because you only knew through her existence what you had perceived. For you can also arrive on a wrong path to a pinnacle, see well that it is a pinnacle, but then, without knowing how it happens, lose your way from it again. Even the purest love is a torturous path if it does not lead you entirely along the path of your spirit, and last of all, in their depths no person may belong to anyone else but God alone.

So, if you do not want anymore, as you say, to collect dust, then you must now acquire for a second time, and now with your own powers, what you possessed through the blessed child. For I believe myself that your little Lena was a blessed person. For that reason, do not be sad and despondent anymore. All life both within us and outside of us must constantly disappear, since it is the way of waves to come and to go. But yet the sea remains, as you yourself wrote in your notes. We men, however, as long as we travel on the currents of this dancing earth, must build ourselves up ever higher from our souls, with ever purer spirit and will, we, the bright shadows of God."

During these words, they had emerged from the forest, and arrived again at the house.

Sintlinger stood there with lowered head, while Faber was already preparing to climb up the steps to the verandah.

It looked as if the blessed farmer wanted, overcome by new sorrow, not to go to sleep, but to escape into the forest again.

For that reason, Faber took his hand, and said affectionately, "No, Sintlinger, now straight to bed! Believe me, you will sleep with your greatest happiness, wall to wall. Tomorrow I want to speak with you further, and then depart."

Only the blessed farmer had been overwhelmed by his old lack of peace, and desolation, and when Faber had shut the door behind him, he left the garden, and ran into the forest, where he wrestled with his malign spirit until the morning.

It seemed to him as if Faber had now more than ever trodden down his entire life through the demand that he should hold himself aloof even from the spirit of dead little Lena as if from a folly.

But when after long hours of night, the first silvery grey of the morning finally awoke over the treetops, the burrowing of obstructiveness towards Faber began to leave him, and it occurred to him that, during all those hours, just like the long period before, he had reared up actually against the sense which, in injured pride, he had placed arbitrarily on Faber's words. How would the great man have otherwise been able to talk of Helene as a blessed person! He pulled himself together with a firm grip so that it would not happen to him again that he came to a pinnacle by mistake.

He freed himself from the vanity of his spirit and the self-infatuation of his heart, and saw that the truth was not true because someone spoke it, but because it was the truth, and that it must be from the beginning in all men, since otherwise it could never have been recognised by anyone.

When the blessed farmer stepped out of the forest, he saw his house lying transfigured in the first brilliance of the morning.

He saw that as a comforting auspice, and the handful of sleep which still remained for him refreshed him as deeply as the peace of calm years, and the coming together of the two men on this last day turned then into an elevated, memorable celebration of the soul.

Faber noted happily the pure open mindedness and freedom which Sintlinger met him with, and talked with him about all the secrets of his life and the lives of all men.

In the afternoon, Faber pressed for an end, for he wanted to spend one more evening in Querhoven with the weaver Staupitz in the circle of poor forest villagers, whom he called wonderful people, before his departure from the district.

He declined with a hearty thanks all the requests of Sintlinger to stay longer. For he must not indulge himself in any rest. Smiling, he stood up, and walked a few times to and fro about the room, happy with love for the blessed farmer and his Johanna. Finally he stepped to the window, and gazed over the garden into the countryside through which he had once fled by night in hardship as an outlaw, and now, after twenty years, he lingered here as a bringer of peace.

Meanwhile, as he stood and pondered raptly, the farmwife also entered quietly, and sat down silently by her husband at the table. The two were attached with looks of veneration to the tall figure of the wise man turned in on himself, until he slowly turned around, and looked at them with a face which was beautified by a deep blessedness.

"Oh yes", he said beaming, "life is beautiful! How glorious everything difficult is in truth when we men accept and overcome it in the proper way!"

After this exclamation, he was quite overcome and enraptured by his spirit, and continued speaking, "See, both you dear, dear people, I must again depart. I am happy that I was with you, and yet am also happy that I must go away again. For my spirit drives me to bring a new gospel to men, not that in chasing it, I must first acquire it myself. No, I possess it. In the middle of the desolation, I am myself indestructible. It is a different thing to what men have believed until now. For whoever talks still of salvation, talks words stripped of their shells, lives in the vanity of sin, offends God, and bakes the bread of his days in the oven of the fear of death. On the standard which I unfurl, there is no painting of an animal and nor of a corpse, but the image of a happy, living man. The entire universe with its countless objects, all the teachings of the churches which were and will still be, all the truths of the sciences are only symbols of his being, everything by and in him, even his domestic activity, his families and states, and even his sins themselves. For time is only in our talk, and space through our thought. Every word of distinction is only an allegory on earth.

The unnamable being which forms the foundation of the world, it is also our deepest being before which a stalk is as large as a mountain. It does not know more and less, not big and small, not here and there, not today, tomorrow, and yesterday. Birth and death are only notes of its eternal song. The dance of the stars causes ebb and flow; but it also tolls our little heart. And everything together is yet no more than the back and forth movement of the clock on the wall in the house of man.

That depth is the eternal being which we call within ourselves soul, and outside ourselves God.

After death, we are undivided. Here, in the state which we call life or existence, everything is shrouded for us by the spirit and its thought, so that we see upside down like the images on the surface of the pond or in the pupils of our eyes.

But even here, shackled by the phantoms of space and time, we can reach into it, into that house without walls that a few call the other side, others call heaven, and yet others the void, because it is everything.

When a bird sits on the tip of the outermost branch, it experiences only the movements of that branch. When it moves deeper within the tree on the branch, it embraces the movements of a hundred branches, and yet sways only a little. But when it chooses its place in the inner crown, hard by the trunk, it experiences the movements of the entire tree, and is itself no longer shaken.

Even more like this bird is how it happens with a man who sinks right to the depths of his soul. For there he experiences all life, the entire universe, all of God with all His mysteries, because this foundation of ours is also God's foundation.

But for everyone who knows this, from them every sorrow is taken, and the transience vanishes before the immortal.

Rejoice! Here is the peace, the happiness, the light, the beauty which nobody can take from you anymore.

That I give to you in parting. Deliberate on it in your hearts when I am gone, and act on it accordingly with vigilance and fidelity. Farewell!"

When Faber had thus spoken, he stepped up to the farmer and his wife, grasped their hands, shook them vigorously, and then left them with his quickly snatched things, hurriedly, almost in flight.

The blessed farmer and his wife had been numbed by the unexpected breaking forth of the torrent of Faber's wisdom as if by a storm, blinded as if their eyes had been seared by the high sun, in such a way that they relied to the squeezing of the departing man's hand, said words too, even moved after him for a few steps, and yet did not actually know what they were doing.

When they awoke from this unearthly dream, they found themselves standing opposite each other on the threshold of the door to the same room into which the last stirrings of Faber's words had now vanished as well. They looked at each other, and noticed that their faces were quite pale.

Sintlinger stepped back, and slowly began pacing about the room. Johanna hurried out, down the verandah steps into the garden, and constantly called Faber's name out loudly, to move him if possible to come back once more. But he was nowhere to be seen anymore.

When she returned to the living room, she found her Andreas standing at the window, his forehead pressed against the pane. He stood there so that his face could not be seen, and gazed motionlessly into the distance.

She stepped up to him, placed a hand on his shoulder, and gazed out too, still breathing heavily from the quick run and the agitation.

After a while of gazing, the blessed farmer said softly, "Do you see, now he is climbing up over the Querhoven hills."

And Johanna also caught sight of Faber now, as he climbed the rise, hat in hand, and with a lusty gait. His hair and his beard wafted white about his massive head.

Now he had arrived at the ridge, looked back for a moment at their house, and then vanished into the light of the sinking sun between the spruces. When the blessed farmer turned away, Johanna noticed that his eyes were still shimmering with tears.

But he did not touch on his deep emotion at all, instead saying with a smile, "Now Faber has taken my writings with him. And I also forgot then to ask him about his life."

With that, he went, sat himself down on a chair at the table, and said softly to himself after some deliberation, "Well. yes, yes. It is surely so. If you constantly think merely of your own life, you lose it, and when you give, you receive. And any one of us is ever only the sound of the steps of a greater one who comes after us."

After Faber's visit, the blessed farmer entered his last transformation.

He opened up in ever greater love and kindness to all people. He even approached the Querhoveners more and more, and supported the forest villagers in every way inwardly and outwardly. Gottlieb Meixner, however, he loved like his own son, and little Meier, who had become his wife, like his daughter-in-law, since he had learnt that, in the night before Helene's gaining her sight, the couple had been married, and blessed by his child. And when the first child, a boy, was born to the couple, it seemed to him as if a part of his and Helene's being, also the heart of his dear wife, was blossoming still at the farmstead of his fathers.

Nevertheless he yearned ever and ever after for his dead child, and he continued tolling the bell of his house so that little Lena's voice awoke and talked to his soul from between heaven and earth. But never again did the wild, hoarse raving come over the bell in its blessed corner. It tolled from now on always cheerfully like the voice of a child, and now, when its notes swung melodiously through the valleys over the hills, the people said to one another in their houses, "Listen, the blessed little Lena is singing", stopped talking, stepped to their front doors, and listened moved until the bell's ringing had faded away.

About the Publisher

Our mission is to provide translations into English of the complete works of neglected major European writers. We do not cherry-pick works that seem the most marketable, but rather seek to provide a complete collection of each writer's works so that readers can follow the writer's development and decide on its merits for themselves.

http://www.kanitzpublishing.com

http://www.facebook.com/KANitzPublishing